TWIST
OF FAITH

STAR TREK
DEEP SPACE NINE®

TWIST
OF FAITH

S. D. PERRY
DAVID WEDDLE and JEFFREY LANG
KEITH R. A. DeCANDIDO

Based upon STAR TREK® created by Gene Roddenberry,
and STAR TREK: DEEP SPACE NINE created by Rick Berman & Michael Piller

POCKET BOOKS
New York   London   Toronto   Sydney   B'hala

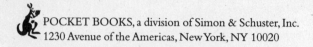 POCKET BOOKS, a division of Simon & Schuster, Inc.
1230 Avenue of the Americas, New York, NY 10020

This book is published by Pocket Books, a division of
Simon & Schuster, Inc., under exclusive license from
CBS Studios Inc.

ISBN-13: 978-1-4165-3415-0
ISBN-10:   1-4165-3415-6

First Pocket Books trade paperback edition May 2007

10 9 8 7 6 5 4 3 2 1

Cover art by Cliff Nielsen
Cover design by Alan Dingman

Manufactured in the United States of America

These titles were previously published individually by Pocket Books.

For information regarding special discounts for bulk purchases,
please contact Simon & Schuster Special Sales at
1-800-456-6798 or business@simonandschuster.com.

What you leave behind is not what is engraved in stone monuments, but what is woven into the lives of others.

—PERICLES

And all but their faith overthrown.

—WILLIAM WETMORE STORY, *IO VICTIS*

Contents

Introduction
Deep Into That Darkness Peering
by David R. George III

Deep into that darkness peering, long I stood there wondering, fearing,
Doubting, dreaming dreams no mortal ever dared to dream before....

—EDGAR ALLAN POE, "THE RAVEN"

Nearly a decade and a half later, I still vividly recall watching that first episode of the then-newest *Star Trek* television series. Its development had been announced months earlier, to both fanfare and skepticism. Unlike its forebears, this show would include among its cast of characters numerous non-Starfleet personnel, and they would interact not on the *Starship Enterprise* or on any vessel at all, but on a space station. The producers also noted that this latest incarnation of *Trek* would unveil a darker side of Gene Roddenberry's optimistic creation. It would be called *Deep Space Nine*.

The name of the show, I remember, did not fill me with anticipation. Just a few years earlier, a B movie had been released with a similar name—*Deep Star Six,* I think—and the resemblance between the titles seemed unfortunate. Of greater significance, I heard fans wondering whether a series that did not include the *Enterprise* could even properly be considered *Star Trek*. How would that work from week to week, some asked, curious about the prospect of adventures having to visit the space station again and again, rather than the new crew boldly going, seeking out new life and new civilizations?

With the very first episode of *Deep Space Nine,* the answer became immediately clear that it would work the way that *Star Trek* had always worked, the way that much good fiction works: as a combination of expert storytelling, compelling characters, and meaningful themes. Cocreator Michael Piller's teleplay for "Emissary" provided all of that and more. The two-hour pilot supplied viewers with an astonishingly textured milieu in which future tales would unfold. Protagonists and antagonists came bearing histories and flaws, the setting offered alien architecture and technology, and two subjects often anathema to series television—politics and religion—entwined their way through that initial episode. From its inception, *DS9* explored the realities and effects of occupation and liberation, of détente and entente, of faith and orthodoxy, of deliverance and charity. The Cardassians maintained a stratocratic government, the Bajorans kept both a provisional secular authority and a religious hierarchy, and the Federation stood between the two peoples, on the side of one and as a buffer against the other.

And yeah, the show was dark. Physically, the space station contained hard, shadowy surfaces and gloomy passages. Dramatically, the tales often ventured out of the brilliant, well-lighted areas of life and into complicated gray areas. Characters and situations changed over time, not always for the better, and themes and stories sometimes reached not merely from one episode to the next, but from one season to the next. *Deep Space Nine* presented a gloriously complex tapestry of diverse, fascinating threads, quite a few of them weaving in unexpected directions. In some ways, the show demanded a lot of its audience, but for those who stayed with it, their viewership paid handsome rewards.

It seemed evident to me, right from the start, that the series could play out for years and never exhaust the surfeit of detailed material that had been built into its foundation. Indeed, through seven seasons, under the leadership of its head writers—first Michael Piller, and later Ira Steven Behr—*DSN* developed the potential initially invested in it, then fulfilled and exceeded it. One episode after another, the show explored human issues in intriguing and accessible ways. This might not have been your parents' *Star Trek,* but it was most assuredly *Star Trek*.

The series came to a close after one hundred seventy-six hours, bringing resolutions to numerous storylines, some of which had begun as far back as the show's pilot. A war ended, heroes and villains died, others moved on to the next stages of their lives. As with the first installment of the series, I very clearly remember watching the last one, entitled "What You Leave Behind." I found the experience bittersweet. While I had thoroughly enjoyed both "Emissary" and "What You Leave Behind"—not to mention the years worth of episodes between—the former had promised a future of quality dramatic fiction, while the latter left all of that in the past. No more would I or anybody else be treated to wonderful new tales set in the *Deep Space Nine* universe.

Enter Marco Palmieri.

Some readers may be familiar with Marco because they've occasionally seen his name on the cover of a *Star Trek* book, or perhaps because they've read his posts on the Internet at various sites devoted to the discussion of *Trek* literature. I suspect, though, that many readers may not know who Marco is or what he does. As an editor at Pocket Books, a part of Simon & Schuster, he shares the responsibility for managing the *Trek* publishing line. Marco hires writers, approves and edits stories, and helps mold the overall direction of the books. Included in a list of his numerous accomplishments is the omnibus edition you now hold in your hands, as well as each of the works it comprises.

After *Deep Space Nine* departed the airwaves in the spring of 1999, Marco, himself a fan of the series, saw a means of keeping it alive by continuing the saga forward in print, picking up where the final episode had ended. Yes, many plotlines had been resolved in *DS9*'s finale, but others had not: Bajor still had not joined the Federation, Ben Sisko remained in another reality, and Kasidy Yates had yet to give birth, just to identify a few of the loose ends. More than that, "What You Leave Behind" had actually offered up springboards for new tales: for example, Kira Nerys had taken over command of the space station, Odo had finally rejoined the Great Link, and Garak had at last returned to Cardassia Prime, now a devastated world.

So Marco imagined relighting the torch and carrying it onward. He crafted a proposal for an ongoing series of *Deep Space Nine* books. In the tradition of the show itself, Marco envisioned new characters and further evolution for the existing characters. He foresaw intricate, dramatic storylines, some of which would be introduced, explored, and brought to fruition in one work, while others would stretch across multiple tales. As on television, twists would abound.

One of those would turn out to be a twist of *faith*.

But first, as the rights holder for *Star Trek* at that time, Paramount Pictures had to approve Marco's pitch. (As of this publication, CBS Studios holds those rights.) Paula Block has long functioned as a gatekeeper in this regard, somehow managing to expertly serve the interests of both her employers and the readers of *Trek* literature. Far from being an obstructionist, Paula appreciates creativity and keeps herself open to new ideas and methods. After working through Marco's innovative proposal with him, and after offering her own observations and suggestions, she endorsed his plan.

The first of the new books, Marco knew, would have a great deal to accomplish. It would need to reintroduce readers to Deep Space 9 and to the changes that had taken place at the end of the series. Captain Sisko had vanished, apparently to reside with the nonlinear aliens in the Bajoran wormhole—or with the Prophets in the Celestial Temple, depending upon your point of view. Kira Nerys had been given command of the space station, which consequently created an opening for an executive officer. Ezri Dax and Julian Bashir had finally begun a romantic relationship. Miles O'Brien had left the station and gone back with his family to Earth, allowing Nog to be promoted to DS9's chief of operations. Odo had left as well, going back to the Great Link, and Worf had accepted a position as Federation ambassador to the Klingon Empire. Damar, Winn Adami, and the last of the Weyoun clones had each met their demise. The Dominion War had come to a close and the wormhole had once more opened to nonmilitary traffic.

But the tale that resumed the chronicles of *Deep Space Nine* would also have to do far more than deal with all of the changes wrought during the last episodes of the series. It would have to introduce new characters and launch new adventures, and it would have to do so in ways worthy of *DS9*. To achieve all of that, Marco wisely turned to S. D. Perry.

As with my watching the superb pilot and finale episodes of *Deep Space Nine,* I clearly remember reading *Avatar,* the two-volume set that relaunched the series in book form. At some point, Marco had begun talking with me about the possibility of my contributing to the new line, and so he sent me prepublication copies of those first two books, which I immediately devoured. I was—if you'll pardon the phrase—transported. Under Marco's guidance, S. D. Perry had crafted an involved story that stood as an exemplar of what

Deep Space Nine had on television given to its audience. Her fine prose revived for me the characters of Kira Nerys and Julian Bashir, of Jake Sisko and Ezri Dax, of Nog and Quark. Ro Laren, who had betrayed Captain Picard when she had abandoned her post aboard the *Enterprise*-D to join the Maquis, returned as well. I also met Commander Tiris Jast, a Bolian woman assigned by Starfleet as the station's new first officer; Elias Vaughn, a centenarian with eighty years of experience in Starfleet Intelligence; Ensign Thirishar ch'Thane, a young Andorian and DS9's new science officer; and a surprising arrival from the Gamma Quadrant: a Jem'Hadar elder.

All of these characters—along with still other familiar faces reappearing and even more new faces joining the saga—fit perfectly into S. D. Perry's absorbing story. While some characters still deal with the fallout of the Dominion War, time and life have moved on. Deep Space 9 and its crew face new threats, military, political, and religious. So much of what invested *Deep Space Nine* as a riveting television series finds its way into S. D. Perry's novels, where it is given even greater lease to engage the audience. Fans of the show could not have been better served by this accomplished writer.

As I read *Avatar,* I quickly realized that, as high as the dramatic potential had been for *DS9* on television, the stakes had been raised in these new books. The limitations of sets and budgets no longer applied, nor did the restrictions imposed by the structure of a television episode. The availability of actors no longer mattered either; any character could be brought back to these new tales, or even resurrected for them. Anything that could be imagined could be included in these stories without regard to the practicality of filming it. Further, with the series off the air and no apparent prospects for a *Deep Space Nine* feature film, real-life production considerations no longer protected the characters. That is, an actor's multiyear contract would not prevent their role from being written out of the show. Coupling all of that with Marco Palmieri and Paula Block's commitments to publishing compelling *Star Trek* literature, I suddenly understood that Kira Nerys could quit her post on the station, perhaps chasing after Odo or going home to Bajor to pursue a spiritual life. She could find another love, suffer a debilitating injury, even die. I knew the professionalism and creativity of Paula and Marco, could see on the page what the talented S. D. Perry brought to the table, and it seemed clear that anything could happen, so long as it contributed significantly to the tale being told. Kira and all the rest of the characters were at risk in ways they hadn't necessarily been during the run of the show.

It took almost no time at all to have such suspicions confirmed. Not every character survives S. D. Perry's story, and of those who do, some confront major changes in their lives. As gripping as *DS9* had been on television, it had become even more so in print.

I anxiously awaited the next book in the series. Just as *Avatar* had carried *Deep Space Nine* forward from the show's last episode, when it arrived in bookstores, so too did *Abyss* pick up the baton from S. D. Perry's two volumes. David Weddle, a former staff writer and executive story editor on *DS9,* teamed with Jeff Lang to bring back the nefarious Section 31. But while the secretive organization provokes all the DS9 crew to action, it is Dr. Bashir who must face his own demons when he meets the brilliant physician Ethan Locken, like himself a genetically enhanced genius. In a story that thrusts Bashir, Ezri Dax, and Ro Laren into harm's way, readers are treated to deep explorations of each character. The nature of the chemical-dependent soldiers bred by the Founders to form an army, the lethal Jem'Hadar, is also put at issue. In *Abyss,* as in *Avatar,* the fates of the characters—who would live, who would die, who would *change*—remained fluid and uncertain.

From Locken's laboratory on the planet Sindorin, Keith R. A. DeCandido then took readers in *Demons of Air and Darkness* to the world of Europa Nova. There, an ecological disaster threatens the independent human colony, and the crew of DS9 lead the rescue efforts. More new characters are introduced, including Andorian Councilor Charivretha zh'Thane, who also happens to be one of Ensign ch'Thane's parents, and a woman named Treir, who long before the television series *Enterprise* premiered offers up a distinctive new take on Orion "slave girls." As well, other characters from *Star Trek*'s past return, including an unexpected appearance by a particular Cardassian.

While Quark embarks on an unlikely mission to address the cause of the environmental threat on Europa Nova—a suddenly functioning Iconian gateway that connects the Alpha Quadrant with the Delta Quadrant—Kira directs the evacuation of the population. But then she and another of the regular characters is seriously imperiled in a thrilling sequence that culminates in an unforgettable confrontation between a Jem'Hadar warrior and a Hirogen hunter. While one character's fate is decided in the novel's closing pages, Kira's is not. Instead, her predicament takes readers directly into Keith DeCandido's follow-up to *Demons,* the novella *Horn and Ivory.*

For me, it seems appropriate that this omnibus edition of post-*DS9* fiction concludes with *Horn and Ivory,* a high point among a range of tall peaks. Here, Kira Nerys unexpectedly embarks on a major spiritual journey—an *action-packed* journey, but one nonetheless deeply spiritual. The story presents a fascinating portrait of this woman who grew up beneath the weight of oppressors, who fought even as a girl for the freedom of her people. Keith's tale impresses as he uncovers and explores the complicated facets of Colonel Kira's personality.

I loved the *Deep Space Nine* television series, and I felt sorry when it came to an end. But Marco Palmieri and Paula Block and these writers have worked hard to craft a continuation of the saga worthy of the wellspring from which it flows, and for me, as a fan, they have succeeded far beyond my expectations. To this point, I have contributed two entries myself to the ongoing chronicles of *DS9,* including *Twilight,* the novel that immediately follows the pieces contained in this volume. As a writer, I could not have been provided with a better foundation upon which to build my own work, but that bears little on why I continue to read these additions to the ongoing Deep Space Nine opus as they are published. These tales engage me just as the show did, with strong stories and themes, with dynamic characters, with rousing action and unexpected twists and turns. I am unabashedly a fan, and I cannot recommend these works highly enough.

So I've read all of the stories contained in this volume. For those of you who haven't, I'm envious; I recall well how much I enjoyed becoming reacquainted with the *DS9* characters and meeting the new ones, how much I loved rejoining this saga I'd once thought ended. For those readers coming back to these tales again, I know how you feel. In the course of penning this introduction, I returned to these works myself, taking pleasure once more in the vision of Marco Palmieri and the storytelling of S. D. Perry, David Weddle and Jeffrey Lang, and Keith R. A. DeCandido.

So what are you waiting for? On the heels of his father's disappearance after the end of the Dominion War, Jake Sisko has for weeks now been working at an archeological dig on Bajor, exhausting himself each day with his toils, allowing him to sleep deeply and peacefully each night.

Except last night. For last night, Jake dreamed.

Why don't you join him?

Historian's Note

These stories unfold over the month of April in the year 2376 (Old Calendar), beginning approximately three months after the events of the *Star Trek: Deep Space Nine* series finale, "What You Leave Behind."

Linear Time

The Distant Past

- Over the course of ten thousand years, the people of Bajor discover nine mysterious artifacts that sometimes convey prophetic visions. Called "Tears of the Prophets" or "Orbs," they are believed to have originated in the Celestial Temple, the legendary home of Bajor's gods, the Prophets.

2328

- The Cardassian Union conquers Bajor. Eight of the nine Orbs are confiscated for study. The ninth, the Orb of Prophecy and Change, is successfully hidden by Bajor's spiritual leaders.

2332

- On Earth, Benjamin Sisko is born, the child of Sarah and Joseph Sisko. Unknown to anyone at this time, Sarah is actually the host for a noncorporeal entity from the as-yet-undiscovered Bajoran wormhole, who has brought about the exact circumstances necessary for Benjamin Sisko to exist.

2345

- A liquid life-form of unknown origin is discovered adrift in the Bajoran system's Denorios Belt. It is later found to be a shape-shifting sentient being, and accepts the name Odo.

2346

- The Cardassians complete space station Terok Nor in orbit of Bajor. It becomes the seat of the occupation under Gul S.G. Dukat.
- To ensure the survival of her husband and children, Kira Meru becomes the comfort woman of Dukat. She is never reunited with her family.

2347

- On Bajor, seven-year-old Ro Laren witnesses the torture and murder of her father by the Cardassians.
- Richard and Amsha Bashir subject their six-year-old son Jules to illegal genetic enhancement. The boy later changes his name to Julian and keeps his enhancement secret for many years.

2354

- Ensign Benjamin Sisko meets joined Trill Curzon Dax at Pelios Station. Their friendship continues through Dax's next two hosts.

2355

- On Bajor, twelve-year-old Kira Nerys, daughter of Meru, joins the Shakaar resistance cell to fight the Cardassian occupation.
- Jake Sisko is born to Benjamin and Jennifer Sisko.

2358

- Ro, after growing up in Bajoran resettlement camps, attends Starfleet Academy.

2360

- Quark opens a bar on Terok Nor after spending eight years as a cook on a Ferengi freighter. Among his staff is his brother Rom, and Rom's young son, Nog.

2364

- While serving aboard the *U.S.S. Wellington,* Ensign Ro disobeys orders during a mission on Garon II, resulting in the deaths of eight members of her away team. She is court-martialed and sentenced to the Starfleet stockade on Jaros II.

2365

- Odo comes to Terok Nor and begins arbitrating disputes among Bajorans, leading Dukat to recruit him for a murder investigation. In the process, Odo meets Kira, with whom he will eventually fall in love, though he keeps that secret from her for many years.
- Dukat makes Odo the station's chief of security, replacing a Cardassian named Thrax.

2367

- The Battle of Wolf 359 between a Borg cube and forty Federation starships claims 11,000 lives—including Jennifer Sisko. *U.S.S. Saratoga* first officer Lieutenant Commander Benjamin Sisko and his son Jake both survive. Sisko is subsequently assigned to the Utopia Planitia Shipyards on Mars, where he becomes part of the *Defiant*-class Development Project, the goal of which is a starship designed specifically to fight and defeat the Borg.
- Curzon, seventh host of the Dax symbiont, dies. The symbiont is transferred to Jadzia.

2368

- Ro is freed from prison in order to carry out an illegal covert mission for Starfleet Admiral Kennelly aboard the *U.S.S. Enterprise.* Instead, she exposes Kennelly's duplicity. At the request of Captain Jean-Luc Picard, her rank is restored and she is assigned to the *Enterprise.*

2369

- The Cardassian Union withdraws from Bajor and abandons Terok Nor. As Bajor regains its independence, a provisional government and an armed militia are formed. Bajor applies for Federation membership, and invites Starfleet to administrate the station as a Federation starbase with an integrated Starfleet and Bajoran crew. Terok Nor is renamed Deep Space 9.
- Cardassian exile Elim Garak, former intelligence agent of the Obsidian Order, is left behind on the station during the withdrawal. He remains an enigmatic station resident, living as a tailor.
- Commander Sisko is made commanding officer of DS9, with Major Kira reluctantly serving as his first officer and liaison with Bajor. Lieutenant Jadzia Dax is assigned as science officer. Lieutenant (j.g.) Dr. Julian Bashir becomes chief medical officer. Former *Enterprise* transporter chief Miles O'Brien is made chief of operations. Odo stays on as chief of station security.
- Sisko meets Bajor's spiritual leader, Kai Opaka, who tells him he is the Emissary long foretold in Bajoran prophecy, the one who will open the gates to the Celestial Temple.
- After experiencing the Orb of Prophecy and Change, Sisko and Dax discover a stable wormhole in the Denorios Belt, linking the Alpha Quadrant to the Gamma Quadrant. The wormhole is also found to be the home of noncorporeal entities who exist outside of linear time. DS9 is moved to a position proximate to the wormhole, and becomes a major center of commerce and the launch point for the exploration of the Gamma Quadrant.
- The Bajoran faithful come to believe the wormhole is the Celestial Temple, and that its inhabitants are the Prophets. Sisko is recognized as the Emissary, a role with which he is never completely comfortable.
- Opaka is killed on a planet in the Gamma Quadrant. Nanomachines previously introduced into the planet's biosphere revive her, but also make it impossible for her to leave.
- Ro leaves the *Enterprise* to receive Starfleet advanced tactical training.

2370

- Minister Jaro Essa and Vedek Winn Adami conspire to seize power on Bajor and oust the Federation. The coup fails, and Jaro is disgraced, but Winn emerges unscathed.
- Kira and Vedek Bareil Antos become romantically involved.
- Ferengi trade expeditions to the Gamma Quadrant first encounter rumors of a powerful civilization known as the Dominion.
- The Federation and the Cardassian Union sign an historic peace treaty, leading to the creation of a "Demilitarized Zone" between the two powers. As a result, several Federation colony worlds are ceded to the Cardassians, but many of the colonists refuse to be evacuated.
- In response to Cardassian hostilities against Federation colonists still living

in the DMZ, and believing they have been abandoned by the Federation, some of the colonists organize an armed resistance and become known as the Maquis. They consider themselves freedom fighters, but are generally regarded as terrorists.

- Winn is elected kai of the Bajoran faith.
- Lieutenant Ro returns to the *Enterprise* and is assigned to infiltrate the Maquis. Finding herself sympathizing with their cause, she turns against Starfleet and joins them. Over time, many other Starfleet officers do the same.
- The Dominion makes first contact with the Federation when Sisko is detained by Jem'Hadar soldiers in the Gamma Quadrant. At the same time, a Jem'Hadar strikeforce destroys the Gamma Quadrant colony of New Bajor and the *U.S.S. Odyssey*.

2371

- To meet the Dominion threat, Starfleet assigns the prototype *U.S.S. Defiant* to DS9. To assist in the defense of the Alpha Quadrant, the Romulan Star Empire equips the *Defiant* with a cloaking device.
- The Federation attempts unsuccessfully to open relations with the Dominion. The Founders' homeworld is discovered, and Odo learns that the Founders are his own kind, a species of changelings.
- Bashir learns that the Jem'Hadar are a genetically engineered species dependent for their survival upon a crucial isogenic enzyme that their physiology cannot produce naturally. The enzyme can only be obtained through the intravenous delivery of the chemical compound ketracel-white, which is created and rationed by the Dominion to maintain its control over the Jem'Hadar.
- The Cardassian Union and Bajor sign an historic peace treaty, negotiated by Bareil, who dies during the final stages of the negotiations.
- With Sisko's sponsorship, Nog becomes the first Ferengi to apply to Starfleet Academy.
- Grand Nagus Zek of the Ferengi Alliance obtains the Orb of Wisdom from the Cardassians and returns it to Bajor.
- The Cardassian Obsidian Order and the Romulan Tal'Shiar intelligence agencies hatch a covert plan to destroy the Founders' homeworld. The Founders learn of it and annihilate the combined attack fleet.
- While hunting sabre bear on Kang's Summit, Klingon General Martok is abducted and replaced by a Founder.
- Jake Sisko introduces his father to Kasidy Yates, a civilian freighter captain. Sisko and Yates later become romantically involved.
- Former resistance fighter Shakaar Edon is elected First Minister of Bajor.
- Sisko is promoted to captain.
- To save the *Defiant* and prevent the outbreak of a new war with the Tzenkethi, Odo kills a Founder impersonating a Federation ambassador. It is the first time that one changeling has killed another.

- Dax and Bashir are promoted to lieutenant commander and full lieutenant, respectively.
- On Cardassia, the civilian Detapa Council seizes power from the Central Command and what's left of the Obsidian Order.

2372

- At the instigation of the Founder impersonating Martok, the Klingon Empire invades Cardassia. The Federation objects, and in response the Klingons withdraw from the Khitomer Accords, ending their alliance with the Federation. Hostilities between the Klingons and the Cardassians, and between the Klingons and the Federation, continue for over a year.
- Lieutenant Commander Worf, former security chief of the *Enterprise,* is assigned to DS9 as strategic operations officer and commander of the *Defiant.*
- Bashir discovers that it is possible (though exceedingly rare) for a Jem'Hadar to be born without a dependency upon ketracel-white.
- Nog leaves DS9 to attend Starfleet Academy.
- Fear of changeling infiltration leads Admiral Leyton to attempt a Starfleet *coup d'etat*. It is thwarted by Sisko.
- While on Earth, Odo is surreptitiously infected by the autonomous covert organization Section 31 with a virus intended to wipe out the Founders.
- Kira and Shakaar become romantically involved.
- Yates is arrested for smuggling supplies to the Maquis. She is convicted and sentenced to six months in a Federation prison.
- A pregnant Keiko O'Brien is seriously injured. Bashir is able to save the unborn child, but only by implanting it in the body of Kira, who volunteers to carry the child to term.
- Odo is found guilty of murder by the Founders and, as punishment, is made a "solid." In the process, he unknowingly infects the Founders' Great Link with the genocidal virus created by Section 31.

2373

- The Founder impersonating Martok is exposed and killed on Ty'Gokor.
- Worf and Dax become romantically involved.
- The Cardassians return the Orb of Time to the Bajorans.
- Bashir is abducted by the Dominion and replaced by a Founder.
- Cadet Nog returns to DS9 as part of his academy training.
- Yates completes her prison sentence and returns to DS9.
- After suffering a neural shock, Sisko experiences visions that lead him to unearth the Bajoran city of B'hala, lost for millennia. At the same time, premonitions of disaster compel him to persuade Bajor to delay its imminent entry into the Federation.
- Kira gives birth to the son of Miles and Keiko O'Brien, who name the child Kirayoshi.

- Odo finds an infant changeling, but it dies of radiation poisoning. Upon its death, its remains are absorbed into Odo's body, turning him back into a changeling.
- The Cardassian Union joins the Dominion after months of secret negotiation between the Dominion and Dukat. A massive Dominion fleet enters the Alpha Quadrant to assume direct control of Cardassia. The Klingon Empire and the Federation renew their alliance. An attempt to destroy Bajor's sun by the Founder impersonating Bashir is thwarted.
- Worf and Garak rescue the real Martok and Bashir from a Dominion prison in the Gamma Quadrant. Martok becomes the Klingon Empire's official representative on DS9.
- Bashir's genetic enhancement is exposed, but he is allowed to retain his status in exchange for his father's voluntary imprisonment.
- Kira and Shakaar end their romance.
- Working together, the Cardassians and the Jem'Hadar exterminate the Maquis, leaving few survivors.
- Open war with the Dominion breaks out. At Sisko's urging, Bajor signs a non-aggression pact with the Dominion. As Dominion forces take DS9, all Starfleet personnel withdraw from the region. The station is renamed Terok Nor and put under the joint command of the Vorta Weyoun and Dukat, with Kira, Odo, and the rest of the Bajoran staff still intact.

2374

- With the aid of a resistance group led by Kira, Starfleet forces retake DS9. Dukat is captured. At Sisko's insistence, the Prophets prevent Dominion reinforcements from coming through the wormhole, but the entities warn Sisko that their intervention carries a price.
- Dukat's former aide-de-camp Damar is promoted to legate and made the new leader of Cardassia under the Dominion.
- Nog earns a battlefield commission of ensign.
- Martok is made Supreme Commander of the Ninth Fleet.
- Worf and Dax marry.
- Dukat escapes Starfleet custody.
- Section 31 attempts to recruit Bashir. Although he refuses to join, the organization will continue to consider him an operative.
- Betazed falls to the Dominion.
- With the aid of Garak, Sisko manipulates the Romulans into allying with the Federation and the Klingons against the Dominion.
- Kira and Odo become romantically involved.
- Dukat makes a pact with the Pah-wraiths, the enemies of the wormhole entities. Using Dukat as their instrument, they seal the wormhole, killing Jadzia in the process. The Dax symbiont survives.
- En route to Trill aboard the *U.S.S. Destiny,* the Dax symbiont takes a turn for the worse, necessitating an emergency implantation into Ensign Ezri Tigan,

a Trill who never intended to be joined, but reluctantly becomes Dax's ninth host.
- Kira is promoted to colonel.

2375

- On the planet Tyree, Sisko discovers the Orb of the Emissary and learns that the wormhole entities were responsible for his very existence. This previously unknown tenth orb also reopens the wormhole.
- Ezri Dax is promoted to lieutenant (j.g.) and is assigned to DS9 as a counselor.
- The disease created by Section 31 starts to manifest among the Founders.
- Ensign Nog loses a leg in battle on AR-558. The limb is subsequently replaced by a biosynthetic leg.
- Dukat has himself surgically altered to pass as a Bajoran in order to turn Winn against the Prophets, and to use her to unleash the Pah-wraiths.
- Sisko and Yates marry. Shortly thereafter, they conceive a child.
- The Breen ally with the Dominion. Fearing for Cardassia, Legate Damar rebels against the Dominion and forms a Cardassian resistance.
- Sisko sends Kira, Odo, and Garak to the aid of Damar's resistance. To help Kira gain the Cardassians' acceptance, Sisko grants her a Starfleet commission with the rank of commander.
- The *Defiant* is destroyed in battle against the Dominion and the Breen at the Chin'toka system.
- Odo begins to manifest symptoms of the disease ravaging the Founders.
- Worf kills Klingon leader Gowron in honorable combat and names Martok the new chancellor of the empire.
- Bashir extracts the cure to the Founder disease from the mind of Section 31 operative Luther Sloan. Sloan commits suicide, but Bashir succeeds in curing Odo.
- The *Defiant*-class *U.S.S. Sao Paolo* is assigned to DS9 under Sisko's command. Special dispensation is granted to rechristen the ship the *U.S.S. Defiant*.
- Bashir and Dax become romantically involved.
- Zek retires and appoints Rom his successor as Grand Nagus of the Ferengi Alliance.
- Federation, Klingon, Romulan, and rebellious Cardassian forces fight to retake Cardassia from the Dominion and the Breen. In retaliation for the Cardassians' betrayal, the Female Changeling orders the entire planetary population put to death. Odo provides the cure for the disease and his return to the Great Link in exchange for the Dominion's surrender, but at least 800 million Cardassians have already been executed.
- Dukat and Winn go to the fire caves of Bajor to unleash the Pah-wraiths. Sisko stops them, but at a cost. Winn is killed, and Dukat becomes trapped

with the Pah-wraiths. Sisko joins the entities in the wormhole, but promises to return.

- O'Brien transfers to the faculty staff of Starfleet Academy on Earth. Worf is made Federation Ambassador to the Klingon Empire. Garak returns home to aid in the rebuilding of Cardassia. Nog is promoted to lieutenant (j.g.). Kira returns to her Bajoran rank of colonel and becomes commanding officer of Deep Space 9.

AVATAR: Book One

S. D. Perry

For Mÿk, who puts up with me on deadline.

One meets destiny often on the road taken to avoid it.

—FRENCH PROVERB

2376

Three Months Later

Prologue

At night, when the tunnels of B'hala were empty, dust swept through on tireless winds. The night breezes were relentless in their irregular keening, the soft, lonely sounds trailing over heaps of dry and crumbling soil, lingering in the corners and dark spaces of the long lost city. Like the gentle cries of shades and spirits lamenting the daily disturbances of their tomb.

Sometimes, particularly at night when he couldn't sleep, Jacob Isaac Sisko thought he might like to write about those ancient spirits—a short piece of fiction, or even a poem—but those instances were few and far between. For the first time in years he had put aside his writing padd, and for the time being, at least, he didn't miss it much. Besides, by the end of each day, he was usually too exhausted to do more than eat, pull off his boots, and crawl into his cot, the sheets heavy with dust in spite of the air recycler. His sleep was deep and peaceful, and if he dreamed, he didn't remember upon waking.

Last night, though . . .

He wasn't quite ready to think about that; he concentrated instead on the small patch of dry and faded earth beneath his fingers, on the feel of the brush in his hand as he carefully dusted. Behind him, Prylar Eivos droned on about some of the recent discoveries in the southernmost section of the dig, his ponderous voice seeming to draw the very life out of the tunnel's cool, recycled air. Eivos was a nice enough man, but probably the most dreadfully dry of all the student overseers; the aging monk seemed to be perfectly happy with the sound of his own voice, regardless of whether or not the content was relevant to anything. Jake tuned in for a moment, still brushing at what would almost certainly turn out to be yet another pottery shard.

". . . but there was one figurine among the rest that was carved out of jevonite, which is nothing short of extraordinary," the prylar said, his tone suggesting that he'd devoted great thought to the matter. "As you know, it has always been believed that jevonite could be found only on Cardassia . . ."

Jake tuned out again, paying just enough attention to know when to nod respectfully. From farther down the tunnel he could hear the soft hum of the solids detectors and the repetitive *chunk* of manually worked picks and shovels. They were pleasant sounds, a bright counterpart to the nights of ghostly crying from ancestors not his own. . . .

He *was* feeling a bit on the poetic side lately, wasn't he? It was strange, unearthing fragments from an ancient culture, and stranger still that the culture wasn't even his—

—Dad's, though, in a way, and in the dream—

He shut that thought down before it could get any further, afraid of the concomitant feelings, afraid of what he might uncover. And he realized that, beneath the soft bristles of his brush, a sliver of color had appeared, a dull red against the lighter soil.

Jake waited for a break in Prylar Eivos's oratory.

"...but then, quantum-dating of the jevonite artifacts unearthed at the site proves indisputably that they actually predate the First Hibetian civilization," the monk stated firmly, and took a deep breath.

"I think I've found it," Jake said quickly.

The prylar smiled, stepping forward and crouching, using the tunnel wall as a support. He pulled his own brush from a fold in his robes and whisked the remaining soil from around the piece with practiced ease. As Jake suspected, it was another broken clay shard. For every intact relic that was uncovered at B'hala, there seemed to be about a billion broken ones.

And they all have to be catalogued.

"Let's see what we have here ... ah, very good, Jake!" The prylar stepped back, reaching for one of the innumerable trays on the nearby cart. "And how gratifying—it's kejelious, one of the most important materials used during the Sh'dama Age. Have I ever told you about kejelious? I don't know if anyone truly appreciates how versatile it can be, when the liquid ratios are altered ..."

Jake nodded, smiling, seeing no point in reminding the monk that he'd already heard all about the virtues of the stuff, twice. Eivos really was a nice old guy, and seemed to be genuinely excited about the work—though for the first time in all his weeks at B'hala Jake found himself feeling disappointed, gazing at the slender fragment as the monk eased it from the ground.

Maybe because it's not what you came here to find, his mind whispered, and it was another thought that he pushed away—but not so quickly as he might have only a few days before. Things were changing whether he liked it or not, and though he knew it was inevitable, had known for some weeks, a part of him was still fighting to avoid the next step.

Acceptance.

When the prylar suggested that they break for a meal, Jake was relieved. He hurried away, suddenly eager to be out of the tunnels where the dead were dust and wind, where his father was a ghost that could only be longed for.

It was late in the afternoon before he thought of it again.

The dream, Jake. Last night.

He felt a tingle at the back of his neck, a subtle shiver of remembered dream-reality—something about the wormhole ...?

Jake sighed, still not sure he wanted to remember. Not sure he was ready, in spite of the fact that he'd been having trouble concentrating for the last several days, really. He was alone in one of the smaller catalog rooms, a constant, soft drone of activity filtering in through several openings that had once been windows; he leaned back in his chair and closed his eyes, breathing deeply.

As far down as they were, second level up from the tunnels, it was always pleasantly cool, and although a lot of the volunteers preferred to work in the larger, climate-controlled areas, he liked the fresh air. Usually it kept him alert, but he'd been daydreaming since lunch. Well, since breakfast, technically, although working with Prylar Eivos would make an android's mind wander....

Jake opened his eyes and returned his attention to the shard he'd been handling, one of several from the area he thought of as the Kitchens, over at the northeast end of the partially unearthed city. Number, 1601; Designation, C/Utensil. The familiar numbers and keys of the database portable flew; he hardly had to look at the container tag, knowing from the curve and distinctive blue color that it was another one of the goblet sets. He'd catalogued at least thirty of them in the last few days, all from the same coordinates. Standard estimation comments from Prylar Krish, noted date of extraction . . .

. . . and had he been in the wormhole with his father? It seemed so distant, but he thought that the dream had been about him and Dad, together, flying . . .

Jake set the piece of clay aside, knowing that he had to stop dancing away from the truth of things. Away from the gentle physical and mental repetition that his time at B'hala had been about, and toward why he had come.

To accept the fact that I have to go on without him.

The hesitant thought, so simply worded on the page in his mind's eye, struck him as a little trite—but no less true or powerful for that. When no paralyzing sorrow came, he allowed the thought again, accepting the heaviness in his throat and chest. For now, at least, he had to make a life for himself.

It hurt, but there was also a forced quality to it. Or, not forced, but . . . deliberate. He knew what had to happen, what he was supposed to do, but he didn't *feel* it yet.

But Dax said that's normal, didn't she? That it could be a gradual thing, or all at once. Ezri had been very straightforward about what he might experience, telling him not to underestimate or belittle his loss, and to keep his expectations to a minimum. He'd talked to her a few times, before and after leaving the station, carefully skirting any real conversation about his father. When he'd told her about his intention to join the B'hala excavation, she'd suggested that not thinking for a while might be exactly what he needed; in the almost nine weeks since he'd started, Jake had come to agree wholeheartedly.

He'd been invited just about everywhere on Bajor after his father's disappearance. Like Kas, Jake had politely turned down each hopeful request—to speak at schools, to lead prayer groups, to extend blessings over everything from local harvest festivals to the openings of new business ventures. Kasidy had received twice as many offers; he was the Emissary's son, but Kasidy was carrying the Emissary's unborn child, a somehow more miraculous connection. They'd shared a quiet laugh about it the last time they'd talked, some small joke that was more affectionate than funny. Jake loved her for that, and had been glad to see how well she looked. Kasidy had the celebrated pregnancy glow about her, even if her eyes were a little sad.

You're still dancing, Jake, avoiding the inevitable—

Jake scowled at his inner voice. If it was inevitable, why rush? It wasn't like he was on a schedule.

Although he hadn't realized it at the time, getting away from the station had been the best thing he could've done. The initial invitation to visit B'hala had been extended by a branch of the Order of the Temple, the prylars who primarily worked the dig, and had been offered as a chance to experience Bajoran history firsthand. Being the Emissary's son surely had plenty to do with it, but Jake appreciated the less-obvious wording. He knew that B'hala had been a special place for his father. And the fact of it was, the station had been too empty without Dad, and the looks of sympathy—or worse, the well-meant platitudes from the Bajoran segment, about the Emissary's great calling—had only served to remind Jake of just how much he missed his father. Kas had been great, and his friends, especially Ezri and Nog, but B'hala had been what he needed. He'd heard about the volunteer program—usually open only to religious initiates—on the second night of what had started as a four-day visit, and had only been back to the station once, to pick up a few personal items.

He'd had time here. Time to not think, to categorize shards and books, to run artifacts between scholars and techs and prylars and vedeks. In the mornings, there were the digs, while afternoons were usually for cataloguing. Occasionally he helped out the students who hand-cleaned and preserved the crumbling stones from the many small temples that dotted the city, each etched with secrets from thousands of years past.

For all the sense of community, there were enough people milling around for Jake to feel anonymous—well, more so than on the station, anyway. Besides the initiate program, there was also a large, semi-organized group of research scientists on site. Mostly they were Bajoran archeologists, although there was a handful of recently arrived Vulcan chronologists and a few assorted off-world theology groups—not to mention a constant trickle of the faithful, devout sightseers who came to pray and meditate in the long shadow of B'hala's central *bantaca*. Jake generally avoided the spire during the daylight hours, as uncomfortable as ever with being recognized—

"Jake Sisko?"

Jake blinked, then smiled amiably at the small Bajoran woman in the doorway. *Speak of the devil,* as his grandfather liked to say. He still felt uneasy with the semi-reverent attitude that so often accompanied his name—when spoken by a Bajoran—but it was actually a relief to have his meandering self-analysis interrupted.

The stranger wore a prylar's robes, and was very obviously a member of the dig; short, silver hair contrasted sharply with her deeply tanned skin, and she had the look of leathery strength that he'd come to associate with the lifelong archeologists who had come to work at B'hala. She didn't look familiar, but there were always new people coming to the city.

"Yes?"

The monk stepped inside, and in the few seconds it took her to cross the room, Jake decided that she was nervous about something. She walked stiffly, her expression polite but blank, her hands clutching at the shoulder strap of a well-worn satchel.

She stopped in front of him and seemed to study his features, her pale eyes intent with some emotion he couldn't place. Jake waited for her to speak, interested; a break in routine, with a vague air of mystery. . . .

Give it up. She probably wants directions, or an entry reading.

The prylar smiled, revealing small white teeth and deeply etched laugh lines. "My name is Istani Reyla. I'm—I was one of the main overseers with Site Extension."

Jake nodded. Beneath the seemingly casual working atmosphere at B'hala was a well-organized system of committees and unions; Site Extension made the decisions about where to dig next and sent in the first documentation people, mostly scientists or vedeks with years of archeological experience. Interesting job; Jake had heard they'd recently excavated the oldest shrine yet discovered, in the ruins beneath B'hala.

"Nice to meet you. What can I help you with?"

The prylar reached into her bag and pulled out a narrow, loosely wrapped bundle, vaguely tube-shaped. The careful way she handed it to him suggested that it was exceptionally valuable or fragile. The package was very light, the cloth it was wrapped in organic and extremely soft.

"It's a . . . document of sorts. Very old. If—it may be—I believe it's important that you—" She grinned suddenly, and shook her head. "I'm sorry, it's been a long week." Her voice was low and musical, and Jake noticed how tired she seemed. There were dark circles under her eyes.

So much for intrigue. He smiled, setting the bundle on the counter in front of him. She seemed nice, if a little odd; *scientists.* "I understand. I have these dishes to go through, and there's a tray of jewelry ahead of you, but I can run it through the translator after that. There's kind of a backlog for the main computer, but if you don't mind a simple text, I should have it done by—"

Prylar Istani shook her head, her grin fading. "No, it's for you. It was written for you, for the son of the Emissary. I believe that unequivocally. Please, don't share it with anyone until you've read it. Whatever you decide to do after that . . ."

She took a deep breath, meeting his gaze squarely. Her own was bright and sincere. "Read it, and think about it. Trust your heart. You'll know what to do." Without another word, she turned and walked out.

Jake started to stand, then sat down again. *That* was interesting. After nine weeks of quiet and routine, he wasn't sure what to do . . . besides the obvious.

He peeled back the soft, fibrous covering, conscious of his heart beating faster at the sight of the tattered parchment inside. "Very old" was an understatement, though Istani surely knew that. Jake hadn't become an expert by any means, but from his weeks of cataloguing, he'd seen enough to make a layman's evaluation. By the uneven texture of the single page and the light shade of ink, it was the oldest document he'd yet handled. And he'd dated writings 23 millennia old.

He looked back at the suddenly boring sprawl of pottery bits he was supposed to finish and decided he couldn't wait. There was a text translation program back at his field shelter, the very one that Jadzia had augmented during that crazy "Reckoning" business over a year ago; new symbols were being added all of the time. He was ahead of schedule, anyway, and it wasn't as though anyone was waiting urgently for his next filing.

He marked where he'd left off with a tag and quickly straightened the work counter, excited about the mini-adventure—until he realized that he was looking forward to telling Dad about it. To seeing his eyes light up with interest, and the slight smile he'd wear as he listened to Jake recount the facts.

Jake took a deep breath, releasing the sorrow and anger as best he could, deciding that he'd worked on his acceptance of truth enough for one day. He had a mystery to unravel—and though he would not have admitted it out loud, he could not help the small but desperate hope that somehow, in some way, whatever he uncovered might tell his heart something about why his father had had to go.

> *. . . battles fall and fail, and there is a time of waiting, the space between breaths as the land heals and its children retire from war. The Temple welcomes many home, the faithful and the Chosen.*
>
> *A Herald, unforgotten but lost to time, a Seer of Visions to whom the Teacher Prophets sing, will return from the Temple at the end of this time to attend the birth of Hope, the Infant Avatar. The welcomed Herald shares a new understanding of the Temple with all the land's children. Conceived by lights of war, the alien Avatar opens its eyes upon a waxing tide of Awareness.*
>
> *The journey to the land hides, but is difficult; prophecies are revealed and hidden. The first child, a son, enters the Temple alone. With the Herald, he returns, and soon after, the Avatar is born. A new breath is drawn and the land rejoices in change and clarity.*

Jake rubbed his eyes, wincing at the hot and grainy feel of them, too excited to care much. It was late, hours after he normally went to bed, but he couldn't sleep. He sat at the ancient chipped desk in his small field shelter, the translation and the original in front of him, writing and rewriting the text's story in his mind. He'd lost count of how many times he'd read it, but if it was true . . . if he decided to believe it . . .

. . . everything changes, and how can I not believe it? How can I deny what's in front of me?

He'd already verified an approximate age, making it a credible artifact. To get an exact date, he'd need access to equipment in B'hala's lab complex; they had a sensor there for detecting the degradation of cytoplasmic proteins in plant cells, used specifically for pounded root parchment. It was amazing, how well-preserved most of the ancient Bajoran writings were, the materials treated by some method long lost to Bajor of the present; even the oldest books seemed to have held up better than many stone carvings from only a few centuries ago.

The remnant in front of him was way beyond "old." His tricorder had only been able to run a basic biospectral analysis, but that still put it as written between 30 and 32 millennia ago—putting it in the era of the tablet that had correctly foretold the Reckoning.

And what it says . . . the son goes into the Temple and comes back with the Herald, the lost messenger who communed with the Prophets—and in time to witness the spiritually significant birth of an alien child.

The translator's dictionary said that avatar meant "embodiment of revelation" in the document's context. The word for herald, *"elipagh,"* could also be translated as messenger or proxy, as carrier or bearer of news—and as *emissary.*

The son, him. The *elipagh,* Benjamin Sisko. The Avatar—Kas and Dad's baby, conceived in wartime, due in . . . five months, give or take. He'd have to get a ship, go into the wormhole by himself . . .

" 'Prophecies are revealed and hidden,' " he said softly, and rubbed his eyes again. Was that meant for him? Did it mean that a revealed prophecy would be hidden, or that there were things that wouldn't be revealed? Maybe it wasn't a prophecy at all; a lot of the ancient writings contradicted one another, or foretold things that had never happened.

But . . . it feels right. True. He wasn't Bajoran, and didn't share the Bajoran faith—but he'd seen and experienced enough not to doubt that the Prophets, whatever they really were, had an interest in the destiny of Bajor, and he knew from his father's encounters with the wormhole beings that feelings counted for a lot. It *felt* true, and he couldn't shake the distinct feeling that he was meant to see it.

Jake shook his head, not sure where to put such an overwhelming thought—that millennia ago, someone had foreseen *him.* And written about it.

He'd already tried to track down the prylar, but she was gone, or hiding. He wanted to know more, to ask her so many things. According to Site Extension, Prylar Istani Reyla had signed herself out for an indefinite leave of absence the day before. She'd been working alone in a newly excavated section of the tunnels, beneath B'hala's foundation. The ranjen Jake had talked to obviously thought highly of her, commenting several times on both her dedication to the Order and her reputation as a scientist. Jake had been careful not to ask too many questions; until he decided what to do, he planned to take Istani's advice.

Think about it, and trust my heart. Easier said than done, when all he could think about was that his father might be waiting, expecting Jake to come and bring him home.

He was too tired to think about much of anything anymore. Jake carefully wrapped the ragged parchment up and slid it into the top drawer of the desk, then stood and stretched. He had to try to get some sleep.

He crawled into bed, tapping the manual light panel at the head of the cot and pulling the dusty coverlet to his chest in the sudden dark. He doubted he'd be able to fall asleep right away, but it was his last coherent thought before he drifted off into an uneasy slumber—and he dreamed again of Dad, dreamed that the two of them were flying through space without a ship, his father laughing and holding his small child's hand as they swam through the infinite black.

Chapter One

The freighter was Cardassian, of an older class, and everyone on board was about to die.

I'm dreaming, Kira thought. She had to be, but the awareness brought no relief. The details were too real, the sensations too vivid. She stood at the entrance of a large cargo bay, the curved and heavy lines of the ship obviously Cardassian, the kind once used to transport laborers and plunder during the occupation. And in front of her, sprawled amidst the broken crates and overturned bins, were a few dozen raggedly dressed Bajorans and a handful of Cardassian soldiers, gasping for air, many of them already unconscious, bathed in the dull glow of the ship's emergency lights. Life-support failure.

She clamped down on a flutter of panic, inhaling deeply—and though she could breathe easily, she had to clamp down even harder, her senses telling her that she couldn't possibly be asleep. The air was cold and sharp, and she could smell the fading scents of sweat and fear and watery katterpod bean gruel, the smell of the Bajoran camps where she'd spent her short childhood. It was dark, the only light coming from emergency backup, casting everything in deep red shadow, and the only sound—besides the pounding of her heart—was the hopeless, laboring beat of slow asphyxiation, a chorus of strained and pitiful hisses.

She stepped into the storage bay, afraid, struggling to stay calm, to try to make sense of what was happening.

The clothes, the Cardassian's weapons, the very status of the Bajorans—occupation. And from the bulkiness of the guard's uniforms, probably from before she was born.

Kira stepped further inside, feeling old defenses rise to the surface, grateful for them. Though bloodless, it was as terrible a death scene as any she'd witnessed. Except for the struggle to breathe, nobody moved. Most of the Bajorans had huddled into couples and small groups to die, clinging to one another for whatever pitiful comfort they could find. There were several children, their small, unmoving bodies cradled in the thin arms of their elders. Kira saw a dead woman clutching a pale infant to her breast and looked away, fighting to maintain control. The Cardassian soldiers were in no better shape; they still gripped their weapons but were obviously helpless to use them, their gray, reptilian faces more ashen than they should have been, their mouths opening and closing uselessly. The image of fish out of water came to her, and wouldn't go away.

Kira turned in a circle, dizzy from the helpless terror she saw reflected in so many eyes, so many more glazing as they greeted death—and saw something so unlikely that the disaster's full impact finally gripped her, sank its dark teeth into her and held on tightly.

Two young men, slumped together against the wall to her right, their stiffening arms around each other in a last desperate need for solace, for the consolation of another soul with whom to meet the lonely shadows of death. One was Bajoran. The other, a Cardassian.

What's happening, why is this happening? Her composure was slipping, the things she saw all wrong—foreign to her mind and spirit, a nightmare from without her consciousness. She was lost in some place she had never known, witnessing the final, wrenching moments of people she'd never met. *Stop, this has to stop, wake up, Nerys, wake up.*

A new light filtered through her haze of near-panic. It filled the room, coming from somewhere above and toward the back of the cavernous space. It was the pale blue light she'd always thought of as miraculous and beautiful, the light of the Prophets. Now it threw strange shadows over the dying faces of the doomed men, women, and children, combining with the emergency lights to paint everything a harsh purple.

She felt herself drawn toward the source of the light, breathing the air of her youth. For some reason, she couldn't pinpoint the light's origin. It was bright enough, and well defined—but there was a sort of haze at the back of the bay, obscuring the exact location. It was like looking at a sun from under deep water, the light source shifting and unsteady, far away. Kira walked on—and then she was in the haze, like a mist of darkness, and the light was as bright as a star's, only a few meters in front of her.

Nerys.

A voice, spoken or thought, she wasn't sure, but there was no doubting its owner—and there he was, emerging from the dark like a spirit, like a *borhya*. He stepped in front of the light and was enveloped by it, his face serene and aware, his deep gaze searching for hers. The Emissary, Captain Sisko. Benjamin.

He's been waiting for me. . . .

Colonel Kira . . .

Kira, this is

". . . is Security. Colonel?"

"Go ahead," Kira croaked, and opened her eyes as she bolted up, instantly awake. Her room. Her bed. A man's voice on the com . . . Devro?

Dream, just a dream but it was so—

"*I'm sorry to wake you, Colonel, but there's been an attack on board the station.*" It was definitely Devro, newly assigned to security, and he sounded excited.

Kira sat up, blinking, forcing herself to leave the dream behind. "What happened?"

"*Ah, I don't have the details, Colonel, but it appears that at least one person was killed, possibly two. The lieutenant said that she'd meet you at Medical D.*"

Autopsy facilities. Kira felt a rush of anger. Quark's, it had to be, and he was going to be sorry this time. There had been several drunken riots in his place in the past few months; no fatalities, but it had only been a matter of time. Just two weeks before, a female Argosian had stabbed one of Quark's servers for mixing up a drink order. He'd been lucky to survive.

I told him to start cutting them off earlier . . . and where the hell was security? After I specifically ordered higher visibility on the Promenade?

"On my way," she said, and Devro signed off. The computer informed her that it was 0530, only a half hour before she had to get up, anyway. She swung her feet to the floor but sat for a moment, eyes closed. Bad news after a bad dream, after a whole series of bad days. Frustrating ones, anyway, with the station's overhaul running past schedule; she had enough to do without having to worry about the continuing stream of die-hard revelers on the station, still looking for a party to celebrate the end of the war. Or having to babysit her new security chief, a woman to whom inconstancy was no stranger.

She dressed quickly, her anxiety growing as her mind began to work, as she woke up and considered the possibility that Quark's had nothing to do with the incident. Maybe she should talk to Jast about trying again to request a few additional security details from Starfleet, just until things settled a little. . . .

. . . *wishful thinking. Might as well have her ask for a few dozen Starfleet engineers while she's at it, and the backup tactical and science cadets to fill out the duty rosters, not to mention medical.* They'd have as much luck requesting a new station made out of gold-pressed latinum. The Federation's postwar reconstruction efforts meant that Starfleet's resources were spread thin, almost to the point of being ineffectual in some places. Not to mention their humanitarian work, the aid being extended to independent worlds and cultures that had been damaged by the war. Politically, it made sense—the new allies and friends they were making meant potential new Federation members, and if that meant that facilities like DS9 had to run overextended and understaffed for a while longer—well, those facilities would just have to make do with what they had.

Some of us more than others. As if they didn't have enough to do, DS9 had also been designated the official coordinator for the multi-societal relief efforts to Cardassia, which meant extra work for everyone on staff. With supply and aid ships from over a dozen worlds arriving and departing daily—supplemented by an ever-changing number of freelance "ships for hire"—there seemed to be a near-constant stream of problems great and small. Add to that a strange new emotional climate on the station, like nothing the colonel had ever experienced. Although Kira had faith in the good intentions of her people, with the overwhelming majority of the station's nearly 7,500 inhabitants being Bajoran, she wasn't so certain that DS9 was the best choice for the restoration effort, regardless of their position and capacity.

First Minister Shakaar had disagreed, arguing that Bajor's willingness to take point in the relief efforts would be an important step toward rapprochement with the Cardassians . . . as well as in Bajor's renewed petition to join the Federation. "Besides, Nerys," Shakaar had said, "you were there. You saw what it was like. How can we *not* help them?"

The question, so gently asked, had left Kira unable to argue as she recalled the carnage and destruction the Dominion had wrought. There was a time, she knew, when she might have looked on Cardassia's fate as a kind of poetic justice. But thinking back on the blackened, smoking ruins, the corpses that lay everywhere, the shocked and vacant faces of the survivors . . . It was no longer possible to view them as the enemy that had raped Bajor for half a century.

But while convincing Kira of the role that Bajor, and DS9 especially, was to play in the healing of Cardassia had been relatively easy . . . the Bajoran populace was another matter. A Bajoran installation providing aid to the Cardassian homeworld? Irony was seldom so obvious, and the atmosphere of reluctant, often grudging charity from some of the Bajorans aboard the station was less than ideal.

At least Starfleet had given her Tiris Jast. The commander had already proven herself able to work miracles when it came to administrative matters, among other things; after a somewhat rocky start, Kira's new first officer had turned out to be a definite asset.

It wasn't until Kira checked herself in the mirror on the way out the door that she thought about the dream again, and was surprised by the sudden loneliness she felt, the loneliness she saw in her tired reflection. *Was* it just a dream? And if it wasn't, what meaning was she supposed to take from it?

It would have been nice to talk to Benjamin again, under any circumstances. . . .

"Get moving, Colonel," she said softly, straightening her shoulders, her gaze hardening. She was the commanding officer of Starbase Deep Space 9, arguably the single most important outpost in the Alpha Quadrant, and there was a matter on board requiring her immediate attention. How she felt about it—or anything, lately—was of secondary consideration.

Will of the Prophets, she told herself, and taking a deep breath, she stepped out of her quarters and started for mid-core.

The colonel marched in looking alert and fully rested, like always, making Ro Laren wonder—and not for the first time—if the woman ever slept. Ro herself had been dragged out of bed on four hours of sleep, and was feeling it; her days of catching a few moments here and there and calling it even were long gone.

"Report, Lieutenant."

Brisk and efficient, undoubtedly Kira's finest qualities; Ro could respect her, at least. Too bad it didn't seem to be mutual.

"At this point, it appears to be a botched robbery attempt," Ro said. "Two dead, the victim and the perpetrator, both Bajoran civilians. Dr. Bashir is conducting the autopsies—"

"Where did it happen?" Kira interrupted. "The attack?"

"Promenade, in front of Quark's. I've got people talking to the witnesses now . . ."

The colonel's eyes had narrowed slightly, and Ro hurried on, remembering their last terse encounter. "There was a strong security presence in and around Quark's, as you, ah, *suggested,* but it didn't seem to matter. He stabbed the woman in front of a crowd, took her bag, and ran. Two of my deputies chased him to the second level, where he attempted to jump one of the railings. He fell badly, he died."

Kira nodded. "Who was he?"

"We don't have an ID yet. He came to the station yesterday, but apparently he was using a false name. He wasn't much of a thief, whoever he was; there was nothing in her bag but a few personal items. The woman was a monk, a Prylar Istani Reyla; she'd only been here two days, which makes me wonder if he somehow came after her specifically—"

Ro broke off, surprised at the change in Kira's demeanor. The color had drained from her face, and her eyes were wide and shocked.

"Reyla? Istani Reyla?" Kira whispered.

Ro nodded, uncomfortably aware that Kira knew the victim. "Yes. Colonel . . . are you all right?"

Kira didn't answer. She turned and walked away, headed for the door that led into the autopsy room. Ro hesitated, then followed her, wondering if she should say something else. Something comforting. She and Kira didn't get along, but they weren't exactly enemies, either. Shar had been pushing the idea that they were too much alike—both strong, stubborn Bajoran women with histories of following their own rules. . . .

. . . and if I was also judgmental and blindly pious, we'd definitely have something in common.

Ro sighed inwardly as she stepped into the autopsy room, reminding herself that she'd rarely been accused of open-mindedness. Besides, she'd only been on the station for six weeks, and although she didn't feel the need to prove herself to the many doubters on board—and doubted herself that it was possible—she was aware that even a grudging acceptance would take time.

Dr. Bashir was speaking softly, standing over Istani's body as Kira stared down numbly at the woman's still face. Ragged circles of blood radiated from several wounds in the old woman's chest, staining her monk's robes a dark, shining crimson.

". . . several times, and with an erose blade. The atrioventricular node was destroyed, effectively severing neuromuscular communication between the chambers of the heart. Even if I'd been standing by with a surgical team, it's unlikely that she could have been saved."

Ro saw the pain in Kira's wet gaze and immediately regretted her unkind thoughts. It was the first time she'd seen the colonel display any emotion beyond impatient irritation, at least in front of her, and it had the instant effect of making her want to leave, to allow Kira some privacy with her pain. If Ro had just lost a friend, she'd hope for the same consideration.

Kira reached out and gently touched Istani's face with the back of her hand. Bashir's demeanor changed abruptly, from subdued respect to open concern.

"Nerys, did you know her?"

Kira's hand trembled against Istani's slack cheek. "At the camps, when I was a child. At Singha. She was a good friend to my parents, and after my mother left . . . she was a good friend. She watched out for us."

The doctor's voice became even softer. "I'm so sorry. If it's any help to you, I don't believe she suffered."

The three of them stood for a moment, Bashir's words lingering in the cool, sterile air, Ro feeling out of place as a witness to Kira's grief. She was about to excuse herself when the colonel began to speak again, almost to herself.

"I've been meaning to contact her, it's been . . . five years? The last time we spoke, she was on her way to Beta Kupsic, for an archeological dig."

Ro couldn't stop herself. "Do you know when she got back?"

Kira looked up and seemed to collect herself, straightening away from the body. "Just before the Peldor Festival, I think, for the Meditation for Peace; the Vedek Assembly called everyone home. That was five months ago."

Ro nodded, biting her tongue. She knew when the Peldor Festival was. "Did you know she was coming here? To the station?"

Kira shook her head. There was another awkward silence, for Ro, at least, and then the colonel turned to her, seeming entirely in control once more. "I expect a full investigation, Lieutenant, and I want to know what you find as soon as you find it. I'll expect your initial report before the end of the day."

"Yes, sir," Ro said. Her first real case; a flutter of anxiety touched her and was gone. She was ready.

"If there's anything I can do . . ." Bashir started.

The colonel managed a faint smile. "Thank you, Julian. I'll be fine."

She nodded briskly at Ro and walked out of the room without a backward glance, as composed as when she'd entered.

She had to admire the woman's self-control. Ro had lived through resettlement camps, and knew something about the kinds of bonds that could be forged under dire conditions. When she was with the Maquis, too . . . the friends she had made and lost . . .

"Was there something else you needed, Lieutenant?"

Not impolite by any means, but the doctor's voice had lost its former warmth. She supposed she should be grateful it wasn't open hostility; her history with Starfleet wasn't going to win her any friends among its personnel.

"No, thank you, Doctor. I'm sure your report will answer any questions I might have."

Bashir smiled civilly and picked up a padd, turning away. Her cue. Ro started to leave, but couldn't help a final look at Istani Reyla. Such gentle character in the lines around her eyes and mouth; to have survived the camps and the war, to have lived a life devoted to humble faith, only to die in a robbery . . .

What would a prylar have worth stealing? Worth being murdered for?

That was the question, wasn't it? Istani's bag was locked up in the security office, and Ro decided that she needed to take a closer look at its contents. She wasn't going to give anyone a reason to doubt her appointment to DS9; they didn't have to like her, any of them, but she *would* do her job, and do it well.

"Doctor," she said, as way of good-bye, and left him to his work.

Kira was on the lift to ops when it hit her. She acted without thinking, slamming her fist into the wall once, twice, the skin breaking across two of her knuckles. No pain, or at least nothing close to the boiling darkness inside of her, the acid of sorrow and loneliness grasping at her heart. She was sick with it. Reyla, dead. Murdered.

She let out a low moan and sagged against the wall, cradling her wounded hand. For a second, it threatened to overwhelm her, all of it—Reyla; the dream, like some dark omen; the fading memory of Odo's arms around her when she felt alone, so alone . . .

. . . *deal with it. You don't have time for this, and you* will *deal with it, and everything will be as it should be, have faith, have faith* . . .

Kira took a few deep breaths, talking herself through it, letting go . . . and by the time she reached ops she was through the very worst of it, and prepared to bear the weight of another day.

Chapter Two

Although he was only three minutes late, Kasidy was already waiting when Bashir got to the infirmary, sitting on the edge of one of the diagnostic tables and chatting with Dr. Tarses.

"...and I'll want to do some planting in the spring," Kasidy was saying, her back to Bashir as he approached. "Kava, I think. If I'm not too fat to bend over by then."

Bashir noted the readout over the bed with a practiced eye as he joined them, pleased with the slight weight gain since her last checkup. Perfectly within normal human parameters. "In five months you'll be big as a runabout, I imagine," he said. "Bending over shouldn't be a problem, though standing back up might take work."

His listeners laughed, and Julian felt his spirits lift. Getting up early to conduct autopsies was not his idea of a pleasant morning, and for Kira's friend to have been murdered ...

Poor Nerys. Bad enough to lose someone important, but practically, the timing couldn't be worse. Kira wasn't always good at delegating responsibility, too often overburdening herself, and the current upgrades to the station were no exception. With the Federation and Bajor both re-organizing their resources and personnel—along with practically everyone else in the Alpha Quadrant—DS9 had been operating understaffed anyway; technical support personnel were in short supply, and even with Jast to take over arrangements with Starfleet, Kira wasn't smiling as much as she used to. The look on her face when she'd touched her friend ...

... Ezri should speak to her, professionally. Assuming she can find the time in the next year or two.

The slightly sour thought surprised him, although only until he remembered the reason. Ezri had already been gone when he'd gotten the call that woke him, off to help Nog with some engineering conundrum. Again. Funny, how quickly he'd gotten used to having her beside him when he woke. And how much he missed her when she wasn't there.

Tarses handed over the shift report and said his good-byes, leaving them in relative privacy. Both nurses on duty, Bajorans, stayed a respectful distance away—although he would have to speak to them about the beaming glances they couldn't seem to help shooting in Kasidy's direction. He knew that the Emissary's wife didn't care much for the attention, resigned to it or no.

Julian pulled up a chair and sat, calling up Kasidy's charts on a widescreen padd. It had been two weeks since he'd seen her last, for a topical rash she'd picked up on her last run to the Orias system. It had turned out to be an extremely mild allergic reaction to a shipment of Rakalian *p'losie* that had gone bad, thanks to a malfunctioning refrigeration unit.

"So. Tell me how you're feeling these days." He glanced at her hands. "No more bumps, I see. I assume you're staying away from Rakalian fruit?"

Kasidy nodded, smiling. "Absolutely. In fact, I'm staying away from the cargo holds altogether. Other than that, let's see . . . I feel pretty good, I guess. Still no more morning sickness. I'm a little tired, even though it seems like I'm sleeping at least ten hours a night. Oh, and I've recently developed a craving for anything made with ginger root, of all things."

Julian ran the bed's diagnostic against a hand-held tricorder's as she spoke, careful to keep the screen away from her line of sight; Kasidy insisted on keeping to a family tradition regarding ignorance of gender prior to birth. The child's sex was listed in the upper left corner, along with the series of numbers that suggested textbook normal development for the fourth month. Both she and the child were doing remarkably well.

"I guess I shouldn't be surprised," Kasidy continued. "Ben loved ginger. He said . . ." Her smile faded slightly, her hands moving to her belly. "He said there was no such thing as a good stir-fry without ginger."

Julian nodded, setting aside his tricorder and focusing his full attention on Kasidy. "I remember. He made it for me once, with Bajoran shrimp. It was wonderful."

Kasidy smiled crookedly, still holding her lower belly. "I've been thinking I should take up cooking. I never wanted to, before, but I set up the kitchen just like he wanted. It seems a shame to let it go to waste."

Sisko's dream house, in the Kendra province on Bajor. He'd bought the land just before the end of the war, and Kasidy had decided to build the home he'd designed and live there until his return. Through Kira, Julian knew that she'd agonized over the kitchen, about everything from whether or not to put in a dividing wall to what kind of appliances Sisko would want.

"It's finished already?" Julian asked. "Last I heard, there was some problem finding the right kind of, ah, cooking device."

"Quark came through," Kasidy said. "Don't ask me where he found it, either. Original wood stoves are hard to come by these days. As for the rest of the house, you'd be surprised how quickly things go when everyone on the planet wants you to get settled in."

"That's all right with you, isn't it?" Julian asked gently.

"Most of the time. They care about him, too, in their own way."

She seemed a bit melancholy, but not actually depressed. Under the circumstances, it was the best he could hope for. Having one's love whisked away to fulfill his own spiritual destiny couldn't be easy, particularly with a baby on the way. Love could be such a tenuous thing, running from emotional ecstasy to fear of loss and back again in a matter of days, hours, really. There were times he felt so connected to Ezri, so elated with what they had, that it was hard to accept the distance that could grow up between them sometimes, as sudden and strange as . . .

". . . a robbery on board. Julian?"

He started. "I'm sorry, I'm a bit distracted this morning. You were saying?"

"I said that the station seems different now. Even dangerous sometimes. Did you hear about the robbery?"

"Yes. Two people were killed, I'm sorry to say."

Kasidy shook her head. "There are just so many strangers here, lately. I really think this move will be good for me. For us."

Julian smiled. "I think that anything that makes you happy will be good for you, and the baby."

She patted the swell beneath her fingers. "Me, too. Another two weeks and we'll be setting up house. We'll be visiting a lot—I'm still part-time with the Commerce Ministry, at least until the big day—but Bajor will be home."

A positive note to end on. He stood up, and was about to tell her to check in before she left, when she asked him a question he wasn't sure how to answer.

"So, distracted, huh? How *are* things going with Ezri?"

"I'm—fine. Well, I think." He felt suddenly flustered, and sat down again. Kasidy's kind expression was inviting, and he hadn't really had a chance to talk about his relationship since—since Miles had left.

Has it really been that long? He shared so much with Ezri, it hadn't occurred to him to talk *about* her with anyone. And things were going well, weren't they?

Julian took a deep breath, and started talking. And quickly discovered that he had more to say than he thought.

As usual, there was a lull in business as the last of the late-night drinkers straggled out and the early breakfast crowd chirped in, but there was a fifteen percent drop from the day before, which meant Quark wasn't happy. It was those damned security guards, hassling his clientele and the staff for details about the murder. Not only had he lost half of his breakfasters to T'Pril's—although why someone would dare Vulcan cuisine first thing in the morning was anyone's guess—he'd had to offer several of his less reputable customers free drinks just to keep them from fleeing. So when he saw Ro Laren walk into the bar, he wasn't nearly as charming as usual; as entirely awe-inspiring as she was, fifteen percent was enough to shrivel his lobes.

"How about you tell your people to leave my customers alone?" he snapped, in lieu of a greeting. "If I remember correctly—and I do—the incident occurred *outside,* on the Promenade. Not in here."

Ro sat at the bar, her lean body bent toward him, a slight, curling smile playing across her lips. "And a good morning to you, Quark. Would you do me a favor and take a look at this?"

Still smiling, she dropped a slip of paper on the bar and leaned back, crossing her arms. Quark ignored the slip and studied her for a moment, not sure what she was up to. He'd heard a lot of interesting things about Ro, of course, practically everyone on the station had, but he hadn't had much of a chance to interact with her on a professional level. From the stories that had preceded her arrival, he'd expected DS9's new head of security to run around throwing tantrums, stealing Federation supplies, and shooting people—but so far she'd been a disappointment, employing almost Odo-like tactics to interfere with his less than legal enterprises. She'd already managed to re-route several contraband shipments, and with Rom gone and Nog too busy to help his own uncle, Quark had been forced to actually buy a program to further randomize his security code generator.

At least Ro doesn't gloat about it. And unlike her predecessor, she's not in love with Kira. Nowhere close. The friction between the two women was already well-established, a definite point in her favor; between that and her looks, Quark wasn't quite prepared to write her off as a liability.

"Of course," he said, picking up the slip of paper and mustering his most seductive smile. "Anything for you, Lieutenant—"

He saw what was on the slip and his smile froze; his name and a series of numbers, written by that Bajoran monk. She'd promised that she would commit her storage code to memory and destroy the hard-copy scrap, but it seemed she'd gone and died before getting around to it. Aware of Ro's close scrutiny, he casually dropped it on the bar and shrugged, silently cursing. The woman was dead, but there was his reputation to consider.

"Doesn't mean a thing to me. Where did you say you found it?"

"I didn't."

He waited, but she didn't elaborate any further, only gazed at him serenely, ever smiling. Quark shrugged again, wondering how much she actually knew. *And to think, my nephew could have been security chief . . .*

"I really have no idea," Quark said finally. "Maybe she was going to meet someone here, that's why it says my name, and those numbers—could mean a time . . ."

He realized his mistake before Ro could point it out, and did his best to cover. He had to start getting to bed earlier; these late nights were killing him. "I mean, I assume this is something about that murdered woman. Isn't it?"

"Give it up, Quark. I found it in her bag and you know it, and you also know what it means." Her dark eyes sparkled. "You already owe me for not telling Kira about that shipment of phaser scopes."

Quark feigned innocence. "What phaser scopes? Really, Lieutenant, I don't know—"

Ro moved so fast he didn't have time to react, reaching across the bar and taking a firm hold of both his ears—not hard enough to hurt, but pain was imminent. Quark froze, shocked, afraid to breathe. She leaned over, so close that her soft voice tickled his left tympanic membrane, arousing in him a strange combination of excitement and terror. Her tone was as firm and unyielding as her grasp.

"Listen carefully, Quark," she half-whispered, sweet and deadly at once. "I don't have a problem with your petty schemes to make money, and unless you're dealing in something dangerous or unethical, I'm often as not willing to look the other way. I'm not Kira and I'm not Starfleet and a victimless crime is just that, right? But if you don't tell me what I want to know when I ask for it, I'll teach you new meanings of the word 'sorry.' And what I want to know right now is what *you* know about Istani Reyla. Make no mistake, this is not open to negotiation."

She abruptly let go, leaving him stunned but unhurt, and in the time it took him to catch his breath, Quark decided two things: one, that it was in his best interests to tell her about the monk—she'd really only paid him a pittance, anyway—and two, he was halfway in love.

Kasidy walked back to her quarters slowly, thinking about Dax and the doctor. She didn't know either of them as well as Ben had, especially Dax. . . .

. . . but some things never change, and probably never will. Ah, love!

Kasidy grinned. The look on Julian's face had been so sincere, so entirely heartfelt as he talked about Ezri, and the "problems" so normal. He worried that they thought differently about some things, and said she sometimes seemed bored by his work. He felt lonely sometimes, and didn't know what she was thinking. He said she wanted to be alone occasionally, and that he did, too, but was afraid for them to spend too much time apart. Every now and then, he felt overwhelmed by emotion for her—and every now and then, she got on his nerves, and what did *that* mean?

The brilliant doctor was certainly clueless in some ways, and Kasidy suspected that Ezri, for all her lifetimes, was probably on the same ship. They were in love, that was all. In love and finding out what that meant, once the initial shine wore off. Falling in love was easy; maintaining a relationship was work, no matter how emotionally or intellectually developed the participants were, and it wasn't always fun.

"I just want us to be happy. I don't want things to become dull for her. Or me," Bashir had stated, so honestly that Kasidy had been hard-pressed to keep a straight face. And he'd been visibly distressed by her advice, that there was no way to set everything up in advance, to avoid mistakes before they happened— that it would take time to learn about each other, to let things unfold.

In a way, being smart probably made it harder; Kasidy imagined that they were both trying to reason out their differences, to logically define their roles in each other's lives. To decide how to feel.

And nothing's more frustrating than having feelings you didn't decide to have.

Kasidy stopped walking, struck by the intensity of the memory. Ben had said that, not long after they'd become a regular thing. He'd been teasing her about something, she couldn't remember what, exactly, although she recalled that they'd been in bed together, talking. He had a way of doing that, of gently pointing out to her the most basic truths in life—things that she'd learned, that they'd both learned but sometimes misplaced. It was the miracle of their time together, that capacity for understanding the truth that they'd been able to share. . . .

The sense of loss flooded through her, so like a physical pain that she had to close her eyes. *Oh, baby, I know you had to go, but I miss you so much, I want you here, with me—*

Kasidy felt tears threatening, and hurriedly walked on, firmly telling herself that she would not cry, would *not,* not in public. She even managed a smile and a nod for a Bajoran couple passing by. She'd had no real choice in the matter about giving Ben up to the Prophets, but her feelings about it, at least, she could keep as her own.

My feelings. As if anyone else would want them.

It had become a full-time job for her just to keep track, so many things were changing. The connection she already felt with the baby wouldn't allow her to be truly unhappy; she was already in love with the small life, and that love kept her from descending into real sorrow—but in all, it was a very strange time for her. Most days she felt strong, positive about a future that would allow for her and Ben to be with each other, with Jake and with their child. But there were also moments that she felt a kind of emptiness inside, a fear for what could be—that too much time would pass and he would return a stranger to her, their paths so far apart that they wouldn't even be able to see each other. He was with the Prophets, after all, experiencing things she couldn't begin to imagine. And as the Emissary, what if he came back and then was called away again? What further sacrifices might they have to make? When those thoughts welled up, she felt like everything she was doing was madness—leaving her job, moving away from everything she'd known to wait for a man who might not return for months, even years....

...and that's okay. That's okay because my life will be as full as I want it to be, because I had a life before I met Benjamin Sisko and I have a life now. Two lives, she amended happily, and felt the slow, heavy warmth in her lower belly, where their child slept and grew....

Her hormones were certainly in an uproar. She felt vulnerable to herself, to the wanderings of her own mind in a way she never had been before. It was almost funny; from amusement to tears and back again, in the time it took her to walk from the turbolift to her quarters. She thought she might be able to relax once she actually moved off the station and got settled on Bajor. She could hope, anyway.

As she walked into her quarters, she realized suddenly that she was tired. Tired and in a state of mild chaos. She was a strong, independent woman, on the verge of beginning a new life for herself—but at the moment, she thought she might like to go back to bed.

Maybe with a cup of tea, and some of those ginger cookies . . .

That sounded good. Kasidy yawned, and decided that there wasn't anything on her slate that couldn't be put off for another couple of hours. If she could nap, get away from her own turbulent moods for a little while, so much the better.

"Oh, kid," she said, smiling, patting her lower belly as she headed for the replicator. "You're really something else."

Chapter Three

The colonel had not been happy with the status reports, although Shar had the impression she just wasn't happy, not this morning. He'd hardly finished listing the various systems and subsystems that were still off-line before she'd disappeared into her office, and she hadn't come out again. Not that he could blame her, given how things were progressing.

Short-range shield emitters, down. Tractor beam emitters, down. Six of the RCS thruster modules were being re-paneled, almost half of the ODN system still needed re-wiring, and the entire computer network was running on one processing core without backup. In short, the station was barely functional.

Shar sat cross-legged on the floor of the engineering station next to a partially disassembled console checking plasma power levels and half-wishing he hadn't offered to work a double shift. He didn't need as much sleep as most—about half as much as a human or Bajoran—but it had been a long week and he was tired. The constant low-level drone of conversation, of tools clattering and the occasional soft curse, was making him sleepy, and he could honestly say he'd run enough system diagnostics to last him a lifetime. Everything had to be checked and triple-checked.

This climate isn't helping much, either. The station's common areas were set to 22 degrees Celsius, 18 percent humidity; cold and dry by Andorian standards, making him long for the comfort of his quarters. Even after Starfleet Academy and a year on the *U.S.S. Tamberlaine*—with a primarily human crew—he still couldn't get used to the environmental conditions.

Shar tapped a key on the padd next to him and saw that he still had two hours to go. He briefly considered finishing with the console and leaving early—Kira and Jast had both urged him to take on half-shifts, if he insisted on working extra hours—but a look around made him decide against it. Everywhere, stacks of partially wired sensor panels leaked from gaping console chasms, the men and women in front of them certainly as tired as he. They were already three days past the original deadline for finishing, and he estimated it would be another four before everything was back up and running. And that wasn't including the *Defiant;* Lieutenant Nog's last report had suggested at least another week.

If the S.C.E. would just send a few more people . . . Typically, DS9 boasted thirty-five resident engineers from the corps, plus an affiliate group of almost as many techs from the Bajoran Militia. But in spite of Starfleet's assurances about more help coming soon, the station had been running with less than half that number since the war's end. Anyone with any engineering experience was being put to work.

Including Ensign Thirishar ch'Thane, science officer; if that isn't desperate, nothing is. He wasn't an egotistical person, or at least he hoped not, though he was aware of his worth in his field—top of his class, already published several times over, and assigned to DS9 just four weeks earlier; only his second assignment, too. When he'd first graduated from the Academy, he'd been fought over by some of the best Starfleet scientists working. But he wouldn't pretend to be any mechanical genius; when it came to the physical application of his abilities, he thought "clumsy" was probably most apt.

"Taking a break from your troubles, Ensign?"

Shar started, realizing he'd been staring blankly. He looked up into the teasing gaze of Commander Jast and smiled, pleased to see her, to hear her distinctively accented voice. Although she was considered cold by some, he liked Tiris Jast; there was something about her, something inspiring. She projected strength and confidence, as would any good commander, but there was also an unapologetic frankness in her manner that was rare in higher-ranking Starfleet officers. She openly discussed her feelings as well as her ideas, and not for any effect; she appeared to simply believe in expressing herself, whether or not it was diplomatic to do so. An interesting person and a superb officer, Shar considered himself fortunate to be working with her.

Besides which, she knows what it's like to suffer these conditions. Jast was Bolian, but came from a similar environment. In the short time that he'd been aboard, they'd commiserated more than once over the chill aridity of the station.

"Commander. No, sir. I'm just a little tired, nearing the end of my shift."

Jast shook her head. "Your second, I imagine. What have I said to you about working doubles?"

Shar nodded, trying to recall the exact phrasing. "That I'll end up freeze-dried if I don't get back to my quarters occasionally. Sir."

"That's correct." Jast glanced around, then leaned closer to Shar, speaking low. "I know things are in disarray . . . but I think you could probably slip away, if you hurry. No one is looking."

Shar grinned, fully aware that she was granting him permission to end his shift early, and relieved that he was starting to recognize it when she was being humorous. Jast was like that; she could be as officially Starfleet as they came when necessary, but didn't flaunt her rank once she became acquainted with those under her command. Or at least in his observation.

"If it's all right, sir, I think I'll stay. The colonel wanted to get as much of ops finished today as possible."

Jast nodded toward the science station, where several people were working. "Remind me why you're not handling the sensor arrays, Shar."

Shar held up his hands, flexing his long—but somehow incapable—fingers. "The work is a bit too delicate for me. I'm sort of acting as a . . . technical consultant."

"Sir," Jast added, her eyes twinkling. "You'll get better with practice, Ensign. Perhaps you should take up a musical instrument, or some sort of cloth-weaving. Work on improving your dexterity."

"Yes, sir." Now he wasn't sure if she was being serious or not. Humor was still difficult for him. Andorians smiled often, but primarily looked upon it as a diplomatic tool; they were a serious-minded people, and he was no exception.

From his time in Starfleet, however, he'd come to appreciate humor in other species, whereas most Andorians viewed too much laughter as frivolity. Or witlessness.

The commander certainly *seemed* amused. "Carry on, Ensign. And no more extra shifts for a few days, all right?"

"Yes, Commander. Thank you, sir."

Jast headed for Kira's office and Shar picked up the diagnostic padd again, glad that she'd taken the time to speak with him. Although still quite new to the station, he already liked everyone he'd met—Jast, Colonel Kira, Ro Laren, Ezri and Prynn and Turo Ane . . . Even Quark, whose hard-hearted reputation preceded him, had been very friendly, going out of his way to offer discounts on Andorian delicacies in his bar. Shar was pleased with his assignment to DS9, and hoped very much that he wouldn't be forced to leave.

The thought was a shadow, a darkness. He pushed it away and went back to work, losing himself in the simplicity of the display screen's tolinite matrix, tired but happy to be where he was.

Kira was on an audio channel with the *Aldebaran*'s first officer, a pleasantly efficient woman named Tisseverlin Janna. After giving the lieutenant commander an update on station repairs and a rundown on expected arrivals and departures, Kira dutifully listened as Janna briefly went over the day's scheduled off-duty boarding parties. She also had several questions about the station's environmental control capabilities, particularly in the holosuites. The *Aldebaran*'s two Denebian crewmembers were up for leave, and were hoping to be able to get out of their suits for a while; it seemed the *Aldebaran*'s holo facilities couldn't manage the intense conditions they required for more than an hour at a time.

"I'm sure Quark has a program," Kira offered, her voice sounding far away, as if someone else was speaking. "We had a freighter crew come through just a couple of months ago, and they had a Denebian on board. He spent a lot of time at Quark's."

Janna said something about how grateful the two ensigns would be, and started telling an anecdote about one of their suits leaking heated slime in the captain's ready room, but with their business concluded, Kira's thoughts were already elsewhere. She liked Janna, but she wasn't in the mood to talk. She needed to work, to move, to not dwell on Reyla. A friendly chat would bring her too close to letting her guard down, and having to force polite laughter was probably beyond her current capabilities. Although she'd gotten a lot better at it since taking command, diplomacy had never been her strong suit.

When Jast showed up for their daily progress meeting, Kira, relieved, apologized for having to cut Janna's story short and quickly signed off. Jast waited patiently, padd in hand, looking as composed and calm as always.

"Good morning, Colonel," Jast said. "I'm sorry I didn't get here sooner, I spent the last few hours dealing with the *Defiant*'s computer refit. Have you had a chance to look over Nog's proposal for expanding the tactical capacity?

You know, I was concerned when I first met him, he's so young, but his ideas are quite innovative."

Kira nodded. "He inherited something of his father's technological genius."

"Ah, the Grand Nagus. Rom, isn't it?"

Kira nodded again. *What do I say about the murder? How do I start?*

Jast accidentally saved her, her bright countenance fading to solemn. "I haven't had a chance to read any reports on what happened this morning, but Ezri mentioned it. Terrible. Anything Starfleet should know, or was it a civilian matter?"

Kira cleared her throat. "Ro is looking into it. At this point, there doesn't seem to be any motive beyond robbery."

"Good. It's a sorrowful affair, but with the state of things, we don't need another Federation complication. I've already worn out my welcome with Starfleet on our behalf; they keep telling me that we'll just have to wait for more techs, that with the *Aldebaran* keeping watch we don't need to hurry with the weapons arrays . . ."

Kira felt she was putting up a good front, but Jast must have seen something. She frowned, the raised ridge that ran down the center of her face wrinkling. "Colonel . . . what is it? What's wrong?"

With the huge responsibilities that they shared, the commander had become a friend in a relatively short period. Jast had been hard to get used to at the beginning, their relationship initially somewhat adversarial, but Tiris had finally relaxed. She'd made an effort to see how things worked at a deep space station, and started accommodating. Kira had come to respect the woman's honesty and sincerity, and thought Jast was coming to feel the same.

On the other hand, she and Jast were still at the foundation level of a friendship, and . . . it just didn't feel right, not yet. Besides, Kira had come to pride herself on the high degree of professionalism she had reached with all of her new officers; it made things easier, having a clean separation between the private and professional areas of her life. Bad enough that she'd already slipped in front of Ro Laren, of all people, who had been obstinately unfriendly since the day she'd arrived. . . .

"I don't know if Ro can handle the investigation," Kira said abruptly, answering Jast's question with a partial truth. "She's never done anything like this before, and what if it wasn't a robbery? I thought security would work out for her, but I may have been wrong. She hasn't even been able to identify the killer yet."

Expressionless, Jast watched her for a moment—and then spoke slowly, as if choosing her words carefully. "She is new . . . but maybe you should see how things progress before you consider replacing her."

Kira was surprised. "You're in Starfleet."

"Yes, and I know her history," Jast conceded. "Her Starfleet file actually makes rather interesting reading, especially once you realize what's missing from it. But there are multiple truths to a story, and for all of Ro's . . . missteps, she's also not afraid to cause a disturbance in order to reach her objective. That's why she was sent here, wasn't it? It would seem to me that you'd want someone in security to be headstrong, even aggressive sometimes. And she does have the tactical background."

She had a point, though Kira found herself reluctant to recognize it. It wasn't just Ro's past, although Kira was anything but reassured by her record—her Starfleet career had been a disaster, marked by bad calls and questionable choices. Many of the Starfleet people in the crew considered her a traitor and a criminal twice over, and being forced to work alongside her because the Bajoran government had insisted on her assignment to DS9 was doing nothing good for the tension level on the station. There was also her abrasive manner, and her obvious disinterest, even scorn, for her own heritage, her own cultural beliefs.

Our cultural beliefs. Ro didn't hide her rejection of the Prophets, in everything from conversation all the way down to deliberately wearing her earring on the wrong side, as if she was daring anyone to object . . . maybe Kira *was* letting her personal feelings about Ro influence her ability to evaluate her performance.

Kira sighed, deciding that it could wait for further analysis. Picking herself apart after the morning she'd had was more than she could stand.

"I want to be fair," Kira said. "And it's not as if we have anyone to replace her with." They didn't, either. Nog had acted as head of security for a couple weeks after Odo's departure, but it had been a temporary measure . . . much to Quark's eternal disappointment. Nog was much better suited to engineering, anyway.

"It's your territory, of course," Jast said. "As for our ongoing upgrade frustrations, why don't we go to an early lunch and work through a new schedule? Nog insists that things will progress faster if we regulate the EPS conduit outflow for the next few days."

Jast smiled suddenly. "Maybe we can have Quark make us up a couple of Black Holes. Just to enhance our creativity, of course."

In spite of how very wrung-out she felt, Kira found herself smiling back—and thinking that perhaps it wasn't too soon, after all, to think of Jast as a good friend. The Prophets knew she needed as many as she could get.

With the *U.S.S. Aldebaran* working its sixth day of sentinel detail for the space station, the bridge wasn't overly crowded or overly busy. The helm and science officers weren't present, and communications was represented by a second-year cadet, one of several trainees currently earning hours on the *Aldebaran*. Captain Robison was in his ready room, probably catching up on paperwork, and although Tiss Janna occupied the captain's chair, she looked as distant-eyed as everyone else on duty—excepting the cadet, of course, who stared intently at his console, watching for any incoming calls. Trainees; it was sometimes hard not to pat their heads, they were so adorably vigilant.

Thomas Chang, the *Aldebaran*'s counselor for just over seven years, wasn't officially on duty, but he spent a lot of his off hours on the bridge. He enjoyed the atmosphere of efficiency, liked watching the people he'd come to know so well as they applied their talents. Of course, watching them during downtime could often be just as interesting . . . but then, finding people interesting was how he'd come to be a ship's counselor.

Pretending to be absorbed in the contents of a science digest, Chang surreptitiously watched the men and women around him, occasionally tapping at the padd in order to deflect suspicion. He didn't want to make anyone uncomfortable . . . and besides, it was part of the game, trying to figure out what someone might be thinking about just by watching them, their gestures and body language. Shannon liked to joke that it was the Romulan in him, driving him to spy on the unwary. Because he was falling in love with her, Chang always laughed—but he couldn't help feeling a vague sadness when the topic came up, recalling the story of his great-grandmother's capture, and how that story had haunted him as a child. That the Romulans eventually released her, and that her life had been happy and full ever after . . . it couldn't take away the memory of hearing the awful truth for the first time, that a brutal man had once hurt her—and that that man's blood ran in his own veins. . . .

It seemed that he wasn't above a little daydreaming himself; Chang let the unhappy feelings go, letting his attention wander back to the pleasantly directionless analysis of his friends and co-workers. Tiss Janna, for example; from the softly calculating gleam in her eyes, the way she kept pulling on a lock of her curly dark hair, Chang imagined that she was thinking about those green opal-and-quillion earrings that the Ferengi bartender had shown her the first night they'd arrived at DS9. She wanted them, but wasn't willing to pay the obnoxiously high price that the bartender had quoted. Even now, she was thinking of a counteroffer . . . and perhaps imagining what Lieutenant Commander Hopping Bird would say about them on their next date.

Chang shifted in his chair, casting a sidelong glance at the officer in question. Mike Hopping Bird, chief tactical officer and Tiss's recent love interest. Only a few people knew, of course; Chang had heard it from Mike himself, and had been pleased. Mike and Tiss were a good match, and although they probably wouldn't let their romance be widely known, Mike was going to give it away if he didn't stop gazing at her with such obvious and ardent affection. It wasn't much of a jump for Chang to guess what Mike was thinking about, particularly considering his own developing relationship with Shannon.

There was a definite rise in the number of romantic relationships on board . . . and, Chang imagined, all across the Alpha Quadrant. There were innumerable statistics and psychological studies he could cite to prove his point, but put simply, as Captain Robison himself had said, "It's an end-of-the-war thing."

Not that everyone was after romance. Kelly Eideman, the dynamic young woman currently slouched comfortably at the engineering station, had already been to DS9 three times to play *dabo,* and had done fairly well ... although Chang couldn't rule out a romance there, either. Some of the *dabo* girls at Quark's were extremely attractive. As practical as the junior grade lieutenant was, however, he imagined that the slight smile she wore was for the clacking spin of the wheel, and the delighted cries of the watching crowd over each *dabo* win.

He didn't care much for *dabo* himself, but Shannon had been pushing for them to try out one of DS9's holosuite programs, one recommended to her by Dr. Bashir. It was for some sort of combined gambling-restaurant-entertainment center, set on Earth in the mid-20th century, and there was a game called baccarat that Shannon very much wanted to try. Shannon, a researcher on the *Aldebaran's* medical staff, had been corresponding with Bashir off and on for several years, debating something or other about chromatin formation, and had been excited to meet him. The doctor had turned out to be a very personable young man, and was apparently involved with the station's counselor, one Ezri Dax. Dax was Trill, a species that Chang found to be highly perceptive as a general rule, and although he hadn't met her yet, he was interested in hearing her take on Vanleden's newest theories about focus charting—

"You're just pretending to read, aren't you?"

At the sound of Tiss's voice, Chang looked up guiltily. Tiss was smiling playfully.

"What an odd question," he said. "What else could I possibly be doing?"

He tried, but couldn't keep a smile from creeping up as he spoke. As well as he'd come to know so many of the crew, they had come to know him. The thought was warm, inspiring a sense of belonging, and although he'd been caught out at his guessing game, he didn't mind a bit.

Tiss started to answer—and then Lieutenant Eideman was standing and turning, running to the helm even as Mike Hopping Bird's usually calm voice was rising to a near shout.

"Commander, the wormhole—it's opening!"

Then Tiss was moving, calling for on-screen, calling for bridge personnel as Captain Robison strode from his ready room, head up and eyes bright as he moved to his chair.

Chang felt an instant of cold shock, watching numbly as the brilliant colors spread out in front of them. The wormhole hadn't opened since the last of the Dominion forces had returned to the Gamma Quadrant three months ago, and although the *Aldebaran* had been assigned to guard DS9 against any possibility of attack during their repairs, no one on the ship had really expected anything to happen.

Thomas Chang swallowed his disbelief, hoping desperately that nothing *would* happen, refusing the idea that they might be in trouble. And even as he accepted that he was in denial, the first of the ships came through.

They were just finishing up their informal meeting when both of their combadges trilled at once. Outside Kira's office window, men and women were jumping to their feet, dropping tools and running to their half-assembled stations. On Kira's desk, an incoming call blinked urgently; the *Aldebaran* was hailing.

Kira and Jast both stood, turning to look out at ops. Shar's voice spilled into the room, the young officer speaking quickly as he looked in at them from his position on the main floor.

"Colonel, Commander—three Jem'Hadar strike ships have just come through the wormhole in attack formation, weapons and shields up, and they—they're heading for the Aldebaran."

No.

It was the unthinkable, the reason she'd put off upgrades for so long. Now, after three months of dead silence from the Dominion, it seemed that someone had decided to make contact, just when the station's defenses were at a minimum.

"Red alert. Battle stations," she ordered. "Shar, send out a distress call, lock off nonessential systems and get me everything on our weapons. I need to know where we are *exactly*. Implement emergency shelter protocols, try to get us visuals on the main screen, and tell Nog to get the *Defiant* ready, *now.*"

She nodded at Jast, who took her cue and hurried out of the office and across ops, toward its transporter stage. Kira reached for the blinking light of the *Aldebaran*'s call, already calculating the kind of damage they could expect if the ship couldn't stop the fighters, her mind flooded with too-recent images of burning starships and a growing dread. *No tractor beams, limited shields, all of the new tactical systems that aren't even assembled yet—*

Kira felt sick and put it aside, praying that things weren't as bad as she feared, suspecting that they were worse.

Chapter Four

"...and, considering all of *that,* do you think it could increase the energy dissipation effectiveness of the hull plating, in the event of shield envelope disruption?"

Ezri sighed, wondering if she could just pretend to be asleep. Probably not; she was on her back beneath the flight control console, but Nog could see her face if he turned around ... and she *had* encouraged him into a conversation.

Next time, I'll be sure to suggest a topic. Nothing so vague as, "What's on your mind, Nog?"

"Honestly, I'm not sure," she said, reaching up into the ODN bundle that swayed above her face and twisting two of the wire patches together. Ensign Tenmei would have to integrate them, she had the fiber torch, but she was below, working on the pulse phaser assemblies. It would have to wait. "It sounds good to me, Nog, but that's really not saying much."

The problem was that Tobin Dax, her second host, had been a theoretical engineer two centuries ago; not only were the memories hazy, technology had progressed more than a few running steps past Tobin's experience. And yet, as often as Ezri had told Nog that, he continued to ask questions and run his every idea past her, delivering each as enthusiastically as possible, the salesman in him shining through. As if she was actually an engineer, or possessed Jadzia's natural ability toward technical problem-solving. Even with all of the symbiont's experiences to draw upon, she wasn't going to win any physics awards.

"But you think it'll work?" he asked, turning around to look at her, his sharpened teeth bared in a sincere grin. "You don't see a problem with the numbers, do you?"

Be patient, he's under a lot of pressure.

Despite assurances to the contrary, Nog seemed to insist on holding himself personally responsible for how slowly things were going. Technically, he had taken over Miles O'Brien's job. And while there were certainly more experienced engineers in Starfleet, none of them knew the station as Nog did, and no other engineer had received his formal field training on both DS9 and the *Defiant.* He was still terrible at the administrative aspect, often relying on Kira or Jast to deal with master reports to Starfleet, and he didn't have the easy self-assurance about his ideas or work that the chief had, but he was determined, talented, and *extremely* eager.

"No, I don't see a problem with the numbers," Ezri said truthfully. She'd already forgotten the numbers. "I think you should write it up and meet with Kira about it—but if I were you, I'd wait a few days."

Nog turned back to the bridge's less than whole engineering station, nodding. "You're right. And that would give me a chance to, ah, iron out the details. I still haven't calculated the density of the subsequent particle cloud, which could interfere with shield harmonics ..."

She listened with half an ear, her wandering thoughts moving back to Kira. Ezri wasn't one to push counseling, but she thought it'd be a good idea to seek the colonel out later, to at least make herself available. Even with half the communications systems on the station operating sporadically, at best, word had gotten around about the murder—although she supposed not many knew that Kira had been a friend of the murdered prylar. Julian had told her that.

And so soon after losing Odo. It's so unfair. Kira projected a comfortable understanding of Odo's choice to return to the Great Link, but Ezri suspected that it still hurt her—and having to deal with the murder of a childhood friend would reinforce conscious and subconscious stresses of abandonment. That was the psychological standard, anyway; Ezri had been acting as station counselor for long enough to know that emotional reactions weren't exactly set in titanium. *I hope she'll talk to someone about it, though. Before she has time to bury the pain.*

She would have gone to see Kira already, except for the incredible workload that had practically everyone on the station occupied; as disheartening as it was, Kira undoubtedly needed Dax's engineering skills more than her ability to listen. The original plan, pushed for by the Federation and Bajor, had seemed feasible enough—take it all apart with the *Aldebaran* keeping watch, refurbish the *Defiant*'s tactical systems and armor, rewire communications and most of the subspace systems for the station, and put it all back together again in one short and brutal push. An updated *Defiant,* but more importantly, no more endlessly overlapping maintenance shutdowns for the station, no more makeshift patches between Cardassian and Federation technology that only seemed to last until it was really important for them to work. . . .

. . . and if ninety percent of the S.C.E. techs weren't off repairing war damage, we could have gotten away with it, too. They just didn't have the staff they needed to get everything done in a reasonable amount of time.

Nog's combadge chirped, and he sat up a little straighter as he answered, drawing Ezri's attention. The obvious pride he took in his position was good to see; they'd all suffered in the war, and deserved a little happiness—

—and the strangest thing happened. She was still on her back and was looking up at Nog, and the change that came over his upside-down face—a flash of pure panic that started in his eyes and seemed to spread, contorting his rounded features—had her believing, just for a second, that he was having some kind of a convulsion.

"Nog, what is it?"

He couldn't seem to catch his breath. He stood and stumbled to communications, running his hands over the console, and as she squirmed out from beneath the flight controls, Shar's voice spilled out into the bridge.

"—is on her way, but power up now. I repeat, the station has gone to red alert. We need the Defiant*'s interface on-line, and a full status report. Commander Jast is beaming over, but the colonel says to get ready immediately, attack ships are—they're firing on the* Aldebaran*!"*

Nog looked positively ill. He ran back to where he'd been working and started digging frantically through his tools, calling for the computer to assess the *Defiant*'s current condition. There was a sudden flurry of movement behind them, as the three other techs on the bridge rushed to various unpaneled consoles and started powering things up.

"*. . . in-line impulse system operating at forty-two percent. Secondary subsystems for engineering interface, reaction control, science control, and torpedo launchers, inoperative. Primary subsystems for . . ."*

As the computer's calm voice continued to list all that was wrong with DS9's best defense, as only a handful of engineers raced to put it back together again, Ezri was suddenly quite sure that people were going to die. She tapped the flight control interface and scanned the numbers, Nog yelling for an interphasic coil spanner over the computer's growing index of problems.

Maybe a lot of us.

It happened faster than Shar would have thought possible.

Only minutes ago, he'd been trying to stay awake, vaguely wishing for the warmth of his quarters. Now he stood at the central ops table amid flashing red lights, relaying orders to Nog and trying to activate the display screen at the same time, about to call for an engineering status on the shield emitters— when the station's sensors registered a hit on the *Aldebaran*. Even as the ship's data flow fluctuated wildly, the screen that dominated ops spun to life, displaying the fierce battle.

The trio of fighters were pulling away from their first run, flashes of brilliant light sparking from a series of shield deflections across the rapidly approaching *Aldebaran*'s bow. The *Nebula*-class starship seemed slow and lumbering as the three Jem'Hadar peeled away and looped back, strafing the saucer's underbelly, their tactical choreography almost like hunting—a pack of vicious carnivores attacking some mammoth beast.

All around Shar, techs were calling out instructions in low, tense voices, moving about purposefully and quickly, making room for the small crowd that erupted from the turbolift. Status reports started trickling in from all around the station, appearing on the table's master display. Shar ran a collation and fed it to Kira's office, channeling his body's elevated awareness and need for action—stimulated by the situation, his antennae fairly throbbed with it—into lending him greater speed.

When he looked up next, he could only see two of the darting fighters. Both twined back and forth in front of the *Aldebaran* as if taunting it, narrowly dodging a series of phaser blasts, the energy streams dissipating harmlessly into the darkness. He tapped at the table's display, looking for the third ship, but there were problems with several of the station's short-range sensors. He could only get a partial read, a suggestion of functional energy behind the *Aldebaran*'s starboard flank—

—and there was an explosion low on the ship's structure, a misty spray of light and escaping gases forming behind what could only be the *Aldebaran*'s main engineering decks. The third fighter flew down and away.

"Their shields are gone!" someone behind him shouted, and a glance at the *Aldebaran's* interface confirmed it. A second later, the interface blanked out, but the station's sensors picked up evidence of the powerful blast, much more powerful than could have been caused by a Jem'Hadar striker's phased polaron beam. It was some type of quantum warhead, and even as Shar sent the newest data into command, Kira burst out of her office, a look of angry shock on her face.

"We've lost contact with the *Aldebaran*. Tactical, can we get targeting for quantum torpedoes?" she called out, turning to face the main screen. All three of the ships were starting another run at the *Aldebaran*. The starship was turning, but slowly, much too slowly.

Lieutenant Bowers was tapping frantically at his station's console. "Negative. Launcher sets three, four, and seven are down, and the station's internal locks are unreliable on five and six."

"Shar, establish communications with the *Defiant,* and try to get our interface with the *Aldebaran* back, at least text," Kira said. "Mr. Nguyen, take your team and get to engineering, I want you and Terek's crew on the shield-emitters. If we can get the *Aldebaran* close enough to one of the docking pylons—"

But it was already too late. Even with the visual dampening, the cascade of light that flashed through ops from the main screen was blinding. Shar was suddenly too busy struggling to compensate the station through the shockwave to see it, but enough of the sensors were working to tell him the terrible, improbable truth, as hundreds upon thousands of pieces blew outward from where the *Starship Aldebaran* had been.

No. Oh, no.

Just over nine hundred people on the *Aldebaran,* and Kira couldn't allow herself the luxury of disbelief or sorrow. It didn't matter that it shouldn't have happened, that an outgunned trio of tiny fighters shouldn't have had a chance; the ship was gone, and the second they finished dodging what was left of the *Aldebaran,* the Jem'Hadar would be back to run at the station. Their intent couldn't be clearer, and her options were limited. Shar called out that the majority of the wreckage from the starship probably wouldn't affect the station, but she barely heard him, her thoughts racing to get ahead of what was happening.

Shields practically nonexistent, weapons arrays are out—if we could commandeer the docked ships— She rejected the idea immediately, remembering what was around. Four freighters and a couple of survey ships, maybe a dozen personal craft, and even with the runabouts and the evac pods, they wouldn't get a tenth of the population out before the attack, *think, think—*

Shar's usually melodic voice was strained, rough. "Sir, we're receiving a response to our priority distress call from the *I.K.S.—*"

"How far away?" Kira interrupted, not caring who it was, hoping wildly.

"Ah, 22 minutes."

In 22 minutes, it would be over. She'd seen the report that Nog had flashed, knew that the *Defiant*'s crew wouldn't have made it to the ship yet, and it didn't matter; they had no choice. She tapped her combadge.

"Commander Jast," she said, silently hating Starfleet and herself for letting this happen, cursing the false security that they'd all been lulled into. "The *Aldebaran* has been destroyed. The *Defiant* is the station's best hope for defense; are you ready?"

Jast didn't hesitate. "We're ready."

"Do what you can," Kira said, and with a silent prayer, she turned to watch the screen, men and women calling out numbers and names behind her as they fought to keep the station safe, as pieces of the *Aldebaran* began to hammer at their shields.

A few seconds later, the Jem'Hadar started their first run at DS9.

Chapter Five

After Ro's not-so-gentle persuasion, Quark had produced a Class One isolinear rod that he'd been storing for Istani Reyla; he had immediately followed up with an invitation to dinner, ostensibly to ensure no hard feelings, which she had refused—but pleasantly, for the same reason. She saw no reason to make an enemy of the Ferengi . . . and, she had to admit, she had a soft spot for people who didn't strictly abide by the rules.

She had just gotten back to the security office when the red alert hit, and the computer instructed her to implement emergency shelter protocols due to an unnamed threat to the station; it wouldn't or couldn't elaborate any further. She had the computer display a checklist as she calmly locked the data rod away, hoping that her staff was better prepared. They had to be—though prepared for what, exactly, she didn't know. Communications between ops and the security office were down, Shar wouldn't answer his combadge, and she didn't feel comfortable bothering anyone else during a crisis.

Doesn't matter anyway, the plan's the same for me. Direct civilians to the reinforced areas, evacuate and secure prisoners if there were any. There weren't, and a locator check for the security officers on duty informed her that she was the only one who wasn't in position.

Ro locked the office and stepped back out into the river of people rushing through the Promenade, finally unable to continue denying her own fear as she saw it all around her. A small child was sobbing somewhere in the crowd, a terrified sound of irrepressible angst, inspiring in Ro her own.

Is it war, again? Is it ever going to be over?

She was no stranger to battle. After the Dominion had effectively obliterated the Maquis, she'd led a small team of independent guerillas against the Cardassians and the Jem'Hadar, and later the Breen. Her group had held no allegiances other than to each other, earning no accolades for their efforts, nor needing any—as with the Maquis, the righteousness of the cause had been enough. She had been in as many conflicts as any Federation officer, if not more, and had done so with fewer people, less powerful weapons, and no outside support.

The difference is, I'm not in control here. I'm one of many, and the decisions aren't mine to make. It wasn't battle or even death that frightened her, it was feeling helpless. The station was under attack, and all she could do—all she was supposed to do—was try to limit casualties. And trust that someone else would make the right decisions, when trust was the one thing she'd never given lightly or easily.

However she felt about it, it was happening. Ro spotted two of her deputies working to control the crowd and moved to join them, wondering if she would ever feel like she belonged on DS9 . . . or anywhere else that required her to put her faith in others.

• • •

Bashir hurried past lines of muttering, frightened people filing through the corridors of the habitat ring, his emergency kit slung, his heart pounding with fear. Ezri was on the *Defiant*.

Where I should be. If they'd only called a moment earlier. He'd been seconds too late, and the first explosion had hit the station even as he'd turned away from the sealed airlock. He'd seen a half dozen *Defiant* crewmembers on his run back to the Promenade, all of them as unhappy as he was to have missed the ship's hasty departure. Unhappy, and not a little anxious; the *Defiant* had disembarked, presumably to go into battle, with a crew of techs.

Since he'd been unable to join the *Defiant's* crew, his next priority was to coordinate with the other doctors on board, to help activate all of the contingency medical stations and prepare for trauma cases. He reached the Promenade and saw Ro Laren and her security team directing groups of civilians to the designated shelter areas mid-core.

As he approached Ro, the station rocked again, the thunder of another blast resounding through the hull, drawing startled cries from the hurrying crowd. The air was charged with fear, the constant bleat of alarms promoting urgency rather than calm.

"Lieutenant, do you know what's happening?" All he'd gotten from ops was the order to report to the *Defiant,* and that the station was under attack.

She seemed surprised by the question. "Don't you?"

There was no point in stating the obvious as the station trembled anew with power flux; they were being fired upon by someone, communications were down all over, and their defenses were negligible at best. And with what Ezri had been telling him about the *Defiant* . . .

"We're in trouble," Bashir said, and Ro nodded grimly. There was nothing else that needed to be said.

Ezri, be safe. The force of feeling behind the thought was so powerful that he felt short of breath, an intensity that startled him. They had slept together for the first time just before the last great battle of the war against the Dominion, and going to fight then had been difficult, fearing for her as well as himself—but things had still been so uncertain, and at least they had been together. In only a few months, so much had changed. . . .

"Ah, Doctor, I have to go make sure the shops have been evacuated—" Ro began.

"Of course. I . . . good luck, Ro. Be careful," Bashir said, and saw that he'd surprised her again, although he wasn't sure how. He didn't have time to consider it, either, or how his feelings for Ezri had complicated his life, or all of the things that could go wrong; he had his own duties to see to.

With a nod to the others, Julian turned away and ran for the infirmary, thinking that he would give anything to be on the *Defiant,* anything at all.

When Kira gave the command to engage the enemy, Nog tried to keep an open mind, to work the problems rather than consider how disastrous the situation was, but it wasn't easy. He knew better than anyone just how pitiful their defenses were right now, how many systems were down, how many weapons off-line—and with the *Aldebaran* destroyed, their chances of coming away unscathed had dropped to a negligible percentage.

Focus, stay focused, reassign pulse phasers two and four to manual, got to divert partial impulse to shields—

Commander Jast took control the second she beamed aboard, assigning positions and prioritizing system checks, but she was making decisions in part based on what he told her. Nog stepped between the engineering station and tactical, trying desperately to direct power where it was needed most, while Ezri struggled with the partially disabled communications interface—the science station was mostly dismantled, sensor arrays routed through tactical—and Prynn Tenmei sat at the helm. With the exception of the commander, Ensign Tenmei was the only person aboard who was where she was supposed to be—not a reassuring thought in spite of her piloting skills, because that was it for the bridge crew. The other techs were below, grappling with the weapons systems. The standard operational crew was forty; they had fourteen.

At least they weren't relying on the cloaking device, although that was small comfort. After the war, the Romulan government had agreed to let the *Defiant* keep it. As the Alpha Quadrant's first line of defense against anything that came through the wormhole, it only made sense—even to the characteristically skeptical Romulan Senate—to provide DS9 and the *Defiant* with every possible advantage. Unfortunately, like virtually everything else on board, the cloak wasn't even functional at the moment.

—try to transfer the transporter EPS tap to the navigational deflector, I can do this, I know this ship. Another thought that wasn't particularly reassuring, considering the state of the *Defiant,* but he was too busy to come up with anything better.

The Jem'Hadar scored their first hits against the station even as Kira gave the word. Nog had had nightmares worse than what was happening, but not by much.

"Ensign, take us out," Jast said. "The armor over the warp nacelles is still temp, so try to keep the targets below and in front of us. Nog, what can we do about the lag time on beam launch?"

Nog stumbled over to tactical as Tenmei disengaged the docking clamps and tapped thrusters, the ship's AG lurching with the power flux. "Ah, not much, sir. Point six-five seconds, minimum."

Jast took it in stride. "We'll just have to fire early, then. Shields up. Stay with tactical, Lieutenant."

She spoke casually, as if the Jem'Hadar ships would hold still, waiting for the *Defiant*'s phasers to catch up. Nog had been intimidated by Jast's generally cool disposition since she arrived, but considering the situation, her calm was a definite asset.

The main screen showed a blank expanse of space until the *Defiant* swung around, just in time for them to see the station take another series of hits. Nog struggled to quash feelings of panic; all three of the attackers were apparently concentrating on the fusion reactors, at the base of the lower core. He could see dark streaks of polaron damage all across the section's hull, visually warped by the disrupted shields.

They'll hold, they can take a lot more than that. They could . . . except with the upgrades, a heavy percentage of the station's power was tied up in bypass circuiting, and nothing was certain; the short-range shield emitters were essentially down, running with no backup. If the strike fighters continued to hit any one area, they could inflict serious damage.

"Could," they already have. Taking out a *Nebula*-class starship hadn't proved much of a problem.

"Positions, Lieutenant. And run course probabilities. Without targeting, it may be the best we can do."

Most of the directional sensors were working. Nog read the numbers aloud, tapping in trajectory calculations as he spoke. The Jem'Hadar had turned back toward the station, wheeling into a loose formation, point high.

"Dax, how's the station doing?" Jast asked.

"Unable to establish a full interface," Ezri said. "Their shields are down at least forty percent."

Jast seemed unfazed. "Let's see if we can tempt them away, people. Ensign, get us as close as you can to point at full impulse, bearing two-two-seven mark nine, and be prepared to run evasive pattern Theta Sixteen at my word. Lieutenant Nog, when we're twenty kilometers out to range, lay down a calculated phaser spread in front of the lead ship, firing at will. Better they think we're a bad shot than underpowered." Nog could hear the grim humor in her voice. "Who knows, enough runs and we may get lucky."

It was a clever scheme. The Jem'Hadar could be fanatic about following point, and although the computer predictions had a minimal chance of scoring a hit, the phasers would come close enough to be threatening. The evasive pattern would turn the *Defiant* back to run a two-degree parallel to its "strafing" course, keeping the well-shielded front of the ship facing the attackers.

The *Defiant* sped away from the station, angling into the path of the point ship. The instant they went to full impulse, Nog could see they were in serious trouble. At the unmanned engineering station, a bank of lights started to flash. All across the bridge, lights brightened—and abruptly dimmed, filling the tool-strewn deck with shadows.

"Sir, the mid-hull RCS thrusters are bleeding power from the electrical system!" Nog shouted. He knew the danger would be obvious to Jast; an electrical crash would shut everything down.

With a full crew, it would have been noticed immediately. *Or if I'd bothered to look closer. I should have checked that, I should have—*

"Compensate! Cut impulse to half and run a tap," Jast snapped.

"Sir, if we boost it from here without checking the source—" Nog began.

"I know," Jast said. "We risk an overload, but we don't have a choice."

Nog stepped away from tactical, but the commander was already out of her chair and headed for the engineering station. "Stay at your post, Lieutenant, I'm on it. Ensign, report."

"One hundred ten kilometers and closing," Tenmei said tensely. "Intercept projected course in eleven seconds."

As Nog knew from experience, experience he'd hoped never to revisit, those seconds seemed to stretch into eternity, time slowing, his senses recording it all. The trio of Jem'Hadar ships streaked toward the station, their flat, insectile shapes shimmering like water mirages beneath heavy shields. The low hum of the bridge systems increased, the lights strengthening as Jast manipulated the power flow. Ezri called out the stats from DS9, confirming the loss of shield efficiency to thirty-seven percent and severe energy surges in every major system. Nog laid in the phaser directionals, intensely conscious of the sweat trickling down the back of his neck, the hot, acrid smell of scorched optical cable—and the crawl of numbers on the console that told him the *Defiant* was being targeted.

Forty . . . thirty . . . now.

Nog fired, a series of layered shots that responded with agonizing slowness to his command—and as the bright pulse bolts shot out into space, he could feel that they were lucky, the triumph blossoming in his gut, visual proof following an instant later.

Yes!

The right flank ship took a massive hit to its port side and fell away, spinning out of control as hull plates tore and atmosphere escaped. A veil of light and mist trailed behind the dying ship like a comet's tail, a pale streak lost in the brilliance of the final explosion a second later.

Everything sped up then, as if making up for the eternity of waiting, happening too fast for Nog to absorb all at once. He started to call out the information to Jast, who was still at engineering; Tenmei was shouting at the same time that the lead ship was shifting position; and, from the pulse phaser mains below, Turo Ane was trying to tell him something about the hull, her voice filtering through the com in a haze of sudden, violent static—

—because the Jem'Hadar point ship was firing, scoring a jagged hit across the *Defiant*'s bow. A terrible light filled the screen. Nog hugged his console as the gravity net pitched, as the ship bounced and jerked, and Jast let out a short, sharp scream.

The commander flew back from the engineering station in a shower of sparks and fell heavily to the deck. Nog stared at her for a half second before snapping his attention back to his screens, tapping up damage reports and checking their shields—but that half second was enough, the image of her face clear in his mind.

Commander Jast was dead.

Chapter Six

The two remaining Jem'Hadar ships continued toward the station, apparently uninterested in the faltering *Defiant* as it rapidly angled away from them. The commander wasn't moving, and for a second, in spite of a thousand small indicator alarms, it seemed strangely quiet on the bridge.

Because someone should be giving orders.

Ezri was on her feet before she considered what she was doing, her heart pounding, a number of powerful memories strong in her mind—mostly from Jadzia, confident and in control, moving about the *Defiant*'s bridge, speaking as firmly as she was now.

"Nog, report."

Nog was obviously flustered, practically shouting the information. "Single intensity polaron, shields down to eighty percent! There was an electrical surge straight through the ship's structural body, warp plasma injectors are down, and we've lost communications with the station!"

Electrical surge. Ezri had crouched next to Jast and touched the woman's brow, running her finger along the central vertical ridge. A Bolian's pulse could be detected there, something she hadn't known she knew; the memory was Curzon's, vague, holding a Bolian baby at a political dinner, feeling the flutter of life through the ridge of flesh and bone. Tiris Jast had no pulse. Her eyes were wide and fixed, and there was a settling of her features that Dax had seen often enough to recognize—life had left them, transforming the strong and delicate face into a waxy likeness of Jast's, into a mask.

Even if there was *still a chance* . . . No doctor aboard, they couldn't transport her, and no one on the *Defiant* could be spared for the shuttle. As quickly as that, the decision was made; she could doubt it later. Maybe. If they were very lucky.

"Tenmei, execute evasive pattern Theta sixteen," Ezri said, standing, stepping in front of the captain's chair. Jadzia had commanded the *Defiant* on more than one combat mission, which made her the only person on board with the experience for it. *It'll have to be close enough.*

"Nog, shut down the bridge's engineering console, route it down to Turo. Is the shipwide working?" She was surprised at how calm she sounded, and it seemed to have a positive effect on Nog. He took a deep breath before answering.

"Negative."

"Then comm them directly, tell them to put everything they can into repairing the phaser lag—we need them more than shields or thrust. And keep trying to reestablish contact with the station. Tenmei, get ready, we're about to go on the offensive."

The *Defiant* swung back toward DS9, Ezri's stomach reeling as the inertial dampeners wavered. Both of the strike ships had reached their objective and were firing, brilliant arrows of light flashing up against the dark, glowing hull of the lower core. The ships dropped down and split as they completed their run, each darting away in a different direction, spinning and curving between pieces of the *Aldebaran* like strange, deadly fish.

They were smaller than the *Defiant,* and faster, but only in sprints. *If we can bear down on them one at a time, refine phaser accuracy through constant bombardment and hone in . . .* The *Defiant* would probably take heavy fire from the second ship, but it was a solid plan and they had to do something immediately. The station was practically defenseless.

"Hard to port, close in, and fire as soon as we're in range," Ezri said, feeling too many things to sort through, hidden among them a tiny astonishment as the full realization hit—she was commanding the *Defiant* by memories of Jadzia, but with a confidence all her own.

Except for the docking ring and the upper pylons, ops was situated at the point farthest from the attack on the lower core, but each hit resonated through all of the structure's segments. Ops trembled, lights and consoles wavering, streams of information lost as backup networks crashed—but enough came through Shar's console to show him how fortunate they were compared to other parts of the station. Damage reports from the lower and mid cores were serious, bordering on critical, and the *Defiant* had only managed to destroy one of the fighters. Unless Jast stopped them, another attack could prove disastrous to the already fluttering shields.

Kira shouted orders to divert power, to shut down noncritical systems, to evacuate everyone into the upper core. Even occupied as he was, Shar couldn't help but notice how well Kira handled herself. Her reputation for being indomitable under pressure was well-deserved.

As the tremors subsided and the Jem'Hadar coursed away, the *Defiant* veered sharply after the point ship.

"*Defiant's* status?" Kira called.

"Unable to lock sensors, and there was an energy surge after they were hit that wiped out the interface." Shar resisted the urge to extrapolate aloud on the state of the subspace sensors. He felt very focused, very alert, his ability to absorb and process information at its peak. He didn't glory in conflict or seek it out, but he couldn't help his body's natural response, an Andorian's response; the stimulus of the situation was now profound enough that he had no fear of injury or death. And though he was deeply anxious for the station and horrified by the loss of life that the *Aldebaran's* destruction represented, he couldn't help his objectivity or his exhilaration.

The peace broken so soon; cruel and impractical. We're witnessing the creation of new woes. The obvious implications of the Jem'Hadar's actions had not been voiced, there was no benefit to it, but Shar silently lamented the breaking of the treaty. Wars of ignorance benefited no one.

On the main screen, the *Defiant* maneuvered into position behind the point ship and fired, multiple pulses that went wide, the striker gliding easily among the untargeted beams. The second ship was streaking back to join the battle, the *Defiant* and the point ship roughly two hundred kilometers from the station at varying planes of altitude.

As the lead ship continued to elude the *Defiant's* attack, the second ship reached its weapons range and opened fire. The *Defiant's* rear shields sparked violently, but she held her course, closing on the target. Shar was impressed by Jast's commitment to their course of action, the *Defiant* taking several severe hits from behind as they continued their pursuit.

The tension in ops built upon itself, every spare glance on the main screen, every awareness at least partially tuned to the *Defiant's* conflict. She fired again and again on the point ship as it swerved and dove, each series of shots coming closer, accuracy improving in costly increments as the second ship blasted mercilessly away.

Within the data stream that flowed across his console, an alarming series of numbers caught his full attention—a partial sensor read on the *Defiant* that he hoped was faulty. If it was correct, Jast was about to lose her shields. And if that happened with both Jem'Hadar still in commission, it was all over.

"Colonel, we're picking up the *Defiant,* they're losing their shields," he said, as there was another volley of shots from the second Jem'Hadar, brutal and effective that proved his words out. The *Defiant's* shield envelope burst, the only visible sign of her imminent demise a brief, brilliant flicker of her aura—

—and the Jem'Hadar point ship exploded, becoming an expanding wave of energy and debris. Jast's gamble had paid off; the *Defiant* was certainly damaged, but even without shields, they stood a likely chance at victory over a lone strike ship. The *Defiant* sailed up and over her victory, the last Jem'Hadar ship retreating rapidly as their target turned to confront them.

Nobody cheered. People had died and there was still an enemy to deal with, but the atmosphere in ops expressed a release of tension, a partial conquest understood. Techs returned to their work with renewed fervor. Shar was warmed by the release physically, his skin flushing in reaction to the elevated bioelectrical charge in the air. His left antenna itched madly.

Colonel Kira stood a few meters away with her fists clenched, watching the screen with an expression of total concentration, her body rigid.

"They're going to attack us again," she said, almost to herself, startling Shar. Of course they were, but somehow, it hadn't occurred to him until she spoke. The ship wasn't retreating from the *Defiant;* it was coming back for another run at the station.

The Jem'Hadar had to know they wouldn't survive, they shouldn't even have made it this far. Why would they stop firing on the station now, just because they'll certainly die?

"Put everything into shields, everything," Kira shouted, as the Jem'Hadar set its course back for the station—

—and as if some unloving god had decided to put a stop to their hopes, the *Defiant* died in space. Shar didn't need to look at whatever scant information the station's sensors could tell him; it was there on the screen in front of them all.

The suddenly dark *Defiant* plummeted on momentum alone after the Jem'Hadar ship, no longer firing as the attacker closed on the station.

The money was all safe, of course. No good businessman would leave his latinum box or account access codes behind just because a few shots were fired. But in all the excitement, Quark had forgotten the kai wager sheet in the bar's hidden floor compartment. An easy mistake, considering how hectic evacuations were, securing the bar, having to keep track of each fleeing customer's bill, but a mistake all the same. He'd been two steps from his heavily fortified storeroom when he remembered, and had been forced to risk life and limb to come back for the hard copy.

At least the firing seems to have stopped. I could probably just wait it out here. The bar was silent and empty, a depressing sight but strangely peaceful. Extending the bar's hours had been a wise decision, the profit margin respectable, but he sometimes missed the quiet times, the silence of the *dabo* tables when the lights were low. . . .

I have got *to get more sleep.* Maybe his stress level was higher than he thought. The station *was* under attack, after all, and his nephew was unaccounted for— although Quark figured Nog was probably slaving away on an engineering level somewhere, wishing he had taken the advice of his elders and kept the security assignment. As for the attack, it was probably a pack of drunk Klingons, or some random terrorist element . . . the station had been fired upon more than once in recent years, and hadn't blown up yet.

And if there was even a whisper of war in the air, I would have caught it. The proverbial "grapevine" enjoyed a healthy offshoot at Quark's, and he couldn't help overhearing a few things. Quite simply, nothing vast was brewing anywhere, or at least nothing within a troubling distance.

Quark replaced the floor panel behind the bar and stood, tucking the paper in his jacket. Kira had been adamant about no more pools when she found out he was taking bets on Winn's successor (as it had turned out, her timing couldn't have been more fortuitous; he'd given easy odds on Ungtae, who was barely in the running anymore), and since he didn't want to spend any time in a cell, he'd decided to keep that one, at least, on paper. Programs could always be traced; anyone could draw up a list, if they remembered to use DNA-resistant paper.

Although considering who would arrest me, maybe I should let myself get caught . . .

"What the hell are you doing here?"

Startled, Quark looked up—and saw the source of his budding prison fantasy glaring down at him from the balcony.

"Lieutenant Ro!" He smiled up at her, pleased with the opportunity to interact with her again . . . assuming she hadn't seen him pocket the list. "I was just making sure that everything is secured here. You know, it's my responsibility to maintain Federation and Bajoran safety standards during all emergency procedures—"

"Fine, don't tell me," she said dismissively, heading for the stairs. "But whatever it is, it's not worth risking your life over."

Quark nodded, simulating agreement. The wager sheet was worth a few bars of gold-pressed latinum, easily. "Why are you here, if you don't mind me asking?"

"I had to check the holosuites," she said, starting down. "They're empty, by the way. Now if *you* don't mind, I think we should get—"

There was a sudden, violent quake, knocking Quark off his feet. The already dimmed lights flickered, and there was the sound of glass breaking in one of the unshielded cabinets behind him, a high, clear sound over the heavy, threatening rumble of uncertain machinery.

Please, let that be machinery!

He stayed where he was for a few seconds after the rumbling stopped, waiting for the station to evaporate around him in a ball of flame—but other than his stomach, which seemed to be in serious disagreement with his breakfast, nothing seemed to be broken.

He stood up, brushing at his coattails, suddenly quite anxious to get to a better-shielded area. "Lieutenant?"

No response. Then he heard a low groan, from the shadowy recess at the bottom of the stairs. Quark hurried to the end of the bar and out onto the main floor, worried about Ro, about the attack, wondering if he could be held liable somehow for any injury she might have incurred—

—and saw her lying on the floor, far enough from the stairs that she had to have been pitched off. Her eyes were closed and she groaned again, the sound half-conscious.

Quark hesitated, thinking it might be better if he went to the nicely reinforced infirmary and organized a few rescue personnel to come back for her. It made more sense, really; he didn't have the appropriate training, and she *had* seemed angry that he'd risked his life to come to the bar; she certainly wouldn't want him to remain in an unsafe area. . . .

Before he could decide, the station was hit again, and more fiercely than any previous attack. Quark grabbed a table and held on as the room teetered wildly all around him. The lights went out completely as more bottles crashed behind the bar, emergency lights powering on a second later, the floor settling back to level in one sweeping, nauseating lurch. All was uncommonly quiet, even the distant blare of the red alert finally silenced.

Quark stood up, wincing at the depressingly sharp scent of spilled liquors, still clutching the table tightly with one hand as he looked around for Ro. Her body had tumbled several meters from its original position, coming to rest against a bolted chair. She'd stopped groaning.

The internal argument was brief but to the point, both positions clear. He had to get out immediately. And if he left her there, and the station took another hit like that, she was going to get hurt a lot worse.

Plus, what are the chances she could ever love the man who left her behind? And heroically saving the life of the head of security . . . contrary to popular belief,

Ferengi were not cowards; the benefits just needed to outweigh the risks in some value, if not latinum. Latinum, of course, was preferable, but for Ro, he'd be content with her undying gratitude.

Quark hurried to her side and knelt down, numbly aware that he'd hugely underestimated the seriousness of the situation.

"Lieutenant? Can you hear me?"

Ro's eyes cracked open, then closed again. Her voice was weak but clear. "Quark? Hit my head, on the stairs . . ."

"Yeah, I figured. Come on, we've got to get out of here." He slipped his arm beneath her shoulders and lifted, pulling her into a sitting position, relieved that she was conscious enough to help.

With Quark supporting her, they managed to stumble through the bar toward the door, barely staying upright as the station trembled yet again. Quark steeled his nerves with pride at his own good deed and the pleasantly firm pressure of her body leaning against his. If they survived, he had no doubt that this would be the beginning of a lucrative relationship.

Chapter Seven

They had run through their few ideas in thirty seconds, discarding each as quickly as they were said out loud; they just didn't have the resources or the time to implement any of them. It wasn't a matter of routing power or clever rewiring. The final hit from the strike ship had effectively destroyed the main plasma transfer conduits, from which the warp core operated. That, in turn, had instantly taken the drive off-line, creating a surge that had pushed the impulse fusion reactors into overloading . . . which had basically killed absolutely everything. There was simply nothing they could do to make the *Defiant* have power that it didn't have.

Except for the viewscreen, of course, Nog thought bitterly. No gravity, no light except for a few charged emergency spots—but a working viewscreen with a near perfect picture, because holographic systems on Starfleet vessels operated from an independent power grid. Fate had apparently decided that it wasn't enough to just kill everybody; that would be too easy. No, fate had also deemed it necessary to keep the *Defiant* around as an audience for the grand finale, and had given them a primary vantage point from which to see it happen. The explosion would blow them apart, of course, but they'd get to see their friends and families die first.

Alone on the bridge, Ezri and Nog watched silently as the tiny strike ship battered the station. After gently securing Commander Jast's body, Tenmei had gone below to tell the rest of the crew what was happening . . . assuming there was anyone left to tell.

The *Defiant* continued to coast forward. DS9's shields seemed to be holding, but Nog figured it was only a matter of moments before they went—and once they were gone, the station would go even faster than that.

Ezri's strategy had almost worked—taking a beating in order to halve the attack forces wasn't necessarily inspired, but it was a sound enough plan. If the shields had lasted just another minute, it *would* have worked. . . .

Without a word, Ezri reached out and took his hand, squeezing it with her own. Nog was grateful, and glad she didn't say anything. In the face of what was happening, of the sheer enormity of the imminent apocalypse, words would be useless. The station was now obviously faltering, tilting, the translational controls probably down, the lower core's lights all gone.

After everything we've been through, for it to end like this . . .

He couldn't complete the thought, and as the screen suddenly flared, a wash of light enveloping the station, Nog almost convinced himself that he was seeing the end—until he realized that the brilliant blue light wasn't nearly brilliant enough to be an explosion.

The wormhole had opened, and something was coming out.

Kira felt her responsibility like a deadweight as the Jem'Hadar ship continued its attack, as the station beneath them went critical—shields down to eight percent, structural damage throughout the lower core, environmental systems on the brink of collapse. She should have rejected the ridiculous upgrade schedule, or demanded additional engineers, or fought harder for a second guard ship.

Should have, and didn't.

"Evacuate the station," she said, knowing the failure to be hers. "Civilian priority for runabouts and escape pods, everyone else to docking ring airlocks three, four, and six—make sure the freighters are full and prepped for warp, and program the ops transporter for the impulse shuttle at upper pylon three. Seal off everything else."

If I had handled things better, I could have prevented this. The idea, that a trio of strike fighters could successfully disable the *Defiant,* could actually destroy the *Aldebaran* and DS9 . . . she wouldn't have believed it possible, and now, all that was left was to flee—

—and it's probably too late for us but we have to try, we have to keep trying—

There was another solid blow to the station. A second later, Lieutenant Bowers said the inevitable, horrible words Kira had dreaded hearing, the sound of them worse than she could have imagined.

"Colonel, we've lost shields."

She nodded, not trusting herself to speak as he continued.

"We can't expect more than a few minutes before a full breach in—sir! The wormhole, it's opening again!"

Kira's heart skipped a beat, sudden thoughts of the Prophets filling her with a manic hope. "On screen!"

The view was angled badly and blurred, a testimony to the station's dying power, but it was clear enough. They saw a small ship bursting out of the wormhole, riding the funnel of swirling light into the Alpha Quadrant. It streaked past the helpless *Defiant* toward the station, as small as one of the attack fighters—

Damn it, no!

It was another Jem'Hadar strike ship, and though it appeared to be damaged, much of its starboard hull black and crushed, it was obviously prepared to fight. How many more Dominion ships were waiting on the other side, they'd never know; with a second ship firing on them, there wouldn't be enough time for any kind of evacuation.

If even a quarter survive, we'll be lucky. Most—if not all—of the departing ships and escape pods would be caught in the explosion.

The station rocked, and Kira called out for Shar to send the new information to Starfleet on the long range, the thought that it was her final report a dagger to her heart. She prayed for time, furious with herself for not starting an evacuation earlier. It didn't occur to her that there hadn't *been* an "earlier"; she felt too guilty and desperate to allow herself such consolation.

"Anything on sensors?" Kira asked. Perhaps the fourth ship to exit the wormhole was too damaged to fire.

"Negative, external banks are all down," Shar said. "I can attempt to transfer power from one of the auxiliary generators."

"No," she said, and raised her voice, aware that the newest strike ship would be within range in seconds. The battle was lost; it was time to let go, and hope there might still be a chance for some to survive.

"We have to evacuate now. Everyone stand down and get to the transporter—"

Lieutenant Bowers interrupted, pointing at the screen, his voice hoarse with emotion. "Colonel, the second ship!"

Kira turned, sick with sorrow; she could at least face the final moment—and watched, stunned, as the newest arrival fired upon their attacker.

"It's *fighting* them," Nog breathed.

He let go of her hand, pulling himself closer to the viewscreen, looking as shocked as Ezri felt. She barely dared to hope that the damaged ship could stop the attack; it was obviously in bad shape, only one of its weapons firing, but maybe it had a backup weapon, an override code for the attacker's ship, tractor beam capabilities . . .

. . . *or some kind of warhead.*

Ezri suddenly felt like her mind was being flushed with heat, the realization and the possibilities coming so fast that she could barely think. It was impossible, the strike ships were too close to the station and it had never been done—

—*but if they move away . . . and if the command codes will work . . .*

"Nog," she said, the hope taking a definite shape even as she spoke. "I have an idea."

The damaged striker only appeared to have one of its polaron weapons functioning, but it was as fast and agile as the attacker, managing to score several hits to the aggressor's port weapons array. The attacker stopped firing on the station, turning to dart after the damaged ship as it dropped into an evasive maneuver.

No one spoke, staring in mute disbelief as the two strike fighters engaged. They tagged each other around and beneath the station, firing and dodging. Kira refused to think about how close they were to an irreparable breach, or why the damaged Jem'Hadar ship would attack one of its own. What mattered was what was being played out in front of them.

Their protector was good, the pilot well-trained and bold, but they couldn't overcome their handicap; after a few hits from the attacking ship, its daring moves became stilted. It limped around the lower core, still firing—but another hit from the enemy stilled even that, knocking out its last polaron array.

The damaged fighter didn't retreat. Kira stared at the screen, unable to believe what she was seeing as it placed itself in harm's way, actually moving to block the attacker from firing on the station.

The attack ship didn't hesitate, blasting pitilessly at the interloper. Their protector suddenly barreled straight into the fire, apparently planning for a suicide collision—and streaked up and over the aggressor at the last second in an unexpected burst of energy, speeding away, heading back toward the wormhole.

Without another shot to the dying station, the point ship wheeled around and took off after it, firing intermittently. It seemed determined to finish the interloper off before doing anything else—although while the actions were clear, the motivations were anything but. Kira couldn't begin to guess at either pilot's reasoning, attack or defense.

Don't care, Prophets be praised, we're still alive—

The two ships raced toward the wormhole, the mostly undamaged attacker quickly gaining, scoring one hit, then another. They circled around, spinning back and racing forward again, gradually moving closer to the wormhole as the damaged ship worked to save itself, as the attacker tried to take it out. Their protector wasn't going to make it, it had taken too much damage—and as soon as it was gone, the point ship would be back.

Silently, Kira began to pray.

There was no way to gain access from the bridge. Nog got through to Ensign Tenmei on his combadge, filling her in as he and Ezri dropped into the turbo shaft that would take them down to deck two—one step closer to warhead control. It was a room Nog had been in only once, when Chief O'Brien had given him his first full tour of the original *Defiant*. The memory was sharp in his mind as he and Ezri hurriedly swam through the dark, the air already growing cold in the lifeless ship.

"Neat, huh?" O'Brien said, looking around at the tightly packed, tiny room with something like love. "Part of the autodestruct system . . . The whole thing can be launched from here in a worst-case combat scenario, though I doubt it ever will be. Come on, let's head back. I want to show you the pulse phaser system. . . ."

Not much of a memory, and although he'd studied the schematics more than once since that long-ago day, Nog still only had the most basic understanding of how the deployable warhead operated. He decided that he would gladly pay his future inheritance as the only son of the Grand Nagus if the chief was on his way to the control room instead of him.

The warhead module—that foremost section of the *Defiant*'s hull that also housed the navigational deflector—was equipped with its own impulse engines for propulsion as well as an independent power supply, plus a magazine of six photon torpedo warheads. As the chief had told him, it was meant to be used only in the most dire circumstances, which was probably why it hadn't occurred to Nog at all—their current circumstances were probably as dire as any ever got, but he'd just never expected to be in them.

He dredged up what he remembered, making mental notes based on what needed to happen. This close to the station, they would only arm one of the torpedoes, he'd have to punch in a safe-distance shutoff and a single signature target into the guidance system. It was dangerous, but it could work. . . .

. . . assuming I don't mess it up, like I messed up the repair schedule— Nog swallowed the thought, concentrating on remembering the codes they would need, anxious and sweating in spite of the cold.

They reached deck two, Ezri leading the way as they kicked off bottom and swam fore, the combined sound of their breathing seeming incredibly loud in the featureless dark.

"Don't worry, we're almost there," Ezri said, and the firm, calm tone of her voice made Nog feel infinitely better. Not the sweet, laughing voice of Ezri Dax, but the determined, reassuring pitch of a leader. He was too relieved to feel any surprise; a commanding officer was present and all he had to do was listen and carry out her orders.

They hurried on, Nog breathing more evenly, feeling his own spark of determination. He was still scared, and they were still probably going to die, anyway—but at least they wouldn't be sitting around waiting for it.

The damaged Jem'Hadar ship managed to draw the chase out longer than Kira would have thought possible, the pilot maneuvering well, the tiny ship like some wild animal running for its life. It had lured the aggressor away from its attack, at least—but as they looped ever closer to the wormhole, another hit spun the devastated ship around, pieces of its tattered armor bursting outward into space. It sprinted forward, back toward the station—but the enemy ship was on top of it, mercilessly blasting away, and Kira could see that it was over.

The final blow came a split second later, and the ship that had tried to protect DS9 shattered, a small but sparkling fan of wreckage and gases exploding from where it had been.

Kira's gut knotted as the people around her gasped and cursed and softly cried out in muted despair, as the attack ship started back to finish off the station.

What did I expect, some kind of miracle, some beam of celestial light to shoot out of the Temple and save us all?

Maybe she had, maybe—

—*what is that?*

From offscreen, a tiny blur of motion, a glowing streak chasing after the moving strike ship. The ship apparently saw it coming at the same time she did. It picked up speed, diving down and away—and that tiny smear of light followed it, catching up—

—*torpedo*—

—and Kira understood what was happening just as it hit the diving Jem'Hadar ship, as the light of a small sun blossomed and expanded from the tiny craft, the light becoming everything.

"*Got it, we got it!*" Nog shouted, and Ezri pounded the control panel with a triumphant fist, the fire of victory surging through her heart, filling her up.

Yes!

"Hang on!" Kira shouted, and suddenly ops twisted and shook around them, people crashing into consoles and one another as the unshielded station suffered the force of the warhead explosion. Kira grabbed a railing, forgetting to breathe, seeing only the bright destruction on the screen in front of them.

Please let it be over—

—and in a few seconds, the short and violent ride ceased, the station coming to rest. For a moment, nobody moved or spoke. Kira imagined she could feel DS9's wounds, could feel the loss of power and the compromise of integrity all around her as the people in ops slowly crawled to their feet, returning to their stations.

With a silent prayer of thanks, to the Prophets and Jast's tactical brilliance, Kira set her mind to what came next. The *Aldebaran* had been destroyed, the *Defiant* and the station had been brutalized; the treaty between the Dominion and the Federation was broken. An act of war.

We have to regroup. Jast needs to confer with Starfleet, we have to oversee the repairs, we'll need Bajor to send in more techs, and we'll have to talk about establishing a defensive line here. . . .

"Bowers, launch the *Rio Grande* and the *Sungari*. I want the *Defiant* crew beamed off before they freeze to death. And arrange for the ship to be brought back for repairs. Shar, status report." Kira suddenly welcomed the incredible amount of work ahead as the reprieve that it was; with so much to do, she wouldn't have to analyze anything for a while, or consider how much of the fault was hers. She already knew the answer, anyway.

Shar read off damage reports as the ops crew struggled to manage their posts, sending people out to assess damage and carry messages to those who had been cut off. The initial communications were daunting; the hull had been breached in several places in both the lower and mid cores, most of the damage done by the aggressive point striker. Two of the fusion reactors had been impaired to the point of shutdown, reducing the station's power by a third . . . and at least thirty-four people were dead. Dozens more were unaccounted for.

Even as Shar tapped and spoke, trying to organize the flow of information, he found he couldn't stop thinking about the sensor readings that had flashed across his screen in the final seconds of the battle. They probably meant nothing, but still . . .

Kira was at the command station, her expression dismal as she scanned readouts from the lower core. Shar joined her, waiting until she looked up before speaking.

"Colonel—I should tell you that the internal sensor array suggested a transfer of energy to the station as the last strike ships were destroyed."

Kira frowned. " 'Suggested'?"

"It's not possible to verify any of the readings," Shar said. "And it's likely that they were all false, created by the power surge through the EPS system or—"

"How many such readings did you pick up, exactly?"

Shar shifted uncomfortably. "Seven hundred eight, sir."

Kira nodded slowly. "I see. As soon as the *Defiant* is brought in, you can try running our sensor logs against their externals, but I think you probably picked up radiation pulses from the explosions . . . or, like you said, random surges through the network itself from direct damage."

"I think so, too, sir, but I felt it was my duty to tell you."

"Thank you, Ensign. I'll include it in the master report. If that's all . . ."

Kira returned her attention to the table, and though Shar didn't know her well, he suspected that she was angry with herself over the near-success of the strike ships. It was a ludicrous notion, but she was radiating enough heat to suggest some strong emotion.

Perhaps if I engage her further, encourage her to talk about the battle . . . He had so admired her poise during the fight, he wished to offer some measure of his deference, however small. And he *was* genuinely interested in her perception of events.

"Sir, have you given any thought as to why the fourth ship attempted to protect the station?"

When she looked up again, he could see anger in her gaze—but her voice was calm and controlled, her manner almost formal. "No, I haven't. Perhaps you could hypothesize on the question for a later briefing. Right now is not a good time."

Shar nodded, wondering if he'd made a mistake in his approach. In his own culture, asking someone's opinion without offering one's own was a gesture of respect, and it had worked well with the captain of the *Tamberlaine*, a human male . . . maybe Bajorans were different. Or females.

Kira's combadge chirped.

"Colonel, this is Dax, on the Defiant."

"Good to hear from you, *Defiant*. And good work. We have runabouts on the way. Tell Commander Jast and Nog to report to ops when you get here, and have Nog look at our damage reports en route. We're going to have to work out a repair schedule immediately. How's everyone on the ship?"

There was a long pause, and Ezri's voice, when she spoke again, was uncharacteristically solemn. *"Two people were killed, three others wounded. Commander Jast and Turo Ane are both dead. I'm sorry, Nerys."*

Shar stared at the colonel, who stared back. He could see his own feelings reflected in her face, but found no solace in the awareness that she, too, had sustained a loss.

He grasped at his training, struggling not to lash out physically in his pain, and saw in Kira the same fight—anguish warring to become violence. It was in the set of her jaw and in the tremble of her hands.

In other circumstances, discovering that they shared similar reactions to an event might have made him proud. Now, he turned and walked stiffly back to his station, understanding only that, like himself, she needed now to be left alone.

Chapter Eight

There were seven, including himself; each a high-ranking member of the Vedek Assembly, each of the other six as openly anxious as a vedek could be while still maintaining some semblance of piousness. It all rested in the hands of the Prophets, after all—though to look at their pinched faces, one might think otherwise. One might think, in fact, that the Prophets had deserted them, leaving each alone with his or her own fears.

Such uncertainty, because of what's happened. How difficult it must be. Yevir Linjarin understood the pain of doubt, and he ached to see it in others, particularly the six other men and women in the great chamber. That there was great change coming, there was no question, but the Prophets would provide. As They always had.

The man who'd called the meeting, Vedek Eran Dal, seated himself at the head of the long stone table, nodding to the attendant ranjen to close the doors of the great hall. The incense-scented chamber was cold, the meeting called too hastily for a single fire to have been built—although the secret nature of their small alliance surely had something to do with it. The traditional fires were lit only for the Assembly entire, and there would be no evidence of this meeting once it was dismissed.

Seated here were the seven most influential, the most doctrinally inclined, the men and women who would use their powers of persuasion to carry the rest of the Assembly in the direction best for Bajor. Kai Winn's sudden disappearance had necessitated the formation of the unnamed council; with First Minister Shakaar offworld, lobbying the Federation on Bajor's behalf, the people needed guidance, and not the endlessly turbulent sort provided by the Assembly entire, with its share of politicians and sycophants and deals.

Here, though . . . here sat the careful hands that would lead the way. The shared anxiety on their faces saddened Yevir, reminding him of the passage in Akorem's *A Poet's Flight*:

> To doubt Their wisdom is to deny Them the pleasures of due faith, and to deny oneself the joy of being—and being, to be loved.

When the doors had rumbled closed, Eran began to speak.

"I thank each of you for coming with such little notice. I'm sure you understand why I've called this session. Before we discuss our options, I would ask your impressions of the crisis before us."

Vedek Frelan Syla, a small, highly opinionated woman, was the first to place her hands on the table. For reasons of poor health she had refused to be considered for the recent nomination to kai, much to everyone's relief; no one wanted another Winn Adami, and of all the possible candidates, Frelan was easily the most politically prone.

"Vedek Frelan," Eran said, opening the discussion.

"Early this morning, Deep Space 9 was attacked," she said, her statement of the obvious a clear sign that she was warming to a speech. "The last report I received from our contacts within the Militia told of sixty-one dead in all—not including the crew of the guardian starship, or the wounded—and severe damage to the power core . . . making it, I believe, the deadliest offensive yet waged against the station. Even in the time of war there was not so much damage, nor so many lives lost.

"My firm conviction is that the heresy was destroyed during the battle—and therefore that the battle itself was sanctioned by the Prophets. Did the attackers not travel through the Temple gates? I put forth that we have acted with unnecessary haste, presuming too much, and that we should now await further guidance from the Prophets."

Yevir saw, with no real surprise, that everyone now had their hands on the table, except for himself. He wanted to hear the opinions of the others before speaking; after all, it was likely they would look to him for the last word, and though he did not consider himself to be gifted politically, he knew that every notion should be heard. No one liked to feel dismissed, even if their ideas were rejected in the end. He accepted the fact of their acquiescence with no pretensions of humility, just as he accepted the reality that he would one day be kai—perhaps not after the upcoming election, but it *was* inevitable. His path was clear.

The discussion went around the table, Eran calling each vedek by name, each stating his or her thoughts in turn, no two alike. Scio Marses believed that the matter should be opened to the Assembly, or at least the part of it that they could openly claim. Kyli Shon wanted to consult the Orb of Contemplation; Sinchante Jin, the Orb of Wisdom. Bellis Nemani insisted that they send a covert team to the station, to gather data, and Eran put forth the idea of allowing Kira Nerys into their confidence. She was, he pointed out, a devout woman, though Vedeks Kyli and Bellis disagreed strongly with the idea, reminding them all of how difficult Kira had proved to be in the past. The discussion, if not heated, was quickly becoming antagonistic. Gone were the traditional formalities of hands-on-table.

"We mustn't trust any information we don't collect for ourselves," Bellis argued. "Isn't it obvious? And Kira knew Istani, from Singha. For all we know, they were acting in collaboration—"

"—and you think she wouldn't come to the Assembly for confirmation, if she had talked with Istani?" Eran asked. "We need Kira. She runs the station and the people trust her. Granted, she can be obstinate, but her faith and loyalty to Bajor aren't in question—"

"Faith, perhaps not, but loyalty? You know the stories of her and Kai Winn," Kyli interrupted, his face flushed.

"Forget about Kira, and Istani," Frelan said. "The Prophets will show us the way, when the time is right!"

Yevir had heard enough. He placed his hands palms up on the table and closed his eyes, breathing deeply, turning his face to the high ceiling, to the sky beyond.

Their intentions are true and right, but they argue their own opinions. What is the way? How can I be a vessel of Your wishes?

He listened, to the small voice at his deepest core, the voice of his *pagh,* vaguely aware that the debate around him was finished, the angry words giving way to silence. When he opened his eyes, he saw that everyone watched him.

"Vedek Yevir, you wish to speak?" Eran asked. His tone was hushed and respectful.

"Thank you, I do." Yevir smiled, gazing at each face with warmth. "We all want to do what we think is right. Because we love the Prophets, and we love the people of Bajor. I know that each of us feels that the Prophets speak to us through our emotions, but I ask that we set aside anger and dissent at this moment, and meditate on what we share. On our love."

He had their full attention. Only a few years ago, he would have marveled at the concept that he, Yevir Linjarin, would someday lead such important people through a crisis, but all he wanted now was to share his vision.

"We have too often become entrenched in politics . . . but simply loving is also not enough. Like all matters, this is one that calls for action as well as faith. As we have all agreed, the heresy must be contained—but our course so far has not been worthy of us, and I feel regret for what has happened. I grieve; I feel shame. But I know too that the Prophets forgive us, because They know our hearts, and know that we mean only to express our love."

They were smiling back at him now. They understood, and it made him happy to see the self-doubt washed away, to see their faces shining with restored purpose. They hadn't forced Istani Reyla to run away, after all.

"What would you propose?" Eran asked.

"As you all know, I once served on the station during my days in the Militia. I could approach Kira, and talk with her as a friend—but discreetly, a day or two from now. I wouldn't reveal so much as to burden her with the kind of decisions we're facing, of course. But if the tome is on board, and she has knowledge of it, I'm certain she would tell me."

They were nodding, pleased with the moderate and reasonable plan—and with having the immediate responsibility for what to do taken from them. It made him feel cynical to think such a thing, but he could not pretend blindness. Yevir knew each of them to be a worthy vedek, but he also knew that they missed having a kai to make the difficult decisions.

"I know it's asking a lot, but if you would place your trust in me, I believe that I could further our interests here, and thus the interests of all of Bajor," he finished, fully aware that their trust was already his. He didn't enjoy playing the politician, but there was really no choice, and he *was* deserving of their confidence. He had been chosen, after all.

As they gazed at him lovingly, he thought of the Emissary, of all he had done for Bajor—and all that Bajor was becoming because of the Emissary's work.

I won't let it fall apart because of some heretic's scratchings. I owe that to the Emissary, for choosing me, and I owe it to the Prophets, for Their boundless love—and to all of Bajor, because I am here to serve.

The seven were in agreement, all as one. Yevir would go to Deep Space 9 and make things right. He would find the heresy and burn it, and scatter the ashes so that no one else could be tainted by its evil ever again.

Hopefully, no one else would have to die. He would pray for it, anyway.

Chapter Nine

After a full day of triage and surgery, of making calls that meant life or death with only an educated hope that his decisions would prove sound, Bashir was exhausted . . . but as his backlog of critical cases wound down, he found himself wishing for more to do. So many lost, so many that no one had got to in time, who could have been saved; not only was it painful to review the incredible waste of life, having no pressing matter to attend to meant that there was nothing to keep him from what he thought of as the death watch—those cases for which there was no reasonable hope.

And nothing I can do, nothing at all. For all I've researched and studied, for all my abilities, I may as well wish them better.

There had been six in all. Now there were three in the infirmary's ICU, the room quiet and still but for monitor sounds and the stifled tears of the visitors. A nurse moved lightly between the beds, assuring that there would be no more pain for the dying.

Bashir stood in the doorway from surgery, looking at them, struggling to believe that he hadn't failed. He'd beaten Death throughout the day, through proper diagnosis and delegation and surgery, cases he tried to keep in mind as he gazed out at the ICU ward. Mostly he thought about the operations, because he had been able to touch the problems, to physically heal them. A sternal fracture that had caused a mediastinal bleed in a Bajoran girl, only 11 years old, healed. A compound fracture had nicked the femoral artery of a Bajoran security officer, who would have bled out if Julian's hands hadn't been fast enough. The flail chest on the visiting Stralebian boy, the open-book skull fracture of the human ensign who had been on leave from the *Aldebaran*—they all would have died if his skills had been lesser.

But that doesn't help these people, does it?

It was faulty reasoning, of course, and logically he had no cause to feel guilt. But feelings weren't necessarily logical. He couldn't blame himself for the majority of the deaths that had occurred on the station, because most of them had been instantaneous—forty-six plasma burn fatalities, a single rush of energy that probably hadn't even been experienced as pain. The rest of them had been lost to broken seals at the main lower core hull breach, except for two blunt trauma cases, victims of falling debris. There had been nothing that anyone could have done.

Of the nearly two hundred people injured, twenty or so had been critical, and only eleven of those had required immediate surgery or stasis. With the help of Dr. Tarses and the Bajoran surgeon, Girani Semna, they'd gotten to everyone. Three compartment syndrome cases had been treated and released; all three would be shipping out to the advanced medicine facility at Starbase 235 for biosynthetic limbs. Except for some head traumas, a few incidentals, and those recovering from surgery, the immediate crisis was past—

—but for the three of you. Six, and now three, a death watch because I don't know enough.

In the cool, antiseptic air, the three patients were silent, sleeping or comatose. Woros Keyth, a Bajoran man who had worked in the admin offices, lay waiting for his brother to come from Bajor, to say good-bye. Keyth might have been saved, if he had been treated sooner. A subdural hemorrhage, the resulting intercranial bleed too far along by the time he'd been brought in, the brain damage irreparable. The blow was from a desk clock, of all things, when the AG had shifted; Keyth had been alone in his office, and hadn't been found for almost three hours. Too late.

Two beds away, the sleeping Karan Adabwe was watched over by her betrothed and one of her closest friends. Karan, an engineer, had been both burned and frozen, caught in the major plasma leak and exposed to an area of hull breach. It was a wonder that she was still alive, so much of her skin and muscle tissue had been affected. Her lover and a friend each held one of her poor, wretched hands, both crying, both certainly in more pain than Karan. She was beyond that, at least.

Prynn Tenmei, the new Starfleet pilot, sat next to the last case, Monyodin, a lab tech. Bashir didn't know if they'd been dating or were just friends, but either way, it was over. Monyodin was a Benzite, and had been in mid-core when a cloud of chemical polymer gases had been released from a temp bank of atmospheric regulators. The alveoli of his lungs had liquefied. In a non-Benzite, Bashir would have tried stasis and an eventual transplant; for Monyodin, for any Benzite, there was no chance. With their cellular growth patterns, even external transplants rarely took. All that could be done was to make him comfortable . . . and watch him die.

It's not my fault. There's nothing that anyone could do.

It was true, and it didn't matter, not to the core of him. They were alive, but he couldn't keep them that way.

Bashir turned away, knowing that there were others to see, rounds to make, people he could still help. Knowing that the names and faces of the death watch would stay with him, as clear and crisp in his memories as he'd just seen them, until the day he died. He was aware that people on the station were starting to debate the long-term consequences of the Jem'Hadar attack, but if they could see what he had seen . . . he could personally testify to the tragedy of the short-term. It was more than enough.

"... then perhaps I should come back at another time. How long will she be here?"

Familiar, a familiar voice. Friendly. *Shar, that's Shar . . .*

"It shouldn't be long, but I can't really say; the doctor wanted her to wake up on her own," a woman answered. "He said she could leave then, assuming her responses are normal. The concussion wasn't severe, but we don't take chances with head injuries."

"I understand. Would it be all right if I left these with you?"

Ro opened her eyes, wanting very much to see Shar, understanding from the tone of the exchange that he was about to leave. She was in the infirmary, most of the beds around her full, the woman talking with Shar one of the nurses. Ro wasn't sure what was going on, and the fact that Shar appeared to be holding a bouquet of bright green flowers only added to her disorientation.

"Shar?" She rasped, and coughed, her throat dry.

Both Shar and the Bajoran nurse turned toward her, the nurse immediately moving to her side. Ro sat up a little, light-headed but in no pain.

"What happened?" Ro asked, and coughed again. The nurse miraculously produced a container of some mildly sweet beverage and stood by while Ro drank, gratefully.

"There was an attack on the station, and you were brought to the infirmary with a head injury," the nurse said kindly. "But your readings suggest a full recovery. I'll go get the doctor."

Shar stood next to the bed as the nurse went off to find someone. He held up the rather exotic-looking bouquet of waxy, tubular blooms with a slight smile.

"These are from Quark. I saw him on the way here and he insisted that I deliver them; he said he was too busy ordering new inventory for the bar to stop in, although he might later. He says that flowers are a customary gift for the ill or diseased. These are Argelian, I think."

Ro smiled in spite of her confusion, not sure if she was more amused by Quark's gesture or Shar's uncertain explanation. "I'll be sure to thank him. Shar, what happened to the station? What happened to *me?*"

Before he could answer, Dr. Bashir appeared from another room, walking slowly and looking harried, his hair uncharacteristically rumpled. The smile he gave her seemed genuine, though. He glanced at the bed's diagnostic before moving to her other side, across from Shar. "Lieutenant, Ensign. I have a few questions, if you don't mind."

"So do I," Ro said, propping herself up on her elbows. "Chief among them, why is Quark sending me flowers?"

Bashir grinned, the expression as sincere as his smile—but she could see the strain behind it, could see that he was hiding some pain behind the sparkle. With how full the infirmary was, she guessed he'd had a rough day.

"Oh, I can imagine," he said. He opened a medical tricorder and passed the scanner over her head, his intense gaze shifting from the readout to each of her eyes as he spoke, his smile quickly fading. "Tell me, what's the last thing you remember before waking up a few minutes ago?"

She frowned, thinking. "There was . . . a murder on the Promenade. I remember meeting with you and Kira. And then I, ah, talked to Quark a little later about it, I remember that."

She'd gotten an isolinear rod from him, she'd gone to her office, and afterward . . . she recalled feelings of unease, even distress, but she couldn't pinpoint the reason. *Something about the holosuites?* "I don't know what else, I can't remember."

The doctor nodded, setting the tricorder down. "I saw you on the Promenade not long before you were brought in; I'd say you've lost less than an hour of your memory. An amnesic gap is perfectly normal with this type of concussion, nothing to worry about. Your cranial blood pressure is stable and your neurographic scan shows no disruptions. You can return to duty . . . but if you find yourself feeling nauseous or dizzy, or unwell in any way, you're to call for assistance and report back here immediately, all right?"

Ro nodded, a little surprised at his excellent bedside manner. She really hadn't interacted with him since coming to the station, and had assumed him to be generic Starfleet medical, patronizing and probably arrogant. "How did I get hurt?"

"You fell from the stairs in Quark's," Bashir said. "Quark saw it happen, and brought you here. It's lucky he did, too. With the way the station was bouncing around, you could have been seriously injured."

She started to ask about the station and the doctor hurried on, nodding toward Shar. "But I'll let your friend fill you in on all of that. If you'll both excuse me, I have rounds to make."

Ro thanked him and turned to Shar, who spent the next few minutes filling her in. She was amazed at all she had missed, and appalled by the station's death toll, not to mention the loss of the *Aldebaran*.

And Commander Jast. Hearing about her death hit Ro harder than she expected. A lot of Starfleet officers on board had a cold attitude toward Ro. Not surprising, really. She suspected most of them bitterly resented her presence on the station and were probably dismayed that Starfleet Command hadn't made a move to arrest her for her past offenses. How the provisional government had persuaded the Federation not to exercise its rights under its extradition treaty with Bajor was a mystery. The end result, though, was that the Starfleet personnel on the station were forced to work alongside someone many of them believed belonged in prison. Or worse.

But Jast had been different. The commander had gone out of her way to be amicable. At first, Ro thought it was because Jast also seemed to be awkward at making friends . . . but, just in the last few days, she had been starting to feel that the commander actually liked her.

". . . and with incoming communications basically inoperative, the only messages from the Federation have been relayed through Bajor, telling us to wait," Shar continued. "Colonel Kira has all of the senior officers on standby for a briefing as soon as she gets word."

"What are we doing for defenses?" Ro asked, finally sitting up. Physically, she felt perfectly fine, but their conversation was making her stomach knot.

"The *I.K.S. Tcha'voth* got here just after the attack, and six Bajoran assault vessels arrived a few hours ago, so we aren't entirely defenseless," Shar said, "but there's great tension on the station, and the fear that war is once again imminent. It doesn't help that the wormhole has opened three times since this morning, triggered by debris from the *Aldebaran.*"

He lowered his gaze, speaking softly. "There's to be a service at 0700 tomorrow, in memory of all those lost. If you're not well enough to attend, it's going to be broadcast station-wide."

Listening to his gently lilting voice, she could sense a change in him. He was tired, she could see that, but there was more—something deeper, more fundamental.

Shar had probably liked Tiris Jast as much as Ro had, and had certainly known a majority of the station residents who had been killed. Though she wouldn't call him extroverted, exactly, Ensign ch'Thane was one of those rare people who seemed to honestly enjoy listening to and learning about others. He had quickly found himself a place in DS9's community, well-liked because, unlike herself, he never seemed to pass judgment. So different were their personalities, in fact, Ro had wondered more than once why he seemed to seek out her company. She'd finally decided that the old saying about opposites seeking out one another was probably true.

Shar was quite young and, though obviously brilliant, relatively inexperienced, both in his career and in his life. His only assignment before DS9 had been on a survey vessel, primarily collecting information on the Vorta. He'd seen little or no battle, and although he didn't seem the type to shy from it—Andorians, as a rule, were combat-ready—she doubted very much that he'd savored his first figurative taste of blood. Shar was too inherently decent, and she found herself mourning what he could not—the addition of a kind of tense wariness to his electric gray gaze, a look she knew too well from years of watching innocents return from their first real fight.

"I should return to ops," he said. "The sensor arrays are operational, but Colonel Kira wants them at peak efficiency now that we're focused on the wormhole."

Ro smiled at him. "I'm glad you came to see me, Shar," she said, and was faintly surprised at how much she meant it. He was the closest thing she had to a friend on the station.

Except for Quark, maybe, she thought, as Shar handed her the flowers. They had a pleasantly spicy scent.

"I hope that you will continue to mend properly," Shar said sincerely.

And I hope we're not about to go to war.

The unbidden thought frightened her, reminding her of all that was at stake—but it was a strangely compelling thought as well. She was only barely conscious that the prospect of battle had sparked her interest.

They made tentative plans to meet later and he departed, leaving her to consider all that had happened and to wonder what would happen next. So, the station's residents were scared, but fear wasn't all that hard to inspire in a primarily civilian population. The soldier in Ro couldn't get behind the idea that the Dominion truly wanted another war, not with what Shar had told her about the nature of the attack—and for all of Kira's faults, Ro didn't think the colonel was dense enough to think so either, not when it came to matters of conflict. Though, what Starfleet was convinced of was another thing entirely.

Forget it, Laren. None of your business. She had her own duties to worry about, reports to make and listen to, security measures to be reviewed and evaluated. And pointless as it suddenly seemed in the face of the larger tragedy, there was still that investigation into the prylar's death.

Ro stood up, Quark's flowers in hand, and though she'd already decided it wasn't her concern, she suddenly found herself wishing very much to know what Kira was thinking about, what she would say when she finally spoke to Starfleet—and what Starfleet would have to say to her.

There was more than enough room in the cargo bay for the coffins and urns and memorial plaques, but it was no less crowded for the dark and cavernous space. She'd left the main bank of lights off, the barely lit shadows much more appropriate for her lonely visit . . . and somehow, it reinforced the vague feeling that she'd never seen so many of the dead in one place. It wasn't true, of course, but the blank rows and stacks of sealed containers seemed to go on forever as they disappeared into the dark, an endless testimony to all that had gone wrong only a single day ago . . . and to her own place within that series of events that had left almost seventy of her people dead.

The memorial service had gone well, she supposed, as if any such thing could be said to describe a few simple prayers and a shocked moment of silent remembrance. It would have been better to wait a few days, but Kira knew from experience that reality assimilation often took time—which was an uncertain variable until they knew exactly why the Jem'Hadar had attacked the station. Better to say a few words when there was opportunity to say them, and hope that the survivors could manage their own personal closure in the days to come.

The service itself had been brief, the Promenade overflowing but still, everyone who could leave their work for a few moments standing en masse like a tide of lifeless dolls, watching her speak with flat and barely responsive gazes. After staying up all night walking the damaged station and personally taking reports from every section and subsection chief she could find, standing in front of the mostly silent assembly had seemed unreal, a disjointed dream filled with realistically unhappy details—the pale faces of the *Aldebaran* crew, knowing that only an assigned leave had spared them while their friends had died. The way Nog's proudly raised chin had trembled, or the soft sigh of an elderly woman who had lost her son. Kira had heard tears and seen the hard, set lines of faces that reflected emptiness, for fear that even acknowledging the pain would be too much to bear.

Kira rested her hand on the cool, smooth surface of a keepsake box, destined for a family in the Hedrikspool Province of Bajor, a few personal items that their daughter had left behind. Setrin Yeta, one of Ro's junior deputies, a bubbly redheaded girl with a high-pitched laugh. Gone. To be with the Prophets, surely, but would her family feel any less pain?

Will I? Will any of us?

Tiris and Turo Ane, Kelly and Elvim and McEwian and T'Peyn and Grehm and the list went on, some of the faces only known in passing, all of them real people with real lives, and if she had only done something more, if she'd made a decision a few seconds earlier, or later . . .

Without consciously deciding to, she had gone straight from the ceremony to the cargo bay, almost as if guided by some invisible hand. Even with all there was to do, her sense of responsibility wouldn't allow her to avoid it; to understand what had happened, to really understand what had been lost, she needed to see them. To witness the reality of them.

As she'd stepped into the bay, her early morning dream from the day before had come back to her, from what seemed to be millennia ago. It was the environment that did it, bringing a flash of imagery—a cargo bay, and she'd been surrounded by dying people on the Cardassian freighter, the fleeting glimpse of Ben as she'd walked into the light of the Prophets . . . had it been an omen, even a warning? Had she been too quick to dismiss it as a dream?

Now, she was surrounded by the dead, but she knew that there would be no saving grace at the end, no friendly voice or affirmation of divinity. She wasn't going to wake up, and although she'd been responsible for the deaths of others in her time, there was no real way to prepare for it, or work out moral rationalizations. It would always be something so vast and shocking that there was little to be done but to weather it, to let it be. There wasn't anything that could make her less responsible; better to accept the consequences and move on than to waste time wishing things were otherwise.

She walked slowly between two of the rows, letting her fingers slip across the various containers of nondescript black metal, hurriedly replicated that afternoon. She'd had some vague idea about looking for Tiris to say good-bye, but she couldn't simply walk past the others. She thought that Jast probably would have understood.

Here were two humans bound for home, two Federation diplomatic trainees—both male, bright, fresh from the Academy and excited to study in the field, observing Cardassian aid relations. During his first day on the station, the older of the two had actually tried to flirt with her; he obviously hadn't yet learned how to read Bajoran rank insignia, and flashed a grin that told her that her eyes burned like the stars. She'd actually considered not telling him her name when he had asked, amused and secretly flattered by the ignorant attempt; in the end, she'd been unable to resist. The young man had blushed furiously and then studiously avoided her, right up until the day he'd died.

Eric, and his friend was Marten. She touched the black lines of code at the heads of their containers, wondered what Asgard and New Paris were like, the places where their families unknowingly waited for notification.

Next to them, a small, sealed pouch of liquid that would be sent to Meldrar I, blood from Starfleet Ensign Jataq'qat's heart that would be poured into the Meldrarae sea by its siblings. Jataq'qat had challenged her to a game of springball not so long ago, a date they would never keep. Kira walked on. A row away, a long line of small ceremonial urns bound for various Bajoran cities and townships, some containing earrings—the symbols of family, of the victims' devotion to the Prophets and the spiritual community to which they belonged—others with small pieces from the lives that had been taken.

She sighed, her mind so full of masked recriminations that she didn't want to think—not because she feared the pain, but because it was too distracting. Balancing between remorse and the cold, linear reality of the future was a cruel and terrible thing; she couldn't even allow herself the questionable relief of wallowing in guilt, because the station needed her, it needed her to be at the top of her game and she couldn't afford to shoulder the presumption of incompetence, no matter how much she thought she should.

"Why did you come here, Reyla," Kira said softly, her voice almost lost in the soft hum of the air coolers. She wasn't sure if it was a question, wasn't sure what she expected, but the death of her long-ago friend meant something, it had to mean something, didn't it? All of this had to mean *something*.

Kira felt her throat constrict and took several deep breaths, inhaling and exhaling heavily, clearing her mind. With each new breath, the tide of sorrow crept back, giving her room, reminding her that she was whole and alive and had a lot to do, too much to be standing around weeping in the dark.

Just as she felt herself reaching safer ground, her combadge signaled.

"Colonel Kira, there's an incoming message from Bajor, routed from the U.S.S. Cerberus—*"*

Ross's ship.

"Should I send it to your office?" It was Bowers, in ops, and he sounded tense. Everyone on the station understood that Admiral Ross's call would set them on a definite course of action, to comply with whatever the Federation decided. What that course would be, Kira wasn't certain; at one time, she would have called for immediate action, but she wasn't so quick to assume the worst as she used to be.

And not so quick to fight, if there's even a possible alternative. As far as she was concerned, the attack should be quietly investigated through diplomatic channels, at least until something solid turned up . . . and although Kira *believed* that the Federation wouldn't act rashly, that they probably wouldn't even whisper the idea of a counterattack before careful consideration, she wasn't positive. That was bad, but what really scared her was the possibility that she wouldn't have any way to influence their decision if they had, in fact, decided on some sort of retaliatory action. Deep Space 9 sat at the Alpha entrance to the wormhole, the first outpost that any Gamma traveler—or soldier—would encounter. Without question, the Dominion could not be allowed back, not if they meant to fight—but how could she allow one more life to be lost, when she might be able to prevent it?

My job here isn't about me, and it's not just about the state of the Federation. It's also about trying to do what's best for the people on this station, and for Bajor. She believed that, and it gave her strength, it was direction when she needed it—but as Bowers waited for her response, she gazed out over the sad remains of her friends, of her wards and peers and the semi-remembered faces of just a few of the thousands who depended on her, and she didn't feel it.

I'll be as strong as I need to be.

"Yes. I'm on my way," Kira said, gathering her defenses as she turned toward the doors that would lead her back to the world of the living. She didn't hurry and she didn't look back, the possibility of tears already a memory.

Chapter Ten

Whirling plumes of light spun up from wavering plains of fire, the radiant shapes lengthening thousands of meters until they grew too vast to sustain themselves. The funnels collapsed, disintegrating back into the amorphic ocean of red and orange before rising anew, the dance of the storms beautiful, threatening, and eternal.

After watching for what seemed like hours, Commander Elias Vaughn finally broke the silence. "Are we done yet?"

Captain Picard smiled, not looking away from the incredible lightshow. "Done watching?"

"Done looking, for the Breen. They're not here, Jean-Luc. I don't think they ever were."

Picard's smile faded. "I've come to agree with you, but we have to be thorough. Another run through the thick of it, and we'll have completed a second grid. We want to be able to declare a reasonable certainty, after all our efforts."

They stood before the viewport in the captain's ready room, the ever-shifting view of the Badlands spread out in front of them in shades of flame. For the last several days, the two men had taken to meeting there as the ship completed each run, to watch the plasma storms together.

The *Enterprise* had been searching the treacherous area for nearly three weeks, the constant atmospheric disturbances making it necessary to pilot and investigate manually, their sensors useless beyond a very short range. Vaughn had come aboard to advise the mission on Breen tactics . . . though even if their supposed presence had turned out to be true, he doubted he'd have been of much use. The captain and crew of the *Enterprise-E* were more than worthy of their distinction, and Vaughn was certain they could handle themselves against a few Breen.

It's been nice to spend some time with Picard and his people, anyway. Vaughn liked Picard, having met him on more than one occasion in the past. He'd always thought the captain bright, if a bit dry, and surprisingly well-rounded. His tactical instincts were superb, and he carried his command well, with distinction and grace. A little formal, perhaps, but not offensively so, his politeness clearly stemming from a respect for others rather than some self-promoting mechanism. But Vaughn had worked with this particular *Enterprise* crew only once before, at the Betazed emancipation over a year ago—a mission that had earned them his profound respect.

The intercom beeped, Will Riker's voice interrupting his musings. *"Captain, the new course is plotted. Allowing for the predicted plasma currents, Commander Data suggests that we begin immediately, and that we start out at one-quarter impulse for the first two million kilometers."*

"Make it so," Picard said, and as the ship eased toward the shimmering Badlands, Vaughn thought again about the coded transmission he'd received only a few hours before. Even the dramatic beauty of the plasma storms wasn't enough to distract him entirely. He was bone-tired, and not from three weeks of chasing a rumor.

"I'm thinking of retiring, Jean-Luc," Vaughn said abruptly, a little surprised at his own impulsiveness as the words left his mouth. He'd been considering it for months, but hadn't planned to tell anyone until he'd decided. And he didn't even know Picard all that well. . . .

. . . *although he probably knows* me *as well as anyone*. Vaughn didn't know if that was good or bad, but it was the truth.

Picard also seemed surprised. He turned to look at Vaughn, eyebrows arched. "Really? May I ask why?"

"You may, but I'm not sure I have an answer," Vaughn said. "I suppose I could just say that I'm getting too old. . . ."

"Nonsense. You can't be much older than I am."

Vaughn smiled; he'd never looked his age. "I'm a hundred and one, actually."

Picard smiled back at him. "You wear it well. But you still have decades ahead of you, Elias."

"I suppose I mean old in spirit," Vaughn said, sighing. "Since the end of the war, I find myself thinking differently about things. After eighty years of charging off to battle . . ."

He paused, thinking. He'd never been an eloquent man, but he wanted very much to define the path of his feelings, as much for himself as for Picard. After so long a war, so little time for pleasures or luxuries, he felt out of touch with the delicacy of his self-perceptions.

"I've always been a soldier," he said. "I was trained for it, and have excelled at it—and for a long time, I've felt my role to be an integral part of the peace process. Now, though . . . just lately, I've been thinking of the universe as an unending series of conflicts that doesn't need another aging warrior to help circumscribe them."

Vaughn shook his head, searching for more words to explain what he'd been feeling. "Wars will always be waged, I know that. But I'm starting to think of myself as a participant in war, rather than someone working toward peace. And the difference between the two is immeasurable."

Picard was silent for a moment, and they watched as the *Enterprise* slid effortlessly into the bright and turbulent space of the Badlands. Vaughn felt strangely relaxed, at ease with the captain's silence. He suspected that what he'd said was being carefully measured by Picard, scrupulously considered, and the thought was oddly comforting.

"Perhaps you need a change of vocation," Picard said finally. "Do you know the story of Marcus Aurelius?"

Vaughn smiled. A great warrior of ancient Rome, a general who'd lost his taste for battle in spite of his successes. The original soldier-philosopher of Earth. "You flatter me."

"Not at all. And I'm not suggesting that you turn to writing your meditations on war and peace . . . though perhaps that's not such a terrible idea. You have more strategic and tactical experience than any career officer I've ever known, Elias, but that doesn't mean you have to use it as a soldier would. You could write, or teach."

Picard faced him, his expression earnest. "Of course, you can do whatever you wish. But—forgive my presumption—I don't think you're the kind of man who would be content to sit back and watch the worlds go by."

Vaughn nodded slowly. "You may be right about that." He took a deep breath and expelled it heavily, finally reaching the foundation of his thought, the essence of what he was trying to express. "I don't know. I just know that I don't want to fight anymore."

Picard leaned back, looking out at the fiery storm once more. "I understand," he said softly, and Vaughn believed that he truly did. The captain's ability to empathize was perhaps his most admirable trait. It was a rarity in any species, and most particularly in upper echelon Starfleet.

The intercom signaled again. *"Captain, Commander—we may have something."*

That was a surprise. Vaughn left his personal thoughts behind as he followed Picard toward the door to the bridge. He'd been so sure about the Breen, had already decided that perhaps the Klingons had picked up *something*, but that "possible Breen warp signatures" wasn't it. Following the treaty, the Breen had withdrawn to their home space for the most part. But though they were certainly capable of deceit, building a military presence in hiding didn't fit with the Breen's cultural psychology. . . .

. . . *although it does fit in with a few other reports I've heard of late* . . . Reports that were still on a need-to-know basis. It was a funny thought, though Vaughn was too aware of the *Enterprise*'s current position to find any humor in it.

They stepped out onto the bridge and moved to their seats, Vaughn taking the advisory position to the captain's left. All they could see on screen was the rolling sea of unstable plasma.

"Mr. Data, report," Picard said.

The android consulted his operations console as he spoke. "Sir, the ship I am detecting is not Breen. It is a freighter, and it appears to be Cardassian in origin."

Picard frowned. From his other side, Riker spoke softly. "What's a freighter doing out here?"

Data answered him. "It is caught between two conflicted masses of pressure. Sensors indicate that the freighter is powerless, and there are no life signs aboard. Also, that they have been trapped in this area for an extended period of time."

"Estimate? How long?"

"Considering the relative consistency of both pressure fronts and initial reads on hull integrity, I would estimate that this particular eddy has existed for thirty years or more."

Picard's frown deepened. "Can you get a visual?"

"Trying, sir."

A few seconds later, the main screen's view changed, and Vaughn caught his breath, fascinated. The long, dark freighter tumbled slowly end over end against its bright backdrop, as it apparently had for decades, dead and alone. Vaughn felt his earlier exhaustion dropping away at the sight, barely noticing his relief that there was no battle to be had.

Haunted, it looks haunted.

"Captain, if you have no objection, I'd like to lead an away team to investigate," he said, not sure why he was so intrigued, not caring particularly. It seemed to be a day for impulsiveness.

Picard glanced at Vaughn and smiled, so slightly that it was barely visible. He looked back to the screen.

"Commander Data, is the ship's hull intact?"

"Yes, sir."

Meaning it's possible to initiate an atmosphere, at least temporarily. AG's a must, but we can suit it against cold, wouldn't have to wait for an environmental toxin analysis then, either. . . .

Picard nodded, and turned again to Vaughn. "Commander, I hope you'll allow Commander Riker to accompany you, and advise you in your selection of team members."

"Of course. Thank you, Captain."

Vaughn and Riker both stood, Riker asking for Data to join them, recommending that La Forge and an Ensign Dennings meet them at the transporter. Vaughn found himself unable to tear his gaze away from the exanimate freighter, and finally understood why he was so interested, the reason so fundamental but so odd that he'd almost missed it.

Somehow, looking at the lifeless freighter, he felt quite strongly that his future was inexorably tied to whatever they would find there.

I am *getting old.* Such fanciful thinking and daydreaming adventure wasn't his style. Vaughn shook himself mentally and headed for the turbolift, but in spite of his own best efforts to act his age, his excitement only grew.

Chapter Eleven

Ensign Kuri Dennings was the last to arrive at the transporter room, slightly breathless in her environmental suit and obviously excited to have been asked along. As she hurriedly donned her helmet, Riker introduced her to Commander Vaughn, making a point to mention the anthropological study she'd done on Cardassia's occupation of Bajor. Vaughn asked several educated questions about the occupation as they stepped onto the transporter pad, all of them making minor adjustments to their helmets before pressurizing their suits.

"Is everything ready?" Riker asked La Forge, his own voice sounding annoyingly strange in the confines of the headpiece. Irritating, SEWGs. No matter how streamlined the suits got, they still felt bulky and restrictive.

"Yes, sir. Our tractor beam is holding her steady. Gravity's been established, there are some emergency lights . . . though it's going to be a little cold, even with the suits. Negative 80° C at last check."

They could handle cold, but not dark. "How long will we have before the portable's cell runs low?" Riker asked.

Vaughn answered. "Considering the size of the freighter, I'd say about two hours. It's a standard cargo model, isn't it? 220?"

He directed his own question at La Forge, who nodded, looking distinctly impressed behind the thick lens of his faceplate. "That's right, Commander."

Vaughn smiled. "Sorry. I should leave the engineering matters to the expert."

Riker was also impressed, though not because of Vaughn's awareness of portable generators; the commander seemed to know a little bit about everything, but used it well, also knowing when to defer to others.

And when to shut up. The elder commander didn't seem to ramble, ever. Riker didn't know that he'd be so reserved with eighty years of war stories under his belt, and his taciturnity only added to his appeal; Vaughn wasn't mysterious, exactly, but there was an impression of great intensity behind his genial exterior, of levels operating within levels.

"Shall we?" Vaughn asked, and then nodded to Palmer at the controls. "Energize, if you please, Lieutenant."

A sparkle of light, and they were standing in the well of a large control room, littered with random debris and dusted all over with glittering frost. There were no bodies; the crew had probably sealed themselves in whatever areas were easiest to seal, to retain atmosphere for as long as possible. The freighter's bridge was cold, empty, and dimly lit by a handful of emergency lights, reminding Riker of nighttime on the mountains of Risa. He'd camped there last before the war, alone, huddled in front of a small fire as a cold plateau wind ruffled his hair. . . .

. . . *where did* that *come from?* A weird connection, to say the least. Risa was light-years away, literally and figuratively.

Vaughn stepped away from their group, surveying their surroundings. Ensign Dennings and Data both held up tricorders and started to take readings, and La Forge turned toward what had to be the engineering console with his case of adapter components, his silvery eyes glinting in the low light.

"Anything we didn't expect?" Vaughn asked, addressing no one in particular. Data answered, his voice startlingly clear. Physically, he didn't need a suit, but the helmet comlinks were still the best way for him to stay in contact with the rest of them.

"Tricorder readings are consistent with those of the Enterprise *sensors,"* Data stated. *"This ship was caught in a plasma storm approximately thirty-two years and four months ago. The structural damage in evidence would have made it impossible for them to break free from this pocket of space. Their power and life support would have failed in a matter of days."*

"There were at least three Cardassian ships lost in the Badlands around that time," Dennings added, *"but all military, no record of a freighter."*

Geordi had plugged into one of the consoles and was reading from a small screen. *"I think it's called the* Kamal,*"* he called. *"Ring any bells?"*

Kamala. The smell of her hair, and the way she tilted her head ever so slightly when she spoke . . . Riker blinked, taken aback by the sudden vivid memory of the empathic metamorph. He hadn't thought of Kamala in *years*.

Seems like I'm determined to let my mind wander. Deanna said I've been less focused lately, guess I should have paid more attention. . . .

He also knew from Deanna that the crew desperately needed some time off, that stresses were high and productivity low. Since the end of the war, the *Enterprise* had been inspecting defunct military installations, transporting supplies and emergency aid, chasing after possible terrorist groups—in short, wrapping up the loose ends to a war. It was almost the *Enterprise*'s turn for a much-needed break, and considering his lack of concentration, he abruptly decided that it couldn't be too soon.

Dennings was checking a padd she'd brought with her. *"There* was *a transport freighter* Kamal, *but no record of it being lost. Of course, the Cardassians aren't exactly famous for sharing that kind of information. Not then, anyway."*

Not much of a mystery here; the freighter had gotten stuck. For some reason it reminded him of an abandoned ship they'd come across when he'd been on the *Potemkin*, though that had been a personal craft, caught in a natural soliton wave. . . .

Snap out of it, Will!

Vaughn turned to address them, his eyes glinting with interest. *"Well. I know it's not standard procedure, but if no one objects, I'd like very much to poke around a bit, see what there is to see."*

He looked at Riker. *"Commander, I know there are safety protocols to consider. . . ."*

Riker smiled at the half question. Vaughn certainly didn't need his permission, but was gracious enough to ask, acknowledging his status as executive officer. "I think an 'unofficial' inventory would go much faster if we split up."

"I think so, too," Vaughn said, smiling in turn. *"I thought I'd head for the*

aft cargo bays . . . perhaps we could each take a direction, and check in every fifteen minutes?"

Everyone nodded, and Riker found himself feeling relieved, looking forward to having a few moments to collect himself as he assigned sections to Dennings and Data; La Forge wanted to stay on the bridge and download whatever information he could. Riker wasn't tired, but felt as though he was suffering the symptoms of too little sleep—although of course he *had* stayed up too late, catching up on reports, and then a very late dinner with Deanna . . .

. . . curled up together afterward and talking about work, her eyes as dark and shining as when we met . . .

She'd had a sleeveless yellow dress that she often wore that first summer he'd been stationed on Betazed. He remembered the crisp feel of it brushing against his arm when they'd held hands and walked through the university's grounds, laughing about some random observation and enjoying the sun against their youthful faces—

God. He had to get some downtime, and soon.

There were dead Bajoran civilians in the cargo bays, corpses crushed beneath long-worthless boxes of supplies or sprawled atop broken sections of hull and deck. Prisoners of the occupation, their sad, frozen bodies were too thin, a testament to the suffering they'd experienced in life—and though there were a number of Cardassian soldiers among the dead, the oppressors and villains of the occupation, Vaughn found himself unable to work up any anger. They were all dead. The occupation was history, and dead was dead. He wasn't always so unfeeling, so uninterested, but the reality of the *Kamal* had become a veil, a mist through which his life was being played like a holodeck program.

The memories had started small at first, shadows of experience that touched him and were gone. But the memories grew in detail as Vaughn continued to walk through the dark and cold, becoming more than vague images, becoming brighter than what was in front of him. Having never experienced a spiritual epiphany—and from the oft-heard tales of such experiences, he assumed that was what was happening—he wasn't sure what to expect, but perhaps the memories were part of it. Part of letting go . . . ?

Violence and death and rationalizations. It was hard, the truth; he'd seen and done many things that he wished he hadn't. He walked on, and the memories came faster, the intense feelings striking like lightning. People he'd loved, long ago; a dog he'd had as a child; the first time he'd kissed a girl. But overriding the touches of fond nostalgia were the battles, the substance of his life as a soldier. He couldn't stop remembering other tragedies, deaths as needless and terrible as the ones laid in front of him now. He'd witnessed innumerable wars, he'd documented the bloody aftermath on dozens of worlds—and he'd participated in more sorrows than he wanted to count.

My life has been about death. In the name of preventing it, I've killed so many, and seen so many killed. . . .

The civil war on Beta VI, where over eleven thousand men had beaten each other to death with sticks and rocks on one catastrophic afternoon, and all his team had been able to do was watch. The genocidal holocaust on Arvada III. The Tomed incident, in 2311; he'd been a lieutenant then, only in his thirties, back when he'd still believed that evil was doomed to fail simply because it was evil.

Vaughn walked slowly through connecting corridors as he'd gone through the lower cargo bays, his mind light-years from where each leaden step carried him. The desperate and hungry faces of Verillian children, orphaned by war. The mad, hopeless cries of fear and warning that had echoed down the halls of the Lethean veteran asylum. The terrible assassination of the Elaysian governor that he could have stopped, if only he'd known the truth even moments earlier. . . .

Vaughn was so caught up in the barrage of memories that he was slow to recognize the change of light. It wasn't until he stepped into the next bay that he noticed; the dim red of the emergency lighting was different here, the massive hold bathed in a purplish glow.

It wasn't as important as the images that held his mind, that battered him mercilessly as he walked inside. A dying scream. A crying woman. Friends lost. Feelings of triumph and pride, hate and fear.

The light grew brighter, illuminating the faces of the dead cast about like debris, and Vaughn stopped walking, trapped by a lifetime of memory.

On the bridge of the *Enterprise* they had very little warning before the giant wave hit them from behind, its intense burst of radiation shattering across their shields in a sparkling halo of light. The truly powerful ones were very rare, and because the surges of energy traveled like tsunami beneath the surface of their plasma ocean, they were hard to foresee; the sensors didn't pick it up until six seconds before impact.

"Sir, there's a sudden concentration of highly charged plasma radiation behind us at mark, ah, hitting us now."

Even as the words were leaving Lieutenant Perim's mouth, the *Enterprise* was reacting, struggling to spread out the concentrated phenomenon, cutting sharply into the ship's power supply as the shields automatically prioritized their energy use.

Picard knew what it was before Perim had a chance to finish her sentence. The experienced physical effect was surprisingly mild, lights brightening suddenly and then lowering in strength, less background noise as nonessential equipment powered down, but he wasn't encouraged. A shield drain big enough to tap into something as insignificant as the lights had potentially devastating consequences.

"Engineering, report," Picard snapped, nodding to Perim at the same time. "Hail the away team, and put the freighter onscreen."

Status from Lieutenant Achen in engineering was fast and mixed. The last of the concentrated energy flux had traveled past them and wasn't dragging a secondary current, which meant they weren't in immediate danger of being hit again; all systems and their backups were suffering severe power shortages, but there was nothing irreversibly damaged except for the subspace communications array—it had been scrambled, and could take days to recalibrate and realign. Their shields were operating at substandard levels and wouldn't be up to par for several hours, which shouldn't be a problem so long as nothing else rammed them anytime soon—and the power to the tractor beam had been cut, releasing the freighter.

"No answer from the away team, sir," Perim reported, sounding tense and frustrated. "It looks like our short-range is down, too."

"Do we have transporters?" Picard asked.

"Negative, but that's temporary," said Achen. "They were just knocked off-line, so as soon as they've got enough power built up for the fail-safe, they'll automatically reinstate."

Picard watched as the magnified freighter settled across the main screen, weighing and measuring the possibilities. Nudged by the turbulence of the power wave, the freighter was slowly moving away from the *Enterprise*. Perim called out the approximate rate of four meters a second.

At their rate of movement . . . say, five to ten minutes until they move far enough to completely dissolve the conflict of pressures, less if they're caught in a heated current.

Re-establishing a tractor lock would take too long. Factoring in the accompanying glitches to transport failure, Picard calculated that they'd need anywhere from four to nine minutes, assuming there was no trouble with the fail-safe charge.

"Get the transporters working immediately, priority one," he said. "Helm, can the sensors read anything beyond lifesigns?"

Perim shook her head, running able hands over the console pads. "Four living humanoids . . . no beacon read on Commander Data, no distinctive biosignature capacity from here."

"I can't get their combadge overrides to signal, sir," communications added.

For the well-shielded *Enterprise,* the random plasma tsunami had acted as an energy leech, no permanent damage done. But the freighter was no longer shielded by the tractor beam, had in fact been pushed toward possible danger by the beam's dying surge—and the away team might not even know it.

We can't talk to them, and at the moment, we can't pull them out. There was also no way to easily dock a shuttle, not without someone operating the freighter's lockdown controls. Blowing out a chunk of bulkhead was possible, but it would take time to do it safely.

Will was due to report within the next few minutes, and was decidedly punctual as a rule; when he realized that the *Enterprise* couldn't be contacted, he'd have the team initiate their communicator emergency signals. The transporters should be working by then.

"Prep a shuttle, and have a rescue team standing by," Picard said, not liking that he had to include it as one of the better options, knowing that he wanted as many contingency plans available as possible. "Security, send someone to transporter room one, have them suited and briefed. Have Dr. Crusher standing by with a medical team as well."

Less than two minutes after the wave had come and gone, Picard had done what he could to influence the outcome of the situation. He watched the freighter as it slowly drifted away from safety, wondering what could be keeping the away team from noticing that their tricorder readings had changed.

Kuri Dennings had been thinking about her days at the Academy as she walked, feeling fondly nostalgic and a little irritated that she couldn't seem to pay attention to her surroundings. To see an occupation-era Cardassian freighter as it had been during those years . . . it was the chance of a lifetime, and yet she couldn't stop reminiscing about people she'd known, remembering names and faces she thought she'd forgotten. She had signaled in at fifteen minutes or so without thinking about it, too intent on her memories to care much about what everyone else was doing.

Kelison, with that silly hat he always wore to dinner, until Stanley hid it. The birds that nested outside the dorm. And Kra Celles, who could impersonate Lieutenant Ellisalda dead-on, from her facial mannerisms to that high, wavering voice. . . .

When she finally stopped walking, she realized she had found the weapons store, directly beneath the bridge. It was connected to a *yeldrin,* a kind of hand-to-hand-combat practice room common on older Cardassian ships. In the corridor between the two rooms were a dozen dead men, all Cardassian— after thirty years of weightlessness, they'd been cruelly dumped to the floor by the *Kamal's* sudden gravity. She'd avoided looking at them, disturbed by the blank, ice-lensed gazes and stiff and awkward poses. They reminded her of the time she'd gone fishing with her brother on Catualla. They had stored their catch in a refrigeration unit that had malfunctioned, turning the fish into blocks of gray, lumpy ice. At the time, it had been funny. . . .

. . . and we joked about it, we called them ichthysicles, and Tosh was still laughing about it the last time we talked. When he called to tell me he'd met someone, a woman, and he thought he was falling in love.

A transmission in the middle of the night from her father, seven months after their vacation to Catualla. She'd been half asleep until she'd seen his face, seen the horrible struggle not to break down in the way he blinked, the way his chin trembled. He was the bravest, strongest man she'd ever known, but his son, her brother, was dead at the age of 26, victim to a freak cave-in at one of the mines he surveyed.

"Tosh is dead, baby," and he'd wept openly, tears running down his tired, tired face.

Nine years ago, but the pain was suddenly as fresh as it had been that very moment, and Dennings slumped against the icy wall of the *yeldrin* and clutched at herself weakly, trying to hold herself against the terrible pain.

Tosh is dead, baby. Tosh is dead. . . .

Ensign Dennings slid to the deck, sobbing, lost to the memory.

• • •

After Miles O'Brien had transferred to DS9, he'd kept in intermittent touch with the *Enterprise*—sometimes to say hello, to catch up with how the crew of the "D" and later the "E" were doing. In the early days he would contact La Forge just as often to complain good-naturedly about his new job. DS9 had once been the Cardassian "Terok Nor," a uridium processing station—and, as Miles was quick to point out, Federation technology simply didn't function very well when plugged into machines built by Cardassians.

Not without a lot of rewiring, and some very imaginative bypass work. It wasn't that the technology was that much more or less advanced—only a two-point difference on the Weibrand logarithmic developmental scale, at least when the *Kamal* was built. But the fundamentals were distinct, from the positioning of warp engines to the computer's defense capabilities, and La Forge found himself appreciating O'Brien's troubles, seeing them in a whole new light. Even the mission last year to Sentok Nor hadn't prepared him for this. He was having a hell of a time figuring out how to get around in the freighter's most basic systems. It wasn't helping that he couldn't seem to get anything to power up properly.

I should get Data back up here, see if he can make sense of some of these translation disparities . . . La Forge scooped a .06 laser tip out of his tool case and sparked it, deciding to weld two of the console's EPS processing wafers together, see if he could boost efficiency—and hardly aware that he was doing it, he found himself thinking about how Leah would tackle the *Kamal*.

She'd be able to get a handle on this, no problem. Together, they'd be able to manage it easily . . . if it was the Leah he'd known on the holodeck, his own personal version of the engineer. . . .

La Forge felt a sudden flush of shame, remembering how she'd found his private program, his small fantasy of working with the brilliant engineer cruelly exposed. He'd never exploited her image, using the holographic program as a kind of confidence-builder—but he *had* made Dr. Leah Brahms much friendlier than she was comfortable with. He remembered the look on her face when he'd walked into the holosuite, too late to keep the real Leah from seeing the Leah-projection . . . he remembered the anger and embarrassment in her eyes, remembered thinking that *he* had caused those feelings, that she probably thought he was some kind of perverted miscreant when all he'd wanted was to be with her, to work side by side with a woman who respected him as much as he respected her—

La Forge frowned and shook his head, wondering why he was rehashing that particular aspect of their relationship. He'd found out she was married, she'd realized he wasn't a creep, and they'd ended up parting on friendly enough terms. . . .

This place is getting to me. Old ship, old feelings.

He'd been daydreaming since they arrived, running through all kinds of personal history as he worked. No harm done, he supposed, although he was usually better at focusing himself.

He lowered the bright torch tip to the processing chips, concentrating on the fine web of filaments. There was a spark, a wisp of smoke, the gentle swirl claiming his awareness.

—blind and alone, the smell of smoke thickening—

He'd been five years old, still too young for the VISOR implants that would allow him sight, and the fire had been started by a short in his bedroom's heating unit.

I didn't call out at first. I thought that if I stayed very still and quiet, it would go away. A blind child alone in his room at night, fists clenched and sweating, silently praying as hard as he could that there was no smoke smell, the air was clean, and that wasn't the crackle of flames, *wasn't-wasn't-wasn't—*

It wasn't until he actually felt the building heat that the little boy had screamed finally, screamed until he'd heard running footsteps, his father's gasp and mother's curse and more running. He'd burst into tears when he'd felt strong arms lift him up and away, the voice of his excellent father soft and soothing in his ear, *it's okay, Geordi, shhh, everything's okay now, shhh, my son, it's over and everything's okay . . .*

Feelings of love and remembered terror welled up in his heart and stomach, reminding him of how he'd loved them, of how dark his life had been except for their light, remembering . . .

After her hurried briefing, Deanna Troi reached the bridge as quickly as she could, the intensity of the atmosphere immediately setting her teeth on edge. The *Enterprise* was shadowing the freighter, which was apparently only minutes from hitting a strong current that would toss them, unshielded, into the whirling, deadly spumes of light. Will's report was officially overdue, and the transporters were still off-line . . . there were still too many variables for exact predictions, but simply, if they couldn't make contact with the away team soon, they would be lost.

Deeply frustrated, the captain was listening to an engineering update and leaning over the helm's console, watching stats. Deanna took her seat, breathing deeply as she opened herself up, first acknowledging and then tuning past the people directly around her. She felt for Will, searching for the familiar presence in a radiating arc of awareness, but couldn't find him; she couldn't find anyone. She hadn't really expected to, the Badlands disrupted all sorts of sensors, even her innate empathic sense, but she'd had to try.

Having nothing to report, Deanna stayed silent, watching the freighter, hearing status revisions and possible solutions to the problem—but her concern for her lover and friends wouldn't allow her any real objectivity. She gave into it instead, recognizing her own need to feel productive in the face of such frustration.

Nothing to lose, anyway.

Deanna closed her eyes for just a few seconds, seeing herself, seeing a sense of warning expanding from her presence, mentally speaking words of alarm. *Will, you're all in danger, look out, receive, understand that you're in trouble.* She knew that it was probably useless, she wasn't much of a sender outside her own species, but her faith in their connection gave her hope—that by some chance he would feel the fear in her thoughts and understand what was happening, before it was too late.

Riker walked until the silence got to him, and then he remembered. He remembered, and was afraid.

There was death everywhere, Cardassian bodies stiffly jumbled like stick dolls and no sound but the sounds of his own body, his heart and respiration, the rustle of his uniform against the inside of his suit. It was as though the ship was holding its breath, waiting, in between what had come before and what was coming next, the silence a secret in the empty space.

Quiet and secret, secret and hidden . . .

He'd reached the living quarters. The *Kamal* had small, individual rooms for her crew, the entries dark and open, the bodies here all heaped at the end of the main corridor. He was at the opposite end, his back to a corner where another hall intersected the one filled with bodies, his hand on his phaser. He shouldn't be afraid, he knew that, and so he wouldn't draw his weapon . . . but his envelopment in the memory was complete, his outrage and horror was new.

They'd come for him at night, to perform medical experiments. Years ago. Secret experiments conducted on the sleeping crew by a secret race, the constant, random clicking of their voices or claws like insectile rain, like a black, evil thaw. They'd been solanagen-based entities, and they'd killed Lieutenant Hagler, replacing his blood with something like liquid polymer, and surgically amputated and reattached Riker's arm for no reason he could ever know or comprehend. . . .

. . . and I volunteered to stay awake, to carry the homing device so that we could seal the rift between their space and ours. I took the neurostimulant and I waited, waited for them to take me, knowing that they would dissect me awake and not care as I screamed.

Laying there in bed, seconds like hours in the dark, twitching from the hypospray, waiting in perfect silence, wondering if he'd make it back. And then the abduction, and feigning semi-consciousness as they'd clicked and muttered from the darkness, telling their secrets in an alien language. . . .

He knew he had to act, he had to do something, but the feelings were overwhelming. Paralyzed, Riker hunched further into the corner, listening to the past.

Data stood in the *Kamal*'s communal eating area, accessing seemingly random personal information. Although he had experimented with daydreaming in the past, the spontaneous nature of the experience was unusual, particularly under the circumstances. A self-diagnostic did not inform him of any problem. Still, it was perplexing; the occurrence of memory recall did not normally interfere with his ability to function, but he found that his designated task—to observe this specified section of the Cardassian freighter—did not seem as important as the examination of his previous experiences and aspects thereof, which seemed to occur to him in no particular order.

The sentience of Lal, stardate 43657.0. Learning to dance, stardate 44390.1. Meeting Alexander, son of Worf, stardate 44246.3. Deactivating Lore, stardate 47025.4. His attempt at a romantic relationship with Ensign Jenna D'Sora, stardate 44935.6. His return to Omicron Theta, stardate 41242.4. Commanding the *U.S.S. Sutherland,* stardate 45020.4. Sarjenka, stardate 42695.3. Kivas Fajo, stardate 43872.2 . . .

Data's understanding of each memory's relevance to his current situation was lacking, and the only common element was that he seemed to be present for each one. He decided he would return to the *Kamal's* bridge and speak to Geordi about it—but thinking of Geordi called to mind an entirely new set of experiences, and he paused to consider them, interested in his apparent ability to direct the focus of his memories.

Geordi's unnecessary funeral assemblage, stardate 45892.4. The disappearance of the *U.S.S. Hera,* on which Geordi's mother was captain, stardate 47215.5 . . .

"Captain, the transporters will be ready in two minutes or less."

The freighter would only be safe for another four minutes, at most. Not enough time for a rescue team to find anyone, and he didn't want to risk it without knowing if the away team's comm units were operating. Beyond that, it was unlikely that a transporter beam could pull them out in time, the interference of the storms too great.

Last resorts. They could try to use low-power phasers to nudge the freighter onto a new trajectory . . . but given its condition, there was no way to be sure it wouldn't cause catastrophic damage. Even if it worked, they might conceivably end up sending the freighter hurtling into the path of another plasma flare.

"Is security ready?" Picard snapped.

"Yes, sir. Mr. Dey is fully suited and standing by in transporter room one," a voice over the comm called from security. *"He's been briefed to objective."*

Beam in, call an emergency, beam out. They'd have to hope that all the away team members still had working comm units, and weren't somehow restricted from using them. It was the last realistically possible option; if they couldn't get the team out through the steadily closing time window, there might not be any way to save them.

Something was wrong. Vaughn's internal journey through the past was starting to include events outside of his experience, or one series of events, specifically—the loss of the *Kamal,* and the deaths of the people surrounding him. The integration of memories not his own was gradual at first, but his alarm grew with each unfamiliar experience.

The woman on Panora who cursed us for letting the Jem'Hadar come. A stand of dead garlanic trees, poisoned by biogenic gas. A plasma storm, bursts of powerful energy buffeting the freighter, the impulse engines knocked out in the first wave of burning light . . .

Not me. That never happened to me.

Vaughn struggled to understand as the memories kept coming, so strong that he was nearly incapacitated. He forced himself to take a step forward, then another, practically blinded by the persistent wash of feelings and images, fewer and fewer his own.

The brilliance of exploding Jem'Hadar ships over Tiburon. The Cardassian captain shouting, ordering for power to be diverted to the shields. The controlled terror on the faces of the men guarding the prisoners, when they realized that life support had been cut by half.

The purplish light was growing in intensity, brightening, becoming bluer, and Vaughn sensed a familiar odor, comprised of unwashed bodies and desperation and overcooked soup; it was a prison smell, or that of a refugee camp. Sadly, he'd known enough of both to be certain. He took another step forward, remembering the soulless gaze of the first Borg he'd ever seen, and the soft prayers of a Bajoran couple who'd asphyxiated less than ten meters from where he now stood, and the ashy gray faces of the gasping Cardassian guards, still grasping their rifles—

—this is not some personal catharsis I'm having, I have to stop this—

—and there, at the back of the cargo bay, the source of the light. A twisting, fluid shape in an open box, less than a half meter in size, propped up on a broken crate. The object itself was barely visible behind the shining, pale blue rays of light that it emitted, the dark red of the emergency lights drowned out by its radiance. He stumbled toward it, suddenly sure that the light was creating whatever it was he was experiencing.

Dying, they were all dying, Cardassian and Bajoran alike, suffocating—

—the Cardassian occupation. Bajoran history . . .

Orb. The Orbs of Bajor.

Another memory, but this time, there wasn't another to push it away, as though it was a memory he was supposed to have and keep. The Orbs were religious artifacts, supposed to generate spiritual visions or hallucinations of some kind; the Bajoran faithful believed that they were gifts from their gods. *Read about them somewhere . . .*

It was still the past on the *Kamal,* the strained hisses of death all around him in the cold bay, but Vaughn felt stronger, clearer. And when he reached the box, studded frosted jewels or reflecting ice, he thought for just a moment that there was someone with him, standing at his side. A tall, dark human, a man who seemed to radiate a kind of serenity as strongly as the Bajoran artifact radiated light—

—and then Vaughn closed the box's intricately carved door and he was alone, standing in the cold, silent peace of the long dead *Kamal.*

Only a few seconds later, an unfamiliar male voice sounded in his helmet, identifying itself as a security officer and demanding that everyone on the team trigger his or her emergency signature immediately.

Vaughn quickly hefted the box and set it by his feet before tapping the contact on the forearm of his suit, motivated by a strangely compelling certainty that the Orb was ready to leave the icy, floating tomb where it had rested for so long.

Chapter Twelve

After some thorough scans by Dr. Crusher, the away team reported to the observation lounge for debriefing. As soon as the captain finished reviewing the final damage assessments, he would join them there.

Standing in front of the door, Deanna received a depth of chaotic and disturbed emotion, a feeling of darkness. She took a few deep breaths, relaxing, centering herself. Allowing any personal distress to enter her mind at this point would only hinder her effectiveness, which would inevitably make it harder to communicate, to listen and hear. It was a fundamental truth of effective counseling.

Still, she was concerned. The freighter had disappeared into the Badlands a full two minutes after the away team had returned, certainly close enough to trigger post-traumatic responses, but it was the discovery of an uncased Bajoran Orb that worried her. No one on the team would have been prepared for the kind of effects such an artifact produced.

She walked in and took her place at the table next to the captain's empty seat, the agitated feelings in the room assigning themselves specifically to each member of the team, except for Data. They were all confused, but in keeping with the history of the Orbs, the base feelings suggested personalized experiences. Geordi was emotionally exhausted, wrung out, but other than bewilderment and an uncharacteristic vulnerability, he was well. Kuri Dennings was similarly exhausted, but from pain. Kuri had visited Deanna a few times concerning the death of her brother, but had been handling her grief well; the raw depth of it had been revisited, and Deanna decided immediately to call in on her later.

Will . . . She could feel his strength, his desire to be brave for her, but he was struggling against a post-adrenaline low. . . . And something like self-doubt, possibly even shame.

He was scared, and quite badly.

She had to resist an urge to hone in on his feelings, to probe deeper for how the experience was affecting him. It was an important element in their relationship, to maintain a firm boundary between their private and professional lives, but there were times that she found it difficult. Now, with the crisis past, she did what she could, accepting her personal concerns for him and setting them aside for later.

She turned her attention to Commander Vaughn just as the captain walked into the room, and was surprised by what she found there. She'd come to like Elias, very much, since they had first met, and though she still didn't know him well, she appreciated the weight of the unknown responsibilities he seemed to shoulder. He was a thoughtful man with a strong sense of decency and compassion, but he'd also been troubled since he'd come aboard for this mission. She'd sensed great uncertainty beneath his polished confidence, the kind generated by meticulous soul-searching. In that capacity, the commander was like Captain Picard . . . but where Jean-Luc's foundations were solid, Elias had seemed to be in doubt of the very structure of his belief system. As he was an extremely private man, Deanna had not approached him about it. But the highly charged energy coming from him now was so fundamentally different. . . .

. . . his doubt is essentially gone. Whatever he was struggling to decide about himself, he's decided.

She couldn't know what the decision was, but he was sending out waves of exhilaration, and she found her curiosity about the nature of this particular Orb soaring.

Vaughn waited until Picard finished telling them what had happened during their absence before delivering his simple, concise report of their ordeal aboard the freighter. Everyone on the away team, even Data, had experienced vivid and incapacitating memories while separated, which had stopped as soon as the Orb had been shielded. Data provided a brief explanation of the Orbs themselves, describing them as "energy vortices," but admitted that the Orbs that Federation scientists had so far attempted to study had consistently defied a more meaningful analysis. Of the original nine, only four were accounted for. Eight had been taken by the Cardassians during the occupation; one had remained hidden on Bajor. Three of those stolen had been returned to Bajor over the five years following the Cardassian withdrawal, but the whereabouts of the remaining five were still unknown. And given the present turmoil on Cardassia Prime, the Bajorans' expectations of recovering them anytime soon were low. A tenth Orb, previously unknown, had been discovered off-world only a year before, but that one had vanished after it had apparently fulfilled its purpose.

The captain was excited about their find, though he was outwardly calm. "It seems we've found one of the missing ones. And I think it's reasonable to speculate, from your experiences, that this is the Orb of Memory. It was originally discovered in the Denorios Belt more than two thousand years ago."

"What exactly *did* we experience?" Will asked. "How do they work?"

Captain Picard nodded toward Deanna. "Counselor?"

"As Data said, there's very little scientific information on the Orbs," she said. "Except that they transmit an energy that works directly on neural pathways, affecting chemical and electrical balances. They're quite powerful. At least one has been known to function as a time portal. In most cases, however, the effect is more . . . personal. Having an Orb experience is often life-changing for those of the Bajoran faith; many believe that it offers a line of direct communication between themselves and the Prophets, the wormhole entities said to watch over Bajor."

The discussion continued, the decision made for Data to immediately begin work on the delicate realignment of subspace communications, the captain announcing that they would be moving away from the Badlands to run full systems diagnostics and to reassess options. The *Enterprise* needed a dock so that the shield-emitters could be properly tested, and access to Starfleet command as soon as possible, to make their report. Will suggested that they plot a course for Deep Space 9, the closest starbase to their current position and conveniently owned by Bajor; they could turn over the Orb to the Bajorans and await new orders as they carried out repairs.

Deanna could feel the flagging concentration in the room and decided to speak up before the captain started assigning responsibilities. He was unaware that Will and Kuri, at least, had been adversely affected by their encounter. "Captain, Orb experiences are generally quite draining. I strongly recommend at least six hours of rest for the team members before they return to duty."

Picard nodded, the natural concern he always felt for his crew intensifying slightly. Deanna had often wondered if he knew how paternal the tenacity of his feelings was.

"There's no immediate crisis, is there? Let's make it a full night," he said lightly, and stood up, smiling. "Data, I hope you won't mind the extra hours. I'd like the rest of you to contact your teams and tell them that they'll have to do without you, that you're officially off duty until 0800 tomorrow. Rest well, everyone."

They all stood, Deanna deciding that she would walk with Kuri back to her quarters. She made eye contact with Will, and both saw and felt that he was holding up well; like Geordi, he wanted only to sleep at the moment.

Not Elias, though. He was very much awake, she could get that much from the spark in his sharp blue eyes.

"Captain, if I could have a moment . . ." he asked, and Picard nodded. Both men lingered behind as the rest of them filed out, Data telling the weary La Forge which self-diagnostics he planned to run while he worked on communications, the others silent with fatigue. The counselor felt a twinge of wistfulness as she followed, wanting very much to hear what Elias would say to the captain, if he would talk about his newfound sense of determination and purpose. Intellectually, the change was only a simple shift of attitude—but the simplest were often the most profound emotionally.

Deanna sighed inwardly before turning her full attention to Kuri Dennings's sweet, anguished heart, starting the search for the words that might help.

Commander Vaughn didn't seem to be nearly as tired as the others had—nor did he seem as tired as he'd been only a short time ago, discussing his retirement as they'd watched the storms. In fact, he seemed positively invigorated.

Perhaps I was right about that change of vocation, leading an exploration team seems to agree with him. That, or his experience inspired this somehow; he was closest to the Orb.

Picard couldn't help feeling vaguely sorry that he hadn't insisted on going along. To have found such a historically and culturally valuable object . . . it would certainly have put a spring in his own step.

"Captain, I just wanted to thank you for our conversation earlier today," Vaughn said, firmly meeting his gaze, even sounding different. Gone was the slight hesitancy, the careful measure of each sentiment expressed. "It set the stage for one of those 'powerful experiences' that Deanna mentioned. I feel that things are much clearer now."

"My pleasure," Picard answered, pleasantly surprised at the man's mood for freedom of expression, part of him thinking that Vaughn was about to say he'd reconsidered retirement. Something had certainly changed; the commander no longer seemed to have that cautiously watchful quality that had drawn deep lines at the corners of his eyes and mouth.

"You seem to be in high spirits," he added, raising an eyebrow, not wanting to pry but curious about the transformation.

"I am," Vaughn said, folding his arms and leaning against the table. "The memories I experienced—I was reminded of things that I'd forgotten, of people I used to know, of events and the feelings I had when I was experiencing them. And I realized that since the end of the war, I've been . . . I've been preparing to be old, if that makes sense. Because I'm tired, I'm sick of death and the destruction that accompanies it."

Picard nodded, understanding perfectly.

"Jean-Luc, do you know why I joined Starfleet?"

Picard considered his response before answering. "I suppose I always imagined it was out of an honest sense of duty, an earnest desire to serve and defend the Federation."

Vaughn shook his head. "That was why I *stayed*. I became a floating tactical operative very early in my career because I was good at it, and I was needed. It wasn't a career path I chose; it chose *me*. And when I was on the freighter, I remembered that, and how differently it all started for me, and for a moment I felt . . . I felt like the young man that I was, when what I really wanted to do with my life was clear in my mind."

Vaughn brushed at his neat, silvery beard, smiling. "I want to learn, Jean-Luc. I want to explore, and live in each moment, and feel excited about my experiences—not because I want to recapture that blush of youth, but because it's what I've *always* wanted, and I'm too damned old to put it off for one more minute."

"*Come, my friends, 'tis not too late to seek a newer world,*" Picard thought, smiling back at him. "Does this mean you're leaving Starfleet?"

Vaughn shook his head. "I don't know. And the amazing thing is, I don't know if it actually matters. If what I want to do doesn't fit in with Starfleet's agenda, I'll leave."

"Bravo, Elias," Picard said warmly, amusedly considering Starfleet's reaction to the news that one of their most capable officers, with clearance that probably went higher than the captain dared to speculate, might be quitting in order to find himself. He instinctively offered his hand, which the commander promptly shook. "I'm happy for you."

"Thank you, Captain."

They decided to meet for breakfast, and Vaughn left, his shoulders definitely straighter, his head held higher than Picard had seen previously. It was a real pleasure to be witness to such a shift of spirit; discovering a renewed sense of purpose at his age—at any age, really—was cause for celebration.

Picard suddenly felt an odd wave of déjà vu, wondering when he'd witnessed such a startling transformation before. Then he remembered.

Seven years earlier, another Starfleet commander he'd known had come to a crossroad in his life's journey, and its course also had been determined by an unexpected encounter with an Orb of Bajor.

The captain stood for a moment longer in the quiet room, thinking about Deep Space 9 and how Colonel Kira would react to their "surprise" visit. Knowing that the Cardassian relief efforts were being routed through the station, he hoped she'd be amenable to accepting unannounced guests. Now that he thought of it, he was actually looking forward to the stop; perhaps Vaughn's enthusiasm for new experience was catching. It would be interesting to see what had changed since Captain Sisko's departure, see how the staff and residents were building their post-war lives—and it would be a chance for the crew to see a few old acquaintances.

And considering that we'll be presenting them with a prominent instrument of their faith, lost for decades . . .

It was likely to be a most engaging visit.

Still thinking of the sharp new brightness in Elias Vaughn's gaze, Picard straightened his uniform and headed back to the bridge, unaware of the faint smile he wore.

Chapter Thirteen

Kira walked slowly to the briefing, collecting her thoughts, trying to relax. Her conversation with Ross hadn't gone well, but she saw no point in expressing the depth of her anger and disquiet to her crew, so she took her time. She'd gotten a lot better at controlling her temper through the years, but as tired as she was, she wanted the extra few moments to refocus. No one would like the news, and it was her job as commanding officer to provide a realistic example of calm leadership, regardless of her personal feelings.

Just before she reached the wardroom, she realized someone was walking right behind her. Startled, Kira stepped to one side and turned around—and saw nothing, a few meters of empty corridor and a wall.

Getting paranoid now, that's just wonderful. One more thing to put on her list of nervous-breakdown topics.

The meeting room seemed too empty, even though everyone was there—Bowers, representing tactical, Nog and ch'Thane, Bashir, Dax, and Ro. No Tiris, of course . . . and Major Wayeh Surt, the Bajoran government's administrative liaison, had just gone on an indefinite leave. His wife of nearly thirty years had been one of those killed during the attack. Wayeh had offered to stay, but Kira had insisted that he go home to be with his children, promising that she'd take care of things until a replacement was found.

Maybe they should find a replacement for me, too, at least when it comes to talking with Starfleet from now on. It was one more way that Jast would be missed; the commander's ability to effectively represent the station's interests to Starfleet had never been so badly needed.

Dax threw a slight, encouraging smile at her as she moved to the head of the table, but Kira couldn't manage to summon one of her own.

"I've just come from speaking with Admiral Ross," Kira said without preamble, taking her seat. "At this time, Federation and Allied forces are on full alert throughout the quadrant. After an emergency council of the Allied leaders that lasted until a few hours ago, the Federation has organized a task force to investigate yesterday's attack on the station. Members of the Romulan and Klingon governments will be joining the task force, which will leave from here, and everyone—Federation, Romulan, and Klingon—is sending military backup. Their plan is to send a well-armed contingent of ships to the Gamma Quadrant in order to make contact with possible Dominion forces."

For a few seconds, no one spoke, but she could see that their reactions were much as hers had been. Incredulity to uncertainty to frustration.

"When are they coming?" Dax asked.

"And what does this mean for us?" Nog added. "What are we supposed to be doing?"

"Three days from now, maybe four, depending on how soon they can assemble," Kira said. "Their rendezvous point is the Gentariat system, a day and a half away at high warp. And because of our current status, we're not officially expected to do anything beyond what we were already doing—repairs and upgrades, coordinating relief aid, cleaning up the mess. Bajor will be sending us several teams of Militia engineers to help—the first shuttles should arrive later today."

"Do they really think that the Dominion is about to wage another war?" Shar asked, an anxious set to his features.

"Ridiculous," Bowers said, shifting in his seat. "If they really wanted to start something, they wouldn't send only three attack ships. It was a rogue attack, we've run across that before with the Jem'Hadar."

Dax was nodding. "And there was that fourth ship, the one that tried to stop them. It doesn't make any sense."

"It's been suggested that the initial attack was deliberately staged, either to directly lure the Federation into battle or to distract it from noticing a buildup of forces elsewhere," Kira said woodenly, not bothering to point out the rather obvious holes in such an attack plan. She'd pointed out a few to Ross, who had countered each neatly with reminders of the Dominion's war record.

Tell them the rest, they may as well know it all. Her allegiance was to Bajor and to the people she worked with first, not to Starfleet.

"There is currently a motion before the Council to establish an Allied peacekeeping force within the Gamma Quadrant," Kira said quietly, "which doesn't leave this room, for the time being. Officially, it's a rumor I heard."

"They can't be serious," Bashir said, his brow furrowed in disbelief. "They can't believe that the Dominion will tolerate an armed force that close to their borders even for a single day, let alone as an ongoing presence. It could spark another war."

"It's definitely not going to promote opening diplomatic relations," Ezri said. "They already don't trust us."

Kira had said pretty much the same thing to Admiral Ross, and his answer was still clear in her mind:

They broke the treaty, Colonel, and in less than three months. The Allied leaders are in full agreement on this. If the Dominion wants another war, we take it to them, and the first step is to do exactly what they've done; we're going in to assess their current capabilities, and we're going in prepared to defend ourselves.

The worst part was that she could understand that point of view. Strategically, the idea was sound, especially if they could secure the other end of the wormhole against further intrusion. Unfortunately, it was also rash and inappropriate, but she could see how the logic of defense, fueled by resentments and bitterness over a long and terrible war, could sway a crowd of politicians and admirals into making such a choice. She saw how the Klingons and the Romulans might push for an excuse to redress what they saw as deficiencies of the treaty—neither had been happy with the noninterference provisions—but Kira was stunned and not a little disappointed that the Federation was willing to spearhead it.

And there's Odo. She hadn't brought it up with Ross, aware that it would seem like an emotional argument coming from her, but she couldn't believe that Odo wasn't being figured into the equation. After his celebrated role in ending the war, he had gone back to the Link partly with the hope of teaching the Founders tolerance—and she believed that he could, that if it was possible, Odo would do it. But if the Allies undermined his efforts by sending troops, if they'd already withdrawn their faith in him, she had little doubt that he would lose tremendous ground with his people.

All of this flashed through Kira's mind in an instant, rekindling her anger, but she stamped it solidly down. She wasn't going to encourage dissent just to validate her own opinions. Besides, preaching to the converted would take energy, and she couldn't spare it.

"Admiral Ross was sympathetic, but he has his orders. I've registered my protest, and will urge the Bajoran provisional government to do the same, but there's nothing else we can do."

Again, there was a brief silence, looks of anger and worry, and Kira pushed on to station status. Whatever the Federation planned, it wasn't going to be resolved by any of them, not here and now, and there were more immediate problems to discuss.

An exhausted Nog gave them a rundown on reconstruction efforts, glumly listing the most critical first and quickly descending into a morass of minor disasters, everything from roaming power failures to industrial replicator malfunctions. Dax, back on temporary engineering duty, helpfully threw in a few that he'd forgotten before briefly touching on station morale. There wasn't much for her to say outside of the obvious; people were moving from shock into depression and anxiety.

Bowers and Shar both briefly reported on technical aspects of their respective departments—with everything powered down and no tactical capacity, not much was happening beyond hands-on manual work, cleaning, testing, or recalibrating. Bashir's medical report was even shorter, statistics and supply needs delivered in a soft, tired voice, dark circles beneath his eyes . . . and Ro basically had nothing—rehashed security measure reviews from the handling of the crisis, final effectiveness assessments, recommendations for new drill procedures. Kira was hard-pressed not to let her irritation show.

"Anything yet on the investigation into the Promenade deaths?" she asked.

"It's ongoing," Ro said blandly. "I'll file a report as soon as there's any progress."

Her tone was inflectionless, but the way she glanced away gave Kira a sense that she wasn't being entirely forthcoming.

"Do you have any leads?" Kira encouraged, hearing an edge in her voice and not able to stop it. "Anything?"

"Colonel, as soon as there's any progress, I'll file a report," Ro said, this time firmly meeting Kira's gaze, her own unflinching.

For a fraction of a second, Kira had a satisfyingly clear mental flash of throwing Ro against a wall. Aware that Bashir and Dax were exchanging a look over the tense interplay, Kira let it go—but only for the moment; it was past time for her and Ro to have a private conversation. "Fine. Let's move on."

They spent the next few minutes running through priorities and plans, Kira making her recommendations as they went along. She pushed Nog into agreeing to delegate more responsibility, and they talked about coordinating with the arriving technicians. Bashir and Dax were going to start collaborating on an agenda to help station residents in emotional distress. Kira emphasized the need for the station to continue coordinating Cardassian relief efforts in spite of the present situation; ships would continue to pour in for inspection and certification, and too many lives were depending on them to let that process be disrupted. The Federation-sanctioned task force wasn't mentioned again, or included as a factor in their immediate agenda; they needed to worry about making their own environment livable and working again.

The meeting was about to break when Kira remembered the one decent piece of news that Ross had given her. "I almost forgot—Starfleet commendations are pending for Nog and Prynn Tenmei—and Lieutenant Ezri Dax's name has been submitted for, let's see if I remember this right . . . the Starfleet Citation for Conspicuous Gallantry, I believe it's called."

Everyone smiled, even Ro. Dax rolled her eyes.

"I assume you'll be switching to command now—congratulations, Captain," Bashir joked, earning another round of smiles. Ezri saluted him. It wasn't much, but it was the only light moment Kira expected to have for a while, and she was grateful for it.

She hadn't planned to say anything else, but as they stood up to leave, Kira realized she wasn't quite finished.

"Listen . . . this is a difficult time, but we'll get through it. We've come through worse. I just wanted you to know that I'm glad you're all here."

Not overly inspired, perhaps, but Kira felt better for having said it. This was her crew, these were her friends, and she'd do right by them no matter what it took.

It was late for lunch, and Quark's was mostly empty. There was still plenty of activity going on around the station, but the majority of those visiting on personal business—Quark's clientele, mostly—had decided to depart for safer seas following the attack.

They had the right idea, Kasidy thought. *The quiet is nice though, for a change.* They sat on the balcony, looking over an agreeably subdued Quark's. Kas was relieved not to be shouting over the blitz of a *dabo* tournament, and thought that Kira was, too; her friend was obviously in need of some peace. As it was, she'd only been able to spare enough time for a single *raktajino*, and Kasidy was ready to bet that it was the first break she'd taken in hours.

". . . but other than that, things are looking up," Kira was saying, the haggard tightness around her eyes and mouth indicating otherwise. Considering the list of the station's ongoing technical problems—and what was brewing with Starfleet—Kas wasn't surprised. "The Militia techs will stay at least a week, maybe longer."

"Things will go much faster with all the help," Kas said. She was trying to be helpful and supportive; Kira had certainly been those things for her since Benjamin had been gone, but the truth of it was, she was impatient to leave the station. If it was just her, it would be different . . . but with young Rachel Jadzia or Curzon Tye (*maybe,* she silently reminded herself; a week ago, she'd been absolutely fixed on Sylvan Jay and Joseph Cusak) to consider, her priorities had undergone a major shift. During the attack, in the reinforced corridor where she'd crouched and waited with the other frightened residents, terrified that she'd be injured in some way that might affect the baby, she'd made her decision—to turn down the next couple of assignments with the Commerce Ministry so that she could move as soon as possible. The station wasn't safe, and not far away was the quiet patch of land where home waited, sunlight streaming in the windows, an herb garden freshly planted out back. . . .

". . . don't you agree?"

Kas blinked, quickly replaying the conversation she'd missed. She'd read that a lot of women suffered lapses of concentration during pregnancy, but she couldn't blame everything on hormones. *Some friend I'm turning out to be.*

"Yes," Kas said firmly, picking up the thread again. "By the time they get here, everything will be different. They'll have to reconsider once they cool down a little, put things in perspective. Hey, look at the bright side—at the very least, there will be a few more Starfleet engineers running around for a couple of days while the brass sorts everything out. Between them and the Militia techs, the station will be taken care of, finally . . . and then maybe you can get away for a few days. Like we talked about."

Kira stared down into her cup of *raktajino,* surely lukewarm by now. "I don't know, Kas. It sounds wonderful, it really does, but you'll be getting settled in, and there's just so much for me to do now that Tiris is gone. . . ."

"Well, forget about that 'getting settled in' stuff, you know I'd love the company," Kas said firmly. "And you've been so great—without you, the house wouldn't be half finished by now. Really, you deserve to come down and spend a few days just sitting around and reading books, or wandering around in the garden. . . ."

Kira shook her head, and Kas trailed off, wondering why such a strong, brilliant woman insisted on making things so hard for herself. Kas waited until Kira looked up and held her gaze, determined to get through. She was going to push, and hope that she wasn't overstepping the bounds of their friendship.

"Nerys, the strain is showing. You haven't had a break since the day you took command. I know things are a mess right now, but you're going to have to schedule a few deep breaths now and then, or you're going to burn yourself out."

Kira looked away, and after a moment, she started to speak in a quiet, low tone, indirectly responding to Kas's question. "I hadn't seen Istani Reyla in years, or talked to her. I didn't even know she was here until after she was killed."

Kasidy already knew that Kira had been friends with the monk who'd been murdered on the Promenade, one of the Commerce secretaries had mentioned it at the morning admin meeting, but it was the first Kira had talked about it. *Probably to anyone.*

"That must have been terrible," Kasidy said softly.

Kira nodded. "I'm going to miss her. We haven't stayed close, but I'm going to miss knowing that she's out there."

"I know what that's like," Kas said, not elaborating. Kira didn't need to share, she needed to get it out.

"If she was just someone I knew from before, it would be bad enough," Kira said, finally looking at Kas again, a wrenching expression of wounded confusion in her eyes. "But she was such an amazing person—at Singha, at the labor camp where I met her . . . she was a prylar then, and she must have known what I was doing with the resistance, but she didn't care."

Kira shook her head, wearing a faint, incredulous smile. "I mean, here was this woman who truly believed that all life was sacred, and I was just a child, and I'd already *killed* people . . . and she used to tell me the story about how the Prophets filled the oceans and painted the sky, and she taught me how to braid my hair, of all things . . . she tried to encourage me to be a child, in spite of what my life was. Or maybe because of what it was."

"What a gift," Kas said quietly, sincerely.

Kira nodded, her face working as though she were trying not to cry, but her voice was as strong and clear as ever. "Truly."

Patiently, Kasidy sipped her tea as Kira got hold of herself, aware that she would withdraw from a gush of sympathy. Considering that Nerys prided herself on her near-perfect autonomy, Kas had some idea of the effort it had taken for her to talk about her feelings.

Time to pull out the fail-safe, a simple but perfectly wonderful trick that Kas had recently discovered.

"So, are you still going to be godmother to this baby, or am I going to have to find someone else, 'cause you're too busy?" Kas asked.

The lines of tension on Kira's face almost magically lifted, her whole demeanor changing, a more positive outlook reflected in her very posture. Kasidy had asked her almost a month ago, explaining the honorary term and receiving an enthusiastic *yes.* They'd only been close for a relatively short time, but their friendship had come to mean a lot to Kasidy. Inviting her to be godmother was Kas's first real solo decision regarding the baby, too, so it felt good to talk about it, to remind herself that she was moving forward instead of simply waiting.

"Don't you dare," Kira said. "I promise I'll take a vacation, okay?"

Kas relaxed. Just seeing Kira smiling again, really smiling, was enough to put any real concern to rest. For Kira, the birth would be doubly blessed; she'd be godmother to Kas and Ben's baby, but also an important figure to the child of the Emissary . . . although that wasn't a part of it that Kas liked to think about too much. Attention, even fame, was going to be unavoidable—they were going to be living on Bajor, after all—but she meant to do what she could to see that their child was protected from the kind of religious fervor that had surrounded Ben.

Kira took another sip of her *raktajino* and grimaced, pushing the cup aside as she stood up. "I have to get back to ops. But thank you, Kas. Really."

She already seemed less exhausted, less stressed. Kas smiled, glad to have been able to help, watching Kira move down the stair spiral with a satisfied feeling. It felt good to have a close female friend again, to know that she could give support as well as be supported when things weren't ideal. It made maintaining a grounded approach to her life a lot easier. . . .

Kas happened to glance down as Kira was leaving the bar, in time to see the colonel freeze in her tracks—and shoot a startled, suspicious glance all around her. It was only for a second; Kira seemed to realize that she was in public, such as it was—only Morn at the bar, less than a dozen patrons scattered throughout Quark's—and then she turned and quickly walked out before anyone noticed her behavior. But Kas had seen it, and felt her good mood stilled by that odd look. Because it meant that Nerys might be in trouble, real trouble.

Now who's paranoid? Hormones again. Kira had heard something, that was all, or . . . she only thought she had.

Kas drank the last of her tea, running through her mental packing lists, refining plans for the move . . . and found herself unable to ignore the small knot of worry that had bloomed in her mind.

Ro Laren was in the security office, absorbed in something on her desk console, the drab setting still so thoroughly *Odo* that Quark decided immediately he would give her a discount on remodeling accessories. She was simply too magnificent a gem to be surrounded by such . . . *Odo*-ness.

He straightened his coat and stepped into the office, as uncomfortable as ever in the environment of the law, but determined. He hadn't seen Ro since leaving her at the infirmary; he'd wanted to visit her, but besides having to oversee the repairs to his much-too-empty bar (Broik had actually attempted to replace some of the broken shelves with a higher grade of Foamet, trying to justify the expense in terms of durability, the witless slug), he'd felt strangely reluctant to go to her quarters. As if she *didn't* owe him her life, and wouldn't be thrilled to see him. . . .

. . . *so why so worried?* He wasn't sure—but no, not true. He was simply a hopeless romantic, eternally doomed when it came to a pretty face and a nice set of hands, and Ro Laren made him quiver with all sorts of foolishness. Love made idiots of men, common knowledge—and thank the Great River for such stupidity, lovers loved to spend—but *being* the idiot wasn't a strong position from which to bargain. Making his intentions obvious would give her an advantage, and if he wasn't very careful, someone like Ro could embezzle his very soul. Not a big deal in and of itself; souls were too ethereal to be worth much. But his willingness to offer her genuine discounts, *that* was frightening.

When she finally looked up, the smile she favored him with very nearly paid for the flowers he'd sent. "Quark! Come in, have a seat. I was going to come by and see you later."

He smiled winningly and sat down in one of the chairs across from her, unable to remember a time when he'd been welcomed into DS9's security office. "I can't stay long. I just wanted to stop by and see how you were feeling . . . and see if you got the tube orchids."

He considered telling her how expensive they were, but decided it would be wisest to hold his tongue. She wasn't a *dabo* girl, after all; in fact, he suspected she was the type who didn't care about such things.

I always seem to fall hardest for the crazy ones. . . .

"I did, thank you," she said, still smiling warmly. "And I'm feeling fine, thanks to you. Dr. Bashir said that you rescued me after I was thrown off the stairs."

Quark cast his gaze modestly to the floor, saying the words he'd rehearsed in his mind on the way over. "It was a considerable risk, of course—but even with the station falling to pieces all around us, I knew I couldn't just leave you there to die. . . ."

He looked up at her, gauging her reaction. She was still smiling, still receptive; he kept going. ". . . because that would have been a tragedy beyond all measure, Laren. May I call you Laren?"

Her smile grew. "I believe you just did. Seriously, Quark, thank you. There's a good chance that you saved my life, and I'll always be grateful to you for that."

He grinned back at her, his heart singing, thinking of all the shipments that wouldn't be inspected, all the time he'd be able to save not having to sneak around to conduct business (time wasn't latinum, but they *were* interdependent), of how she'd look draped on his arm wearing something slinky—and then she opened her mouth again, and his dreams fizzled into so much smoke.

"Of course, I'm not going to let you get away with anything because of it," she continued brightly, a bit *too* brightly. "Now that I think of it, I'll have to watch you even more closely than before. We wouldn't want anyone to suspect that there was some kind of favoritism going on. Because of my appreciation for your bravery, I mean."

She was still smiling, and smiling back at her, he scrambled to salvage what he could, the 285th Rule of Acquisition running through the back of his mind like a curse. *"No good deed ever goes unpunished."* It was always the 285th that got him, he could have it tattooed on his forehead and he'd still forget it.

Think, think, you want this woman on your side— He hadn't been prepared, foolishly assuming that his selfless heroism would pay off, and—as was his everlasting luck—it had backfired. But as long as she was being amenable, he should do whatever he could to further the bond between them.

—not the flowers, and the bribe window is closed—work the Kira angle. Allying

himself against the colonel might help things along; any opportunity in a storm. He'd actually come to respect Kira's shrewdness over the years, a fact that only threat of severe torture would force him to admit to the woman's face—but she was still a headache. Besides which, she made the big decisions, but it was Ro who'd be enforcing them, and therefore Ro he wanted to side with.

"You're probably right," he said, sighing. "I know the colonel would love nothing more than to catch the two of us falling short of her high moral standards."

Ro's smile faded, and he hurried on, not wanting to be *too* obvious. "Don't get me wrong—I like Kira, she's a fine commander and all that . . . but her self-righteousness can be a little trying at times."

"I don't suppose I know her well enough to say," Ro said neutrally, watching him carefully now. "Is there a point to this, Quark?"

"No, no, of course not. Making conversation, I suppose." He was about to let it drop, deciding that he'd totally misread the opportunities here, but a real curiosity struck him about the two women, something he'd wondered about since the first day Ro had come to the station.

And it's not like I have anything to lose, he thought sourly.

"If it's not too personal, may I ask why you wear your earring on your left ear?" Every other Bajoran he'd ever known always wore it on the right.

Ro's smile crept back. "May I ask why you're asking?"

Quark shrugged. "Honestly, because I've noticed that it seems to bother some of the other Bajorans on board."

Particularly Kira. And "bother" was a serious understatement, but he saw no point in giving her a complex.

Ro seemed almost pleased. "That *is* honest. All right, Quark, I'll tell you. I wear it in memory of my father. He loved his culture, and in my own way, I suppose I do, too. But I've never been very religious. Not all Bajorans are, you know. Wearing my earring on the left was the best way to discourage the random vedek from wandering up to feel my *pagh* . . . which, you may know, is traditionally felt by taking hold of the left ear. For different reasons, of course, the practice was also taken up by the Pah-wraith cultists. . . ."

". . . which explains why people don't like it," Quark finished, and though his hopes for having the head of security in his pocket were still dashed, his romantic interest had rekindled explosively. She'd actually gone out of her way to annoy, upset, and alienate her own kind.

What a woman.

"Right."

She didn't continue, only sat with that amused expression on her fine face, and though he felt a sudden, wild urge to profess the seriousness of his intent, Quark decided that he'd better leave before he offered her something expensive. He needed time to work out a new strategy.

"Well, I suppose I'd better let you get back to work," he said, standing. "Drop by the bar later, if you like. I'll . . . buy you a drink."

"Thank you, I'll do that," she said, and with another bright smile, she turned her attention back to whatever was on her desk monitor.

Quark walked slowly back to the bar, his heart full, his lobes tingling, Rules battling through his mind. The 94th Rule, *"Females and finances don't mix,"* was one he'd ignored to his own disadvantage on more than one occasion . . . but the 62nd Rule was louder, drowning out his concerns by its simple, love-friendly truth:

"The riskier the road, the greater the profit."

Oh, yes; quite a woman.

Chapter Fourteen

It had been some time since they'd made love, their lives too hectic, too rushed for anything but sleep . . . and since the attack on the station only two days before, Ezri had seemed distant, or at least preoccupied. Julian didn't mind, particularly; he'd been preoccupied himself with a second wave of minor injuries, from pulled muscles to stress headaches. And although the death watch was finally, thankfully, over, he still had the incidental cases he'd discovered while treating first-wave problems. Most had already been dealt with, but there was one he couldn't seem to "leave at the office," as it were, and he'd woken up thinking about it.

While cauterizing a scalp laceration on a Hupyrian freighter cook, a standard blood scan had picked up a fairly rare genetic disorder specific to the species—not lethal, but potentially debilitating at some future point, similar to what would have once been called rheumatoid arthritis in a human. The medical database didn't have much on it, but Julian thought he saw a few possibilities, assuming he could keep the sequences in proper order.

It was early, both of them in bed, more than an hour before he had to get up. Ezri was still asleep and Julian was working through one of his sequencing ideas, staring absently at the padd with the cook's chart. He'd gone to her quarters late the night before and they'd both been exhausted, falling comfortably asleep not long after his arrival.

Julian was just deciding that altered nucleic material re-injected into the Hupyrian's secondary pituitary-like gland might be the answer when Ezri reached out to him. The gently playful smile on her face as she touched his arm, stroking it, suggested that she'd been awake for at least a few moments.

"And what do *you* want?" he asked lightly, smiling back at her, setting the padd aside. Eight days, fourteen and a half hours, give or take a few minutes, and he carefully ignored the precise thought, reorienting his focus from the literal to the feel of her hand.

Ezri grinned, snuggling closer against him, twining her fingers through his. "What do you got?"

"I hope that's rhetorical," he said, and slid down so that he was facing her. Still holding hands, they kissed, slowly and gently, with love more than passion—at first. With his eyes closed, he still saw her, the soft warmth of her smile, the perfume of her hair and her skin enveloping him. Ezri was a physically beautiful woman, but her looks didn't matter, not here and now. It was her presence, it was the feel of them together that fired his senses, thrilling each part of him.

They shifted, breaking their kiss long enough to reposition themselves, Julian moving over her, looking down at her sweet, flushed face, her slightly dilated eyes, as excited by the awareness of being with her as by his own physical sensations. For so long in his life he'd only known shadows of such feelings, never understanding how much more there could be, what was even possible.

He bent and kissed her again, the thinking part of him falling further away as she closed her eyes, pulling him closer . . . and in another shift of limbs they were together, and it was wonderful. He watched her smile widen, heard the soft murmurings from her throat that he'd come to cherish, the tousled bangs across her brow, feeling love, feeling completely embraced by the friend he knew in her—

—and she opened her eyes, and everything changed.

For a split second, his mind couldn't grasp what he suddenly knew, but the sound of her voice brought it all together.

"Julian," she breathed, and her voice was deeper, sultry and languid. It matched the darker blue of her eyes, and of course she was Ezri . . . but she was Jadzia, too. Jadzia, gazing up at him in passion's abandon.

When they finally displaced his shock, the feelings were complex, multi-layered and overwhelming—fear and confusion, mainly, but there was also a sense of betrayal, glimmers of excitement, of nostalgia, of loneliness.

His response was much simpler. He instinctively pulled away from her, wanting to be covered, to protect himself. Trembling, he rolled over and sat up, pulling the rumpled bedclothes around his waist, his body forgetting the flush of sex as if no such thing existed. His thoughts were in chaos, his heart pounding. He felt like he'd been hit.

A few seconds later, a tentative hand on his shoulder, and Ezri's clear voice, gentle with concern.

"Are you okay?"

He tensed away from her, not sure how to feel about her touch for the first time since they'd become lovers.

"What just happened?" he asked, his voice harsher than he meant it to be, quite aware of what had happened, if not how. "The way you looked at me, I—what happened?"

He turned and saw Ezri, her wide, worried gaze, the curves of her face soft with compassion—

—but maybe that's Audrid, or Emony. Or any of them.

"I'm . . . I was—" She frowned, her body language changing abruptly. She pulled her knees to her chest and held them, staring down toward her feet.

"I'm not sure," she said, but it was all wrong. She didn't sound sorry, or afraid, or unhappy. The look on her face, the tone of her voice, was deeply thoughtful.

"I was thinking about the time that you let Jadzia sleep in your cabin, on the Defiant," she said slowly. "Remember? When you gave up the top bunk for her . . . she thought about that later, and I was—"

She looked up at him, her expression unreadable. "I felt like Jadzia would have felt, just for a few seconds," she said intently. "I mean, it was me, but she was—it was different, it was—it wasn't the same, it was . . ."

She trailed off, staring into his eyes. And still, she wasn't a bit sorry, he could see it, as if she'd forgotten his reaction.

Or as if she doesn't care.

"Different," he finished, and reached down for his clothes, a rumpled heap on the floor. He stood and started to dress, not wanting to be in bed with her for where things were going.

"I'm *sorry,*" she said, and surely she meant it—but was there a touch of exasperation in her tone? Could he trust that there wasn't?

"I was making love to *you,*" he said angrily. Scooping up his boots, he moved to the edge of the bed and sat, not looking at her. "Can you understand that I might not want to change partners in the middle of it?"

Her voice was much cooler than his, verging on cold. "You didn't, Julian. I'm Ezri *Dax.* Can you understand *that?*"

"Right," he snapped, jerking on his second boot and standing. "Got it. Why don't you bring Tobin along next time, see how he feels? Or Lela, or Curzon?"

"Why don't you grow up," she retorted, "and try to see past yourself? I'm a joined *Trill,* and that's not going to change, ever. Why can't you see that all of me is Ezri, that I'm a whole being? That I don't have to limit myself to some species-specific concept of individuality?"

Her tone had changed from angry to near pleading, but he was too worked up to stop, unable to believe how insensitive she was being, furious at the implications of her words.

"Sorry to be so simplistic, *Dax,*" he said, regretting it even as he spoke. The look of hurt that flashed across her eyes almost quenched his anger. Almost, but even if he wanted to take it back, he wasn't sure how.

"You should leave," she said, face pale except for two hectic spots of color, high on her cheeks.

"My thoughts exactly," he said, and turned for the door. He didn't look back, and as he hit the corridor and started for his own quarters, a part of him marveled at how quickly things could change, as quickly as a look in someone's eyes.

Nog's hands were filthy, streaked with ash and blackened bits of melted polymer. He'd just finished replacing yet another in a series of torched computer boards and found himself staring down at his hands, noting each dark, chemical smudge, knowing if he raised them to his face, he would smell burning destruction. It was mindless work, shifting boards, but responsibilities were delegated for the moment, and he couldn't do much more with the *Defiant* until the shipment of parts arrived from Starbase 375. The new warhead module would have to come directly from Utopia Planitia itself, and that might take weeks. And the truth was, he'd chosen the one area no one else wanted to work in because he felt like it was the least he could do. It was the smell, he thought, that the other engineers hated so much, a reminder of what had happened. The lower core's atmosphere had been blasted clean through stacked filters, but the burn smell was still there, coating every twisted wire, caked on every fire-blown component.

You're not responsible, Nog, none of this is your fault. . . . Ezri's heartfelt words from after the briefing echoed in his mind, words he almost believed, but her voice was far away. Down in this subsection, working with a few grim-faced and silent techs in the broken spaces where forty-six people had died, a lot of things seemed far away. He knew that nobody blamed him; earlier, after the memorial service, he'd been stopped by at least a dozen people who'd gone out of their way to tell him as much—

—but if I had organized everything better, if I'd pushed harder to get things done on time . . .

It was useless thinking. At the Academy, he'd taken PTP 1 along with everyone else—post-traumatic psych was a requisite course, even the Klingons had a version of it—and they'd hammered on the concept of useless thinking, and how guilt was essentially worthless beyond a certain point. But thinking about that only made him feel worse. Not only had he failed as an officer, contributing hugely to how effective the Jem'Hadar's attack had been, now he was wallowing in worthless guilt. Even when he'd lost his leg, he hadn't felt so terrible. At least then, he alone had been the one—

"Sir?"

Nog looked up and saw Shar standing over him, his dusky blue face uncharacteristically sober. The ensign held a tool kit.

"I thought we agreed you'd call me Nog from now on," Nog said. Maybe he'd get used to it someday, but he still didn't feel like a "sir." Particularly not today. He and Shar had actually been at the Academy at about the same time, but had never met before Shar's assignment to the station.

The Andorian nodded, speaking in his strangely formal way. "You're right, Nog, forgive me. Colonel Kira thought you might be able to use me down here."

Nog frowned. "I thought you were working on the sensor arrays."

"I was, but only because no one else was available. I miswired the secondary cilia circuits for the short-range particle samplers. It was an accident, I knew the correct sequence, but it will take several hours to restring. The colonel said that replacing circuit boards might be easier for me."

Nog couldn't help a small smile. Shar was the most mechanically inept Andorian he'd ever met. "Okay. You can help me test these. I'll trigger, you check."

Shar crouched next to him and opened his tool kit, pulling out a diagnostic padd. Nog waited until he was situated and then started turning on the replaced boards, making minor adjustments as they went.

After a few moments, Shar broke the near-silence hesitantly. "Nog, may I ask you a question?"

"Sure."

"Were you a witness to Commander Jast's death?"

Nog had been expecting a technical question, or something about the Federation's plans, and felt new guilt crash over him, remembering that Shar had been friendly with Jast.

"Yes," Nog said dully, feeling his ears flush.

Shar looked at him curiously. "Nog, are you all right?"

"What's your question, Shar?" Nog asked, wishing he was a million light-years away, wishing he was at Vic's, balancing the books and drinking two-olive martinis, wishing he was anywhere but here.

"I only wanted to ask if you thought she died without pain," Shar said softly. "But I see now that I have upset you. I'm sorry. Were you and the commander close?"

Nog stopped working and shook his head miserably. Before he could stop himself, he blurted out the truth. "No, we weren't, but it's my fault she's dead."

Shar stared at him. "How is that possible? I thought she was killed by an electrical surge when the *Defiant* was under attack. . . ."

Before Nog could say anything, Shar nodded his comprehension, answering himself. "You're attempting to assume responsibility because the upgrades were unfinished. I believe Colonel Kira feels the same way. Also, Lieutenant Bowers, Lieutenant Nguyen, and Nancy Sthili feel similarly, judging by their behavior. I'm fairly certain they all feel some measure of guilt for not performing more efficiently, either before or during the attack."

Nog was totally surprised. "Really? Why do *they* feel guilty?"

"Why do you?" Shar asked. "It was the Jem'Hadar who attacked us."

Nog opened his mouth to respond—and then closed it again, frowning. It wasn't as though some awesome truth had dawned on him suddenly, setting him free from all self-doubt—but he thought Shar had a point. Maybe the station could have been better prepared, but the real responsibility for what had happened didn't lay with anyone on the station.

Not with us. With them. The reminder instantly shifted his guilt, transforming it. The thought of their spiky, emotionless faces filled Nog with a powerful hatred that had become all too familiar in the last year, a mix of rage and fear unlike any he'd ever known. They were monsters, brutal, evil monsters.

"Have you ever dealt with the Jem'Hadar, face to face?" Nog asked, hardly recognizing his own voice. It was so old, so very old and wise and deadly soft. The Jem'Hadar had given him that voice.

"Not directly," Shar said. "I know something about their chemical and genetic makeup, through some of the Vorta research we did during the war, but I've only ever seen them from a distance."

"If you're lucky, you'll never have to get any closer," Nog said. "They shouldn't exist, anyway, they aren't even a real species, they're . . ." He searched for the description he wanted and found it in a single word. "They're *abominations*. They're bred to be merciless killers, *murderers*. The Federation should have demanded their breeding programs stop when the treaty was being negotiated." It didn't even occur to him to wonder how such a thing could be enforced; he was too caught up in his own rage. "Maybe it's not so bad after all, this task force. If the Jem'Hadar attack now, they'll get wiped out."

Shar looked around suddenly, turning to face the empty, broken room behind them—and in the same instant, Nog heard something. A very faint sound of movement, like the creak of settling equipment . . .

. . . but I've been hearing that all day, it's the supplementary bulkhead sections shifting, that's all.

"It's just all the new materials getting settled," Nog said, surprised that Shar had noticed. He'd never heard anything about Andorians having especially good hearing.

"It's not that," Shar said, still peering around the room, his expression puzzled. After a moment, he turned back to Nog, shaking his head. "It's gone now, whatever it was. That's the third time today."

Nog frowned. "You heard something?"

Shar reached up to scratch at one of the two short, stout antennae that grew from his head like horns, pushing his thick white hair away from the base of the left one. "No, felt it. These are sensory, but not like ears. Andorians can detect some kinds of electrical fields, through changes in air density and temperature. But they're not exactly reliable . . . strong emotions, surges of adrenaline or teptaline, even an overheated piece of equipment can register analogously."

Hatred is a pretty strong emotion. Shar must have picked up his feelings about the Jem'Hadar. Interesting; Nog had met several Andorians at the Academy, but had never realized that their antennae weren't auditory. But now, as he focused his gaze past the bizarre white locks that seemed to hang randomly from Shar's head, he saw that his friend did indeed have ears.

Shar sighed. "Twice yesterday I felt something, too, and both times there didn't seem to be anything close enough to stimulate them."

"Maybe you're just getting old," Nog said, smiling so that Shar would know he was kidding. The Andorians he'd known had needed a little help when it came to humor.

Shar smiled back at him, but seemed distant as he picked up the diagnostic padd again. "Perhaps."

After a few seconds, Shar glanced up at Nog and asked, conversationally, "I've read that in popular Ferengi culture, attaining material wealth is one of life's predominant goals—is that correct?"

Nog was surprised into a chuckle. There were understatements, and then there were understatements. "Yes, I'd say that's correct."

"Would you mind if I ask, then, why you've chosen to join Starfleet?" Shar asked.

Nog shook his head. It was a personal question, but the way Shar asked made him want to answer honestly. "I don't mind at all, but it's kind of a long story. I can tell you that it isn't easy to make a choice where, for the most part, you're going against your culture. What they expect of you, you know? My uncle insists it's just a phase—he says that many a young entrepreneur has to experience debt before he can understand the necessity of expansion planning, but I'm betting that he's wrong."

Shar nodded. "Because you feel like it's important, what Starfleet and the Federation are doing."

"Right, exactly." Shar really seemed to understand.

"I'd like to hear the long story, if you want to tell it," Shar said. "I was going to take a meal break in the next hour, at your Uncle Quark's establishment. Would you like to join me?"

Nog barely hesitated. He *was* busy, but he also instinctively liked Shar, and was grateful for the point about responsibility. And Uncle had been giving him a hard time lately about granting free favors—but also lately, Nog had come to enjoy disappointing his uncle, a fact that had pleased Father to no end the last time they'd spoken.

"You're on, Shar," Nog said.

After managing to get a few hours of sleep, Kira felt ready to sort things out with Ro. She'd meant to get to it after the briefing, but there had been too much else to do, and she'd been too exhausted. Before she'd finally collapsed for the night, she'd put it near the top of her list for the morning's agenda. A crisis was not a good time to have the social system break down; Kira needed to feel that she could depend on all of her people, and she needed Ro to understand that. After checking in with her department heads, she'd started for Ro's office, hoping that they could have a reasonable conversation about attitudes and expectations.

If not reasonable, I'll take conclusive; at least that way I'll have something resolved before the Federation shows up. Although they weren't behind on the current revised schedule, the first Allied ships should be arriving in three days, and neither the station nor the *Defiant* were anywhere near as functional as she'd hoped. Even with the new techs on hand, the intermittent and random crashes that seemed to be plaguing the station's every system were making everything twice as difficult as it needed to be. And it didn't help that she wasn't feeling particularly functional herself, either. If she crashed, she might end up locked in a room somewhere, mumbling to herself.

Not funny, Nerys. She felt emotionally blasted, which was bad but not paralyzing, she still felt functional and sane enough ... but she'd had the experience four times now, of suddenly feeling that there was someone behind her. And twice, she'd felt that she was being watched when there was no one around. Shar's internal sweeps since the attack had turned up a few random energy pockets, but nothing out of the ordinary, considering the station's structural damage ... which meant Kas was probably right to insist that she take a vacation. When she was with the resistance, she'd heard of several people in other cells who'd succumbed to paranoid episodes, eventually hurting themselves or others to avoid being caught by "them." And they probably thought they were sane, too.

In any case, one thing at a time. The big picture could be overwhelming, worrying about everything from trying to convince the Federation to stand down to her own mental quirks—and after all that had happened in the last few days ...

. . . just keep moving, get things sorted out. Introspection can always wait. An attitude that generally worked well for her. She'd reached the security office, and was more than ready to establish a few ground rules.

Steeling herself against memories of Odo, and reminding herself again that Ro Laren deserved a chance to explain her position, she pasted on a friendly expression and walked in. Even knowing what she would see, Kira felt her tension level rise a notch; it was irrational, she knew, but the woman was sitting in Odo's chair.

Ro looked up from whatever she was studying and Kira saw her gaze harden slightly, her defenses obviously triggered by Kira's mere presence.

Make the effort. She had to get better at handling difficult people, now that she couldn't just throw up her hands and start shouting. Well, she still *could,* but if the last seven years had taught her anything, it was that that approach only got you so far.

Kira glanced around the office as she spoke, realizing it was still exactly as Odo had left it. "I thought I'd stop by, see if you have a few minutes to talk."

Ro nodded, waving her hand in a go-ahead gesture. "By all means."

There were other chairs in the office, but Ro's attitude made Kira feel like standing. She decided not to wait for a better opening.

"I'm going to be honest with you, Lieutenant. I'm not happy with how your posting here is working out, and I think a few changes are in order."

Ro nodded again, a sour look on her face. "I see. You're relieving me of duty. Any specific reason?"

Kira sighed inwardly, annoyed. She was trying to give her a chance. "Why do you make things so difficult, Ro? Is it me, or are you just absolutely determined to make everything impossible?"

"Of course it's not *you,*" Ro snapped. "It's me, *I'm* the one with the problem, because I don't look to you every time I make a decision."

Kira stared at her. "What are you talking about?"

"I understood when I took this job that how I conduct the day-to-day operations of this office would be left to my discretion," Ro said, "but by the way you've been acting, you seem to think I'm a complete incompetent."

In spite of Ro's heated tone, Kira refused to be baited. She was being reasonable, dammit. "I know you have the skills, but you've got to understand—although there's a lot of traffic coming through here, we live in a community, and it's important that everyone at least *tries* to work together. Especially department heads and senior staff, because we have to support each other through what it takes to run DS9, *and* try to set a positive example while we're doing it."

"Does that include conversations about being transferred?" Ro asked, her face flushed.

Kira ignored her. "If you've made any effort to fit in, I haven't seen it," she said. "And you act like I'm some kind of monstrous authority figure who's out to oppress you. What will it take for you to stop turning everything into some kind of a . . . a contest of will?"

Ro stood up, facing her directly across the desk. "Maybe if I was human, there wouldn't be a problem."

Kira frowned. "Human? I don't see how that could—"

"Yes, you do. Without accepting the Prophets as divine, I'm not a real Bajoran, isn't that right?"

Reason only went so far. Kira could take a lot, but what Ro had just implied was insulting. Yes, she'd disliked Ro's pompous agnosticism, but had also gone entirely out of her way to be fair to Ro because of it.

"That's right, Ro," Kira said, her voice quickly raising to a near shout. "That's it exactly, I can't work with anyone who doesn't believe the same things I believe, and it has nothing to do with your constant, obvious disrespect for me as commanding officer of this station, which is both unfair and childish!"

She took a deep breath, blew it out. "Look, this obviously isn't working out. I think it would be best if you put in for a transfer, immediately."

"I couldn't do my job, so I put in for a transfer," Ro said. "That's ironic, when if you would stop second-guessing my every move, I could actually get something done."

Kira felt her anger reach a boiling point. *She wants to get booted on a disciplinary, fine—*

—when it dawned on her. From all appearances, that was exactly what Ro wanted. For some reason, she had accepted a posting she didn't actually want.

And why would she? She hasn't lived on Bajor since she was a child, she seems to despise our faith, she's either withdrawn or openly challenging most of the time—

"Why are you here, Ro?" Kira asked, her anger ebbing, remembering the Starfleet file that Jast had told her about. Ro Laren had a history of disciplinary problems, of being bright but resentful of authority, of not being a team player. But was that really the whole story? "Why did you take this job?"

Ro seemed shocked by the question, a flash of panic displacing the fury in her eyes for just a fraction of a second. For the first time Kira recognized what Ro had been doing, the bluff and bluster of insecurity and defense. She'd been a master of it herself at one time.

"Why, Ro? What do you want? What did you expect?"

Her eyes wide, Ro shook her head, and Kira could actually see her work to dredge up her anger again, could see her grabbing for something to say that would make Kira wrong, that would win the confrontation. All to avoid confronting whatever it was that was hurting her.

Kira cut her off before she got started. She had sympathy for Ro's confusion, but she didn't have all day to hold her hand through it. "Part of this job means that you will have to work with people, me included, and it means that you aren't always going to have things the way you want them. I've been there, I know it's not easy—but you have to decide what you want to do, and then do it."

"Colonel, I don't need your advice," Ro said, eyes still wide and angry.

"Lieutenant, I think you do," Kira said, and when Ro didn't respond, Kira turned and walked out.

· · ·

Ro sat down after Kira left, furious, then a little less so. The question kept replaying, and she wasn't finding an acceptable answer.

Why, why did you take this job, why are you here?

Arrogant woman. Ro supposed that some part of her had been prepared for their fight since her first day on the station—but then, why did she feel so disappointed, so unhappy?

You know.

Did she? Kira was as condescending as ever, she knew that, acting as though she had personally earned Ro's respect, that she deserved it. Ro's lieutenant pin and gray special forces uniform were honorary, awarded to her—along with her assignment to DS9—by a government that, while grateful for her efforts during the war, hadn't known what else to do with her.

And Kira knows that, and she still can't stand it that I don't seek out her wisdom—

—why, then? another part of her asked, the same part that had told her she knew why she was disappointed. *Forget Kira, she doesn't matter in this. Why are you here?*

Because. I've got nowhere else to go.

And you resent it. Why are you disappointed?

Because . . . because she had been prepared to leave the station as a result of the inevitable argument, to declare herself unappreciated and undervalued, and to seek a life for herself somewhere far from Bajor and DS9. She was angry because her little refuge of self-righteousness had been taken away, at Kira for taking it, and at herself once she understood that it had been there all along.

She hadn't belonged in Starfleet. No; that wasn't quite true, was it? She *had* felt like she belonged there once, before Garon II changed everything. And after years of running with the Maquis and then her own group of anti-Dominion fighters, she'd wanted nothing more than to return home, to the world whose air she hadn't breathed since she was a child. Word had gotten around Bajor about some of the things she and her team had accomplished during the war, and in recognition of that, the Militia had offered her a commission, hoping to make further use of her tactical experience.

But post-occupation Bajor was an alien world to Ro; she realized almost from the start it wasn't going to work, that she no longer knew how to sit still, that she'd been living on the run and fighting for too long. Militia HQ had quickly come to the same conclusion, and informed her that her skills would better serve Bajor aboard Deep Space 9.

All I wanted was to come home . . .

And the agonizing truth was still that, unless she meant to run off and find another war, she had nowhere else to go.

I always said I wanted a life beyond the fight . . . and I finally got it, and I've been waiting for it to fall apart since day one. Wanting it to, because I no longer know how to do this.

Ro closed her eyes for a moment, recognizing her fear as useless, and understanding that Kira's question had changed things. Maybe she'd stay on the station, maybe she wouldn't, but she would no longer have the luxury of believing that it wasn't her choice to make.

Damn her.

Ro opened her eyes and looked back down at the desk screen, where the complete contents of Istani Reyla's isolinear rod were displayed—a few seemingly random numbers, with no clue as to their meaning—and abruptly realized she was more determined than ever to solve this minor mystery, to wrap up the murder of Kira's friend. She felt that she wouldn't be able to rest easy until she proved to the colonel that she was competent, until she proved to herself that she could do this job.

3, 4, 24, 1.5, 25. A code? The numbers could mean anything, but the fact that Istani had paid Quark to hide the rod—rather than storing it at the assay office—suggested to Ro that the prylar was afraid of someone finding those numbers, or finding out that she had access to them. Ro had already checked them against every combination the computer could come up with, from mathematical theorems to replicator item adaptations, but nothing she'd seen looked right.

She stared at the screen, thinking about the colonel, about sparring with Quark and Shar's friendship and Istani Reyla, and realized that for a while, at least, DS9 was going to be home. She'd lived a life of loose ends; it was time to see where the threads of these new relationships would take her, time to stop being afraid of the kind of life she'd never known.

Chapter Fifteen

"Doctor! May we join you?"

Bashir looked up and smiled, wondering why some people seemed to think that if you were reading, they weren't interrupting anything. Standing over him were Nog and Shar, both obviously taking a meal break during what must have been another difficult day. The lunchtime seating in Quark's was limited; there were a lot of people coming off shift and looking to get a little uninhibited, to talk.

Bashir set the padd aside, nodding, wistful for the second reading but happier to have company. Ezri wouldn't be by for another twenty minutes, at least. "Of course. Have a seat."

He had been fortunate enough to grab a table by the front wall, not in a main traffic area, and had been waiting for Ezri to get off her shift. When he'd called her a few hours ago, she'd agreed to talk, and he had heard relief in her voice; he'd felt some of that himself. He regretted their fight, he missed feeling that they were friends, even for a day.

"What are you reading, Doctor?" Shar asked, noticing the padd.

"Julian, please. We're not on duty. It's a letter from a friend of mine."

The Andorian smiled, nodding as he sat down. Julian hadn't spent much time with Shar, but liked him very much. A very unassuming young man—

Person, he mentally amended. Andorian biology was unique, another reason Bashir was glad Nog had asked if they could sit at his table; he'd wanted very much to ask a few questions. Except for Erib, whom he'd known at medical school, Bashir hadn't been around many Andorians.

Nog was looking at the paused text, frowning. "You're on page 256 of a *letter?* Who wrote it?"

"Garak," Bashir said, smiling again at the nervous look that suddenly appeared on Nog's face. The Cardassian tailor had intimidated a lot of people during his years on the station. Having already read the autobiographical letter once, Bashir thought that if they'd known even the half of it, they might have moved off the station themselves.

"So, what are you two up to today?" Bashir asked, picking up his glass of tea, remembering that he'd seen the two of them having dinner together last night, too.

"Ah, nothing," Nog said casually. "Just dealing with the mess in the lower core when Shar suggested lunch."

Nog has a new friend. The young Ferengi was trying very hard to be nonchalant, a young man's favorite game. Basir found himself feeling fondly nostalgic about O'Brien suddenly, remembering the stories they'd swapped of their reckless youth.

Back when I was a brash young officer . . . He was all of 34, not exactly ready for retirement. Now that he was thinking about it, though, he abruptly remembered one of the correlations common to all of the papers he'd read about Andorians, regarding age.

"Shar, if you don't mind me asking—how old are you?"

Shar looked up from his plate of vegetables. "Twenty-three."

"Are you married, then?"

As soon as Bashir asked, he could see that Shar was uneasy with the question, and trying to hide it. He dropped his gaze, his face flushing a darker blue; only Bashir noticed, the flush too slight to be obvious. "No, I'm not."

Shar's distinct discomfort dissuaded Bashir from pursuing the matter. Perhaps he didn't want to discuss it in front of Nog—or perhaps he didn't want to talk about it at all.

Still, 23 and not married . . .

Erib—whose full name was Shelerib th'Zharath—had avoided questions about relationships, though he'd once said that the unique biology of the Andorian species necessitated certain . . . expectations of its members. Bashir understood the biology, but not the sociology or the culture. But as interested as he was in understanding Shar's particular situation, it wasn't really any of his business.

"How would you boys like to try a little *fa'ntar?*" Quark had swept up to their table, holding a tray of glasses and a pitcher filled with a distinctly noxious-looking, deep orange brew. "It's tonight's discount special, a rare but intoxicating blend of exotic fruits and spiced leaves from—"

"—from a vat in the storeroom," Nog broke in. "Last month, you called it *tarf'an,* but it's still what you make from rotten fruit shipments, and no one ever buys it."

Quark's smile had disappeared. He leaned in, teeth bared. "You want to keep your voice down? What's wrong with you? I sell plenty, and it is rare, you can't get it anywhere but here."

Bashir shook his head. "Thanks anyway, Quark, but I think we'll probably—"

"Starfleet," Quark spat, obviously warming up for one of his tirades, still glaring at Nog. "They are sucking the Ferengi right out of you, you know that, don't you? You *never* ruin another man's sell, not unless you can profit from it. The Federation, though. They *say* that they want to help people, that they have a clear directive not to interfere with other cultures, but look at how you're turning out. And do you think they've given one thought to how another war might affect the rising tourist interest in this area?"

Quark appealed to the whole table, the very picture of sincere outrage. "I've got to say, and no offense, I'm getting pretty sick of the Federation's attitude. I mean, who made *you* keepers of the universe? What does the small businessman get out of it?"

Bashir considered responding, but decided that between withholding his own opinion and prolonging the conversation, the latter would be the greater evil. Quark wasn't interested in anyone else's opinion, anyway. Besides which, Bashir suddenly felt a headache coming on.

"Uncle, please," Nog said pleadingly, growing irritated or embarrassed by the reddening of his ears. Shar didn't seem to be paying attention at all; he scratched absently at his left antenna, his expression blank.

Quark wouldn't be stopped. "I blame your father for this, Mister I'm-so-proud-you're-going-to-the-academy. Why you chose him for your role model I'll never understand, not when you had me—"

As the last syllable left Quark's lips, Shar was suddenly in action. He lunged across the table and snatched the pitcher away from Quark, his reflexes brilliantly fast. He spun around, balancing himself in motion, and threw the contents of the pitcher at the wall behind them. He completed the action so quickly that the upset tray of glasses was still hitting the ground as the spiced fruit concoction flew—

—and before any one of them could react, the air became solid and somebody screamed.

Quark's interruption saved Shar from any more questioning by Dr. Bashir, for which he was grateful. He still hadn't decided how to respond to such inquiries, and even the thought of trying to answer them made him feel somewhat anxious.

He was still thinking of where the questioning might have led when Quark and Nog began to get angry. Shar was a little uncomfortable about the strife between the two Ferengi, but the amusement on Bashir's face suggested that there was no reason for concern.

A complicated relationship. Family dynamics often seemed so; Shar was starting to believe that it was a universal constant. There were many subtle intricacies within his own family's communication.

His left antenna itched, and he scratched it—and froze, feeling it again, the same itch and flush of heat he'd already felt several times since the attack on the station.

Someone is here.

Between their table and the wall. Shar concentrated, holding very still. Although his ability to differentiate specific energy types was limited, he couldn't help feeling that he was sensing bioelectrical energy. It was similar to the sensation of hearing two sounds of a similar pitch and volume, one made by a machine, the other by a person.

Tingling heat, and he could see that there was no one there. He thought again about the internal sweep that Colonel Kira had asked him to do, and the random pockets of collected energy he'd found.

And if someone wanted to hide . . .

All of this flashed through his mind in an instant, and he accepted it as truth by the preponderance of evidence, not the least of which was his physical reaction.

Before he could properly consider his options, the tingling started to fade, and he made his decision. As fast as he could, Shar snatched the pitcher from Quark, turned, and threw the thick liquid at what he believed to be an organic being, watching them.

A meter in front of him, the liquid hit, splashing across the head and torso of a very tall humanoid. Someone shouted as the air shimmered and curved, becoming solid, becoming a Jem'Hadar soldier.

He was imposing, his sharp, reptilian face somehow blank and malevolent at once. Quark let out a high-pitched squawk, and Bashir stood and shouted for security as Nog tried to pull Shar out of harm's way, clutching at his arm with fumbling, desperate fingers—

—but the Jem'Hadar had no weapon and only stood, watching, as fear and confusion pushed the crowd back. Shar allowed Nog to pull him away, barely able to keep himself from beating at the unexpected intruder with the empty pitcher, his body prepared to fight.

Then the Jem'Hadar spoke, and his words stilled everyone who heard them.

"I am Third Kitana'klan, here on an errand of peace," he said, his voice deep and inflectionless. "I would speak to your Colonel Kira Nerys. You can tell her that I was sent by Odo."

Ro was waiting for Kira at the entrance to the security office, her expression thankfully professional. A shrouded Jem'Hadar soldier had popped up in Quark's bar; Kira didn't have any interest in dancing around with Ro again.

"What have we got?"

"Ensign ch'Thane found him at Quark's. He's making his statement now. I've got a team working with the internal sensors, to see if there are more."

As she spoke, they started through the door that led to the holding cells, Ro leading the way. Kira was glad to see a pair of armed security guards flanking the entrance to the hallway; Ro had the presence of mind to lock down the facility, at least.

"The soldier was unarmed, and offered no resistance; he was carrying a pack of ketracel-white cartridges, but nothing else. He says his name is Kitana'klan, and asked to speak to you, claiming that he's here on a peace mission—"

Kira couldn't help a sneer as they turned into the holding cell area. *A peaceful Jem'Hadar. Right.* At least she knew now why she'd felt watched, but that small relief was heavily overshadowed by thoughts of what he could have been doing all this time; he had to have been hiding on the station since the attack.

"—and that Odo sent him."

They stopped in front of the only occupied cell, Ro nodding at the guard, excusing her with a few words of direction—but Kira barely heard them. She could only stare dumbly at the soldier, overwhelmed with feelings of loss, of anger and disbelief—and a tiny seed of hope.

Odo . . .

The Jem'Hadar stood stiffly, as if at attention. When he saw Kira, he stepped closer to the force field.

"Colonel Kira. I am Third—I am Kitana'klan," he said, his deep voice betraying no emotion. The fact that he'd faltered over his designation gave Kira pause; as long as they were supplied with white—and this one was, she could see the isogenic enzyme sputtering through a slender tube at his throat—the Jem'Hadar simply did not falter.

Just looking at him inspired a dozen unhappy memories—the first Jem'Hadar she'd ever seen, telling her that the slaughtered settlers of New Bajor had fought well, for a spiritual people; the violent and untamable Jem'Hadar child that had been found on the station—even without enemies, he'd been unable to stop fighting, or to curb his hatred for anyone who was not Jem'Hadar, Vorta, or Founder.

In that order, too. The Vorta keep them, the Founders are their apathetic gods, and everyone else deserves death. The Jem'Hadar grew from genetic envelope to maturity in a matter of days. Born to a martial code of blood lust, the vast majority died in battle before the age of ten.

Kitana'klan looked like every other Jem'Hadar she'd ever seen—tall, muscular, his heavy, pebbled gray face studded with pearly spikes like tiny claws, his eyes piercing and sharply intelligent. His vestigial tuft of long black hair was knotted in typical Jem'Hadar fashion. He stood perfectly still, staring straight ahead as she studied him. If he felt anything at all he didn't betray it, and appeared to be waiting for her to speak before saying anything else.

Where to start . . .

"Explain your presence on this station, Kitana'klan," she said finally.

"I have been sent by the Founder, Odo, to serve you," he said, his gaze still fixed straight ahead.

Right, sure, that's so like Odo—

"And to learn about the cultures and lifeforms that coexist here," he continued. "I am to study everything I can about the synergy among peaceful peoples, so that I can bring this knowledge to the other Jem'Hadar. The Foun—Odo believes that this will be an initial step toward helping the Jem'Hadar evolve beyond our genetic programming."

Kira stared at him, remembering how hard Odo had fought to keep that Jem'Hadar orphan on the station, even after the "child" had proved to be incapable of forming nonaggressive tendencies.

He wanted so much to believe that the Jem'Hadar didn't have to fight, that they wouldn't fight if given other choices, other options. . . . Kira had strongly disagreed, and in the end, had been proved right—but suddenly, Kitana'klan's presence didn't seem so improbable. It *would* be like Odo to keep trying; his conscience had been deeply disturbed by the very existence of the Jem'Hadar, created by his people to have no aspirations higher than killing for their keepers.

"Go on," she said quietly, vaguely aware that Ro had taken the security guard's position behind her—and glad that there would be a living, breathing witness to this unprecedented conversation. She was willing to hear him out, but doubted there would be much truth in what he had to say. *The entire Dominion knew about Odo, they knew what kind of a man he was. Is. It wouldn't be all that hard to come up with a story like this one.*

But if he *was* telling the truth . . .

"The attack on your station was not sanctioned by the Founders," he said, finally turning his gaze to meet hers, and although it was exactly what she wanted to hear, she had to physically suppress a chill. His eyes were pale and unbelievably alien, incapable of any mild or gentle emotion. It was the gaze of a pure predator.

"There were a small number of Jem'Hadar who sought to redeem themselves for losing the war against the Alpha Quadrant," he continued. "They planned to destroy this station, in the hope that this might initiate hostilities once again."

"How do you know?" Ro asked abruptly. Kira didn't mind; she was wondering the same thing.

"Because I was told," Kitana'klan said, still looking at Kira. "I was overtaken by these rogue soldiers on the other side of the Anomaly—the wormhole—and they attacked me, disabling my ship. First Javal'tivon, their leader, had been my First at the end of the war; he told me of their plans so that I might understand the reason for my death."

"Quite a coincidence, you and these rogue soldiers headed for the station at the same time," Kira said.

"No. I believe that learning of my mission inspired their attack, and that they followed me from Dominion space."

Kitana'klan looked away, as if remembering, and his toneless voice grew cold and sharp. "It was their mistake to leave me still alive. A few of my crew survived, and we were able to repair the ship enough to follow after them. We defended you as best we could—but when the destruction of my ship became inevitable, I had to board this station. My instructions were clear."

"Why didn't you announce your presence then?" Kira asked. "Why have you stayed shrouded all this time?"

Kitana'klan seemed surprised by the question. "Your station had just been attacked by Jem'Hadar. I did not think I would be welcomed here."

"So you thought it would be better to skulk around, hiding in energy vents and spying on us? Exactly how long were you planning to wait?" Ro asked, and again, Kira had no objection. She'd worried about losing her mind, thanks to Kitana'klan's choice of actions.

If he was bothered by Ro's obvious scorn, he gave no sign. "I was watching for a reasonable opportunity in which to present myself. Odo gave me no instruction on what to do in the event that the station was attacked by my people. . . ."

Kitana'klan lowered his gaze, almost as if ashamed. ". . . but I understand now that my decision was ill-considered, and that I have made myself untrustworthy by my actions."

Kira was unmoved by his performance, but there was a ring of truth to his story that she couldn't deny hearing.

The fourth ship was damaged. And it backs up everything about the nature of the attack.

"You said the Dominion didn't sanction the offensive. . . ." Kira prodded.

"Yes. When Odo joined the Founders, he brought with him experiences unknown to them. The Great Link is in contemplation of Odo's life; it is . . . thinking, and surely does not know even now what has happened here. At this time, the Founders wish only to remain in reflection."

Kira glanced back at Ro, and saw on her face the same skepticism that she was feeling—but she didn't seem as openly incredulous as Kira would have thought, and she realized that Ro was also uncertain. Kira didn't like the Jem'Hadar as a species, and trusted Kitana'klan about as far as she could pitch him one-handed—but his story actually made sense.

"Can you prove any of this?" she asked, turning to look at him again.

Kitana'klan shook his head. "I cannot. There was a transmission of introduction and explanation given to me by Odo, but it was destroyed along with my ship and crew."

Of course it was. He's lying.

He's telling the truth, and the Federation has to listen now; Odo sent him, Odo sent him to me.

Before she could argue with herself any further, Kitana'klan abruptly fell to his knees. Forgetting the force field, Kira instinctively dropped into a defensive stance, and behind her, Ro was on her feet, pulling her phaser—

—and Kitana'klan ripped at the neck of his uniform, tearing it enough to reveal his ketracel-white cartridge, a small, flat rectangle in a sewn pocket beneath his knobby collarbone. He unfastened the cartridge from the implanted throat tube and pulled it free, holding it up toward Kira.

"I was sent here to serve you. I offer you my obedience and my life."

Realistically, the gesture meant nothing. He was unarmed and in a holding cell, and Ro had said they'd taken his additional white cartridges; his life was already in her hands—but the symbolic display was effective anyway, because he was Jem'Hadar. They were merciless, competent killers, not prone to drama. Without the enzyme and trapped in the cell, he would be driven into a useless, murderous rage before dying in great pain.

"I'm not sure I want either," Kira said. She stepped back from the force field, entirely unsure of what to think. "Keep your white. I'll get back to you."

She looked at Ro, who half-shrugged, obviously as perplexed by the Jem'Hadar's behavior as Kira was.

"Have Dr. Bashir run a scan when he's done with his statement, and . . . keep a watch on him," Kira said, feeling strangely helpless. For the moment, it was as far as she was willing to go. Whether or not Kitana'klan was lying, his presence on DS9 would be a major factor in the station's future. If he was telling the truth, there would be no reason for the Allies to go into the Gamma Quadrant—and there would be a Jem'Hadar living on the station, a disruptive situation at best. If it was all a lie, if he came from one of the attack ships or from somewhere else entirely, then there was no telling what he or the Dominion was planning. In any event, it was going to take her a little time to sort through the possible consequences—and to figure out how to prove his story out, one way or the other.

Kira started to leave the area, glancing back at Kitana'klan a final time before she stepped into the corridor. He was still on his knees, and again, that feeling of helplessness hit her at the improbable sight. A Jem'Hadar soldier, claiming a mission of peace. If Odo had done this, either he had made real progress with the Founders and the Dominion . . . or his sense of humor had taken a serious turn toward the inexplicable, which Kira could not find it in herself to believe.

Chapter Sixteen

Although he'd assumed she would be seeking him out eventually—she'd already talked to everyone else on the away team—Vaughn hadn't actually decided to speak to Deanna Troi until she approached him in Ten–Forward, a full day after they'd left the *Kamal* behind. He'd been enjoying the feelings he'd been having, and felt protective of them, not sure if he wanted them analyzed. He would not have sought her out, in any case—he had too many secrets to ever feel entirely comfortable around a Betazoid, let alone someone he'd known as a friend's child—but since finding the Orb, he'd also felt open to trying new things. Like talking to a counselor.

"Elias. May I join you?" She stood in front of his table, a small one near a viewport where he'd been sitting alone, remembering all sorts of things. Outside, the Badlands erupted and shimmered wildly. Soon, they'd be on their way to DS9, leaving the plasma storms behind; he'd wanted to get his fill.

"Please," he said, gesturing at the seat across from his, thinking that Ian had been a lucky man; his daughter had grown into a bright, intelligent, lovely person.

Troi sat down, smiling somewhat shyly, a touch of color in her cheeks—and he realized that she had probably detected some of what he was feeling. Only a few days before, his mind had been too preoccupied with feelings of self-doubt and confusion to feel anything clearly.

"Is it uncomfortable for you, to sense how others perceive you?" he asked, intuitively feeling that the question would not be inappropriate.

"That depends on who it is, and in what context."

"How do you mean, context?"

Deanna grinned. "I mean, if they like me, I try to pay more attention."

"Always a good plan," Vaughn said, smiling.

"Does this mean I get to ask you a few questions?" Troi asked.

Vaughn hesitated only a second, thinking of how he'd been feeling since the freighter. Strange and chaotic, definitely, strong memories continuing to appear randomly in his thoughts—but not at all unpleasant.

"You can if you can tell me what I'm feeling right now," he replied, honestly curious as to what she would say.

Troi took a deep breath, studying him. "Confused. Elated and uncertain. Contemplative. You are out of your emotional comfort zone, but not afraid, and . . . you're still experiencing flashes of your past, aren't you?"

Vaughn nodded. "Excellent, Counselor. And I assume you know why . . ."

"The Orb experience," she said, and he sensed *her* excitement now. He could see it on her face. "It was very different for you than for the others."

"Yes, I think it was," he said lifting his glass of synthale, then putting it back down, not really in a drinking mood. "I had memories on the freighter, too, good and bad—but when it was over, when I closed the door on the Orb, I felt . . ."

He shook his head. "It's hard to explain. It wasn't so much a feeling as a comprehension, if that makes any sense. For just a second, I . . . I *remembered* who I was. Who I am. And just like that, all of my concerns and fears about the future, about *my* future—gone."

Deanna nodded, looking pleased. "Yes. I can feel some of it even now. I don't know that you had a *pagh'tem'far*—that's the Bajoran concept of a sacred vision—but I think you definitely experienced a moment of clarity, catalyzed by the Orb. Perhaps because you were already questioning some aspects of your life, and you were open to a change of direction."

He hadn't thought of it that way, assuming instead that it had been a matter of his proximity to the Orb, but she was right, of course. Ironic, that a spiritually skeptical person like himself could have such an altering experience with a religious artifact.

Although there was that Linellian fluid effigy. The dream of small death when you touched it, followed by a brief, brilliant vision of swimming through milky-white waves . . . He'd been only 24 then, charged with returning the stolen container to the embassy, and hadn't known that such peace could exist. . . .

"These memories you've been experiencing—are they troubling to you?" Troi asked, watching him carefully.

"No," he said, thinking that her perceptions were even clearer than he'd first thought. "A little distracting, perhaps, but nothing too terrible."

Even as he said it, he realized that she, of all people, would know better. He smiled, shrugging.

"Nothing I can't handle, anyway."

Deanna leaned closer, lowering her voice slightly. "If there was anything you wanted to talk about, I could get a security clearance waiver . . ."

Vaughn felt a sudden fondness for her, wondering if she had any idea how impossible that would be for someone like him. The past was the past, but promises had been made, orders given that he could never set aside. There was a saying, something about aging tigers still having teeth . . .

. . . *and it holds true for some memories. Several of those tigers still have very sharp teeth, and claws that could inflict serious injury* . . . As long as they remained in the cage of his mind, there was no danger. He meant to keep it that way.

"Thank you, Counselor, but that's not necessary. Really, I'm all right."

At her slight frown, he thought again of how lovely she was, how compassionate, and suddenly recalled a clear image of an infant girl he'd held long ago, looking into her sweetly exotic eyes and feeling that his heart was so full it might cease to beat from the weight of his feelings. He concentrated on the memory, knowing that Ian Troi had certainly felt the same way when he'd first held Deanna, and was rewarded with another warm smile from the young woman.

"Of course you are," she said, and stood, still smiling. "Thank you, Elias. I'll leave you to your reflections."

After she was gone, Vaughn turned his attention back to the Badlands, letting himself drift again. Whether it was a Bajoran religious epiphany, or a passing mind-set, or some spiritual, emotional truth that he had been destined to learn, it didn't matter; he knew what he wanted, and knew that he would figure out how to get there as he went. He'd read a saying somewhere once, about how when you knew who you were, you knew what to do; it was more true than he'd ever suspected. It made him wonder how many people in the universe simply let their lives slide into some comfortable pattern, forgetting that they could do anything they wanted to do, that they could change direction if they could remember how easy it actually was.

Isn't life a strange party, Vaughn thought, looking out at the raging storms and feeling as young and free as a child.

Vedek Yevir arrived early for the shuttle to the space station. His luggage was taken by a pleasant young man who saw that he was comfortably seated before hurrying off to attend to other duties. The young man—Kevlin Jak, he'd introduced himself as—said that the shuttle would be full, a contingent of Militia technicians having booked flight two days before in addition to a number of regular passengers. Remembering how boisterous Militia folk could be in company, even this early in the morning—he'd been one himself not so very long ago—Yevir settled into his chair and closed his eyes, taking the opportunity of his early boarding for a few moments of silent meditation. It would be his first trip back to Deep Space 9 since he'd left to pursue his calling, and although he felt mostly positive about his return, he was not calm. Even the reason for his trip could not dampen his excitement.

And why shouldn't I be excited, considering what happened for me there? Behind his closed eyes, he remembered—the touch on his shoulder, warm and strong. The soft voice, ringing with truth. The sudden complete awareness of his own path, and the tranquility that had enfolded him, that had surrounded him ever since.

It was a story he'd told time and again, to anyone who wanted to know why he'd walked away from his old life to embrace the teachings of the Prophets—and it unfolded to him now like a story, almost as if it had happened to someone else. Perhaps because he'd told it so many times, or perhaps it was because his younger self was so very different from who he was now that he could no longer relate to him. No matter; the story of his life was an inspiration, and one he was proud to own.

Yevir Linjarin, Lieutenant in the Bajoran Militia. A man barely 40 at the end of the occupation, his family dead and gone except for an aunt he'd never known, assigned to the small but industrious Bajoran off-world operations office on Deep Space 9. He'd been a minor administrator in a sea of minor administrators following the Cardassian withdrawal, his specific task to help relocate some of the thousands of Bajorans returning home—families and individuals who'd managed to flee before or during the occupation. It was gratifying work, he supposed, but he'd taken no real joy in it. He had been a lonely man, a man with plenty of acquaintances and no real friends, a man who ate his dinners alone. It was a gray life, not the constant celebration he'd promised himself all those years in the camps; it was the life of a survivor, who'd forgotten how to do anything but survive.

He'd had faith, of a sort, attending weekly services along with everyone else—but he'd never really felt or understood the nature of the Prophets, even after Benjamin Sisko had come to the station. His relationship with Them had been perfunctory, his feelings for the Bajoran Gods a kind of vague, mental appreciation; he likened it to the way some childless individuals felt about children—glad that they were there, but only because that was the appropriate response to children, whether or not one actually enjoyed them. The Emissary's arrival was just another "prophecy" fulfilled that would make no real difference in his life, interesting but essentially inconsequential.

Except he was *the Emissary* . . .

One day, shortly after B'hala had been rediscovered, in fact, Lieutenant Yevir had been on his gray, unassuming way to the station's Replimat for something to eat when he'd been caught in a crowd of his people—and seen light in their eyes, their faces glowing as they watched the Emissary walk among them, touching them, telling them what the Prophets whispered in his ear. Yevir hadn't known the captain beyond being someone to nod to, but on that miraculous day, he'd seen and felt the spiritual power of the man for the first time. It had radiated from him like heat, like a thousand bright colors, and Yevir had understood that something was going to happen, something vast and wonderful. The Emissary told an aging couple not to worry about the harvest, and everyone in the crowd had known it was the truth—and suddenly, the Emissary had been standing in front of him, in front of *him*.

And he touched my shoulder, and I felt the power. "You don't belong here," he said, and I understood that my life was gray and wasted. "Go home," he said, and I knew the truth. I knew that I would serve; I knew that I had been touched by the Prophets through his hand . . . and I left the station that very night.

The story went on—there was his newfound tranquility, and his acceptance as a religious initiate back on Bajor, and his rapid rise into and through the Vedek Assembly—but it was his contact with the Emissary, that single, life-altering moment of total reality, that was the point. It was as though he'd been awakened from a very long sleep, one that had lasted his entire life, and that he would be kai one day was only a natural extension of that rapturous moment.

Is it any wonder that I'm excited to see the station again? To see the people I used to know, to walk through the same places I used to walk, but to see everything through new eyes, through eyes opened by the Prophets' love?

Just thinking of it, he was pulled from the depth of his contemplation, a slight smile touching his lips. He should enjoy his anticipation; pretending some distant calm he didn't feel was unworthy. It was funny, how he still so often worried about how a vedek *should* behave—

Yevir opened his eyes, curious. People had been boarding the shuttle for some time, their shuffle and conversation faint to his ears—but as he tuned back in to his surroundings, he realized that something had changed. An excited murmur swept through the compartment, men and women talking in rapid whispers, smiling and nodding at one another.

Kevlin Jak, the shuttle attendant, was striding past his seat. Yevir reached out and touched his arm, not even having to ask before the young man happily chattered the news.

"The son of the Emissary has just boarded," Kevlin said, his eyes wide and shining. "He asked the captain if he could sit with the other pilots in front—you know how modest he is, of course—can you believe it? The Emissary's son, on our flight!"

"It's a blessing," Yevir said, smiling at the attendant, sure now that his decision to travel to the station was the right one. He'd had doubt, that to so directly involve himself in pursuit of the heresy might not be what the Prophets wanted.

This is a sign, a portent for the righteousness of my cause. His own son, returning from the ruins to share my journey. . . .

Yevir closed his eyes again, praising Them, knowing Their wisdom in all things. The book of obscenities would be found and destroyed. The will of the Prophets would be served, in this as in all else.

Ro slowly walked the cool, quiet corridors of the habitat ring, deep in thought. She could have just as easily done her thinking in the security office, but something about knowing that the Jem'Hadar soldier was close by made it difficult to concentrate. She had Devro watching him at the moment, probably with one hand on his combadge and the other on his phaser, which was fine by her. She *hoped* he was scared; she'd had more than a few fights with the Jem'Hadar during the war. Letting one's guard down, even when the soldier in question was behind a good, sturdy, planar force field, was suicidal behavior.

Of course, the soldier in question seems content to stare off into space and wait for Kira to decide his fate. Kitana'klan hadn't said a word since the colonel had walked out, at least during Ro's watch. Which was also fine by her; not only could she not imagine making small talk with a Jem'Hadar, her mind had been otherwise occupied. Even as strange and possibly singular as Kitana'klan's sudden appearance was, the investigation into Istani Reyla's death was still stalled, and she was finding it more and more difficult to think about anything else.

3, 4, 24, 1.5, 25 . . . The scant information from Istani's isolinear rod had become an endlessly cycling loop, underlying everything. It was like a game, one that wasn't particularly fun but was entirely addictive: find out where the numbers go. There were three main processing cores in the station's computer network, environmental controls were polled at level four once each hour, twenty-four variations of hasperat at Quark's; the habitat levels ran one through five, and there were twenty-five personnel and cargo transporters distributed throughout the station. As soon as she found a place for each number, the cycle started over again—three spokes within three crossover bridges, four work shifts a day, and on, and on. It was tiring and annoying, and she couldn't seem to stop; something had to fit and she knew she would find it, if she could just come up with the right combination.

After Kira's peculiar conversation with Kitana'klan, Ro had spent several frustrating hours scanning recorded images from the station's security monitors, trying vainly to trace the movements of the prylar and the mysterious thief. Thanks to the upgrades, the ODN lines for the monitors had been on a revolving track, the only constant surveillance on engineering, ops, and the Promenade—so while she'd been able to get clear images of the murder and subsequent "accidental" death, there were several time spans completely unaccounted for, most for Istani. She'd been on the station almost a full 52 hours longer than her killer.

And she spent a fair amount of that time in the habitat ring—but not all of it in her quarters, according to the reads from her door monitor. And there was no way to tell where, exactly. Of course. So Ro walked, counting her steps, counting doors, running through the few facts she had and theorizing wildly.

The killer had yet to be properly identified, a frustration unto itself. He had booked passage from Bajor under the name Galihie S., from the Laksie township just outside of Jalanda, and listed his reason for coming to the station as personal business—in other words, shrine services. A lot of Bajorans came to be near the Prophecy Orb. His ID card was apparently a forgery, since there was no one at the Laksie township with his name—the Bajoran net listed 227 Galihies on- or off-world, only 17 with the given initial S, and every one of those were accounted for. The woman who sat next to him on the shuttle said he was uncommunicative and seemed preoccupied. And Dr. Bashir's autopsy report listed him as a healthy Bajoran male, approximately 41.5 years of age, no distinguishing marks. He'd obviously worn an earring, probably for his entire adult life, but none had been found . . . and he hadn't eaten anything for at least 12 hours before he died. Ro had sent tissue sample scores to the Central Archives, but with their backlog, it was going to be another twenty-six hours minimum . . . and that was assuming that he was on file somewhere.

So, Istani Reyla, an archeologist with a spotlessly clean history, came to the station with something valuable, perhaps even stolen, and she'd been chased by Galihie. Istani had been working at B'hala . . . although it was hard to imagine that a prylar would take anything from the holy ruins without permission. On the other hand, why would she have any dealings with someone like Quark, unless she'd been up to something less than legal? And why would Galihie S. have gone to such pains to hide his identity, unless *he'd* meant to perform some criminal act? Maybe the two of them had been working together, some kind of smuggling operation, a partnership gone bad . . .

22, 24, 25 . . .

She was on level four of the habitat ring, corridor E, when the first glimmering of an idea struck her; she stopped in front of the next schematic she saw posted, scanning it. In the Bajoran alphabet, the analog of 'E' was the seventh letter; the fourth was 'C'.

So I'm at 4, 7. Istani could have meant Level 3, corridor C. Three and four, and . . . something between the 24th and 25th sets of rooms? It was simple, undoubtedly too simple, but she found herself jogging back for the turbolift, anyway, silently urging it to hurry after she pressed the call button.

It was ridiculous for her to get her hopes up, but as she stepped off the turbolift on three and walked quickly along C, she hoped anyway. She'd been overthinking the numbers, trying to make a complicated code out of what may have been Istani's simple reminder to herself.

Even as she reached the rooms, she knew that she'd figured it out. Running the entire distance between the designated doors were a series of small removable maintenance panels, angling up from about a half meter off the floor to about a half meter from the height of the corridor. Environmental control overrides, for the quarters on this level.

Tense but exhilarated, Ro measured up what she imagined to be a meter and a half from the floor, the most obvious application of 1.5, and popped the panel loose. Behind the narrow rectangle was a circuit insert next to an empty space, room to reach in and manipulate the wires. There was nothing else— but there *was* something behind the panel directly to the left of her first choice. The dark bundle stuffed behind the panel was perhaps the most welcome sight she'd seen in a long time.

I did it, I figured it out! She felt deeply satisfied, almost giddy with it.

She considered running back to the office for a tricorder for about two seconds, then reached in and carefully pulled the bundle free; if it was a bomb or equivalent, she would at least die having solved the mystery. Narrow and weighty, about the size of two padds side by side, the object was wrapped in some kind of pounded fiber cloth.

Grinning, Ro looked up and down the corridor, wishing there was someone to share her excitement with before she unwrapped the package. It was a book, and a very old one, practically falling apart. The thick, leathery covers were pitted and stained, but unmarked by writing. She turned it over in her hands, brushing at the soft covers, noting the uneven ruffle of aged parchment pages sticking out.

This is from B'hala. It was too old to have come from anywhere else. In spite of her general agnosticism, Ro felt a tiny thrill, aware that she was handling something probably thousands of years old. She carefully opened it, a faint scent of cool dust emanating from the tattered but sturdy root-paper pages . . . and frowned, disappointed. Even to her untrained eye, she could tell that it was written in ancient Bajoran.

Well, obviously. It didn't matter, anyway. Although a few of the particulars had yet to be resolved, she now held the reason for Istani's murder in her hands, she was sure of it.

Except . . . why had Istani hidden the book, unless she'd thought someone would come after it? Ro turned a few of the uneven pages, saw that many were loose, and that others had been ripped out or lost to time. While it might be historically valuable—though considering the hundreds of artifacts being uncovered every day at B'hala, even that seemed unlikely—the shabby tome couldn't be worth much as a collector's piece, no matter how old it was.

Maybe it's the text itself that's valuable. A bizarre thought; anyone could copy words out of a book, or even replicate the thing. So what was so important here that two people had died for it?

Ro closed the age-worn covers and rewrapped the book slowly, thinking about her promise to Kira. About going to her as soon as she turned anything up.

But really, I don't know what I've got here. It could be a book of recipes, for all I know—and Kira will have it translated, anyway. . . .

There had to be a translation program somewhere in the station's network; Captain Sisko had been the Emissary, after all, supposedly off living with the aliens now, and he'd spent a fair amount of time playing around with the Bajoran religion. The discovery of B'hala was even attributed to him. If she told Shar that the book was part of her investigation, which it was, and asked him to pass it quietly through the system . . .

. . . I could take the translated text to the colonel. I wouldn't be breaking any promises, just running a thorough investigation.

Her mind made up, Ro tucked the book under one arm and went to find Shar, sure that she could count on his discretion—and feeling quite pleased with her resourcefulness. She'd found the answer to Istani's death; now, all she had to do was figure out what it meant.

Chapter Seventeen

"So . . . what's up, Doc?"

Vic was smiling as though he'd told a joke, and Bashir smiled back at him, having learned a long time ago that asking the lounge singer to explain himself usually wasn't worth the effort, his references period-specific and occasionally unimaginable. Bashir liked hearing them regardless, charmed by the "hip" sound of each alien allusion.

They sat together at one of the small tables near the stage, Bashir drinking tea, Vic drinking something he called *cuppajo* that smelled very much like coffee. It was morning, the lounge empty except for a handful of casino workers at the bar who had apparently just finished their shifts. Bashir had been relieved to see that Vic was up so early; since his program had gone full-time, there was always the risk now of waking him up, or finding him preoccupied with something else.

"Lots of things, I suppose," Bashir said, noting that his friend was making a point of not asking outright the reason for his early visit—as if he didn't already suspect. Vic Fontaine was remarkably tuned in to people when it came to relationships, particularly romantic ones, but he also didn't interject without being asked. The hologram was special, and not just because he was self-aware, or could transfer his matrix into other programs at will; Vic Fontaine knew about women and what they wanted, he knew how a man's heart worked, and he was willing to share his thoughts on either subject without seeming didactic.

Vic sipped at his *cuppajo*. "I guess so. A few people who came to last night's second set were telling me that one of those Jem'Hadar goons turned up. Bad pennies, you know?"

Bashir nodded, although he had no idea. Mid-twentieth century Earth was a complicated time. "Yes, one did, and he made some fairly amazing claims. Ezri is assessing him even as we speak, to try to see if he's telling the truth."

"Because of all that Starfleet investigation hubbub, right," Vic said. "It was the first thing I heard about when we came back on, after the power short. That and the *Aldebaran,* those poor kids."

Bashir started to ask who'd told him, but since Vic could access the station computer without much trouble, he'd probably just tapped in to see what was happening after his program had blinked. Vic was definitely exceptional. Even Miles hadn't been able to figure out how he worked, not entirely.

Bashir nodded again, thinking about how to start the conversation he wanted to have, thinking about his and Ezri's discussion the night before. They had both apologized, but hadn't talked any further about the incident itself—

"So, doll-face is running the talking cure with a Jem'Hadar," Vic said, casually leaning back in his chair. "That's quite a gig. Say, you two still making the music?"

Bashir had to smile at the man's seemingly innocent segue, matched by a guileless expression. "I think so," he said. "Things are good, overall . . . but I guess you could say we've run into a bit of dissonance."

"Stepping out bad?" Vic asked, frowning.

Bashir shook his head, not sure. "Ah, hurt feelings bad."

"Yours or hers?"

"Both. We were—there was a problem, and she didn't seem to care about how it affected me, and I got angry about it."

Vic ran a hand through his silver hair, his handsome features set in an exaggerated wince. "Ouch. You make it up to her yet?"

Bashir sighed. "Yes. We both apologized . . . but we haven't really resolved the issue. I started to bring it up, but she changed the subject. We're having dinner tonight, though, and I thought I might try again."

Vic drank more of his beverage, a thoughtful look on his face. "Sometimes things don't get resolved until you're ready to resolve them, pallie. And even then, they don't always shake out the way you expect."

Bashir wasn't so sure he liked the sound of that. "You think she doesn't want to work this out yet?"

The singer grinned brilliantly. "Hey, you make it sound like a bad thing. The beauty of the long-term is that you get some elbow room, a little time to breathe—and taking it doesn't have to mean you're ready to call it quits."

Bashir nodded slowly, accepting the information and feeling better. Vic had a way of quickly uncovering the core of a problem; Ezri just needed some time to herself. That was fair, wasn't it?

Fair to her, since I'm the one who doesn't know what's going on.

The spurt of petty anger surprised him by its intensity, and he decided immediately that it was juvenile—but he couldn't entirely discount it. As much as he wanted everything to be good again, there was a part of him that felt *disregarded.* And childish or not, he was angry that she hadn't noticed.

I'm sorry and angry. And I want to fix it, but I don't.

"Crazy thing, love," Vic said. "All kinds of twists and turns, a real Coney ride."

Bashir thought he could grasp that one from context.

> *. . . and considering the subject's doubtful ability to experience guilt, the computer's interpretation of frictive patterns and syllabic emphasis points can not be relied upon to detect truthfulness (extension subtext 4).*
>
> *In short, beyond the brief personal history he supplied upon request (extension subtext 2), I am unable to offer any information about Kitana'klan that he has not volunteered, or that isn't already widely understood about the Jem'Hadar's cultural psychology. . . .*

Wonderful. She hadn't really thought that Ezri—or any counselor—would be able to figure out whether or not the Jem'Hadar was trustworthy in a single session, but Kira had hoped, regardless. Sighing, she scanned the rest of Ezri's summary, seeing pretty much what she expected—until they knew more, they couldn't know what to do with him. Ezri did suggest that he be moved to a secure area other than the holding cell, pointing out that even such a small extension of trust might help things along later. Assuming he was telling the truth.

Kira dropped the padd on her desk and rubbed her eyes, wishing she knew what to do about their surprise guest. Not so much what to do—putting him in one of the reinforced cargo bays, under guard, and letting Ezri work with him was a plan, at least until Admiral Ross showed up—as what to *think*. If only Kitana'klan had managed to hang on to that transmission chip from Odo—

"Nerys?"

Startled, Kira looked up—and saw a tall, dark-haired vedek standing in the doorway, smiling at her with an easy familiarity. He looked so different that it took her a second to place him, even though they'd worked together for a couple of years. Yevir Linjarin.

"Yevir—Vedek Yevir," she stumbled, and stood up, grinning. It was strange to see him wearing the robes, but they suited him. He looked tanned and healthy, and beamed with that inner radiance that so often accompanied late faith. She'd heard the stories after he'd left the station, and could see now by his open, glowing face—so different than the solemn Yevir she'd known—that he had truly been Touched.

"Please, Yevir will do just fine," he said. "It's what you always called me. May I come in? If you're busy . . ."

"No, not at all," she said, stepping around her desk to greet him. He must have come in on the early shuttle, which had docked only thirty minutes ago. "It's so good to see you!"

He opened his arms, and Kira embraced him readily, vaguely amazed to find herself hugging Yevir Linjarin. The man she remembered had been pleasant enough but extremely reserved, even awkward. It *was* good to see him; she didn't know that she had ever felt really close to him, but she had considered him a friend. And at the moment, she could use a few friends—and cynical though it made her feel, she couldn't help but think of his political standing. Reestablishing contact with a man favored to be kai someday—perhaps soon—could be beneficial for the station.

She stepped away, motioning for him to join her at the long, low couch at the office's far corner. "So, what brings you back to DS9?"

Yevir smiled, dropping comfortably onto the padded bench. "Part business, part pleasure. I don't know if you were aware of it, but I'm with the Vedek Assembly now—" At Kira's nod, he continued. "—and with everything still so unsettled on Bajor—politically, I mean, with the First Minister still on Earth, and no kai, and the government caught up with the Cardassian aid project . . . well, I suppose you could say the business aspect of my visit is to see how things are going here, at least on behalf of the Assembly."

He gazed at her sorrowfully now, and with great empathy. "We were all

132 TWIST OF FAITH

shocked and saddened by the news of the attack, of course . . . and by the death of Istani Reyla. It must be a difficult time for you."

Kira nodded again, not sure how to respond. For the depth of the friend-ship they'd had, she didn't feel right discussing her personal feelings. But he was a vedek now, and from all accounts, an inspired one. Even sitting close to him, she could feel a kind of spiritual electricity emanating from him, as though his *pagh* was too vast to be contained.

Like Benjamin, after the pagh'tem'far *that led him to B'hala.* Which was also when the Emissary had spoken to Yevir, and forever changed his life. A miracle of the Prophets.

"It's been hard for all of us," she said finally, giving in to her instincts, and to a lifetime of faith. Vedeks counseled, and she couldn't imagine hiding any-thing from one who had been Touched. "Reyla's senseless murder, then the attack . . . people I knew and cared about were killed. And now the Federation is coming because they believe the Dominion was behind it."

"But you don't . . . ?"

"My gut tells otherwise. And this morning we turned up a shrouded Jem'Hadar soldier hiding on the station, who insists it was a rogue aggression." Kira shook her head, feeling very tired. "Unfortunately, he's not what I'd call a credible source of information."

He continued to hold her gaze, his own soft with kindness and understanding. Again, she felt mild disbelief—Yevir Linjarin, of all people— but she also felt encouraged to continue.

"I'm feeling a lot of stress these days. It's not that any single thing I do is that hard—dealing with a difficult member of my crew, keeping the relief ships on schedule, making sure repairs are made—individually, any part of my daily routine is just something I have to get done. But when I think about running the station, I feel—overwhelmed sometimes. As though it's something much harder than the sum of those individual parts. Does that make sense?"

Yevir nodded. "It does. Because this is also your life, Nerys. And no matter how important the station is to you, you can't make it your entire life. You can't, because what will happen—what is happening—is that even the thought of it will become a terrible burden. It will make you tired and discouraged, and that's not how the Prophets meant for their children to live."

She took a deep breath and blew it out heavily, nodding. It was what Kas-idy had been trying to tell her—and Ezri, and Julian, and even Tiris, in a way. Why was it so hard for her to grasp, that she needed to maintain a more bal-anced life?

"Forgive me for my presumptuousness," he continued quietly, "but may I say that the Prophets have blessed you with great strength and courage. Every-one I've spoken to within the Assembly agrees that you are managing Bajor's interests here wonderfully. However difficult things may be, I hope that know-ing you have our full confidence is some small comfort to you."

He smiled then, his expression compassionate and caring. "As I hope our friendship will be. I know it's been a while, and that thinking of me as a vedek might take some getting used to . . . but when I heard about Reyla's death, I wanted to come and see you. It's one of my personal reasons, I suppose—to offer my prayers for you and for those recovering from the tragedies that have occurred here. I've already spoken to Vedek Capril, and he's agreed to let me lead services this evening. I hope that you'll attend; I mean to speak from *Songs of Dusk.*"

A lovely, lyrical meditation on age and dying. Kira's face broke into a smile, touched by his thoughtfulness. "Of course I'll come. It's an honor for the station."

"And perhaps, afterwards, we could talk some more," he said, standing. "I have to admit, I was hoping to ask you a few questions about the Emissary. About what his life and transcendence have meant for Bajor . . . and what it was like to work with him."

Kira stood also, noting with a touch of amusement that he suddenly seemed a little shy. She could understand; although she and Captain Sisko had finally developed a good working relationship, separating her commanding officer from the Emissary . . . she supposed she'd never managed to do that, not with any consistency.

"His son was on the shuttle, you know. I took his presence as a positive omen for my—"

"Jake?" Kira couldn't help interrupting. "Jake's here on the station?" *Kas will be so happy* . . . And Nog, and Dax, and a half dozen others, not least herself.

Smiling, Yevir nodded. "I gather you didn't know he was coming."

"No, but it's wonderful news, we've really missed him around here." Kira shook her head, delighted.

"I would imagine. He *is* the son of the Emissary," Yevir said, still smiling—and although Kira didn't say anything, she felt the faintest whisper of irritation.

He's also his own person. But of course, Yevir hadn't really known Jake, or the captain, and it was only natural that he felt some reverence for the man who'd led him to the Prophets. A lot of people felt that way about the Emissary, even though Benjamin had done his best not to encourage it.

Yevir slowly raised his hand to her ear, and Kira remained motionless to allow the touch. He closed his eyes, and after a moment, the hand withdrew. He smiled gently at her. "Walk with the Prophets, Nerys."

She walked him to the door, promising again to see him at services. She was glad Yevir had come, and grateful that he'd be around for a little while . . . and Jake, returning unexpectedly—nice to have a little good news for a change.

As she returned to her desk, a loud and abrasively urgent voice squawked from her console. *"Colonel Kira? This is Quark, and I have a proposal for you."*

"Get off the comm," Kira said, scowling. "Now."

"I wouldn't have dared," he intoned earnestly, *"except it's come to my atten-*

tion that Captain Sisko's son has come home to us, and I feel that he deserves a proper welcome back. And although I'd like to throw him a lavish party, the kind of reception he truly merits, the financial burden is really too great for a single businessman—"

"Off, Quark, I mean it," Kira warned. He was strictly prohibited from official channels unless it was an emergency.

He went on as if he hadn't heard her. "—and, of course, it would also be a chance for everyone on the station to come together, to reestablish a sense of community in these uncertain times . . . and it occurred to me that since you've always been so generous, so unstinting when it comes to providing for the emotional needs of the people who live here, I thought that you would want to lend your support to my humble gathering."

Kira sighed. She hated to admit it, and she certainly wouldn't to him, but Quark's idea wasn't all that bad. Not a party, but . . . a connection. A reminder for everyone that they weren't alone, and that even after all they'd endured, there were still good things to share.

"Bottom-line it," she said, sighing. Quark's tone instantly hopped from wheedling to mercenary. He knew he had a sale.

But after all, he is the son of the Emissary. Smiling, Kira let Quark try to talk her into a few things, thinking about positive omens and old friends.

After a quick shower in his quarters, Jake put on fresh clothes—clothes that seemed too clean after B'hala—and went to see Kasidy, walking briskly along level three of the habitat ring and checking the numbers over each door. Level three, corridor C . . . he'd only been to her place a few times before, and when she didn't answer her door signal, he thought he'd forgotten, after all. The computer had said she was in her quarters, but maybe it was 0246, not 0426.

No, I remember the enviro panels, she's two doors down. I haven't been away that long. He signaled again, frowning, thinking that maybe he'd just missed her—

—when the door opened, revealing a bleary, tousled Kasidy Yates. He grinned as her eyes lit up, as she stepped forward and hugged him tightly.

"Jake! Why didn't you tell me you were coming?" She leaned back, gazing up into his face with a look of sheer happiness. "Did you just get in? How long are you staying? Oh, it's so good to see you!"

Her hair was sticking up, and Jake playfully patted it, smoothing it down. "Just wake up, Kas?"

She laughed, releasing him and stepping back, touching her hair and straightening her loose dress. "You got me. It's what, five o'clock? I must look a mess . . . come in, come in and tell me things."

He followed her inside, happy to see that some things never changed; there were five or six empty tea cups sitting amongst several partially filled packing containers, a few random articles of clothing strewn across chairs and countertops. The woman was not a cleaner. Dad used to complain good-naturedly about it, having to pick up after her visits.

Kas settled into a chair across from the couch, and as he sat down, he saw for the first time how big she'd gotten. Her jawline had softened, the curves of her body definitely thicker, and there was a noticeable swell in her stomach. She looked fantastic, and distinctly pregnant.

"Are you going to tell me whether that's my brother or sister in there?" he asked, gesturing at her belly.

Kas laughed, touching the soft curve with both hands. "No way. It's going to be a surprise for everyone, you know that. And don't go asking Julian, he's sworn to secrecy."

"Yeah, right. I bet I can get it out of him."

She laughed again, a bright, familiar sound. "Well, if you find out, don't tell me. Now fill me in, kiddo. What's up?"

He didn't want to lie to her, he didn't want to lie to anyone, but especially Kasidy. The story he'd worked out *could* be the truth, depending on what happened after he left the station. . . .

. . . just say it. If the prophecy turns out to be true, no one is going to be mad . . . and if it's not, there's a good chance nobody will ever know, anyway.

"I guess I got tired of working in the dirt," he said, surprising himself by meeting her gaze evenly. "I've decided to go see Grandpa." He smiled, shrugging. "See if I can get tired of working in a kitchen for a while."

Kasidy's smile faded, but only a little. "So you're not staying?"

"I'd like to. But no, I just came to find myself a ride." He grinned at her again. "Don't worry, though, I'll be back in plenty of time to help you get ready for the baby."

She nodded. "Well, I can't say I'm not disappointed for my sake, but I know Joseph will be thrilled."

She looked at him seriously, and for just a second, her calm, caring expression was so like Dad's that he felt a chill. "And I'm glad you're going to see him for *your* sake. Family's important, Jake. So, tell me—what's B'hala like?"

Jake relaxed. He'd expected . . . actually, he wasn't sure what he'd expected, but not such an easy acceptance of his plans. It made him feel guilty, but only a little. It was best this way; if things didn't work out, he *was* going to go to Earth, and he wouldn't have to feel like a jerk for getting anyone's hopes up.

He told her a few anecdotes about B'hala, about some of the artifacts he'd handled and some of the people he'd worked with. She listened attentively, even though he caught himself telling her a funny story he'd told her before, in one of their transmissions. The fact that she laughed just as hard the second time made him feel lucky to know her; she was going to be a terrific mom.

The conversation meandered around to the house, to plans for a garden and a few questions from Kas about final touches for his room. From there, she chatted about changes in station personnel and the aftermath of the attack. He tried to appear casual and interested, but considering what he was planning— what the possible consequences could be—it was hard to sit still.

Maybe I'll leave early tomorrow. Maybe even tonight. He wanted to see a few people, Ezri and Nog and Kira at least, but only so they wouldn't feel slighted

if he ended up going on to Earth. *And I won't be, because it has to be true. My fa-*
ther is waiting for me in the wormhole, the prophecy was clear.

"*The son enters the Temple alone. With the Herald, he returns.*" He saw it every
time he closed his eyes, felt the truth of it every time he thought the words. In
the days since the prylar had given him the ancient writing, he'd been able to
think of little else.

"... and I never thought I'd end up being happy about having a Jem'Hadar
on the station, but I was getting worried about Kira—"

"What? There was a Jem'Hadar, here?"

Kasidy glared at him in mock reproach. "You haven't been listening. There
is a Jem'Hadar here, his name is Kitana—something ... really, you'll have to
get the story from someone else. All I know is that he turned up in Quark's
yesterday, and that they've got him in a holding cell now."

That was news. "Did he attack anyone?"

"No, but it gives me the creeps, knowing he's been wandering around
ever since their strike on the station. That's why I was worried about Kira, she
was acting a little strange, and after everything she'd been through, I thought
maybe she was suffering some kind of paranoia. A friend of hers was actually
murdered on the Promenade, just a few hours before the Jem'Hadar ships
hit. And it turned out she thought she was being watched because she *was* being watched."

"Murdered. That's terrible," Jake said, shaking his head, feeling very much
like an outsider. He'd missed all of this. "Who was it?"

"An old friend of hers who'd just come up from Bajor, a prylar. Someone
stabbed her during an attempted robbery, some crazy man who grabbed her
bag and then ended up falling off the second floor balcony and breaking his
neck. You know, she might even have been at B'hala—she was an archeologist,
I'm pretty sure. Istani Reyla?"

Stunned, Jake stared at her, at a complete loss for anything to say. Istani
Reyla, murdered, here on the station. It was all he could think, and the thought
repeated itself several times as Kas moved to his side, frowning, gently taking
one of his hands in hers.

"You knew her."

Jake nodded mutely, new thoughts coming in, none of them comfortable.
The woman who'd given him the prophecy, one that had surely been buried
for thousands of years, murdered only a few days later by a thief—or someone
who knew that she had taken something extremely valuable from B'hala. It
couln't possibly be a coincidence—

—but you don't know *that. You don't know anything about it, and she seemed*
like a nice lady, but it probably doesn't have anything to do with what you're here for—

It was the voice of rationalization and he clung to it, desperately hoping it
was true and suspecting that it wasn't. He couldn't change plans, he
wouldn't ... but she was dead, somebody had *killed* her—

"Jake?"

He looked into Kasidy's worried, searching gaze and forced himself to speak, more determined than ever. If she knew what was going on, there was no way she'd let him go.

"Yeah. I didn't know her, exactly, but I met her once. She seemed really nice. It's just a surprise, you know?"

It was the best he could do, and it was enough for Kasidy. Still holding his hand, she murmured a few words of comfort and then delicately eased the conversation into less troubled waters. Jake let her, comforted by her careful maneuvering to make him feel better, telling himself that he'd be bringing Dad back to her and that everything was going to be okay, very soon.

Chapter Eighteen

"You're finished already?"

Ro Laren's first words upon answering her door. Smiling, Shar held up the wrapped Bajoran artifact in one hand, a padd with the translation in his other, and Ro quickly stepped back, motioning him inside with a somewhat anxious expression.

Shar stepped into her quarters, looking around with interest; his first invitation to see inside her rooms. Like the security office, there was not a single personal item in sight. Disappointing, but not really a surprise. The lieutenant didn't strike him as a particularly sentimental person. He didn't see Quark's flowers anywhere.

Ro took the book and its translation from him and sat down at the small table next to the replicator, scanning the padd's content numbers.

"Have a seat. Can I get you anything, a drink?" The offer was absently given, her attention fixed on the padd.

Noting how distracted she seemed, Shar shook his head. "If you'd rather, I could excuse myself so that you might have an opportunity to read the text," he said. "It seems to be of primary interest to you."

Ro looked up him and smiled, setting the padd aside. "I'm sorry, Shar. Please, sit down. I just wasn't expecting it so fast . . . how did you do it? You didn't use the main computer, did you?"

She seemed concerned by the prospect, apparently forgetting that she had specifically asked him not to upload the text. "No. It seems that one of the station's previous science officers—Jadzia Dax, in fact—made a number of improvements to a translation program the Bajoran archeologists had already been utilizing. It's been in a near-constant state of update and revision on Bajor since then. There are two vedeks on DS9 who regularly record new changes in the program for their own use. I copied the file to the terminal in my quarters and scanned the pages manually . . . though I'm afraid the translation is only about 94 percent accurate, and parts of the text are missing."

"That's all right, Shar. I appreciate what you've done . . . and knowing that I can count on your discretion."

Shar nodded. "As you said, it's evidence in an investigation. I understand your desire for caution . . . although considering the material, I'm not sure that I understand the need."

"What are your impressions of what you read?" Ro asked.

"It seems to be a book of prophecies, written in a religious context. The few I read were very old, and I don't know enough of your history to know whether or not they were accurate."

Ro nodded slowly, a look of resigned displeasure on her face. "I figured as much. We Bajorans seem to be lunatics when it comes to prophecies."

Shar wasn't clear about her meaning, but didn't think it was appropriate to ask about the evidence, which he assumed had something to do with the two

Bajoran deaths on the Promenade. He was curious about her attitude, however.

"Laren, I have noted before that you don't seem to share the same religious enthusiasm as other Bajorans. Is there a particular reason?"

She didn't answer for a moment, and Shar was about to rescind his question, afraid that he'd overstepped social boundaries, when she finally spoke. He was relieved. Ro's forthright manner was one of the reasons he so enjoyed her company. It continued to mystify him that there were those on board the station who avoided her, apparently perceiving her bluntness as unfriendliness; he welcomed the opportunity to be around anyone who avoided deceit.

"I don't think that there's any one specific reason," she said. "I had a hard childhood, but so did just about every other Bajoran currently living, and it didn't stop them from believing . . . the weird thing is, I *do* believe in the Prophets. I mean, they obviously exist, and I even believe that they watch out for Bajor, after a fashion. But just because there are some mysterious beings living in the wormhole, that occasionally interfere with our people—I don't think that's enough of a reason to worship them as gods."

She smiled, a small and bitter smile. "And it doesn't help that the prevailing attitude among the faithful is that if you don't worship, there's something wrong with you, or that you're missing out on some great truth. Maybe I'm just contrary, but I don't like the suggestion that I'm somehow less of a person, just because I don't want to do what everyone else does. Whether or not the Prophets are gods, I'd like to feel that I'm free to make my own choice and not be judged because of it."

Her smile changed, becoming the half-whimsical expression he recognized as an attempt to lighten the severity of her statement. She used it often. "Does that make any sense at all?"

Shar's heart was pounding. He understood, better than she knew. With few changes, it was a speech he could have made concerning his own life, the feelings expressed the same as his own—the desire to be independent from what was expected, to make choices deviant from tradition. The difference was, he had never dared to speak his thoughts aloud.

Nor are you at liberty to do so now. The time, the place, even the person was inappropriate.

"It does," he said slowly. "And I support and applaud your decision, Ro Laren."

She raised her eyebrows, surprised perhaps by his sincerity, as she couldn't possibly know the cause. "Well, that makes one of you. But thank you, Shar, that's nice of you to say."

He stood, feeling a strong urge to be alone for a while, to ponder the importance and relevance of Ro's statements. It was with an effort that he remembered what else he'd meant to ask her.

"I was informed by Ezri Dax that there's to be a celebratory gathering at Quark's later this evening, about 2130 hours," he said. "The son of Captain

Sisko is being welcomed back to the station, and Ezri says he's an exceptional young man. I thought I might attend . . . perhaps you'd like to meet me there? Ezri suggested that I bring a friend."

"Actually, I think I'll stay in tonight, see how much of this translation I can get through," Ro said. "But thank you for asking—and please don't talk about any of this prophecy business to anyone, all right?"

Shar nodded, and after Ro thanked him again, he left her spare quarters for the cold solitude of the corridor, feeling hopeful and reflective and very much afraid of the thoughts that their talk had inspired.

Alone in one of the engineering offices, Vaughn sat looking through files on some of the *Enterprise*'s past missions, a cup of cooling coffee at hand. The warp drive was still faltering, but they'd be headed for DS9 as soon as it was on-line; less than a day, surely. And officially, without another assignment waiting, Vaughn's time was his own.

He supposed it was awfully boring of him, but reviewing the tactical history of different commands was a pastime he'd always enjoyed, probably due to all of the years he'd spent out on loan as an adviser. Hopping from ship to ship, most without the holodeck facilities that had become standard these days, meant finding a hobby that didn't require lugging around a lot of equipment, one that he could take up anywhere.

And no matter how I've come to feel about my participation in battle as of late, I can't deny the interest. It had been his life for too long not to have become a part of him, and a change of perspective didn't mean that everything had changed; reading mission reviews relaxed and entertained him.

Only a few years out, and the *Enterprise*-E had already been involved in a number of extremely interesting tactical situations, and reading about them inspired memories of his own, conflicts and resolutions that he hadn't thought of in years. It was ironic—the Orb's influence had worn off, but his taste for reflection seemed to be growing.

He'd just finished perusing a number of entries about Picard's decision to defy the Federation's initial stance during the Ba'ku affair. It was fascinating material, but he was finding it hard to concentrate; he kept thinking about the fact that they still had no subspace communications, and what it might mean for the *Enterprise* and her passengers once they reached DS9. The coded transmission he'd received two days ago wasn't one he could talk about, but Picard would undoubtedly have been notified by now, if communications were working. Until Vaughn had official word of declassification, his hands were tied.

"Commander Vaughn?"

Vaughn looked up and saw Will Riker in the doorway. He smiled at the young man; even though he'd chosen the small office to avoid being sought out, he was happy for the reprieve from the darkening nature of his thoughts.

"There's no one around, Commander. Elias will do."

Riker smiled back at him, stepping into the small office. "Elias, then. I'm sorry to interrupt, but the captain asked me to keep you apprised of our situation."

"Which is . . . ?"

"We've set a course for DS9, but the warp drive is still a concern. A diagnostic on the core shows a slight imbalance in the antideuterium levels, probably because of the extended exposure to plasma radiation. It's not serious, but Commander La Forge has recommended that we don't exceed warp four until we can dock and perform a thorough inspection. We're looking at twenty hours, maybe a little less. ETA is 1500 tomorrow."

"Have you ever been to DS9?" Vaughn asked.

The first officer nodded. "A few times. The first was just after the Cardassian withdrawal. Commander Sisko had just taken charge of overseeing Bajor's preparedness for Federation membership."

"Captain Sisko of the *Defiant*?"

Riker nodded. "He ran the station for the last . . . seven years, I guess. You never met him?"

"No. I know the name, of course." Everyone in Starfleet knew about Sisko; he'd been a key player on the frontlines, one of the Allied force leaders in the final days of the war against the Dominion.

Vaughn frowned, trying to recall something unusual he'd heard about Sisko's command. He'd had some kind of connection to the Bajoran religion, though Vaughn couldn't remember in what context. "Didn't he retire recently? Or . . . was he killed?"

"Neither, actually," Riker said. "He disappeared. I don't know the specifics, but I know that Starfleet decided not to pursue an investigation, for some reason. Something to do with Bajor . . . the Bajorans considered him to be some kind of religious figure, I believe. Maybe they're investigating, or he stepped down in private and joined their religious council. . . ." Riker shook his head. "I'm not sure. I could have someone look it up for you."

Vaughn smiled. "Thank you, but that won't be necessary. It'll give me something to do on the way, now that we've got some extra time to kill."

"Which reminds me, the captain and I are having a working dinner in about an hour, with Commander La Forge," Riker said, "to talk over our repair schedule. He specifically asked me to invite you. It's an informal meeting in the captain's quarters. Can I tell him you'll be joining us?"

"Please do," Vaughn said. "Thank you, Will."

Riker grinned. "You're welcome, Elias."

With a nod, the first officer departed, leaving Vaughn alone once more. His curiosity piqued, he decided to see what he could find out.

"Computer—show me the current personnel file for Starfleet Captain Benjamin Sisko."

The computer's consistently efficient female voice filtered into the room. "*General access to personnel files in the ship's database is limited to—*"

"Whatever you have will be fine," Vaughn interrupted.

A second later, a brief history of Sisko's career popped up on the screen in front of him, a list of honors and decorations, of postings and dates—but Vaughn only saw the small head shot in the upper corner of the screen, a standard optical capture from about the time Sisko had made captain.

It's him.

When Vaughn had reached the Orb and stepped forward to close the doors of its ark, there had been someone with him for a few seconds, a calm and smiling presence he had discounted as a random Orb-induced hallucination. He saw now that it was Benjamin Sisko who had been with him on the *Kamal,* a man he'd never met or even seen before.

"Computer, show me the rest of this file, authorization Vaughn-alpha-zero-seven-zero."

"Access to specified files is restricted to Level Fourteen security clearance or above."

That *was* classified. "Recognize, Vaughn, Elias A., Commander, security clearance Level Twenty."

A new file hit the screen with multiple category options, everything from medical records to personal history. Vaughn called up pictures and found a good one, a full face shot taken only days before the end of the war.

Vaughn leaned back in his chair and stared at the picture, unblinking, the seconds spinning into minutes. It was definitely the same man he'd seen on the freighter, suggesting that there were forces at play that extended far beyond the reality he was most familiar with. He could only hope that they were favorable ones.

Returning to the personal history file, Vaughn opened the first chapter and started to read.

" '. . . and singing, taken to Their eternal home.' "

Finished, Yevir took a deep breath and looked out over the gathered faithful, gratified to see tears on almost every face, mingled with smiles and nods of acceptance. The piece he'd chosen to read was a powerful one, an affirmation of life and existence beyond life; it had been the perfect choice.

The Prophets guide my hand, he quickly reminded himself, knowing how easy it was to become lost in pride. It was a powerful experience for him, too, being the focal point of so much faith, even for a few moments. Every seat was taken, many standing against the back wall, and he knew from Vedek Capril that the reading had been broadcast to several private gatherings throughout the station, so that every Bajoran on board could listen.

Yevir was silent for a moment, aware of the chance he was being given—not just to comfort and lead, but also to put out a few subtle feelers for the missing book. It was hard not to be able to ask outright, but considering the nature of the text, the fewer who knew of it, the better; his small deceit was for the greater good.

"I want to thank you, to thank all of you for this opportunity," he said, nodding ever so slightly at Kira Nerys, sitting in the second row. He saw that she, too, had wept; he sincerely hoped that it wasn't her conscience that had inspired her tears. Earlier, he hadn't sensed any disingenuousness on her part, but he knew that making faulty assumptions could prove disastrous. Until he located the book, he had to remain vigilant.

"It's a particular honor for me to be able to speak to you here," he continued. "As many of you know, it was just outside this very shrine where I received the Touch that led me into the service of the Prophets, only a few years ago. The Emissary was Their tool, as he was for so many of you, for reaching me. For showing me where I belong in the grand Tapestry that is our culture. It is a tapestry that we weave, with the choices that we make, with the lives that we touch—but it is incumbent upon us to always remember that it is the Prophets who provide the threads."

Nods among the gathered, smiles of acknowledgment. Yevir went on, choosing his words carefully now. "As the Emissary showed us all, one does not have to be a vedek to serve. I believe, with all my heart, that we can each do our part—and that it will take each of us doing our part to continue creating that Tapestry. We best honor the Prophets by always seeking Their will, in every thing we do . . . by choosing love, instead of hate. By seeking to understand, instead of staying in ignorance. By rejecting all forms of heresy, raising our hands to the Prophets and turning our backs to the unclean words and thoughts that seek to pull us away from Their wisdom."

In the sea of glowing faces, Yevir saw acceptance and agreement. It was the best he could hope for; if someone listening had knowledge of the book, perhaps he had reached them. At the very least, he had made himself known to them all by leading a well-attended service. It would make his task easier, if he didn't have to introduce himself to everyone he meant to question.

"This concludes tonight's worship; thank you all for coming. *Tesra Peldor impatri bren. Bentel vetan ullon sten.* Walk with the Prophets."

He glanced at the prylar to his left, who softly tapped the gong that signaled the end of the service. Immediately, people rose and surged forward to greet him, talking amongst themselves about their pleasure with the service, many actually reaching out to touch him. Yevir smiled and nodded as he stepped off the riser, thanking them, receiving their kindness and working to keep it from swelling his pride.

Kira was suddenly in front of him, her eyes shining. "That was beautiful," she said, briefly squeezing his hand.

"Thank you, Nerys." He leaned toward her, lowering his voice slightly. "I hope that means that you'll buy me dinner. I haven't eaten since I got here."

Kira grinned. "Absolutely. I was just on my way to Quark's, and was going to ask if you were free. I wanted to introduce you to someone—"

There were more people eager to speak to him, standing patiently by. Yevir nodded at Kira. "I'll meet you there."

A second later she was gone, a half dozen smiling men and women pressing forward in her place to be near him. For a few seconds, he forgot about the book, forgot about Kira and the Assembly and even the Emissary, instead allowing himself to be enveloped by their faith and happiness. Surely, the Prophets wouldn't begrudge him a moment of complacency, a single moment to enjoy what his position inspired. He was only a man, after all.

Yevir opened his arms, accepting their goodwill, accepting their love.

Chapter Nineteen

Bashir signaled at Dax's door promptly at 2120 hours, to walk with her to the welcoming party. Ezri was still trying to make her hair do something interesting. The sound of the door's tone started her heart beating a little faster.

"Come in!"

The door opened and Bashir stepped inside, smiling when he saw her in front of the mirror. She frowned, running her fingers through her hair, brushing it forward and then pushing it back.

"It's short, Ezri," he said, moving to stand behind her, speaking to her reflection. He slid his arms around her waist, resting his chin on top of her head. It always amazed her, how well they fit together. "There's just not that much you can do with it."

Dax smiled, still fussing with her bangs, happy to be in his arms. "Says you. I'm going to dye it purple and green, and spike it like a prong flower."

She turned around, leaning back to kiss him hello before stepping away. "Are you ready yet?" she asked, teasing.

"I'm always ready," he said, his stock answer, but his smile was a little thin . . . and although she knew exactly why, she wasn't prepared to get into it. She knew he was hurt by what had happened, but his response had hurt, too, and she wanted a little more time to figure out what she wanted to tell him.

I need time to figure out what I'm *trying to tell* me. Since commanding the *Defiant,* she had discovered new kinds of memories, feelings of confidence and possibility that she'd never felt before. She felt strong and excited and a little bit confused, and she knew that things were changing.

But that's good, change is a good thing . . . and he loves me. He'd understand, he'd be patient and understanding—

—*like he understood about Jadzia?*

Dax ignored the vicious little thought, reminding herself that he'd been surprised into anger.

"Listen—about tonight . . ." Ezri smiled up at him, feeling strangely nervous. She trusted him, but was feeling a little uncertain about his mood. "Would it be okay with you if we moved dinner to tomorrow?"

Bashir's smile faded. "Why?"

"I really need to do some serious prep work, for my next session with Kitana'klan. I'd been planning to do it after our dinner, but then Kira called about Jake, and I guess he's only going to be here for a day. . . ."

At the tensing of his jaw, she gave up. "I do need the time for work, but I also want to be alone tonight. Not because of what happened yesterday, but because . . . I just do."

Bashir stared at her, and for a moment she thought he would be angry, a thought that both distressed her and opened the door to resentment. She loved him, but she was also unhappy about his reaction to what had occurred between them. She'd reached out for understanding, for empathy and support, and he'd turned away.

"I understand," he said finally, obviously doing his best to mean it. "Tomorrow it is, then."

"Hey, we've still got a party to go to tonight, right?" Ezri smiled encouragingly at him.

"Right." His smile seemed a little forced, but she appreciated the effort.

"I love you," she said, and his face brightened a little, the lines of tension around his mouth and eyes relaxing.

"And I love you," he said, so warmly that she almost regretted changing their plans. Almost, but she had so much to think about, so much to consider. She'd known that a joined Trill had lifetimes of experience to draw upon, obviously, but except in specific instances, she hadn't really *felt* it before, not as something that could define her. But since the *Defiant* . . .

All of them, and me; Dax.

"Shall we?" Ezri asked, taking his arm, and Julian nodded, leaning down to kiss her again.

They started for Quark's, and although they walked touching and in love, their arms closely linked, smiling at one another, Ezri could feel the distance, and wondered if they'd be able to keep it from growing.

It was a beautiful thing, Quark decided, the kind of thing that made him believe in miracles.

Trays of hors d'oeuvres and sliced *hasperat* and stick sandwiches, enough to feed 600 with orders to replenish as needed. An open bar for two full hours, no maximum, and half price cost thereafter. And with shrine services ending, a wave of spiritually satisfied but certainly hungry and thirsty customers headed in his direction; all that worship could be rough on a body. It had been too short notice to get the hype up, but he was betting that at least 2,000 people would manage to drop in throughout the evening, at least for a drink. After days of drying profits, caused by those nasty Jem'Hadar driving away the last of his postwar revelers, Kira's acquiescence to a catered event—at his bar, and one that was open to the entire station—was like a blessed rain.

After a few final words to his staff—"keep it coming" prime among them—Quark stepped out from behind the bar and started encouraging the arriving patrons to eat, drink, be joyous, and then eat and drink more. He made a point of telling all who entered that everything was free, and that on such a lucky evening, they should consider trying a hand at *dabo* or *dom-jot*, perhaps even a late night game of *tongo*. As the 9th Rule promised, "Opportunity plus instinct equals profit."

He was saying as much to an elderly Bajoran woman when he saw Colonel Kira arrive, looking much happier than he'd seen her in a while. She had that bounce in her step that had been missing lately, and she actually smiled and nodded at him after looking over the accommodations. He'd had Frool hang a few streamers around the main food table, left over from Rom's going-away party. The decorations added that special festive touch, and since Rom had paid for them, it didn't cost Quark a thing to appear the consummate host; what could be better?

The bar slowly filled, more and more people wandering in, helping themselves to food and drink. When Jake Sisko and Kasidy Yates walked in together, a small cheer went up. Quark was too busy to see to them personally—that damned replicator of his was still blinking out, requiring him to constantly stay on top of his employees, keeping them running to and from the kitchen—but he had Broik go over with a glass of synthale for Jake and ginger tea for Kasidy. It was the little touches, he knew, that made Quark's the place to spend money on DS9.

Quark was fully occupied—keeping the *dabo* girls smiling, pushing his employees to hurry, advocating merriment—but not so engrossed that he couldn't keep his eyes and ears open. Sensing and reacting to the emotional undercurrents of his customers' interactions was the mark of any good entrepreneur. When he saw Shar come in alone, he mentioned to Morn that the new science officer probably knew all sorts of tricks for generating hair growth, and sent Morn over with a fresh pitcher of high-grade ale to share with the Andorian. When the adorable Ezri came in with her silly doctor, Quark noticed that there was definitely trouble in paradise, at least on Bashir's part. The doctor was faking his laughter, no question; Quark specifically assigned Frool to keep the doctor's whiskey glass full, as he had for so many troubled lovers through the years. Sometimes misery was even more lucrative than happiness.

Quark kept watch on the new vedek, and wasn't particularly impressed with what he saw. The mostly forgettable Yevir Linjarin had always been a man of simple, inexpensive tastes, and it seemed that getting bit by the Prophet bug hadn't changed anything. He ate a single slice of *hasperat* and drank only water, setting a bad example for his small flock of beaming followers. Kira seemed to like Yevir, though, making a point of introducing Jake and Kasidy to him soon after he walked in. Quark noticed with some interest that meeting Sisko's family was the one thing that actually wiped the pious smile from Yevir's face; nice to see a little humility in the religious, particularly those who didn't know how to enjoy free food. Rumor had it that he'd only be staying a short time on the station, at least.

In all, the party was proving to be a success, the only sour note being that Ro Laren hadn't put in an appearance. *Yet,* he reminded himself; it was still early. It was frustrating, particularly considering he had promised to buy her a drink the next time she dropped by. With Kira picking up the tab, he could have plied the lovely Laren with plenty of high quality liquor, saving himself a few slips of latinum.

Can't win 'em all, he thought, feeling uncharacteristically easygoing, ducking behind the bar to scrounge up another pitcher of Andorian ale after noting that Shar and Morn were running dry. He was in a good mood; people were eating and drinking and betting, the sound of laughter and conversation filling the air, the bill steadily climbing. Besides, Ro wasn't going anywhere; he had plenty of time to work his magic.

"Hi, Quark."

Quark stood up, pitcher in hand, and saw Jake Sisko leaning across the bar. Quark plastered on a bright smile, a little surprised to find that he actually meant it. Not only was Jake's presence responsible for Quark's profitable night, he . . . well, Quark had a soft spot for the gangly young man. He was Nog's best friend, after all, and unlike his nephew, Jake had shown the good sense not to go into Starfleet.

"Jake! Welcome home. Enjoying your party, I hope? You should try the stick sandwiches, the fruit ones are especially crisp." They also weren't going as fast as everything else, and leftovers didn't keep.

"Thanks, but I'm not planning on—" Jake started.

"Say, where's that nephew of mine?" Quark interrupted, his grin fading. Jake Sisko was important to the people of Bajor; it would be just like Nog to destroy his only good contact.

"Ensign Chavez said he had a few more repairs to oversee in one of the defense sails, but he should be here any minute," Jake said. "Anyway, like I was saying, I wasn't planning to stay on the station—"

"Oh? Where are you going?" Quark asked eagerly. If he could talk Kira into a going-away party . . .

"Earth," Jake said, apparently frustrated about something. "And I'd actually like to travel alone for a change. So I need a ship that'll get me there. Do you have one?"

Quark stared at him for a moment, then laughed. He had more of a sense of humor than his father had, Quark had to give him that much. "Very funny."

"It's not a joke," Jake said. "And I know you had a couple of unregistered shuttles stashed in one of your cargo bays before I left for B'hala. Nog told me you picked them up cheap at an auction, after the war. Do you still have one?"

Nog had a big mouth. Quark sighed, lowering his voice slightly. There were a lot of people around. "Maybe I do. But I don't run a rental agency."

"Oh, I want to buy it. How much?"

As he spoke, Jake unfastened a small pouch from his belt and dug into it. Quark could hear the dully musical, telltale *clink* of latinum slips, the slightly deeper sound of a strip or two.

Right. Sell a shuttle for *strips*. Being the Emissary's kid apparently caused hallucinations.

"Forget it, Jake. Even if you've got a bar in there, there's no way you could afford it. Now if you don't mind, I see some empty glasses out there—"

"Wait," Jake said, and finally rummaged out a personal account card. He thumbprinted the access key and handed it over.

Quark took it from him, trying to decide if he should bother letting the kid down gently—and then he saw the number on the tiny display. Frowning, *that can't possibly be right,* he expertly tapped a few keys, *has to be in Cardassian leks, or Tarkalean notch-rocks . . .*

Gold-pressed latinum. Not just bars, but *bricks* of it, enough to buy ten shuttles. Twenty.

"Give me a couple of hours," Quark said, a little breathlessly. "You can take possession at airlock 12, 2500."

Jake plucked the card from Quark's numb fingers and slipped in back into his bag. "I'll want to see the merchandise before we agree on a price—though I'm sure it'll be fine. Nog said he checked them out, and you got a good deal."

Jake turned to walk away. Still stunned, Quark found his voice again; he had to know.

"How? How did *you* end up with that kind of latinum?"

Jake looked back at him and shrugged. "It was my dad's."

Quark shook his head. "Jake, your father worked for the *Federation*."

Jake grinned, a bright and sunny smile. "Remember how Jadzia used to win at *tongo?*"

Quark nodded, suppressing a shudder. The woman's luck had been uncanny. Six years of it, too.

Still smiling, Jake delivered the punch. "She lost most of it to Dad, wrestling him on the weekends."

Jake returned to his party, and for a moment, Quark could only stare after him, trying to think of an applicable Rule. Something about irony. He kept coming up blank, and those glasses out there weren't filling themselves.

Well, at least he'd be getting some of it back; he'd be sure to charge as much as he could get away with for the shuttle. *Sisko's kid or not, he can afford a little gouging. . . .*

Shaking his head, Quark spotted Frool and Broik loitering by the bar and went to yell at them.

Nog didn't get to Quark's until almost 2300. He'd been working with a crew of the new techs, slogging through the last bit of repair work on the weapons arrays, and had been afraid he'd missed everything; he was relieved to see that there were still plenty of people milling around.

He stopped at the bar for a root beer, eagerly looking around for Jake. Uncle was in fine form, ordering the servers around and table-hopping with a vengeance, and as Nog searched for Jake, he saw that most of his friends were still in the bar. Shar, Morn, and Ezri sat together, laughing about something, and at the table next to theirs, Kas and Kira were chatting away. Dr. Bashir was playing darts with Ensign Tenmei. A table of engineers saw Nog and waved, raising cups and glasses, and Nog held his root beer up in turn, thinking that he felt really good for the first time all day.

Hard to relax, when you know there's a murdering monster on board, an unhappy voice whispered in his mind, helpfully reminding him. It had even been hard to concentrate on work, and for the first time in months, he'd had twinges of pain in his leg.

"Hey! You made it!"

Nog turned, and saw that Jake had managed to sneak up behind him. Grinning, Nog set his drink down and impulsively hugged Jake, heartily slapping him on the back before letting go. Nog already missed him; Colonel Kira had already told him Jake was probably leaving in a day or so, off to see his grandfather.

"Sorry it took me so long," Nog said. "You wouldn't believe how much stuff there is to do around here. How's the party going? Do you want to sit down somewhere?"

Smiling, Jake jerked his head back toward the Promenade. "What do you say we go to our spot? For old times' sake?"

Nog hesitated for just a second, wondering if it was appropriate for a Starfleet lieutenant—then nodded, unable to resist. He *was* off duty. "That sounds great."

Jake glanced around the bar and then raised a finger to his lips. The old let's-keep-it-quiet sign reminded Nog of earlier times, days when his only responsibilities were going to Mrs. O'Brien's school and helping out in the bar, when his biggest worry was that Odo would catch them exploring the station's old service ducts. It was a fond, wistful feeling so sudden that it made his throat ache.

The two of them slipped quietly out of the bar, taking the long way around to the small lift that went to the second floor balcony. They headed for "their" bridge, the one that crossed between the viewport and the upstairs level of Quark's bar. Without ceremony, they flopped to the floor, sitting with their legs dangling over the edge. Although there was some noise from the bar, the Promenade itself was mostly deserted and quiet, the low, eternal hum of the station audible in the near silence.

For a moment, neither spoke, Jake gazing out the windows, Nog thinking about all the hours they had spent sitting there, talking about their plans for the future as they watched people walk the Promenade below. Jake seemed distant, and Nog supposed he was thinking about his father. It had to be hard for Jake, missing his dad. Nog missed his father, too, but Rom was on Ferenginar; he could always call him, collect, even. Rom had changed the law first thing, just so Nog would be sure to stay in touch.

"So that's what's left of the *Aldebaran*," Jake said quietly, surprising Nog. There was a wide field of scattered debris far beyond the window, glittering in the light of Bajor's distant sun. Jake had apparently been looking at the floating wreckage, not thinking about Captain Sisko.

Nog nodded. "It's been a problem, too. Some of the bigger pieces have been triggering the wormhole, and they're putting out enough radiation to confuse the sensors. The only way we can tell a ship isn't coming through is to scan for incoming neutrino bleeds, and that takes a few seconds." A few terrifying seconds, not knowing if the first wave of another Dominion aggression had just come through.

"Why don't you just blast them?" Jake asked.

"The *Defiant* is still under repair. I suppose we could use runabouts, but they aren't an immediate threat, and Starfleet will want to examine the remains once the task force gets here."

"When are they supposed to show up?"

Nog sighed. "Sometime in the next day or two, I guess. Not soon enough for me."

"Why?" Jake asked. "I thought Kira didn't want them to come at all."

"Because they'll probably take that Jem'Hadar with them when they leave," Nog said, hearing the bitterness in his voice. He couldn't help it, but wasn't sorry, either. Just because the Federation said they weren't official enemies anymore, that didn't mean they were friends . . . or that Nog had to accept one of them.

Jake frowned. "I thought—Kira told me that Odo may have sent him. And that he could end up staying, if that turns out to be true—"

"I'll quit," Nog spat. "I'll quit before I work on a station with one of those things aboard. And Odo didn't send him. There's no way he would have sent a Jem'Hadar soldier here without some kind of, of *credentials.*"

He shook his head, the anger a sharp, hot needle in his gut. "And even if he did, he wouldn't have sent *that* Jem'Hadar. If you saw him, you'd understand. He's just like the rest of them, he's a murderer, you can see it in his eyes—"

Jake put a hand on his arm. "Hey, you don't have to convince *me.*"

Nog saw that he was sincere, and exhaled heavily, nodding. "Right. I'm sorry, I just—I've been thinking about it a lot, you know?"

"I understand. Maybe . . . well, I probably won't be around, but maybe you should talk about it to Ezri, or Vic—"

"What's to talk about?" Nog snapped. "They're all killers, nobody disputes that. I don't need to talk about it, I need for that thing to be off the station, and the sooner the better."

Jake nodded, his expression mild. "Yeah, okay."

They were quiet for another minute, Nog feeling somehow like he hadn't made his case properly. He *was* upset, maybe more than he should be, but he was also right, and didn't want his anger to confuse the issue. On the other hand, he hadn't seen Jake for a while, and probably wouldn't again for at least another few weeks. It would be a waste to spend their time together talking about the prisoner in the holding cell—

"I'm probably going to leave tonight," Jake said quietly, looking out again at the debris field hovering beyond the windows.

"Why? It's pretty late . . . why don't you stay for a couple of days?" Nog was a little hurt by the news, immediately wondering if Jake's decision had to do with his tirade against the Jem'Hadar.

Don't be ridiculous. He just needs some convincing.

Nog forced a grin, revealing as many teeth as possible to promote enthusiasm. "If you're here when the Federation ships arrive, I bet we can get a *dom-jot* game going with some of their crew. Maybe even a tournament." Just about everyone on the station knew better than to play against them; Nog was good, but Jake was practically a master. "We make a great team."

Jake smiled, but even that seemed far away. "That's true. But there are things I need to do . . . and I'd kind of like to get away without making a big deal out of it. I mean, I've seen everyone I wanted to see. They'll understand, if I just kinda sneak out of the party early."

Jake grinned. "And I *will* be back, you know. Maybe even in time for part of that *dom-jot* tourney."

"I thought you were going to Earth for a couple of weeks, at least," Nog said.

Jake shrugged. "Plans change."

For just a second, Nog had the idea that Jake was concealing something, his childhood friend's expression too innocent to be genuine . . . but he dismissed the thought, deciding he was being paranoid. They weren't children anymore, trying to get away with some minor indiscretion without Odo or their fathers finding out. Besides which, he and Jake were partners; Jake wouldn't hide anything from *him*.

"Well, I hope they do," Nog said sincerely. "I miss you, Jake."

Jake nodded somberly. "I miss you, too."

After another second, Jake smiled, and batted his eyelids. "So, you want to kiss now, or what?"

Nog laughed, and punched Jake on the arm. "You should be so lucky, hew-mon."

He thought Jake would punch him back, and for a second, he had a strong flash of nostalgia for it. Even a couple of years ago, an exchange of punches would inevitably have them rolling on the floor, giggling like children as they struggled to pin each other down.

Jake suddenly looked a little down, and Nog thought he knew why. Things had changed, they'd been changing for a long time, and the reminder of how things had once been was both sweet and sad. It seemed like they'd both just figured out that they couldn't go back.

Jake started talking about B'hala, and the moment was gone. Nog wasn't sure if that was good or bad, and finally decided that it didn't matter. It was good to see his best friend again.

Chapter Twenty

Ro wasn't as knowledgeable as some about her planet's history, but she certainly knew the high points—and it seemed that almost all of them were in the book that Istani Reyla had hidden just before her death, the events written about thousands of years before they happened.

And the way it's *written* . . . With as much truth as there was in the text, its secular nature could be considered a threat to Bajor's religious structure. Could be, although Ro wasn't sure; between the bizarre, often twisted metaphors and the occasional rantings about persecution, whoever had written it had almost certainly been insane.

Insane but eerily accurate. Eyes burning and shoulders aching, Ro flipped to the next page on the padd, fascinated and more than a little awed. The writings in the book were almost random in terms of significance, from the grand building of B'hala, to a good kava harvest in 1423—but so far as Ro knew, all of it had come to pass. She'd checked out a few things against the station's library, and hadn't managed to find a single discrepancy. A lot of the names were different, the translation program unable to decipher quite a few of them, but the descriptions of the events were so clear that it didn't matter. They were even roughly chronological, beginning with the adversarial relationship between the Prophets and the Pah-wraiths, and their war over the Celestial Temple. ("Temple" and "Prophets" seemed to be very close to the actual written words, but the term used for the Pah-wraiths translated to something like "fire-living spirits.") It continued through the dissolution of the *D'jarra* caste system with what the book called "the coming of the gray warriors."

Ro was just getting into the occupation—the domination of the land and its children, in book-speak—when she realized she'd been sitting still for too long. She leaned back and stretched, rubbing her eyes, feeling excited and afraid and uncertain all at once.

"Computer, what time is it?"

"The time is 2512."

Ro blinked, thinking it was no wonder she was so sore. She'd been hunched over the book for well over four hours. She stood up and walked to the replicator, ordering ice water and a small fruit salad with sugared protein sauce. She ate standing up, gazing blankly at the ancient book itself, her thoughts all over the place.

Istani knew how important it was—whether the writer was crazy or not, it's a book of prophecy in which the prophecies are actually consistent and precise. She stole it from B'hala, and someone who knew it came after her and killed her for it, because . . .

Ro frowned, mentally backing up a step. How did anyone know Istani had taken it? The prylar had gone out of her way to hide it once she reached the station—but was that because she knew it was valuable, or because she knew someone was coming for it?

She signed out of B'hala, but didn't get to the station until a day and a half later.

Maybe she showed it to someone—Galihie S., for instance—before she left Bajor. And maybe Galihie wasn't all that thrilled about her keeping the book for herself. He could have been an artifact collector, or a religious fanatic, or a business partner . . . maybe he was her lover, and he killed her simply because she left him.

Until I know something about Galihie, I can only guess about why he did it. Unless—

—unless it was something in the text itself, something that Galihie didn't want to be known. Something that had happened and been written about, that could damage him somehow . . . or something that hadn't happened yet, that he'd wanted to keep hidden.

Ro carried her half-finished salad back to the table and set it aside, picking up the padd again, her aches forgotten for the moment. She skimmed through the occupation, pausing only long enough to read about what had to be the Kendra Valley massacre before reaching a series of prophecies regarding the Dominion war . . . and a man who could only be Captain Sisko. Several pages from the book had apparently been torn out from the time period immediately following the war, but a few pages were intact. Ro skipped around, hoping that something would catch her eye—and something finally did.

Ro read and re-read the prophecy of the Avatar, her stomach knotting, feeling really afraid for the first time since picking up the translation. Two of the pages leading up to the prophecy were gone, but there was enough—and if there was even a chance that it was true. . . .

It was late, but there was no getting around it. It was time to talk to Colonel Kira.

After Quark left him at the airlock—the bartender walking away with a few more strips of latinum than he deserved—Jake stepped aboard the *Venture*, a little shocked at how easy things were turning out to be. After about an hour of hanging around with Nog, Jake had returned to his quarters and packed a few necessities, reaching the airlock without running into anyone. Quark had overcharged him, but hadn't asked any questions, either, and had managed to scrounge up a temporary registration license for a few extra strips. Although the personal craft was a little run-down accommodation-wise, its warp and impulse engines were in decent shape.

It's perfect. Or good enough, anyway . . . assuming I keep the lights down. Jake sat his bag down on a padded bench, smiling as he looked around at the gaudily upholstered cabin—everything was striped purple, gold, and green, even the floors. According to Quark, the twenty-year-old Bajoran-built *Venture* had been the private shuttle of a humanoid gambler once upon a time, a woman who had made some poor investment choices during the war and had been forced to auction her assets. In spite of the opulence of the décor, tired though it was, the replicator could only churn out simple proteins and carbohydrates and the bed was a string hammock, but it would get Jake where he needed to go.

Soon, Dad.

Just thinking it gave Jake a chill. It hadn't seemed real before, working out his story back at B'hala, coming to the station and carefully stating his mistruths to the people he cared about. Throughout, it had all felt like some fantastic but distant dream. Even now, there was a dreamlike quality to the moment—he, Jake Sisko, was standing in a ship he had bought to take into the wormhole, to fulfill a prophecy written thousands of years before. "Crazy," as Vic might say, and not for the first time, Jake had to wonder if the more popular connotation didn't apply.

But if I'm wrong, so what? I'm out a few bars of latinum and maybe a little bit of hope, he reminded himself. *Nobody gets hurt.* Maybe it *was* crazy, but his feelings said otherwise. His feelings said that something big was going to happen when he reached the wormhole, because the prophecy was real. It was destiny, *his* destiny, and he wasn't going to let it pass by just because it seemed like a crazy thing to do—

—not when a woman probably died because she gave it to me, or because someone was trying to stop her from giving it to me.

No, he didn't *know* that. Maybe her death was because of something else she'd found, it was possible . . . but he couldn't begin to convince himself of it, as hard as he tried. He was appalled by her death, and he was afraid that the prophecy was the cause, and he didn't want to think that. Because he didn't know what it meant, exactly, or what he should do about it.

Nothing, for now. Later, you can think about it later. Or perhaps he could talk to his father about it, a thought that drove his fears away.

Jake walked to the pilot's seat and sat down, looking over the flight controls. For the most part, they weren't that different from those of a *Danube*-class runabout, which he had learned to pilot not long after his disastrous science project adventure in the Gamma Quadrant. Then, he and Nog had been essentially trapped on the *Rio Grande,* unable to return to DS9 to get help for Jake's father and Quark, who were being held by Jem'Hadar on the planet below. Though he'd only been a kid, Jake had sworn to learn basic piloting skills when they finally made it back to the station. He had, too, and the *Venture* was a much simpler version of the Federation ships he'd learned to pilot. There weren't any weapons or complex sensor arrays for him to worry about, and it had everything else he needed—gravity net, a single transporter, and a standard Bajoran filter/recy life-support system.

He powered up the engines and the onboard computer, and spent a few minutes punching in numbers, double and triple checking coordinate possibilities for what he had planned. He'd had some concerns about getting into the wormhole without everyone on the station knowing about it, but like everything else so far, circumstances seemed to be working in his favor. His conversation with Nog had supplied him with the information he needed, and the wreckage from the *Aldebaran* would provide the means. It was almost as though he was being helped along in his quest, as though . . . but no, that really *was* crazy.

Why? The Prophets watch out for Bajor, and he's with them. Why couldn't he be watching out for me, influencing things so that I can get to him?

It was far-fetched, but perhaps no more so than what he was doing, no more than a dozen things he could think of that he had experienced growing up on the station. It was certainly no stranger than having one's father turn out to be the Bajoran Emissary to the Prophets.

Or having him take off to live with the Prophets, leaving me alone.

Not for much longer.

Jake plugged two flight plans into the computer, ordering the autopilot to kick in with the second one as soon as he was out of the station's sensor range. Avoiding the Klingon patrol ship would be tricky, but the debris field should be helpful there. After a few deep breaths, he transmitted the first flight plan, a mostly straight shot to Earth along a couple of major shipping lanes, to the departure log in ops. A few seconds later, he received vocal confirmation and clearance from an unfamiliar Militia officer who was working the panels. And just like that, he was ready to go.

He hesitated for a moment, the sane, rational part of his mind telling him that it still wasn't too late. He could forget all this nonsense and just head to Earth, or go back into the station and see his friends, or even return to B'hala, to the pleasant monotony of dust and data entry. But he knew better. It had been too late the instant that poor, doomed Istani Reyla had walked into the catalog room where he'd been working and handed him the prophecy of his father's return.

"Shuttle *Venture* departing from airlock 12 at 2524 hours," Jake said. "Course confirmed, bearing oh-one-five mark two."

"Received," the male voice responded, and in a softer, quieter tone, he added, *"Walk with the Prophets."*

Jake felt an instant of surprise and concern as he signed off, that the officer knew something of his plans—but realized in the next second that the man was simply a Bajoran wishing him luck. It was quite doubtful that he had any idea of how appropriate the farewell was.

The shuttle lifted smoothly away from the bay and eased out into space, carrying Jake a step closer to his reunion with his father. He could hardly wait.

Kira had stayed late at the party, later than she probably should have, but she returned to her quarters feeling like she might actually get a decent night's sleep for the first time in almost a week. Even considering Kitana'klan's arrival, it had been a good day; Yevir Linjarin had conducted a beautiful, uplifting service and Jake's party had been a success, even if he had ducked out early.

He was probably tired, Kira thought, as she sat on the edge of her bed and kicked off her boots. Or just readjusting to station life, or preparing himself to leave for Earth. Any one of those would explain why he'd seemed so oddly distant. In any case, the party hadn't been just for him. She didn't expect one broadcast and a few free snacks to fix everything, or to make up for the losses that so many of the station's residents had suffered, but it had been a step on the path to recovery.

She undressed, changing into a loose, woven shift before laying out clothes for the morning. Wiping her face and hands with a cleansing cloth, she thought about how even a few small things could change one's entire outlook on life. Knowing that she had Yevir's support, sharing a few glasses of spring wine with Kas, seeing the hardworking men and women of DS9 relaxing and unwinding . . . it all made her feel that she was doing her job. She felt ready for the Federation and its allies, ready to make her case and make it stick; Kitana'klan's presence helped, but more than that, the strong, positive feeling she had, that things were under control, was enough to allow her some peace. Everything would work out.

Pleasantly exhausted, Kira crawled into bed, determined not to let herself latch on to the things that had been keeping her awake. She needed to rest, and all of the sorrows and problems and complications of her life would still be around in the morning. She closed her eyes, offered a silent prayer of gratitude for the good things in her life, and was right on the verge of sleep when someone signaled at the door.

Dragging herself awake was painful. *The station had better be on fire. . . .*

"Who is it?"

"It's Ro."

Ro. Her sleepy anger dissolved and was replaced by a small knot of anxiety in her stomach; there was simply no way that Ro Laren would bother her at this hour unless it was important.

Reyla. She found something.

"Come in," Kira called, sitting up and reaching for a coverall. She pulled it on in record time and stepped out of her bedroom to greet Ro, who seemed distinctly agitated. The lieutenant was pale and disheveled, her body language uncharacteristically tense.

"I'm sorry it's so late, but I felt I needed to come to you right away," Ro said. She held out a bulkily wrapped object, a padd sitting on top. "It's a book, and a translation. The book was Istani's. I believe she took it from B'hala, and that she was killed because of it."

Kira took them from her, frowning as she set the padd aside and unwrapped a decidedly ancient tome from a soft piece of cloth. The cover was unmarked, but the ragged pages inside were covered in Bajoran from millennia past, the ink faded with time. "Where did you get this? And why do you think someone would kill her over a book?"

"It's a book of prophecy. Istani hid it just before she was attacked, and I found it. I had it translated this afternoon—"

"This afternoon?" Kira interrupted, feeling a surge of anger. "Why didn't you come to me earlier, Ro?"

Ro shook her head. "I didn't know if it was important. I thought it was, but—maybe I should have, all right? If I made a mistake, I'm sorry. But this book . . . Colonel, the prophecies it contains have all come true. *All of them."*

Kira's anger subsided. Bajoran history was full of prophets and prophetic writings, most notoriously contradictory, but even the best of them had only been correct part of the time. "All of them?"

"Take my word for it. Or read it yourself," Ro said. "But read the passage I have marked there, first. The first part of it's missing, but I think it's pretty clear."

Kira leaned against the divider that separated the dining area from the rest of her living room and picked up the padd, reading from where a small cursor slowly blinked.

> . . . *with the Herald attendant. A New Age for Bajor will begin with the birth of the alien Avatar, an age of Awareness and Understanding beyond what the land's children have ever known. The child Avatar will be the second of the Emissary, he to whom the Teacher Prophets sing, and will be born to a gracious and loving world, a world ready to Unite. Before the birth, ten thousand of the land's children will die for the child's sake. It is destined, but should not be looked upon with despair; most choose to die, and are welcomed into the Temple of the Teacher Prophets.*
>
> *Without the sacrifice of the willing, the Avatar will not be born into a land of peace. Perhaps the Avatar will not be born at all; it is unclear. That ten thousand is the number, it is destined. Ten thousand must die.*

Kira looked up into Ro's unsmiling face and shook her head, unable to believe it. "This isn't possible," she said.

"Colonel, I'm not prone to leaps of faith, you probably know that," Ro said. "But so far everything in that book has come true. Everything."

She sat down opposite Kira, her face almost sick with unhappiness. "For better or worse, I'd be the first person to disregard a Bajoran book of prophecy. But this book . . . whoever wrote it was in touch with something real. They knew about the great war, and B'hala, and the occupation. They even knew about the Founders, and the outcome of the Dominion war. And here it says—absolutely—that ten thousand people have to die before Kasidy Yates gives birth."

Kira shook her head again, but inside, her gut was churning, explosions of darkness and fear going off in her mind and in her heart. She looked at the padd, at the book, and at Ro, still shaking her head, wanting more than anything to believe she was asleep and dreaming, painfully aware that she was wide awake.

Her earlier feelings of peace and possibility were gone, and Kira felt like she might never sleep again.

Epilogue

After the call from Starfleet, Ross stepped from his ready room onto the bridge, nodding at communications.

"Anything?" he asked.

Ensign Weller shook his head, certainly knowing what the question was; Ross had asked more than once in the past day since the *U.S.S. Cerberus, Prometheus*-class, had led the Federation fleet to the rendezvous in the Gentariat system. "Negative, sir. Still no acknowledgment from Captain Picard."

Damn. Lieutenant Faro had pointed out that the Badlands were notorious for garbling communications, and Ross hoped very much that he was right, that it was radiation interference keeping Jean-Luc from calling in—because the *Enterprise*-E had apparently fallen off the edge of the universe, and they couldn't wait a moment longer. The Klingon and Romulan fleets had already departed.

The admiral moved to his chair and sat, wishing that things were different, feeling sick with irresolution and dread. The nightmares from less than fifteen weeks before were still perfectly clear for him, haunting his every waking hour and many of his sleeping ones. Another war was unthinkable; the idea of new devastation raining down on societies still in ashes . . . the apocalyptic breadth of such a sin was enough to drive a man mad. Standing with Ben on Cardassia, he'd seen how easy it could be to lose one's mind from horror.

Standing with Ben on Cardassia . . .

Ross had seen many terrible things, but the sheer magnitude of the destruction and loss of life on Cardassia had been brutal beyond words. Mangled bodies littering the streets, buildings burning, the oily, grim dusk of choking smoke and dust settling over it all like a fetid shroud. It was Cardassia that Ross saw in his dreams; Cardassia was the realization of war, and he didn't know if he could bear for it to happen again.

Which is why this investigation is so very important, why it must be carried out immediately and forcefully. He could never let himself forget that the Dominion had been responsible for the holocaust he'd witnessed, and he would do everything in his power to stop them from creating another.

Violence begets violence. Peace at any cost. The two contradicted and confirmed one another, battling for higher ground, but Ross had his orders, however he felt about it; the Federation Council had spoken.

"We can't wait," Ross said, settling back into his chair, hoping beyond hope that they were doing the right thing. "Open a channel to the fleet; we're moving out."

Book Two

For Steve, Dianne, and Gwen
For Home

Prologue

Odo sat on the speck of rock in the great golden sea, on the barren island where he had last seen her face, watching the ocean glimmer and wave. There were times when he had to wonder if the loneliness of Odo was worth holding on to, gazing out across the living surface; it was forever, and even in chaos, it was beautiful.

But with the loneliness always came memories of his life, and they reaffirmed his purpose. He sat on the warm rock where she'd last stood, where she'd smiled in love as he'd descended into the Link. He remembered feeling himself expand across their ocean, his ocean, feeling exhaustion and despair become peace for those he reached, as they reached others. Feeling hope, and experiencing possibility. It was a good memory, its beautiful, idealistic imagery making him want to remember others—times of mirth and confusion, feelings of friendship, and Nerys, always Nerys. He held on to his memories, sharing but never relinquishing them, keeping them as treasured proof that she had loved him.

Now he sat looking out at the beckoning sea because there were things to consider. When he was Odo instead of One with the Link, he could organize his thoughts the way he'd always organized them, to make them understandable in a linear way . . . and more simply but no less important, he had taken form to help keep track of time, which was very different within the Link. Events were unfolding, and it would serve him well to be watchful.

The Link had not been at peace since the war's end, its unrest growing as each member rejoined, bringing information of their defeat's continuing outcome. News of the Dominion's grand failure had sparked rebellious disturbances on some of its subject worlds; the Vorta had been instructed to use the Jem'Hadar to maintain the Dominion's cherished order. Odo had extended the thought that force was only one of many alternatives, but it was being roundly ignored.

He told himself that the Great Link was just beginning a period of transition, that hurrying through it was impossible, but some of their beliefs and practices—violence against their subjects, the continued mistrust of solids, desires for retaliation and fear of reprisal—were frustrating and upsetting. The Link could examine and accept information easily enough, but there was still great trouble understanding.

Behind Odo, a sound of liquid taking form. He glanced back and then looked out over his family again, steeling himself for whatever reason Laas had come. It was usually Laas, when the Link wanted to reach Odo as solid; it was as though they thought Laas's temporary stay on DS9 made Odo more receptive to him. Odo was, in fact, mostly indifferent; Laas wasn't going to convince him of anything.

"It's decided that the Vorta will take soldiers to abolish unrest," Laas said.

Odo nodded, sighing. It had never really been in question, but he would keep proposing peaceful options, even knowing that they might fail. That was certainly one reason there was still such resistance to his thoughts; many had already decided his interests made him unreliable, unstable, and refused to listen.

Laas stepped closer, his own opinion clear in his voice, toneless but somehow slightly sneering. "We still don't think that anything will come of your plan," he said.

Odo scowled, turning to look up at him. "You speak for the Link now, Laas?"

"Most of it." The changeling didn't back down, but Odo noted that he didn't presume any further, either. "They're willing to wait and see what happens . . . but they believe the Alpha Quadrant will strike, as soon as they see an opportunity. The treaty was our death warrant. Solids are incapable of changing their prejudices."

Odo had heard it before, and it never ceased to amaze him. "It's as if they forgot who started the war," he scoffed.

Laas was getting angry. "We didn't attempt genocide. We didn't try to murder them all with disease."

It was a point often argued within the Link, its form at times distorted by the discord. Odo shook his head, always disheartened that he had to explain it again.

But if I repeat it often enough . . . He hoped, he proposed and reasoned, and until his persistence bore fruit, it was the best he could do. They would eventually get tired of his arguments and their own fear, it was inevitable, and then some would try listening to reason. The Link was stubborn, and it was angry and hurt . . . but he didn't believe that it was incapable of change.

"We are not all alike, as fragments of the Link—do you judge the Link by my actions?" Odo asked. "The disease was the work of extremists, a very few among very many, and only then because the Link had aroused the very fears and prejudices you ascribe to them. Inciting wars among the Alpha powers, abduction, terrorism, invasion . . ."

Laas frowned, the pity on his face infinitely worse for Odo than his contempt. "They tried to destroy the Link, Odo. Your obsession with promoting them, it isn't right. *We* are One, and you are One."

"And 'we' were also part of the Hundred, Laas," Odo said. "The Founders sent us out to seek and discover, to find and learn, in the hope that we would bring knowledge back to them. I've come home knowing that the solids are neither inferior nor evil, they're just not like us. Peace is possible."

Urged by feeling, Odo got to his feet, facing Laas. "This is the knowledge I've brought home to the Great Link, that I was sent away for. Shouldn't I be permitted to show them how things really are?"

"Your 'knowledge' is being heard," Laas said, his pity turned to resignation, his voice heavy with it. "That the solids deserve our respect. You introduce this to us when we've lost so much by their hands . . . but we still listen, because we are Linked with you. All of this the Link does for you, and still you plead for *them.*"

Odo turned away, looking up and away from Laas and the shimmering gold sea, looking into the sky. Laas stepped from the rock and was gone.

They would listen. They would learn.

Odo saw stars, pale in the dark and far away, and thought of Nerys. He was concerned for her. She was the reason that he was here, she was how he knew that the Link was wrong, and she was out there now, dealing with what he'd set in motion. Events that might eventually provide evidence for his cause, for *their* cause—but that might also be hard on her. She was the strongest person he'd ever known, but he couldn't foresee all the possible consequences of his actions.

Odo sat down again, leaning back against a raised formation of rock so he could keep looking at the sky. He could only keep telling the truth; he would have to wait for news.

Chapter One

After Ro left, Kira sat down, staring at the book and its translation, feeling strangely numb. It was almost as though Reyla's murder had triggered a chain of miseries, as though the man who had killed her had introduced chaos and disaster to them all.

Within the last three days, Reyla's murder, then the Jem'Hadar attack. Now the Federation is coming, weapons ready, we've got a Jem'Hadar locked up who says that Odo sent him here on a mission of peace . . . and now this.

As unhappy and tired as she was, the thought almost made her smile, a giddy reaction to the unlikely summary of events. It sounded ludicrous, the details and circumstances only adding to the implausibility of it all.

Yes, and people have died.

The thought sobered her instantly. She picked up the translation, scrolling through a few pages. She opened the book's front cover again, looking at the strangely flowing symbols. No author's mark.

Ro's voice, the open worry on her face. *Colonel, I'm not prone to leaps of faith, you probably know that, but everything in that book has come true. Everything.*

Kira concentrated on the translation, moving back to the text that Ro had shown her, considering her security chief's credibility as the words skipped by. Whatever the difficulties between them, Ro had presented her findings clearly, her deductions sound: Istani Reyla had brought a book of Bajoran prophecy to the station and hidden it, perhaps because she knew that someone wanted to take it from her. The as yet unidentified killer had stabbed her for the bag she carried, and had almost certainly fallen to his death believing that he had the book. All of this suggested that the artifact was extremely important.

Kira wasn't sure about a lot of things when it came to her new security officer, but Ro's intelligence had never been in question. Nor had her reading skills.

Kira read the marked passage again; according to the padd, it was the last complete prophecy. Pages from before and after the text were gone, ripped from the book.

> . . . *with the Herald attendant. A New Age for Bajor will begin with the birth of the alien Avatar, an age of Awareness and Understanding beyond what the land's children have ever known. The child Avatar will be the second of the Emissary, he to whom the Teacher Prophets sing, and will be born to a gracious and loving world, a world ready to Unite. Before the birth, ten thousand of the land's children will die. It is destined, but should not be looked upon with despair; most choose to die, and are welcomed into the Temple of the Teacher Prophets.*
>
> *Without the sacrifice of the willing, the Avatar will not be born into a land of peace. Perhaps the Avatar will not be born at all; it is unclear. That ten thousand is the number, it is certain. Ten thousand must die.*

Kira read it again, then closed her eyes. There were over a thousand documented prophetic writings accepted by the Vedek Assembly and the Chamber of Ministers as having been influenced by the Prophets, easily several thousand more that had been rejected; Istani Reyla would surely have taken it before the Assembly, if she'd actually believed that it was real. Or to a vedek, at the very least. Ro could have read exaggerated importance into a few vague predictions . . . and even as complicated as a twenty-plus-millennia-old book would be to create, it surely wasn't impossible.

Kira felt a new ache. The idea that the sweet and compassionate Reyla might have been murdered over some kind of a fraud scheme, something so useless, so trivial, was a dismal one. It made her wish that the clumsy killer were still alive, so that she could kill him herself.

If it *was* true . . . but no, with the seeds of doubt planted, she couldn't swallow it. Not without reading it herself, first.

I should get back to bed. The station repairs were unfinished, their defenses unreliable, and the Allied task force would be coming within the next twenty to thirty hours, give or take, planning to charge into the Gamma Quadrant to see what the Dominion was really up to. It was a decision that no one on the station agreed with, whether or not they could get DS9 operational in time to defend against the probable outcome; the task force was a bad idea.

The Allies feared that the isolated strike on the station was a Dominion ploy; Kitana'klan, their Jem'Hadar mystery guest, claimed that the Founders hadn't sanctioned the attack. She wanted to believe it . . . but Kitana'klan could be lying. It didn't help that the station's internal sensors were still uncertain, and the manual sweeps were inconclusive; for all they knew, there could be a dozen more of the damned soldiers lurking around, and one was already over Kira's limit.

Kira had more than enough insanity to deal with without crediting a probable forgery . . . but she couldn't dismiss it, not yet. If Ro was as right as *she* thought she was, they were headed for a very dark place.

Sighing, Kira touched the command that sent the translation back to its beginning and started to read.

Jake piloted the shuttle *Venture* back toward the station, carefully watching the radiation levels that hid his approach. He was probably being overly cautious; Nog had said that the destruction of the *Aldebaran* had irradiated the station's immediate vicinity, making it nearly impossible to detect a ship—certainly a personal shuttle the size of the *Venture*—but Jake wanted to be sure that he couldn't be tracked. The departure log would show that he'd left DS9 headed for the most common route to Earth, assuming anyone wanted to look, and if what Nog had said was true, the sensors shouldn't be able to pick up his return.

Or me going into the wormhole, if I'm careful. And lucky. He'd been incredibly lucky already; the circumstances couldn't be better, with so much of the station still being repaired or upgraded, and the wormhole still being triggered by remnants of the *Aldebaran*. Once the Federation showed up, they'd start investigating the wreckage, then transporting the remains away. That would close his window of opportunity; once they arrived, there'd be no way for him to get into the wormhole undetected.

He was still out of sensor range, but could see the tiny dot of DS9 on the viewscreen, and even imagined that he could see the cloud of destruction that billowed near the station, an invisible aura of hazardous energy studded with great, ragged pieces of the *Aldebaran*.

Although there were at least seven ship remnants large enough for what he had planned, there were only two that seemed to be on a trajectory that would trigger the wormhole. Jake meant to ease in behind one of them, carefully keeping it between him and the station as he fired a couple of low-power thruster bursts to help it along, low enough that the radiation should cloak him completely. The Klingon patrol ship, the *Tcha'voth,* might spot some of the energy bleed, but they were guarding against attack *from* the Gamma Quadrant; they'd go with the station's assessment in the end, because the bleed would dissipate too fast to be coming from a cloaked ship. A frag trigger explained things nicely.

And then I'll find him. I'll find him and bring him home.

The thought gave him flutters of anxious hope. He knew the prophecy almost by heart, of course, but it was a comfort to see it, to hold it in his hands; keeping an eye on the *Venture's* careful progress, Jake reached down into his bag and pulled out the small bundle that Istani Reyla had given to him. It seemed like a million years ago, but it had been less than a week—and the prylar had been killed only days after their meeting, a fact that Jake still hadn't fully digested. He focused instead on the ancient page of writing that he unwrapped, that told him what he had to do.

Jake traced the symbols of the dead language, the words of the translation clear in his mind, the parchment waxy and soft beneath his trembling fingers.

> *A Herald, unforgotten but lost to time and removed from sight, a Seer of Visions to whom the Teacher Prophets sing, will return from the Temple at the end of this time to attend the birth of New Hope, the Infant Avatar. The welcomed Herald shares a new understanding of the Temple with all the land's children. Conceived by lights of war, the alien Avatar opens its eyes upon a waxing tide of Awareness.*
>
> *The journey to the land hides, but is difficult; prophecies are revealed and hidden. The first child, a son, enters the Temple alone. With the Herald, he returns, and soon after, the Avatar is born. A new breath is drawn and the land rejoices in change and clarity.*

Herald. Or Emissary. And who else could the first son be, if the Avatar was Kas and Dad's baby? Istani Reyla had given the prophecy to him because she knew that it was true, and he knew it, too. He could feel it, and that everything had gone so smoothly—buying the *Venture* from Quark, the readiness with which everyone had bought his story about going to Earth to visit his grand-father, even the fact that the *Aldebaran* had been destroyed and would effec-tively shield his movements—all of it had fit together in a way that was almost frightening, that suggested there were greater powers at work. Powers that wanted him to succeed.

Except for Istani Reyla, his mind whispered. *Where did she fit in?*

He didn't know, and didn't want to think about it. At the moment, there was nothing he could do about it anyway, not without abandoning his mission. When he got back, he'd tell Kira everything, he'd tell her about the prophecy and what he suspected—that somehow, Istani had been killed because of it.

Or I'll tell Dad. He'll know what to do.

It was hope talking, but that was okay; he thought he deserved a little hope. And if he was wrong about everything, no one would ever have to know what he had attempted. He could make up a story about the shuttle being faulty, that it had been nudged into the wormhole by some of the debris as he was returning to the station; he could make up anything he liked, if the proph-ecy turned out to be false.

It won't be.

On the screen, the space station slowly grew, its tiny lights glittering and bright against the fathomless dark. Jake tucked the aged paper back into its wrapping, excited and nervous. He was going to bring his father home.

Chapter Two

Captain Picard found Elias Vaughn in cargo hold D, standing over the closed ark that held the Orb of Memory. It didn't surprise him, really; the commander had been quite taken with the Bajoran artifact. Understandably.

Vaughn glanced up as Picard approached, perhaps pulled from his reverie by the sound of another's footsteps. The cargo hold was still and peaceful, the low lights making it seem even quieter, a dark and silent place far from the bustle of a starship.

"Captain," Vaughn said lightly, tilting his head. "You're up early this morning."

"Commander," Picard returned, smiling. "Yes. I hope I haven't interrupted your—meditation, but I thought you might like to join Dr. Crusher and myself for breakfast. It may be our last chance." They were running a few hours late on original estimates, but if nothing else went wrong with their engines, they'd now reach DS9 in just over fourteen hours. Picard expected that the commander would take a shuttle to Starbase 375, to whatever new assignment awaited him, once they'd concluded their business at the station.

Vaughn smiled back at him, but seemed distracted. "Kind of you to ask, Jean-Luc, but I'm not actually hungry. It's a little too early for me . . . or late, rather."

Picard hesitated, not sure if Vaughn was asking him to leave or inviting further conversation. The man he'd known as Elias Vaughn had always kept his own counsel, not secretive so much as reserved, although he surely had his secrets—a Starfleet officer with an eighty-year career in strategic operations had probably forgotten more clandestine information than Picard would ever know.

But after his Orb experience, Elias had seemed renewed in spirit, an enthusiasm and openness to his manner that hadn't existed before. He'd described to Picard a sense of rediscovered purpose, and he had fairly glowed with it. Deanna had equated it to a spiritual awakening of sorts, a shift of his fundamental perceptions.

Vaughn was gazing down at the ark, the lines of his face now drawn into an unreadable mask. Picard continued to be intrigued by Vaughn's change in manner, but he wasn't one to pry; he had just decided to leave when the commander spoke, his strong voice soft in the still air.

"Strange things happen, Jean-Luc. Things that can't be explained away. That you know will probably never be explained."

Picard nodded. "I agree."

Vaughn grinned, and shook his head as he looked up from the ark. "It's nice to meet another realist. As long as we're agreeing on philosophical matters, I have a hypothetical question for you, a kind of moral dilemma."

Picard folded his arms. "How hypothetical?"

"Completely," Vaughn said. "Say that a high-ranking officer on your ship had received classified information about upcoming circumstances."

Picard nodded. Before they'd lost their subspace array, the commander had received several coded transmissions while on board.

"Say that the information regarded a space station, that your ship might now be headed for," Vaughn said, looking down at the ark again. "And say that this officer believes that if communications were working, you would have heard a declassified version by now. Unfortunately, you won't have the subspace relays operational before you get to the station. And the officer doesn't know what he *can* tell you, beyond the simplest of recommendations."

The charade of the hypothetical was obviously cursory on Vaughn's part, as if he'd only bothered with it at all to get their conversation started. Picard nodded again, stepping carefully. "Would this information be about anything that could jeopardize the safety of my crew, or this ship?"

"Chances are extremely low," Vaughn said. "You'd want to be on guard, that's all. You'll be able to talk to Starfleet about any possibly developing concerns once you reach the station."

Vaughn met his gaze, then, his own clear and perfectly reasonable, matter-of-fact . . . and it occurred to Picard that Vaughn was violating an entire career's worth of security status just to tell him that he should be wary. However else the Orb had affected him, he had clearly shifted his priorities regarding Starfleet.

"Dust is settling, Jean-Luc, that's all," Vaughn said.

Picard nodded, relaxing a bit even as he began reorganizing his own priorities. The kind of dust that settled after a war was fairly consistent, at least, everything that Vaughn said suggesting a minor skirmish, or perhaps another semi-organized protest by non-Federation activists. Almost inevitably from Alpha Quadrant worlds that hadn't been touched by the Dominion, their "passive" resistance had included some minor sabotage to a few Starfleet vessels, all performed on ships docked at non-Federation stations.

Supplement shield emitters, engineering and tactical to yellow, reinforce security procedures before docking . . . They would arrive at DS9 around 2100 hours ship time, but their plans for a midrange maintenance layover might be subject to change, depending on what had happened. Vaughn didn't seem to think it was too serious, but he wouldn't have warned him without cause, either.

"I think I will take you up on that breakfast," Vaughn said abruptly. "We have a busy day ahead, don't we?"

"That we do," Picard said, as they left the hold together, the captain noting that Vaughn's gaze lingered on the Orb for as long as it was still in sight.

". . . and Ezri *recommended* that he be moved to one of the cargo bays, so he wouldn't feel like a prisoner," Nog said. "And when I asked her about it last night, she started on about building *trust,* and getting him some privacy. There are only two guards posted outside, *two.* Like there's any chance that a Jem'Hadar soldier isn't planning to kill us all, like he could ever be trusted. Can you believe it?" Just saying it out loud filled him with a renewed sense of angry betrayal; no one was taking the threat seriously. Nog shook his head in disgust.

Vic Fontaine sighed, running a hand through his rumpled hair. They sat on the couch in the singer's hotel suite, the first glimmers of a holographic dawn forming outside the holographic balcony. It was early, but Nog had hardly been able to sleep, too angry, and his first shift started at 0630; he needed to talk about that—that *creature,* and with Jake having run off to Earth and Ezri siding with the enemy, waking up Vic had seemed like the best choice.

"That's rough, pallie," Vic said, yawning, pulling his robe tighter as he stood up. "Listen, I'm going to order up coffee, maybe an omelet, side of home fries—you want anything?"

He wasn't positive about "home fries," but Nog remembered what an Earth-style omelet was made from, from his time at Starfleet Academy—bird eggs and flavored mold. In a word, revolting. How his father had ever developed a taste for the stuff was beyond him. He shook his head as Vic stepped to the phone, a little hurt that Vic hadn't reacted much to the news.

He knows *what they did to me,* he thought . . . but also remembered that Vic had never dealt with Jem'Hadar; he didn't understand what they were like.

Vic returned to the couch and flopped down. "Sorry, kid, I don't mean to be a drag. You know how I am mornings . . . and we did two encores last night," he said, shaking his head with a little smile. "My axeman—you know Dickie— he was trying to impress this skirt, a real looker, so we ran through the whole shebang. They were making eyes like you wouldn't believe. He made some points, though, got her number and a date for next week. Got to keep the boys happy, right?"

Nog nodded, deciphering the slang easily as Vic talked. It took some getting used to, but he thought he was probably better at it than anyone else on the station. When he had stayed with Vic for a few weeks, he used to love watching people tap anxiously at their translators when they entered the program. The universals didn't have much memory for period slang.

"So this Kitana'klan," Vic said casually. "Have you actually talked to him?"

"*No!* Are you kidding?" Even thinking about it terrified Nog, his palms suddenly spiked with sweat, although he did his best to bluster his way through. "I don't have anything to say to a Jem'Hadar. They're bred to kill, it's all they know how to do. And it seems like everyone suddenly forgot that, like they forgot how many people died because of them."

Vic nodded, but didn't look convinced. "Way I heard it, he had a chance to hurt a lot of people when he was hiding out," the singer said lightly. "And that he didn't put up a racket when you and Shar and the doc found him . . . maybe everyone thinks this one's different because—"

"He's not," Nog interrupted, hardly able to credit what he was hearing, feeling his ears flush with hurt and disbelief. "He was on one of those attack ships, Vic! I can't prove it, but he can't prove that he wasn't, either! Why is everyone so ready to believe him?"

"Easy, kid, easy," Vic said soothingly, raising his hands in conciliatory surrender. "You gotta remember that most folks are ready to put the war behind them. And this guy turns up saying that Odo sent him, and that the attack on the station was a fluke, and that the Dominion has hung up its gloves and wants to make nice. I'm sure a lot of people feel like you do about it, it's just—they're tired, that's all."

Nog nodded slowly, frustrated but thinking he could understand being tired. When the Jem'Hadar on AR-558 had shot off his leg, when he'd run from the reality of the war into Vic Fontaine's innocuous and engrossing world, there had been times he'd woken up in the small hours and lain there, remembering, over and over, staring at the ceiling that wasn't really there, his new leg aching. Struggling with his first real understanding of his own mortality, a terrible gift given to him by the Jem'Hadar. The faces of dead Federation soldiers fresh in his mind, in the dark . . .

I was so tired then that I couldn't leave the holosuite. The same kind of deliberate ignorance to reality as the people he'd talked to last night at Uncle's; it made sense when he thought about it. They *wanted* to believe Kitana'klan's story, because the alternative was to consider new deception by the Dominion. And no one wanted to think about the Dominion at all.

"So what do I do?" Nog asked, his anger subsiding to a grudging understanding of what he was up against.

"If you think he's bad news, kid, you stick to your guns," Vic said firmly. "Talk to some more people, find out how the scene is sitting with them. Stay cool, though, try to keep in mind that everyone has a right to an opinion . . . and keep your eyes open."

There was a knock at the door, presumably Vic's breakfast. Nog and Vic both stood up, Nog finding a smile for his friend.

"I have to get to work," Nog said. "But—thanks, Vic. I feel better. Sorry about waking you up."

Vic smiled back. "Anytime, kid. I mean that; I still owe you for rent."

Nog held his breath as he brushed past room service, a young simulated hew-mon holding a steaming plate of noxious food, and headed for the exit, feeling stronger about his position. It was a relief to know that at least one other person on the station hadn't lost his reason. Nog wasn't overreacting; everyone else was *underreacting.*

Kitana'klan was bad news, no doubt about it, and Nog also had no doubt that behind that scaly, spiky face was a mind calculating how to destroy them all.

Ezri nodded at the guards outside the cargo bay, shifting the two staffs she carried as she approached the door, praying that she wasn't making a huge mistake.

No. Trust has to start somewhere, and this is as good a beginning as any. She hoped.

Yesterday's initial interview with Kitana'klan had given her very little to work with; he had only repeated the story he gave Kira, that he had been sent by Odo to act as a kind of cultural observer on behalf of the Jem'Hadar. Of the four strike ships that had come through the wormhole, he claimed to be the pilot of the one ship that had tried to protect DS9 from the other three, all supposedly rogue Jem'Hadar fighters. He said he'd transported to the station even as his ship was destroyed, and remained shrouded for fear that his motives would be suspect following the attack.

It was a good story, and it certainly explained a lot. If it was true, if the Dominion wasn't behind the attack, then there was no need for the Allies to send a battle-ready fleet into the Gamma Quadrant. If he was lying, he was an enemy.

Which means it all comes down to whether or not I can figure out if he's telling the truth. No pressure, Ezri. Her inner voice sounded a bit amused; she was actually eager to see how her rapidly evolving self-image would affect her insight.

A few deep breaths and she nodded at one of the two security guards, who tapped at a control panel, unlocking the bay. The door slid open and a second guard, Corporal Devro, preceded her inside, phaser drawn.

Ezri had to admit to herself that she was relieved to have an escort. Fear wasn't the issue; the extra set of eyes meant she could relax more, to start seeing how he said the things he said, to try and get a better understanding of his capabilities. There wasn't enough known about Jem'Hadar behavioral psychology for her to assume much of anything.

And Julian will certainly be glad to know I didn't do this alone. He had expressed some concern with her new assignment, although he hadn't pushed, not with the current tension between them. They weren't fighting, but they weren't talking enough, either . . .

. . . and now is definitely *not the time.* Ezri cleared her mind, feeling the whole of her come into balance.

The Jem'Hadar soldier stood in the middle of the cavernous bay, empty except for a few stacks of broken-down storage containers and some shelving. As instructed, Devro remained near the door as Ezri approached the Jem'Hadar, still holding the two staffs. Each was about two meters long, made from a light but dense alloy—a sparring weapon with a decent heft, common to many martial arts. Jem'Hadar fought, it was what they did, and although she wasn't as physically capable as some of her predecessors, she thought she could hold her own with Kitana'klan in an exercise. Long enough to earn his respect, anyway.

The staffs were safer than *bat'leths,* or the Jem'Hadar's usual blade weapon of choice, the *kar'takin* . . . but she wasn't going to kid herself; a Jem'Hadar could kill with whatever was at hand. She was counting on the fact that, whether he was telling the truth or not, it would be against his purpose to kill her here and now.

She stopped in front of Kitana'klan, who looked down at her with an absolutely unreadable expression. As usual. He hadn't expressed any emotion that she had understood, although Kira said he'd been quite adamant about swearing his loyalty to her, even offering the colonel his ketracel-white cartridge. As long as they had white, Jem'Hadar didn't need food or sleep to survive, but they died horribly if their supply of the enzyme ran out. Most of the time, at least; she knew that Julian had once met a soldier who could survive without white, but he had been a genetic anomaly.

"I thought you might be restless," she said, carefully keeping her expression neutral. "My last host once trained with some Jem'Hadar for a joint mission, before the war. So I'm familiar with a few of your hand-to-hand combat drills." She tossed him a staff, and he scarcely moved as he picked it out of the air with one hand. "Let's dance."

He hefted the staff with one hand, not taking his dark, ambiguous gaze from hers. From what she knew about them, Jem'Hadar were both intelligent and inquisitive. They also responded to directness, and Ezri hoped that by challenging him to a physical contest, she would finally make meaningful contact.

"Agreed," Kitana'klan said, and backed up a step, crouching slightly.

Ezri held her staff loosely in both hands, one hand facing up, watching as he took a few sliding steps to his right. He held his staff the same way, suggesting that he was familiar with the weapon . . . or maybe for a Jem'Hadar it was instinctive, coded into their genetic sequencing. Neither would surprise her.

Ezri summoned up all of her Starfleet combat training. Then she reached within herself, first to Jadzia's experience battling Jem'Hadar on Vandros IV, then to her sparring sessions with Worf. She tapped into Curzon's lifelong study of the *mok'bara,* and further back still to Emony's athletic prowess. She then extended her awareness outward, reaching with her senses to take in all of her opponent; his face and body, stance, which muscles were flexed. The chest and the waist were crucial; staff action would begin in one of those two areas. Looking into your opponent's eyes was a mistake, a look could be faked, and Kitana'klan certainly knew—

—*slap,* a blur of motion, and the back of her right hand was stinging, the move so fast that he was already back and away as she registered the pain.

Uh-oh.

She nodded in acknowledgment, startled and not a little impressed; he could have broken her fingers just as easily.

They circled, Ezri turning off her consciousness as much as she could, letting her observations take its place. What she thought wasn't important, because it didn't matter; the first rule of Galeo-Manada was not to worry about what your opponent might do, but to flow with what he or she *did* do.

Except Jadzia was the wrestler, not me—

—*relax, dammit!*

She was Ezri, and their memories were hers. She held the staff at a slight angle in front of her body, watching and waiting, circling as he did. She had no plans to attack, for physical as well as psychological considerations; he was better than her, obviously, but she also thought an attack by her might reinforce his negative beliefs about—

—a thrust, aimed at her gut. Ezri parried, knocking the staff down and

away, but it was an effort. He was strong. It was all she could do to avoid his fol-
low-through—

—and as he leaned into his thrust, Ezri spun into her dodge, wheeling
around and raising her staff for a blow to his shoulder, but he was already gone.
He'd stepped away, moving faster than any being she'd ever fought, only a
breeze across her face.

She continued the turn, putting a leap into her spin as he stepped back
into her range, crouching even lower, *feint for his head and come in low*—

—and in a single, brutal movement, Kitana'klan raised his staff with incredible force, knocking her own out of one hand. She lost her balance for a
split second, but it was all he needed—if he even needed that to beat her. He
brought the staff around, low, sweeping her feet out from under her, the
weighted stick cracking painfully against the side of her left ankle.

She went down, slapping the ground with her free hand, vaguely aware
that the security officer was shouting something. The light was blocked,
Kitana'klan towering over her, staff aimed for her throat—

—*his eyes, look at them*—

—and she felt the cold metal tap at her windpipe, so slightly that it was
almost a tickle. The Jem'Hadar stepped back, lowering his staff.

"It's okay!" Ezri called, breathing deeply as she sat up, afraid that young
Corporal Devro might open fire. Kitana'klan looked down at her, his face as
blank as ever as he reached out to help her up.

"You fight well," he said, his voice without inflection.

"You lie poorly," she answered. "I respect your greater skill, and appreciate
your mercy. Perhaps we can talk, once I put away these weapons."

Kitana'klan nodded dismissively. Ezri collected both staffs, thinking of
how he'd looked at her, thinking of the killing rage she'd seen in his eyes at
her moment of complete vulnerability. He hadn't just wanted to kill her; he'd
craved it.

*He's Jem'Hadar, he can't help what he is. And he could have easily done it, if he
wanted to. He restrained himself, that's what matters.*

Another mental voice, just as loud. *Of course he restrained himself, killing me
would only hurt his situation. He didn't strike because he has other plans.*

She didn't know what to think. All she knew was that she wasn't going
to plan any more therapeutic sparring sessions, certainly not any in which
she was an active participant. However positive she was feeling about her
other skills, Kitana'klan was clearly superior in a fight . . . and that look in
his eyes . . .

She had her opening to ask questions, it was what she'd wanted. Aware
that he was watching her, she did her best not to limp as she walked to the
door, Devro covering her. Kitana'klan simply stood there, needing nothing
from any of them.

Chapter Three

It was time to enter the wormhole.

The *Venture* had been floating in the shadow of a massive section of hull from the lost *Aldebaran,* on the off chance that the wormhole was being visually monitored . . . and according to his shuttle's course reads, it was very close. Close enough that he shouldn't have to do any more than tap the piece with his shields.

This is crazy, Jake thought, manually setting the controls to ease the shuttle forward, wondering what his friends would think of what he was doing, knowing that his father would understand. It was a charge from a prophecy that Jake wholly believed, because his heart told him it was true; how could he possibly do anything but try to fulfill it?

You could have stayed on the station, he told himself. *You could have talked it over with someone a little more objective. You could have helped your friends deal with their losses, helped with the investigation into Istani Reyla's murder, helped Nog deal with having a Jem'Hadar on board—*

"It's a little late for that now," he murmured, unblinking, his gaze glued to the navigation screen—

—and a funnel of swirling energy blossomed around the tiny shuttle. He felt a trickle of sweat run down his back, hands on manual, hoping that his good luck would hold, that he could have just another few seconds as the *Venture* edged incrementally through the wormhole's brilliant entrance. Hoping that he wasn't about to totally humiliate himself in the process of botching his mission.

Help me, Dad, help this to happen.

And then he had crossed the threshold.

Nog was watching his boards in ops with only half an eye, working up another repair-time estimate on the *Defiant,* when the sensor alerts flashed. Tactical and science jumped to attention.

Nog put the wormhole on the main screen before Lieutenant Bowers could ask for it. A frozen field of debris was illuminated across the screen, standing in harsh silhouette contrast to the blinding beauty of the lights.

"No trails, no increase in energized particle count . . . and I'm not reading any displacement in the field," Shar said, and Nog realized he'd been holding his breath when he blew it out in a rush. Another fragment.

"It *is* one we were tracking . . ." Shar continued, his long fingers running across science's control board. "But it shouldn't have tripped the entrance yet, not for another three hours, twenty minutes. It wasn't moving fast enough."

"Is the disparity within a reasonable range, counting for probable collision factors?" Bowers asked.

"Affirmative."

Bowers nodded, looking relieved. Nog didn't blame him; Colonel Kira had called in to say she had some other business to see to before coming up, which meant the lieutenant would have had to make any necessary split-second decisions. It wasn't a responsibility that any of them wanted, not with how things currently stood.

"Communications, contact the *Tcha'voth* and see if our readings match up," Bowers said.

Looks like we're not being invaded quite yet, Nog thought, smiling uneasily at Shar and shrugging. Shar nodded, composed as always. Nog had always heard that Andorians didn't succumb to pressure as easily as others, that they actually got even calmer in crisis situations—until they got violent, anyway. As if he needed any more proof, after the way Shar had handled the Jem'Hadar at Quark's. . . .

"Ah, they say they might have a signature reading—" Shoka Pian, at communications, her terse voice snapping Nog back to attention.

Shoka placed one hand to her earpiece, listening, everyone in ops watching her. She was a volunteer from Bajor, a Militia communications consultant who had shuttled in with some of the engineers to help fill in shifts. Nog strained to hear what was being said, but could only hear a tinny crackling sound.

"—wait, they've lost it," she said, her tone relaxing. "If it was there, it's gone now."

Bowers smiled. "Because they were picking up residuals off the fragment. Again. Please ask them to continue monitoring, unless they wish to pursue the possible reading."

They wouldn't. Nog swallowed heavily, wondering how many more of these they had to look forward to before the Federation showed up. Sciences said only two more ship fragments would trigger the wormhole, but they obviously weren't perfect. He felt bad, thinking of the *Aldebaran* as some kind of nuisance, but the station's tension level was high enough without surprise wormhole openings.

Nog picked up his *Defiant* report again, his stomach a little fluttery, thinking of how much he despised the Dominion and their damned soldiers for teaching him to be so afraid.

Ro had slept poorly, half listening for the computer's voice to tell her that the colonel was calling. Kira finally contacted her just as Ro was getting dressed for her morning shift, asking her to come to the security office.

Ro hurried to get ready, wondering if Kira had already contacted the Bajoran government, wondering who else might be waiting in her office. A vedek or two, maybe someone from the Chamber of Ministers. She ran her fingers through her hair as she left her quarters, not really caring how she looked but wanting to appear sane, at least.

Ro had no idea what anyone could possibly do to prevent a prophecy from happening, but imagined that it would be handled like a natural disaster of some kind. She had given it a lot of thought while not sleeping. As far as she was concerned, the wormhole aliens weren't gods—but no one could deny that they possessed godlike powers. And there were too many actualized prophecies in Bajoran history to ignore one this specific, not with the entire book to back it up.

She was a little surprised to see only Kira waiting for her at the door, holding the cloth-wrapped book and its translation in one arm. Her expression was impassive, and she looked tired. They stepped into the office together, Ro thinking that she might learn to get along with Kira, after all. She took her job seriously, which Ro could respect.

The thought was wiped away with Kira's first words.

"It's not valid," she said, holding the items out to Ro, actually smiling a little. "I'll admit, I was a little scared reading this, at first; there are several writings in here that are incredibly close to actual historical events. But the Prophets didn't have anything to do with this."

Ro took the book and the padd, frowning. "How do you know? What did the lab find out about its age?"

Kira's smile faded. "I didn't take it to the lab. I know because of the content."

Ro stared at her, not sure what she was hearing. "In what way?"

"In that the Prophets never Touched the person or persons who wrote this book," Kira said, as though she were stating some kind of fact. "Who was obviously insane. And it's too obvious, with just enough metaphorical twisting to make it seem halfway credible. It's fallacious and heretical."

Ro had known that the devout Kira wasn't going to like the book's secular theme, but had convinced herself that when it got down to it, the colonel would do the right thing—that she would know the truth when she saw it, and act accordingly. Ro had also considered the possibility that the book was an elaborate fake, written for some unknown purpose, but she seriously doubted it—although until they had it looked over by an expert, there was no way to be sure.

Now she opened her mouth to tell Kira who the insane one obviously was, but realized that what she was going to blurt out would shut the conversation down before it even got started. She snapped her mouth shut, counted to three, and tried not to seem furious. She was a thread from losing her patience.

"Did you read all of the translation?" Ro asked. "Because there were some very unclear parts, but—"

"I read all of it," Kira interrupted. "I know you're not . . . one of the faithful, Ro, but I've read every accepted prophecy, some from the same era as this book—and there's no mention of anything like this, or any acknowledgment of this prophecy being made. The Prophets would never ask for anyone to die, or condone it as destiny. They convey messages of life, not visions of death."

It was Kira's tone that did it, the faintest hint of gentle sympathy for poor, faithless Ro. The thread snapped.

"Are you being deliberately ignorant?" Ro asked, words spilling out sharp and fast, angry disbelief lending heat to her voice. "Everything in that book has happened, and you don't think it's a fake any more than I do. Just because it hasn't been verified by some religious *authority* doesn't make it any less true, it doesn't change what's in the book, and excuse me, but don't you think it's a little presumptuous for you to decide what the Prophets would or would not condone?"

She had stepped over the line, but barely cared. Kira had too much responsibility to indulge her religious biases; it wasn't appropriate and it was maddening, besides.

High color flooded Kira's cheeks. In contrast to the fire in Ro that had made her snap, that bloomed even now in the colonel's face, Kira's manner was deep-space cold.

"Give it to me," she said, thrusting one hand out. "I'm turning it over to Vedek Yevir, to take to the Assembly. If they say it's authentic, we'll move from there. And if not, they have enough experience with false prophecies to take suitable action."

Denounce it loudly, of course. And then maybe set it on fire.

Ro turned and placed the book and translation on her desk before answering, aware that she was probably about to be dismissed from duty as she faced Kira again.

"This book is a key piece of evidence in an ongoing murder investigation," Ro said, keeping her tone as even as she could. "Once the investigation is over, you can lay a claim to it; until then, it stays here."

She hurried on before Kira could respond, just trying to get some kind of point across, something that would make the colonel reconsider her position. "If the artifact *is* genuine, do you think the Vedek Assembly is the only Bajoran group who should have access? You know it's from B'hala, it has to be, which means it belongs to everyone. Do you honestly believe that the Assembly will even consider keeping it as a historical document, let alone opening any part of it to debate?"

Kira didn't seem to be listening. She looked at Ro with something like pity, but her voice carried that no-nonsense tone of absolute belief that to Ro, at least, represented the dogma of the pietistic.

"I don't expect you to understand."

Never underestimate the power of faith. Ro hated that one. It was a tenet of the shrine, as if faith were *always* a good thing.

"But I *do* expect a bare minimum of respect, as the commanding officer of this station," Kira said, meeting Ro's gaze squarely. "Think of it as a courtesy, if you'd rather, but don't forget it if you want to continue working here."

Ro looked away. She was still angry, but Kira was right about that much. She was too old to be indulging her temper, having long seen it as one of her shortcomings.

"Yes, Colonel."

Kira nodded briskly. "Fine. I'll expect a progress report on your pending research results this afternoon, in person. We can talk about a few other matters then, too."

"Are you going to show it to Captain Yates?" Ro asked, her voice flat with resignation. Without the colonel's support, there would be no independent investigation into the book, except for how it related to Istani's murder. Whatever happened, Yates should know that she was an indirect part of the investigation before anyone else did.

Kira seemed startled by the question. "I suppose I should," she said, after a brief hesitation. She reached past Ro and picked up the translation padd. "Is there anything else, Lieutenant?"

Ro shook her head, and Kira turned and walked out without another word. Ro stared after her for a moment, then sat down at her desk, crossing her arms and leaning back in her chair. She gazed absently at the book, thinking, frustrated and alarmed by the situation, surprised at how leniently Kira had responded to her outburst; if their positions had been reversed, Ro would certainly have dismissed her.

Mostly she thought of how comforting it must be, to really believe that the Prophets held every Bajoran in their all-encompassing hands, that they saw every Bajoran as a child to be loved and guided. It had its advantages . . . not the least of which being that if she really did believe, she'd be able to dismiss the book as easily as Kira had.

Ro sighed and turned to the morning security reports, still not sure if she truly belonged on DS9.

Chapter Four

Kasidy was sitting at the small desk in her quarters' living room, revising a list of things to do for her stay at the house. She wasn't leaving for another two days, and would only be staying on Bajor for three, but she loved making lists. Having moved to part-time with the Commerce Ministry, she had a lot of free time to "putter," as her grandmother had liked to say—make lists, catch up on correspondence, take naps.

And eat, she thought sheepishly, glancing over at the small stack of empty plates on the table. Boy or girl, it was going to come out the size of a four-year-old if it didn't slow down.

. . . see about hiring field equipment for spring, check vineyard possibilities(?), check new channel reception . . . This would probably be her last short trip before the move, and she wanted to be organized, to make sure that she took care of as many house details as possible. Jake would probably be back in time to help her unpack, but she'd like to keep the move as stress-free as possible for both of them. He missed his father a lot, she could see it in him every time they talked about the house or the baby, and she wanted to spend a few days with him just being friends. Puttering.

She was seriously debating whether or not to order up another plate of gingerbread when her door signaled. It was Nerys, just in time to save her.

"Come in," Kas called, standing. "Good morning! Did you get enough sleep? You were still at Quark's when I left, and that had to be after 2400 sometime."

"Did Jake really leave?" Kira asked. "Nog told me he did, but I haven't actually looked at the departure list since last night."

Kas smiled, shaking her head. "Well, you know Jake and the limelight. That, and I got the feeling he was in a big hurry to get to Earth."

Kira nodded, but didn't seem to be listening. Kas noticed she was holding a padd at her side, and seemed a little edgy.

She doesn't want to tell me something.

"So what brings you by this morning?" Kas asked, dropping one hand to her lower belly without even thinking about it.

Her nervousness must have showed. "Kas, it's probably nothing at all, really," Kira said, and Kasidy tensed even further. "Let's sit down, all right? There's a story."

Kas sat, and Kira explained. Kira's lost friend, the monk, had been carrying a book with her when she came to the station, and had hidden it soon after arriving. Ro Laren had found the hiding place—coincidentally, less than ten meters from Kas's door—and believed that there was a chance the book had something to do with the murderer's motive for killing Istani Reyla.

Kas's initial unease slowly deepened—it was as though a part of her had expected this, had been waiting for it. As soon as the word "prophecy" cropped up, she had to interrupt, ready to get it over with.

"Is it a prophecy about Ben?" Kas asked, afraid that it was . . . but even more afraid that it wasn't. *Not the baby, please, not the baby*—

"Kasidy, listen to me—I don't believe that anything in the book can be verified as coming from a credible—"

"Nerys, *tell me*," Kas interrupted, really starting to worry.

"One of these alleged prophecies says that your baby will be an important figure in the lives of the Bajoran faithful," Kira said, quietly and directly. "And although I absolutely believe the entire book is a fake, I thought you should know."

Kas was nodding, trying to accept what she was saying, her heart pounding. Her baby, the little somebody who liked ginger and made it hard to sleep comfortably, whom she already loved and was committed to, a religious figure for the Bajorans.

You knew this was a possibility when you got married, take a breath. She'd had the wonderful but rotten luck to fall in love with the Emissary, after all, and had come to a slow, careful acceptance of what that entailed . . . for herself. She'd avoided thinking about what would happen to the child of the Emissary, hoping the baby would take toward her side of the family. Her distinctly normal, pleasantly nonmystical family.

She thought she could deal with it. It wasn't what she wanted, but she understood that everything wasn't up to her. And she'd come to some very positive realizations about herself, about her feelings for the little somebody; she would protect her, or him. Kas had never been a violent person in any way, but in just a few weeks, she'd come to understand the capacity for it in her life—no one would hurt the baby, or they wouldn't be around long enough to regret being born.

"Okay," Kas said, still nodding, taking another deep breath. "Okay, it could be worse. What does it say, exactly?"

Kira held out the padd, presumably the translation to the book. "Kas, I think you should read it. I'm sure this is going to turn out to be some kind of elaborate hoax, to deceive an artifact collector, or extort gain somehow . . . but it may mean that you'll be in the public view again, until the official denunciation is made."

Kasidy took it from her, suddenly realizing that some of the tension in Kira's stance was from fear, whether she admitted it or not.

She's trying to convince me that it's not real, because she doesn't want to believe it, either.

"I've never known you to shy away from the truth, Nerys," Kas said softly. "What does it say?"

Kira hesitated, but must have realized that she wasn't making things any easier. "The book says there will be a sacrifice made before the birth, to ensure that everything will be ready when the baby comes," Kira replied, searching Kas's face for a response. "A Bajoran sacrifice."

Kasidy was starting to feel sick. "What? A person?"

"Ten thousand people."

Kas's fingers were numb, holding the padd. "Ten thousand Bajorans are supposed to die before the big miracle, is that right? Is that what you're telling me?"

"I'm telling you that either some unknown lunatic nonbeliever wrote that down a long time ago, or someone made it up entirely, Kas," Kira said firmly. "And now it's a piece of evidence in a criminal investigation, and that's the only context it belongs in."

Get away, protect the baby.

Kasidy made the decision as the words were leaving her mouth, giving over to a sudden surge of protective instinct. "I'm going to be moving sooner than I expected," she said. "I was planning on going to the property, anyway. To finish up, I mean."

To visit my new home, to finalize a few last details. On a planet that worships the beings who keep taking things from me, and the more I give, the more they demand. My husband, my peace of mind, a normal childhood for our baby.

Maybe she shouldn't be moving to Bajor at all.

"Kas, I'm going to resolve this as soon as I can," Kira said. "The investigation won't take more than another day, I'm sure. Ro is expecting some test results on Reyla's killer, to make an identification, and then it should be over. Please stay."

Kas was unhappy with all her choices, but it wasn't Kira's fault. And Kira had been a good friend to her, asking nothing in return for helping her make Ben's house a reality.

"I'll stay, but I want to read this," Kas said, looking down at the padd and then back at Kira again. "All of it. I need to know what else it says."

Kira nodded reluctantly, and stood up. "Of course. I should be in my office most of the day, if you want to talk."

After she'd gone, Kas stared at the padd for a long time, wishing there were someone to blame for such craziness, someone to hold responsible for the things that had happened in her life since she met Ben Sisko. He was worth it, she believed, most of the time; other times, she had to wonder.

After breakfast, Vaughn decided to see if there was a holodeck available. Picard had called for a senior staff meeting, probably to suggest a few defense adjustments, and Vaughn was feeling restless.

He was in luck, two rooms open. It was a luxury he rarely indulged in, holodeck time, generally preferring to read—but he'd decided over breakfast that he'd like to relax with his thoughts for a while. He felt a need to analyze some of what he'd been going through.

"Computer, do you have 'Life Cycle Meditation/Old Growth Forest'? Program number 06010, I think." Vaughn doubted the *Enterprise*-E would carry it; it was one of the earliest holoprograms.

"Affirmative."

"Run it," Vaughn said, smiling as he punched in his visitor code and a time call. It had been at least ten years since he'd used the program, but he'd thought about it several times since his experience with the Orb, remembering it wistfully.

He stepped onto the holodeck just as spring was taking hold and started walking, wanting to get to the clearing before summer.

All around the trail that led into the thickly shaded woods, buds were forming on branches, flowers were springing up, saplings were becoming young trees. He saw a trio of baby rabbits, and heard fledgling birds crying. The sound and imagery were perfect.

By the time he reached the fully enclosed clearing he remembered, fresh young life was maturing. Plants were reaching their life peak, fuller and darker, their blossoms most brilliant, insects lazily buzzing past; half-grown animals darted through the trees, killing, mating, rolling on the ground in the sun. There was a sloping, grassy rise in the middle of the open space, a perfect place to sit; Vaughn flopped down comfortably, crossing his legs, watching as the forest evolved.

Summer, then fall, things dying, changing color, holing up for winter in small spaces. In the winters, it usually snowed. Vaughn didn't feel the cold air or the gentle sting of the snow, for the same reason it never got too dark to see, or some things grew disproportionately fast or moved disproportionately slow. The point of the program wasn't to simulate reality, or to simply show a speeded-up loop. It was a backdrop for meditation, the soft sounds becoming a drone of occurrences, nothing so jerky or loud as to distract attention from anything else.

He saw a white rabbit slaughtered by a white fox, then a thin deer, nosing for something to eat. He heard tree branches snapping, and thunder. And a moment later, the trickle of thaw, and a smattering of pale green crept up across the clearing. The forest evolved for about twenty years, the full program running over two hours.

Vaughn watched, letting his mind wander. Thinking that he was starting to settle into his new mindset, feeling less exuberant and more thoughtful about his future. Interesting, that he was enjoying his introspection as much as he'd enjoyed his initial flush of vitality. It seemed that being born-again young made everything interesting, the heaviness of his past dropping away like cut ballast; he felt like he was looking up and out after years of staring straight ahead.

Midsummer, the grasses weaving in a simulated wind. Vaughn was glad he'd decided to tell Picard that the environment at and around DS9 might be unstable. Jean-Luc was more of a straight arrow than Vaughn had ever been, but he was also the kind of captain who lived and died for his crew and ship, a mentality Vaughn respected. Picard had appreciated the warning, and it had cost him nothing.

And admit it—you enjoyed telling him because you weren't supposed to. Although he had more discretion in clearance matters than a lot of admirals, the Vaughn of a week ago probably wouldn't have done it. Because Starfleet officers didn't do things like that, the chain of command broke down when people didn't do their jobs; it wasn't the *code*.

Vaughn got to smiling as the autumn rains started to fall once more. At the age of 101, he had decided to stray off the path of absolute righteousness and military ideology because ... because he wanted to, and it turned out that wanting to was enough. The cycle playing out all around him reaffirmed his confidence, the feelings of clarity and contemplative objectivity. Life went on, whether he was fulfilled or not; why not do as he wished?

He thought about what had happened on the freighter just before he'd closed the ark, wondered how it was meaningful. Assuming that approaching the Orb hadn't caused hallucinations, why had Benjamin Sisko been there? Vaughn couldn't remember having ever seen an image of him before, and there had been nothing familiar about him at the time. Was it coincidence, that he'd seen the missing captain standing beside the Orb, and that the *Enterprise* was now on her way to DS9, the station he'd commanded? Of course not. The files Vaughn had been able to access on Sisko had an extremely detailed report about the captain's disappearance, and where he was presumed to have gone; friends in high places, so to speak. Vaughn was very much looking forward to exploring the noncoincidence a little further, and to meeting some of the people who'd worked with Sisko.

And with what will be happening at the wormhole entrance in a day or so, unless things have changed. . . .

The tragedy behind it was too vast to contemplate for long, and he'd known a lifetime of such tragedies—misunderstandings, acts of revenge or simple malice that created more tragedy, by encouraging mistrust, by encouraging hate, always in the name of necessity. Vaughn didn't think it would come to that; he expected there to be a lot of chest-thumping for a few days among the Allied forces, but saner heads would certainly prevail in the end, no matter what the political climate. They simply didn't have the energy or the resources to consider anything else.

The seasons changed, and Vaughn stopped thinking after a while, the low, persistent hum of life lulling and sweet to his ears. Rot and rebirth and rot, hope springing eternal, the end always near. He'd never been much of a philosopher, but some things seemed pretty obvious.

They had decided to have lunch together in his quarters, Julian knowing the second she walked in that she was ready to talk. Her posture and a microexpression of anxiety beneath her smile gave her away.

Don't push, let her get to it on her own.

Ezri picked up the plate of salad he'd already replicated for her and sat down on the couch across from him, her shoulders tight. He wished that he understood his own feelings better. He thought about what Vic had said about giving her space, and then about his own frustrations with Ezri's distancing tactics; she was going through some kind of an emotional change, and he wanted to be supportive, but she'd consistently avoided talking about it—and hadn't taken any great pains to consider his feelings in the matter, either. Which hurt.

Julian set his own untouched plate on the low table that separated them. "You okay?" he asked.

She nodded. "Still sorry about the other day, though," she said, and Julian relaxed a little.

"I am, too," he said.

"It must have been so strange for you—"

"It really was," he said, relaxing a little more.

Ezri smiled. "I guess you've noticed that I've been thinking about some things since the attack on the station."

"Since you saved the station," Julian said, smiling back at her.

Ezri nodded vigorously, grinning. "Exactly, that's exactly right," she said. "Since I took command of the *Defiant*. Julian, it was such an amazing feeling, tapping my memories for leadership qualities and finding them. It wasn't a decision, to take command; it was more like a . . . a reflex."

"My" memories. Not Jadzia's, or one of the other hosts.

"And as soon as the immediate danger was past, it really hit me," she continued. "I knew it before, logically, but I'd never really experienced the power of who I am now. Even when I drew from Joran's personality to help me in that murder investigation last year, I treated him as something separate and apart from me. Now, though . . ."

Julian nodded, happy for her excitement. "That's wonderful. So you're feeling . . . more *integrated,* if that's the right term."

"More integrated, more confident," she said. "In the last couple of days, I've started to get used to the idea, that I'm not limited to the life goals Ezri Tigan set for herself. Not that those were bad things—a nice home, a family, my own counseling center someday. It's just that I can be so much *more.*"

Julian felt his friendly objectivity slipping just a bit. "So, you don't want those things?"

Ezri shook her head. "It's not that, I *do* want those things, but I have so much to figure out first."

Still smiling, she reached over and took his hand, squeezing it tightly. "You know I never prepared for this life, Julian. Ever since I was joined, I've been struggling to figure out who *I* am, trying to understand where Ezri fit in the totality of Dax. That first year, I honestly didn't know if I could survive as Ezri Dax, I felt like I was being crowded out by eight strangers whom I somehow knew as intimately as I knew Ezri Tigan. I didn't know what to do with them. And worse, I was in constant fear of what they'd do to me.

"But when I took command on the *Defiant,* I had this kind of emotional realization—that 'I' means so much more for a joined Trill. But I wasn't just thinking it, for the first time I really *felt* it—Ezri is all of them, and Dax, *and* who I was before I was joined."

She shook her head again, releasing has hand. "I've just come to realize that I've been given this incredible chance, to see beyond the reality I grew up believing—that fulfillment comes only through our relationships to others. I never realized how alone I was then, not even *considering* the internal relationships that being joined could create."

Julian felt himself tensing. He didn't want to drag her away from enjoying her new insights, but it was as though she'd forgotten the nature of their relationship . . . and was continuing to overlook his feelings, about what had happened during their lovemaking, in what she was saying now. Being in bed with her, looking down to see Ezri open her eyes, to see Jadzia looking back up at him . . . he couldn't think of a word to describe how it had been, to feel that she had gone away and left him so vulnerable. That she had frightened him.

He kept his tone light, but couldn't entirely erase an edge from his words. "No more internal relationships sneaking up on me, I hope."

Ezri frowned, a half-smile still on her face. "What do you mean?"

"Nothing. It's just . . . the other night, I was caught off guard, and honestly, I'm not getting the feeling that you understand why that bothered me."

She wasn't smiling at all now. "I understand perfectly. And I said I was sorry, Julian. It wasn't like I planned it."

He could see the fight coming and he made a last effort to stop it. "I don't want to fight with you, Ezri. I love you. I just want you to tell me what's happening with you when it's happening, so I'm not surprised like that again."

"I love *you*, Julian, and I really am sorry. But if you're asking me to define myself for you . . ." Ezri folded her arms, and took a deep breath. "I've got to figure out what I'm capable of, before I can share it with anyone else."

Julian shook his head, amazed, not sure he was hearing what he was hearing. Only a few days ago, they'd made plans to take a small vacation together, still three months away. "Ezri, are you telling me that you want to end our relationship?"

"No, of course not," she said, but he was suddenly sure that she was holding back. Her instant of hesitation, the shift of her brow, something.

"Well, is it that you feel like I'm limiting you?" he asked, starting to get confused.

"No. I'm—I just want you to let go, a little," she said, no longer angry, the soft plea in her voice even worse. "Let me decide some things. I want us to stay together, I just need to think about how things are changing, I need—I need you to be patient for a while. To give me some time."

He couldn't be mad at her for wanting his support, but he couldn't help being hurt by how she wanted it. Time alone, time away from developing their relationship, so that she could decide whether or not she wanted to develop it any further.

Are we back to kisses on the cheek? To close friends? What were the rules, the boundaries? Julian opened his mouth, not sure what he was going to say, amazed that the simple truth came out.

"I want you to be happy," he said truthfully.

It seemed to be the point, that keeping love meant maintaining a constant awareness that it couldn't be kept.

Chapter Five

Nog was starting to really like Shar, so when he saw the Andorian sitting at the bar by himself, Nog eagerly joined him. Shar seemed to be just as happy about it, although Nog now knew his smile to be fake; he'd told Nog only yesterday about how humor and expressions of pleasure weren't big in Andorian society, that smiling was a learned behavior. Nog thought that was weird, but also entirely fascinating.

It felt good, to feel like Shar enjoyed his company. Nog knew that he was mostly well liked on the station, but his ability to make new friends had never been his strongest selling point. A lot of people in the universe looked down on Ferengi, for their mostly deserved reputation as a devious, swindling species, and it was nice to know that Andorians didn't appear to be among them. It wasn't like hanging around with Jake, but Shar was so curious about everything, and he seemed to cast judgment on no one. It made spending time with him kind of fun.

It was early for dinner, and the restaurant was barely half full. They took a table next to the bar, Nog noticing that Frool seemed to be working alone when he stepped back up to order drinks and food. Shar had agreed to try a root beer.

"Frool, where's Uncle?"

Frool shrugged, turning to get the beers and mugs. "He keeps walking out in front for some reason, staring down the Promenade at something. This is the fourth time today."

"What's he staring at?"

"I don't know. It's down near the security office, whatever it is."

Nog turned and set the drinks down on the table, shaking his head. Uncle Quark had been strangely anxious ever since the attack, but not in a way that Nog would expect. If he was worried about another war, why hadn't Uncle liquidated any assets or sold any stocks, why hadn't he asked Nog to find him a new escape route? He seemed to be smiling too much, too, acting as though he was . . .

It hit him as he sat down, and he laughed out loud. Not anxious, *interested*.

"Why are you laughing, Nog?" Shar asked, his soft voice uncertain, as if he was afraid he'd missed a joke.

Nog leaned over the table, lowering his voice. "I think my uncle Quark might be in love."

Shar looked at him seriously. "His love is a source of humor?"

"The way he experiences it, definitely," Nog said. "I'm sorry, Shar, I was exaggerating. My uncle doesn't fall in love, exactly. It's more like . . . it's like he gets very excited about a possible temporary merger. He told me once that he knew he was in trouble every time he caught himself smiling for no good reason. That, or he buys flowers retail."

Shar tilted his head to one side, frowning. "He bought flowers for Lieutenant Ro."

"Really?" Nog laughed again, lifting his mug. "He's farther gone than I thought."

"You believe he wants to temporarily merge with Ro Laren," Shar said, and Nog actually choked. Sputtering, he put his drink down and shook his head at Shar, who was perfectly deadpan.

"That's *exactly* what I believe," Nog said, and Shar nodded. Nog had no idea if Shar had made a deliberate joke or not, but decided not to pursue the conversation any further; they were about to eat. The last thing he needed was to be thinking of his uncle Quark's romantic hopes for Ro Laren.

Shar tried the root beer, and liked it. As they waited for their food, Nog recounted a few of the minor adventures that he and Jake had gone through . . . although talking about his youth on the station reminded him of Jake's and his science-project field trip. It had been the first time Nog had ever seen a Jem'Hadar.

He finished his story about the self-sealing stem bolts and fell silent, unhappy that he couldn't seem to get away from thinking about *them*. He thought about Vic's advice, to find out what other people thought about the Jem'Hadar being on the station, but he and Shar had already talked about it. Unfortunately, the mild and pleasant Shar didn't seem to form strong opinions about much of anything. He had commiserated with Nog about his anger, but he hadn't expressed any of his own feelings, beyond saying that war was always unfortunate.

In fact . . .

"Shar, why don't you ever talk about yourself?" Nog asked. "It seems like you're always listening and asking a lot of questions, but you don't talk about what you like to do, things like that."

Shar blinked, his expression impassive. "I'm not sure what you mean."

"Well, do you have any hobbies? Things you enjoy?"

"I enjoy learning about different cultures."

Nog nodded; not *dom-jot* but it was a start, at least. "What's your culture like?" he asked.

Shar blinked again, and although his expression didn't change, Nog had a sudden impression that he was reluctant to answer.

"The Andorian culture is complex," Shar said, after a few beats. Then he fell silent again, as if considering how to proceed. Or maybe if he should at all. "Andorians have a genetic predisposition toward violent behavior, but socially, within our own communities, we're extremely structured. I would say we are a serious people, and adaptable. Compared to many other species, Andorians excel under difficult circumstances; like the human fight-or-flight response to danger, our biochemical reaction is to either fight or to increase our sensory input levels, which lends greater power to our analytical and reasoning skills."

So it *was* true. "That's very interesting."

Shar nodded. "All cultures are interesting," he said. "Your own, for example . . . you were telling me about your rules of monetary acquisition last night. Do all Ferengi know them, or just the males?"

Nog was deep into explaining the feminist revolution on Ferenginar before he realized that Shar had neatly sidestepped being asked any more personal questions. It was a common enough business tactic, a safe answer before turning the questions back on the customer, getting him to talk about himself. People loved to talk about themselves, there was a whole subset of rules on it. But why Shar felt he needed to divert him . . .

Maybe he's not all that thrilled about his roots, either. Nog was proud to be a Ferengi, but that didn't mean he was proud of everything the Ferengi people had ever done, and that definitely included plenty of his relatives. If Shar didn't want to talk about himself, that was fine by Nog.

Shar excused himself to get a drink he wanted Nog to try, and Nog sipped his root beer, his mind wandering. Thinking about troubled pasts, and wondering if Jake was having a good trip. He carefully avoided thinking about the station's uninvited visitor, or wondering what he would actually do if the Jem'Hadar's story was accepted as truth . . . and when Shar brought back two Andorian citrus drinks, Nog found that he had managed to keep himself in an optimistic mood. They both had hours of work to return to, hours of having to face the aftermath of tragedy in many of its dispiriting forms; a few minutes of not talking about how bad things were . . . well, that wasn't a bad thing.

Nog sipped from his new drink and thought he did a pretty good job of keeping a straight face, although the beverage tasted like a clear, fizzy version of a smell he'd once experienced, at an animal preserve on Earth. Goat, he thought it was called. In some kind of lemon oil.

Nog decided that they'd had enough cultural exchange for one day, reminding himself to discreetly ask Frool to clear the bar before bringing their meals. Maybe Shar wouldn't notice.

Quark tripped into the bar, imagining Ro's sweet breath in his ear once more. Only not threatening him this time, of course.

Well, maybe just a little, Quark thought dreamily, thinking of how she frowned when she was concentrating, that dangerous curl to her lips. Thank the River for transparent aluminum office fronts.

It was both exciting and disturbing, the way he was feeling, like an awestruck, passionate youth, like he was playing the market with his own money. Oh, there had been brief affairs over the years, what he believed to be mutually beneficial exchanges—no one had complained, anyway—but his serious infatuations were fewer and farther between than most people thought. He flirted with a lot of females, true, but actually thinking about them was a different kind of commitment altogether.

There had been Natima Lang back during the occupation, and once briefly after the withdrawal, the first woman he'd purchased a gift for at retail. The Lady Grilka, now, *she* had been something; one of his closed deals, and he had the scars to prove it. There had been the magnificent Jadzia, of course, and by extension, Ezri—although his feelings were very different for the two incarnations of Dax. Ezri had a youthful quality that encouraged protective feelings, in addition to the occasional less-than-noble ones; but Jadzia . . . even getting shot down by Jadzia had been a pleasure, because she smiled and batted her lashes throughout, inspiring continued dreams of winning the lottery.

Ro Laren, now, she had Natima's passion, but Jadzia's sense of humor, she had Grilka's fire, plus a very appealing, haughty defensiveness that was all her own. She had a rebellious streak that could be profitable, considering her position. She was independent, headstrong, and antisocial, her inclinations didn't seem too expensive, and she had a shady past—not to mention, the kind of hands that men paid for. Ferengi men, anyway. She was exquisite.

To work on his growing mental file of her tastes and habits—research for expanding negotiations—he'd been randomly stepping out of the bar to observe her in her office. He noted what she was doing, collecting any information on her preferences that might work to his advantage. It was business, of a sort, but he was finding that it was a pleasure, as well. Her ironic smiles, her long legs, her habit of scowling to herself when she was deep in thought. Not only did he now know her preference for a hot beverage late in the day, information he could capitalize on, he'd had the extra enjoyment of watching her curse violently when she spilled it across her desk, leaping from her seat like a lithe but delicate jungle creature, mouthing words that would embarrass a Vicarian razorback wrangler.

Quark was snapped from his reverie when he realized that Nog and Shar were sitting next to the bar, eating. Love was something, but free labor was a lot harder to come by. Quark swept up to them, putting a big smile on for the Andorian's benefit. The boy had alerted them to a shrouded Jem'Hadar, after all, a talent too handy to frighten away . . . and he *was* a friend of Ro Laren's.

Quark had learned long ago that getting Nog to lend a hand was easiest to do with guilt, no raised voices or angry accusations, no threats. The fault was entirely Rom's, as usual, for refusing to discourage Nog's conscience when he was younger, but it was certainly too late to fix; anyway, until it stopped working, the guilt card saved the most time.

"Nog, Shar, how nice to see you," Quark said, turning his attention toward Nog, manufacturing a hopeful tone. "Say, Nephew . . . I know that you're busy making everything look nice for when the Federation shows up, but do you think you might take a look at replicator three for me while you're here? It's malfunctioning again, and I wouldn't ask except that I can't afford to hire anyone, not after the beating I took on your best friend's party yesterday."

Quark shifted his smile to Shar. "I probably lost thousands of strips in inventory alone, but Jake Sisko means so much to my nephew, I knew it was the right thing to do. I just couldn't turn away from family. Now that his father's gone, we only have each other."

Shar smiled back at him, his bright gray eyes sort of dazed. Andorians were a strange bunch, although Shar seemed mostly okay. He didn't gamble but he liked imported ale, which wasn't cheap.

Nog sighed dramatically, as if he'd been asked to shovel dung. "Uncle, my team has to rebuild the *Defiant*'s venting conduit system tonight, *and* finish inspecting the lower core shield emitters."

Quark slumped his shoulders. "With all I do for you . . . that you could refuse me a scant moment of your time, just to offer an opinion on a simple replicator . . ?"

Nog rolled his eyes, and Quark gave up. Threats rarely worked, but sometimes a flat demand did the trick. "Nog, just look at it, would you? I'm your *uncle.*"

"Fine," Nog said, sighing again. "I'll look at it before I go back to work. Can we finish eating now?"

Finally. "You're too kind," Quark said, not working too hard to keep the sarcasm out of it. He turned to move back behind the bar, when Shar's combadge bleeped.

"Ensign ch'Thane, this is Ensign Selzner, in ops. You have a call waiting."

Selzner, the Starfleet communications officer with the overbite; she sounded very excited. Quark moved a few steps away but kept his head turned to catch the conversation, interested in what could make the intense, toothy Selzner sound like a teenager.

"Put it through," Shar said.

"It's straight from the offices of the Federation Council, on a directed channel," Selzner said. *"And it's authorized for immediate uplink. Where do you want to take it?"*

Quark forgot that he was pretending not to listen and turned, wide-eyed. Nog was also staring at the expressionless Shar, who answered calmly—but with a lifetime of experience staring into the faces of gamblers to back him up, Quark would have bet the bar that the Andorian was bluffing.

He's rattled, and he's not all that good at hiding it.

"I see. Would you send it to my quarters, please? I'll be there in five minutes."

"Ah, right. Affirmative."

Even as Selzner fumbled off, Quark was back at their table. "Why is someone at the Federation Council calling you, Ensign?"

Shar took a last drink from his glass and stood up, dabbing at the corners of his mouth with his napkin. Definitely anxious. "My . . . ah, mother works for the Council."

Quark nodded, starting to feel hopeful. "Oh, *really?* That's very interesting. What does she do? Secretarial work? Chef? Consultant?"

Shar shook his head, then smiled at Nog. "I apologize for having to leave, Nog, but I've been expecting this call . . ."

Thirishar ch'Thane, Andorians have . . . four distinct sexes, surname prefix denotes gender, 'Thane, that seems familiar . . .

Nog was standing up, too. "Hey, that's all right. I always take my father's calls, and—"

"Your mother is Charivretha zh'Thane?"

Quark blurted it out louder than he'd intended, amazed that this had slipped past him. A few arriving customers turned to look, to see Shar's obvious discomfort and Quark's elated shock. Zh'Thane held the Andorian seat in the Federation Council, very bright and very sharp, a woman who spoke her mind about everything. She was so influential, in fact, that her speeches and stands were often cited as vote-swingers, and thus influenced a vast number of possibilities—from election outcome pools all the way up to interplanetary resource contracts, the real big time.

This could bring a whole new dimension to the concept of inside information . . . the blue kid science officer is zh'Thane's son.

Shar was already walking away, acting almost as if he was embarrassed that his mother was one of the Alpha Quadrant's top political figures. A big part of Beta, too.

He probably thinks people will treat him different, if they know. If they were smart, they would. Quark certainly planned to; the lovely Laren still pulled at his heart, not to mention his lobes, but Thirishar ch'Thane had his feet in the Great Material Continuum, and he probably didn't even know it.

Quark was definitely going to have to find out more about his nephew's new friend. The son of the Emissary, now the son of Charivretha zh'Thane; Nog apparently had an instinct for choosing powerful friends . . .

. . . and if he doesn't want to exploit it himself, why shouldn't somebody else benefit?

All this and the task force would be arriving soon, fresh blood for his *dabo* girls and many a merry Klingon getting roaring drunk on bloodwine. It seemed he'd been mistaken about something he'd said, only a day or two ago; the Federation really did care about the small-business man, after all.

The conversation went well until the very end.

Shar had expected the call, although he had hoped that his *zhavey* would have remembered to contact him directly. Charivretha didn't fear the stain of nepotism, reminding him time and again that he had achieved everything on his own, but he knew that; it was the look on Nog's uncle's face that he'd been trying to avoid, a look that said he had changed in Quark's estimation because of his parentage. Shar wanted to be valued or ignored on his own merits, and now he would have to wonder; he had little doubt that the word was being passed along already.

Zhavey expressed concern over the attack and asked how his assignment was working out, listening with interest to his responses. By mutual agreement they didn't discuss politics, because there were too many facets of it that *Zhavey* couldn't talk about. They briefly touched on contacts with his other parents, leading up to what Shar had dreaded, to the inevitable topic of his future.

Shar listened calmly, looking into Charivretha's wide, lovely face, agreeing appropriately with tilts of his head. As his *zhavey,* she was his closest relative biologically and socially, and it shamed him to see the concern he had caused, the seeds of worry beginning to take root in *Zhavey's* deep gray eyes.

Just as he thought he might get away without having to talk about it, Charivretha stopped her now by-rote speech, gazing at him with love and the thing that he feared most, the threat of losing it.

"Thirishar, you are our only child. We didn't bear and raise you to have doubts about your obligations."

"No, *Zhavey.*"

"You are part of a Whole. The covenant broken by one is lost by all."

"Yes, *Zhavey.*"

Zhavey studied him another moment, searching his face for something that didn't seem to be there.

"There's nothing for you to resolve," Charivretha said, and Shar couldn't disagree, he couldn't, not in the face of his *zhavey's* unspoken anxiety—that he would disgrace all of them for the sake of his own selfish pursuits.

"I know, *Zhavey.*"

Zhavey looked away from him, and he could see the struggle for control. Charivretha zh'Thane was a person of great character and control, but she was also deeply unhappy.

Because of me.

"You'll call very soon," she half-asked, turning to look at him again.

"As is my duty and privilege, *Zhavey,*" Shar said, recognizing that she was letting him go, finished for now. It was both a relief and a sorrow. "Until then, I find you Whole in my thoughts."

"As you are in mine."

The transmission ended and Shar's mind went blank for a moment, feeling something coming, his blood like a hot river crashing into his body.

With a low, primal hiss, Shar leapt to his feet and snapped a powerful kick at the logoed screen, boot heel cracking into the thick support post, the impact shuddering back through his body. The monitor burst into sparks, pieces of clear glass and dusky casing material shattering outward, clattering against the desk and floor. The fierce sense of triumph that accompanied his decisive action lasted only until he realized what he'd done.

Seconds later, when the computer asked if he needed assistance, Shar was able to answer in a mostly even tone, deeply remorseful and very much alone.

Chapter Six

When Vedek Yevir finally called to tell her he was on his way to her office, Kira put the report she'd been reviewing aside and stood up, taking a couple of deep breaths. Ro Laren had kept the book, but Kira believed that Yevir should be told, to be prepared . . . and as a member of the Assembly, he would eventually be dealing with the book anyway, once Ro finished her investigation. Kira ignored the small voice at the back of her mind that told her she sought reassurance, that she desperately wanted to hear Yevir denounce the book.

Just because it hasn't been verified by some religious authority doesn't make it any less true, it doesn't change what's in the book. . . .

Ro Laren's voice, and it had a few other things to say, but Kira wasn't interested. Right or wrong, Ro had used up all her chances. One more challenge to Kira's authority, one more disrespectful outburst, and she could go find another job. And if Yevir wanted access to the heresy, Kira would see that he got it, however Ro felt about it.

She thought this just as the ops lift rose into view, Vedek Yevir standing tall on the platform. The quiet, unassuming man he'd been when he'd worked on the station had changed when the Prophets had reached him, through the Emissary . . . and Their gift to him had been a future in which he would undoubtedly someday be kai; Yevir Linjarin shone with the Prophets' light.

He'll know the book as false. He even said something about heresy at last night's service. . . .

Kira crossed her arms, frowning, watching Yevir step from the lift. It had been a moving service, well read and interpreted, and what he'd said at the end in his affirmations . . . something like, Reject all kinds of heresy, turn your back to unclean—

"Unclean words," Kira said absently, the framework of an unpleasant idea suddenly clicking into place. Her mind listed the pieces, bits of conversation and thought, fitting them together with the man who was walking toward her office.

He arrives only a few days after she was killed, to offer guidance.

The book is from B'hala.

She would have taken it to be recognized by a vedek, at the very least.

Turn our backs on unclean words. Reject heresy in all its forms.

It was a terrible thing to think, but now that she'd thought it, she was stuck with it—the possibility that Yevir knew about the book already, that he had known before he'd come to the station.

That he came here to find it.

Yevir reached the office door and smiled at Kira as it slid open, an honest, curious smile on his face.

"I'm sorry I didn't get back to you immediately," Yevir said, as they both moved toward the low couch at one side of her office. "I was talking with

Ranjen Ela about a doctrinal difference currently being contested among members of the Assembly . . . Nerys, what is it?"

Kira sat down across from Yevir, deciding what she wanted to say. She was too distracted by the possibility of his deceit to talk about anything else, and wanted it cleared up.

So I embarrass myself. It won't be the first time.

"Vedek Yevir, were you aware that Istani Reyla brought an unverified prophetic artifact with her, to this station?" Kira asked, keeping her voice low, nonconfrontational.

Yevir wasn't a natural liar. He flushed, but held her gaze evenly and answered as though he'd been expecting the question. "Yes. It's one of the reasons I came. Have you found it?"

Kira nodded, taken aback by the admission, hoping he would continue talking, because suddenly she couldn't think of anything to say. His admission wasn't what she'd expected; Yevir was being discussed seriously as the next kai.

At her nod, Yevir became eager, his relief obvious. "Where is it? Has anyone read from it?"

Kira found her voice, but not to answer his questions. A vedek and a friend had lied to her, or at least withheld the truth.

"What's this all about, Linjarin? I think I have a right to know."

Yevir nodded slowly. "Of course. I should have told you already, but I was hoping that you would never find out about the book. I hoped I could find it and steal away, before anyone else was touched by its poison."

He smiled ruefully. "You must be angry with me, Nerys . . . and my only defense is that I wanted to avoid bringing attention to my search. The book is dangerous, and should have been destroyed millennia ago."

Thank the Prophets. She'd been right about the nature of the book. She thought she had convinced herself that the artifact wasn't credible, but hearing Yevir say it made her realize she'd been unsure, in spite of her declarations to the contrary. Whatever anger she felt toward him was more than made up for by the relief of finally knowing the truth.

"Tell me," she said quietly.

Yevir hesitated, then started to speak, his tone clear and direct. Again, it was obvious that he had given some thought to what he would say.

"The unnamed book has long been rumored to exist, through generations upon generations of the Vedek Assembly," Yevir said. "The story is that a man named Ohalu wrote it, a very sick and determined man, who plotted in his disease to sway people from the Prophets. He claimed that the Prophets spoke to him, and that they were a benevolent, symbiotic race of beings, learning from Bajorans just as we learn from them. He claimed that there was nothing sacred about them. Ohalu said that his truth would one day be recognized, because his prophecies would prove that he'd been contacted by the alien race."

Teacher Prophets, Kira remembered from the book, and shivered. She knew that a lot of non-Bajorans believed the Prophets to be an alien species. Even Benjamin, who had been Touched by them . . .

. . . but if the book isn't a hoax . . .

She'd read it, and been convinced that it was a fake because of how accurate the alleged prophecies were; skewed against faith and lacking any moral context, but factually correct. Kira felt an odd emptiness in the pit of her stomach, thinking about the prophecy of the Avatar.

"He managed to snare a few who'd lost their way with his sacrilegious views," Yevir continued, "forming a cult that existed to protect his heretical book, to keep it safe. They tried to promote their sickness, but the vedeks of that time put a stop to it. And that's where the story ends. The cult disappeared with the book.

"Once B'hala was discovered by the Emissary, the Assembly began to watch the digs for a number of things, Ohalu's book among them."

"To officially denounce it," Kira said slowly, wishing that she hadn't been so quick to give the book to Kasidy.

Yevir's eyes widened, and he shook his head. "To destroy it, Nerys. Don't you understand how dangerous it is? Istani Reyla read it, and brought it before the Assembly—and tried to convince us to turn the book over to the wife of the Emissary, saying that she should be told about one of the prophecies."

Oh, no.

"Prylar Istani was shouted down, but refused to surrender the artifact. She ran from the Assembly hall, surely driven to madness by whatever she found in that book. We have no idea what she planned to do with it, but if she could believe even a part of it . . ." Yevir shook his head. "The book destroyed her."

But I read it, too. Kira was shocked and concerned and confused, but she felt sane enough. For the moment.

"Where's the book now? How many have seen it?" Yevir asked, as Kira looked past his shoulder and saw both Kasidy and Ro at the door to her office, Ohalu's book in Ro's hands. Neither woman looked happy.

"My security officer found it during her investigation into Istani's murder," Kira said, no longer sure how she should feel about what was unfolding. All she could do was tell the truth now, as Yevir had done. "She and I both read it, and probably my science officer, who had it translated . . . and so did Kasidy Yates. I gave it to her."

"The Emissary's wife," Yevir said, his face pale. "We must pray, Nerys, that she's not infected."

Abruptly, Kira stood up, motioning for Ro and Kasidy to come in. It was time to straighten this out. The Allied task force was on the way, and there was too much work for her to do to continue wasting time on unnecessary etiquette. If everyone had been up-front in the first place, things wouldn't have gotten this far.

"As to where it is now, and what we're going to do about it . . . Vedek, allow me to make introductions," Kira said. "I believe you've already met Kasidy Yates?"

There had been a match. The man who had stabbed the monk and then fallen to his death now had an identity, thanks to Bajor's Central Archives. Ro picked up the book and started for Kira's office, wanting to deliver the news personally.

Ro had just reached the ops lift on the Promenade when Kasidy Yates hurried to catch up to her, a padd in hand. Ro barely knew Captain Yates, but knew exactly what was on the padd; nothing else could account for the deep uneasiness on her face, the nervous tension in the set of her shoulders.

She must be on her way to see Kira, too.

They were the only two on the lift. Ro held the wrapped book tightly and nodded at Kasidy, not sure if she should say anything. She didn't want to be drawn into a conversation about the book before she had a chance to talk to Kira.

"Lieutenant Ro . . . is that it?" Kasidy asked, nodding at the book. Instead of the fearful hush Ro might have expected, Kasidy's voice was calm and clear.

"Yes," Ro said uncomfortably.

"May I ask why you're taking it to ops?"

Ro was still rummaging for a response when Kasidy shook her head. "Never mind. I suppose I'll know if I'm meant to know, isn't that one of the tenets?"

The tense, hostile tone wasn't directed at Ro, although she thought it was, at first, because the alternative seemed impossible; Kasidy was the Emissary's *wife.* Ro had heard that she wasn't a follower, but had never suspected such a depth of disdain for the faith.

A non-Bajoran, left alone to raise their baby, left alone to face a world of believers.

Now that she actually thought about it, Ro realized that Kasidy didn't have much cause to celebrate the Bajoran faith. Which made the prophecy even worse, the unfairness of Kasidy's situation making Ro wish she'd never found the damned thing.

"Captain Yates, I'm sorry," Ro said, sincerely meaning it. "If there's anything I can do . . ."

"It's Kasidy. And you can book me passage into another system," she said, and although she actually managed a faint, sarcastic smile, her tone was serious.

The lift opened into ops and they both stepped off, both walking toward the colonel's office. There were three Bajorans on shift, and Ro noticed that they each visibly brightened when they saw Kasidy. The wife of the Emissary either didn't see it or didn't care, her attention focused on Kira's office. Ro saw through the front window that Kira was talking to a vedek, and felt a conflict of emotions—disappointment, curiosity, and a kind of dark anticipation that she would want to think about, later. It was a childish response to the circumstances.

"That's Vedek Yevir, I think," Kasidy said, as they stopped on the platform outside her office.

The popular vote to be the next kai. Ro knew he was on board, but hadn't seen him yet. His back was to them, but from his hunched shoulders, he was definitely worried about whatever they were discussing.

And I wonder what that could be . . .

Kira stood up and waved them in. Kasidy immediately stepped to the door, Ro right behind her.

". . . allow me to make introductions," Kira was saying as the two women entered the office. "I believe you've already met Kasidy Yates?"

The vedek stood up and faced them, nodding respectfully at Kasidy. "Of course. It's so nice to see you again, Captain."

Perfectly calm, except he didn't seem to want to look directly at Kasidy's face for more than a second. Ro realized from the flush beneath his tan that he was reacting the same way the other Bajorans had reacted, only more so.

It's like they think they're in the presence of royalty.

"This is Lieutenant Ro Laren, our new chief of security. Lieutenant, this is Vedek Yevir Linjarin."

She saw him glance quickly to her left ear, but he was discreet about it. "A pleasure, child."

Ro didn't answer, but Kira was already talking to Yevir again, her firm tone suggesting that she was following a course of action. Ro decided to see where she was going before she delivered the news.

"Lieutenant Ro appears to be holding Ohalu's book. Lieutenant, Kas . . . Vedek Yevir has just confirmed that the book was written by a dangerous heretic from the time before B'hala. The Vedek Assembly wants it destroyed, and considering the nature of the text, I'm inclined to agree with them—"

Ro started to protest, and Kira raised her voice slightly, talking over her, staring directly at Ro as she finished. "—to agree with them, because the members of the Vedek Assembly are the leaders of Bajor's spiritual community, and this artifact falls under the scope of their authority."

Yevir was standing taller, reinforced by her blind trust. "Thank you, Nerys."

Kira ignored him. She looked between Kasidy and Ro, nodding at each. "As I said, that's my inclination. But I want to hear what you have to say about it . . ."

Her gaze sharpened on Ro, her expression sending a clear message—*I already know what you have to say. Stay in your territory.*

". . . because it's evidence in an inquest, and Kas, because the final prophecy concerns you directly. Lieutenant Ro, do you have anything new to report on your investigation?"

Ro nodded. There was no way to say it but to say it. "Yes. The bio results from the Archives just came in. The killer's real name is Gamon Vell. He was a vedek."

Ro had half expected to feel some satisfaction, telling Kira that one of her perfect religious leaders in her perfect religion had been responsible. But the shock in Kira's eyes, the look of betrayal behind it—

Ro had to look away, and she looked at Vedek Yevir . . . who didn't appear to be the least bit surprised by her revelation.

Yevir Linjarin felt great shame as the lieutenant revealed the truth, but reminded himself that he was right to feel shame. The Assembly had chosen an unwise path, and trying to cover for one's own responsibilities was not what the Prophets taught. And because he'd concealed the truth, the Emissary's wife had been exposed to lies and turmoil.

The faithless security officer stared at him. They all stared, and he accepted their anger and disbelief, taking it in and releasing it to the Prophets, accepting his own part. Best to tell it all, and bring an end to the matter as best he could.

"When Istani fled the Assembly, we knew she would come here," he said, taking a deep breath. He looked at Kasidy Sisko, praying that her distress wouldn't upset the Emissary's child, hoping that she would understand. "She believed in the prophecies, and wanted to show you part of the book. She said that you should know."

He turned to Kira, knowing that of all of them, she would understand best. Her belief was strong, her *pagh* untainted.

"By the time we decided we should try to intercept her, she was already on her way here," he said, looking into Kira's wide eyes, not shying from her feelings. "Gamon Vell, one of the strongest proponents of the idea, volunteered for the task, and left immediately. We didn't know that he was unbalanced, that his commitment to keeping this poison bottled would drive him to hurt her. There was never any intention to cause her harm, you must believe that, but we had to stop her from showing the prophecies to anyone else."

Kira's wounded gaze lay heavy in his heart. "I can't believe this," she said.

"Ohalu's book is like a spiritual disease, you surely know that," Yevir continued, not certain that Ro or Kasidy understood the gravity of what Istani had threatened, not like Kira. What he'd heard at the Assembly had been more than enough to convince him.

"Over thirty millennia ago, its influence polluted thousands of people, turning them away from the Prophets," Yevir said. "They were outcasts, pariahs, and still, they clung to their sickness of ego and fatalism. Through thousands of years, cults of this 'philosophy' rear up time and time again, like new strains of a virus, and that book—" He pointed at the bundle in Ro Laren's arms. "—is the source, the original flaw. It's dangerous, it teaches that the Prophets aren't deserving of Bajor's love, and we must stop it from infecting anyone else, no matter what the cost."

"Including Istani Reyla's *life?*" Kira asked, incredulous in her anger. "And the life of Gamon Vell?"

Yevir shook his head. "No, of course not . . . but don't you see, this only proves how treacherous Ohalu's prophecies are. If she hadn't been contaminated by the book, she wouldn't have run from the Assembly, and—"

"Are you trying to tell us that she caused her own death?" Ro Laren interrupted, speaking quickly, her tone heated. "That she *made* you send somebody after her, because she had a book that *offended* you?"

"*Ro.*"

The warning in Kira's voice seemed only to fan the lieutenant's anger, but it also silenced her. She looked away, glaring, her head turned so that he could see her misplaced earring again. Yevir felt forgiveness in his heart for the hostile young woman, who so openly touted her inability to accept the Prophets. The book had probably only reinforced her estrangement.

"Excuse me," Kasidy said, her voice surprisingly mild for the depth of the anger in it, a thread of steel running through her demeanor that demanded attention. She dropped the padd she'd been holding to Kira's desk and crossed her arms, staring at Yevir as if he'd suddenly sprouted wings.

"Excuse me, but I read it. And I have to say, compared to some of what you consider to be *legitimate* prophetic writings, it's more accurate and a lot more complete. So maybe you're telling yourself that you're actually scared for the spiritual purity of Bajor, and maybe that's true . . . but maybe it's also true that the Vedek Assembly wouldn't look so good, if people knew about this book. Because that could mean that all those so-called heretics you've worked so hard to eradicate through the centuries . . . it could mean that you were wrong. That all along, you've persecuted people who had a justifiable belief system, just because it contradicted yours."

The security officer had reigned herself in on the surface, her tone angry but less accusatory. The viciousness came out in what she chose to say. "The suppression of a divergent religion, because its credibility is a threat to your own."

"It's wrong, but I don't know that I'd call lack of faith a religion," Kira said uncomfortably. "Lack of faith doesn't support any kind of spirituality."

Kasidy pulled her arms tighter. "Nerys, that's not exactly the point here."

"I wasn't trying to make a point. I'm just saying that the Bajoran faith is what has unified our planet. It defines us and our culture. It's what has carried us through our darkest times."

"Most of us," Ro said, almost under her breath.

Yevir felt cold to the marrow of his bones, seeing their faces twist in fear and suspicion, the tension in their voices and bodies as their words sharpened.

"Don't you see?" he asked, raising his voice to be heard. "Look at how the book's sickness has already touched you, turning you from the face of the Prophets. What do you think would happen to Bajor?"

All three women fell silent, and for a few beats of his heart, he believed that they had finally grasped the nature of the disease—

—and then Kira, with a kind of furious determination about her that he'd never seen before, firmly pulled the book away from Ro Laren. She turned and thrust it at him, the book actually hitting his chest before he could fumble his hands into catching it.

"Nerys—" Yevir started, but she was already stalking from the room.

Ro and Kasidy both seemed shocked, and Yevir felt no less so. He thought he'd finally helped her to understand. Perhaps she felt torn between her spiritual and professional selves, which was a hard place to be . . . but he had faith in her. She had always turned to the Prophets for guidance.

She had given him the book, at least. Yevir was sorry for the things that had happened, but the Prophets had surely sanctioned the end result: the Vedek Assembly had possession of the unnamed thing, and would deal with it appropriately. For the peace of the Bajoran people, and to the glory of the Prophets.

Chapter Seven

So, I think I'm a little confused. I haven't written in a while; it's almost as though I forgot how important it is, being able to talk to myself. There have been times that I've written pages of words, just to narrow my feelings down to a single sentence. I know my recent lack of interest is because I haven't wanted to talk to myself about Dad, but time is what I've got right now, time and a few questions I should already have asked.

I'm on the Venture, *drifting inside the wormhole. The sensors are a mess, not that I care much. It's funny, that now I find the time to think about what I'm doing a little more carefully. When I finally decided to do this, back at B'hala, I knew—absolutely— that I would stay for as long as it took, and that if I actually made it this far, I would spend every minute anticipating our reunion.*

Ah, naive youth. And hope. Because I wanted so bad to believe that he isn't gone, that these last few months have been just another adventure, another wild and seemingly desperate situation that all gets worked out in the end. Another situation that ends with my father and me, together, because I love him and I miss him in my life. When I trans- lated the prophecy, it was an answer. A solution.

I've been here a single day, and with each hour that passes, my doubt flourishes. This is what I'm starting to think: The prophecy is an answer because I haven't been able to let him go. I was putting off the inevitable acceptance, and Istani Reyla showed up with a way out before I had to face my loss.

That's kind of a harsh summary, and not the whole truth. The prophecy itself, the parchment in my hand—there's power in it. It gives me a sense of the incredible, of the possible. . . . I'm not saying that the prophecy is false, just that my reasons for jumping right into it were certainly influenced by my hope.

Put like that, it seems too obvious. I've missed writing. I tell stories because I want to tell stories; I write because I want to understand.

The prophecy is real, I still believe that. I believe there's something genuine about it, anyway. But I also believe that if it isn't, if the whole thing turns out to be only madness and hope, I'll be okay. There's enough of me to take it.

I'll wait. Time is the one thing I have too much of.

Chapter Eight

Finished with her meditation, Kira opened her eyes and shifted position, from kneeling to sitting cross-legged. She reached out and extinguished the candle atop her *mandala,* feeling much clearer about the events of the day.

She sat on the floor of her darkened living area, thinking, feeling more relaxed than she had in a while. She'd decided that she would actually break for a late dinner rather than pop another ration pack in her office, to have a few moments at the small shrine in her quarters, and she was glad she'd made the effort. The updated ETA for the first Allied ships was less than ten hours from now, it wasn't as though she had a lot of time to spare, but a connection had been essential.

Because of what I've learned. Because of what I needed.

Ro, Yevir, Kasidy, the book, Reyla. Sustenance, faith was; although personal meditation wasn't as powerful as group, when she and her siblings all chanted their love together, there was nothing better for regaining a sense of guidance, of objectivity. In prayer, Kira was reminded that all would be well in Their eyes, as it ever was and ever would be. It also gave her a chance to step back and take account of her own thoughts and motives in everything that was happening, to review and improve, to try and understand other perspectives.

Kira smiled a little. She'd included a thought for Ro Laren in her meditation, which would probably really irritate the lieutenant if she knew. Someone like Ro couldn't seem to understand that faith and prayer didn't necessarily mean slavish devotion to ignorance. Ro exasperated her, but Kira couldn't help feeling sorry for her, too. If it was simply indifference she expressed, an apathy toward religion, no big deal. It was Ro's active anger at the faith that was distressing; something had driven her from the shrine, something that had made it a negative experience for her to trust in her own spirituality.

And as to Yevir . . .

She remembered Winn Adami too well to be surprised by duplicity within the Assembly, but Yevir didn't seem to be politically motivated; there was no question that he genuinely believed, and not for his own sake, but for Bajor's. It was the veracity of his love for Them that had clouded his judgment, and that passion had the potential to be too much for him, too much for anyone so deeply committed. To put such a man in a position of power could prove disastrous; people who believed in the righteousness of their every decision often stopped worrying about the consequences. The Prophets had faith in them all, but Kira was only mortal; she thought that Yevir's appointment to kai would be a mistake, and hoped that he wouldn't stay at the station much longer. With the task force and the Jem'Hadar and still, *still* the repairs, she didn't need to be worrying about how to interact with him at random intervals—

"*Ops to Colonel Kira.*" It was Shar.

Back to the world. "Go ahead."

"*The* U.S.S. Enterprise *has just popped out of warp. They've flashed a text mes-*

sage requesting docking clearance. requesting an immediate upper pylon docking clearance."

And so it begins.

Kira was on her feet, tapping at the closest light panel, looking for her boots. The *Enterprise* was the Federation flagship, but she hadn't expected anyone from the task force to arrive so soon, and she was surprised that they wanted to dock. Why hadn't they signaled hours ago? And a *text* message?

"Give them upper pylon two," she said, reaching for her uniform jacket.

"They report having suffered minimal but disabling damage from a plasma wave," Shar continued, *"and list mid-level maintenance requirements in their request."*

Plasma wave? The Badlands? That might explain their comm troubles. "Status of DS9's senior officers?"

"Lieutenants Bowers and Nog are on the Defiant, *working on the venting conduits. Dr. Bashir is in the infirmary . . . Lieutenant Ro is at the security office, and Lieutenant Dax is at cargo bay 41C, with the Jem'Hadar."*

Kira could drag them all away from what they were doing, but she thought Captain Picard would understand if she greeted them by herself. She didn't want to wait, either, to find out how the *Enterprise* came to be docking for maintenance a full ten hours earlier than the fleet of "investigators" were expected.

"Inform Captain Picard that I'll be on hand to meet him personally, at the inner port, in ten minutes," she said. "Send two security guards to meet us there. And advise the *Enterprise* of our current supply and capacity status. Also adjust ETA for the Allied task force through them, as soon as possible."

She left her quarters immediately, smoothing her hair back as she walked, thinking about seeing Captain Picard and his fairly exceptional crew again; the *Enterprise*-E hadn't been to the station in some time, and despite the situation, she realized she was looking forward to it. Worf and Miles O'Brien had served with that crew, albeit on the *Enterprise*-D, and both men had some fascinating stories to tell. She knew that Ro had left the *Enterprise* to join the Maquis, another point of interest. The android Data was their operations officer, and unless there'd been a change, Will Riker was the ship's second-in-command. Kira had only met Will once since her tragic run-in with Thomas Riker, and had been fascinated by the personality differences between the two. And Jean-Luc Picard . . . she remembered that she'd been a little intimidated by him, in a personal sense. He was formal, well educated, and well spoken, all qualities that tended to make her notice her own roughness.

But that was before I made colonel. Picard was sharp, too, and always spoke admiringly of Bajor. She wanted to know what he had to say about the Allied decision, and hear his opinion on Kitana'klan's story. In fact, the *Enterprise's* counselor was a Betazoid, Deanne, or Deanna Troi . . . perhaps she'd be able to tell them more about the Jem'Hadar's motives.

She walked quickly through the habitat ring to the turbolift, wondering what else the *Enterprise* was about to bring to her entirely unprecedented day. At the moment, she felt like she couldn't possibly be surprised . . . and she knew from experience that feeling that way was usually when the universe decided to shake things up a little more, to try and find out what a person was created from, clay or sand, adapt or crumble.

As the lift started to rise, Kira thought she'd do best to keep her expectations to a minimum. Things were about to get hectic and she needed to keep her calm, to keep letting the Prophets lead, to keep knowing herself in the face of disorder so that she might lead others. All she could do was her best.

The station's air was cool and cleanly scented, the airlock room spotless, the lights lower than on the *Enterprise.* As much as Picard loved his ship, it was nice to set foot in less familiar territory every now and again. He wished the circumstances were different; the shock of seeing the debris field while approaching the station still hadn't worn off, nor the news from DS9's operations center that it was all that remained of the *Starship Aldebaran* and all who had been aboard her.

"Captain Picard," Kira said, stepping forward to shake his hand. Two Bajoran security guards were with her. The young colonel seemed tired, but calm, considering. "Welcome to Deep Space 9."

Captain Picard smiled politely, remembering her as the Bajoran intermediary under Sisko. Although they'd met before, most of what he knew about Kira Nerys had come from accounts of her actions during the war. She had been deeply involved in the Cardassian resistance against the Dominion, which by itself was impressive; Kira had grown up during the Cardassian occupation of her world.

"Colonel Kira, it's a pleasure to see you again," he said. "May I present Commander Elias Vaughn, on special assignment from Starfleet . . ."

Kira shook his hand as well. Vaughn smiled charmingly, but his eyes seemed to be studying the colonel's face intently. Kira smiled back at him. "A pleasure, Commander."

". . . and I believe you've already met my first officer, Commander William Riker."

Kira nodded, still smiling. "Of course. Hello, Commander."

"I'm sorry to hurry through the pleasantries, but my communications officer has just filled us in on your status, as well as news about the Allied task force," Picard said, "which I'm afraid is all news to us. We were hit by a wave in the Badlands, and haven't had the use of our subspace array for the last three days. We came here primarily for maintenance and repairs."

Kira nodded. "That explains it. I thought you were too early."

Riker stepped forward. "If I could get to a private room with a conference screen . . ."

"Of course," Kira said, nodding at one of the guards. "Sergeant, please escort the commander to the 3–3 conference room. It's the nearest."

As Will went to see what Starfleet had for them, Picard and Vaughn both expressed their sympathies. Kira accepted with grace, and explained their current shortages and deficiencies. Picard agreed to lend his chief engineer's services to Kira as soon as the *Enterprise* was pronounced fit, and the colonel offered ship leave for his crew, explaining that the Promenade was actually fully operational. As soon as the immediate plans were covered, the colonel brought them up to speed on the Allied response to the attack on the station.

"What's the word on establishing a peacekeeping presence in the Gamma Quadrant?" Vaughn asked.

"Ah, nothing new, that I've heard," Kira said, and Picard could see that she was surprised. He was, too; he'd assumed that Vaughn knew what was happening, but hadn't suspected that particular development himself. He supposed he should have; both the Romulans and the Klingons had wanted it when the treaty was being negotiated.

Although he shouldn't have said anything about it in front of me, or the colonel. And he seems positively enthusiastic about meeting her.

"If you haven't been in touch with the task force, you don't know about the Jem'Hadar soldier," Kira said. "I—excuse me, would you gentlemen like a drink, or dinner? Forgive my manners, I've had quite a day."

Vaughn accepted the offer for both of them. "The task force isn't going to get here any faster, no matter what we do," he said casually. "I think we can spare the time . . . although why don't we take a walk, instead? I've heard a lot about your station, I'd like to see some of it."

He looked at Picard. "That is, if you don't mind, Captain."

"Of course not," Picard said. "Although I hope you'll let me catch up to you in just a few moments. I need to make some arrangements with my senior staff."

"Of course, Captain. Would you care to see the Promenade, Commander?" Kira said. "We can walk the main floor."

"Elias, please," Vaughn said, following her away from the airlock. "Tell me about this Jem'Hadar."

It wasn't until after they left and Picard was back on the *Enterprise* bridge that it occurred to him—Vaughn had made no mention of the Orb, and neither had he. Entirely understandable, he supposed, given the circumstances. The news of the Jem'Hadar attack and the approaching task force had been quite a shock, and certainly overshadowed the far less galactic import of recovering the Orb of Memory.

After making arrangements with Counselor Troi to begin ship leave rotations, Picard found himself impatient for Will to report back, wanting to rejoin Vaughn and Kira quickly; he didn't want to miss Kira's reaction to learning about the Orb. After hearing about the *Aldebaran,* being part of something positive would do him good.

Ezri was just finishing the notes on her conversation with Kitana'klan when Kira signaled, asking her to come to the Promenade. It seemed the station had just received a visitor who knew something about Jem'Hadar development, and wanted to meet her.

Ezri hurried through the outer rings but found herself slowing when she reached the main floor, the turbolift exiting within sight of the infirmary. She stepped out and stood, looking at it, thinking.

She was a little worried about Julian, afraid that he'd been hurt by her desire to slow things down a little. It was strange, she actually had a memory of telling him that joined Trill tried to avoid serious romantic relationships, not long after she'd met him, as Jadzia. She'd only been half joking; although it wasn't discouraged in any way for the joined, it was widely accepted that other people could be a serious distraction from fulfilling personal potential—something else she already knew, but that she had only started to understand—

Julian walked out of the infirmary, adjusting his med kit on its strap. When he looked up and saw her, he barely hesitated, his expression moving from surprise to a kind of cordial ease as he approached. She knew him well enough to know better.

"Hello, Ezri." Polite, happy to see her, that unconscious stiffness in his manner. He made no move to touch her.

"Hi," she said, not sure what to do, standing with her arms at her sides. She wanted to reach out to him, to reassure him that they had time, that things would turn out for the best, but she didn't want to assume anything about what he was feeling. She'd asked for space and his patience, and he'd given it to her; it wouldn't be right to confuse things by trying to take care of him now, not when she was the cause of his discomfort.

Julian seemed to understand, and quickly said, "I'm on my way to see Kitana'klan, to replenish his ketracel-white. Didn't you see him today?"

"Just finished," she said, grateful for a safe topic. "He's the same, facts without interpretation, either won't or can't extrapolate meaning from environment . . . he maintains that Odo sent him to observe, and that he'll continue to cooperate with our restrictions until we're certain we can trust him."

"Where are you off to?" Julian asked. "It might be helpful for you to watch him interact with someone else. . . ."

"Actually, Kira asked me to meet her at the east platform. She says someone who just arrived with the *Enterprise* may be able to help shed some light on Kitana'klan. Maybe you should be coming with me."

"Can't," he said, smiling, looking into her eyes just long enough for her to be reminded of how beautiful his were, liquid and probing, always watching. "I don't want our guest to be suffering any withdrawal symptoms when I finally get there, thank you very much."

She smiled back at him, and before she could find a way to end their conversation, Julian headed her off again.

"Well. I'd better get to it," he said. "See if Kira's acquaintance wouldn't mind stopping by the infirmary later, to fill me in."

"Sure," she said, and then he was gone, striding briskly away. Ezri took a deep breath, turned, and walked out onto the crowded main floor, reassuring herself that she'd made the right decision, for both of them. People changed all the time, and as much as she loved him, she was going through a big transitional period. She didn't think she could focus on him as much as he wanted . . .

and she was afraid that she might end up really hurting him. What had happened in her bedroom had been an accident, and maybe she hadn't handled it properly, but his reaction had been deeply painful to her; how would he react if something like that happened again? She wasn't human, and she didn't want to restrict herself by pretending that she was, just so Julian would feel more comfortable.

All of this proving that I'm spending too much time being distracted by him, by us, when I should be thinking about—

"Ezri!"

Ezri looked to the shout and there was Kira, standing with Jean-Luc Picard and . . . Elias Vaughn. *Vaughn,* of all people. Still alive. There was no mistaking him, even though he was obviously much older. She'd never expected to see him again. As she approached the trio, she randomly thought that at least she wasn't distracted anymore.

"Lieutenant Ezri Dax, Captain Jean-Luc Picard," Kira said, stepping back into a nook so that they weren't blocking foot traffic, "and Commander Elias Vaughn. Lieutenant Dax is our counselor, and has been working with Kitana'klan."

Picard smiled, extending his hand. Jadzia had thought him attractive in spite of her feelings about him, and Ezri could see why. He had a strong presence, one that matched his finely chiseled features and the natural eloquence of his manner. "I believe I met a Dax when I was here last. And are you . . . I hope I'm phrasing this correctly—weren't you also Curzon Dax?"

"That's right," she said, noting that Elias didn't seem surprised at all. Either he knew already or he'd gotten even better at hiding his reactions.

Ezri felt a vague unease as she took Picard's hand; she knew that Benjamin had made his peace with it, and knew also that it hadn't been Picard's fault . . . but Locutus of Borg had been responsible for the death of Jennifer Sisko, Jake's mother and Benjamin's first wife. And both Curzon and Jadzia had been around to see what that had done to Ben, and to Jake. "It's good to see you again. Sir."

"Dax, it's been a while," Vaughn said, smiling. His hand was warm, his grip as firm as Curzon remembered.

"You're right, it has," Ezri said agreeably.

She suddenly realized Kira and Picard were both watching them.

"You two know each other?" Kira asked.

Ezri nodded, letting Vaughn respond. He was the one who'd brought it up, which meant he was obviously prepared to field questions.

"Long story," he said simply, and Ezri nodded again; worked for her. She thought he looked good for a human who had to be around a hundred now, still full of life.

"It seems that Commander Vaughn has a wide knowledge of what Starfleet has collected on the Jem'Hadar," Kira said. "He was telling me about a new study on individual personality traits, when it occurred to me that you should be hearing this."

Ezri nodded, not bothering to point out that Starfleet hadn't done any such study, at least not officially; she'd spent the better part of two days reading everything she could find, starting with Starfleet's complete research. Included were outlines of results-pending hypotheses, and none of them involved psychological-sociological studies on individuality.

Vaughn will be Vaughn. . . .

Still the enigma, it seemed, although something had changed. He seemed taller, literally and figuratively, the literal coming from the fact that Ezri was easily Dax's shortest host. Julian thought it was funny, but changing stature made a huge difference in one's perception. It had always been strange, seeing the same people through different eyes, particularly when it had been more than a lifetime ago.

"It's easy to misjudge the Jem'Hadar," Vaughn said, off Kira's cue. "Because they're bred to fight and obey, most people assume that they're all alike, simplistic and solely driven by engineered instinct. In fact, it's coming to light that no two are the same. Their social status is partly based on it, on the strengths of individual character based on action and decision making. The most successful squad leaders are exceptional at reading the degrees of these qualities in their men."

"Is the status being considered as ascribed or achieved?" Ezri asked. The sociological equivalent of nature or nurture, and she was fascinated by the possibility that the Jem'Hadar were as complex as he was insinuating.

"Both," Vaughn said. "And there's a suggestion of personal evolution, especially among the older ones, of which there are understandably few. There's even a possibility that the need for ketracel-white decreases over time. It's still theory, but a series of autopsies on Jem'Hadar over the age of ten showed that some of them may actually have been producing a small amount of the enzyme. It's not consistent, or certain; the current thinking is that it's an age-related mutation, although it's also possible that there was simply a bad batch of genetic material around that time, and that the flaw has since been worked out."

Goran'agar, the one Julian tried to help on Bopak III, had been no younger than seven or eight. Julian was still firmly convinced that Goran'agar's freedom from the white had made him less violent. There'd also been Omet'iklan and Remata'klan . . . both of whom Jadzia had been able to observe up close. Both had seemed much more thoughtful and disciplined than the typical Jem'Hadar soldier. And both had shown signs, as had Goran'agar, of a nagging dissatisfaction with "the order of things." It was a sobering thought; if Vaughn's theory was correct, the longer a Jem'Hadar lived, the more likely he'd be able to overcome at least some of his genetic programming.

But Kitana'klan is barely three . . . if it's true that some older Jem'Hadar don't need ketracel-white, the Dominion would know about it . . . why would Odo pick such a young representative, if age actually matters?

"Have you dealt with any Jem'Hadar personally?" Kira asked.

"A few," Vaughn answered. "Enough to know that if your changeling friend actually chose this soldier for the reasons he gave, he wasn't chosen at random. Perhaps he represents the Jem'Hadar ideal. . . . Would it be possible for me to speak to him?"

Kira looked at Ezri, who nodded. It certainly couldn't hurt.

"Lieutenant, Commander Vaughn will be staying with us while he awaits his next assignment. Will you arrange quarters for him, and then take him to meet Kitana'klan?" Kira asked.

"Of course," Ezri said. "Captain, will you be joining us?"

Picard shook his head. "Actually, I was hoping you might show me to one of the station's Bajoran shrines," he said, addressing Kira, then glancing at Vaughn. "I understand an Orb is usually kept there."

"An excellent idea," Vaughn said, nodding at Picard before turning to Kira. "Colonel, I hope we'll be able to spend some time together later. I'd like very much to ask you some questions about the Bajoran faith, if you wouldn't mind talking to me about it."

"Not at all," Kira said, but Ezri thought she detected a slight edge to her voice, a stiffening of her smile. "I'd be happy to."

They split up, Ezri leading Vaughn toward the guest officers' quarters in the habitat ring. Strange, how small their corner of the universe actually seemed after a few hundred years. There did seem to be an inordinate number of recurring faces throughout Dax's experience, lending credibility to the idea that destiny or spirit decides who will be drawn to you.

Ezri wondered if they'd run into Julian somewhere along the way, and wondered, after eight lifetimes of love and loss and change, how it was that she could be missing him already.

Julian missed her already, but knew better than to let his focus wander as he reached Kitana'klan's cargo bay. The Jem'Hadar hadn't acted in a threatening manner yet, but Julian didn't want to take any chances. He asked both security guards on duty to accompany him inside, one to stay at the door and the other to stay with him; both would keep their phasers trained on Kitana'klan.

The soldier was standing in the far corner of the room. When he saw Bashir enter, he walked slowly to meet them, careful to be nonthreatening.

"Kitana'klan, I'm Dr. Bashir," he said, searching for something he could identify as emotion in the soldier's face, finding nothing. "We met yesterday for a few moments. I ran the physical scan."

"You were also at the table," Kitana'klan said. "With the Andorian who exposed me."

"That's right," Julian said, carefully and obviously reaching into his bag, his motions exaggerated. "I've brought you another white cartridge. I'd like to scan your metabolic fluctuations as you receive the enzyme, if that's all right with you."

"I have no objection," the soldier rumbled, still moving slowly as he knelt in front of Julian and the guard, Militia Sergeant Cryan. Devro was at the door. Julian prepped his tricorder as Cryan stepped around behind the kneeling Jem'Hadar, phaser ready.

Kitana'klan pulled the neck of his stiff clothing open, revealing a sputtering tube. Julian started to hand him a fresh cartridge as he ejected the old one, thinking that he might want to reset the numbers to account for stress factors—

—and then he was flying backward, and without his enhanced senses he might have missed what else was happening, it all happened so very fast.

Kitana'klan had grabbed the fresh cartridge and then dropped flat, pushing out and kicking at the same time, managing to knock both the guard and Julian down before rolling up into a crouch.

A phaser blast from Devro, at the door, high and outside, the scared corporal's hand skittering on the trigger—and the double *thunk* of white cartridges hitting flesh was impossibly fast, *thunk-thunk,* both hitting his right temple, the empty one not as loud, Devro falling—

—and only now was the pain registering, because Julian hadn't managed to save himself from hitting the ground in the two seconds that had elapsed, and because Kitana'klan was leaning over him, pulling at his upper chest, the pain immediate and wet, jagged bits of glass being dragged through his flesh, catching on muscle fiber too deep, too deep.

Julian pushed at the sneering monster with one hand, reaching for his combadge and not finding it, his heart pounding. His right shoulder was in agony and he was bleeding quite badly, his neck and upper chest hot and sticky-wet, the air metallic with the smell.

Kitana'klan hit him, a stunning punch to his temple, the blows that followed hazy and painful. At some point the soldier went away, and Julian opened his eyes. There was blood in them.

He concentrated; he had to diagnose the injuries before he could treat them. He felt weak and heavy, impossibly tired, his senses not gathering enough information. His right arm was losing sensation, and his right clavicle was surely broken, he could feel the crepitation. He'd lost a lot a blood.

Nicked subclavian, maybe. Two minutes perhaps before he bled out, if he could trust his own diagnosis.

Julian managed to roll his head to the side, and there was his med kit, less than a meter away. Harder to think, his mind wandering. There was a cauterizing seal patch in the kit, he always carried one. The patch would keep him alive for a few extra moments, assuming he hadn't suffered a hemothorax. Without a team standing by, a breach of the pleural cavity meant he would certainly die.

Julian wanted to reach for the kit but then it was gone, kicked away by the boots that walked past his flickering gaze. He thought that he should at least apply pressure to the wound, but couldn't feel either hand anymore. Didn't matter, he'd just bleed out internally. . . .

Blood was splashing and getting darker, ebbing away into the encroaching swarm of blackness. His brain was starving; he'd lose consciousness and then die. The thought seemed uninteresting and distant . . . except he wished he had seen Ezri one last time, the thought of her face making him sad, and he thought of Kukalaka, his stuffed toy from childhood, and then he thought nothing at all.

Chapter Nine

Kira found that Picard was a lot less intimidating than she'd remembered, although it probably had a lot to do with the respect he showed to Vedek Capril, and to the Orb itself. The Orb of Contemplation was now in a private room that adjoined the shrine, and Captain Picard had asked to see it in a truly reverent tone, confessing an interest in Bajoran artifacts.

Vedek Capril left them alone and Kira watched as Picard walked in a circle around the supported ark, hands behind his back as he leaned in closely, examining the carved detail. She knew he'd seen it before, but wouldn't have guessed from looking at his face; his gaze was very bright, the slight smile he wore a genuine expression of wonder. His few questions indicated that he knew as much about where and when the Orbs had been found as most Bajorans.

When he finished his scrutiny of the ark, he stood straight and adjusted his uniform, still smiling. "Colonel, it seems to be a matter of fate that the *Enterprise* comes to be at your station."

Kira nodded, a little puzzled at his choice of words. Picard's ship needed repairs and access to subspace communications; she wasn't sure that qualified. *Probably means to meet with the task force.*

"May I arrange to have something beamed directly to our position from the *Enterprise?*" Picard asked, looking at the ark again, obviously fascinated by it. "It was actually Commander Vaughn's discovery, but I think he expects me to present it. Kind of a surprise gift, to go along with our surprise visit."

He looked at Kira again on the last, and she had the impression that beneath his pleasantly placid exterior, he was grinning. His eyes sparkled with good humor.

"Of course, Captain," she said, feeling slightly apprehensive.

Picard gave their coordinates to someone on his ship, and a few seconds later, a small object materialized at their feet. Kira couldn't credit what she saw for a few blinks, thinking that she'd somehow mis-seen it, but it didn't waver. It was an ark for a Tear of the Prophets.

"We believe it's the Orb of Memory," Picard said as Kira moved toward it, reaching out to touch it, knowing that it *was* the Orb of Memory as a sigh escaped her. The design at the opening was a series of curved lines radiating out from a central sphere, a design that every Bajoran child knew as belonging to the missing Orb.

She was speechless for a moment, so struck with awe that she forgot Picard was present. The mystical, beautiful connection to the Prophets that each Orb represented was always cause for joy, but to see one that had been taken away early in the occupation, lost to Bajor for so many years . . . to know that it was with them again was a blessed, precious knowledge, and for just a few seconds, it filled her up.

"Where did you find it?" Kira asked finally, unable to take her hand from the closed ark.

"In the Badlands, actually," Picard said. "On a derelict. Commander Vaughn led the away team, so I'm sure he can better describe the exact circumstances."

Kira straightened, the depth of her gratitude and joy inexpressible as she turned to Picard. She floundered for an appropriately diplomatic response to his miraculous gift, aware that words were insufficient but that they were all she had.

"Captain, on behalf of the Bajoran people, please allow me to thank you and your crew for what you've done."

Picard nodded, a deeply satisfied look on his face. "You're welcome, Colonel. I have some idea of what this means to Bajor, and I'm delighted to have played even a small part in returning it to you . . . though it really is Commander Vaughn you should be thanking."

"I will," Kira said, gazing at the Orb, deciding who she should contact first, thrilled to have such a decision to make. Shakaar was still on Earth, she thought, but that might be the best—

Her combadge signaled, and her bright mood immediately darkened. She stepped away from Picard and the beautiful ark, expecting the call to be trouble; she couldn't imagine the day bringing anything else at this point, and although she'd planned to keep her expectations to a minimum, it was turning out that she couldn't expect her plans to work out, either. . . .

Keep it together, you haven't slept in at least twenty-six hours.

"This is Kira."

"Colonel, this is Ro," Ro said, sounding out of breath. *"I've got a situation here with Vedek Yevir, and Kasidy Yates is also present, and I, ah, request your immediate presence at the security office. Sir."*

Not just out of breath. Ro sounded like she was about to kill someone.

"On my way," Kira said, looking back at Picard as she tapped out. Ro's office was close, but she didn't want to leave the Orb unattended, and it didn't sound like she had time to track down Vedek Capril, he'd been on his way home . . .

. . . the candle cabinet. There was an indiscreet panel on the south wall of the small room, a space where extra candles were stored. The shrine was closed for the evening, but she wanted to take the extra precaution, at least until she had time to tell one of the vedeks about it.

Perhaps after Yevir leaves . . . An unkind thought, but sincere. She wasn't feeling particularly trusting toward her old friend's motives.

"My apologies, Captain," Kira said, "but I'm needed somewhere immediately. Would you mind terribly if we put off announcing the Orb's return for the moment?"

Picard smiled, shaking his head. "The Orb belongs to you now. And I should be returning to my ship, to prepare my own argument against what the

Allies have in mind. I'm sure you've got enough to do without having to escort me around."

Kira asked Picard to open the cabinet for her, and she gently lifted the ark, putting it on a low shelf. It would be safe. The Prophets had wanted it brought back to Bajor, or it wouldn't be here.

Kira suggested that they walk together toward the security office; there was a turbolift directly across from it. Picard nodded, and they walked out onto the Promenade, Kira just putting one foot in front of the other, moving toward the next event in line. The Prophets knew that she rejoiced inside for the return of the Orb, but she had the station to consider, and the idea that Ro might stab Vedek Yevir with something had to take precedence over her own elation.

Things were bad, and they were probably going to get worse. When she realized that there was no point in trying to tell Yevir anything, Ro called Kira and then held her tongue, letting the man quietly poison the air. Captain Yates had arrived only a few moments after the vedek and had watched their exchange silently, her arms crossed, her face drawn. When he'd started his monologue, she'd turned away.

Hurry up, Kira, Ro thought miserably, fighting an urge to leave the office and an even stronger one to start yelling. Yevir was exactly the kind of man she most disliked, so convinced he was right that he believed the entire universe was backing him up.

"—worse than malicious, it was immoral and criminal," Yevir was saying, calm and absolutely furious, his polite words dripping with threat. "I'll see to your immediate dismissal, and that you're remanded to the custody of the Militia's justice department. I can only hope that you'll find the love of the Prophets in the end, to beg their forgiveness for what you've done . . ."

Where is she? Ro looked past Yevir, and—

—oh.

Yevir was still talking, but Ro didn't hear him. Standing not two meters in front of her office was Jean-Luc Picard. Kira was with him, but that didn't seem as important, *I knew a starship had docked but not yours . . .*

Picard, who had once trusted her because she'd given her word. Ro hadn't seen him since she'd broken it, but had spent many a moment in the years that followed wishing that things had been different. Regardless of the necessity of her actions, she knew she'd disappointed him, and being a disappointment to Captain Picard had easily been the worst consequence of her decision. The intensity of her feelings seemed too obvious, her own father had died badly when she'd been a child, but Ro wasn't sure what it was; she'd just always wanted his respect.

The captain looked past Kira, glanced at Ro—and quickly found her gaze, his own as sharp as blades as he studied her, frowning. Yevir was still telling her how much trouble she was in, and Kira had turned away from Picard, heading for the office door, but Ro was frozen, feeling herself flush with shame, hoping it wasn't showing. How many years had it been? Long enough for her to have forgotten what a hard place it was to be, standing in the path of his scrutiny, *knowing that you're being inspected and are about to be found wanting—*

Picard held her gaze a second longer and then turned his back to her, walking to the turbolift. He didn't look at her again.

Great, her defenses mustered, laying on the sarcasm. *This is just wonderful, a real experience. I needed a reminder that I don't belong anywhere, that I don't measure up. . . .*

Kira stepped into the office and Yevir immediately turned his attention to her, demanding that Ro be dismissed, that she be disciplined severely. Poor Captain Yates looked as though she wanted to be physically ill.

Kira didn't even look at Yevir, fixing her gaze instead on Ro, completely ignoring the vedek's apoplexy. "Report, Lieutenant."

"Colonel, it appears that approximately three and a half hours ago someone with access to the translation of Istani's book uploaded it, in its entirety, into the Bajoran comnet. Reports are being filed to the station from every province, asking about it."

Kasidy finally spoke, looking at Kira pleadingly. "I just got a call from the Commerce Ministry; they want to know if they can issue a release saying that I believe the prophecies are false. They said they've received over a thousand direct calls in the last hour from people asking to speak to me."

Kasidy lowered her voice, but Ro could hear her. "Nerys, I don't want to deal with this, not now."

Kira took Kasidy's hand and squeezed it, looking into her eyes. "Everything is going to be okay, Kas."

"I don't see how you can say that," Yevir said, still managing to keep his voice down, still playing the part of the angry victim. Maybe he actually felt that way. Ro figured it didn't make much difference, in the end; he was a fanatic.

"All moral issues aside, a crisis has been deliberately unleashed, and all because an admitted opponent of the Vedek Assembly was given access to sensitive materials," Yevir said. "She used her position to promote her own intolerance, with no thought as to how it would affect anyone else."

He was glaring at Ro as he spoke, and she decided that she was ready to end this particular party, hopefully with Yevir's apology. Seeing Picard had left her off balance, but she was still confident that Colonel Kira would believe her word over Yevir's. Ro knew she didn't come off that well with a lot of people, but even her enemies knew her to be honest, and she had never lied to Kira about anything.

"Colonel, I absolutely did not," Ro said. "Vedek Yevir is mistaken. I haven't seen the translation or the book since we all met in your office this afternoon, and I had nothing to do with its transmission to Bajor's communications network."

Yevir smiled, a small, sanctimonious smile. "The word of a nonbeliever, that certainly holds its own with a lie."

"Please don't call me a liar," Ro said, just tired of listening to him.

"I didn't, child, I just don't understand why you won't admit to it," Yevir said. "You're the only one here with a reason. That treacherous book validated your damaged beliefs, and you couldn't stand to be alone anymore, could you? A nonbeliever from a world that embraces spirituality—"

Kira was nodding along, her expression neutral. When he hesitated long enough to draw breath, she spoke quickly, looking directly at Yevir for the first time.

"I did it," Kira said. "I uploaded Ohalu's book."

Yevir finally shut his mouth, but Ro felt her own hanging open.

Kasidy didn't believe her. They all stared at her, and Kas saw her own feelings in their faces—Ro's eyes were wide with incredulity, and Vedek Yevir looked like he'd had the wind knocked out of him.

"You're joking," Yevir said. He seemed smaller, somehow.

Kira's chin was raised, her head high. "I gave a lot of thought to what you said earlier. You asked me what I thought would happen to Bajor if the book were made public, and after I considered it carefully, I came to the realization that you don't know the Bajor I know."

Yevir was the very picture of injured confusion. "Nerys, I don't know what you're talking about."

"The Bajoran people aren't children," Kira said. "They don't need anyone to censor information on their behalf, and frankly, Vedek, I'm surprised and a little offended by the Assembly's attempt to do so. It's patronizing, it suggests that you don't think the Bajoran faith is strong enough to tolerate a different perspective."

"And this is your answer?" Yevir asked. "To send blasphemous and offensive words into people's homes, like some kind of . . . of *test?*"

Kira didn't hesitate, her manner angry but controlled. "And are you that desperately afraid that they'll fail? I'm tired of wondering whether or not I'm being manipulated by people who say they speak for the Prophets. I have my own relationship with Them, and I trust my own judgment. And whatever you think about that, what gives you the right to decide what's bad for me, or what's best for anyone besides yourself?

"I see it as an opportunity for all of us. Here it is, over seven years since the occupation ended, and we still haven't found our balance. I see our world as a place that's trapped in transition. I see a struggle to integrate the cultural spirituality of thousands of years with what we've learned in the last century, and I think a good look at ourselves is exactly what we need to get through it, to create an atmosphere of positive change. To let every Bajoran reevaluate what the Prophets mean for their lives."

Yevir was aghast. He ran one hand through his silvering hair, mussing it, his face screwed up in distress as he took a half step back.

He's not faking it, he really thinks this is a holocaust. Kas could understand his reaction, could see perfectly why he felt so betrayed. And she could see why

Kira might have done it; the politics couldn't be plainer. The thing was, Kas still didn't actually believe it.

"I love the Prophets," Kira said seriously, still addressing Yevir. "And it doesn't matter to me what anyone thinks of my faith, because I know the truth. Reading that book only confirms for me that the love of the Prophets can be interpreted in other ways. I prayed about this, and I truly believe it's the right thing for Bajor. I've been given a sign, that the Prophets support us. Ohalu's book belongs to every Bajoran, Vedek; please, have faith in *us,* have faith that each individual can only grow as the Prophets intend."

Ro seemed almost to smile, and for some reason, that look of approval finally did it for Kasidy's belief problem. Kira Nerys, who had been there for her, who had helped her find workers and apply for permits on her new home, who had been a real *friend* to her . . . Kira Nerys had just created absolute chaos for her and the baby. And she had done it on purpose.

Kasidy hated public confrontation, but there was no help for it, she needed to understand and she needed it *now.*

"How could you do this to me, Nerys?" Kas asked, and Kira turned away from Yevir, finally, her head not quite as high. She at least had the decency to look ashamed, but at the moment, Kas didn't care a whit for Kira's shame. What good did it do her?

"Kas, I'm so sorry," she said, and it certainly looked like she meant it. "It was just—it was the right thing to do, I had to do it."

"That's fine, good for you," Kasidy said tightly, folding her arms, and then she took a deep breath, *baby, it's okay, relax,* then another. The kind of anger she was feeling couldn't possibly be harmless. After another deep breath, she started again.

"So you and the Vedek Assembly have now each made a grand statement of how right you are," Kasidy said, making the anger and pain become words instead of heat, struggling to keep her body from reacting to her distress. "I can appreciate that. But I didn't ask how you could do this, I asked how you could do this to *me.* To be honest, I don't care why, because all of this means that if I want a moment's peace for the rest of my pregnancy, I'll have to go into hiding."

Silently watching her, Kira was obviously unhappy, her expression guilty and apologetic—which for some reason seemed to make things worse. How convenient for Nerys, that she could betray her friend and then feel sorry about it, knowing all the while exactly what she was doing. Kas knew she wasn't being entirely fair, but decided that she was allowed.

She looked at Yevir, at the way he was practically wringing his hands, his thoughts as clear as if they were written in the air above his head, *The mother of the Emissary's child is unhappy, oh, dear, what can I do?*

Relax. Breathe.

"I'm sorry, but this is not okay," Kas said slowly, talking to herself as much as to Kira and Yevir, her words gathering speed as they poured out. "I can't stay here if this is what it's going to be like. I'm a person with a *life,* I'm not some indirect religious figure in a cause, and if you think I'm going to let my child be involved in any part of this particular dilemma, think again. Ten thousand Bajorans, dying so that my baby will be born into peace, so that he or she can be worshiped as some kind of spiritual embodiment, as some *thing?*"

Kas folded her arms tighter and then deliberately relaxed them, so tuned to the second life inside her that she almost reflexively protected it now. It wasn't a matter of choice, her current priorities didn't allow for choice; she just couldn't have this in her life.

"I'll leave," she said calmly. "I'll get as far away from here as possible. In fact, my things are already packed."

I could *leave.* It sounded so possible, so easy. So tempting. *Just . . . fly away, and never come back.*

Her pronouncement was followed by silence. All three of the Bajorans in the room looked mortified, but as far as Kasidy was concerned, Ro was the only one with any credibility, the only one who hadn't actually done anything wrong.

Before anyone could speak, a man's unfamiliar voice spilled out of an open comm on Ro's desk, deep and clear and very fast.

"*Security alert, the Jem'Hadar soldier has killed at least two people and is no longer in containment. Starfleet medical officer down, needs emergency transport to medical facilities, Dax is with him. We're at cargo bay 41C or C41, this is Commander Elias Vaughn, acknowledge.*"

Kira hit her combadge as the last words were spoken, calling for medical transport, already striding for the door; Kasidy barely had time to get out of her way. Ro acknowledged and hit the security alert, and Yevir Linjarin stood uncertainly, perhaps wondering who he would complain to now.

Worried and wounded and afraid, Kas left immediately for her quarters, planning to throw the manual at her door as soon as she got there. No matter what else happened, she was moving away from DS9 as soon as possible.

Chapter Ten

A monster, looming. Troubled sleep, and pain. Someone calling his name. A bone-deep *ache,* so pervasive that his own body was a stranger to him, numbed flesh warming up just enough to scream at the cold, cold air.

But I'm dead.

It was Julian's first whole thought in a while, and the paradox exhausted him. Kitana'klan had killed him, but he couldn't remember dying so he couldn't be dead. The pain was terrible, it made his next breath into a cry for relief that emerged as a helpless whimper.

That tiny sound of pain and he was *with* the pain, the sound bringing him closer to full consciousness as it defined him from the dark. He couldn't think, the level of awareness too much, the totality of the pain making him afraid that he might lose himself—

—and then Ezri was there, talking softly, explaining that he'd been hurt and that they were going to the infirmary. He couldn't see her, didn't know if she was touching him, but her voice was enough. It was clear and firm and she told him that she loved him. Julian fell asleep before she finished, but he wasn't afraid.

Vaughn should have called the alert as soon as he saw that there were no guards posted outside the bay. Neither he nor Dax carried a weapon, and if there was a situation inside with the soldier Kitana'klan, going in unarmed meant no chance. As opposed to a slim one.

His instincts telling him that the Jem'Hadar had escaped, Vaughn didn't bother to think about procedure. With a curt nod from Dax, they walked through the unlocked door, Vaughn in the lead.

He took in as much as he could as soon as they were inside, wasting no input that could help his assessment. Smells of scorched material and blood, phaser fire, exposed insulation. There was a splash of blood on the inside of the door, and a trailed smudge leading to the first body, a Bajoran Militia corporal, young. Throat cut deeply after the body was moved, from the pool of it he lay in now.

Another young man at eleven o'clock some distance away, Starfleet medical lieutenant, still alive but in bad shape, deep claw marks seeping across his chest, a cauterizing pack at the base of his throat. There was a med kit close by, adrift in the doctor's blood.

Bajoran Militia sergeant, the third victim, not far from the doctor. Another kid, his head twisted around at an angle that counted him dead.

Within a few seconds, Vaughn had all the information he needed to get things going. He stepped back to the door and hit the companel as Dax ran to the survivor, snatching up the bloody med kit before crouching next to him.

Vaughn relayed the prioritized facts quickly, spotting a dropped tricorder on the floor as Dax and the wounded doctor sparkled away to a medical facility. A Lieutenant Ro acknowledged, telling him to secure the situation as best he could, that security and Colonel Kira were on their way.

DS9 had underestimated the soldier, but it hadn't been their fault. In the war, the Allied troops had mostly faced off against soldiers only weeks old, deadly but untrained, unfocused.

A Jem'Hadar who'd had extended training for hand-to-hand and small arms wasn't nearly so easy to kill as a violently impulsive youth, however. The Jem'Hadar got faster and better at everything with practice, so even at a year or two of age, depending on how often they used their skills, the studied soldiers were effectively unbeatable without weapons. Their reflexes were simply better than those of most humanoids.

Obviously, there were species who could hold their own physically against the Jem'Hadar—Klingons, for example. But whereas Klingons' code of honor could make them respect, even admire an enemy, the Jem'Hadar were bred to see every opponent as inferior; no respect, no mercy, and for a Jem'Hadar, victory was life. They weren't interested in glory or lasting honor, just the win. How they got it didn't figure into the equation, and that made them extraordinarily good at killing.

As soon as he'd signed off, Vaughn ran to the tricorder and scooped it up, setting the readings with one eye while he searched for a phaser. The Jem'Hadar soldier certainly had one of them, but perhaps not both—

—there, near a stack of empty boxes by the door. Vaughn paused in the tricorder adjustment long enough to grab it, the sharper sounds of his movement resounding through the cool air of the dead and empty bay. Only seconds later, the station went to red alert, a light panel on the bay wall starting to flash, a distant alarm sounding.

Vaughn ignored it, working on the tricorder. A shrouded Jem'Hadar standing still could be detected easily enough, almost all energy was observable, but to track one you had to be exact, *and better at running science equipment than I am, dammit, what's the formula* . . . Vaughn knew a lot of theory, but rarely had to practice.

As with a ship's cloak, gravitons were produced by a Jem'Hadar shroud aura. There was a way to pattern the residue, to follow it, but the trail dissipated quickly. Vaughn assumed that Kira would want to track Kitana'klan from ops, but he'd also gathered that the station's internal sensors weren't a hundred percent, and he knew that a full sweep on a station the size of DS9 would take time. It was unlikely that the sensors could even pick up such a delicate trace; from the reports Vaughn had read about the process, a tricorder was definitely the tool for the job. If he could follow the soldier for long enough to narrow the search perimeter even a little, it could make a big difference.

He was just finishing with the tricorder when the colonel walked through the door, followed only seconds later by a Bajoran security lieutenant and five noncom guards, all of them armed. Good. He didn't mind the idea of having an escort; it was highly unlikely that the Jem'Hadar wanted to be followed, and the more of them, the less likely he was to attack.

Vaughn rapidly outlined the residue-pattern theory, explaining that he'd never tried it firsthand. Kira liked it, recommending that they coordinate the effort with ops, letting the station's sensors take over when they picked up a definite direction. She put a call in, absolutely on top of things, not looking at the two dead boys but not looking away, either. Vaughn was impressed.

One of the Militia guards volunteered that she'd worked as a sensor array tech and operator. Vaughn gladly turned the tricorder over to her and waited for Kira to finish her instruction to a science officer named Shar, in ops. Vaughn assumed it was zh'Thane's child, Thirishar; he'd accessed DS9's current personnel files before the *Enterprise* had docked, gaining all sorts of highly classified insight into some of the people on the station.

"Colonel, I'd like to apprise Captain Picard of this situation," Vaughn said, as soon as Kira tapped out. "And ask him to stand by to assist."

"Please," Kira said. "And tell him I'm open to suggestions on how to resolve this thing before it goes any further."

The tech/guard held the tricorder up, motioning at the door. "I've got it."

They fell in around her, Kira and the tech taking the lead, Vaughn hanging back to talk to Picard. As he filled the captain in, he found he couldn't stop staring at the dead corporal's open eyes, his clawed throat, the fan of thickening blood on his forehead from a pair of deep cuts. He looked surprised, caught off guard by the end of his life. He looked dead.

If they didn't find and stop the Jem'Hadar ASAP, a lot more people were going to end up the same way. Vaughn could think of a dozen ways that one determined person could destroy a space station without too much trouble, and that was without being invisible . . . or a Jem'Hadar soldier, who was always willing to die if it meant he could take out his enemy in the process. To them, death meant nothing, but it was a victory if they didn't go down alone.

Five minutes. If they didn't have a clear idea of Kitana'klan's intent by then, Vaughn was going to start pushing for a full evacuation. They couldn't afford anything less.

Ezri acted unprofessionally. She didn't reflect or consider. As soon as she stepped into the bay behind Vaughn, she saw Julian. And there was so much blood, what seemed like bucketfuls splashed across his face and chest, puddles of it all around him, that she knew he was dead. Knew it. And that was when she saw his chest rise, and when she took action.

Not thinking about the possible dangers, not thinking about anything but how important he was, how she had to make him stay with her, Ezri ran to him, grabbing the med kit off the bloody floor before dropping to his side.

He was so pale, the blood seemed ludicrously bright against his skin. His tattered jacket and the shirt underneath were soaked with it, but the gashes on his chest were only oozing. The seal patch on his collarbone might have stopped the major bleeding, she didn't know, and she didn't want to make anything worse by jumping to medical assumptions—

"Julian, can you hear me? Julian?" Ezri asked, not expecting a response, wondering why they weren't already at the infirmary—and he let out a semi-conscious moan, so soft that she barely heard it.

He winced, his mouth twisted, an expression of hopeless suffering, and Ezri started talking, reassuring him. Comforting him. She took his hand, noting with alarm that his fingers were scarcely warmer than her own, keeping the alarm from her voice; she told him that she loved him, and that he would be all right.

She was looking at his blood-spattered face as the environment around them changed, as they were transported to an emergency table, flush with the floor on one side of the infirmary's operating theater. Ezri quickly stumbled away and someone touched a command, the section of floor rising, Julian's devastated body rising up to meet the waiting, healing hands of Dr. Girani. He wasn't conscious, and his eyes were partly open, and Ezri didn't know if he would live.

Ezri called up her memories, Dax's memories, searching for an appropriate response to her fears, some relief, something she could *do* . . . and couldn't find one. Dealing with life and death on an emotional level was one of the very few things that all hosts had handled in their own way, because the feelings were so complex, so intimate, so specifically tied to each relationship. There was no simple concept to grasp, nothing from their past that could help her.

So, I'll deal with this as Ezri, she thought, and as she thought it, she realized what she wanted. It wasn't a choice from fear, although she was afraid . . . it was that she just knew now, it had hit her and she couldn't deny the strength of it. Ezri could spend the rest of her life contemplating possibilities that others had created, or she could create her own, by choosing to follow her heart.

The joining of Ezri Tigan and Dax loved Julian Bashir, very much. If he survived, and he would, *he will,* she was going to make a place for him in her life, period; she could find her space to grow, but she couldn't find another Julian. If he died, she would lose her closest friend, and a lover who made her feel good about herself, who loved Ezri Dax.

That can't happen, it can't.

Shaking, Ezri held her blood-smeared hands together against her abdomen, watching as two nurses and a doctor fought for his life. After a moment, someone else gently asked her to wait outside, and Ezri managed to make her legs carry her away, telling herself that he would be fine, that everything would be fine now.

Chapter Eleven

With Geordi and Data leading the maintenance teams and the captain in the station's wardroom, talking to Starfleet, Will Riker really had nothing to do on the bridge but stand around as CO of a communications noncom and an engineering tech. He was impatient to take his own leave, looking forward to winding down, still not recovered from the news about the *Aldebaran*. He stared at the blank main screen, waiting for the captain to return.

The *Enterprise* was officially inactive, the warp cores undergoing a definitive diagnostic, the subspace arrays still offline. The captain hadn't liked it any more than Will did, the nearly complete power down with the wormhole so nearby, but the *I.K.S. Tcha'voth, Vor'cha*-class, was still standing guard, and repairs had to be made.

Particularly if we're going to join up with this task force to the Gamma Quadrant. Riker hadn't liked that much, either; an armed investigation into the Gamma Quadrant seemed like a monumentally foolish idea. No one knew how the Dominion was taking their defeat, and it seemed to him that moving aggressively into the Gamma Quadrant to confront them after three silent months wasn't going to make things less tense.

And there's the Jem'Hadar's story. Picard had told him about it upon his return to the *Enterprise,* and had gone to talk to Admiral Ross about the news. Deanna had just left to see who to talk to about offering assistance in an assessment. They were all keeping their fingers crossed that the Jem'Hadar was telling the truth.

The captain seemed to be in full agreement about the task force, after he heard Will's report on the update from Starfleet. Although he hadn't given a final opinion, wanting to hear the Federation's decision directly from Ross, Picard had clearly stated that he was leaning toward Kira's view of things, much the same as Will's. A few rogue ships on a suicide run had gotten lucky, turning a postwar skirmish into an interstellar incident. Such things needed to be handled carefully.

He was still thinking about it when Mr. Truke spoke up, his voice high with urgency, the fur on the back of his neck ruffling.

"Sir, I'm receiving multiple reports from crew on the station, that DS9 has just gone to red alert," he said, and Riker was up and moving, going to stand behind communications, watching the flatscreen for details. The crew members on the station would already be on their way back to the ship to sign in, standard procedure for an emergency while on leave.

Behind them, the door to the bridge opened and the captain walked in, finishing a call on his combadge. Although he wasn't speaking loudly, his voice resonated, his commanding tone at full force.

"... than those we discussed, and inform her that we'll be standing by for anything else she needs," Picard said, striding toward his chair. "Thank you, Commander, Picard out."

The captain didn't sit down, turning to Riker instead. "That was Commander Vaughn. The Jem'Hadar soldier killed two guards and has escaped. The station is at red alert. Contact Data and Geordi, Number One, tell them we need our impulse engines back up immediately. I want us prepared if the need to provide evacuation transport arises. I'm going to ask Dr. Crusher to lend a hand at the station's infirmary, as it seems that the chief medical officer has been wounded. I want armed security teams standing by, to be called in if Lieutenant Ro requires them, she's chief of security. Make sure everyone understands that they're to accept direction from the station officers, rank notwithstanding; we want to assist, not get in the way."

—Ro? Common name, someone else—the thought barely rose from Will's subconscious before settling back.

Picard left him in command, going to his ready room. Riker hit his badge for Data, letting his organizational skills come into play as he reflexively broke down the orders, deciding how best to fulfill them through a series of mental directions—get updated DS9 schematics to the transporter rooms, process sign-ins and -outs back into the duty roster, yellow alert status to override shift changes and standbys but not to battle stations, get an exact time for the impulse drive to be fully functional . . .

His deeper thoughts were of Deanna. She wouldn't have gone to see the Jem'Hadar before working things through with the station's counselor, he was sure of it, and she hadn't been gone for that long. Not long enough to be anywhere near a Jem'Hadar on a killing spree, one who might recognize a Betazoid as a threat—

Riker let it go, throwing himself into the work. Relaying orders successfully was a skill, and he could best contribute to the resolution of a crisis by managing the system, by making things happen appropriately. And the faster he worked, the sooner he'd be able to call Deanna, and make sure she was all right.

Deanna Troi had only just reached the Promenade when the station went to red alert. Although she was usually fine with her defenses, the mass emotional response to the alarm signal and flashing panels was incredibly loud, solid and fast—there were something like 7500 people on board—and she felt herself tensing, the smash of anxiety digging at her with prickly fingers, looking for a way in.

She stepped to the Promenade's outer wall between a meeting hall and the station's infirmary, leaning against it, taking several deep breaths. She was fine, she just needed a moment to reestablish her filters. A recorded loop explained to the hurrying streams of people that it was an internal security alert, to act accordingly.

For all of the *Enterprise* crew that meant an immediate return to the ship, but Deanna closed her eyes and centered herself instead, running through a minute or two of shield visualization, picturing herself wearing armor made of light. She wasn't minimizing the importance of what was happening; she had to keep herself well, or she wouldn't be able to function. If the *Enterprise* had urgent need of her, they would call.

A few more deep breaths, and Deanna opened her eyes, ready to go. There was a turbolift almost directly across from where she stood, to the right of a Spican jeweler's. She started toward the lift just as the doors opened, and Beverly stepped out. She was carrying her med kit and was unhappy, her energy brightening only a little when she saw Deanna approaching.

"Beverly, what's happening?"

Dismayed but not distressed, Beverly acted perfectly calm. "A Jem'Hadar soldier is loose on the station. He's killed two people and injured the CMO, he's in surgery now. Dr. Bashir, you remember him?"

Arrogant, childish, entirely charming and off-the-scale bright. He'd worked with Geordi to help Data "diagnose" his first dreams . . . seven years ago? It was the last time she'd seen him, anyway. Deanna nodded.

"The captain thought I might be able to help," Beverly said, a flush of concern coming from her, its nature . . . the doctor was afraid that more casualties were coming, Deanna thought.

"Why don't I come with you," Deanna half-asked, following an instinct, sure she could be useful in some capacity. Beverly was glad for the offer, which was enough of a reason.

As they walked across to the infirmary, people hurrying by on either side, Deanna called in to the bridge. Will picked it up, and sounded relieved to know where she was. He didn't object to her continued absence from the ship, although he quietly told her to be careful after relaying the order of deference to station staff. She returned the sentiment and followed Beverly into the infirmary.

There were three medical attendants and a doctor from the Bajoran Militia in the infirmary's front room, loading hypos and bandages into med kits. A lone patient was being seen to by a fourth nurse; it appeared minor, the patient sitting on the edge of an exam table. A young woman with a liberal amount of blood on her uniform stood stonily near a set of doors to the right, which presumably led to surgery. She had smears of blood on her face. Deanna couldn't make her rank, but she was dressed in Starfleet sciences . . .

. . . *and she's obviously a friend of Dr. Bashir's.*

As Beverly approached the group packing med kits, Deanna let her emotional barriers soften toward the bloody young woman. She was traumatized and afraid, but also seemed to be incredibly focused, much too focused for her emotional state, or her age, for that matter. There was something strangely familiar about her, too, though Deanna felt sure that she'd never seen her before. The young woman stared straight ahead, her profile to Deanna, her arms crossed, expressionless.

Deanna took a step closer and saw that she was Trill, which explained the woman's precision of spirit; the distinctive markings were partly obscured by the bloody smudges on her face . . . and Deanna realized with a start that it had to be Dax.

Deanna and Worf had parted ways amicably enough, and although they hadn't faithfully kept in touch, she'd always wished him well. She'd met Jadzia Dax once, the woman who would eventually become his wife, and had liked her very much; she'd been pleased by the news of their wedding, the expected pang of jealousy lasting only a short time. The marriage itself had ended tragically, when Jadzia had been killed. Deanna had seen Worf only a month after that, during the mission to Betazed, and she had wanted to reach out to him, to offer him that friendship they still shared; but as with so many other things, the crisis of the moment had made it impossible. She'd found out later from Keiko O'Brien that Worf had recently returned from a battle he'd fought in Jadzia's name.

And Keiko also mentioned that there was a new Dax aboard . . . and that she was a counselor.

Deanna didn't want to invade Dax's privacy; she sensed that the young woman was . . .

. . . in hope, in desperation, bargaining and affirming. In love . . . Her lover was in surgery. This incarnation of Dax was with Julian Bashir, it seemed, and she was working hard to believe that he was going to survive; Dax wasn't looking for company, she was trying to concentrate.

Deanna had just decided that she might be most useful back aboard the *Enterprise* after all, when a familiar female voice boomed over the Promenade comm system, ordering the immediate evacuation of Deep Space 9.

Chapter Twelve

After an overlong meal break, Shar had returned to ops feeling a new heaviness in each step, imagining that people were already looking at him differently. He knew that it was unlikely in so short a time, but couldn't help it. It had happened at the Academy, and again on the *Tamberlaine,* as soon as it got around who his "mother" was.

You ignore the real issue, he scolded himself, entering ops without looking at anyone, going straight to the science station. He hadn't wanted anyone to know his relationship to Charivretha, but what he wanted wasn't all that important, not to his family. There were times he felt it never had been.

He wished he had more time now, that he could afford to continue avoiding thoughts of his future, but knew that he was being irrational. *Zhavey*'s call, the first since he'd come to the station, had forced him to face the immediacy of his situation. He didn't like it, but couldn't pretend any longer that it did not exist.

I can, however, avoid thinking about it while I'm on shift. It was inappropriate for him to bring personal troubles with him to his work; it was what the Academy taught, and Shar thought it was sound instruction. He was in ops to keep working with the internal and external sensor arrays, to fine-tune and test all of the readjustments that had been made in the past few days. People depended on him to do his job well; he would not founder because of his own problems.

As soon as he finished looking over the array results from the past few hours, Shar logged a requisition for a new console to be installed in his quarters. He didn't list a reason, and hoped he wouldn't be questioned about it. As Nog had pointed out over their drinks, Shar didn't talk about a lot of things . . . but he didn't lie, either.

Ops was quiet, most of the manual repair work finished, the stations occupied but the colonel's office empty. He considered visiting the *Enterprise* after his shift ended. It was, after all, the ship that Data, Soong's son, served on, and Shar had always wanted to meet the android. But the idea failed to excite him; his violent outburst after the call from *Zhavey* had been draining, but the shame that had followed had been much worse, stealing even the carefully restrained satisfaction he took in his work. For the first time since he'd come to the station, he hadn't wanted to go to his shift. He knew it would pass, but knew also that until he could tell his family what they wanted to hear, the situation would only get worse. . . .

Shar felt his chest constrict with unhappiness, and he did what he could to forget all of it, his family, home, what was expected of him. If he could not enjoy his work, there was no point to all of his struggling.

He was almost an hour into checking the external sampling arrangement, so focused that nothing else existed, when Kira called tactical, issuing an internal security alert—the Jem'Hadar soldier had escaped.

Ops was suddenly in motion, everyone contacting their department teams and securing orders, struggling with backup communications as each worked to account for his or her people and equipment.

Within seconds, Shar went into a state of calm efficacy as his body adjusted to the circumstances, his thoughts refocusing to the tasks at hand. Tracking the Jem'Hadar could best be done from his console. Ignoring the internal visual arrays, he worked with the station's sensors to focus on energy fields and spatial displacement, starting from the cargo bay where the soldier had been held and extending outward. Unfortunately, without knowing which way the Jem'Hadar had gone, he couldn't exclude most of the station, nor could he rely decisively on what he was getting; there was nothing keeping the soldier from doubling back to an area that had been scanned, it was the same problem they'd had running the internal sweeps after Kitana'klan had been discovered, and with the station's energy shortages, blanketing large areas was practically impossible.

"*Kira to sciences.*"

"Ch'Thane here," Shar answered.

"*Shar—we're going to attempt to pick up Kitana'klan's trail by manually testing for graviton residue. I want you to focus on us, and stand by to search for Kitana'klan's shroud signature as soon as we establish direction.*"

"Yes, sir," Shar said, finding the team at the cargo bay before she'd finished speaking. There were eight life signs, one human and seven Bajorans, and they set out almost immediately, heading for the cargo transfer aisle that ran to the outer habitat ring.

Kitana'klan had been held in one of several storage areas at the base of pylon one, and when the team passed the pylon's main turbo shaft, Shar removed it from the search zone. It made no sense for the Jem'Hadar to go up pylon one, as there were no ships docked there . . . although that was assuming he actually meant to escape.

"*Shar, are you still with us?*" The colonel again.

"Yes, sir."

"*Take upper pylon one off the possibility list, and start—wait, just a minute . . .*"

Shar waited, the reason for Kira's hesitation glowing on his schematic in soft red. The team had reached a maintenance tunnel in the crossover bridge, moving toward the hub of the station. When Colonel Kira spoke again, he could hear the gathering apprehension in her voice.

"*Stay with us. Keep narrowing the perimeter.*"

Watching the path they were following, Shar understood her trepidation. He heard Ensign Ahzed, at the engineering station, tell Kira that Lieutenant Nog was standing by at one of the cargo transporters, only waiting for the word to send the team to Kitana'klan's location.

Which is becoming clearer with each step they take. Shar made no assumptions, but the trail was unwavering in its course, and he was fairly sure even before the colonel told him where to concentrate his efforts.

The Jem'Hadar was almost certainly in the lower core, where the fusion reactors were, where the multiple plasma conduits were still being repaired; the station had been on the less secure secondary system since the attack, the engineering teams creating a single central conduit surrounded by a forcefield. It wouldn't take too much effort to completely obliterate the station by explosive overload, assuming one was so inclined; an increase in plasma density in the deuterium slush flow could create a cataclysmic overload in a matter of minutes.

It only took a minute and a half for Shar to find the Jem'Hadar, but he'd already had more than enough time to tamper with the reactors; it had been nearly six minutes since the red alert panels on Shar's console had started to flash, and he didn't know how long Kitana'klan had been free before his absence was noted.

In his current state of enhanced objectivity and heightened awareness, Shar wasn't capable of fear for himself. But for the rest of the station, he grew more worried by the moment.

They were in a scarcely used service corridor at lower mid-core when Kira found she could no longer avoid the obvious. She halted the team, realizing that if she was right, they needed to start a full-scale evacuation immediately.

"Search the lower core," Kira told Shar. "Concentrate on paths to and from the reactors, and around the fusion core."

Kira turned to face the others, calculating time and necessity, hoping that she was wrong but seriously doubting it. Kitana'klan was going to try and blow up the station; she could think of no other reason that he would have run to the lower core. He'd lied about everything, and she'd wanted so badly to believe him that she hadn't taken enough precaution. And they were all going to suffer for it.

Blame yourself later.

"Ro, head to ops," she said, working out plans as she spoke. "I want you to begin emergency evacuation procedures on the way. Call in everyone you need to get it done as quickly as possible. Have communications contact every ship in our immediate vicinity except for the *Tcha'voth* and tell them to get out of blast range, assume full-scale. Have Shar coordinate with the *Enterprise* and the *Tcha'voth* for whatever evacuation transport they can provide, we've got seventy-five hundred on board, and between the two of them, they can . . ."

Kira trailed off, staring at Ro, who gazed back at her with a kind of terror-struck awe, her usually impassive face expressing a depth of feeling that Kira had never seen before. Seventy-five hundred, give or take. Something like a thousand on the *Enterprise,* nearly two thousand on the *Tcha'voth*—

"Ten thousand," Ro breathed, and Kira felt a deep chill hearing it said aloud, one that went into her bones. She'd assumed the prophecy had meant ten thousand *Bajorans*—it said that ten thousand of the land's children would die, but between the two starships and the station, the number was too close. If only a half-dozen escape pods made it out, the number might even be exact.

But it's heresy, part of her objected, *and Kasidy is on the station, the rest of the prophecy can't come true if she dies.*

Maybe she won't die. Maybe she'll be saved. Maybe it'll just be the rest of us.

"Go," Kira said. It was the only answer. They had to stop Kitana'klan, whatever he was doing. DS9 was not going to be lost because of one soldier. Or one heretical prophecy.

Ro nodded, her anxious expression hardening to determination. "Yes, sir."

She turned and hurried away, already talking into her combadge.

Kira turned to Vaughn. "Commander, it might be a good idea if you—"

"All due respect, Colonel, but I may know more about the Jem'Hadar than anyone else here," he interrupted, his jaw firmly set. Kira wasn't going to argue.

"Colonel, I have him," Shar said, and the five guards immediately moved closer together, Vaughn and Kira both stepping in with them.

"It appears that he's at the fusion core, on grid twenty-two," Shar added.

Where the primary reactor banks are.

"Get us to twenty-one," Kira said, pulling her phaser, nodding at her team. "Set phasers on maximum."

Seconds later, the corridor sparkled away.

When Ahzed in ops told him that the soldier had escaped, Nog didn't feel vindicated. He felt nauseated and angry and afraid, telling the ensign that he would handle the security team's transport personally before hurrying from the *Defiant* to the closest docking-ring transporter system. He informed ops that he was standing by at one of the larger cargo transports, and someone sent him the team's signature signals, and then he could only wait and worry, alone. He felt cold and shaky, his stomach strangely empty-feeling, the rims of his ears burning with anxiety.

I was right, nobody listened but I was right all along, he told himself, staring blankly at the CPG controls, his hands trembling just a little. Still, no sense of self-righteous indignation, no glimmer of smarmy satisfaction beneath his fear. As he waited for the word, he thought that he would happily forswear all material wealth for the rest of his life to have been wrong. The monster was loose, and when the destination coordinates for the team flashed across his console's screen, Nog actually groaned out loud.

The core! And only one level above the main reactor banks. With the six reactor conduits still offline, the energy flow to the station was coming from a single, central channel. Easier to sabotage and with more explosive results.

"Energize," Ahzed said, and Nog did it, promising himself that he would never again back down when he knew he was right, wishing that he'd learned that particular lesson a long time ago.

Chapter Thirteen

As soon as they transported, Kira raised one hand, circled in the air with her finger, then pointed down. The grid they were on was exactly that, although the holes were small and spaced far apart; they would have to move to the edge and look over the railing to see the level below.

They had materialized on grid 21, one of the many mesh walkways that surrounded the secondary plasma channel in a series of reinforced metal arcs. The brilliant, glowing mass of moving energy was gigantic, an elongated column suspended through the middle of the lower core shaft and held in place by forcefields. The combined energy from the reaction chambers was still only two-thirds of what the station was used to, it had been since the attack, but the destructive potential was no less. If the core were to overload, the station and anything within a hundred kilometers of it would be blown to atoms.

The twenty-first level of open walkways and platforms was closer to the base of the channel than to the top; the clear conduit extended high over their heads, at least eighty meters of it, and another twenty below. The air was cold, the vast chamber strangely lit by the brilliant spire of white-flame-colored, pulsating power. A deep, throbbing hum resounded throughout the shaft, providing a blanket of white noise that seemed to vibrate the very air.

Together, Kira and Vaughn leading the way, the team sidled toward the railing, only five or six meters from the outside of the glowing tower. At various intervals up and down the core shaft, red alert panels flashed silently, their blinking crimson light barely noticeable in the vivid blaze of the massive conduit.

Kira darted a glance over the side, looking down and to the left, tightly gripping her phaser—

—and there he was. Unshrouded, kneeling in front of the first bank of reactor panels, Kitana'klan had his arms thrust into an open vent near the bottom of the system capacitance section. A phaser lay on the platform next to him . . . and only a few meters away, the broken body of an engineer, obviously dead. A male Bajoran she didn't recognize, probably one of the techs who'd come in on the shuttle.

Kira felt a sudden surge of hate for the Jem'Hadar, sick with the fact that she had been even partially fooled by such a creature; he'd surely been on one of the attack ships, already responsible for mass murder. He had killed two young officers and perhaps Julian in his escape, and now a civilian, a man who had voluntarily come to the station to lend his skills, to help rebuild what Kitana'klan had already tried to destroy once.

And there he is, efficiently working away to finish us off, oblivious to everything else. Kira had tried hard in her life to learn forgiveness for, or at least understanding of, her enemies, but Kitana'klan didn't deserve his life. She wanted him dead, and the sooner the better.

She looked at Vaughn, who held up his own phaser, nodding, his eyes narrowing as he took another look at the unknowing saboteur. Safest to kill him outright, then undo whatever he was doing to the reactors.

Kira jabbed a finger at Sergeant Wasa, beckoning for him to take aim; Wasa Graim was probably the most accurate shot on the station, and had trained half of the security force. A mostly solemn man in his early fifties, Wasa edged to the railing, carefully raised his phaser—

—and before he could fire, Kitana'klan was moving, scooping up his own weapon as he threw himself sideways into a shoulder roll, so fast that he almost seemed a blur as he disappeared under their grid. Wasa took a shot before the Jem'Hadar was entirely out of sight, missing the soldier's heels by scant centimeters. The phaser blast skidded harmlessly across the metal grating.

Damn! She didn't know how he'd known, but it didn't matter now, they had to—

It happened so quickly.

Kitana'klan was suddenly in sight again, dancing out from beneath the grid just long enough to fire, disappearing before any one of them could get off a shot—or get out of the way.

Wasa went down, dead before he hit the floor, a blackened circle appearing almost dead center on his chest. And with a single running step back across the platform, Kitana'klan ducked among the banks of machinery again. If he stayed low, they wouldn't be able to spot him from their position.

"Back, get back," Kira whispered harshly, thinking fast, remembering something that Vaughn had said when they'd first started talking, about the superiority of a Jem'Hadar's reflexes. He was fast, and deadly with a phaser, and now Graim was no more; they couldn't hope to outshoot him.

A trap, something he won't suspect . . . She looked down at Graim and offered a silent prayer, fighting not to think of his two teenaged daughters.

Kira huddled with Vaughn and the four security guards against the shaft wall, silently commending the team for the determination she saw in their grim faces. Vaughn spoke first, his voice low and hurried as he addressed Kira.

"He's going to stay there, to protect his work for as long as he can or as long as he feels is necessary. If you can distract him, draw his fire up here, I might be able to circle down and get behind him."

"My thoughts exactly," Kira said. "But I'm going." The walkway they stood on led to platforms on either side, those connecting to more extensive passages across the core—and several runged ladders, in addition to the four half-caged lifts that ran the length of the shaft.

"We should both go," Vaughn said. "Or three of us, but not together. He'll expect one or all of us to go straight at him, not two or three coming from different directions."

So if he kills one, he'll think he's safe. She didn't want anyone else to die, but if it meant saving the station, she was ready.

Kira nodded, glancing at the others, deciding that she and Vaughn would try it alone; more people meant more noise.

"Make it look good, revolving shots, not a constant barrage," she said. "Don't hit any equipment. Keep firing until we get to the banks."

They were all nodding, but she could see the question in their eyes, as plain as stars at night.

"If we don't make it, call for additional security," she said, answering what she knew no one would ask. "We have to stop him, we have to disable whatever he did to the main controls."

Although if Vaughn and I don't get him, it may be too late. She wasn't sure what Kitana'klan had done, but he must have known they'd find him within minutes of his escape. Whatever his exact plans, he was obviously confident that he wouldn't be stopped before he saw them to fruition.

With a silent prayer that the evacuation was going well, Kira and Vaughn separated from the team, heading away from Kitana'klan's position toward the other side of the cavernous shaft. Behind them, the team began to fire.

When they reached the first of the wall ladders across from the team, hoping that the tower of transforming matter would block them from the Jem'Hadar's sight, Vaughn signaled that he would take it, that she should pick another route down. Whoever reached the lower platform first was more likely to be hit. He didn't have a suicide wish, but one of them had to go first, and Kira commanded the station, her survival was more important than his.

Kira must have realized it, too. She didn't look happy but she didn't hesitate, either; she nodded, pointing at herself and then at another ladder several meters away, near one of the lifts. If she was afraid, he hadn't seen it. Kira Nerys was cooler under pressure than some Starfleet admirals he'd known.

Still holding his phaser, Vaughn stepped down onto the rungs, quickly and quietly one-arming it to the bottom. When he reached the lower grid he turned, deciding the best approach to the reactor bank area. Neither way looked promising, the walkways and platforms all open, the only real cover provided by the power conduit; heading to the right seemed fractionally safer, there looked to be a secondary reactor station, a few solid control banks that could act as a temporary screen.

Vaughn looked up, and saw Kira waiting to see which way he would go, her face a pale, half-shadowed oval by the light of the central conduit. He pointed to himself and then to the left; she nodded, then disappeared from view. Above them, more phaser fire erupted. Kitana'klan wasn't firing back, and Vaughn seriously doubted it was because he'd been injured or killed.

Let's do this. His heart was pounding, his body itching with adrenaline. No matter how many times he'd walked into deadly situations, it was never something that one could get used to. He'd known other humans who'd insisted they felt no fear, but as far as he was concerned, they were either lying or fools.

Crouching, Vaughn sidestepped his way to his left, alert to even a hint of sound or motion. The constant thrum of the reactors would cover any small sounds, but even well-trained Jem'Hadar weren't known for their subtlety. If Kitana'klan took him out, he'd make enough noise so that Kira would at least have an idea of his location. And even a shrouded Jem'Hadar couldn't hide from a phaser sweep.

Vaughn edged around the conduit, the main reactor banks sliding into view. He could see the dead man and the console that had been tampered with, but no Jem'Hadar. Another volley of brilliant phaser fire stabbed down from above, the shots still too wide; the security team hadn't happened across their target yet.

Go, now!

While they were firing, Vaughn ran, taking advantage of the fact that Kitana'klan wasn't likely to stick his head up to take a look around. There was a narrow storage locker only a few meters from the reactor bank platform, situated at a widened section of the walkway. Vaughn reached it and squatted in its shadow, darting another look at how the reactor banks were situated.

Three long rows, say seven meters each and four individual units, nothing taller than two meters . . . Kitana'klan would either be somewhere he could fire on anyone approaching his handiwork, or close enough to the front row to attack physically. Either way, going straight in was definitely a risk, and one they had no choice but to take. Time was a factor.

So take a risk. He could run past the ends of all three rows, firing down each. If he stayed low, he might get lucky . . .

. . . but the odds are a lot better that he'll get me, first. Vaughn would have to hesitate before each shot, just long enough to be sure that Kira wasn't in the line of fire—but that fraction of a second would be all that Kitana'klan needed.

And my death would be all that Kira needs to find him. He wasn't sure where Kira was, but she was certainly close by now. If his sacrifice meant saving thousands of lives, the choice was simple.

When all of the security team members started firing again, he launched himself from behind the cabinet, crouch-running for the rows of equipment, phaser ready.

Vaughn had just reached the first machines when he heard Kira cry out in surprise and pain, the sound cut off a second later when he heard a deep and loud, echoing *crunch,* and something landed heavily on the platform.

Kira was behind a low console not far from the main banks, and was just readying herself to make a run across the open platform when she saw Vaughn. The commander was making a break for the equipment banks, crouching low, a look of fierce determination on his face.

If they both ran at Kitana'klan, wherever he was among the reactor instrumentation, he could only kill one of them at a time.

Go! Kira launched out from behind her shelter—

—and felt brutal, shocking pain as invisible claws punctured her waist on either side, the crushing force of the grip stealing her breath.

Kira swung both of her arms forward, hitting only air, *behind me*—

—and before she could fire into the space behind her, before she even got her arm up, she heard at least one of her ribs snapping as the shrouded creature squeezed, a terrible, internal bone-sound. She started to cry out and then she was in motion, flying, the console rushing up to meet her face as Kitana'klan threw her into the secondary bank. She felt the right side of her head hitting solid plasticine, she felt something in her upper right arm give way in a wave of dark pain—

Vaughn spun around, the sound coming from near the secondary station where he'd sent Kira so that she might have a better chance—and that was also effectively blocked from the security team's line of fire. They'd stopped firing anyway, as soon as Vaughn had reached the main banks.

He leaned against the end of the front row and shot a look around the corner, silently cursing when he saw Kira's boots sticking out from behind the low console. Acting on reflex, he triggered his phaser and swept it across the open platform a meter and a half off the floor, the bright beam searing the shaft wall before crackling brilliantly across the conduit's forcefield.

Nothing. Kitana'klan would have unshrouded if he'd been hit. *Behind the console? Circling around the core?* Vaughn couldn't randomly fire, couldn't risk damaging the vital controls of the fusion reactors, and the soldier could be anywhere.

He needed to get to the machine that Kitana'klan had worked on, his instincts screaming that time was running out. He'd have to call the security team down, even knowing that some or all of them would be killed trying to get to the sabotaged controls. Beyond that—

—*beyond that, I call Picard and Ro and tell them to get the hell away from here.*

Vaughn reached for his combadge—and felt a hot breath on the back of his neck, and knew he was as good as dead.

With at least twenty platforms to descend, he'd been too late to stop Kitana'klan from hurting the Bajoran Kira Nerys. Once again, he had not anticipated correctly. His failures had already caused enough death; the obvious recourse was to cease failing. Taran'atar quickly moved to be near the silver-haired human, understanding that the whelp would try to kill him next. The human's uniform indicated he was a Starfleet commander with a specialty in command or strategic operations, and therefore a priority target.

Only Jem'Hadar could sense the *di'teh,* the aura of the shrouded, and even then only if they were physically very close. But he remained undetected as he held his position next to the commander; Kitana'klan was too distracted, too intent on his next victim to sense Taran'atar's presence. It was as close as they'd been since their arrival, the best opportunity he'd had with the consistently wary soldier; even as the Starfleet human tensed, Taran'atar was in motion.

He unshrouded as he grabbed Kitana'klan by the throat, holding on tight and diving for the floor. The unsuspecting young soldier was thrown off balance. He hit the platform awkwardly, half on his back, becoming visible as he struggled to get free of Taran'atar's grasp, his concentration faltering.

Kitana'klan was strong and fast but too young, unaware that his lethal rage wasn't enough. Still holding him by the throat, Taran'atar swung himself over the youth's thrashing body, straddling his chest.

Kitana'klan snatched at Taran'atar's throat and face, kicking at his back, his pale eyes shining with murder. The blows were powerful but poorly executed, barely effective. Taran'atar looked down into the young soldier's twisted, ignorant face, and saw himself a long, long time ago.

"Accept death," Taran'atar said, but Kitana'klan still fought. A good soldier. Taran'atar moved his hands to the sides of Kitana'klan's pebbled skull, took a firm grip, and twisted, hard. There was an audible *crack,* a sound of tearing muscle, and Kitana'klan ceased to be.

The battle had lasted only seconds. Taran'atar smoothly rose to his feet, nodding at the silver-haired commander, whose eyes never wavered from his.

"I take it you're on our side," the human said.

"I am," Taran'atar confirmed, matching the commander's scrutiny. Silver hair usually represented older age in humans, he thought. Perhaps he was wise.

"Good to know," the commander said. "We can talk about it later."

The man shouted up at the four others not to fire as he hurriedly dropped to his knees in front of one of the machines, opening a wide panel. Taran'atar crouched next to him, ready to offer his assistance. He thought they might be too late to stop whatever destructive plan Kitana'klan had set in motion; the light of the power channel had started to change, getting brighter, and there was a growing sound, a sound like machinery that was dying, but perhaps the commander could stop it in time.

Taran'atar hoped that it would be so. He could not atone for his mistakes if they all died.

The machine was Federation and it adjusted plasma density. Looking at the numbers on the small internal screen, Vaughn saw what Kitana'klan had done almost immediately. Behind them, the light was growing stronger, and Vaughn thought that the chamber's powerful hum was incrementally higher than before.

Damn damn damn!

The Jem'Hadar had instructed the system to increase density by twenty percent and then shorted the boards, including the alarm sensors. The structural integrity of the fusion reactors had been compromised, and the data indicated that the station's power grid had ceased to accept the unbalanced flow of energy. A buildup was already under way, but if Vaughn could get to the venting system, there might still be time to release the mounting pressure.

The Jem'Hadar who was not his enemy squatted at his side, and when Vaughn stood, so did he. Vaughn shouted up at the security team as he ran to the second bank of machines, the Jem'Hadar still with him.

"Evacuate!" Vaughn yelled, recognizing that they probably only had minutes, wondering why there weren't a hundred other alarms going off. "Get out of here, now, and tell everyone at least two hundred klicks away from the station!"

He didn't bother to see if they'd gone, hunting for the exhaust cone controls. He wasn't familiar with DS9's setup, but the equipment was all recognizable, and the hum *was* getting louder; it might already be too late to vent before the core went supercritical.

"I will aid you," the Jem'Hadar said, just as Vaughn spotted the controls for the cone.

"See if Kira's alive," Vaughn snapped, scanning the console's panels, feeling sweat run down his chest. *There,* emergency functions! Vaughn hit the key and a grid of options scrolled across the monitor. He saw the overload strip and jabbed at the touch square, praying for success—

—and the screen went blank.

No.

Vaughn saw the board access panel and yanked it open, already knowing what he would see. From the convoluted tangle of broken cables, he was surprised that the monitor had worked at all. Alarms weren't going off because it seemed that the Jem'Hadar had smashed the reactor sensor arrays all to hell, or at least the ones that would have triggered an overload alert.

Vaughn couldn't know how much time they had, he didn't know the core capacity or how well the station's systems worked, but he guessed five or six minutes at the outside. They still had time to get to a ship, to get away, but he could hardly see the point; even if the evacuation had been running like clockwork, he doubted very much that more than a few thousand people had managed to get out. Leaving the doomed station, leaving thousands more to die as they commandeered a private ship, seemed cowardly and arrogant.

Vaughn slammed his fist against the useless console, feeling just as useless.

There was no way for anyone to stop it. DS9 was going to explode.

Someone was touching her face.

Kira swam up from the dark sea, feeling terrible, feeling as though she was going to vomit from the pain in her head. The left side of her body felt strange, far away, and when she tried to move, her right arm went white-hot with agony.

She opened her eyes and saw Kitana'klan bending over her, the back of one cold, scaled hand pressed against her forehead. She tried to move away, but her body wasn't listening, her motor skills malfunctioning.

Kitana'klan spoke, but his voice was garbled, only a few clear words reaching her.

"... station ... not ... killed the ... fusion ..."

The station. She remembered parts of what had happened, but her head hurt so much, and she didn't understand what Kitana'klan was saying, let alone why he was talking to her at all, and there was a high-pitched whine in her ears—

—*hum, rising hum, Kitana'klan was at the reactor banks*—

—*overload?*

The thought was more important than her pain. She struggled to sit up, ignoring the torment of her upper right arm, and there was Commander Vaughn, next to her, next to Kitana'klan.

"Help me up," she said, but her voice didn't work, her own words as foreign as the Jem'Hadar's. She tried again, and was now aware that the light around her was getting brighter, that things might be very bad.

"Help . . . up," she managed. Her voice was slurred, and she understood that she'd taken a blow to the head, but didn't care. She didn't care that her assailant, along with Vaughn, was gently easing her into an upright position, and she didn't care about the pain. The station, she had to know what was happening.

". . . core overload, the . . . won't vent," Vaughn babbled.

Kira concentrated as hard as she could, understanding that things *were* bad, they were critical. There had to be something . . .

. . . *get away from it. Get it away.*

If there wasn't any way to stop it from happening, there was only one option left.

"Get me up," she slurred. "Lift. Eject it from the top, my voice. Jettison. Up, we go up."

She must have made sense, Vaughn was talking to the soldier excitedly, and although she didn't want Kitana'klan to touch her, she couldn't stop him from picking her up, cradling her like a child. But she didn't care about that, either.

The station. The station.

Colonel Kira Nerys spoke, her words vague but her voice strong with urgency. Taran'atar understood each word, but didn't know what they meant. The commander apparently did.

"We have to get to the top of the shaft, now," he said, no less urgently than the colonel. "Can you pick her up?"

Taran'atar did so. The colonel was light in his arms, and obviously suffering from a head injury. He could see the swollen flesh just above her right ear, and her eyes were blurred with pain; he thought her arm was broken, too. It was bad, that he'd let this happen.

"*Hurry*, to that lift," the commander said, and Taran'atar held Kira Nerys tighter, running to the caged platform. The rising sound of imminent overload and the now sickly-white light that bathed the shaft lent him speed; death was close for them all.

The colonel gritted her teeth against the jostling motion, but did not cry out or lose consciousness. A good soldier, for a Bajoran.

Odo had not exaggerated her strength.

• • •

Vaughn slammed the lift controls as soon as they were inside—and the open platform, surrounded by a waist-high railing, began to move up, slowly, very slowly. It would take almost a full minute to reach mid-core. He could call for transport, but wanted anyone at the transporter controls to be concentrating on the evacuation. And by the time their moving signals were locked on to, considering the signal interference that was surely being caused by the power build, they'd have already reached the top.

The growing whine of the imminent overload was joined now by a recorded loop, a woman's voice explaining that there was an emergency situation. Her calm voice resounded through the core chamber.

"Warning. Plasma temperature is unstable. Engage liquid sodium loop at emergency venting. Capacity overload will occur in five minutes. Warning. Plasma temperature . . ."

Vaughn tuned it out, willing the lift to hurry.

The Jem'Hadar stood stiffly as if at attention, his impassive gaze fixed on Vaughn, Kira barely conscious in his arms. Vaughn hadn't had time to wonder about the soldier's fortuitous appearance, but as the lift slowly ascended, he remembered Kira's account of the Jem'Hadar strike against the station.

Three ships firing, and one that tried to stop them. All Vaughn knew for sure was that he'd killed Kitana'klan, and that made him an ally.

They were almost to the top, only a few more levels and the lift would reach the base of the station's middle section.

Vaughn reached out and touched Kira's pale face, hoping to any god or prophet who might be watching that she'd be able to function long enough to authorize the lower core break. Her eyes were shut and her forehead was creased, but whether it was in pain or concentration Vaughn couldn't be sure. Her injuries were severe; it was astounding that she'd managed to speak at all. Her solution hadn't occurred to him, DS9 hadn't been built by Starfleet, but her stilted command had been clear enough—although he feared her voice wouldn't be, that the computer might not recognize her faltering commands.

". . . loop at emergency venting. Capacity overload will occur in four minutes."

Even if Kira could pull it off, how long would it take for the fusion core to reach a safe distance?

The lift passed the very top of the straining fuel tower, passed open space, rising through a mostly solid landing. They came to a stop in a circular room lined with blinking lights and flashing consoles. For the first time since coming aboard, Vaughn was struck by the true immensity of the station.

With an obvious effort, Kira forced her eyes open as soon as the lift stopped moving, as Vaughn slammed the low gate open and they stepped out. Ominous light filtered up from the lower core in shafts, the flashing red glow of the emergency panels combining to make unclean shadows.

"Master con," she said, blinking hard. They almost couldn't hear her over the now piercing whine of the overload.

Vaughn looked wildly around the room, spotting the main computer bank at eleven o'clock.

"Over there!"

The Jem'Hadar ran at his side; Kira gritted her teeth against pain as they stopped in front of the master console.

"Down," she said, and Vaughn helped the Jem'Hadar lower her feet to the floor, both of them supporting her.

"... *overload will occur in three minutes,*" the computer noted.

Kira forced her eyes open and saw the controls. The station. The lower core. There was a horrible, wavering sound, high-pitched, like machinery that was about to burst apart from overheating.

My station. My people.

"Hit three-one-four-seven-zero," she whispered, and a hand reached out to the controls, hurriedly punching the code in. She wanted to crumble, to go to sleep, but Kitana'klan held her up and she knew that it was the end. One chance, and then it was over.

Concentrate! The voice of every teacher she'd ever had, every commander, the voice of authority shouting in her aching head. *Do it, get this done, don't fail!*

"Computer, this is Colonel Kira Nerys, initiate ... initiate lower core emergency separation," she said. It took all of her energy to speak. "Authorization Kira Alpha ... One Alpha."

"*Identity confirmed. Request additional authorization.*"

Kira closed her eyes. "Override, Kira Zero-Nine. Disengage and initiate emergency launch ... on my mark. *Mark.*"

Did it, got it done ... Kira's head rolled to her chest, too heavy to hold up, but she kept herself awake; she had to know. And within seconds, she did.

There was a tremendous buckling beneath them, the strange, fierce light from below swirling into shadow with a sound of immense destruction, of meter-thick support beams snapping like twigs, of applied force and ruin. Kira tried to open her eyes and it was dark, she didn't know if the lights had gone out or if she'd managed to open them at all—but that terrible screeching sound had stopped, and she knew that it really was over.

"Did it," she mumbled, so tired that she thought she might sleep forever. And a minute later, when the jettisoned core exploded some 120 kilometers away in a blinding and spectacular blossom of devastation, when what was left of the station shuddered and rocked in the dark, pushed from its position by more than a dozen klicks, Kira Nerys slept on. There were no dreams.

Chapter Fourteen

In all, the injuries from the shock wave had been minor. Crusher had treated three broken arms, a couple of dislocations, and what seemed like a hundred minor lacs and contusions. They'd also had at least a dozen stress patients, all civilian, but nothing a mild sedative couldn't relieve; once Dr. Bashir was out of the woods, Ezri Dax had also lent a few calming words to the frightened men and women who'd dropped by. The other doctors and infirmary staff had been a pleasure to work with . . . most especially Simon Tarses, who, to her delighted surprise, was now a full MD. And as the small hours of the morning crept up on them, all the beds were clear except for three.

Not bad for a night's work. Crusher was tired but content, and although she didn't have to stay, she found herself lingering, enjoying the calm. Word was that everyone was back on the station now, which likely meant no more patients for a while; she imagined that DS9 was sleeping, thousands of people curled up in the safety of their beds. . . .

Crusher yawned, leaning against a wall near the supply cabinets. She knew better. With the station running entirely on backup, there were undoubtedly plenty of people working to stabilize systems and revise repair plans. It was just that curling up in bed sounded so heavenly at the moment—

"Doctor Crusher?"

It was Bashir, again. It was true that doctors made the worst patients. Bashir was pleasant enough about it, but he'd asked twice in the last hour if he could get up.

Crusher moved to the foot of his bed, catching a knowing glance from Dax in the soft glow of the emergency lights. She'd been at his side since he'd come out of surgery, not even leaving to change out of her bloody clothes; at some point she'd grabbed a scrub shirt and donned it where she sat.

"Yes, Doctor," Crusher said, smiling a little.

"My BP and hematocrit are both within normal range, and I'm certain the tissue stitch has set by now," he said, all seriousness. *"I* would release me."

"And if you were on duty, you could do that," she answered. "Another half hour, Julian. Postsurgical standards apply to everyone."

The young doctor sighed dramatically, but didn't argue, turning to gaze up at Dax instead; she smiled, stroking his hair. He'd been incredibly lucky, managing to get a seal patch over his right subclavian artery while he'd been in the process of bleeding to death. He said he couldn't remember it, that he was certain he'd passed out, but there was no other explanation.

Crusher left the young lovers to themselves, wandering over to check on the infirmary's other two patients, both asleep. Another human male, John Tiklak, who'd pitched over a railing when the station had been buffeted by the initial blast, one of his four broken ribs puncturing his left lung, also a fractured navicular of the left wrist; and Kira Nerys, concussion, open humeral fracture, two broken ribs. The concussion had bruised Kira's right temporal lobe, the injury severe enough that she was fortunate not to have suffered any permanent damage. Commander Vaughn had brought her in, explaining that like Bashir, the colonel had been injured by the Jem'Hadar soldier. Crusher hadn't gotten the full story; Vaughn had been in a rush over something and had stayed only long enough to hear that Kira would survive.

Speaking of.

The colonel was waking up, shifting beneath the coverlet, the reads over her bed showing a rise in consciousness. Beverly went to her side, wondering if Colonel Kira would remember that she'd saved the station. From the location of her concussion, Beverly thought it remarkable that the woman had managed to authorize the core ejection; speech, language comprehension, and gross motor skills would have all been affected.

Kira opened her eyes, frowning, and sat up.

"Easy, Colonel," Crusher said, smiling at her, speaking calmly. "I'm Beverly Crusher, the CMO from the *Enterprise;* I believe we met once, several years ago."

Kira nodded, still frowning. "I remember. How's the station? Was anyone hurt?"

Obviously, she was cognizant. "Colonel, everything is fine. You were badly injured by the Jem'Hadar, a concussion and several fractures, but you've been treated, and—"

"Picard to Doctor Crusher."

Still smiling at the young colonel, Beverly tapped her combadge. "Yes, Captain."

"Is Colonel Kira awake? The task force will be arriving in just a few minutes, and Commander Vaughn has called for a briefing as soon as the colonel is able to attend."

Kira was nodding. Crusher would have recommended a full night's sleep, but she was well enough—and Crusher suspected that the colonel wasn't the type to rest when there was station business to be handled. Kira had that in common with Jean-Luc—the belief that unless you were dying, there was no good excuse to delegate your own responsibilities. "Yes, Captain, she just woke up," Crusher said.

"Good. Please inform her that we're meeting in the station's wardroom. Admiral Ross and representatives from the Klingon and Romulan Empires will be meeting us."

Kira leaned and spoke in the direction of Crusher's combadge. "Captain, this is Kira. I'll need a few minutes to confer with my staff before I can be there."

"Of course," Picard said, and Crusher could hear the smile in his voice. *"I look forward to it, Colonel. Picard out."*

"Am I good to go?" Kira asked, leaning back and swinging her legs over the side of the bed. Dax and Bashir both watched from across the room, holding hands and smiling.

"Absolutely. If you feel nausea or any vertigo, I want you back here, though, right away."

"Thank you, Doctor. And thank you for helping out here."

Crusher nodded, thinking of how different Kira looked awake. Asleep, her face had been as peaceful and lovely as a child's. As soon as she'd opened her eyes, her prettiness had become beauty; a level of intensity had been added, a kind of casual confidence and determination that matured her, defining her as a leader.

Kira stood and stretched, then walked over to Dax and Bashir, stopping to talk for a moment. Crusher could see the easy friendship between the three of them, the bond of working and living together in a closed community, and thought of her own friends, and how much she cherished them; Will and Deanna, Jean-Luc, Data and Geordi, her own staff of doctors and nurses and med techs....

She yawned again, smiling at herself. She tended to get sentimental when she was tired. After checking one last time on John Tiklak and seeing that he was already in the capable, caring hands of Dr. Tarses, she put a friendly hand on Simon's shoulder. He looked into her warmly smiling face and smiled back, their shared relief needing nothing more. Then Crusher packed her med kit and went home.

Kira stopped at her quarters for a change of clothes, talking to Shar as she undressed, to Nog as she donned a fresh uniform, and to Bowers as she quickly brushed her rumpled hair. Shar relayed Ro's report, which included the news that the *Tcha'voth* had retrieved the escape pods that had launched; that the partial evacuation and subsequent return to the station had gone smoothly; and that everyone was accounted for. Except for a Bajoran citizen who'd been working in the lower core, a man named Alle Tol. That Kitana'klan had killed only four people during his escape was a small miracle, but Kira doubted that would prove a comfort to Tol's family. She would pray for them.

The upshot of all of the reports was that the station was safe. There had been no new structural damage from the lower core detonation, and although DS9 could operate temporarily with all the emergency generators running at full ... there was still grim reality to face. Unless they could replace the reactor core in the short term, the station would no longer be viable.

One thing at a time.

Kira asked Shar to organize a senior staff meeting for 0900, deciding that they could all use a little extra time in the morning, to recover from the near catastrophe and get some much-needed rest. With Kitana'klan's story having proved to be a lie, she knew they were in for a few tense days or even weeks; the task force would press on with their investigation. If anything, they'd be even more insistent after hearing what Kitana'klan had attempted ...

... except I really thought he was there at the end, with Vaughn. I remember him carrying me. An hallucination, it had to be; she felt fine now, just a little tired, but she'd been in a bad way after the head injury. Julian and Ezri had told her that Kitana'klan was dead, that they'd heard it from Commander Vaughn, who

had also spread the word that she had been entirely responsible for saving the station. As soon as she'd signed off from Shar, Kira was ready to head for her meeting. But as she turned, she caught sight for the first time of the spectacle outside her window.

The Allied task force, a combined armada of Federation, Klingon, and Romulan ships, was far more than she'd expected. She'd prayed she would never again see such a thing in her lifetime . . . because a force like that had only one use, and she knew from personal experience what it was capable of.

Kira hurried out to Vaughn's meeting.

On her way, several people stopped her to ask how she was feeling, or to lend a thought about the generous nature of the Prophets. She'd been unconscious for only a couple of hours, but word had spread—and as much as she welcomed the feelings of community and faith, almost all of the Bajorans she talked to had questions about the book of prophecy. Questions she wasn't prepared to answer.

And now that the immediate crisis of Kitana'klan is over . . .

There was still Yevir, and the book, and the station's strange parallel to the Avatar prophecy . . . what if it *was* meant to come true, in some other way? And while Yevir's patronizing anger hadn't had much of an effect, Kira still had to come to terms with Kasidy's reaction, which had been far worse than she'd expected; she'd foolishly hoped that Kas would be pleased by the upload, happy to see Bajor growing and changing.

There's the Orb of Memory, though. Surely it's a sign, that exposing Bajor to Ohalu's book was the right thing to do.

Maybe it was, Kira thought, stepping into the turbolift. But doing the right thing didn't mean there were only positive consequences . . . and right or not, Kasidy's friendship was important to Kira; she should have talked to her before making any decision.

The turbolift reached the upper core and Kira quickly walked to the wardroom, hoping that Vaughn hadn't held the meeting up for her arrival; stopping to talk to people had slowed her down considerably. She wasn't sure, but thought that Vaughn had probably called the briefing to share his opinions on the task force; she hoped so, anyway. He clearly knew a lot about the Jem'Hadar, and if Picard was any indication, Vaughn was someone whose opinions counted among Starfleet brass.

As she rounded into the conference room's corridor, she saw that she *was* late. Four security guards stood outside the room, a Klingon, a Romulan, and two Starfleet. None of them looked happy to be sharing space with one another.

Nodding to the guards, Kira stepped inside the conference room—and froze, astonished by the scene.

Seated around the long meeting table were two Klingon captains, a Romulan commander, Admiral Ross, Captain Picard, and Commander Vaughn. All of them were looking at a uniformed Jem'Hadar soldier who stood near the head of the table, unrestrained, and no one had their weapons out.

"It's good to see you on your feet, Colonel," Vaughn began, rising from his chair, "but you may want to sit down. I'd like you to meet Taran'atar."

Although they'd asked him several questions, which he'd answered honestly, Taran'atar did not give a full account; Kira Nerys was the one with whom he'd been instructed to meet, and so he waited. When she finally arrived, Taran'atar felt an odd satisfaction that she had survived, of a duty fulfilled. She appeared to be well, and surprised to see him—although no more so than the others in the room had been. The Klingons had drawn weapons before the silver-haired human, Commander Vaughn, had explained his presence to them. Taran'atar thought it fortunate that the commander had intervened. Killing them would have run contrary to his task.

After Admiral Ross quickly made introductions, Vaughn again explained that it had been Taran'atar who had dispatched Kitana'klan, and helped both Kira and Vaughn in their last desperate moments with the lower core. Taran'atar stood and waited for him to finish, noting that Kira watched him almost the entire time.

Vaughn brought his narrative to a close, telling the colonel about Taran'atar's shrouded trip to the wardroom—in order to pass through the station without creating a panic—and Vaughn's decision to call the Allied leaders together, to hear what Taran'atar had to say. Taran'atar found himself wondering about the commander. It was curious; if his information on Alpha Quadrant command structures was accurate, Vaughn was the lowest-ranking officer in the room. Yet the other military leaders, especially the Starfleet officers, gave deference to him. Vaughn clearly did not command them, but they seemed to regard him as an equal, as if his rank were nothing more than a shroud.

"... which brings us to the story of how he came to be here in the first place," Vaughn said. "Which I haven't heard, either. Taran'atar, will you speak to us now?"

"Yes," Taran'atar said, although he'd already decided that preparing for combat was much easier than addressing these aliens.

Victory is life. Conquer this unease, it is your enemy.

"The account Kitana'klan gave of how he came to be among you was partly true," he began, addressing Kira directly. "There was an envoy sent to your station as an envoy of peace, who was attacked by rogue Jem'Hadar who sought to thwart his mission. I am that envoy, chosen by the Founder Odo to live among you so that the Jem'Hadar might come to understand peaceful coexistence.

"After your war with the Dominion, Odo instructed the Vorta to begin a search among the Jem'Hadar for deviants. He believed, based upon knowledge he obtained while living here, that some Jem'Hadar existed who were capable of surviving without the white. The Vorta's search took many weeks, but when it was done, they found only four." Taran'atar lowered his collar, showing them the scar tissue where his tube had once been. "I was one."

"Odo then met with each of us. He asked us questions. He listened. In the end, he chose me to be his messenger."

"Why you?" Vaughn asked.

Taran'atar never took his eyes off Kira. "I am not certain. I think he believed that as the oldest among the four, I was somehow better suited for the task he wished to accomplish. Among my kind, I am an Honored Elder of twenty-two years as you measure them."

Taran'atar saw Kira exchange a look with Vaughn. They said nothing, and when she turned to face him again, he continued.

"I left Dominion space soon after, and had almost reached the Anomaly when my ship was attacked by others of my kind. There are some Jem'Hadar who were displeased when the war ended, and who still believe they need to redeem themselves for their failure to conquer the Alpha Quadrant."

"How many?" Captain Klag interrupted, glowering at him.

"Few," Taran'atar answered. "Among us, disobedience is dealt with quickly and decisively, when detected. The Jem'Hadar follow the will of the Founders, as is the way. And they have not sanctioned any hostilities since your treaty was signed."

The Klingons didn't seem convinced, but the others visibly relaxed.

"Some of these defiant Jem'Hadar learned of my mission before they could be dealt with," Taran'atar continued. "Four strike ships attacked ours, inflicting serious damage, although we destroyed one of theirs. I was contacted by Kitana'klan when our engines failed, who wanted me to know why we had been attacked; he told me that there could never be a peace with the Alpha Quadrant until it belonged to the Dominion, and that by destroying Deep Space 9, a new war would be sparked. A war that the Dominion would win.

"Although our ship was disabled, we succeeded in repairing it enough to pursue the remaining strikers into your space. My crew fought well, but we could not defeat them all. And when I understood that we were about to be destroyed, I transported here."

Taran'atar pulled himself straighter, remembering the courage of his crew. "I would have chosen to stay with my men, who died to bring me here, but death was not my mission."

At this, both Klingon captains nodded, as if they understood. Taran'atar thought perhaps they did.

"What I found out shortly after my arrival was that Kitana'klan had also come here, with a revised plan to destroy you from within. But he knew of my presence, as well, and we remained shrouded, stalking each other as we both sought to draw attention from the station's inhabitants. But Kitana'klan was young and inexperienced. He allowed himself to be detected by the Andorian. Nevertheless, he was able to gain more time to achieve his goal by claiming the peace mission was his."

"Why didn't you reveal yourself when Kitana'klan was discovered?" Captain Picard asked.

"Because Kitana'klan did not transport to the station alone," Taran'atar responded. "Three of his crew were with him, and in the last five days, each has attempted to reach the station's fusion core. I believed my best chance to stop them was to remain shrouded, and watch for them; that is how I learned of their plans, and of Kitana'klan's deception. All three of their bodies can be found in a storage area not far from where the lower section of the station once was. I can show you. I killed the last only a short time before Kitana'klan escaped. But I underestimated his abilities, arriving at the cargo bay too late . . ."

Taran'atar wasn't certain if he should ask about the Starfleet lieutenant he'd tried to help; if he had died, these people might believe he'd inadvertently caused it.

"There was a human in the bay who was bleeding to death," he said, determined to fulfill Odo's expectations of him. "A Starfleet doctor. I tried to stop the bleeding before I went in pursuit of Kitana'klan. Did he live?"

Colonel Kira spoke, for the first time since arriving. "He did."

Taran'atar nodded.

"This is a charming tale," Commander Sartai said, addressing the others, her eyes narrowed with mistrust. "But this creature has yet to offer any evidence that he is what he says he is. For all we know, the real envoy—even if we are to believe there ever was one—could be one of the three he claims to have killed. Where is the proof of his veracity?"

"Here," answered Taran'atar, retrieving from his belt the data chip. "It is from Odo. I was instructed to give it to you, so that you might share the message with others in the Alpha Quadrant."

He held it out to Kira, who made no move to take it. He could see in her eyes that she was unsure of him still. He had failed to convince her. Then he remembered the last words Odo had said to him.

"Hide nothing from them, show them you can be trusted, and only good can come from this."

Taran'atar continued to hold out the chip to her. "I tell you truthfully, Colonel Kira, I still do not understand what I am meant to achieve here, among the same aliens who defeated the Dominion. I was told understanding would come in time, and perhaps that will be so. But for now, all that matters is that a Founder has given me a mission. It is not necessary that I understand, only that I obey. Obedience brings victory. Victory is life. You may be certain that I will do as Odo has instructed me, or die in the attempt."

There was another pause, the people in the room looking at one another uncertainly. Taran'atar knew that all but a few of them had come to discuss retaliation of some kind for the attack on the station; he wondered what he would do if they went forward with those plans.

Everyone was looking at Kira Nerys now, who still hadn't taken the chip from Taran'atar's outstretched hand.

Kira reached out. She accepted the chip, looking at it with a strange expression.

"Let's see it," Admiral Ross said, and Kira handed it to him. Taran'atar found her difficult to read, but sensed a certain reluctance as she parted with the chip. She had been close with the Founder, he knew, in an emotional and physical relationship; perhaps she was angry with him for leaving her.

The admiral plugged the chip into the table's reader and they all turned to look at the viewscreen on the far wall.

Chapter Fifteen

The screen was blank—and then there was Odo, and he seemed to be gazing directly at her, the soft rumble of his voice stirring her deeply, making her throat ache with longing. Everyone else in the room ceased to matter, there was only Odo, and the way he was looking at her.

"This message is for Colonel Kira Nerys of Deep Space 9," he said briskly, but his blue eyes were gentle, the smooth curves of his face as beautiful as she remembered. Behind him, an empty room on a Dominion ship.

Oh, how I've missed you. . . .

"Nerys, I hope that you're well," he said, and she smiled a little. He must have known that she wouldn't be the only person to see his message, and was putting on what she used to call his repressed face. Direct, in control, absolutely on top of things—and beneath it, his kindness and innocence shining through like a bright light he couldn't completely veil. Perhaps she was the only one who saw it, but that only made it more personal for her . . . that she could still read him so easily, that the connection hadn't been severed.

"If you're watching this, you've most likely met Taran'atar by now," Odo said. *"And he has probably explained his presence to you, but I thought you should also hear it from me.*

"You know that ever since we learned how and why the Dominion had created the Jem'Hadar, I've felt a certain responsibility for what my people had done to them. Their lives have only one meaning here, to fight and die for the Founders. And because the majority of them die young, very few of them ever imagine that any other kind of existence is possible. But some do. We've all seen this.

"Among the ideas I've tried to introduce since I returned to the Link is that the Jem'Hadar deserve a chance to be freed of their dependency on ketracel-white, and to evolve without further genetic manipulation." Odo grunted, as if remembering. *"You can imagine the Link's reaction to that suggestion."*

Odo's look suddenly became more intense. *"I have no illusions, I know I can't transform the Jem'Hadar or the Dominion overnight. But it has to begin somewhere. My people once sent out a hundred of my kind into the galaxy to learn what they could, and to bring that knowledge home. I was one of them. It took some doing, but I convinced the Link to let me try the same thing with a single Jem'Hadar.*

"I know the Jem'Hadar aren't all that popular in the Alpha Quadrant, and with good reason, for the most part . . . but I also know that you have nothing to fear from Taran'atar. He's not dependent on white, and he never fought in the war for the Alpha Quadrant. He's there to do as you tell him, Nerys, and to experience living among different life-forms just as I did.

"My hope in sending him to you is that . . . it's a first step, a step toward change. I think you'll find him to be honest and direct, and open to new possibilities. I hope you'll let him stay for a while."

Kira glanced at Taran'atar, his emotions still too alien to be read clearly.

But Kira thought she saw in his face a flicker of something she understood. Acceptance, maybe? Even hope?

"I also want to tell you," Odo went on, "and tell leaders of the Alpha Quadrant, that you have nothing to fear from the Dominion, either. The Link is also in a state of change. We've been . . . they've been considering the insights and experiences that I've brought to them, and will be for some time to come, I expect. You can believe me when I say the Dominion is closing its borders for the foreseeable future. I guess you could say I've given them a lot to think about."

Commander Sartai started to say something, and was hushed by Admiral Ross.

"We stumbled across the Dominion by accident, back before the war started," Odo said. "Most of the people from the Alpha Quadrant simply wanted to explore and to befriend those they encountered . . . and I want you to pass the message along that if the Federation and its allies want to resume that peaceful exploration, the Dominion won't interfere. All the Link asks for in return is to be left alone, until it's ready to initiate contact."

Kira could feel the surprise in the room, but couldn't look away, not now. His repressed face was slipping away, the light breaking through, and he was gazing at her with love and tenderness, the look that had scared her by its intensity in the first weeks of their romance. Now, it filled her with bittersweet joy. She knew that it had been the right thing, Odo returning home to live as he was meant to live, to share with the Founders what he'd learned living among humanoids . . . and it was still the right thing, because she loved him and it was what he wanted.

"Take care, Nerys," he said, his low voice rich with sincerity and a yearning of his own, his gently passionate gaze reaching hers through tens of thousands of light-years.

He reached for something and was gone, the message delivered.

Admiral Ross sat back in his chair, as stunned as he'd been in quite some time. He looked at Colonel Kira first, but quickly looked away, seeing the barely contained emotion on her face. The personal subtext of the message was impossible to ignore, and he felt almost as though they had all invaded her privacy by watching.

The others in the room also seemed surprised, though it appeared that the news had affected each of them differently. Commander Sartai was obviously unhappy, her sharp features set in narrow lines; the Romulan government had pushed harder for the armed task force than any other, so he took her sour face as an indication that she believed Odo's message. Captains Klag and R'taga both glared at the Jem'Hadar, but with less intensity than before, and Captain Picard seemed relieved, his shoulders back, the barest possibility of a smile on his face. Commander Vaughn wore a thoughtful expression, absently stroking his carefully trimmed beard with one hand.

Kira had collected herself, and spoke first. "Is there anyone here who doesn't believe what Odo and Taran'atar have told us?"

A hesitation, the powerful men and women in the room all looking to each other to see. As Ross expected, Commander Sartai answered first.

"I have strong reservations about the supposed truth of this matter," she said, the mildness of her reaction proving that she believed what she'd heard. "I wish to speak privately with the other leaders in my forces before answering."

Both Klingons were nodding, and Captain Klag spoke slowly, his voice gruff but deliberative. "We also choose to confer among ourselves."

Ross thought that both Odo and Taran'atar were telling the truth, but recognized that even if the Romulans and Klingons believed it, they would need to make a show of deciding. With the Federation leading the investigation, he knew his opinion would figure heavily in the final decision—but also that if the other Allies felt pushed, they would resist.

"Considering the evidence, I'm leaning toward Taran'atar's version of events," Ross said carefully. "But we should all meet with our own teams to discuss this new information. Shall we reconvene here in, say, an hour's time?"

"Agreed," Klag said. Commander Sartai and the Klingon captains all stood up, nodding at Ross and at the others—when Commander Vaughn spoke up, seemingly addressing no one in particular.

"Think of it—as long as we don't bother with the Dominion, we'd be free to explore huge areas of new territory. There are unknown worlds to find, new cultures to experience . . . and just think of the untapped resources that would be available to us."

Ross held a straight face, but knew before the others left the room that Vaughn had just decided for them. The calculating gleam in Sartai's gaze, the barely hidden grins of the Klingons—the opportunities were considerable, and too important to ruin with political power plays.

And he knows it. If they weren't a hundred percent before, they are now; the investigation is as good as over.

When they were gone, Colonel Kira broke into a smile. "Well played, Commander. I'm impressed."

Vaughn smiled back at her as he stood up. "Thank you, Colonel."

"Since this is a Federation matter, and you already know where I stand on it, I'll take my leave," she said, and then nodded at Taran'atar. He'd stood silently during the exchange, still watching the blank viewscreen as if he expected Odo to reappear.

"Taran'atar, until I have a chance to explain your presence to the station, I'm going to ask you to stay in one of our guests' quarters. I'll take you to them now."

The Jem'Hadar nodded. "Shall I shroud?"

The colonel hesitated, then shook her head. "We might as well let people start getting used to the idea."

Ross didn't envy her the task of teaching a Jem'Hadar anything, but Taran'atar did seem to be different than most. He told Kira that he'd contact her as soon as the Allies returned, and she and Taran'atar left—after she took the data chip with Odo's message, tucking it into her uniform.

When the three Starfleet officers were alone, Picard turned to Vaughn with a smile. "Nicely done, Elias."

The commander accepted gracefully before turning his sharp, bright gaze to Ross. "Any doubts, Bill?"

Ross shrugged, thinking that Elias Vaughn was one of the few people below the rank of Admiral who could get away with calling him "Bill."

"Personally? No, not really. Though I have to admit, I'd feel a lot better about this if we had some way to test the Dominion's sincerity."

Vaughn smiled enigmatically. "I have a few ideas, but I have to check on a couple of things before I can commit to anything."

The commander excused himself, leaving Ross and Picard alone. They talked casually for a few more minutes about Starfleet business—the rumors about the Romulans making diplomatic overtures to the Breen, the probability of establishing a permanent Allied presence in the Bajoran sector, the mandates currently being reviewed by the Federation Council. Picard mentioned that the *Enterprise* would be leaving shortly, so as not to overtax DS9's limited power reserves . . . which in turn led him to suggest to Ross that every Federation starship in the task force supply one emergency generator to the station. That should carry them through until a permanent solution to the reactor core problem could be found.

Ross approved of the idea, and both officers agreed that Colonel Kira seemed to be handling her command well, stepping into Ben Sisko's shoes without a hitch.

Finally, Picard said he should see to his ship, and Ross decided he should put his call in to HQ . . . and when he stood up, Ross realized that he actually felt physically lighter, as if a weight had been lifted from his chest and shoulders. The nightmare of the last week was over, their journey to DS9 thankfully, mercifully unnecessary—there would be no war, no more Cardassias to mourn.

At least not today, he thought. It was enough.

Once Vaughn made it clear why he was calling, they wasted no time before bringing out their big guns—a four-way conference was quickly set up. Rear Admiral Presley, Vice Admiral Richardson, and perhaps the top mediator/negotiator for Starfleet MI, Captain Lily Shalhib, were online, three people with extraordinary careers in Starfleet . . . and security clearance similar to his own.

Vaughn listened respectfully for a good twenty minutes, faintly amused and a little flattered by how hard they were trying to talk him out of his decision. Captain Shalhib, in particular, was extremely convincing.

"*. . . and security risks aside, it smacks of sheer recklessness,*" Shalhib was saying. "*Really, Elias, I think you ought to take some time to think this through. You're easily one of our best independent operatives, and that isn't something you can expect us to simply do without. . . .*"

When they started to repeat themselves, Vaughn restated his intentions, making arguments of his own. "I'm more than qualified, I have the background, the diplomatic awareness, and the desire."

The nice stopped there. Vice Admiral Richardson shook his head, frowning, and Vaughn could see both Presley and Shalhib steeling themselves for what was coming.

"I'm sorry, Elias, this isn't open to discussion," Richardson said. *"You're too valuable to us, especially now."*

Vaughn's eyes narrowed, thinking that there wasn't a moment in his career when his superiors would *not* have said "especially now." He reminded himself that they were only doing their jobs. "Then I tender my resignation from Starfleet, effective immediately."

They all stared at him, Presley forcing a smile.

"That's a joke, right?"

"Try me," Vaughn said. "I know this puts all of you in an awkward position, but let's not forget, this is my *life* we're discussing. I've made my decision. If you don't like it, I'll take my retirement instead, and go through with my plans as a civilian."

There was a pause, and then Shalhib spoke, suddenly seeming very tired.

"Will you excuse us for a moment, Commander?"

"Take your time," Vaughn said, and the split screen went to standby.

A moment later, they were back—and he knew immediately that he wouldn't have to step down, from the reluctant surrender he saw in their eyes.

"Congratulations, Elias," Presley said. *"Pending final approval from your new CO, I'll have the official order put through within a day."*

Vaughn sincerely thanked each of them and signed off, unable to wipe the smile from his face.

Chapter Sixteen

After the morning staff meeting, Ro walked slowly to her office, thinking over the events of the last few days, both good and bad.

The Allied task force had agreed to stand down in the early hours of the morning, which was good news for everyone. Ro could feel the relief in the air, could see it in the faces of the people she passed. Most of the ships had already left, although a few would remain in Bajoran space, to be on hand for any other surprise visits from the Gamma Quadrant. The news that the Dominion had agreed to allow exploration on their side of the wormhole was already spreading throughout the station; Ro was cautiously optimistic about it, along with just about everyone else.

Three of her officers were dead, killed by Kitana'klan ... who had been killed in turn by another Jem'Hadar, who would be staying on the station. Kira had assured all of them that Taran'atar was atypical, and from his actions so far, there was no argument—he'd saved Dr. Bashir's life and kept the station safe, four times over. Lieutenant Nog had strenuously objected, but after Kira played Odo's message, he'd lapsed into quiet grumbling. The colonel made it clear that she expected all of her senior staff to meet and work with Taran'atar, pointing out that the station population would be looking to them—that his being accepted would depend in large part on how the officers treated him.

Ro had to admit, she was looking forward to meeting him—because of how much she *wasn't* looking forward to tomorrow's memorial service, for the civilian tech and the deputies Kitana'klan had murdered. Wasa, Devro and Cryan had all been good young men, and she'd gladly shake the hand of the man who had taken out their killer, Jem'Hadar or no.

Ro reached the Promenade and started for her office, wondering if Yevir Linjarin was still around. Probably; the prophecy upload debacle hadn't been resolved so far as she knew, and Yevir was definitely not one to let something like that rest. She still planned on filing a report with the Ministry of Justice, but that seemed minor next to Kira's act of defiance. Ro never would have guessed that the colonel had it in her to challenge a vedek, or to choose truth over faith. She knew she was simplifying, knew that Kira still didn't entirely believe in Ohalu's prophecies, but the colonel's belief in the Bajoran people was admirable ...

... though I doubt Captain Yates sees it that way. Unlike the rest of Bajor, Ro didn't particularly care where Yates chose to live, but she sincerely wished the woman luck; she seemed like a good person. If Ro had been in her position, she probably would have lost her mind by now.

Word was going around that Shar's mother had the Andorian seat on the Federation Council, which was quite a surprise. Obviously, he hadn't wanted anyone to know. He'd been uncharacteristically subdued at the meeting, and had seemed reluctant to make eye contact, which suggested he was embarrassed, though Ro couldn't imagine why. She decided she'd seek him out later, just to make sure he was okay.

Ro was so preoccupied with the ongoing complications of life on DS9 that she was actually walking through her office door before she realized that Quark was inside, waiting for her with a steaming mug in hand. She'd been expecting a visit for a couple of days, ever since she first noticed his recently acquired habit of watching her from outside his restaurant.

"Lieutenant, good morning," he said, charmingly formal as he extended the cup to her. "Forgive my presumptuousness, but I've noted that you have a fondness for hot tea, and I've been told that this is an excellent blend. It's very expensive."

Ro paused in reaching for it. "Does that mean I have to pay for it?"

Quark looked faintly wounded. "No, no, of course not! It's a gift. Call it a token of my appreciation for your superb work with the evacuation last night. You know, you really know how to pack a crowd."

She accepted the mug and walked to her desk, smiling at him as she sat down. "Thanks, Quark, that's very considerate of you."

The bartender smiled back, bowing a little and looking up at her over his lashes. "You're welcome . . . Laren."

She sipped the tea, and nodded her approval. "This *is* good; what's it called?"

He hesitated for so long that she was about to ask him again when he suddenly blurted out, "Darjeeling, would you have dinner with me?"

Even knowing that it was coming, Ro felt her heart beat a little faster. How long had it been since someone had asked her to dinner, or looked at her the way Quark did?

"Quark . . ." Ro set her mug down, feeling a little awkward. She was terrible at romantic dealings, having never really practiced. She also actually liked Quark, and didn't want to hurt his feelings.

"Never mind," he said briskly, nodding at her, the open look of hope giving way to a half scowl. "Forget I asked."

"No, wait," she said. "Listen . . . right now I'm going through a kind of—self-evaluation period, I guess you could say, and while I'm flattered by your invitation, the truth is, I really don't want to be involved with anyone right now."

For a split second, she thought she saw disappointment—but then he was grinning, shaking his head.

"Involved? Who said anything about getting involved? I'm talking about eating together, you know, as friends."

Ro was pretty sure she knew better, but if that was how he wanted to handle it, she was willing to play along.

"Oh. In that case, yes. Not tonight, though, I'll be too tired. I've got a lot of work today. In fact, maybe we should wait a couple of days, until things calm down around here."

Quark was entirely too casual, but his eyes were gleaming. "Sure, tonight's bad for me, too. Maybe in a couple of days. Or next week, even."

"Maybe," Ro said, wondering if she'd made a mistake. He was entirely too happy for having just been turned down. "As friends, though, right?"

"Absolutely, you bet," Quark said, backing out of her office, showing most of his teeth in a sharpened grin. "Friends, got it. You won't regret this."

He was gone before she could say anything else. Ro sighed, staring down into her mug of tea, regretting it already. Oh, well; she'd made her position clear, and he'd just have to—

"May I come in?"

Ro looked up, and saw Captain Picard standing in the entrance to her office.

Ro stood up quickly, almost upsetting her tea. "Captain. Yes, of course."

He stepped into her office, standing stiffly as he looked around, and she was more than a little astonished to see him looking uncomfortable. Jean-Luc Picard was *never* uncomfortable.

"So," he said, finally looking at her. "A Bajoran Militia lieutenant, special forces, and chief security officer for the station. It's good that you're putting your tactical training to good use."

There was no spite or animosity in his voice, or in his coolly appraising gaze. Ro nodded, finding that she was still completely intimidated by the man.

"Yes, sir. The rank is honorary. I was appointed here, after the war. Recently, I mean." She mentally slapped herself, her heart pounding.

Picard nodded, still studying her face. "I see. Do you think you'll stay here?"

Again, Ro searched for the anger she expected and again, came up empty. He was simply asking. She thought about his question, thought about telling him she was fine and happy and all settled in, but found that she didn't want to lie. He hadn't come here to condemn her; this was her chance to be honest with him.

"I don't know," she said uncertainly. "I think so, but sometimes . . . sometimes I'm not sure if it's what I want."

"Commitments can be difficult," he said, nodding again. "But there are benefits to following through. You've done well for yourself; perhaps you should stay for a while."

Ro swallowed heavily, no longer able to stand it. "Captain, about what happened—" she began, and he raised one hand, silencing her.

"Everyone has regrets, Lieutenant . . . and the consequences of our actions, of the choices we make, can stay with us for a long time. I only stopped by to say that I hope you won't let your past dictate your future—and to wish you well."

Suddenly, Ro found herself perilously close to tears. She'd betrayed him . . . and it seemed that he had forgiven her.

"Thank you, Captain," she said, struggling to keep a tremor out of her voice and failing, horrified by the thought of breaking down in front of him.

Picard took pity on her. "Well. Good luck, Lieutenant."

He nodded once, then turned and walked out, straightening his uniform as he disappeared into the crowd on the Promenade.

Ro sat down, elated and weak with gratitude, depressed and uncertain of everything. She stared at her cup of tea until she felt the threat of tears pass; it was ice cold before she felt ready to move on with her day.

After saying good-bye to Colonel Kira in her office—and receiving more of her sincerely felt appreciation for the delivery of the Orb—Picard headed for the *Enterprise,* thinking that he was glad he'd gone to see Ro Laren. There had been a time when he'd felt only anger and disappointment at the thought of what she'd done; after the faith he'd placed in her, her abrupt decision to join the Maquis—and to sabotage a Starfleet operation, in the process—had been a surprise, to say the least.

Something about her had always appealed to him on some fundamental level, though he'd never been able to quantify those feelings to his satisfaction . . . and still couldn't, not really. The need for second chances, perhaps. All he knew was that when he'd seen her yesterday, when he'd seen the open self-doubt and shame in her eyes, he'd realized that he didn't want her to carry such sorrow on his behalf. It was as simple as that.

An exciting and unusual day, all in all, he thought, stepping from the pylon turbolift to head for his waiting ship. From the Orb to an evacuation, to a Jem'Hadar ambassador and the changes his presence had wrought, Picard was quite satisfied with their stop at DS9. He was sorry they couldn't stay longer, but the ship needed a more extensive maintenance than DS9 could currently provide; Starbase 375 wasn't too far away, and the crew still needed to stretch their legs. He thought they might stay there for two or three days, let everyone take a few deep breaths before they continued on with Starfleet business. . . .

"Captain, would you mind if I accompanied you to the bridge?"

Vaughn was standing just inside the outer docking port, smiling. Picard shook his head, glad to see him; he'd planned on asking the commander to come to the ship before they disembarked, knowing that Will and Deanna, at least, would want a chance to say good-bye. And he wanted to know if his suspicions about Vaughn's future were correct.

"Not at all," he said, and the two men stepped on to the ship, heading for the turbolift. They stood side by side, speaking without looking at each other as the lift ascended to the bridge. "I suppose you know what I did," Vaughn said.

Picard smiled. "I had my suspicions," he admitted, "especially once you mentioned having ideas about testing the Dominion's sincerity. This puts you in quite an extraordinary position, Elias. You'll be taking point in the renewed exploration of the Gamma Quadrant, if Starfleet approves it."

Vaughn grinned. "Hell, even if they don't approve it," he said, as the lift halted and its doors opened.

They strode together to the center of the bridge, Geordi reporting from the aft engineering station that the *Enterprise* was in good shape for their trip. All of the senior staff were present, and when Vaughn revealed his plans, the reception was overwhelmingly positive. Even Data turned on his emotions just for the experience; he put on a grin and warmly shook Vaughn's hand, congratulating him heartily.

After Deanna had embraced Vaughn, promising to keep in touch, only Picard was left to bid the commander farewell. They walked back up to the turbolift together, neither speaking until they reached the doors.

Picard smiled, extending his hand. "It's been a pleasure, Elias. I sincerely hope we'll have an opportunity to work together again."

Vaughn reached out to clasp Picard's hand with both of his own. "As do I. Jean-Luc, thank you for everything."

"You're welcome, sir."

With a final grin, the commander stepped onto the lift and the doors closed, taking him to his future. Picard went to his chair, and Will began the process of leading them away from Deep Space 9, communications calling ops, Data laying in a course for Starbase 375.

A remarkable turn of events. Picard decided he'd have to make a point of bringing the *Enterprise* back this way in a year or so, time and circumstances allowing. Elias, Ro, the colonel, Taran'atar; it would be interesting to see what developed.

"Take us out," Riker said, and Picard leaned back in his chair, wishing he'd taken Elias horseback riding, deciding that he would indulge himself soon after they were under way; life was too short not to take full advantage.

After Picard left Kira's office, she decided that it was time to reveal the Orb to Vedek Capril. With all that had happened since the captain had presented it to her, there'd been no opportunity—and though she'd wanted to track down Shakaar and tell him first, she now thought that it might be best to let the station's vedeks handle the revelation. Her plate was full enough without having to manage the fervor that a returned Orb would create.

Kira stepped off the lift onto the Promenade, and headed straight for the shrine. She could hardly wait to see Vedek Capril's reaction, or Vedek Po's, or that of the prylars who assisted them. The Orb, Kira was certain, would bring some much-needed harmony to her people, as a sign that the Prophets were still with them.

An account from the Bajoran Chamber of Ministers had come in just before Picard had stopped by, reporting that mass gatherings were being held all over the planet, confused and worried citizens meeting to talk about Ohalu's book. It had been fourteen hours since she'd uploaded it, and although the prophecies had apparently stirred up plenty of unrest, no one was panicking, or rioting in the streets, contrary to Yevir's assertion. A new dialogue had been created, that was all, and Kira believed that the returned Orb would ease any turmoil in that dialogue. She was grateful to the Prophets for allowing the Orb to be found and brought back to Bajor; it was one of the few bright lights in days of darkness, along with the message from Odo. . . .

Kira wasn't ready to let Odo in, not quite yet. The feelings were simple but the thoughts weren't, and she'd have plenty of time to miss him in the days to come, after the station was repaired and its population was at rest. She pushed the image of his well-loved face out of her mind, thinking instead of Taran'atar, of how to introduce him to the station—

"Nerys."

Kasidy was standing near the doors of the temple, her arms crossed, her shoulders hunched with tension. Kira looked around, and saw that a number of Bajorans had stopped in the middle of the Promenade, talking to one another softly as they stared at Kas. Kira felt herself flush with guilt, and hurriedly stepped into the temple, beckoning for Kas to join her.

The shrine was empty and quiet, the attendants apparently all in the back offices, the lights low. Kira turned, looking into Kasidy's face, and saw a careful guardedness in her usually mild brown eyes, a caution that had never been there before. Knowing that it was her fault made Kira's heart ache.

"Kas, I . . . I'm so sorry," she said, wondering if she'd ever be able to make it up to her.

Kasidy nodded. She didn't seem angry so much as resigned, which was much worse.

"You did what you had to do," Kas said calmly. "I wish you hadn't, but I understand why. I might have done the same thing myself, if I were you."

Kira shook her head. "If I'd known what this would do to you, I would have thought twice," she said, hoping that Kasidy believed at least that much. "But all of this will go away, I promise, and sooner than you think. The people of Bajor care about you, Kas, they're not going to turn your life into some kind of a . . . a religious attraction."

"You're right," Kas said, still calm and matter-of-fact. "Because I'm going to Earth, to be with Jake and Joseph, at least for the duration of my pregnancy. I'll be leaving day after tomorrow . . . and I may not be coming back. I don't know yet."

Kira felt her stomach clench, a rush of desperation and denial moving like heat throughout her body. "Kasidy, no! Your house is finished, and all of your friends are here—please, please don't go, not because of what I did. What can I do, how can I fix this?"

Kasidy reached out and touched Kira lightly on the arm. "I don't blame you, and you shouldn't blame yourself. It's just—I woke up this morning to find something like eleven thousand messages posted to me, on the communications net. I read about fifty of them, but it was enough—Nerys, some of those people were offering to *die* for me, to be part of the sacrifice for the Avatar. For my *baby*."

Kira felt sick. "Oh, Kas, I'm so sorry. I'm sure that it's just a few people . . ."

She trailed off, realizing that it wouldn't make a difference. Even one was too many.

Kasidy smiled faintly. "It's okay. I wish I could stay, but I just can't handle this kind of stress, not now. My body can't handle it. This is for the best. And maybe I will come back, once things die down a little."

Stricken by the hollowness of the statement, Kira searched for something else she could say, something to make things right again, but she was grasping at air. Kasidy gave her arm a squeeze before turning and walking out, leaving Kira alone.

Kira sat down on the back bench, closed her eyes, and started to pray.

Chapter Seventeen

Commander Vaughn found Kira in the Bajoran shrine just off the Promenade. When he stepped into the temple's entrance, he didn't see her at first, and wondered if the computer had steered him wrong. The shrine itself was lovely, the complete lack of ornate or lavish trappings adding to the atmosphere of faith and good feelings. A light scent of incense and candle wax lingered in the still air.

Vaughn took a few more steps inside and saw the colonel, kneeling in the back of the room to the far left, where she'd been blocked from sight by the entrance wall. Her eyes were closed, and he realized she was meditating or praying, her still face tilted upward slightly. Not wanting to interrupt, Vaughn started to back quietly out of the room, thinking that he could approach her about the XO position later.

Kira opened her eyes, turning to look at him. Her features were relaxed, but somehow not serene, as though she'd just woken from an unhappy dream.

"Hello, Commander."

Vaughn smiled. "Sorry to interrupt—perhaps we could meet when you're finished . . . ?"

"That's all right," she said, pushing off her knees and sitting back against the rear wall of the shrine. "I'm having a little trouble concentrating, anyway. Have a seat."

Vaughn joined Kira on the floor next to her, wondering what was wrong. She definitely seemed tense, and perhaps a little sad. Kira didn't strike him as someone who would be comfortable sharing her emotions with a virtual stranger, so he didn't ask.

"I never got a chance to thank you, for what you did last night," she said. "If you hadn't been there, a lot of people would have died. You were instrumental in saving the station."

"I really just helped *you* save it," he said, and took a deep breath. "Though as long as you're thinking well of me, how would you feel about keeping me around? I noticed you have an opening for an executive officer, and I'd very much like to fill it."

Kira hesitated, then slowly nodded, smiling a little. "That would be great, assuming Starfleet is agreeable. . . . You're overqualified for the position, if you don't mind me saying."

Vaughn grinned, feeling as though the last piece of a puzzle was fitting into place. "I've already worked that out, actually. My, ah, superiors have agreed to it, as long as you're not opposed to the appointment."

Kira looked a bit puzzled. "I was under the impression that your background is primarily tactical. . . ."

"It is," Vaughn said. "But I had an experience recently that made me want to try something else. An Orb experience, actually."

Kira's eyes widened. "Captain Picard told me you found the Orb, I can't believe I forgot to thank you—you have no idea how much this means to my people."

"Actually, maybe I do, a little," Vaughn said, smiling. "Did the captain tell you that when we found it, the ark was open? Everyone on the away team was affected. For me, it was . . . it changed me. It made me realize that I didn't want to be doing what I was doing, which is a big part of why I want to be your second."

Kira was nodding, a look of real understanding on her face. It was a look that made Vaughn feel safe to tell it all, a look that told him she knew the power of the experience.

"I don't want to fight anymore, Colonel," Vaughn said. "I want to be here. I want to be a part of the changes that are happening, here and now. When I was on that freighter, remembering who I once wanted to be, reliving experiences that I worked so hard to forget . . . I saw that it wasn't too late for me."

"The Orb was on a freighter?" Kira asked. "A Cardassian freighter?"

Something in her tone gave Vaughn pause. "That's right," he said. "The *Kamal*. It was trapped in a conflicted energy mass, had been for at least three decades."

"Were there Bajorans on board?" The look on Kira's face told him that she was more than simply curious.

"Yes."

"Did you . . ." Kira took a deep breath and blew it out. Her expression was almost fearful.

No, not fearful. Awed.

"Did you find the Orb in a cargo bay? With Bajorans and Cardassians?"

Vaughn nodded, wondering if Picard had mentioned it, knowing already that he hadn't. "Yes."

"I dreamed it," Kira said wonderingly. "The day that the Jem'Hadar attacked the station. I dreamed that I was in a lost freighter, in a cargo bay. And all around me were Bajoran refugees, and their captors, and they were dying—"

"—asphyxiating," Vaughn said.

"—and there was a light in the back of the bay—"

"—and Benjamin Sisko was there," Vaughn said, taking a chance. He hadn't told anyone else, but she knew already, not a trace of surprise on her face as she nodded.

They stared at one another, Vaughn not sure what it meant, not sure that he had to know. He remembered telling Jean-Luc only a day before that strange things happened, things that might never be explained.

There might never be an answer to how it had happened, but Vaughn thought he knew why.

"I was meant to find it, and bring it to you," he said, knowing that he couldn't back it up, that there was no proof beyond the dream of one woman and the exceptional experience of one man. It didn't matter. It was true, and Kira knew it as well as he did.

"Welcome to Deep Space 9, Commander," Kira said softly, and although he hadn't been assigned quarters, hadn't even seen a quarter of the station or met more than a handful of people, Vaughn thought that he was probably home at last.

When she was alone again, having sent Vaughn to ops to introduce himself around, to find quarters and get situated, Kira went to the private room where the Orb of Prophecy and Change sat on its low pedestal. She closed the door behind her and went to the storage cabinet where the Orb of Memory was hidden, still waiting to be given back to the people.

Kira gently lifted the precious ark out of the cabinet and placed it on the floor, kneeling in front of it. The Prophets had been trying to tell her something, all along, and she hadn't understood—but she understood now. Vaughn was right; he'd been meant to find the Orb, and she'd been meant to receive it. And the only way for her to find out *why* was to open the ark, to let the Prophets speak to her, if They saw fit.

She closed her eyes for a moment, silently reciting a prayer of thanks for all of the gifts They gave, and opened the ark, the beautiful light of the Prophets filling the room, the room disappearing until there was only Their will, Their strength.

Chapter Eighteen

Yevir had stayed in his quarters since returning from the aborted evacuation. He wouldn't be able to get a shuttle seat for another day—departures to Bajor had been cut in half because of the fuel shortages—so he spent a fair amount of time doing what he could to manage the situation from the station.

He spoke with Vedeks Eran and Frith, who had already called for a full Assembly meeting, to discuss how best to handle the crisis. Over the next few days, Eran said, they expected hundreds of vedeks to travel to the Assembly hall, to collaborate on an official assertion of denouncement. The book of lies had already been publicly condemned by the Assembly, of course, but it would take more than a simple statement to silence the public outcry. Yevir wondered how long it would be before the first Ohalu cults sprang up, growing from the disease like poisonous flowers.

And all because of Kira Nerys.

The thought of Nerys's incredible, terrible act had made sleep impossible, and prayer nearly so. Yevir had spent much of the night pacing his rooms, unable to concentrate on his love for the Prophets, to find solace in Their embrace. He tried to console himself with thoughts of petitioning to take her command away, perhaps even finding a way to force her to leave Bajor, but it didn't help him find peace. The damage had been done, out of blindness or malice, he couldn't be sure, but he knew that guiding Bajor through the resulting spiritual chaos might very well take years.

Which was why, when the companel in his room chimed, the last person he expected it to be was Kira Nerys, speaking without a trace of apology, not even a hint of shame. If he needed any more proof that there was something wrong with her, the obvious self-satisfaction in her voice was it.

"Vedek Yevir, would you come to runabout pad C, as soon as possible? You might want to bring your things with you, too. We're going to Bajor."

She commed off before he could ask any questions.

Yevir considered ignoring her request, but returning to Bajor as quickly as possible was in the best interests of the people . . . and to be truthful with himself, he was afraid that he wouldn't be able to find forgiveness for Kira.

When he'd turned his life over to the Prophets, he'd let go of anger and prejudice and malignity, leaving behind those things that separated him from Their light. He knew he was only mortal, but Their Touch, through the Emissary, had relieved him of pessimism and negativity. His heart had been opened to greater things . . .

. . . but how do I forgive such a staggering disdain for faith, for the Prophets themselves?

He didn't know. What he did know was that he didn't want to wait another day to return home; the Assembly needed him, they needed a strong hand to lead, so that they could lead others. He quickly gathered his things and headed for the bay, wondering why Kira wanted to go to Bajor. She'd already created havoc enough, even insulting the Emissary's wife with her blasphemous designs . . .

. . . which was why he was surprised when he stepped into the runabout airlock and saw Kasidy Yates standing with Kira, near the runabout *Euphrates*. Ro Laren was also there, just inside the ship's entrance.

"Ready to go," Ro said.

Yevir slowly walked toward them, not sure what to expect—and saw that Kasidy and Ro both wore similar expressions of uncertainty. Only Kira seemed to understand what was happening, and as he drew closer, he was shocked to see the light that emanated from her, the blazing eyes and tranquil demeanor of one who has recently been with the Prophets.

How can that be? It didn't seem possible, but the effects of an Orb experience or vision were unmistakable. Her *pagh* radiated both strength and placidity, her gaze on fire with comprehension.

When he reached the trio of women, Kira smiled at him. "I'm glad you decided to join us, Linjarin."

"What's this about?" he asked curtly, not at all sure he liked what he was seeing. How could They speak to her, after what she'd done?

The Prophets are wise in all things, he hastily amended. It wasn't for him to question.

"Funny you should ask," Kira said, still smiling. "Because I'm not really sure myself. We're going to B'hala, I know that much . . . and I believe I'll know what to do when we get there."

Yevir nodded, knowing that sometimes it was like that, still not quite understanding why They'd chosen her—and he realized that his concerns about finding forgiveness for Kira Nerys weren't about his *capacity* for that forgiveness . . . they were about his desire. Prophets help him, he didn't want to see her absolved, because she didn't deserve it.

"Shall we?" Kira asked, lit from within by awareness.

Ro and Kasidy turned and walked to the open hatch, and clutching his bag, Yevir reluctantly followed.

After the strained and silent journey to Bajor—except for Colonel Kira, who was perfectly content to sit smiling to herself—Ro was more than ready to get off the runabout. Yevir had been relentlessly moody, stalking around the *Euphrates* like a troubled child, pausing occasionally to gaze at Captain Yates with adoring eyes. Yates had ignored him entirely, only holding herself and exuding a kind of soft sadness. Ro normally didn't mind avoiding conversation, but the atmosphere had been strangely tiring, and when they finally arrived, she was the first one on the transporter pad.

When they materialized at B'hala, in a clear-front office near the top of the city, Ro was amazed at just how huge the dig actually was—before them stretched a vast pit, filled with levels and layers of unearthed ruins, those at the very bottom so far away that it felt like they were standing in front of an optical illusion.

I had no idea it was so . . . beautiful. Religious significance aside, the crumbling city was magnificent to behold, speaking to the longevity and tenacity of Bajoran culture. The afternoon sun spread across the city in long shadows, dappling all of it in lovely, random patterns of light.

While Kira spent a few minutes talking with someone who worked at Site Extension, whatever that was, Ro gazed down at the ancient buildings and spires, her hands pressed to the cool window. Yates and Yevir stood on either side of her, also looking down, expressionless. Ro wasn't sure exactly what Kira was planning, but decided she was glad she'd come along, if only to have seen such an eternal and glorious thing in her lifetime.

When Kira rejoined them, she carried four light sticks and a small rock hammer. She seemed to have come down a little from whatever Orb high she'd been on, but she was still glowing too much for Yevir's taste, Ro could see it in the set of his jaw.

"What now?" Yates asked quietly, as Kira passed out the lights.

"Now we transport to where the book was found," Kira said.

"Why?" Yevir asked, still endeavoring to wear his pious serenity like some kind of armor. "And why the hammer? B'hala is sacred ground, it's not open to anyone who feels like participating in the dig."

Kira smiled, shrugging. "I still don't know why, exactly. All I know is that there's an answer here, close to where Reyla found the book."

Kira gave the coordinates to the young ranjen who was operating the transporter, clicking on her light stick as they returned to the pad. Ro did the same—

—and was glad she had, when they materialized in a small, dark place a second later, underground cold, the air suffused with the smell of age and dust.

As Kas and Yevir turned on their lights, Ro saw that they were in a small room, empty except for a long, low shelf made of stone, a few broken clay pots—and an open space at the base of the far wall, where someone had recently been excavating.

"That's where she found it," Kira said, her voice hollow in the empty air. Yevir actually shuddered before turning away.

"Come this way," Kira said, walking to the uneven arch that marked the entrance to the room. There was a corridor past the arch, obviously newly unearthed, great piles of dusty, untouched stones randomly strewn throughout.

They walked in a line behind her, Ro bringing up the rear, nervously wondering how far down they were and where Kira was leading them. The darkness was oppressive, swallowing the light, a total blackness reclaiming the ground as they walked on. For some reason, Ro felt very small, as though they were a line of tiny insects crawling through a universe of tunnel.

Finally, the meandering corridor stopped, a dead end of fragile-looking stackstone, the slaty layers eroded by tens of thousands of years. Kira stopped, turning to face them. Her face was eerily lit by the glow of the sticks, her eyes like dark holes.

"Here," she said, almost in a whisper, handing her light stick to Ro. "This is as far as they've dug down; we're at the very bottom of B'hala's very lowest level. The farthest from the city's center, too."

"Do you know why yet?" Yates asked, also keeping her voice low. It somehow seemed obligatory, not to speak too loud in such a deep, dark place.

"I think so," Kira said. "It's about you, Kas. And about the book, and your baby."

Without another word, Kira turned and struck the face of the dead-end wall with the rock hammer, the *chink* of the stone being hit somehow not as loud as Ro would have expected. Layers of gray stackstone, pitted and brittle, fell at Kira's feet as she pounded the wall twice, three times, a fourth—

—and on her fifth strike, she broke through into an open space, the sound of the hammer disappearing into a seeming abyss beyond the wall.

Kira dropped the tool and pulled at the ragged edges of the hole with both hands, the brittle rock coming off in plates. In only a minute or two, she had opened a space large enough to step through.

"What is this?" Yevir asked, not so haughty in the darkness, his voice hushed.

"Let's see," Kira said, still smiling. She took her light stick back from Ro, turned, and stepped through the opening, leaving them no real choice but to follow—Yates first, then Yevir, awkwardly pulling at his robes, and finally Ro.

Kira held up her light as soon as she stepped through, seeing the place to which the Prophets had led her . . . and the full understanding of her Orb experience came into her grasp, the information They'd secreted in her mind moving into her awareness.

In front of her and to either side, stretching away for kilometers, she knew, were corridors upon corridors of rough-hewn crypts, natural and created, openings in the rock where thousands of bodies—ten thousand—had gently mummified or decayed to dust, millennia ago. Each had been sealed by cairns of stone, each closed space undisturbed by time or the elements.

Behind her, Kasidy drew a sharp breath. Yevir said nothing. It was Ro who broke the silence, holding out her light stick, her voice a rough whisper in the echoing dark.

"The prophecy of the ten thousand," she said, and Kira nodded, walking toward the nearest crypt-riddled wall, the truth spilling out as it reached her conscious mind.

"These are the remains of the men and women who kept Ohalu's book safe," she said, her light shining down on hundreds of carefully placed rocks, just for the crypts that were closest. She knew that each individual tomb throughout the extensive network had been sealed the same way, a testament to the binding strengths of their convictions. "They were brought here one by one and in groups, through the centuries, all long before B'hala was lost. Ten thousand of them."

"So many . . ." Yevir said, a thread of discouragement in his soft voice. Kira didn't know if his despair came from the vast number of "diseased" Bajorans, or the realization that the supposedly profane prophecy was true. Nor did she care; Yevir would have to find his own peace with it.

"Despite the prevailing orthodoxy that sought to suppress it, all of these people knew that Ohalu had been Touched," Kira said. "They refused to hide from the truth, that the Prophets could also be experienced as teachers—and they protected the book, because of the prophecy of the Avatar."

She turned to Kasidy, smiling at the absolute wonder—and relief—on her face. "They lived and died for the hope that the birth of your child would one day represent the promise of a new age for Bajor. The birth itself will be a catalyst of a kind . . . but your baby will be your own, Kas, not some symbol, or representation. You don't have anything to fear."

Even as she was speaking, Kasidy walked toward the beginning of the corridor to their left, raising her light stick. There was an opening in the wall that hadn't been sealed, a pile of rocks on the ground next to it.

"Why is that one empty?" Yevir asked tonelessly.

Kira knew, not sure if the final clarity came from the Prophets or her own understanding—but it was Kas who answered, turning back to look at Yevir, wearing the tiniest curve of a smile.

"It's for the last guardian of the book," she said. "It's for Istani Reyla."

Chapter Nineteen

Vedek Yevir Linjarin walked to the center of the small stage, holding his head high. Nearly everyone on Bajor would be watching, he knew, and it was important for them to see that their spiritual leaders had not lost their dignity or their poise.

Yevir ignored the recording cameras aimed at the podium, instead addressing the vedeks and ranjens who had gathered at the indoor arena, placing his hands on the pulpit and gazing up into their ranks. Hundreds of them, yet it was so silent, he imagined that they could hear the beating of his own heart.

Only the truth. The Prophets deserve no less.

"Only two days ago, an unacknowledged book of prophecy was uploaded into Bajor's communications network, anonymously," he began, his voice carrying through the room. A strong voice; the voice of a leader.

"The Vedek Assembly had heard of the book, but until it was placed in the public domain, none of us had read it—and I must admit, some of us were afraid . . . at first. Afraid that the Prophets would somehow be overlooked in the controversy that was inspired; afraid, perhaps, of the Bajoran people finding out that we knew of this book, but had never spoken of it."

Nods from the assembled now, as they heard and acknowledged him.

"I want everyone to know, to understand—it was I who pushed for this book to be condemned," he said, finding strength in sharing his awareness of his faults. "I was afraid, because I looked away from the Prophets. Because for a moment, I forgot how strong, how open the Bajoran people are. I forgot that we have always looked for the truth, no matter what form it takes, and that the Prophets would never—*never*—send us anything we couldn't learn to accept. The Prophets love us; we are Their children."

He could feel himself gaining momentum, could feel it reflected back at him by the men and women watching. His words held power, because they were the truth.

"I was afraid because of my own lack of faith in Them. For all of the boundless love and respect I feel for Them, I followed my first inclination—to protect Them from secular thoughts, from secular ideas. To my shame, I didn't want the Vedek Assembly's authority to be challenged, because I thought that meant some people might turn away from us—and in turning away from us, that they would turn away from the Prophets. I was wrong. I was unworthy."

Hundreds of faces frowning, shaking their heads in disagreement.

"I might have continued on my narrow path, if not for the miraculous return yesterday of the Orb of Memory," he said, wording himself carefully now. "The Orb, which showed us the truth of the book's final prophecy—the prophecy of the Avatar, the Emissary's child, who is not yet born."

Slow, lingering smiles of faith throughout the rows, gazes filled with the knowledge of miracles.

"The Orb has come back to us . . . and I stand before you today to address the meaning of its return, as I see it. People are beginning to criticize the unyielding stoicism, the elitist conservatism that the Assembly has come to represent to so many of you. People are expressing interest in philosophical debate, in new interpretations of truth . . . and what *I* believe is that the Orb stands for more than the Prophets' love. I believe that it's also a sign, a sign that the Prophets choose for us to be open to change. They want us to look into our pasts, to learn from our experiences, and to use our collective knowledge to rise to the challenges of our future."

A low murmur of assent rose from the assembled. Yevir felt humility in the face of such understanding, he felt their trust in him grow as he revealed his mortal flaws. It was right and true, that he should lead the revolution for change, that the Prophets had ordained. Why else had They sent him to DS9? It had all been destined from the start.

"I know it may seem strange, that I would want to tear down the very system that has allowed me this voice, that has made it possible for me to stand here, telling you what I believe," he said. "And I'm not saying it *should* be torn down. All I mean to say is that like all of you, I am here to serve the will of the Prophets—and those among us who turn away from Their light have no place in the Bajor of tomorrow, because our lives and our world, our changing views and our established tenets, everything we do, we do for Them. It is all part of Their loving plan for us."

Yevir smiled, nodding humbly. "Thank you for listening. Walk with the Prophets."

Acceptance flowed from them like water, enveloping him in warmth and forgiveness. Yevir closed his eyes for just a second, knowing that he had reached millions of people the world over, knowing that the Prophets, too, were watching; praise be.

"What a load," Quark grumbled, turning away from the viewscreen. Morn nodded, raising his glass to the observation. At least Kai Winn hadn't hidden her insatiable craving for power; Yevir Linjarin was apparently going for some kind of humility award for *that* little performance, but it had MEGALOMANIAC written all over it. Either that, or he was a serious fanatic; either way, Bajor was in for a ride.

Quark wouldn't have bothered watching, except he knew that practically every Bajoran on the station had been permafixed to their monitors for the duration of the much-heralded speech—and it always paid to know what the zealot faction was up to. Besides, he'd already stopped taking bets on Yevir for kai, and was interested to see the man in action. From the looks of things, the only way he could lose now would be if he got caught beating up children, or delivering a sermon in the nude, something like that.

Morn was starting to get sloppy, talking about how much hair Linjarin had, so Quark casually moved to the other end of the bar, to better indulge one of his two new favorite pastimes: thinking about his impending dinner with Ro. The other was fantasizing about Shar's mother visiting the station and asking for Quark's advice on the Alpha Quadrant's economy—just as exciting, but nowhere near as immediate.

He'd already decided to take Ro to a holosuite, and to wear the new coat he'd special-ordered—off-the-rack was for losers, at least when it came to impressing the ladies; it was one of the very few expenses that he didn't skimp on, often—but he was still debating the perfect environment. He didn't want to be too obvious, so the sex palace program was definitely out . . . but maybe the harem room, minus the harem. Lots of pillows, and plenty of that veil-y fabric hanging all over the place. They could eat toasted tubeworms and drink sweet *p'losie* wine—he had a case of the stuff that was about to turn—a little conversation, a little music . . . she said she didn't want any "involvement," but Quark was a romantic at heart; he'd wear her down. He'd woo her until she couldn't think straight.

He had just formed a perfect mental picture of her in one of those teeny little harem outfits, all delicate and wispy except for a pair of gravity boots and an intimidating sneer, when the bar's companel signaled. His daydream dissolved into Morn's sloppy face, which happened to be in the way of Quark's unseeing gaze. Talk about a lobe shriveler.

Scowling, Quark smacked the panel with one fist. "What?"

"You get more and more charming every day," Kira said, her voice dripping sarcasm.

Quark made a face. "Sorry, Colonel. What?"

"I want to have a senior staff gathering tonight, in the meeting hall across from the jeweler's. Kind of an impromptu welcome for Commander Vaughn and Taran'atar."

Quark backpedaled like mad. "What a wonderful idea! Colonel, I have to say, you're . . . well, just so generous when it comes to showing your staff how much they mean to you," he marveled, throwing his heart into it. "But you know, if you really wanted to make them feel like a part of our small, close-knit community, you'd have your party *here,* where everyone could join in. You know, so that our new friends can really get to know the people they'll be living and working with every single day—"

"Drinks and appetizers for, say, fifteen people, for two hours, 2100 on," Kira snapped. *"Make it nice and I'll see that you get an extra hour of computer time every day this week."*

"You're such a good person, Colonel, I mean that," Quark said, but Kira commed off before he could push the dessert option. Too bad, but the extra time was incentive enough; he'd been having to run the holosuites off his own reserves, which didn't come cheap, and Kira had flat-out refused to reimburse him for the expense. As if she *hadn't* been the one who'd authorized dumping the station's entire fusion core. . . .

Ro was senior staff.

"Grimp!" Quark screamed, the server nearly dropping a tray of glasses at the sound of his own name. Worthless slug.

As Grimp scurried toward the bar, Quark made a mental list of what needed to be done to get ready for the party—and after a discreet sniff, he added taking a shower, or at least splashing some of that special cologne on, the stuff that all the *dabo* girls had commented on. He remembered that even Leeta had been impressed, telling him that she'd never smelled anything quite like it—

At the other end of the bar, Morn let out a huge, gaseous belch and blinked his watery eyes, his upper body weaving back and forth as if in a strong wind. Quark shook his head, wondering how it was that some people managed to get along without even a shred of class or culture.

Some things, even latinum couldn't buy. . . .

Once they reached the meeting hall, Taran'atar stayed near the door, wondering if he was supposed to approach any of the assembled. There were only six others besides himself—Kira and Vaughn, Dr. Bashir and a female Trill, and a Starfleet tactical lieutenant. The sixth was a Ferengi, bearing plates of food and drink. On the way from his quarters, the colonel had suggested that he just be himself, but that meant not speaking unnecessarily; he wanted to follow orders, but after watching the gathering for a short time period, he saw that talking to others seemed to be the purpose.

Still, Taran'atar was unsure of the appropriate action. Colonel Kira had officially announced his presence to DS9's population hours ago, but had explained to him afterward that it might be some time before he was "accepted." He didn't understand how that could be—what was there to accept? He was on the station; it was a fact. Perhaps she had been speaking figuratively—

Two people were approaching, Dr. Bashir and the Trill. They smiled, and were touching hands as they walked. Taran'atar prepared for the confrontation; he was to be himself. They stopped in front of him, and he saw that Dr. Bashir carried a small plate holding slices of unknown fruit.

"Taran'atar, I'm Ezri Dax," the Trill said, her smile fading as she looked up at him. "I want to welcome you here."

Taran'atar nodded, accepting her statement.

Bashir was also serious now, properly establishing sincerity just as the woman had. "Taran'atar, I just wanted to say again that, ah, I'm grateful to you for saving my life."

"You owe me nothing," Taran'atar said firmly, recognizing the burden of obligation Bashir had expressed. This was going well, their interchange.

"Come with us," Dax said. "We can help you interact with the others. If that's your choice."

Taran'atar nodded again, remembering what Kira had said at the meeting of his explanation. An expression of appreciation. "Thank you."

The doctor and the Trill exchanged a look, and then both were smiling again. Taran'atar hoped he had spoken appropriately. Never in all his years had he felt so lost, so far away from the reality he understood best, but he would learn. Odo had singled him out, had spoken his name; Taran'atar would watch and learn, or, as he vowed to Kira Nerys, he would die in the attempt.

• • •

Shar joined the party a few minutes late, wishing that the colonel had been less adamant about attendance. Since the call from Charivretha, he'd spent his off-duty hours alone in his quarters, aware that his parentage had become common knowledge; he didn't want to talk about it, and had begun to avoid social interaction.

Before he'd taken a single step into the room, Quark was at his side, holding up a tray of vegetable pieces. A strange odor surrounded him, though Shar didn't know if it was the vegetables or Quark himself.

"Shar! I'm so glad you could make it, I haven't seen you around for a couple of days. Try these—fresh Bajoran vegetables, marinated in *p'losie* wine. Exquisite, don't you think?"

Shar nervously took a piece and tasted it, aware that Quark was one of those who would be treating him differently since learning about *Zhavey*. "Very good. Do you know if Nog is coming, or Lieutenant Ro?"

"Of course! Are you kidding? They're both your friends, right? Nog is a wonderful boy, I'm just thrilled that the two of you have become so close. Any friend of his, you know? And Ro . . ."

Quark grinned, lowering his voice slightly, speaking in a conspiratorial way. "Why do you think I'm wearing this cologne? It cost me a pretty strip, I don't just put it on for no good reason. What do you think?"

It smelled vaguely like deuterium fumes on a hot day, mixed with something organic and possibly decomposing.

"I've never smelled anything like it," Shar said honestly, and Quark nodded happily.

"*Exactly*. Say, as long as we're talking, I've been meaning to ask you—I had this really incredible idea about establishing new shipping lanes into the Beta Quadrant, and—"

"Hey, Shar."

Shar turned, grateful for the interruption. It was Nog, just arriving.

"Nephew, how nice," Quark said through a gritted smile. "I think Colonel Kira wanted to see you about something. . . ."

Nog pointed across the room. "Look, Lieutenant Bowers is holding an empty glass. You're not catering for a flat fee, are you?"

Quark hesitated, then grinned at Shar again. "If you'll excuse me . . . perhaps we can pick this up again later."

Shar put on a smile for Nog as Quark swept away. "Hello, Nog."

"You'll have to excuse my uncle," Nog said, smiling back. "He thinks that if he can get in good with you, he'll have an inside line to the Federation Council."

Shar felt that too-familiar ache inside, his heart growing heavy and sinking, but Nog wasn't finished.

"Like anyone cares who your mom is. My dad's the Grand Nagus of Ferenginar, but what does that say about me? Nothing, that's what."

Shar blinked, looking into Nog's earnest face—and felt something starting to loosen inside.

"You don't care . . ."

"About your mother?" Nog asked. "Why would I? I don't know her."

Nog abruptly narrowed his eyes, looking across the room to where the Jem'Hadar was standing with Dr. Bashir and Ezri, the three of them talking to Commander Vaughn.

"Have you met him yet?" Nog asked.

Shar shook his head, still feeling that sense of release in his chest, feeling good for the first time since *Zhavey* had called. It didn't resolve the big problem, about what he was going to do—but if Nog didn't care about Charivretha zh'Thane . . . perhaps there were others who didn't, either.

"Well, Kira can make me talk to him, but she can't make me like it," Nog said. "And if he didn't have Odo vouching for him, I would have put in for transfer already."

"You respect Odo," Shar said.

Nog nodded. "Yeah, I guess I do. He scared me when I was younger, always checking up on me . . . but he treated me okay once I grew up a little . . ."

He trailed off, staring at Taran'atar, then looked back at Shar, visibly brightening. "So, I guess we're going to be working together for a while, on the *Defiant*. Kira says that they are going to be refitting it for two science labs, biochem and stellar cartography. It's going to take *weeks* to get everything up and running. Ensign Tenmei is supposed to drop by later, so we can start talking about the new navigation-sensor patch."

Shar nodded, wondering if he would still be on the station when it was all finished, hoping very much that he would.

"What do you think they will do about the station's fusion core?"

Nog broke into a grin. "I can't believe I forgot to tell you—I think I have the solution! I just need to make sure the numbers work, but if they do, and if I can convince the colonel to let me go ahead with it, our power problems will be over in a week!"

Shar was skeptical. "A week."

"Two, tops," Nog guaranteed. "Come on, let's go get a couple of drinks, and I'll tell you all about it."

When finally Julian got back with their drinks—Quark had run out of synthale, and dashed off to the bar to get more—Ezri and Vaughn were smiling at one another like old friends, Vaughn nodding and shaking her hand.

Julian handed Ezri her drink and Vaughn excused himself, taking Taran'atar with him to meet Lieutenant Bowers. Ezri was glowing.

"I take it your conversation went poorly," Julian said, smiling. Across the room, he saw peripherally that Ro Laren and Kasidy had just arrived, and that Quark was practically running to greet them.

Ezri grinned up at him. "I'll have you know that you're looking at *the* unofficial assistant commander for the *Defiant*'s first trip into the Gamma Quadrant."

"Ezri, that's wonderful," he said, meaning it. "And you're sure this is what you want . . ."

"Positive," she said. "And Vaughn's going to include his recommendation along with Kira's, that I'm put on a command track."

Julian touched the rim of her glass with his, feeling a sudden wave of warmth and love for her. They'd had several long talks since he'd woken up from surgery, about needs and expectations. Ezri's sudden decision to transfer to command was something of a surprise, but she said that she was ready to commit herself . . . one of the immediate results being that she wouldn't need *quite* so much space to figure out what she wanted to do.

"I just finally realized that with as much potential as I have, I could stand around for years contemplating my choices," she said, lying in his arms, her ever-cold hands in his. "I want to get on with it, that's all. I'm ready."

Julian had surprised himself by trying to talk her out of it, afraid that she was only reacting to his near-death experience, but she insisted that while her fear had played a part in her resolution, it wasn't the only reason.

"You're worrying again," she said. "Quit it, Julian. I made up my mind, and I'm happy with my decision."

"Yes, but I don't want you to feel like—"

"—I don't," she said firmly. "And it might do you some good to remember that as much as I love you, you're probably going to be calling me 'sir' before too long."

Julian lowered his voice, leaning in. "I can call you sir now, if you like."

Her eyes sparkled as she looked over the rim of her glass. "Ask me again later," she said.

Julian promised her that he would.

Vaughn was enjoying himself thoroughly, talking and watching and relaxing. Kira was in a fine mood—and no wonder, she'd told him all about the prophecy situation and its outcome earlier—and though he'd already been impressed by her command in crisis, seeing her at ease and happy cinched his feelings. He was going to like working for her.

So far, he'd liked everyone he'd talked with. Vaughn had met most of the senior staff yesterday, and thought them a good mix. The only one he hadn't met formally was Ro Laren, and when he saw her talking to the Ferengi bartender, he started edging in her direction. Taran'atar, a little baffled but still game, was listening intently to Lieutenant Bowers recommending sociology texts he should look into.

Quark was smiling up at Ro with the unmistakable demeanor of the hopelessly smitten, shooting an unhappy glance in Vaughn's direction when he approached them.

"Nice party, Quark," Vaughn said. "Though I should probably tell you, that fruit wine of yours is right on the edge of going bad."

"I'll have to look into that," Quark said blankly, then smiled at Ro again. Vaughn noticed an odd smell coming from him.

"So, tomorrow night it is," Quark said, and Ro nodded. With another sullen look at Vaughn, the Ferengi hurried away, a definite spring in his step, taking his odor with him.

"Lieutenant Ro, I'm Elias Vaughn," he introduced himself, extending his hand. Ro shook a little hesitantly, but her grip was firm.

"Commander," she said, only meeting his eyes for an instant before looking away. He wasn't surprised; her disastrous reputation in Starfleet preceded her, and he knew from her files that she was something of an introvert.

"I hear you were top of your class at Advanced Tactical," Vaughn said. "You know, I helped design part of their curriculum. I'd be interested in hearing what you thought of the entire training experience; we should get together some time."

Ro nodded, her surprise showing in the slight widening of her eyes. "Sure. That would be fine. I'm sorry, Commander, if you'll excuse me . . ."

"Of course. Nice meeting you."

Ro quickly walked over to where Shar and Nog were, both young men greeting her warmly. Interesting; Vaughn looked forward to knowing her better. She'd led a life of extremes, and he found that while real adversity destroyed many, it also sculpted its survivors into some of the most intriguing personalities he'd ever known.

He wondered if she had any idea what Picard had done, after word had started to spread that she'd resurfaced on Bajor. Starfleet had been ready to clap her in irons and put her away for good, Bajoran government or no Bajoran government. But something about this woman had affected Jean-Luc profoundly, despite her betrayal. He'd actually lobbied command behind the scenes on her behalf, quietly but insistently, until they agreed to let the Ro Laren matter drop. Starfleet might never go so far as to issue her a formal pardon, but because of Jean-Luc Picard, they would let her be.

Vaughn noticed that Taran'atar was starting to look a touch uncertain as he sniffed the air around Quark and went to rescue him, as happy as he'd been in years.

Ensign Prynn Tenmei ran her fingers through her short black hair and checked one more time to make sure her combadge was on straight as she strode toward the hall. She'd been so busy dealing with the *Defiant,* then the evacuation and its aftermath, that she'd only learned about the new XO and the welcoming reception an hour ago. One shower and fresh uniform later, she felt ready to meet her new commander, and she was determined to make a good first impression.

Tenmei took a deep breath, then another, stepped through the doors . . . and refused to believe what she saw.

Vaughn.

Oh, God. He's the new first officer?

He stood there, talking to the Jem'Hadar with a slight smile on his face. Shaking with rage, Prynn turned before she could be noticed and bolted out the door. She walked quickly away, headed for her quarters. After a few seconds, she broke into a run.

Nerys had gone out of her way to invite Kasidy to the welcoming party. Kas had debated not going, but finally decided that she would stop by at least long enough to announce her decision, maybe longer depending on how she felt. She ran into Ro just outside the meeting hall, and the two women walked in together in a companionable silence. Kas liked Ro; she thought Bajor could use a few more like her.

Ro was immediately all but tackled by Quark, and looking around, Kasidy realized that she didn't want to stay; she wasn't in the mood for light conversation or company, although she had to admit that seeing Taran'atar for the first time definitely captured her attention. It wasn't every day that one saw a Jem'Hadar at a cocktail party.

Kira was talking to Ezri about something, but when she spotted Kas, she quickly extricated herself and hurried over, smiling a little anxiously.

"Kas, I'm so glad you decided to come."

Kasidy smiled, looking into her concerned, searching gaze and seeing how much Kira still wanted their friendship. She was glad for it, but also knew it wasn't ever going to be the same.

"Actually, I'm not staying," Kasidy said. "I'm feeling a little tired ... but I wanted you to know that I've decided to go ahead with my plans to move to Bajor."

Relief flooded Kira's face. "That's wonderful. I just know it's the right thing for you, Kas, after all you've done with the house, and ... and how much you've wanted it."

Kas patted the noticeable swell of her belly, thinking of Ben, thinking that there was just too much tying her to Bajor now. Wondering what her child's life would be.

"You're right," she said, softly. "It's what I want."

Only moments after Kasidy left, Kira got a call from ops; a personal line from Bajor was waiting in her office. Vaughn was in the middle of telling a pretty funny anecdote about having to take the academy flight test with his very first hangover, but Kira didn't like leaving people on hold; she quietly excused herself from the small audience and slipped out of the meeting hall, hurrying across the Promenade to a turbolift.

On another day, she might have been annoyed at having to leave in the middle of such a pleasant gathering, but she was just too happy. Commander Vaughn was going to make an exceptional first officer; he was emotionally balanced, bright, experienced—and his brush with the Prophets made him the perfect choice for a Bajoran station.

An Orb is home, Bajor is opening up to new ideas, I have a great staff and great friends ... and the station is safe.

Kas's plans to leave the sector had been the only thing that had still felt unresolved, and though Kira had hoped that the revelation of B'hala's secret crypts would change her mind, she hadn't been certain. Now, she felt a sense of completion, of things coming full circle—from her early-morning dream of a dying freighter and Benjamin to here and now, riding the lift to ops and knowing that she had a party of new and old friends to return to, she felt like she'd grown. She felt like for the first time in a while, there was nothing dark hiding in her life, waiting to surprise her.

She stepped into ops, nodding and smiling at the evening shift as she walked to her office. Not everything was perfect, of course—but happiness wasn't about achieving perfection. For her, happiness was about hope and feeling loved, about being competent at her job and in touch with herself, with her faith.

Life was good, maybe as good as it got.

Chapter Twenty

Ro saw Kira leave, and found herself talking to Shar with one eye on the door, waiting for the colonel's return. After about ten minutes, she decided it might actually be better if she could have a few minutes with Kira in private. Besides, Quark was starting to circle again, and he smelled like he'd taken a shower in lightly rancid fuel oil.

Ezri said that Kira had been called to her office, so Ro slipped out of the party and headed for a turbolift. When the doors opened into ops, she saw that Kira was sitting at her desk, alone.

As Ro walked closer, she realized that Kira was working, a stack of reports in front of her and one in hand. She didn't want to interrupt the colonel, but Kira didn't know that she'd already filed her investigation report, and Ro wanted to make sure that Kira was ready for any fallout.

When the office doors slid open, Ro knocked on the doorframe and Kira looked up, obviously preoccupied.

"Colonel, I'm sorry to bother you . . ."

"That's all right, come in," Kira said, setting the padd aside.

"I just wanted you to know that I sent my report on Istani's murder to the Ministry of Justice," Ro said, the doors closing behind her. "I included everything, but I kind of figure that with the killer dead, no one is going to want to look too hard at the Assembly's involvement. Anyway, I thought you should know, they may have some questions before they close the file."

"Thank you," Kira said. "Listen . . . I meant to tell you before that you did an exemplary job with the evacuation. With the investigation, too. Really outstanding work."

"I—thank you," Ro said, flustered and pleased. Kira had never said anything as nice to her, and it felt amazingly good, touching off a flush of warm pride.

"I was too quick to judge you, Ro, and I hope you'll accept my apology."

Ro hadn't planned on saying anything, but Kira's praise had caught her off guard, surprising her into it.

"Colonel, I should apologize, too. Being too quick to judge runs both ways, and I haven't made it easy for you."

Kira smiled slightly, but seemed to be looking past Ro, her thoughts elsewhere. There was something different about her, something . . .

"Maybe there comes a point when we all need to start again," she said, brushing her hair behind her ears.

"Colonel, your earring," Ro said, immediately scanning the floor in front of Kira's desk. The clasp must have broken; she'd never seen Kira without it.

"I took it off," Kira said, still wearing that little smile, but Ro saw a profound sadness in her eyes. "It seems that Vedek Yevir got the last word, after all. I've been Attainted."

Ro stared at her. "You mean . . ."

"I mean that I am no longer welcome within the Bajoran faith," Kira said calmly. "I'm forbidden from entering any temple, nor can I study any of our prophecies, or wear my earring, or look into an Orb, or even pray with other Bajorans. Ever."

Kira's voice caught just a little on the last word, and she quickly swallowed it down, not sure why she'd told Ro, of all people, Yevir's calm and self-righteous expression still clear in her mind, his voice repeating over and over again.

"When you chose to go against the word of a vedek, you turned away from Their light, Nerys. I had no choice but to make the recommendation, and the Assembly agreed . . ."

She saw the open compassion and pity on Ro's face, saw that Ro was about to tell her how very sorry she was, and Kira suddenly realized that she couldn't bear it. That the words would kill her.

"Ro, I have work to do."

Ro nodded, seeming to understand, and that was awful, too. Without saying anything else, she turned and left the office. Kira picked up the report she'd been reading and found where she'd left off, concentrating, refusing to be beaten by one petty man, refusing to think of what he'd taken from her.

She still had her work; it would have to be enough.

Epilogue

It had been long enough; nothing was going to happen. It was time to go back.

Jake sat at the shuttle's controls, his shoulders slumped, a few empty ration packets cluttering the console. The flight plan was up on the screen, all set to retrace his path back to the station, and he couldn't help thinking that it looked a lot like failure. Nearly three full days, and all he had to show for it was a pinched nerve in his neck, from falling asleep in the pilot's seat on the second night. He hadn't brought a med kit, and all the *Venture* had on board was a few bandages and a half-empty tube of medicated foot lotion.

Jake massaged the sore muscles, scowling, focusing on the ache because he didn't particularly want to keep thinking about his grandiose washout. He'd already decided that when he returned to the station, he would tell his friends what he'd done. He didn't care anymore about being embarrassed. Dad was still gone and he'd let his own wild hope talk him into a big, stupid fantasy. He'd lied to people he cared about, but he could fix it . . . and maybe by talking to Ezri and Nog, to Kas, he'd be better able to come to terms with how he was feeling about his father.

And not just the good stuff, either. Jake loved and missed him terribly, but there was also a little anger, and some hurt. Dad was off having this incredible, enlightening experience, because it was his destiny . . . but whatever he was to the Prophets, he was also Jake's father, and that relationship mattered. Yes, Jake was old enough to be on his own, but did that mean he was just supposed to let his father go with a smile and a wave?

Maybe so, Jake thought, and for the first time since Dad had gone, the thought wasn't a bitter one. Now that he was about to leave, about to let the prophecy go, he realized that his trip to the wormhole had brought him closer to an acceptance of the situation than all those weeks at B'hala. Maybe part of the reason he'd struggled so hard to avoid dealing with it was because he didn't want to feel angry or hurt . . . and he didn't want to accept that his father had willingly left him behind.

And that's okay. I don't have to be perfect . . . and neither does he.

He was disappointed that the prophecy hadn't come true, no question, and he wasn't looking forward to confessing his bizarre mission—but he *was* looking forward to going home. Maybe he would start another book, or look into the Pennington School again, after Kas had the baby. Maybe he could do a lot of things, and when Dad *did* return to linear space, he'd be proud that Jake had gotten on with his life.

Jake straightened in his chair, feeling okay, feeling hopeful and a little bit excited about all of the possibilities in front of him. Not great, but not so bad, either. Maybe he'd misunderstood the prophecy, or it had never been real, or it wasn't even meant for him. Whatever it was, he suddenly felt like he hadn't wasted the last three days, after all.

"Going home," he said, tapping at the controls, telling the *Venture* to return him to the station. The shuttle had drifted some, but he'd be back at DS9 within the hour.

Jake hit the command key—and the shuttle spun around suddenly, the sensors reading a massive flush of energy surrounding him. They'd been out of whack for his entire trip, but he hadn't seen anything like this.

"Onscreen bow," he said, hearing the quaver of sudden hope in his voice, trying not to read too much into it—

—and what he saw on the screen made him laugh out loud, a pure sound of delight and wonder.

It's true, it's all true!

Swirling, dancing colors filled the screen, red and blue, white and purple, every color he'd ever seen in a kind of flowering mist. It was all around the *Venture,* streams of light flowing past the tiny ship in ribbons and waves. He could feel the power and the presence of consciousness, of an awareness, and his surprise was surpassed only by his joy; he might have been ready to let it all go, but it wasn't necessary anymore, the Prophets had come and he would see his father again, he'd be able to bring him home—

—except the colors were moving faster now, and the sensors told him that the shuttle was going too fast, that it was starting to spin as it was carried deeper into the wormhole.

A second later the artificial gravity went, and Jake grabbed for the straps of his chair, not laughing anymore. The ship was going even faster, he was getting dizzy and an alarm started to flash and beep, then another, then a third. His stomach lurching, Jake stabbed at the controls—and there was no response.

"Stop! Stop it!" Jake shouted, an empty ration pack flying in front of his face, the colors in front of him getting brighter, becoming blinding. The *Venture* couldn't take much more, it was going to tear apart, and his head was spinning along with the colors, they were blazing but things were getting darker, he was sick and he felt like he couldn't breathe—

The shuttle started to shake violently and all of the alarms died at once when the power cut out.

Just before Jake lost consciousness, he saw his father's unsmiling face in his mind's eye, he saw his father reaching out to touch him, and he thought that he might be dreaming, after all.

ABYSS

David Weddle and Jeffrey Lang

To Alexis Quartararo, who showed me that to discover strange alien life-forms I
needed to look no farther than the parking lot of the Woodley Market.

D.W.

For Jim McGuire
Who taught me something about the abyss
and
For Lane Carpenter
Who knew some things about how to get out of one.

J.L.

"For every Julian Bashir that can be created, there's a Khan Singh waiting in the wings."

—STARFLEET REAR ADMIRAL BENNETT

Chapter One

Something was almost ready to come out of warp. Something very big.

It was tripping all of Deep Space 9's proximity alarms, lighting up the sensor board in ways Ensign Thirishar ch'Thane had never seen before. If the readings were accurate—and he was certain they were—a subspace displacement of almost unheard-of proportions was heading directly for the station and playing havoc with the long-range sensor arrays. Shar found himself struggling with his console, fighting back his mounting frustration as each klaxon he muted was quickly replaced by another.

The sudden pins-and-needles sensation in his antennae alerted him to the fact that Commander Vaughn was standing just behind him. Shar tried not to look flustered; the commander had a casual manner about him much of the time, but Vaughn was always an intimidating presence. Most Andorians cultivated a polite, soft-spoken demeanor, even—some might say *especially*—when they were about to slip daggers between each other's ribs, but Shar was still adapting to Vaughn's habit of shifting back and forth between easygoing civility and Starfleet formality.

"Cardassian control interfaces take some getting used to, don't they?" he asked gently, sipping the noisome beverage Shar had learned was called "twig tea."

"Yes, sir," Shar admitted, thoroughly embarrassed. After six weeks as DS9's science officer, he thought he'd finally mastered the idiosyncrasies of his own console. To have the station's new first officer witness his sudden ineptitude was mortifying.

As if sensing his thoughts, Vaughn leaned over for a better view of the readings. "Relax, Ensign," he said. "Given the circumstances, it's no wonder the arrays are going haywire. Stay with it."

Shar let out a breath and concentrated. As he moved his long fingers over the board again, the klaxons finally began to diminish. When the last of them was silenced, Vaughn patted him on the shoulder. "Good. Whenever operating alien technology, I find it's usually helpful to keep in mind the psychology of the people who created it. In this case, extremely detail-oriented, exact, and thorough. Redundancies in the system are a given."

"I'll remember that, sir," Shar said.

"Something coming in?"

Shar looked up to see Colonel Kira standing in the open doors of the station commander's office, her voice echoing loudly in the otherwise quiet operations center.

Returning to his position at the central ops table, Vaughn set up an interface with Shar's sensor board. "Certainly looks that way. Something quite large, coming in at low warp."

"Nog?" Kira asked, coming down the stairs to join Vaughn.

"It had better be," the commander said. "If it isn't, we're going to become a multi-gigaton smear of debris across the Denorios Belt."

Kira ignored Vaughn's commentary as she studied the tabletop display. "But no hail?" The question was directed at Shar.

"No, sir," Shar replied, "but we anticipated this. Something this big coming out of warp, when you consider the disruption to subspace, it's to be expected . . ." But Colonel Kira wasn't listening anymore. She was watching the track of blips on the table.

"Does it look to you like he's giving himself enough room to brake?" Kira asked Vaughn.

"It depends on how much momentum it had when Nog took it into warp," Vaughn said. "Let him do his job, Colonel. He seemed to know what he was doing. The kid is smart. And he has style to burn."

"Style," Kira repeated. "Nog?" She seemed to be having trouble forming an association between the two words.

"Sure," Vaughn said. "His little scheme. His solution for . . . all this." Vaughn waved his hand around the dimmer-than-usual operations center. Many of DS9's nonessential systems had been shut off during the ongoing state of emergency. Ever since the colonel had been forced to jettison the station's fusion core, DS9 had been running on a complex network of Starfleet emergency generators. The measure had bought them time, allowing the station to continue functioning, albeit at only a third of its normal power consumption. But after two weeks of running at full capacity, the system was showing the strain. In the last few days alone, entire sections of the station had been evacuated and powered down so as not to further overtax the generator network. In fact, with the exception of the scheduled aid convoys to Cardassia Prime and the three Allied ships patrolling space near the wormhole, DS9 was currently turning away all traffic.

The pulse of the station had slowed to a sluggish thud since Kira had ejected its great heart into space. The explosion, according to the Bajoran news feeds, had been visible across most of the planet's nightside, appearing like a new star just as the westernmost cities were slipping into evening and those easternmost were turning off their lights for the night. Young children had run outdoors thinking it was fireworks for a holiday while their grandparents, recalling the arrival of the Cardassian occupation fleet, had fought to keep them inside.

Shar was both intrigued and somewhat perplexed by the behavior of some of his crewmates as conditions aboard the station deteriorated. The more the place began to feel like a frontier outpost, the *happier* some of the old hands seemed to be. Dr. Bashir was practically giddy about it sometimes. Shar had begun to form the opinion that these people were in serious need of some leave time, a *lot* of leave time. *This is what happens,* he told himself, *when you associate with prophets, ghosts, and demons.*

Shar's attention swam back to the conversation between the commander and the colonel. "I admit I've been skeptical about this all along," Kira was saying. "But I hate to discourage Nog's initiative ..."

"... and you didn't have any better ideas," Vaughn finished for her.

"Something like that," Kira said. Shar wondered if she minded that the commander finished sentences for her. Then again, he decided, the colonel seemed like the sort who would finish sentences for her commanding officer. He hadn't yet been asked to sit in on a briefing between Kira and her Bajoran superiors. *Now, that would be interesting,* he decided.

So far, there hadn't been any discussion about what would happen if Nog's plan didn't work, but Shar could not find it in himself to be too optimistic about DS9's future. The Cardassian station was thirty years old, and despite all the reengineering that Starfleet had put into it, it had taken quite a beating in recent years. Perhaps it would be a mercy to send the station spinning into Bajor's sun and start over fresh. In such a scenario, considering the strategic importance of the wormhole, it seemed likely that Starfleet would insist on constructing a new starbase, a project that would certainly cause controversy and discord among the Allies, unless Bajor's latest petition for Federation membership were put on a fast track. The Federation was war-weary and its resources were stretched thin. The Council would bend a polite ear to listen to all sides, but when it was done, they would send in the Starfleet Corps of Engineers no matter what anyone said. Shar knew how politics worked. Better, in fact, than he really wanted to know.

"Anything on the short-range sensors, Ensign?" Kira asked.

Shar blinked, then said, "I was told that the short-range array was to be taken offline until further notice. Sir." Shar attempted to project a mental image of Commander Vaughn issuing the order. He knew that Bajorans were no more psionic than most Andorians, but he thought it was worth the attempt.

Vaughn, apparently, had better than average psionic abilities for a human, because he picked up Shar's distress call. "I gave the order, Colonel," he said. "The patrol ships are more than capable of covering our front yard."

"I don't remember authorizing that," Kira said, and Shar felt himself singed by the heat of the glare she focused on Vaughn. He fought the urge to scratch his left antenna.

"You didn't," Vaughn said agreeably. "I decided to shut them down yesterday." He took a sip of tea. "You were busy dealing with the Cardassian liaison at the time. I didn't want to bother you with it. It was an easy choice: short-range sensors or lights."

Shar watched as the colonel held her first officer's gaze for a moment. He knew that Commander Vaughn's job had once been hers. Not long ago, it had been *her* responsibility to know *everything* that happened on the station. Shar had heard that she went through a similar period of adjustment with Vaughn's predecessor, Tiris Jast, and wondered how much Kira still blamed herself for Jast's tragic demise ... and how much that misplaced guilt played on her natural impulse to micromanage the running of the station. Shar knew enough people with command responsibilities to know that one of the worst things about being promoted was coming to grips with the idea that you had to trust someone else to make some of the decisions.

Kira, it seemed, was still making that adjustment. Her apparent frustration didn't evaporate, but it did recede significantly. "Right," she said. "Lights. Good call, Commander."

Shar felt his own tension diminish just in time to hear Lieutenant Bowers report from tactical that he was receiving warning flashes from all three patrol ships, each going to heightened alert status as the monstrous subspace displacement closed on the Bajoran system. Shar shot a questioning glance toward Kira, and waited for her nod before bringing the short-range sensors back online.

He found himself wishing he'd kept them off as he looked at the readings, cursing softly in his native tongue when he saw that the disruption to subspace had intensified markedly. The colonel didn't seem to notice his outburst, more concerned with instructing Bowers to activate the main viewscreen, but Commander Vaughn shot him a warning glance that indicated he might know some Andorii.

The viewscreen came online and Shar tried to divide his attention between the image on it and his console. Space split open with a rapidly dissolving warp field. Time seemed to slow down as the aperture continued to expand, stretching so wide that for a moment, in spite of everything he knew to the contrary about what was unfolding, Shar wondered if DS9 would be pulled inside.

Instead, something emerged. Led by a single runabout, nine assorted Federation starships moving in carefully calculated formation dropped out of warp as one, the bright blue cones of their tractor beams strategically distributed over the tremendous mass of their shared burden. How anyone had talked nine starship captains—not to mention their chief engineers—into even attempting such a thing, Shar couldn't guess. He didn't need to imagine the complex level of calibration and coordination that the operation required, or who was behind it; Nog had transmitted his revised plan before it had been implemented, and everyone but Commander Vaughn had pretty much decided that he was out of his mind. The computer models, not to mention Deep Space 9's increasing desperation, had finally convinced Kira that they had nothing to lose, and Shar privately began to suspect that the colonel shared Vaughn's apparent taste for audacity.

Shar saw the warning signs in the data stream flowing across the board, then looked back up at the viewscreen, expecting to see warp nacelles blowing out, warp cores ejecting, and clouds of white-hot plasma venting . . . but instead he saw something else:

Salvation.

He looked at the colonel. She was smiling—no, grinning—then whooping with triumph as she madly pounded the command station, unleashing the elation of a woman who, he knew, despite everything else she had experienced in her life, never took the miraculous for granted.

Shar looked up at the screen again. It was still there.

Empok Nor, Deep Space 9's long-abandoned twin.

"Colonel, we're receiving a hail from the *Rio Grande,*" Bowers announced.

"It's about time," Kira said, unable to get the smile off her face. "On screen, Lieutenant."

Bowers replaced the exterior scene with the image of Nog at the controls of the runabout. He looked, Shar thought, as though he hadn't slept in days. *"Lieutenant Nog reporting in, Colonel."*

"Nog, I—" Kira started, then faltered and shook her head, words failing her. Finally she took a breath and tried again. "You realize this is going to ruin my view of the wormhole, don't you?"

Nog almost cracked a smile. *"Not for long, Colonel,"* he assured her. *"Once we transfer Empok Nor's lower core to Deep Space 9, we can tow what's left of the station someplace nearby and park it there for the next time we need spare parts."*

"How did the station hold up?" Vaughn asked.

"Even better than the simulations projected, Commander," Nog said. *"Some minor structural damage to two of the lower pylons, but for a ten-day low-warp journey across three light-years . . . not bad. It's like Chief O'Brien used to say about Deep Space 9: The Cardassians built this place to last."*

"You look tired, Nog," Kira said.

Nog shrugged his shoulders, seeming to resist the urge to rub the large black circles under his eyes. *"I'm fine, Colonel. Slept three hours last night. I'll be able to start work on the fusion-core transfer just as soon as we've stabilized our orbit."*

"No, I don't think so," Vaughn said. "See that Empok Nor is stable, but I want you asleep in your quarters when you're finished." Nog began to protest, but stopped when he saw the tilt of Vaughn's head. "Don't force me to make it an order, Nog."

Nog sagged, then seemed to almost smile gratefully. *"Yes, Commander. Thank you, sir. Colonel . . . I want you to know the S.C.E. really came through. This wouldn't have happened without them, or the ships in the convoy."*

Kira smiled. "I'll be sure to note that in my report, Nog."

"I also assured the convoy captains you'd be able to arrange shore leave for their crews on Bajor," Nog said, suddenly looking a little worried.

If Nog expected the colonel to be put out, he was disappointed. "Don't worry, Lieutenant," Kira said, still smiling. "I'll take care of it. And Nog?"

"Colonel?"

"Excellent work."

Nog's face split into a grin. *"Thank you, Colonel,"* he said, and signed off.

Vaughn settled onto a stool and sipped his tea. He looked, Shar thought, as satisfied as he would be if he had just finished pulling the station all the way from the Trivas system himself. "I told you the kid had style."

Chapter Two

It was to be his first vacation in some time, since his trip to Risa with Leeta, Jadzia, Worf, and Quark, before the war. It was also to be his first with Ezri. They were to go back to Earth, back home, so he could show her some bits and pieces of his past, the ones he was willing to share at this early stage in their relationship. And of course, while there, they'd look in on the O'Briens in San Francisco, and drop in on Jake and Joseph Sisko in New Orleans.

But this leave was different for another reason, Bashir reminded himself; Kira had ordered most of the non-techs to clear out, get lost, take a hike. The station needed to be powered down to its lowest threshold before they could transfer Empok Nor's fusion core, as delicate and daunting a bit of surgery as Bashir had ever encountered, and Kira didn't want any unnecessary personnel on board while it was in progress.

"Since when is the chief medical officer considered unnecessary personnel?" Bashir had asked.

"Since now," Kira had replied. "Since I have an *Akira*-class starship nearby with a fully staffed and fully equipped sickbay."

"But you're letting Quark stay!"

"And there are a lot of people remaining on board who are going to need downtime during the next few days. And much as I hate to admit it, the role Quark plays in the well-being of station crew can't be minimized, especially now. I need him, Julian. I don't need you. Have a nice time."

Bashir shook his head as he recalled the conversation, slipping his toothbrush into the side pocket of his luggage and hefting the bag. Ten kilos, he judged, and smiled in satisfaction. Packing a suitcase had developed into a minor fixation over the years, a game to see if he could pack just the right combination of articles to meet any eventuality during his travels. It sometimes made for an oddly shaped bag and good-natured ridicule from his friends, but sometimes his foresight paid off . . . like the time the *Rio Grande* had lost power near a white dwarf star and Miles had been very glad to see that self-sealing stem bolt. . . .

He placed the bag on the bed. Now to collect Ezri and be on their way to airlock seven before their ride, the civilian transport *Wayfarer,* got under way.

Jadzia, Bashir knew, had been a talented last-minute packer. Worf had mentioned how she once yanked a suitcase out of the closet five minutes before a ship was scheduled to leave and was still the first one to the airlock. It was a gift, Bashir hoped, that Ezri had inherited.

The door to her quarters opened as he approached, the sensors encoded to permit him entry. Either Ezri was expecting him or, more likely, she had forgotten to change the sensor key since the last time he had been invited over. He was pleased to see a travel bag sitting on the floor, though it looked suspiciously deflated. She might be traveling light, but there was a more likely explanation. Bashir picked up the strap with one finger and lifted the bag off the floor. Empty.

He sighed.

"Ezri?" he called.

No answer.

He went into the bedroom, where her uniform jacket had been tossed carelessly over a chair, then followed the sounds of movement into the bathroom. Ezri was sitting on the floor working a blob of clay, pinching and pulling it with her fingers. There were several other blobs on the floor around her. Her red command shirt was caked with the stuff. "I don't know if I'll ever get used to seeing you in that color," he commented.

Ezri looked up and said, "Oh," as if startled. "Hi. What time is it?" There were smears of clay on her chin and cheeks. She scratched her nose and left another blotch.

"Almost thirteen hundred hours," Bashir replied, trying very hard not to sound annoyed. "Our transport is leaving in forty minutes."

"Wow. Later than I thought," Ezri said. "Sorry." She set the object she had been working with down on the floor and carefully studied the mess. "Clay isn't as easy as I thought it would be," she said.

"What made you decide to take up sculpture?" Bashir asked. He fought the urge to add, "Especially *now?*"—but lost.

"Well," Ezri said, either missing his exasperation or choosing to overlook it, "I was off duty today and figured that since all I had to do was pack, this would be a good time to work on some of the exercises the Symbiosis Commission recommended."

When they had first become a couple, Bashir and Ezri had lain awake many a night (as new lovers do) discussing their histories, shared and unshared, as well as their similarities and differences. Among the interesting details that had emerged were things like the fact that Bashir liked peanut butter and jelly, but never the two together. Ezri hated yoga and considered lawn bowling a "sport" (it was a family thing). Also, she hated mint chocolate-chip ice cream, which surprised Bashir, because Jadzia had loved it.

They had discussed some more serious things, too, such as how comparable their peculiar situations might be: her joining and his genetic enhancements. Over time, they had come to the conclusion that the circumstances of their transformations were similar only in broad strokes. The change to Bashir's psyche had happened years ago, when he was only a child, and, though frightening, it had been like the thrill one feels emerging from a fog into a clear space with a spectacular view.

Ezri's experience had been almost exactly the opposite in many respects. She had been a mature adult, or, as she conceded, an *adult,* even if not mature on all counts. She had just been coming into a period of her life in which some of its emotional clutter was beginning to sort out, when she was plunged into the mental cacophony of eight other lives.

There had been a time when Julian Bashir had thought that everyone sought out someone like themselves for a partner, someone who would see the world in a similar way. But his relationship with Ezri had changed that, making him realize that he had never needed someone like himself to feel complete. Ezri was someone who could help him bridge the gap between himself and the holes in his experiences.

Dax allowed Bashir to help her up off the floor, then leaned against him for several seconds, steadying herself. Obviously, she had been sitting on the cold, hard tile floor for some time and lost some circulation in her legs. She placed her hands in the middle of her back and stretched, leaving two wet handprints.

Bashir studied the blobs on the floor and saw that they were, in fact, attempts at faces, or, more accurately, masks, since the eyeholes had been left open. He counted eight in all. At least two of them were clearly meant to be males with strong cheekbones and broad brows, while at least three others were definitely women. Bashir recognized one of these, the most clearly defined—with hair pulled back from the forehead and a wide mouth turned up at the corners. Jadzia.

"The previous hosts?" Bashir guessed.

Ezri nodded while looking down at her handiwork, turning her head this way and that. "The idea is *not* to try for something too representational. The exercise is more about impression and emotional response. I think about each host, and the feelings guide my fingers."

"Interesting concept," he said, lightly brushing his finger across the cheek of one of the male faces, where Ezri had somehow managed to convey an impression of triumph and tragedy at the same time. *Torias?* "But is this the sort of project you want to undertake just before we leave for a vacation?"

Ezri turned to the sink and began to run what Bashir suspected was a large percentage of her daily emergency ration of water into the basin. "Don't try to counsel the counselor, Doctor. Former counselor," she corrected herself. "I know my timing is a little off and I know myself well enough to understand why." Shutting off the flow of water, she immersed her hands and began scrubbing. "I admit it—I'm a little nervous about this trip, about leaving the station right now. I feel like I'm running away just when things are in upheaval."

"You were *ordered* away," Bashir corrected.

"I could make a case for staying if I wanted," she said, hitting the sink's recycle setting. Then she looked up at him and grinned. "But I figure they can get along without me for a while and I really *do* want to go see where you grew up. I'm guessing I'll come away with all sorts of *insights . . .*"

"Oh, lord," Bashir groaned. "Maybe it's not too late to convince Kira to let us stay."

After rubbing the worst of the stains off her hands, she threw the now brown towel into the recycler and refilled the basin. "Ha! No way! Now we have to go. And as long as we're doing some short-term analysis, what's with you not saying anything to anyone about your promotion, Lieutenant Commander? When Nog was promoted, the entire station turned out for the party. Not that I'm jealous on your behalf, but no one has ever accused you of avoiding a celebration."

Bashir shrugged, resisting the sudden impulse to touch the new pip on his collar. "It didn't seem appropriate somehow," he said. "I'm not like Nog. He still needs the recognition, the ego boost . . ."

Ezri was splashing water on her face when she suddenly stopped and looked at him. *"Nog* needs an ego boost?"

"My dear ex-counselor," Bashir said, grinning, "I'll have you know that inside that narrow chest beats the heart of a very sensitive young Ferengi."

"Are we talking about the same Nog?" Ezri asked, working the soap into a lather. "The one who watches me every time I walk past?"

"He's just appreciating some of your finer qualities. Again, the mark of a sensitive soul."

Ezri rolled her eyes. Then, she snapped her head around and regarded Bashir carefully. "Hey!" she said. "How did we get off the subject of your promotion?"

"How," Bashir countered, "did we get off the subject of your not being sure you wanted to go on vacation?"

"I'm packing! I'm packing!" Ezri cried, drying her face.

Bashir smiled to himself, then changed the subject again. "I made Nog promise to turn on Vic's again as soon as he's finished."

"You didn't have to do that," Ezri said. Bashir followed her into the bedroom as she pulled off her soiled shirt, remembering to take her rank pips off first, and tossed it in a corner of the room. After donning a fresh one, she began to tear open drawers and toss things onto the bed. "Nog would have done it anyway."

"Vic made *me* promise before we saved his program. I think he was a little worried what would happen if Empok Nor hadn't made it through intact."

"Maybe you should activate him long enough to tell him." She tossed a pile of undergarments onto the bed.

"Just so I can shut him down again until the work's finished?" Bashir asked. "No, it's better this way. And just in case something does go wrong while we're away, I forwarded a copy of his program to Felix."

"Good idea," she said, and to Bashir's abject horror, she gathered the pile of clothes into a ball, obviously intending to carry it out into the living room, where her bag lay. He wondered if this was part of the Jadzia Dax packing technique Worf had never mentioned. "Where's your suitcase?" she asked. "I don't see anything perfect and hermetically sealed lying around here."

"Back in my quarters."

"Well, you'd better go get it if you want to make this flight."

"Yes, ma'am," Bashir said, heading for the door. "And may I say that you've obviously taken well to command." The doors closed behind him before he could hear what Ezri said in reply.

• • •

There was a man in Bashir's quarters, gazing out the window.

Standing in the doorway, Bashir felt an absurd desire to say "Excuse me!" and back out of the room before the analytical portion of his brain kicked in. The man was a middle-aged human, medium height and build. He wore a moderately pleasant expression, the kind of bland, neutral smile that Bashir would feel inclined to return while waiting for a turbolift. His dark hair was extremely close-cropped over a well-formed skull. But the man's most note-worthy characteristic was his eyes, which were a startling emerald green.

"Dr. Bashir," the man said. "It's a pleasure to finally meet you."

There was something about the way the man said his name. He continued to collect data—*the movements of his facial muscles, the constant readiness of his seemingly relaxed hands, the way he carries his weight squarely on his pelvis*—parsed it, then drew conclusions.

Section 31.

The doctor slapped his combadge and spoke quickly. "Bashir to ops, in-truder alert. Request armed assistance in my quarters immediately."

The man's smile didn't waver. "I'm sorry, Doctor. Your coworkers aren't receiving you at the moment. We really can't afford any interruptions. Lieu-tenant Dax is still in her quarters and will remain there for at least another twelve minutes or so. She's having trouble finding a padd she wanted to bring with her. Also, the *Wayfarer* is experiencing some minor engine problems. Nothing serious, I assure you." He didn't offer any explanations, but Bashir didn't doubt his word. "Now that you know where things stand, I'd like to in-troduce myself. Please call me Cole. As you've no doubt already guessed, I'm affiliated with the organization you call Section 31."

"You don't call it that?" Bashir asked.

"I don't call it anything, Doctor. I've found that I rarely need to identify it to anyone who doesn't already know what it is."

Bashir moved to a chair and sat down, realizing he had no option but to indulge his unwelcome visitor, at least for now. "I can only assume this isn't a social call," he said, trying to maintain the flippant but polite tone.

Cole took a seat opposite Bashir. "Courteous, but direct," he noted pleas-antly. "Sloan noted that in his profile. You're exactly what I'm looking for."

"If Sloan mentioned that, then he must have also mentioned that I'm not interested in working with Section 31."

"In fact," Cole replied, "he did mention that. But you might change your mind when you've heard me out."

Bashir rose from his chair, his anger beginning to escape the container of his false civility. He knew Cole was probably armed, probably a trained killer, but he didn't care. All Bashir could think about was lifting the man up by the scruff of his neck and tossing him out of his quarters. Bashir knew it wasn't the most sensible thought he'd ever had, but it was satisfyingly direct.

"Sit down, Doctor," Cole said, not raising his voice. Bashir stopped mov-ing, then found himself settling back into his chair. He realized that his fingers and toes were slightly numb and tingling. "You *will* do me the courtesy of hearing me out."

Against his will, Bashir nodded.

"Good," Cole said, then crossed his arms. "You know, of course," he began, "that you're not the only genetically enhanced human in the Federation. And I don't mean only your little circle of friends—Jack, Lauren, Sarina, Patrick, that lot. There are many others, far more than Starfleet Command knows about . . . or wants to know about, if you want my opinion. One thing I've learned in my line of work, Doctor, is that the best place to hide is where your enemies don't wish to look. Almost four hundred years after the Eugenics Wars, humans are still so terrified of the idea of someone spawning another Khan that they're afraid to admit to themselves that black-market genetic labs exist on dozens of worlds. What do you think of my assessment?"

"I agree," Bashir replied, surprised to hear himself voice the long-held but never-spoken opinion. *Some kind of psychoactive,* he decided. *Not only is it making me compliant, but it's acting as a truth serum.* He quickly reviewed the half-dozen compounds he knew of that would have this effect but would also leave him feeling clearheaded. He decided none of them were likely candidates. *How did he administer the drug? No hypo. He didn't touch me. . . . Aerosol? Yes, that makes sense. Something he sprayed the room with before I got here, something he's immune to.* All of this went on in the analytical portion of his mind while the rest of his attention was fixed on Cole. Despite himself, whatever the drug might be doing, Bashir was interested in what the man was saying.

"And the good news," Cole continued, "from my perspective, at any rate, is that some of these individuals are very happy to have someone acknowledge their existence. One in particular that I came here to discuss with you is Dr. Ethan Locken. Name mean anything to you?"

Bashir shook his head.

"I'm not really surprised. He wasn't in Starfleet, isn't even a researcher despite his astonishing gifts. Doesn't travel in the same rarefied circles as you do, Doctor. He was, I assume, trying to keep a low profile. Sound familiar?"

Unable to fight the impulse, Bashir nodded.

Cole asked, "Do you think it's a coincidence that so many of you—the genetically enhanced, I mean—go into medicine? It really doesn't have anything to do with my . . . my problem, but I'm curious to hear what you think."

"It's not a coincidence," Bashir said. "But don't make too much of it, either. Think about it—anyone who has been genetically enhanced spent a great deal of time around doctors when they were young. Generally, these are favorable impressions, especially if the procedure is successful. If you check the statistics for the general population, I think you'll find that persons who survive a medical crisis when they're young have a predilection for going into the medical sciences."

"Ah," Cole said. "Very well reasoned, Doctor. Excellent point. I can see that I'm going to enjoy many stimulating conversations like this one in the future." He pulled out a compact personal data recorder and made a note. "Very good," he said to himself, then continued, "Where were we?"

"Locken," Bashir replied. He couldn't resist the urge to reply to a direct question.

"Ah, yes. Correct—Dr. Locken. He was a pediatrician. Very popular, I'm told. Very well liked. Had a practice on New Beijing. You've heard of New Beijing, haven't you?"

"Yes," Bashir replied tightly. "Of course I have. *Everyone* has heard of New Beijing. It was a massacre, probably one of the worst of the war, especially when you realize it had no strategic value . . ."

Cole held up a finger, interrupting. "Not exactly correct, Doctor. Terror *always* has a strategic value. Remember that."

Not having been asked a direct question, Bashir could not reply, but he wanted to. Desperately, he wanted to speak, to spew the venom that was clogging his mind and heart.

But Cole wouldn't have been interested. He was already continuing, reciting facts as if he were reading a dossier. "Dr. Locken had no family on New Beijing and his parents were long dead, but he had friends and he had colleagues, and, oh, he had patients. You might have heard the official death toll—five thousand human colonists, all civilians—but it was actually higher than that. Much higher.

"As you might expect, after surviving an ordeal like that, Dr. Locken was somewhat more receptive to our invitation than you've been. He understood the need for an organization like ours in a hostile universe. If only more people possessed his clarity of perception, then perhaps catastrophes like New Beijing might not have occurred."

"Wait," Bashir said, the word ragged, but comprehensible. "I have a question." It was a brutal struggle to speak without being spoken to, but Bashir could feel the effects of the psychoactive beginning to wane.

Cole's eyebrows lifted in surprise. Obviously, he had been expecting the drug to work longer, but he didn't object to Bashir asking his question.

"Did you—did Section 31—know about the plan to attack New Beijing in advance?"

Cole lifted a finger to his upper lip, patted it several times, then said, "You know, Doctor, I'm not sure. I'm afraid none of us knows everything everyone else in the organization knows. Security measure, you understand. It certainly *sounds* like the sort of thing we would hear about long before Starfleet Intelligence. But let's assume we did. What difference would it have made? Enlighten me, sir."

"You could have told someone," Bashir hissed between clenched teeth. "You could have told *me*. . . ."

"And you would have done *what*, precisely? At the height of the Dominion War, would you have tried to convince Captain Sisko or Admiral Ross to have forces reassigned to New Beijing? Say, for example, an *Excelsior*-class starship and a detachment of Starfleet ground troops? What would that have accomplished? The planet was attacked by two regiments of Jem'Hadar soldiers. The starship would have been destroyed, our troops killed, and all those civilians *would have died anyway.*"

Cole leaned forward, warming to his topic. "Oh, and consider this—maybe the Starfleet forces in this hypothetical scenario were needed someplace where they might have done some good, something crucial. Perhaps they'd have been taken from the force that was successfully repelling the attack on Rigel at that time, and perhaps as a consequence the entire Rigel system would have fallen. Think about it, Doctor: Maybe what happened to New Beijing was the best possible outcome that we could have expected."

Bashir's anger was so intense that he wondered why his eyes weren't boiling like two eggs in their sockets. "That," he snapped, "is the most specious, spurious, fatuous sort of sociopathic double-talk I've ever heard! It's exactly that sort of logic that allows people like you to maintain the illusion that what you're doing has some sort of intrinsic value. It's insanity, *Mister* Cole. People *died*—"

Cole rose, a visual cue that had another immediate and involuntary effect on Bashir: he stopped speaking.

"First, *Doctor*," Cole said in cool and collected tones, "never use the word *'insanity'* unless you know precisely what you're talking about. It's an imprecise word. Second, and I wouldn't have thought you'd need me to tell you this, but *people die all the time.* It's simply a question of how many, who they are, and, sometimes, how they died. That's what my colleagues and I try to do: keep the numbers as small as possible, make sure the right ones don't die, and keep the suffering to a minimum. It isn't easy work, but we do the best we can. You yourself have benefited from some of our efforts, so please be very careful about who you're condemning today."

Bashir's eyes narrowed. *He believes it; he believes every word that he's saying.* And worse, Bashir suspected that what he was saying might even be true.

Cole strolled over to the mantel jutting out of a nearby wall. He bent to study a small hologram of Bashir's parents, then gave a quizzical glance to the larger holo of the Deep Space Niners taken in Quark's bar after their triumphant defeat at the hands of the *T'Kumbra* Logicians. Shaking his head, Cole resumed his tale: "After Dr. Locken agreed to assist us, he underwent training to become an agent. Or, to be more accurate, he indulged us as we took him through our program. Not surprisingly, considering his background, he already knew almost everything we could teach him about how to go unnoticed when he desired. I believe he even taught our trainers a few things." He looked over at Bashir. "You could probably teach them a few things, too, now that I think of it.

"And then, just in the last days of the war, we found him a mission. We flattered ourselves, believing it was the *perfect* mission." Cole grinned once more, but there was no real merriment in it. "So, of course," Cole said, "Locken betrayed us."

Chapter Three

Several seconds ticked past during which, Bashir suspected, he was supposed to offer a comment. He decided to be spiteful, and so, finally, Cole continued. "We discovered a Jem'Hadar hatchery on a planet called Sindorin. Heard of it?"

"No."

"A class-M world in the Badlands. Very unusual for that region with the high concentration of ambient plasma energy. We have no idea when the hatchery was established; not even the Cardassians knew about it. Evidence suggests that the Dominion didn't quite manage to bring it fully online. If they had, that last offensive on Cardassia might have gone a little differently. Something to think about late at night, isn't it, Doctor? Calculate how many more ships and soldiers the Dominion needed to turn the tide of that battle."

"It was Odo who ended the war," Bashir said. "He convinced the Founder that the Federation and its allies weren't a threat to the Dominion. He gave them the cure to your damn virus and prevented the genocide your organization sought to achieve."

"Hm, yes," Cole said. "That's certainly an interesting interpretation of events."

"You have another?"

"We're off topic, Doctor. As I was saying, the hatchery we found was abandoned and undefended. Locken's mission was simplicity itself: Tell us whether the hatchery DNA sequencers could be adjusted so that the Jem'Hadar would be loyal to us."

Bashir said, "You bloody fools."

"A comment, Doctor?" Cole asked. "An imprecation?"

"We just finished fighting a war against a totalitarian power that callously used a genetically engineered army of slave soldiers as cannon fodder. How could you think for even a moment that anyone in the Federation—in the *quadrant*—would tolerate you employing the same methods? It violates every principle that millions of Starfleet officers, Klingons, and Romulans sacrificed their lives to protect."

Cole regarded Bashir for several seconds, then slowly raised his hands and clapped them together half a dozen times. "Bravo, Doctor," he said. "I am impressed. You do have a flair for oratory." Cole folded his arms over his chest. "Now, step down off your soapbox and allow me to guide you through a few possibilities you might not have considered. Give me the benefit of your superior intellect and tell me who you deduce will be the group the Federation will be facing in the next war."

Bashir sighed. He had lain awake too many nights calculating exactly these variables. "It's difficult to say precisely because of all the factors involved. Unless Chancellor Martok can solidify his power base in the next six months, the peace between the Klingons and Romulans will likely crumble. If they go to war the victor will likely attack the Federation next. The Breen will be watching our borders, too, making raids, checking for vulnerable areas. From the Project Pathfinder database, we know that there are several species in the Delta Quadrant that may be threats in the near future: the Hirogen, Species 8472, the Srivani, the Vaadwaur . . ."

Cole paced the floor, nodding his approval with each of Bashir's observations. "Very good, Doctor. Excellent analysis. I particularly approve of your read of the Delta Quadrant situation. Many potential threats there. You obviously have been keeping up on current events."

"Admiral Ross has been using some of us here as a sounding board," Bashir said dryly.

"Yes," Cole said. "I can see why. You all have lived through unique situations, haven't you? But you're leaving something out, I think, the most obvious . . ."

Bashir was silent for several seconds, but then relented. "The Borg."

"The Borg?" Cole said. "Interesting. We've beaten them, you know? Twice here and at least once in the Delta Quadrant . . . if you believe the Pathfinder reports. But you think the Borg is the number-one threat. Why is that?"

"Because they're relentless," Bashir said. "Because we still don't know how many there are. Because the fact that we beat them makes us all the more interesting to them, that much more worth assimilating. Because I think they recognize something in us that they might have been themselves once and want to exterminate it. If we survive, if we thrive, it means that some decision they made long, long ago was the wrong one. Because, I think, for all their claims of being emotionless, I think they hate us."

Cole had ceased pacing and was studying Bashir's face carefully, a small, wistful smile playing on his lips. "Thank you, Doctor. Quite excellent. I believe I've learned something important here tonight."

Bashir couldn't resist the urge to ask. "And that would be?"

"You're still a romantic," Cole replied. "We had thought the Dominion War might have burned that out of you, but I see it's still there. That was a marvelously romantic interpretation of the Borg situation, but, I think, essentially correct. They *are* the greatest threat to the security of the Federation, the one we are least able to counter right now. If the Borg attacked *now,* we would be destroyed, even if the Klingons, Romulans, and Breen came to our aid. Computer models don't lie. Oh, and here's another interesting fact that Admiral Ross might not have shared with you: Even if the Dominion were to fight alongside us, we would probably lose. Ironically, the prewar Dominion might have stood a chance against them. If we had allied ourselves with them, but, well . . . never mind *that* option."

Bashir flexed the muscles in his forearms and calves. Yes, definitely some control was returning.

"So," Cole continued, now with a full head of steam, "the question should not be 'How could we contemplate using the despicable methods of our enemy?' but 'What could we learn from our former foes that we might turn to our advantage?' If we continue on our present path, we will not be counting our dead in the millions next time, Doctor, but the *billions.*" He stopped pacing and leaned in close to Bashir. "Have you ever seen what the Borg do to a human body? *I* have. Children, pregnant women, the elderly: it doesn't matter; all just grist for the mill. All just *parts.* Don't you think, as a *humanitarian,* that if there's something we can do to prevent that suffering then we should *do* it?"

Bashir stared at the man, aware of a creeping horror sliding up his spine. How many newly made orphans and bereaved parents had he talked to, tried to comfort, ending up feeling utterly ineffectual? Listening to Cole, Bashir felt his head begin to nod, against his will . . . *Almost.*

"How much more sensible," Cole continued, "how much more equitable and humane it would be if the Federation could mass-produce its own army, genetically engineered soldiers who would be happy to sacrifice their lives for their leaders. The citizenry would be liberated from the barbaric practice of war, allowed to enjoy happy, peaceful, long-lasting lives with their loved ones. With the ability to produce unlimited numbers of professional soldiers, we would never again need fear the Borg, the Romulans, or the Klingons. Who could *ever* pose a threat to the Federation again?"

"Let me remind you of something I think you know all too well, but seem to have conveniently forgotten," Bashir replied. "The history of the Federation is steeped in examples of peoples who were able to successfully battle larger, better-equipped, and more advanced aggressors because the citizen-soldier is always going to be more creative and resourceful, better able to adapt to changing conditions on a battlefield. It was an army that fought for a love of freedom, not a love of slaughter, that defeated the Dominion's genetically engineered legions, Mr. Cole."

Cole stared thoughtfully at Bashir and then, for the first time, a troubled expression passed over his features. "You know, Doctor," he finally said, "I wish we'd had this conversation *before* we sent Locken on his mission. As I implied earlier, things didn't go quite according to plan."

"What happened?"

"He left for Sindorin about ten weeks ago, accompanied by a team of specialists. For the first few weeks, he kept in regular contact with us and indicated good progress. Confirmation from his associates showed that Locken was doing exactly what we asked him to do."

"His associates?" Bashir asked. "You mean a spy."

Cole shrugged. "We had to try to protect our investment."

"And then the messages became irregular," Bashir said.

"That's right," Cole said. "And then we stopped hearing from . . . his associates."

"Then they're dead, all of them. Your spies were probably the first to be killed. If Locken is everything you say he is, he probably arranged to have them kill each other."

"Why do you say that?"

"Because if I were Locken, it's what I would have done."

"I recruited some of the agents who went with him," Cole said. "I knew some of them well. They weren't the sort who could be easily deceived."

Bashir shrugged. "Believe whatever you want. It won't bring them back to life. What do you theorize has happened since?"

"We know that he succeeded in bringing some of the incubators back online and began to grow Jem'Hadar. We can only assume Locken was successful in reprogramming the genetic matrix, and that they're loyal to him."

"Have you done any estimates?"

"We had very little data to work with," Cole said, "but our best guess is between two hundred and a thousand. Worst-case scenario is fifteen hundred. He can't get them all off the planet right now, because he only had one ship, but we think he's found other things for them to do."

"Such as?"

"You've heard about the rumored Breen presence in the Badlands?"

"Yes," Bashir said. "The *Enterprise* investigated and found nothing."

"That's correct. But they couldn't completely rule out that *something* was out there. And since then, a number of ships have gone missing, and at least two former Cardassian holdings have suffered hits by an unidentified attacker ..."

"They're not 'former Cardassian holdings,' " Bashir said firmly. "They're protectorates. The Federation, the Klingons, and the Romulans set them up to safeguard Cardassian Union territories. They'll be returned when Cardassia is able to resume control of them."

Cole smiled. "Fine, Doctor. Phrase it any way you want. The point is that Locken could make all of this political theorizing moot if he isn't stopped. Perhaps he's planning to use hit-and-run attacks to train his warriors and try to collect usable ships. Perhaps he wants to destabilize the truce between the three powers. Perhaps he's only tweaking them so that they'll discover a genetically engineered human has set himself up as the new Khan. . . . *It doesn't matter.* The only thing that matters is that you stop him as quickly and quietly as possible."

"That *I* stop him?" Bashir asked.

"Of course, Doctor. Who better? Our psych profile indicates that Locken can rationalize his actions because he feels so isolated. Certainly, the trauma of his losses on New Beijing can account for much of this, but our specialists are certain that his psychosis has its roots in his belief that he is fundamentally different from everyone around him, *better* than everyone. In his mind, it doesn't matter what he does to anyone else because, ultimately, it's for their own good. He's a doctor to all humanity."

"To what end?" Bashir asked.

"We don't know," Cole said. "If I had to guess, he's decided that he wants to make the quadrant safe for children and other small things by any means necessary. If you really want to know, *ask* him. We want you to go to Sindorin, establish some sort of rapport, use those forensic skills you just demonstrated, and convince him to turn the hatchery over to us ..."

"Like hell," Bashir began.

"Or whatever you think is best," Cole continued. "Our goals are the same in this instance. We do *not* want a superhuman launching a jihad with an army of genetically engineered killing machines at his back."

"Especially not a superhuman who knows everything about you," Bashir added.

A tight smile flickered across Cole's lips. "Nobody knows everything about us, Doctor."

"And if I'm not able to persuade him?" Bashir asked.

Cole shrugged. "I very much doubt," he said, "that anyone who could outthink Sloan would have much trouble with a tyro like Locken. He may be . . . enhanced, but he's still quite naive, I think. Almost as naive as you used to be."

Bashir shook his head in disgust. "How could you believe *for a second* that I would buy into this hideous charade? You've managed to mire yourself in a morass of backstabbing and double-dealing and you're expecting *me* to liberate you? Give me *one* good reason why I should."

"Besides the obvious, you mean?" Cole asked. "Besides the fact that the Federation could be torn to pieces if the Romulans and the Klingons discover what's happened?"

Bashir wanted desperately to be able to say, "There are ways around that," but he knew Cole was right. As they had been talking, he had been running simulations and the numbers weren't encouraging. *And that's what it comes down to,* he realized. *Not right and wrong, moral or immoral, but numbers—counting the quick and the dead.* He didn't want to say any of those things because if he did, Cole would know he had prevailed, so, instead, he said, "There are others who can do what you're asking, most of them better than me."

Cole smiled. "Doctor, you underestimate yourself. In fact, there isn't *any-one* better suited. While there are many more enhanced persons out there than the Federation is willing to acknowledge, very few of them are as—how shall we say it?—well socialized as you are. Most of them, in fact, would consider your friend Jack to be a social butterfly. And, speaking of Jack, what do you think would happen to him and his friends if it became known that a genetically enhanced person was responsible for starting a war? How long do you think it would be before Starfleet would disavow them, cast them to the wolves? A week? A *day?*"

"Starfleet would never do that."

"You don't think so? I won't presume to speak for *you,* Doctor, but one of the things *I* learned during the Dominion War is that under the worst circumstances, even among the best and the brightest, morality can sometimes become a pliable thing. If the conditions are right . . . well, I've heard stories even about the late, sainted Captain Sisko."

Bashir glared at Cole from under lowered brows, thinking, feeling, like a caged animal inside his own skull.

"Damn you to hell," he said at last, resigned to whatever awaited him on

Sindorin. He expected Cole to grin triumphantly, but was surprised to see only a very tired man, a gaunt and bitter man, a man weary unto death.

"Thank you, Doctor," Cole said softly. "When can you leave?"

Bashir shook himself, then said, "I don't know. I have to make some arrangements."

"Of course," Cole said, heading for the door. When he passed Bashir, he dropped the padd he had been holding into the doctor's hands. "Please extend my apologies to Lieutenant Dax for making her miss her vacation. Just out of curiosity—did you *really* want her to go back to Earth with you and visit the old homestead?"

"Yes, I did," Bashir said. "Very much."

"Really?" Cole said, pausing in front of the open door. "Well, then, it must be love." And then he was gone.

When he was certain Cole wasn't coming back, Bashir stood and walked stiffly across the room to where his med kit rested and opened it. He wanted to get a blood sample before the psychoactive was completely dissipated. As he worked, he took a second to try his combadge. "Bashir to Kira."

"Go ahead," the colonel's voice answered.

"Nerys . . . we need to talk."

Chapter Four

Kira felt a headache building behind her eyes and began to massage the ridges of her nose. "Do we have anything on internal scanners . . . ?"

"Nothing," Vaughn said.

"No surprise there, I guess. I'd have been more shocked if we *had* picked up something."

"So would I," Vaughn agreed. "And then we'd have to worry about why he let us know he was here. No, I think it's better this way. He's gone and we can accept his request at face value."

"It sounded more like a threat than a request," Kira noted. "Or a trap." She looked around the wardroom table and attempted to take everyone's measure.

Bashir was angry, of course. He didn't like being backed into a corner, but then, who did? There was something else going on, but Kira couldn't quite piece it together, not yet. Partly this was because when Julian wanted to conceal something, it stayed concealed. It wasn't so long ago when she had considered the doctor an open book, a man who was all too eager to reveal everything about himself. But now Kira understood that this had been a ruse, a persona created to conceal the "real" Julian Bashir.

Ezri, typically, was wrestling with several emotions simultaneously. Kira read fear (primarily for Julian), anger (mostly at Cole, but with a little reserved for Julian), and an edge of excitement. A quirky smile kept forming at the corners of Ezri's mouth, but she managed to keep it under control. Kira recognized it as the skeleton of the smile Jadzia used to wear when she was undertaking some new challenge or digging into a new mystery. Seeing it made Kira feel at once comforted and disconcerted. *Jadzia is in there somewhere,* she thought. *Listening intently to everything I'm saying.* She knew that wasn't exactly how it worked, but Kira had a hard time shaking the feeling that the ghost of her friend was hovering in the room. She found herself wondering if Benjamin had felt the same way after Jadzia had succeeded Curzon.

Vaughn was harder to read, drinking that damned tea, absorbing everything that was being said, and processing it through his eighty years of Starfleet training. Still, Kira sensed something going on beneath the detached calm, something that felt a great deal like anger, though she was having trouble imagining Vaughn being angry about anything.

But where Vaughn was impenetrable, Ro seemed preoccupied. Maybe it was just the shock of learning about the existence of Section 31. Kira and Sisko had both felt that shock, after Julian had told them about his first encounter with Sloan. Ro, however, seemed to be trying to work through something.

"You have something to contribute, Lieutenant?" Kira asked.

Ro met Kira's gaze, and seemed to reach a decision. "Sindorin," she said. "I know the planet. There was a time when the Maquis considered using it for a base. This was almost three years ago, just before everything fell apart. It would have been a good place to retreat to if we'd had the chance." She indicated the planetological file currently displayed on the wardroom screen.

"It's mostly tropical with about two-thirds of the land surface covered with dense rain forest." Pointing at a subcontinent in the southern hemisphere, Ro continued, "This area was particularly interesting to us because some recent volcanic activity has deposited a rare mineral throughout the water table. The trees draw it up into the canopy and it plays hell with sensors. Anything but the most intense scan bounces right off. The forests are teeming with life, but you wouldn't know it from orbit."

Ro touched the table controls and the holographic image of Sindorin receded. "And here's the other reason we liked the place," Ro said. Red and yellow plasma storms erupted just beyond the edge of the solar system. "It's unusual to find an M–class planet this deep in the Badlands, but, well, not impossible. And, let me tell you, it makes for some pretty amazing aurora effects."

"So why didn't you relocate there?" Dax asked.

"Two reasons," Ro said. "The first was the storms. The shielding on most Maquis ships was never that great. We might not have lost one the first or second time we passed in or out of the system, but, sooner or later, something would have gone disastrously wrong. And, second, like I said, we only found the place a few weeks before the Cardassians joined the Dominion. When that happened, we had bigger problems. . . ."

"Apparently, the Dominion didn't feel the same way," Kira said.

Ro shrugged. "Their ships had better shields."

Kira caused the image to zoom back in on the planet. "So, based on what you've told us, this southern continent is the most likely candidate for a base. Any thoughts on how to narrow that down?"

"It depends. What's needed for a Jem'Hadar hatchery?"

"Genetic material, which the Vorta would have brought with them when they set up the place," Bashir contributed. "They must have abandoned it in quite a hurry to leave some of it behind, perhaps during the final offensive against Cardassia. But they'd have needed water, too. Preferably fresh water."

"It's all rain forest," Ro said, "so there's not a lot of open water. It's all invested in the vegetation. During the rainy season, it rained twice a day, early morning and early evening, so regularly you could set your chrono by it. Would that be sufficient?"

Bashir shook his head. "Probably not. Too dispersed."

Kira watched them talk and noticed how they quickly fell into the easy give-and-take of Starfleet-trained information exchange. It was a skill she had always admired in Sisko, Jadzia, O'Brien, and Julian, but hadn't imagined it extended to *all* Starfleet officers, even former ones like Ro. *Klingons don't do this,* she mused. *Or the Romulans or the Cardassians. They have their own methods, their own martial cultures, but nothing that can compete with this.*

Ro pointed at a large blue splotch near the southern tip of the subcontinent they had been discussing. "Here, then. This lake. We didn't give it a name.

Just called it 'the Big Lake.' It's the only large open body of fresh water on this part of the planet."

Julian leaned in to study the map. "It must be a couple thousand klicks around. Big area to check."

"We'll be able to pick up something once we get in close," Ro said.

"But not *too* close," Julian replied, staring intently at the lake, obviously memorizing the shape of the shoreline.

"Well, that's the trick of it, isn't it?"

"Yes, it is, Lieutenant," Julian said absently. "And thank you for volunteering to come along. It'll be good to have someone there who knows the territory. I have a feeling we'll need every advantage we can get . . . which brings me to my next request. Colonel?"

"Doctor?"

"I'd like to ask Taran'atar to accompany us."

Kira could feel her face knitting into a frown at the suggestion. "You realize that if what Cole told you is true, there's liable to be quite a few Jem'Hadar there."

"Which is precisely why I want one there who's on *our* side," Bashir said. "He'll be able to offer us valuable insights about how they think, their possible responses . . ." He paused, studying Kira's face. "I take it you don't care for the idea."

"I don't. This is getting crazier by the second. You're talking about going to a planet in the Badlands with only one or two other people . . ."

"Possibly three," Ezri chipped in.

"We'll talk about *that* later," Kira snapped. "With one or two other people, one of them a Jem'Hadar, so that you can confront someone who has set himself up as the local deity. And for what? To save Starfleet some embarrassment . . . ?"

"No, Nerys," Bashir said. "To preserve the peace. To save some lives. I don't like this any better than you, but it's the lesser of two evils."

Kira felt the pressure behind her eyes building. "All right, I'll speak with Taran'atar and see how he feels about this. He might not be able to do this, you know. Odo told him to obey *me*."

"And if you tell him to listen to me, then he will," Bashir said.

"Or any of us, for that matter," Dax added.

"I'm not sure it works that way," Kira said. "Or, if it does, I'm not sure I want it to."

"He's a Jem'Hadar," Bashir said. "He'll do as he's ordered. That's their raison d'être."

"This one might be different," Kira said. "That might be the reason Odo sent him here."

"Or he might be the purest example of the species," Bashir mused. "Maybe Odo wanted us to better understand what we're going to be dealing with the next time we meet the Dominion."

It was an intriguing question and Kira normally would have been happy to debate the topic with her friends and colleagues, but the immediate issue would be what Taran'atar would say about the idea. "Computer, locate Taran'atar."

"Taran'atar is in holosuite one," it intoned.

Curious expressions all around the table.

"How much longer is he scheduled to be there?"

"His session will expire in twenty minutes."

"Then I'd better get down there soon," Kira said. "Julian, I'll call you when I find out what Taran'atar wants to do. Either way, don't slow down your preparations on his account. I'm guessing he's a quick packer."

"I'll have Bowers assign you a runabout," Vaughn said. "Any preferences, Ro?"

"The *Euphrates*," Ro said. "She handles well in turbulent atmosphere. Sindorin has some heavy storms."

"Good choice," Vaughn said. "Six hours from now sound all right?" Ro and Bashir agreed and Vaughn left the room, followed soon after by Ro. Julian had subtly signaled to Dax and Kira to remain for a moment, so they both made a show of stacking padds until the others had left.

"What is it?" Kira asked when the doors had closed behind Ro.

"I just wanted to note," Bashir said, "that the commander didn't seem terribly shocked to learn that there is a secret covert operations group within Starfleet."

"Ro didn't seem surprised, either," Ezri said. "What's your point?"

"I think Ro expects *every* society to have a secret covert operations group," Kira added. "Odo felt the same way. What *is* your point, Julian?"

"I'm not sure that I have one. But Vaughn's service record isn't exactly full of details, is it? I checked, Nerys. For someone who's been in Starfleet as long as he has, you'd think it would contain more than the few meaningless details I found. And he didn't contribute much to our discussion just now."

Kira chose her words very carefully. "Julian, I may not be Starfleet, but Commander Vaughn has proven himself to me, and to this station. If you want to bring his trustworthiness into question—"

"No," Bashir said, as if realizing he'd crossed a line. "I'm sorry. I guess this Section 31 business is making me suspicious of everything. You're right, Colonel. I won't bring it up again." Bashir looked at Ezri. "See you later?"

Ezri nodded. As soon as Julian left the room, Kira said, "I don't like what I just heard."

"Neither do I," Dax said, still watching the door. "But he has a point."

"In what way?"

"Vaughn plays it close to the vest," Ezri said. "He always did. Even when Curzon met him decades ago he was like that. I don't mean he can't be trusted. I think he's basically a good man. Plus, the opinions of Starfleet Command and captains like Jean-Luc Picard count for something, and they obviously have complete confidence in him. But given the strain Julian's under right now, questioning a lack of information—which is what Vaughn represents to him—isn't unreasonable, or unexpected."

Kira could understand that, and wondered if she would eventually have to address the issue with her enigmatic executive officer. First things first, however. "Can Julian do this?" she asked Dax.

"No question," Ezri said. "But he'll need backup he can count on. I think Ro and Taran'atar are a good start, but I want to go, too."

Kira sat down and leaned back, studying Dax carefully. "Do you remember the mission to Soukara?" she said finally.

"Yes, of course," Ezri replied without hesitation. "Jadzia almost died. Worf had to choose between saving her life or meeting with Lasaran. He chose to save me."

"And do you remember what happened next?"

"Benjamin forbade us from ever going on a mission together again."

"And the lesson I should draw from that is . . . what?"

"Colonel," Dax said, straining to sound reasonable, "these are entirely different circumstances."

"Really? Different how? How is this different from the mission to Soukara?"

"Look at it this way. You and Odo together went to the aid of Damar's resistance group while the two of you were in a relationship."

"Odo and I are not you and Worf," Kira said, and as soon as the words were out of her mouth, she knew she was trapped.

"Exactly my point," Ezri agreed. "Odo and Kira are not Jadzia and Worf. Well, Ezri and Julian aren't Jadzia and Worf, either."

Kira sighed. "What if you're wrong, Ezri?"

"I'm *not* wrong and you know it. We'll do this the right way if for no other reason than to prove to you that we can."

"Have you talked to Julian about this? I got the impression he expects you to see him off, not join him."

"Of course we've talked about it. And of course he wants me to come along. He feels exactly the same way I do about this."

"I don't want you to come along," Bashir said.

Ezri, sitting on Bashir's bed, shivered as she watched him repack his travel bag. The station was getting colder and Julian's quarters, which were always a couple of degrees cooler than she liked, were close to unbearable. "You're not being reasonable," she said, then pulled the afghan off the foot of his bed and wrapped it around her shoulders.

Bashir walked over and pulled the afghan more tightly around her. "How am I being unreasonable? I just don't want you to be hurt . . . or worse."

Ezri shrugged his hand away. She wasn't impressed. "Doesn't work," she said. "I don't want you to be hurt or killed either, but I'm not insisting you stay. I know you have to go. It's your duty."

"Yes," Bashir agreed emphatically. "It is . . ."

"And it's mine, too," she said, not letting him finish his thought. "Or do you think you're the only Starfleet officer with a stake in this?"

Bashir sighed, hating the way this was going. "Of course not. But I probably know more about how Locken is likely to react than almost anyone . . ."

"Except for me," Ezri said matter-of-factly.

"You?"

"Me," she repeated. "Julian, you might *be* an enhanced person, but I, a trained counselor and a lifelong observer of humanoid behavior, *live* with an enhanced person. Don't you think that counts for something?"

Bashir regarded her without comment for several seconds, obviously looking for a flaw in her argument, and finding none. Finally, he lowered his head in resignation. "Lieutenant, I submit to the overwhelming force of your logic. Obviously, one of the previous hosts spent a great deal of time with Vulcans. You'd better go pack."

"Already did once today," Ezri said, trying not to smile too broadly. "Not everyone is as fussy as you are."

Closing his bag and lifting it from the bed, Bashir pointed at the door. "We'll see what you say about that when we get to Sindorin."

Chapter Five

Ordinarily, Kira wouldn't violate another's privacy by entering a holosuite while a program was running, but she was fairly confident she wasn't walking in on anything the Jem'Hadar would consider embarrassing. As far as she knew, Jem'Hadar couldn't be embarrassed. And even if they could be, it wouldn't have stopped her in this case. Time was a factor.

She entered and found herself looking down a dozen meters into a bowl-shaped pit with a floor of loose soil and walls of broken rock. Below her, Taran'atar was fighting a nightmare.

The creature appeared to be insectile—five meters tall, eight long limbs, each one ending in a two-pronged horny claw. The claws at the end of the foremost limbs were more flexible than the others and were holding heavy clubs that looked like they might have been rubbed or shaped somehow for easier grasping.

The insect aimed one of the clubs at Taran'atar's head, but the Jem'Hadar sidestepped a half-meter to the left. The club head was momentarily buried in the sandy soil, and Taran'atar leapt up onto the creature's back, then took a swipe with his axlike *kar'takin* at the soft, flexible part where two sections of the insect's chitinous armor overlapped. The blade bit deep and the joint spurted a thick, purplish ichor. The insect made a strange metallic noise, then tore the club out of the soil. Taran'atar backflipped off the creature and landed softly, knees bent, then tumbled to the side as the club descended again.

The creature, which apparently had poor peripheral vision, didn't see where its opponent had gone and issued another piercing cry as the *kar'takin* landed again. It reared, rolling itself up onto only four legs, waving the claws and clubs of its forelimbs but finding no target.

Taran'atar stepped lightly onto the insect's back again, took three quick strides up its dorsal ridge, and landed a heavy blow on the crown of its head. The carapace didn't crack, but what passed for the creature's central nervous system must have been under that part of the shell, because the blow staggered it, its sapling-thick legs buckling beneath it. Taran'atar used the creature's forward momentum to tumble over the top of its head, curled into a shoulder roll, and came to a halt about three meters from where the insect now lay dazed.

Taran'atar rolled nimbly to his feet, then paused, watching the swaying giant. Kira expected him to approach the insect and end the battle, but the Jem'Hadar was obviously waiting for something. Kira wondered distantly if the Jem'Hadar was simply enjoying having the creature at his mercy and wished to prolong the moment as much as possible.

Then, suddenly, the insect's whole body spasmed and it curled into a tight ball, all eight limbs wrapping around its lower abdomen. The edges of the armor plates on its back lifted and stubby, thorny spikes slid out from underneath. Muscles contracted, the creature shuddered again and the spikes shot out in every direction, some embedding themselves in the loose soil, others shattering against the walls. Kira flinched in spite of herself, startled by the simulated carnage.

Taran'atar leapt lightly into the air, correctly judging the trajectory of the half-dozen projectiles that were heading in his direction. He slipped between the two highest-flying spikes, clearing the other four by half a meter, then dropped to the ground directly in front of the bug's great head. He raised his blade high and Kira braced herself for the sight of split carapace or splattered brain matter, but instead heard only "End program."

A momentary shimmer, and Kira suddenly found herself on the same level as Taran'atar, in the otherwise empty holosuite. Taran'atar was leaning on his weapon, gazing at her fixedly, but without concern. "Good day, Colonel," he said, his loose black coverall as clean as it must have been when he started the program. At Kira's request, he had shortly after his arrival on the station stopped wearing his gray Dominion uniform in favor of the less provocative garment.

"Good day, Taran'atar. I hope my presence didn't interrupt your exercise."

"No," he said. Kira had spoken to the Jem'Hadar a number of times since he had come onto the station, but she still had not grown accustomed to his voice. She always expected something on the order of a Worf-like growl, but his tone was higher, richer, more melodious. She wondered if Jem'Hadar ever sang, and, if they did, could they carry a tune?

"But you shut off the program before . . ." She faltered. "You weren't finished."

Taran'atar studied the edge of his blade, then looked up at her. "The battle was won. I would have killed it with the next blow."

"Well, yes, that was obvious," Kira said. "What was that, anyway?"

"On the world where they live, the natives called it something which, translated, means approximately 'Comes-in-the-night-kills-many.' They lived in burrows and would tunnel up underneath their prey, pull them down, and then consume them."

Something suddenly dawned on Kira. Taran'atar had come aboard the station with few possessions, and holoprograms weren't among them. "Did you create that simulation yourself? From memory?"

Taran'atar inclined his head slightly. "I knew the parameters, and was able to encode them onto a data rod preformatted for the holosuite."

A Jem'Hadar of no small talents, Kira mused. Or were they all as capable as this one, and she'd just never known it? One thing was certain, she was never going to underestimate Taran'atar again.

"That one was using weapons. They must possess some sort of rudimentary intelligence."

Taran'atar tilted his head in the Jem'Hadar equivalent of a shrug. "Perhaps. You may be right. It was not my concern. My orders were to kill them, not to study them. They were decimating the population of a settlement the Founders had assigned to grow food crops."

"And you were guarding them, the settlement? That's what you did before you came here?"

"Not before I came here. This was many years ago, long before I became an Elder. The survey team found them before the settlement was established. My unit was assigned to eradicate them."

"Are you telling me you wiped out a native species to establish the farming community?"

Taran'atar nodded. "It is the practice among the Founders to assign peoples who have proven themselves to be superior tillers of the soil to woi.ds where they may best serve the needs of the Dominion. This group—I do not know what you would call them—was transplanted from another world, one that the Founders had conquered many years earlier. They were a small species, poorly equipped for combat, so my unit was called in to secure the settlement."

"Secure the settlement?" Kira asked. "You mean commit genocide."

Taran'atar took note of her change in demeanor, but didn't hesitate. "Our goal was to completely eradicate the population, yes. This disturbs you?"

"It would disturb any of my people. We ourselves were once enslaved by invaders, too."

"We did not enslave these creatures . . ."

"No, you eradicated them," Kira said. "Can you tell me which is worse?"

Taran'atar asked, "Is it your wish to debate this issue, Colonel?"

Kira felt her jaw tighten. "No, I'm not interested in a debate. That wasn't my intention. In fact, I came here to make a request."

The Jem'Hadar seemed uncertain. "A request?"

"There's something I'd like you to do, but I don't want you to feel *compelled* to do it. You have to decide whether you wish to or not. It is our custom to *ask* our guests for assistance, and to let them make the choice."

Taran'atar clearly wasn't just uncertain now, but agitated and impatient. "I am not your *guest,* Colonel. I am a Jem'Hadar, with a mission to obey, observe, and learn. The Founder . . ."

"Odo," Kira said.

Taran'atar accepted the correction, but his agitation only increased. *"Odo gave me this task, to serve your will as I would serve his. I still do not understand completely how this can be done, but I took an oath and so I will obey you. But he never said anything about making choices. "* And with this, Taran'atar slammed the head of his *kar'takin* into the holosuite floor. The computer that controlled the room's simulated environments sensed the imminent impact and attempted to generate a cushioning forcefield, but was too slow to block the full force of the blow. The blade bit into the deck and a shower of sparks erupted from a pierced EPS conduit. Safeties kicked in and the sparks stopped.

Kira was too surprised to say anything for several seconds and before she could protest Taran'atar's behavior, the room's comm came on and she heard Quark say in diffident tones, *"Ah, hey. Hello in there? Maybe you could take it a little easy on my holosuite? No offense, but since Rom stabbed me in the back and took off for Ferenginar, there isn't anyone on the station who knows how to fix the* frinxing *thing. Okay, Mr. Jem'Hadar? Hello?"*

"Everything's fine, Quark," Kira said. "Don't worry about it. I'll have Nog come down and look at it later."

"Oh, Colonel. Heh, well, so you're . . . ah . . . joining the fun, too. Well, okay. But Commander Vaughn won't let Nog . . ."

"I'll speak to Commander Vaughn," Kira said. "All right?"

"Okay, Colonel. Fine. You two just have fun in there, all right. No problem." He paused. *"There isn't any problem, is there?"*

"Not unless you don't go away," Kira said.

"Right," Quark said. *"Gone."*

Kira and Taran'atar stood looking at one another for a moment or two. Then, Kira reached down, tugged the *kar'takin* out of the deck and hefted it in her two hands. It was heavy, heavier even than it looked. "Did you program a replicator to produce this, too?"

"Yes."

Kira nodded, appreciating the balance of the weapon as she scrutinized it. "By the way," she said. "How much did Quark charge you to use the holosuite?"

Taran'atar looked confused again. Kira was momentarily struck by a guilty feeling that she was using up the Jem'Hadar's lifetime supply of confusion. "Charge?" he asked. "When I learned that this facility existed, I told the Ferengi that I would be using it today. He did not mention anything about a charge."

"Yeah," Kira said. "Okay. Never mind. No surprise here. I'll set up an account for you. Try to remember that there are other people on the station who might want to use things and some of them might be in line in front of you." She handed him back the weapon.

The Jem'Hadar accepted it.

"Now, getting back to my request . . ."

"Simply tell me what you want me to do," Taran'atar said.

"I want you to *consider* accompanying Dr. Bashir on a mission to a planet where a human has taken control of a Jem'Hadar hatchery." Briefly, Kira outlined the story of Locken and their guesses about his plans.

Taran'atar listened without comment until she had finished, then said, "It will be as you say. You may consider the Jem'Hadar serving this human already dead."

Kira shook her head. "I'm afraid you aren't getting this. I'm not asking you to go kill all the Jem'Hadar . . ."

"But there are Jem'Hadar on this planet who have been conditioned to serve this man whom you oppose. Correct?"

"Yes, correct."

"Then I must either kill them or they will kill the doctor and anyone else who accompanies him on his mission."

"Let's get something straight," Kira said. "Your participation in this mission is contingent upon your helping my crew according to their needs. I realize you have a genetic predisposition toward killing your enemies, and use of lethal force may in fact become necessary, but it isn't to be your first option. Am I understood?"

The Jem'Hadar looked down at her. "You wonder at my willingness to kill my own kind. You think because you have fought my species, that you understand what drives it, that it's defined solely by the controlled genetics used to create us. Tell me, Colonel, is that how you feel about Dr. Bashir?"

Kira was taken aback by the question. Taran'atar continued. "You have accepted that he is genetically predisposed to act differently, to think differently, to *feel* differently than you do, even though this disposition was devised by the hand of other beings no greater, no more divine, than yourself."

Kira could see where the logic of the argument was headed, but she was helpless to steer a passage around the upcoming rocky shoals. "Yes," she said.

Taran'atar then said, with surprising calm, "Then please extend the same courtesy to *me.*"

Kira's eyes narrowed. "You make some very valid points," she said. "But we're still going to do things *my* way. So I'll ask you one more time. Am I understood?"

The silence was deafening and seemed to last far too long for Kira's comfort.

"No," Taran'atar admitted finally. "But it will be as you say."

Chapter Six

With less than an hour before the *Euphrates* was to depart, Ro Laren sat in the security office, studying the copious and astonishingly detailed files Odo had left behind.

All but a few of her deputies and supplemental Starfleet personnel were already gone. With so few people on the station, and so much of it currently powered down, onboard security was far less complicated. Ro had decided to use her remaining time to listen to some of Morn's stories, attempt to uncover whatever skullduggery Quark might be engaged in, and read through her predecessor's database. She enjoyed Morn's stories, had managed to quietly sabotage the worst of Quark's indiscretions, and was dutifully amazed at the quantity and quality of Odo's records. There was information buried in the security office that she suspected was unknown even to Starfleet Intelligence.

Shortly after she first came aboard, she had uncovered the first cache of redundantly encrypted files in an innocuous subsector in the office's dedicated mainframe. She wondered if even Kira knew they were there. It had taken Ro five full days of studying the computer system just to figure out what Odo had done to safeguard the hidden files. Then another twelve days to devise a way to access them without tripping the EM pulse that would wipe the data if she'd made a single mistake. Her persistence paid off in the end; the files were hers now, and it was gratifying to know that some of the more subtle skills she'd learned with Starfleet and the Maquis could be combined so effectively.

After she started reading, Ro had been tempted to anonymously contact a couple of the most begrimed individuals mentioned therein and send them a tidbit or two, just to see what would happen. Fortunately, she waited long enough to let the temptation pass. Within a day or two, the wisdom of Odo's designs had become clearer. This wealth of material was meant to be salted away until a moment in the indefinite future—the proverbial rainy day—when it would be most useful. Strangely, that day had apparently never arrived, even in the darkest moments of the Dominion War, but then again, this was not *that* kind of data. It wasn't the sort of information that would save an empire or a world or even an army. It might save one or two lives—special lives, the lives of those who might someday change the luck of armies or worlds or even empires.

If Quark ever learned about this— She smiled at the thought.

Ro noted the time and decided she'd better get to the *Euphrates*. She closed the files and checked the encryption codes again. She'd considered backing up the data, a risky move, but she didn't trust the station core right now for obvious reasons. Instead, she'd taken the precaution of asking Nog to physically retrieve the security datacore in the unlikely event that DS9 had to be abandoned. She was taking a chance trusting Nog, but not, Ro thought, a big chance. Ro liked him. He was an interesting commingling of Federation

Boy Scout and scoundrel, both types she understood and whose responses she could predict, which was as close to trust as Ro Laren ever came.

After making sure everything was secure, Ro reached under the desk and pulled out her travel bag. She never had to look inside the bag, because she always knew exactly what was there: a change of clothes; some basic toiletries and first-aid items; enough condensed rations to last three days; a microfilter for water reclamation; a fully charged hand phaser; a tricorder; a small but powerful palm beacon; and, in a concealed compartment, a porcelain fractal-edged knife. If Ro ever found the last item in the possession of any visitor to DS9, she would have confiscated it immediately. It was illegal in the Federation and on numerous independent worlds, Bajor included. Fractal knives had only one use: they were weapons of terror, because their edges were too fragile for anything else. She had taken this particular blade from the body of a Cardassian "information officer" who had used it while interrogating Maquis prisoners. Someone—Ro had never found out who, having arrived on the scene long after the fact—had used the fractal knife on the inquisitor, extensively. She had kept the blade ever since, considering it the ultimate "you never know when you might need it" tool.

She paused at the door and took a last look around at the blank walls. *Was it like this when Odo was here,* she wondered, *or did someone take away his things when he left?* From the little she had heard about the man and, more tellingly, from what she had gleaned from reading between the lines of his reports, Ro guessed that there had never been anything belonging to Odo in this room. Personal effects would have given the criminals he had brought here more information about himself than he would have wanted them to know.

Ro slung her bag over her shoulder, knowing that the walls of her quarters were as blank as these.

Bashir, Ezri, and Ro had assembled in the airlock outside runabout pad C. It was, Bashir noted, only a little more than eight hours since he and Ezri had told the *Wayfarer* to leave for Earth without them. Taran'atar arrived last, carrying only a soft-sided case of suspicious proportions. "Let me guess," Ro said. "Weapons?"

Taran'atar didn't reply, but only laid the pack down on the deck, unfastened a pair of clips, then unrolled it like a sleeping bag. It contained a standard-issue Bajoran hand phaser, with several replacement power cells affixed; what looked like a dozen or so photon grenades; and a sheathed weapon that Bashir guessed was a *kar'takin*.

"What, no throwing knives?" Ro asked.

Taran'atar indicated a small satchel bound into the case's lining.

"Oh, good. Don't want to forget those."

Taran'atar regarded Ro speculatively, but still did not comment. He rolled up the case again with quick, precise movements so that when he was finished it looked exactly the way it had before he had opened it.

Just as Taran'atar was rising, everyone was surprised to see Commander Vaughn emerging from the runabout.

"Sir?" Bashir said. "We didn't expect to find you here."

"Thought I'd save you some time and run through the preflight," Vaughn said. "She's ready, by the way. Try bringing her back in one piece, please. I recently found out what a terrible record this station has when it comes to runabouts."

Bashir almost smiled. "Thank you for seeing us off."

Vaughn nodded. "Colonel Kira intended to be here herself, but she wanted to be on hand when Nog and his crew began detaching Empok Nor's lower core. The operation started about two hours ago. Are you heading directly for Sindorin?"

Bashir shook his head. "Ro and I have been talking. We're going to take a very indirect route, try to look like a survey ship and bore anyone who might be watching. We'll be skirting the edge of the Romulan protectorate, so we're working on the assumption that there are cloaked ships nearby." Ro handed a padd with a copy of their flight plan to Vaughn, who scrutinized it carefully.

"All right," he said finally. "But avoid going into the protectorate if you can help it. And check in periodically before you hit the Badlands. It'll help keep up the pretense that you're surveying."

"Right. And we'd like to know how things are going here," Bashir said. "If it starts to look like Nog is going to blow the place to pieces, could someone please rescue my ficus?"

Vaughn smiled. "I'll see what I can do. Well. Safe journey."

"Thank you, sir," Bashir said, and started to follow the others into the runabout. Vaughn waited until Bashir was just on the threshold before calling, "Doctor? A moment, please."

Bashir stopped and turned. "Yes, Commander?"

"A word of advice," Vaughn said in low tones. "Don't try to be a hero. Don't think for a moment that you're going to be able to find evidence you can use to expose Thirty-One. Just go in, do the job, and come home. Understand?"

"I understand what you're saying," Bashir said suspiciously, "but not why."

"Because I'd like to see all of you come home alive. Cole needs you to do his dirty work for him, but that's all he's going to allow. Try to go beyond that and I can guarantee there will be unpleasant repercussions." With that, Vaughn turned and walked away.

Bashir stared after the commander for several seconds, wondering not without some smoldering anger what he was supposed to make of all that. The doctor usually enjoyed a good mystery, but this was something else entirely. And as he entered the runabout, Bashir resolved that if and when they returned from Sindorin, he was going to get to the bottom of this particular enigma once and for all.

Chapter Seven

"How long is this going to take?" Ezri asked.

"To make it look good, about eighteen hours," Ro said. "Just long enough for everyone—well, almost everyone—to get some sleep, eat a couple meals and get tired of looking at each other."

Ezri, relaxing in the copilot's seat, made a sour face.

Ro caught the look. "Don't take it the wrong way," she said. "I've been on a lot of these kinds of trips. The best thing to do is try to maintain your sense of humor and don't get in anyone else's way." She glanced over her shoulder toward Bashir, who was just going into the aft compartment with a padd in hand. As he disappeared behind the door, Ro added, "Unless you *want* someone to get in your way."

Ezri grinned. "I don't think that's really an option."

"You'd be surprised what you could do on one of these runabouts. When I was in the Maquis, we had ships much less sophisticated than this—basically just big cans with engines mounted on them—and people used to find all sorts of ways to make private space. You had to, especially if you were spending a lot of time together."

"This isn't really like that," Ezri said.

"Actually, it *is*," Ro asserted. "A *lot.* It's surprising how much, in fact. You people on DS9, from what I've seen so far, have a lot more in common with the Maquis than anything I ever saw on a starship."

"*We* people on DS9, you mean," Ezri corrected good-naturedly. "You're one of us now."

Ro shrugged. "Well, yes and no. I'm not old guard—you, Kira, Bashir, Nog. Don't get me wrong: you seem like a good group, but you *are* a little insular. In that respect, you remind me of, well, another crew."

Somehow Ezri knew Ro wasn't thinking about the Maquis anymore. "You're referring to the *Enterprise,* aren't you?" Ezri asked.

Ro snuck a quick look at Ezri, then returned her gaze to the control board. "You're not part Betazoid, are you?"

"No," Ezri said. "Just a counselor. That, and I read your file."

"Ah, yes. My file," she sighed, as if nothing more needed to be said.

Ezri wasn't quite ready to give up, though. "So, what was it like?"

Ro checked their course and submitted a slight correction while she considered her answer. Then, slowly, she reached out and ran her finger along the edge of the viewport. She showed it to Ezri, who saw it was covered with fine gray dust. "It was very clean," Ro said. "Everything. Even the engine room. I've been in a few engine rooms since the *Enterprise* and I know how hard it is to keep one clean. And it was very well lit except, of course, when you wanted the light to be low." Her expression, which had been set in a soft scowl, softened then and she said, "Life on the *Enterprise* was very tidy."

"So you liked it?"

"Did I like it?" she repeated, as if it was the first time she had ever considered the question. "I suppose I did. For a while, anyway. It was so safe, so secure, so invulnerable. But then I came to be reminded about all the people whose lives weren't so safe and secure and I knew I had to make a choice. Follow my orders, or follow my conscience." Ro lapsed into silence again, then noticed the look on Dax's face. "You want to ask me about Picard, don't you? It's all right. Everyone does eventually."

"All right, you got me," Ezri admitted. "I hate to seem predictable, but . . . what was it like serving with Picard?"

Ro smiled, but it seemed to Ezri that the smile was bittersweet. "He was pretty much what you look for in a captain: Tough, but fair. Committed to high ideals. Intelligent, even scholarly, but not stuffy. And he wore a very nice cologne."

Ezri laughed, delighted.

Ro chuckled, too, but tried to keep a straight face. "No, I'm serious. It was very subtle, but distinctive. If you were working on something, head down to the grindstone, and heard a door open behind you, it was always obvious when it was Picard because of this great cologne. And he has a very nice voice. Oh, that's right—and he was a wine snob."

"I think his family owns a vineyard."

"Right. I'd forgotten that. But I'll tell you something about Picard that you'd never know unless you served with him . . ."

"He's not as tall as he looks in the news feeds?" Ezri asked, remembering the last time she saw him, standing on the Promenade next to Kira only two weeks ago.

Ro shot Ezri a sly glance. "Well, in fact, *no*, he isn't, but that wasn't what I was going to say. It's just that, well . . ." She paused, gathering her thoughts, searching for words. "Maybe the universe seems just as confusing to him as it does to the rest of us. Maybe he feels like it's difficult to decide what he should do, but it never *seemed* that way to the rest of us. He had a gift for looking, sounding, *acting* like whatever he was doing was the exact *right* thing to do . . ." She paused, looked like she was going to continue, then shook her head. "I don't know any other way to put it." Ro looked over at Dax. "Have you ever served with anyone like that? I've heard some stories about your Captain Sisko . . ."

"Benjamin?" Ezri shook her head. "He wasn't that kind of commander, not that kind of man. You know that before I was Jadzia I was Curzon, don't you?"

Ro nodded, watching the controls.

"I knew . . . I've *known* . . . Benjamin for more than twenty years, from the time he was little more than a boy to the day he . . . well, we don't really know with complete certainty what happened to him, do we? You're a Bajoran. What do *you* think?"

"I'm a Bajoran," Ro explained, "but I'm not *that* kind of Bajoran. If you want the religious interpretation, you'll have to ask the colonel. If you want my opinion, I'd say he died in the fire caves."

"If it were anyone else, I suppose I'd agree," Ezri said. "But not Benjamin. Maybe this is all hindsight, but when I look back, I see that Ben's life was like a refiner's fire. Things that would have ground down any other man only made Benjamin stronger and sharper. Hardship *purified* him. He took the heat and he made it his own and at the core of it was the fact that he never ceased questioning his motivations, his desires and fears. He didn't see himself as a prophet or an emissary, not really. But he did what a prophet is supposed to do: he tried to clarify his vision by never allowing himself to think that there was only one path to truth." Ezri stopped speaking, rolling around what she had just said in her head, trying to decide whether she believed it, then finally decided she did. "How does that sound?" she asked.

Ro looked at Ezri and smiled. "Like a hard act to follow."

Back in the runabout's aft compartment, Bashir was removing a bowl of couscous and a cup of broth from the replicator and trying very hard not to let Taran'atar's stony silence unnerve him. Setting the food down on the table, Bashir glanced over at the Jem'Hadar and was surprised to see he was currently showing more interest in the bowl and cup than he had in anything else so far during their trip.

"How's that liquid diet working out?"

Taran'atar looked up. "Adequately."

"I wonder," Bashir said. Shortly after Taran'atar had come to DS9, he'd allowed the doctor to subject him to a complete medical examination. Bashir had put him through a battery of tests, scans, and analyses, in part to verify Taran'atar's claim that he was one of the anomalous Jem'Hadar who wasn't dependent upon ketracel-white for his survival. Withdrawal would never be an issue for him, but without the white to supply all his nutritional needs, Taran'atar needed to eat.

He'd told Bashir that after the Vorta had identified him as having the mutation, they'd devised a liquid diet that would satisfy his nutritional requirements while slowly allowing his digestive system to reassert itself. Taran'atar had committed the formula to memory, and managed to program the station replicators to produce it. Bashir had analyzed a sample, and while it was chemically suited to Taran'atar's physiology, he didn't even want to imagine how vile the stuff must be.

"You wonder what?" Taran'atar asked.

"I'm wondering if you're ready to try something other than that concentrated pond water the Vorta gave you," Bashir said with a small smile. "How long since you ate last?"

"Six days," the Jem'Hadar said. Because his physiology was so efficient, any food he ingested was completely absorbed and converted to fuel, with no waste. Taran'atar only needed to eat once every four or five days. Six, however, was too long.

"Let me guess: You're finding the Vorta's concoction a little hard to swallow." The doctor indicated his bowl. "Do you want to try some of this?"

Taran'atar hesitated. "I don't know," he said finally. "What is that?"

"This is couscous—grain and spices and beans . . ." He held up the cup. "And this is vegetable broth."

"Humans are omnivores. You do not eat meat?"

"Very rarely," Bashir said. "I never make meat for myself, but I'll eat it if someone else prepares it."

"This is a cultural prohibition?"

Bashir shrugged. "Call it a lifestyle choice."

"Klingons eat a great deal of meat," Taran'atar observed.

"Klingons get diseases of the colon a lot, too," Bashir replied, picking up the cup of broth and carrying it to Taran'atar. "Let's start with something simple. Try this."

Taran'atar took the proffered cup and held it to his nose, sniffing. His face wrinkled and he said, "It has an unpleasant odor."

"Try some anyway," Bashir said, then had another thought. "No, wait, let me check something." He pulled his medical tricorder out of his bag and passed the scanner over Taran'atar a couple of times until he was satisfied. "Go ahead. No allergies."

Taran'atar took a small sip of broth, looked for a moment as though he was going to spit it out, but did not. Finally, he swallowed and appeared to roll the flavor around in his mouth for a moment or two. Then he took another mouthful. Then another. After finishing the broth, he gave the cup back to Bashir. "Thank you. How do you know so much about our biology?"

Bashir handed him the bowl of couscous and the fork. "You aren't the first Jem'Hadar I've examined. Some I've studied quite carefully, in fact. You'll need to chew that, by the way."

"Dissections?"

"I beg your pardon?"

"Did you dissect them?"

Bashir shook his head. "No, of course not."

"Vivisection?"

"*No.*"

"Then I do not understand. How could you know so much about my species?"

Nonplussed, Bashir collected himself for several seconds, then replied, "I . . . we . . . found a Jem'Hadar child several years ago and I was able to observe and record much of its maturation process with my medical scanners. Also . . ." But then he hesitated, uncertain whether to continue. "Well, perhaps I shouldn't be telling you this, but I once tried to help free a group of Jem'Hadar soldiers from their dependency upon the white."

Though his expression didn't change, Bashir sensed a sudden tension in Taran'atar's shoulders and back muscles. In measured tones, he asked, "And did you succeed?"

Bashir shook his head. "The actual situation proved to be not unlike your own: a rare and random mutation."

"How rare?" Taran'atar asked.

"You tell me. Didn't you say the Vorta specifically searched for Jem'Hadar like yourself at Odo's request?"

"Yes, and they found only four of us," Taran'atar said. "Or so they said."

"You sound skeptical."

"The Jem'Hadar understand the Vorta better than the Vorta understand us," Taran'atar said. "We obey them because it is the will of the Founders, but if they did not control the supply of the white, if the white were discovered to be unnecessary or, at the very least, conquerable . . . Most Jem'Hadar go their entire lives without ever seeing a Founder, but the Vorta are there every day—watching, prying, *sneering*. You all look like Vorta to us: humans, Klingons, Romulans, Bajorans, Vulcans—some of the Jem'Hadar who fought in the war said it made killing you more satisfying."

"Charming," Bashir said, deciding he was no longer hungry.

Taran'atar seemed to realize he had caused offense. He felt compelled to explain himself. "The Founder who exil—who *sent* me here told me something I did not understand at the time, but now I'm beginning to see his wisdom. He said, 'Exposure brings understanding.' Then, the Founder laughed aloud and said, 'And just as often, familiarity breeds contempt.'"

Bashir nodded. "That sounds like something Odo would say."

"He also told me to be watchful particularly of the one named Quark. I am not sure why."

Bashir laughed. "I am. But never mind. So, do you have any personal feelings about your mission to the Alpha Quadrant?"

"The Founder told me only to obey the colonel as I would obey him. The colonel has told me to obey you. So that," he said, "makes you my Vorta."

"Oh, no," Bashir said. "No, no, no. Not me. I'm the doctor, the man who gives you broth and couscous."

". . . As the Vorta gave me the white."

"Bad comparison. I want you to be well . . ."

". . . So I can fight for you," Taran'atar said. "So I can kill other Jem'Hadar."

Struggling to remain calm, Bashir let out a breath and said, "That's not true. I want you to tell me what the other Jem'Hadar will do so that we can try to find a way to avoid *more* deaths. I'm a doctor. Do you understand what that means in my culture? Our first rule, one of the oldest rules in our recorded history, is 'Do no harm.' It's my role to develop new ways to help, then to teach those ways to others." Then, realizing how pedantic he sounded, Bashir hesitated and tried to shift the conversation back to Taran'atar. "Is there anything analogous to this in the Dominion?"

"There may be," Taran'atar said. "I do not know everything that happens throughout the length and breadth of the Dominion. I am a soldier. *My* role is to defend and, if necessary, to kill. Do you think that makes you superior to me?"

Bashir was surprised by both the question and Taran'atar's matter-of-fact tone. "Better?" he asked. "Well, not better. More tolerant, perhaps. The Federation . . ."

"Not the Federation," Taran'atar interrupted. *"You.* There is something about the way you carry yourself. You wear humility like a shroud. Again, it reminds me of the Vorta."

Bashir knew he was being challenged, that he had to think carefully about what he would say next. There was danger here, but also opportunity. "There were times in the past," he said slowly, "when I felt the need to hide who I was. It's been a hard habit to break. I'm trying to learn new habits."

Taran'atar studied Bashir's face for the space of several heartbeats, then said, "When you think about what you are going to say, you are not nearly so much like a Vorta." He held out the empty bowl. "May I have more?"

Bashir took the bowl. "Yes, of course." Then, he handed Taran'atar a napkin. "Wipe your chin," he said.

Chapter Eight

Bashir's combadge chimed and Ezri called, *"Dax to Bashir."*

"Go ahead."

"We've found something. You'd better come up here." She paused and Bashir heard Ro speak, though her words were indistinct. Ezri added, *"And bring Taran'atar."*

Taran'atar followed Bashir into the runabout's cockpit. Ro had dropped out of warp and was using the runabout's thrusters to edge them into the shadow of a large derelict spacecraft. Neither she nor Ezri looked up when they entered, both intent on their instruments. Though they were too close to the spacecraft for Bashir to make out the ship's configuration, Taran'atar announced, "Romulan *N'renix*-class cruiser. Crew complement: forty-five. Medium shielding, medium weapons, excellent cloaking capability. Maximum speed: warp nine point eight. Can sustain a cruising speed of warp nine point five for over twenty-six hours. Used primarily to transport high-level military personnel and secret technology."

"I've never heard of this class," Bashir said, studying the sensor input. "Has one ever been to the station?"

"No," Ezri said. "This might be one of the classes of ships they didn't want us to know about."

"That is correct," Taran'atar said. "No *N'renix*-class ship ever left Romulan-controlled space during the war."

"Then how do *you* know about it?" Ro asked, giving the thrusters one more nudge. Bashir looked out the main viewport and saw they were so close to the derelict that he could make out the seams where the hull plates were joined.

"The Dominion's military intelligence on the Alpha Quadrant is extensive," Taran'atar explained. "I made a thorough study of it before embarking on my mission."

"What happened to it?" Bashir asked. "Are there any casualties?"

"It's been hulled in half a dozen places," Ezri said, reading off the sensor log. "No life signs. No energy signature. And the engines are gone."

Bashir winced. "Core failure?"

"No," Ezri said. "I mean the engines are *gone.* Someone removed them. Did a good job, too. Wait, let me check something. . . ." She reset the sensors and did a quick scan. "They took the main disruptor bank, too. Ripped it right out of the belly."

"Are you picking up any third-party engine signatures? Maybe make a guess about how long ago this happened?"

"Long enough," Ezri said. "And, no, nothing."

Taran'atar leaned forward and checked the sensor readout. He pointed to the pattern of impact marks on the ship's hull. "This is not a Jem'Hadar attack pattern, but it *is* very well placed."

Ro looked over her shoulder at him and asked, "You guys have patterns for weapons-fire attacks?"

"For every class of enemy craft, yes. Each has its unique weaknesses."

"How about Federation runabouts?"

"Aft shield generator."

"I'll remember that."

"That's enough," Bashir snapped. "Can we board her? Is it holding atmosphere?"

"Let me check," Ezri said. She finished her scan and said, "Not in the cargo bays or weapons-control areas, not without EVA equipment. The crew quarters are . . . well, they're gone. Engineering and the bridge are intact, and I think I could reactivate life-support from here, but the corridor linking them is open to space. I could beam over a forcefield generator and plug the hole. Life-support would need maybe an hour to generate enough atmosphere to sustain us. No gravity, though."

Ro groaned. "I hate zero gee."

"That's all right," Bashir said. "We need you to stay here and mind the sensors. Get to work, Ezri. Taran'atar and I will gather our gear."

"On it," Ezri said, and set to her task.

Bashir was struck by a thought and turned back to Ro. "Lieutenant, how far are we from the space lane for this sector?"

"I was just thinking about that myself," she said. "Not far at all. This isn't a heavily trafficked area, but if you were leaving the Romulan-controlled sector of Cardassian territory, you'd pretty much have to pass by here."

"Could you tell if the ship was towed here?"

"Not unless it was done very recently, but there's one thing that leads me to believe it was."

"And that is?"

"No bodies. If the crew quarters were opened to space, there would be bodies nearby. I don't read any."

Bashir sighed heavily. "Right," he said. "Someone wanted this ship to be found. But why? A scarecrow?"

Taran'atar looked at him quizzically and silently mouthed the word "scarecrow." Then he said, "If I understand the meaning of the word, then, yes, it was meant to incite fear."

"Terror is an effective weapon, Commander," Ro said.

Bashir looked down at Ro, momentarily stunned into silence. Then he laughed disgustedly and said, "I keep hearing that today, so I suppose it must be true. Anything on long-range scanners, Ezri?"

Ezri stopped what she was doing and ran a quick check. "No," she said, "but if a cloaked Romulan ship was approaching, we wouldn't know it anyway."

"Good point. All right, then, we don't have much time to do this. How are you doing with the forcefield?"

"I'd be doing a lot better if you stopped asking me questions," Ezri snapped, but then looked up and added, "sir."

Bashir smiled sheepishly. "Sorry. Come on, Taran'atar, let's go see what Commander Vaughn packed for us."

Ezri waited for Bashir and Taran'atar to leave, then looked over at Ro and said, "He's trying not to show it, but he's enjoying this."

"Yeah, I got that, too."

"He used to play spy on the holodeck."

"Really?" She grimaced. "Never go spying with someone who thinks it's a game."

"I don't think he's played it since he's learned about Section 31. I think it lost its innocence."

"Maybe," Ro said. "Or maybe he lost his."

"The air pressure looks good," Bashir said, checking the sensor readings and closing the front seam of his protective garment. It was a class-B environmental suit—not rated for hard vacuum, but it would be adequate for the conditions aboard the Romulan ship.

"Better than I would have hoped," Ezri said. "We should be all right as long as our air supply holds out." She looked over at Taran'atar, who was checking the charge on his phaser. "What about him? No suit?"

"He doesn't need one," Bashir said. "Jem'Hadar physiology is much better suited for this sort of thing. He'll probably wear eye protection, but not much more."

Confirming Bashir's prediction, Taran'atar pulled a pair of dark goggles out of his equipment belt and slid them down over his eyes. Holding his phaser at combat readiness, he said, "Transport me first in case there is something waiting."

"Sensors say there are no life signs," Ro said.

"Not everything shows up on sensors."

"Good point."

The Jem'Hadar stepped onto the transporter platform. Just before Ro activated it, Taran'atar shrouded, becoming invisible. When Ro reported that he had successfully beamed over, Dax and Bashir stepped onto the platforms. "Energize," Bashir said.

Materializing in the center of a wide corridor lit only by emergency lighting, they saw Taran'atar floating a meter off the deck, bracing himself against the ceiling, his phaser at the ready.

"No shroud?" Ezri asked.

"No need," Taran'atar said. "There's no one here."

Bashir checked the status of his and Ezri's e-suits and was satisfied with what he found. Looking back down the corridor, he saw the blue glow of the forcefield generator that was preventing the air from escaping.

"How long will the batteries maintain the field?" he asked Ezri.

"Two hours. Not much more."

"All right, then," he said, pointing up the corridor. "Let's not waste any time. The bridge is in that direction." He had memorized the ship's schematics just before they had left the *Euphrates*. "Taran'atar, would you mind taking point?"

The Jem'Hadar did not reply, but pushed off the bulkhead with an easy, practiced motion and moved silently up the corridor.

Bashir looked uncertain. Dax guessed he didn't have a great deal of zero-gee experience. "Don't worry," she said. "It's rather like swimming. Just don't move too suddenly." She tapped her foot against the bulkhead and drifted forward.

Bashir watched her movements, studied the details of the corridor, and seconds later he was drifting past her easily.

Ezri rolled her eyes. "I bet you were even good at ice-skating the first time you tried it."

"Well, yes," Bashir said, trying to sound humble, but failing. "In fact, I was."

Ezri braced herself against the bulkhead and pushed Bashir into the center of the corridor as hard as she could. He pirouetted in midflight, landed feet-first against the bulkhead, twisted, pushed off, then sailed after Taran'atar. "I hate you," she called out. He waved in response, then signaled for her to follow. "No, really," she said. "I do."

The doors to the main bridge were sealed, suggesting that the bridge crew might have had time to erect a barricade before the ship was boarded. When Bashir began scanning the doors for a release frequency, Taran'atar laid his hand over the tricorder display, and then pointed at a pair of small hatches in the walls near the ceiling. "Automatic defenses," he said softly, then quickly sketched out a rectangular area on the floor in front of the doorway. "Kill zone." Bashir passed the information to Ezri, who nodded, drew her phaser, and pushed off to the opposite end of the corridor.

Bashir spoke briefly to Taran'atar, then followed Ezri. As soon as they were at a safe distance, Taran'atar shrouded and Bashir reactivated his tricorder, quickly found the proper frequency, and transmitted it to the doors, which opened without a sound. No illumination spilled out, not even emergency lights.

The hatches near the ceiling remained shut. Bashir and Dax waited.

Twenty seconds later, the Jem'Hadar shimmered back into existence before them. "I've deactivated the defense grid," he said. "It didn't require much effort. There was little power left in the system. The bridge controls are dead."

Bashir nodded toward the bridge. "Is there anyone in there?"

Taran'atar nodded. "If we assume that this vessel was carrying a maximum of forty-five crew members and that between one-third and one-half of them were lost when the hull lost integrity, then *everyone* is in there."

Bashir sighed, then set to work, slowly and methodically preparing himself as if for a minor surgical procedure. He activated the work light on his shoulder mount, then set his tricorder to automatic record and fastened it to the clip in the center of his chest harness. "Will you come?" he asked Ezri, who considered the question only for a second before nodding in assent. "Taran'atar?" he asked.

"I will stay out here and watch. I dislike being in a room with no escape route."

"Ro can transport us out," Ezri said.

"Yes," Taran'atar said. "Assuming she is still there." Then he turned, the air around him seemed to fold, and he disappeared.

Ezri winced, but resisted the urge to tap her combadge. Bashir saw her anxiety and activated his own. "Lieutenant?" he called.

"Ro here."

"Just checking in. Anything out there?"

"Nothing that wasn't half an hour ago. How about in there?"

"Yes," Bashir said. "Something in the bridge. We're going in to check it now."

"I'll resist the urge to say, 'Be careful,' because I hate it when people say that to me, but . . ."

Bashir smiled. "Understood. How's the transporter lock?"

"Solid."

"We're going into the bridge now. If you don't hear from us in twenty minutes, beam us all out. If you lose the lock, leave. Quickly."

There was only a moment's hesitation, but then Ro said, *"Understood. Talk to you in twenty. Ro out."*

Bashir looked down at Ezri and asked, "Ready?"

"I think so," she said. Then, incongruously, she laughed. "You know what's strange?"

"No, what?"

She shook her head. "It's just that I know whatever's in there, at some time in one of my lives, I'm sure I've seen something worse. Curzon witnessed the aftermath of half a dozen battles. Tobin saw a woman get shot out an airlock by Romulans. Audrid watched as her husband was killed by some kind of alien parasite. . . . Yet, as much as these were all things that happened to *me,* it's also like something that I've only read about or had described to me in a lecture. . . ."

" 'For now we see through a glass, darkly,' " Bashir said softly.

Ezri hesitated, ran the phrase over her tongue, then said, "I suppose that's it. Yes. What . . . ?"

"It's from the Judeo-Christian Bible," Bashir said, then quoted:

We know in part, and we prophesy in part.

But when that which is perfect is come, then that which is in part shall be done away.

When I was a child, I spoke as a child, I understood as a child, I thought as a child; but when I became a man, I put away childish things.

For now we see through a glass, darkly; but then face to face: now I know in part; but then shall I know even as also I am known.

And now abideth faith, hope, charity, these three; but the greatest of these is charity.

He stared into the middle distance for a moment before shifting his gaze back to Ezri. "When I was a boy, perhaps a month after the gene resequencing, I found that passage in a book—not the Bible, but a collection of essays—and, in that egocentric way children have, decided it was about *me.*" Bashir shook his head and grinned bemusedly. "Odd," he said. "I haven't thought about that in years."

Ezri stared at him for several seconds and then, because she could not kiss him through the e-suit, leaned forward and rubbed her cheek against his. "Every time I think I know everything about you, Julian Bashir," she said, "you find some way to surprise me."

Bashir laughed, surprised and delighted. "Well," he said, "good." Then, he sobered. "But we should go. Ready?"

"As I'll ever be."

Most of the Romulans had been killed quickly and cleanly, a disruptor to the back of the head at very close range. A few, the highest-ranking by what still remained of their uniforms, had died more slowly. Two of them—one obviously the ship's captain and the other an otherwise nondescript woman who Bashir assumed was a member of the Tal Shiar—had been killed by degrees. Whoever had done this had partially melted the walls, then thrust the pair into the molten metal, totally immobilizing them. Bashir guessed that they had been forced to watch the others being killed, even as they themselves had died. The burns would have been fatal, Bashir judged, but not instantaneously.

Bashir could not help but remember the battlefields of the Dominion War, the smell of burned flesh, the sight of bodies pulverized into jelly by concussive sonic blasts. It had been horrible, but there had been something like a reason behind all the terror and death. Here, he judged, there had been no goal except, perhaps, simple sadism, an exercise in power, like a small child who pulls the legs off bugs because no one has told him it's wrong. For the first time, he wanted to leave, to turn his back on the mission and disavow any kinship to the man he suspected was behind it all, though he knew he could not. He wanted, he realized, to be like a child again, and let others make the decisions. ". . . But when I became a man, I put away childish things," he whispered, not even realizing he was speaking aloud.

He was shaken from his reverie when Ezri called, "Julian? Look here." She was scanning the body of the captain, paying particular attention to the man's forehead, which was coated in a crust of blood.

Inspecting the Romulan carefully, Bashir saw that the blood hadn't flowed from a head wound as he had first surmised, but was a scab over a series of shallow cuts. At first, he made as if to scrape the blood away as he might if he were performing an autopsy, but then he felt the weight of death in the room and restrained himself, instead unhooking his tricorder and adjusting it for an epidural scan.

When the image materialized, he cursed, then thrust it at Ezri, who looked at it curiously.

"All right," she said. "I see, but I don't understand. The round figure is the sun?"

"Right."

"And that's a crescent moon superimposed on it?"

"Yes."

She shook her head. "I don't get it. What does it mean?"

Bashir smiled humorlessly. "I'm sorry. Humans *can* be rather self-centered sometimes. We assume everyone in the quadrant knows everything about us, even the things we don't really want them to know. It's an ancient symbol—almost four hundred years old—the sun and the moon together, suggesting totality, everything in the world. It symbolized the rule of Khan Noonien Singh."

"Khan?" Ezri said. "But he's dead. Isn't he?"

Bashir nodded his head. "He is, but apparently his spirit isn't entirely. Locken has appropriated his icon."

"The humans will go mad," Ezri said under her breath. Then, louder, as if remembering that Bashir was human, "Even those who aren't against genetic engineering in principle won't be able to tolerate the idea of a new Khan. It'll send Earth into a frenzy."

"Yes," Bashir agreed. "And frenzied people make rash decisions. Maybe that's what he wants."

"All right," she said, considering. "That fits." She turned away from the victims and began to work the main control panels. "Now let's see what else we can find out about what happened here." She tried to activate the panel, but instead of the control panel lighting up, a prerecorded message began to play on the viewscreen.

There was only a single figure in the recording, a Terran male in his late thirties or early forties. He was neither particularly tall nor physically imposing, though the manner in which he carried himself suggested a feline grace. His hair was red, cut short, and receded into a widow's peak. He wore a simple tunic and a long cloth overcoat, both black, both cut in a fashion like those worn by doctors in civilian hospitals. There was an emblem stitched into the upper left side of the coat front, the same symbol that had been carved into the Romulan's forehead. His eyes, Bashir saw, were a strange color for a man with such a fair complexion, a dark brown, almost black, almost as if his pupils had swallowed his irises.

"My name is Locken," he said, his voice low and reasonable, much more like the family doctor's than a conqueror's. *"And you are trespassing. This is the*

sovereign territory of the New Federation. If you have not come to pay tribute, then leave or be destroyed. There will be no other warning." He paused, still seeming quite reasonable, then added, almost incidentally, *"Don't imagine for a moment that you're a match for me. You're not."*

Ezri tapped a couple of other controls, but nothing happened. Then she reset her tricorder and performed a quick scan of the ship's computer system. "That's all there is," she said. "The panel was keyed to play this message no matter what we did. Everything else has been deleted." She looked up at the viewscreen and studied the image. "There was something very odd about his manner," she said. "Something . . . inhuman."

"He wasn't addressing equals," Bashir said. "He was talking to lesser beings. Something closer to animals . . ."

"Subjects," Ezri added. "Or slaves."

Bashir's mouth tightened, but then he nodded in agreement. "Or slaves."

"And did you see his eyes? Like two coals. Is that normal?"

Bashir shrugged. "It might be natural coloring. Could be a trait linked to his genetic enhancements. Could be colored contact lenses."

Turning back to the control panel, Ezri asked, "So there's nothing else we can do here?"

"Just one more thing, I think," Bashir said, and tapped his combadge. "Taran'atar, proceed to engineering. Lieutenant Ro, two to beam out."

"Acknowledged," Ro answered.

The Romulan bridge shimmered and disappeared, replaced by the runabout's cockpit. "Why'd you send Taran'atar to engineering?" Ezri asked.

Bashir ignored the question and spoke to Ro. "Lieutenant, please take us out to fifteen hundred kilometers and hold position."

Ro turned around in her seat and looked at them. "What's going on?"

"Before Taran'atar entered the bridge, I asked him to be ready to initiate a warp-core overload on my command."

Dax and Ro exchanged looks. "Do we have authorization to do anything like that?" Ezri asked. "Shouldn't we alert Starfleet and have them contact the Romulans?"

Bashir shook his head. "They'd never believe us. The Romulans would come out here and see that a human had orchestrated that massacre, maybe even find evidence that we'd been aboard and decide that Starfleet was somehow involved. Better to destroy it, and without using weapons that will leave Federation energy signatures."

"You realize, don't you," Dax said, "that this is exactly the sort of thing Section 31 would do. Leave no evidence, clean up the trail so no one will know . . . ? And those people, they had families, friends. Someone should tell them what happened."

"The irony isn't lost on me, Ezri," Bashir snapped. "But I don't think we can take the chance."

Bashir's combadge chirped. *"Taran'atar to Bashir."*

"Bashir here. Go ahead."

"Ready to beam back."

Ro hit the transporter controls, and Taran'atar materialized behind them. "The task is completed. The overload should occur in six minutes."

Ro wasted no time and gunned the thrusters. "Moving off to fifteen hundred kilometers," she said, then spun the runabout around to face the direction of the Romulan ship, which had dwindled to invisibility. "Anyone want to say anything?"

No one did, and in the silence a few moments later, a brilliant white light erupted outside the viewport, throwing stark shadows into the runabout cockpit before winking out. The instant it was gone, Bashir ordered Ro to proceed on their original course, then turned and stalked into the aft compartment.

Dax realized then that Bashir hadn't needed to stay and watch the explosion, but had forced himself to, making himself face the reality of his decision to employ the methods of his adversaries in order to defeat their purpose—knowing he'd have to live with that decision to the end of his days.

It wasn't the first time he'd felt compelled to make such a choice. He'd done it before, entering the dying mind of Luther Sloan to extract the cure for Section 31's genocidal changeling disease, to save Odo's life. Part of Julian had died that day, and Ezri knew she'd just witnessed another part of him die now.

The thought made her ache inside. No, this wasn't the first time he'd made such a choice. And she feared for him that it wouldn't be the last.

Chapter Nine

It was hours later that Taran'atar, watching sensors, announced, "Something on long-range."

"Jem'Hadar?" Ro asked.

"No. Engine signature is wrong. Something Federation, possibly Vulcan."

"Probably a survey ship. The Federation hasn't been able to get into this sector without a lot of trouble for the past couple of decades. The Romulans probably don't like them being here, but they can hardly chase them out."

Dax had come up next to Taran'atar to examine the readings herself. "So, nothing to worry about?"

"No, it's something to worry about. We don't want *anyone* knowing we've been here, least of all a bunch of Vulcans. If the Romulans ask them later, 'Did you spot a Federation runabout in the area . . . ?' "

"They'll say, 'Yes,' " Dax said.

"Right." Ro signaled Bashir.

"Yes?" came the curt reply.

"We've got company, Doctor. I'm changing course. Heading for the Badlands now. The ride will probably get a little bumpy then. The plasma storms cause a lot of turbulence, sometimes long before you actually see one."

"Will it damage the runabout?"

"Not if I'm doing my job right."

"All right," Bashir said. "Understood." And then he signed off.

Ro, concerned about Bashir's abrupt tone, looked at Dax, cocking her head toward the aft compartment. "Was it bad?"

"Bad enough," Dax said, understanding that Ro was asking about the Romulan ship. She slipped into the seat next to Ro and started working her panel. "I'm used to the idea of the Jem'Hadar being ruthless and efficient, but this was worse somehow. This was . . . sadism or something calculated to look very much like it."

"Why do you say that?"

Dax considered the question, then said, "Everything was very . . . orchestrated for effect. It was almost like being in a holonovel—all very ominous, but also very structured. The only thing missing was the music."

Ro grinned sardonically. "You'll forgive me for saying this, but *that* sounds a little calculated, too. Situations like this, everyone writes a little narrative in their head as they go along, the story they'll tell when they get back."

"If they get back," Dax said.

"No, not *if,"* Ro corrected. "Once you start thinking about dying, you don't write the story in your head. As soon as you find you're not writing the story anymore, it's time to start worrying."

"You forget," Dax said. "I've already written a number of life stories. I *know* what it's like to die."

"Sorry, but I don't think that's true," Ro said. "You know what it's like for a life to *end*. That's not the same thing as dying. If any of the previous hosts had died before Dax had been transplanted, we wouldn't be having this conversation."

Dax turned to look at Ro. Coolly, she asked, "So what's your point?"

"That you should never say 'if,' " Ro said, "if you plan to live."

She looked at Dax, but the Trill seemed preoccupied. "Something else on your mind?"

Dax hesitated. "We got a look at Locken—a recording he left—and what I saw didn't jibe with the carnage."

"Maybe he's lost control of the Jem'Hadar."

"Maybe . . . But, no, I don't think so. He told them what to do. Might have even been there to stage-manage it. He wanted the scene set exactly, precisely *right*. He wanted it to have an impact and knew what to do to achieve it."

"Doesn't make it any less horrifying," Ro said.

"No," Dax replied. "*More* horrifying. I think that's part of the reason Julian is so angry. I think he feels like it's his fault, that he should have done something. Maybe made an effort to find Locken before something like this could have happened."

"Meaning what? He's responsible for the actions of every genetically enhanced person in the quadrant? That's rather a big load. I'm not sure I'm comfortable sharing a mission with a martyr. I've dealt with them before—the Maquis was full of them—and you know what?"

"What?"

"They always get what they want: they always die."

Dax shook her head. "Julian's not a martyr. He just wants the universe to be a just place."

"Oh, great," Ro said. "So he's not a martyr, he's just crazy. And what about you, the Trill with a half-dozen lives behind you?"

"Eight," Dax corrected.

"Eight, then. What do you want?"

"I just want everyone to come home safe," Dax said.

Ro nodded. "All right, then," she said. "We do agree on something after all."

After four hours, Ro dropped out of warp and they hit the first wave of turbulence. She turned over the pilot's chair to Dax and went aft for some sleep.

It was, Dax thought, like sailing through rough seas: not life-threatening, but requiring a pilot's undivided attention. Dax tried to smooth out the bumps, but the inertial dampeners couldn't compensate for the irregular chop generated by the plasma waves. Twenty minutes later, they hit a high-pressure ridge that tossed Ro out of her bunk. She rolled onto all fours, then ran into the cockpit even as Dax was calling, "Ro!"

"Here," Ro said, sliding into her seat.

"Shields are on full and I'm down to one-quarter impulse."

"Give it a little more than that or we'll be tossed."

Dax did as she was ordered and the surges seemed to even out. After she switched control to Ro's board, she took a second to sneak a look through the viewscreen and saw a huge plasma plume swirl into a funnel, a red-gold streamer bursting from its center.

"Wow," Dax said, a second before the wave of turbulence struck them broadside. She would have, she knew, been thrown from her chair if she hadn't been strapped in. Behind her, Bashir cursed as both he and Taran'atar belted themselves to their chairs.

"Hang on to your stomach," Ro said. "Here comes another one." The runabout pitched and yawed while all around them plasma streamers erupted, flared, then faded, leaving red and green afterimages dancing on Dax's retinas.

"What's our course?" Dax asked, trying to wrestle some usable data off her console.

"Just turn the sensors off," Ro said, blinking, trying to clear her vision. "They're not going to be much use now."

The runabout was swept into a maelstrom of light and energy. Ro did not so much pilot the ship as goad it from side to side, avoiding globes of coruscating energy and ribbons of supercharged plasma. The inertial dampeners were almost worthless and anyone who wasn't strapped in would have been pummeled into unconsciousness in seconds.

Dax stubbornly kept checking the sensor feed, apparently more out of need to keep busy than out of a belief that she would be able to see anything. She was, therefore, able to exclaim triumphantly, "Starboard, fifteen mark seven." Ro had spotted it almost at the same instant and no sooner were the words out of Dax's mouth than the runabout was slipping into calm, open space.

Turning to survey her comrades, Ro asked, "Everyone still here?"

Taran'atar, leaning forward in his seat, was ignoring her, straining against the harness to look out the viewport, obviously preparing himself for whatever threat might be approaching. Dax was mussed, but looked excited. Ro recalled someone telling her that Ezri was prone to space-sickness, but she showed no sign of it now. In fact, she seemed to be actually relishing the rough ride. Conversely, Bashir's complexion was waxy and nearly green. He was holding a full hypo in his shaking hand and now, slowly, carefully, pressed it to his exposed forearm. "I've been trying to do that for half an hour," he said. Then, he looked at Ro. "And the Maquis used to hide in here all the time?"

"Well, yes," Ro said, and was tempted to leave it at that. Having a reputation for reckless courage was occasionally a useful thing. On the other hand, having a reputation for insanity was not. "But I've never been through anything like *that*. Our ships wouldn't have held together. Whatever else Locken has done to his Jem'Hadar, he's bred them to have strong stomachs."

After checking her sensors, Ro fired the maneuvering thrusters and pointed the bow of the runabout toward Sindorin to give everyone a good look. It was a small world, closer in size to Mars than to Earth, a blue-green orb dappled and streaked with graywhite cloud. They were parked over the northern ice cap, which was tiny, no more than the faintest hint of a white bull's-eye in an otherwise blue dartboard.

"What's our approach vector?" Bashir asked, checking the sensor feed.

"The landmass we're looking for is in the southern hemisphere, so we can't see it from here. Hopefully, they can't see us, either. I'm going to go in fast over the ice cap, try to stay low and approach near sea level. Everyone okay with that?"

"You're the pilot," Bashir said.

"That's right," Ro said.

Less than two minutes later, Dax announced, "Something decloaking on the port side. Two hundred meters. It's big. Oh, hell, it's a Cardassian weapons platform." Ro hit the port thrusters and the runabout lurched to starboard. Behind her, she heard Bashir groan. "It's trying to get a lock on us. Shields are up, but . . ."

The runabout bucked and slid to port, the inertial dampeners pushed beyond their ability to compensate. Ro tried to coax the ship back into a semblance of level flight, but the bow kept sliding away underneath her feet, slicing through the atmosphere at a steep angle.

"That was a direct hit on our aft power coupling," Dax yelled over the noise of rushing air. "We've lost deflectors, tractors, environmental . . . everything. Somebody find some power."

Bashir, working the engineering board, yelled, "On it!" Seconds later, Ro's board lit green and she fed as much power as she dared into the shields and stabilizers. The nose lifted, the bumps smoothed, and the air circulators began to clear the air.

Another bolt of energy sizzled into their stern, and the runabout staggered, but did not tumble. "We're out of range," Ro announced. "Where the hell did they get a Cardassian weapons platform?"

"If the damage to the Romulan ship was any indication," Bashir said, "Locken has been pirating whatever technology he can. It wouldn't surprise me if he salvaged that platform from the aftermath of a battle somewhere at the edge of Cardassian space."

"Great," Ro replied. "But they know we're here now. Do we abort?"

"Not an option," Bashir yelled, pointing out the bow viewport.

Three ships were flying in formation up out of a gray cloudbank, weapons firing. In the split second before she threw the runabout into a roll, Ro saw that Bashir's guess must be right. None of the ships had a familiar configuration, but all had familiar elements. One had the hull of a Jem'Hadar fighter, but was armed with Romulan disruptors half-surrounded by a Breen impeller wing. Another was a wingless Klingon bird-of-prey, outfitted with Federation warp nacelles. The third was composed of so many different bits and pieces that Ro couldn't even guess where it all came from. *They shouldn't be able to fly. How could they make all those systems compatible?* Ro dumped all their reserve power into the engines and redlined the thrusters, pressing her back into her seat.

The patchwork fighters' first shot cut through the shields as if they were gauze. Seconds before her control board overloaded and died, Ro set the stabilizers for glide and locked them into position. "Everyone out!" she cried, unlocked her harness, and reached under her seat for her bag even as the runabout's belly slapped into the first layer of cloud cover.

Taran'atar was already standing on a pad, his weapons satchel slung over his shoulder, when Ro took the three steps from the pilot's chair to the transporter. She pulled a med kit from a storage locker and hooked it to her belt, then turned to look for Bashir. It was more important that the doctor get off than anyone else, and Ro wasn't sure that the batteries held a big enough charge for two transports. But Bashir hadn't moved from the engineering board and was only able to stop working long enough to make a second's eye contact. "Go!" he shouted. "The presets are gone. I have to stabilize power to the inertial dampeners and the transporter's compensators or you're going to end up as a couple of smears spread across twenty kilometers of terrain."

"But you should go!"

Bashir only shook his head and manipulated the controls, his hands moving faster than Ro could follow. "You couldn't do this," he said.

"We're closing on the shoreline," Dax said, not looking up from her board, obviously trusting Bashir to do whatever had to be done. "We're almost in range. Get on the pads!"

Ro hissed a curse, then stepped onto the pad next to Taran'atar. "Don't be long!" she shouted. Bashir waved reassuringly; then the cabin disappeared in a haze of silver sparkles. Seconds later, they materialized in a barren patch on a low hilltop surrounded by a ring of tropical vegetation.

As soon as she felt the ground beneath her feet, Ro craned her neck back, scanning the sky for signs of the plummeting runabout. The sun was sinking into the western sea, streaking the sky with bands of ochre, orange, and crimson. Directly overhead, the heavens were already almost black, and though she knew to expect it, Ro was still rattled by the paucity of stars. This deep in the Badlands, only the brightest lights could cut through the thick curtains of plasma particles.

Taran'atar tapped Ro on the shoulder and pointed to the east at a thin streak of silver light. "The runabout," Ro said, then began to count in her head. When she reached sixty, she looked around the clearing for a pair of silver columns forming out of thin air. When nothing appeared, she counted to sixty again. Nothing happened. She tapped her combadge and called, "Team one to team two. Team one to team two. Please respond."

Nothing.

She kept the channel open, losing hope of a reply as each second passed, but unwilling to give up. Just before the streak disappeared over the edge of the eastern horizon, Ro unslung her tricorder, checked their coordinates, and read them off into her combadge.

Taran'atar hissed, "No," threw Ro down onto the spongy ground, and covered her mouth with his hand. When he turned her head to the side, Ro thought he might be about to twist it off, but he was only trying to point out a patch of foliage at the bottom of the hill, barely visible in the deepening gloom. Leaves stirred where there was no wind and Ro thought she detected the barest glimmer of shimmering air.

Taran'atar released his hold on her mouth and Ro whispered, "Did they see us?"

Taran'atar shook his head once, then pointed at a stand of trees out of the line of sight of their pursuers. Taran'atar shrouded and disappeared. Ro sighed, unholstered her phaser, and started for the trees, staying as close to the ground as she could.

Behind her, over the ridge of the hill and far to the west, Sindorin's sun sank below the horizon and was swallowed by the sea. Night came on, moonless and with few stars to light the way.

Chapter Ten

Ezri shouted "They're down!" almost at the exact moment the runabout was slammed by another disruptor bolt. Her stomach dropped as the ship began to roll to starboard, but Julian managed to redirect power from somewhere and stabilized the craft before its descent became too steep.

Ezri checked the sensors again, hoping she could direct the transporter to beam them to within a couple of klicks of Taran'atar and Ro and found . . . nothing. "Sensors are gone," she shouted over the rising shriek of reentry.

"So is the transporter," Julian yelled back. "Get in the pilot's seat. Controlled reentry."

She did as ordered, pausing only long enough to buckle the crash harness and say a prayer. Seconds later, the pilot board flickered on, darkened, then flickered on again. Somehow, Bashir had rerouted all the remaining battery power to one of the only systems that seemed to be fully functional—the runabout's antigravs, usually used only for liftoff and landing. They weren't in free fall anymore—not exactly—but it was a stretch of the imagination to call what they were doing "flying." The problem was that the antigravs couldn't take this kind of abuse over any period of time. They would blow out if Julian kept feeding them power at the current rate and they were still almost ten kilometers up, moving much too fast.

The solution, she realized, was simple, but it made her heart freeze in her chest. "Do you see what I'm going to do?" Julian called over his shoulder.

"Yes."

"Can you handle it?"

Ezri couldn't answer immediately. He was, she saw, going to shut off power to the antigravs—and everything else in the runabout—and they were going to drop like a rock until the antigrav coils cooled off and recharged. Then Julian would fire up the engines again, just long enough to slow their descent to a survivable rate.

"How many times will you have to shut off power?" she called, trying to memorize the panels while she could.

"Three. The last drop should put us about one hundred meters above the canopy."

She closed her eyes then and almost turned to Julian to say, "I'm not a pilot." But something made her stop. Ezri looked down at her hands and saw that she was manipulating the controls, resetting couplings and bypassing presets.

Yes, I am, she thought, *because Torias and Jadzia both were.* Their knowledge, their skills, were *hers*. All she had to provide was her own force of will.

"Ready," she said.

"Good," Julian said, and she could hear the relief in his voice. "When I cut power, count to ten and then fire the antigravs again. Try to keep the nose up . . ."

"Make sure you distribute the power evenly or we'll go into a tumble."

Julian laughed mirthlessly. "You're the pilot. Get ready. Here we go."

The lights went out. Suddenly, there was only the rush of atmosphere around the runabout's hull.

1 . . . 2 . . . 3 . . .

She had never before realized how many different noises runabouts made—the hiss of the air circulators, the ping of the sensor grids, the thrum of the engines—and now there was only this, the sound of gravity doing its job.

. . . 4 . . . 5 . . . 6 . . .

If the antigravs didn't come back on and they reached terminal velocity, at their present height, it would take them about seventy-five seconds before they hit the ground. *Why am I thinking about this?*

The power came back on and Ezri reengaged the antigravs. Her head snapped forward and she felt a shooting pain down her left side. Lights came on and the runabout bucked beneath her.

Lights out. Count. The runabout was sliding to port. *Must be encountering some strong turbulence.* Made sense. It was a tropical area at sunset. Masses of air moving back and forth as the landmass cooled . . .

. . . 7 . . . 8 . . . 9 . . .

Lights on. The shock wasn't so abrupt this time, so they must be moving slower. Either that, or she was ready for it. She fed as much power as she dared into the antigravs and waited for the lights to go out again. Once they were out, she knew it would only be two or three seconds before they hit the canopy and then it would all be luck, a matter of what was underneath them. Ezri wiped something out of her eyes, then realized it was warm and sticky. *Blood?* she wondered. *Why is there blood on me?*

The antigravs died. Ezri looked over at Bashir, whose hands were still racing over the engineering panel . . .

And then the lights went out for the last time.

The station moaned and rumbled beneath Kira's feet. Far below the Promenade, Nog was tearing something loose, something serious enough to vibrate through the station's vast superstructure. She looked around the dimmed Promenade, half-expecting the walls to tumble in. Kira sometimes imagined that there was a nerve running from her inner ear, down through the soles of her feet, and deep into the bowels of the station; it often seemed as if she was more sensitive to the sounds of Deep Space 9 than anyone else aboard.

Shar had just reported that work on installing the new core was going well. Structural connections ruined by the breakaway of the old core were being cut free and replaced in preparation for the new one.

Viewed from the observation port in lower pylon two, the core detachment from Empok Nor had been a sight to behold, as engineering crews in EVA suits and worker bees carried out the complex task of freeing the massive lower-core assembly from its station. The runabouts *Rio Grande* and *Sungari* then gently towed the core right past her, into position for Phase Three of the transfer. She remembered that Dr. Tarses had likened it to a heart transplant, which, she supposed, was as apt a way of looking at it as any . . . especially since it was she who had created DS9's great gaping wound.

Walking toward her, emerging from the shadows of the closed Klingon restaurant, one of Ro's deputies who had remained aboard with the skeleton crew was patrolling the Promenade. She nodded to him, recognizing the deputy as someone she'd seen regularly at shrine services, but he'd already looked away, carefully avoiding any overt display of disrespect as he passed her.

It's there, though, Kira thought, involuntarily reaching up to and feeling bare skin where her earring used to be. *This stops now.* She halted in the middle of the main floor and turned around. "Do you have a problem, Corporal?" she called out, her stern voice booming through the mostly empty Promenade.

The deputy froze in his tracks, startled into an about-face, and came to attention. "No, sir," he responded, still carefully avoiding eye contact with the colonel.

Not good enough. "I thought perhaps you'd forgotten how to show proper respect to your commanding officer."

The corporal flinched almost imperceptibly as her voice blasted him. "Sir! No, sir!"

"Because if there's something causing you to forget who commands this station, I'm quite certain I can find someone else to do your job."

The corporal swallowed visibly. "That won't be necessary, sir!"

She let him suffer under her scrutiny for nearly a full minute more before she spoke again, her voice closer to normal. "Carry on."

"Yes, sir! Thank you, Colonel." The corporal turned on his heel and hurried off.

Damn Yevir and the Vedek Assembly anyway, she thought, resuming her stroll in the other direction. Kira's banishment from the Bajoran spiritual community had effectively made her a pariah among many of the faithful, even those who served under her. She still had all the authority of a colonel in the Militia, her orders obeyed and her command unquestioned . . . but her bond to the people was gone. Not one of them spoke to her when not on duty, and all of them avoided eye contact unless necessary. And civilians made no pretense at all of hiding their disdain, nor vedeks and monks their open scorn. Even Vedek Capril could no longer bring himself to look upon her. To him, to all of them, she was *Attainted.*

Except Ro, she thought. Ro, who, while faithless, seemed to understand better than anyone what being Attainted had done to Kira, although she freely admitted she couldn't understand why the colonel had accepted Yevir's judgment. Kira wasn't surprised. Ro was an outsider to their people by choice, her contrariness and defiance of Bajoran faith something to be worn like a badge of honor, like her improperly worn earring.

But Kira wasn't Ro. She couldn't defy the Vedek Assembly's judgment of her, even though she knew the actions that led to it had been the right ones to take, and proven so. To Kira, being part of a community of faith meant being true to it, even if that same community cast her out. She would accept its judgment; she would put her earring away and stay out of the shrines, she would close her books of prophecy and stay away from the Orbs.

Yevir can take it all away, and I'll accept it . . . because I still have my faith.

"Evening, Colonel."

Kira looked up and saw another member of Ro's security staff patrolling the level-two balcony. Even in the gloom, Kira recognized the man. He was Sergeant Shul Torem, one of the first men Odo had taken on after the occupation. A gruff, solitary man, Shul always seemed happiest working the late hours, when few people walked the Promenade. Odo had always spoken highly of him, mostly, she had suspected, because Shul hadn't given a damn whether Odo liked him or not. She stopped and smiled. "Good evening, Shul."

Shul leaned on the railing and nodded. "Thought that was you I heard."

Kira laughed. "How could you tell?"

Shul smiled back. "Sorry about Corporal Hava back there. I'll give him a stern talking-to."

Kira nodded. "I'd appreciate that. Quiet tonight, otherwise?"

"When they're not down there bangin' away on whatever it is they're bangin' on."

The corner of Kira's mouth crooked up. *So, it's not just me after all,* she thought. She said, "They should be done soon. Then we'll be busy again."

The watchman shrugged. "It could stay this way from the start of one week to the end of the next and that would be all right with me. Fewer people, fewer problems."

Can't argue with that. "If you feel that way, why don't you stay down on Bajor? I'm sure there are lots of places you could work where you wouldn't have to see . . . well, anyone. A farm, for instance."

Shul turned his head from side to side, stretching his neck, apparently trying to restore circulation to tired muscles. "I've done my share of farming, thanks. Besides, Colonel, if I lived down there, I'd always have to be travelin' back and forth to see the old woman and I'm not really much of one for spaceflight."

"The old woman?"

"My wife."

"Oh," Kira said. "You're married?" She didn't mean it to come out as a question, but there was no concealing she was surprised. Shul didn't seem like the marrying sort.

"Thirty-two years," Shul said. "Last month."

"Oh," Kira said. "Well, congratulations."

He shrugged again. "Doesn't take much skill to stay married. Just some patience and the common sense to know when to shut up and listen."

Kira laughed, delighted. "I'll have to remember that. So your wife works here on the station? What does she do?"

Shul seemed surprised by the question. "She's over at the shrine, Colonel. You know her: Aba. Cleans up after the services, keeps the candles lit. Cooks breakfast and lunch for the vedeks."

"Sure," Kira said, picturing a red-faced, jolly woman. "I know her." She held her hand up to the height of her own nose. "About this tall. Laughs a lot."

"That's her," Shul said, nodding, practically smiling.

Kira was having trouble imagining these two people together. As she recalled, Aba would typically talk a blue streak to anyone who came within striking range, though on the couple of occasions when she had been sucked in, Kira had realized that Aba wasn't so much speaking to *her* as continuing a conversational thread that had unraveled when her last victim had moved out of range. "Well," Kira said, "please give her my regards when you see her."

Shul nodded, but there was something about the way his face didn't move that made it clear he wouldn't be passing along Kira's greeting. Aba was one of the faithful.

"Well, good evening then," Kira said, and made as if to continue her walk. Before she moved three paces, she turned and looked up again and was not at all surprised to see that Shul had not moved from the spot by the railing. "You know that I've been Attainted?" she asked flatly.

Shul nodded, then seemed to decide that wasn't enough and said, "Yes, Colonel."

"Aba wouldn't like it if she knew you were talking to me."

"Well," Shul said, "I won't mention it to her if you don't."

"But it doesn't bother you?"

He frowned. "Bother me? Course it bothers me. Seems that vedeks sometimes use an awfully big stick to try to keep people in line. Doesn't seem very prudent to me. When I was a boy, I used to help take care of a herd of *batos.* You know *batos?* Big, smelly creatures, you know?"

Kira nodded. "Sure. I know *batos.*"

"They're the kinda animals that you have to poke along to keep 'em moving. I found out something funny about 'em when I was around seven. If you hit them too hard, they seem to sort of wake up, like they're not so much dumb as they're thinking about something else and weren't really paying attention to you. That's when you're in a lot of trouble, you know?"

Kira nodded again, wondering where this was going.

"I don't think too many vedeks have herded *batos,* Colonel. In my opinion, what they did to you was pretty much the same thing as hitting a *batos* too hard. Maybe not hard enough to wake it up, make it stop thinking about whatever else was on its mind, but almost. You understand what I mean?"

Smiling, grateful in a manner she scarcely understood herself, Kira said, "Yes, I think I do. Thank you, Shul. It's been a pleasure."

"Pleasure's mine, Colonel. Oh . . . the word around the station is that you heard from the constable not too long ago. Is that right?"

Odo's message, given her by Taran'atar. "Yes," she said. "Yes, I did, Shul."

"If you don't mind my asking . . . is he well?"

"I think so."

"If you see him again . . . please say hello for me."

Kira smiled. "Sure thing."

Shul nodded once more and went about his business.

Kira went on, thinking she might drop in at Quark's, when her combadge signaled. *"Ops to Colonel Kira."*

Doesn't anyone see the "Closed for repairs" sign? She tapped her badge. "Go ahead, Shar."

Shar said, *"I have First Minister Shakaar on subspace, waiting to speak with you, Colonel."*

Kira closed her eyes and groaned inwardly. When Shakaar hadn't contacted her immediately after the Dominion and Avatar crises had been resolved, she knew it was a bad sign. That the first minister had been touring key Federation planets on Bajor's behalf for the last month certainly explained it, up to a point . . . but not completely. The more time that went by without contact from him, the more she knew she'd regret his call when it finally came.

Shar's exact choice of words bore out her expectations. Shakaar wasn't "asking to speak with you," or even "requesting the pleasure of speaking with you," but "waiting to speak with you." *Three years certainly have changed a lot of things, haven't they, Edon?* she thought, remembering the days when a call from Shakaar would have created a thrill of excitement and not a wave of anxiety.

"Route the call to my office," Kira said. "Advise him that with the turbolifts offline, it'll take me a few minutes to get there."

"Yes, Colonel. Shar out."

Kira reached her office in just over a minute, some of her tension pleasantly released by her rapid ascent up the emergency stairs. She sat down behind her desk and immediately keyed open the standby channel. "First Minister," she said, trying to sound accommodating. "Thank you for waiting. My apologies, but we're experiencing some technical difficulties until the station's new core is online."

Shakaar looked up from a padd that he'd been studying while waiting for her. Judging from the furnishings she could see behind him, Kira guessed he was calling from his ship of state, the *Li Nalas*. "Hello, Nerys," he said, ignoring her use of his title. *"Yes, I know all about your core. I've been receiving regular reports from my staff on Bajor."* He picked up another padd and glanced at it. *"By the way, that young officer who put me through . . . Ensign ch'Thane, was it?"*

"That's right."

"Ah," Shakaar said. He made a note, then looked up again. *"I met some Andorians while I was at the Federation Council. Interesting people. Very . . . political. I think your officer may be related to their senior representative."*

That's old news, Kira thought. Word of Shar's parentage had already gotten around the station, as did his apparent unease with having it brought up.

"I'm on my way back to Bajor even as we speak," Shakaar went on.

"That's good news, sir," Kira said, wondering when Shakaar was going to get to the point. "I trust your tour went well."

"I think I made a good case to have Bajor's application for Federation membership revisited. We should hopefully know something in the coming days. Although between you and me, all this politicking gives me a headache."

Kira smiled despite herself. She knew Shakaar would much rather be tilling earth than giving speeches and attending diplomatic functions.

"And, speaking of politics, how is the Jem'Hadar ambassador?"

Ambassador? Kira thought, but decided this wasn't the right time to explain what was wrong with that title. "He's fine, First Minister." *I just sent him on a secret mission that he may not survive, but otherwise, he's fine.*

"What's he like?"

Kira was taken off guard by the question. "He's ... old. At least, by Jem'Hadar standards. I suppose you could even say that he's wise after a fashion." *That sounds good,* she decided, then surprised herself by feeling as if it might also be true.

"Well," Shakaar said, *"perhaps I'll get to meet him before too long."*

Kira felt the tension returning, wondering how much longer they were going to engage in chitchat before he came out and told her what he wanted. She knew Shakaar well enough to know that he wanted her off-balance before striking.

"So," Shakaar said, *"the situation with Vedek Yevir went badly, don't you think?"*

Ah, Kira thought. *Here we go.* She said, "I suppose that depends upon your point of view."

"Nerys," Shakaar said, his voice warming with sympathy. *"This is me, Edon. You don't need to play these games with me."*

Oh, but you can play games with me? "It's my problem, First Minister. I'll deal with it."

"I'm afraid I disagree, Nerys. This isn't just your problem. This will affect how every Bajoran on and off the station will deal with you in the future."

Not every Bajoran, Kira reminded herself, thinking of Ro and Shul. "I think I've earned the right to work this out for myself, First Minister," Kira said.

"Earned?" Shakaar asked, his voice rising sharply and, Kira thought, somewhat artificially. *"This has nothing to do with what you've earned, Colonel. This has to do with what you owe. This is about what you should be doing to bring the continuing chaos on Deep Space 9 back under some kind of control."*

Chaos? Kira thought, wondering who might be writing the reports Shakaar had been reading. "First Minister," Kira said, struggling to remain calm. "My station was attacked two weeks ago by rogue Jem'Hadar who managed to destroy a *Nebula*-class starship and sabotage the station's power core. Since then, we've spent twenty-six hours a day, every day, working to restore the station to full operation. And, against all hope, I think we may have found a solution—"

"This attack, Colonel," Shakaar interrupted, consulting his padd. *"Isn't it*

true that during it your first officer, close to seventy station personnel and residents, and over nine hundred crew members aboard the U.S.S. Aldebaran were killed, due in large part to your allowing your upgrade schedule to fall behind, leaving DS9 vulnerable?"

"We were understaffed and inadequately protected. Neither Starfleet nor the Militia took my complaints seriously—"

"—And afterward, no fewer than five Jem'Hadar soldiers successfully infiltrated the station. Correct?"

"Jem'Hadar are difficult to detect while shrouded—"

"—But not impossible. And you had just been attacked by them. Surely infiltration was foreseeable?"

"Their ships were all destroyed, even the one that tried to help us. There was too much damage to our—"

"And just prior to the attack, a prylar was murdered on the Promenade."

"She was assassinated—"

"—After which, your people discovered and withheld a priceless historical document containing, at minimum, potentially explosive information—"

"—evidence in my security officer's investigation of the murder—"

"—which you uploaded to the Bajoran comnet on your own authority—"

"—because the Vedek Assembly was acting to suppress—"

"—And meanwhile, the one Jem'Hadar you detected successfully escaped custody and sabotaged the fusion reactors. And your solution was to eject your entire lower core, a decision which led directly to the station's current woes. Am I up to speed, Colonel?"

Part of Kira wanted desperately to slug Shakaar right through the screen. "Your information seems decidedly one-sided, First Minister," she said coldly. "Tell me, those reports you've been getting from your staff, were any of them by me, or anyone else from DS9 who actually witnessed those events? If not, may I respectfully request that you, your ministers, and the Vedek Assembly all just keep your comments to yourself."

Shakaar wasn't even slightly impressed or intimidated. "Do you understand now why this isn't just your problem, Nerys?" he asked gently. "You're right about the reports. They are one-sided. And not one report from the station in the last two weeks has found its way to me. Do you think I'm an idiot that I don't see that? I'm trying to show you what a dangerous situation you've gotten yourself into. You've made enemies, Nerys, in the Vedek Assembly, in the Militia, and inside my own government. Enemies who will keep doing whatever they can to destroy you, especially now that you've been . . ."

"Attainted," Kira finished quietly, when it was clear that Shakaar could not. "You can say it, First Minister. I've been Attainted." It shocked her to see Shakaar hesitate like that. To some extent, even he thought she'd become a pariah.

Shakaar took a deep breath, then asked the Question Direct. "Do you feel that you're still capable of commanding the station, Colonel? Not your station, but the station. The Bajoran people's station?"

"Yes, First Minister," she said. "I believe I'm still capable."

"*Because,*" Shakaar continued, "*I spoke with an admiral at Starfleet Command who seemed to think there was a captain available who might be the perfect candidate for such a posting. He made a good case for why it might be a good idea to return the station to its previous command structure . . .*"

"*First Minister,*" Kira said through gritted teeth. "I'm fine. Everything is under control. Please don't expend any more energy worrying about us."

"*I'm not 'worried,' Colonel. I'm planning for the future. My job is to be thinking ahead, to see what Bajor might need over the course of the next year, the next five years, the next millennium. Bajor needs Deep Space 9, Colonel. Bajor might not need you in command of Deep Space 9. Do I make myself clear?*"

"Yes, First Minister."

"*I would rather keep you there, Nerys,*" Shakaar said, once again switching tones, switching tactics. "*You know the job. You know the people, but you could stand to learn some lessons in diplomacy. As I said, you have a tendency to make powerful enemies—*"

"Are you one of them, Edon?"

Shakaar looked stung. "*I don't know if you realize how hard some people are working against you, Nerys,*" he said finally. "*This is just the beginning. I can ignore it up to a point, hope that it'll eventually die down and wither on its own. But if it doesn't . . .*"

"If it doesn't?" Kira demanded.

"*This a very delicate time for me, politically, and for all of Bajor. Everything we've been working toward is coming to a head, but it won't take much to make it all unravel, especially if your enemies decide I'm on your side. Do you understand what I'm saying?*"

"Yes," Kira said. "I think I do." *You want my resignation. That would solve this particular political dilemma quite neatly, wouldn't it? Well, I'm not going to make it that easy for you, Edon.*

"It's been an honor and privilege to hear from you, as always, First Minister," she said formally. "Will there be anything else?"

Shakaar could no longer hide his frustration. "*Why do you always have to be so damned impossible?*"

"I'm the commanding officer of Deep Space 9," Kira said forcefully, enunciating each word so he'd know she would never go quietly. "It comes with the job."

They held each other's gaze for a long moment before either of them spoke again. Then Kira repeated her earlier question, "Will that be all, First Minister?"

Shakaar continued to study her face for several seconds; then he actually smiled, not politically this time, but the way she remembered, as if he was satisfied to know that she hadn't lost any of her edge. "*Yes, that'll be all. Be well, Nerys. We'll talk again soon.*" He signed off, and the screen went to standby mode.

It took Kira several seconds to realize that Shakaar hadn't relieved her of her command, that he never intended to. He was simply warning her, in his own very effective way, that there were rough seas ahead, and if she couldn't weather them on her own, she'd lose everything.

In other words, business as usual. Kira pushed her chair away from her desk. Rubbing her eyes, she realized how tired she was, but couldn't remember exactly when she had gotten up that morning. With so many of the station's lights shut down, her internal clock was thrown off. Even the chronometer on her desktop console was wrong, the power having been interrupted so many times in the past two weeks. She could think of only one person who might know exactly what time it was. Kira reactivated her companel and said, "Kira to Quark."

"Yes, Colonel. Lovely to hear from you. What can I do for you today?"

"What time is it, Quark?"

"Why, Colonel," Quark said, *"it's Happy Hour."*

Kira smiled. "Of course it is," she said, and signed off. Then, speaking to an empty office, she repeated, "Of course it is."

Chapter Eleven

"Have I mentioned," Ro asked, wiping water from her eyes, "how very much I hate being wet?"

"Yes," Taran'atar grunted. "You have. Several times. Please don't do it again."

Ten minutes after the sun had set, clouds had rolled in off the sea and unleashed a torrential downpour. Ro remembered the predawn and post-dusk rains from her previous visit to Sindorin, but, she decided, it must have been the dry season—or the *drier* season, at any rate—because she hadn't experienced anything like *this*. The good news was that the deluge was so intense that their trail had been rendered untraceable to anything but the most sensitive short-range sensors.

The bad news was that they were now soaked to the bone in a dark rain forest that was inhabited, Ro knew, by several creatures that could be quite deadly to most humanoids, even, she suspected, a Jem'Hadar. A fire would improve their chances (assuming, of course, that they could light one), but if Locken's Jem'Hadar were still on the prowl, it would be as good as sending up a flare.

Good news and bad news aside, they couldn't move now. Rain was sluicing down off the treetops, transforming game trails into narrow, rushing streams. Ro suspected that Taran'atar might be able to keep his footing, but she knew just as well that she would have her feet swept out from under her before she could take three steps. They weren't going anywhere.

A bolt of lightning crackled across the sky and Ro tried to use the split second of light to get a look at the surroundings, but all she ended up with was a silhouette of drooping, waterlogged vegetation and streaks of gushing water. The crack of thunder crashing down on the heels of the lightning bolt made her teeth rattle and her empty stomach reverberate like a kettledrum.

"Can you see anything?" she asked Taran'atar. She suspected Jem'Hadar had better night vision than Bajorans.

"Yes."

"What?"

"I see rain."

"And what else?"

"Trees. Many trees. Also undergrowth. More importantly, I see no Jem'Hadar. Otherwise, if you mean 'Can you see anything useful?' then the answer is no."

Ro didn't reply.

She kept expecting the storm to reach its climax, for a pause between flash and crash, but the pause never arrived. A hundred meters to the west, a treetop exploded into flames and then was quickly quenched by the downpour. *That could have been this tree,* she thought, *and we could be two tiny little piles of ash being washed down a hillside.* Before the flames died away completely, she glanced over at Taran'atar, who scuttled closer and, through clenched teeth, asked, "When can we move?"

"Soon. As soon as the rain stops. For a half hour after it ends, nothing moves. Except, of course, for the Jem'Hadar."

Taran'atar nodded in agreement. "If they are still out here, we will elude them. They may be Jem'Hadar by birth, but they have not received proper training. Did you see how they pursued us before the rain began?"

"No," Ro said. "I mean, I might have seen a few strands of grass swaying back and forth when we ran through a field . . ."

"Pathetic," Taran'atar said. "And their uniforms. Did you see them?"

"Maybe for a second when they unshrouded. Were they wearing red, some silver trim?"

"Vanity."

Ro was tempted to laugh, but she sensed it would not be well received.

Then, as suddenly as it had begun, the rain stopped. Dark clouds scudded and Ro felt the hairs on the back of her head stiffen when the breeze picked up. Auroral displays from the plasma storms were already becoming evident to the south. Taran'atar stood up. "I'll return," he said, and shrouded. Not a single leaf stirred, nor did a drop of water fall that could not be accounted for by wind or gravity. It was as if he had never been there.

Several minutes passed. Ro shivered in her wet uniform as the breeze picked up. She stood up slowly and tried to peer through the foliage, but the auroral light did nothing to illuminate the terrain. *"Taran'atar,"* Ro whispered, then shivered again. "Where are you, dammit?"

And then his disembodied voice was in her ear: "Someone is out there."

Ro's heart jumped and she almost fired her phaser. She wanted to yell "Don't *do* that!" but refrained. Instead, she opened her pack, pulled out the fractal knife and clipped it to her belt, then checked the charge on her phaser. *"Who's* out there?" she whispered softly. "Jem'Hadar?"

"No," Taran'atar said softly. "Whoever they are, they move more swiftly and make better use of the cover. They know this forest."

Ro felt hope rise within her. "But you didn't get a good look at them?"

"No," Taran'atar replied, now somewhere to her right. "They are ahead of us, moving in the same direction. I came back to warn you. If you draw their attention, I'm certain I could kill them all."

"No!" Ro said, too loudly. "Wait! I mean . . . they might not be enemies."

Taran'atar unshrouded directly in front of her, and Ro suddenly found herself staring into the eyes of a very suspicious Jem'Hadar. "What do you mean?" he asked. "I thought everyone on this planet was an enemy. What has the doctor not told me?"

"Nothing," Ro said quickly. "He told you everything he knew. . . . It's difficult to explain. I was hoping this wouldn't even come up. . . . Damn." She pulled her tricorder out and checked for life signs. As she expected, Sindorin's environment made the readings intermittent and imprecise, but not useless. Pointing to the southwest, she said, "They're about a hundred meters that way."

"There is a game trail leading in their direction," Taran'atar informed her. "If you are careful, you will not make much noise." He was obviously not pleased that she was withholding information, but was still willing to follow her lead for the present.

"Don't get too close," Ro said, rising and stretching cramped muscles. "And try to stay downwind. Their sense of smell is extraordinarily acute. And stay unshrouded. This is going to be hard enough to explain without having you appear out of thin air." She checked the directional reading one more time. "You're sure there are no Jem'Hadar nearby?"

"Considering how loudly you talk, if there were you would be dead by now."

"Fine, I'll be quiet," Ro said. "Let's go."

Taran'atar turned and headed down the slope, walking quickly, but silently. Ro tried to stay right behind him, but slipped before she had gone ten meters. She managed to stay on her feet, but only by grabbing an overhanging branch, which brought a cascade of rain down on their heads. "Wonderful," she sputtered. "From now on, I'm volunteering for *all* the missions."

The slope soon leveled out and they had only traveled a couple of hundred meters before they were in deep forest. It didn't start to rain again, but Ro could hear the breeze whispering through the treetops, shaking the canopy and occasionally loosing sprinkles of fat drops. It was dark, much too dark to see where she was stepping, and Ro had to pull out her beacon, set it on low, and keep it pointed at the ground. If anyone saw the light, she was dead, but it was either use it or wait until morning. Neither was an attractive alternative and Ro worried that Taran'atar would leave without her if she tried to stop. It was wearisome, nerve-racking work, slogging through the muddy undergrowth, every second wondering when the crack of weapons fire would break the nearly silent night.

Two hours later, just as Ro was beginning to feel that the only way she would get any rest was to throw herself down on the ground and pretend she had fallen, Taran'atar stopped to examine an ancient tree. Training her lamp light on the trunk, Ro saw that someone had burned away a meter-wide strip of bark using what looked to her like some kind of energy weapon. The tree was already dead, held upright only by the web of vines and branches connecting its crown to its neighbors'.

"Who did this?" Taran'atar asked. "The ones we follow?"

Ro shook her head. "They don't have energy weapons," she said. "What do you think?"

Taran'atar leaned forward and examined the burns more carefully, then put his nose against the dead wood and inhaled deeply. A large burrowing insect popped out from under a dangling piece of bark and scurried up the side of the trunk. The Jem'Hadar watched it go, but did not otherwise react.

"Romulan disruptors," he said, then looked around at the other trees in the small grove. About half of them, Ro saw, had suffered the same fate. Taran'atar pointed at specific burns. "Breen. Federation phasers. If we assume that the enemy human is pirating much of his equipment, he would arm his Jem'Hadar similarly." There were also large holes in the soil. Someone had obviously expended a lot of energy trying to destroy root systems. "But what were they firing at?" he asked.

"About another half hour and all will be clear," Ro said. "That is, assuming they haven't all been killed."

"No," Taran'atar said. "Someone has been through this grove recently. They stopped for several minutes, too, though I cannot tell why."

Ro looked up at the dead trees, each of them gigantic and probably ancient beyond telling, each now its own grave marker. "I know why," she said. "To pay homage. To remember."

Taran'atar stared at Ro, waiting for her to elaborate. When she didn't, Ro let him walk away while she stood silently for half a minute, listening for voices she knew she'd never again hear among the treetops. Then, dry-eyed and without comment, she followed her companion deeper into the forest.

Ro didn't have to look at her tricorder when they found the next grove of ancient trees, because she knew she was in the right place. Here the trees were unscarred, the root systems undamaged, but in every other important particular, this place was identical with the one they had left behind forty-five minutes ago.

"Come stand near me," Ro said to Taran'atar. "And lower your weapon."

Taran'atar regarded her skeptically, but Ro persisted.

"Look," she said. "You know and I know that you could probably wipe out the whole lot of them with your bare hands. It's not going to make much difference to you if you point your phaser at that ground for five seconds."

He was staring at her again. Ro wondered how long she could continue to press her luck with him. A younger Jem'Hadar would doubtless have killed her by now. But she supposed that was part of Odo's point in selecting *this* one. Having survived years longer than most of his kind, maybe Taran'atar had learned patience, and was less prone to rash action. After a moment, he did as she bade him.

Ro holstered her phaser, then cupped her hands around her mouth and bellowed a low, staccato, hooting call that echoed strangely under the canopy. There was no reply, but the forest, which had been alive with small, rustling noises, suddenly grew still. Ro turned to the east and called once more. Again, there was no reply, so she turned to the south, inhaled deeply, and lifted her hands. Before she could call again, a high-pitched voice called out, "Why are you here? Why is *he* here?" The voice came from directly overhead. There was no question who the voice was referring to when it said "he."

"He's my companion," Ro said. "He won't hurt you."

The speaker, now higher up and to her left, made a noise, an *ack-ack-ack* sound that Ro recognized as laughter, though there was no humor in it. Ro heard another noise, a deep inhaling sound, and only recognized it for what it was when a glob of phlegm dropped from the canopy and landed at her feet. She decided to ignore it.

"Do you remember me?" she asked. "Is there anyone here who knows me?"

"Yes," the voice said, now lower down again and behind her. She began to wish that at least one person she spoke to that night would stay in one spot for more than ten seconds. "I remember you. That is why I was told to come speak with you. You might not remember me because I was a young man when you were here làst and now I am very old."

Ro was confused. "It's been less than three years," she said.

"It has been a *lifetime*," the voice said. The branches overhead rustled and something suddenly dropped to the ground in front of them. Taran'atar crouched, his phaser up and aimed—

Suddenly Ro was in his way. "Put it *down*," she hissed.

Taran'atar's eyes narrowed, the weapon inches from her abdomen. Ro had no doubt that it wasn't set for stun, but she didn't budge. Taran'atar finally lowered his phaser.

She turned around slowly to face their host, who was shaking with terror. The figure crouched in the shadows, small and unthreatening.

"I apologize for my companion, and our intrusion," Ro said. "We'll leave if you wish. We didn't come here to bring you more trouble . . ."

"But you already have," the figure said. "The Jem'Hadar are moving about in the forest, obviously looking for something. It's not—they think we're all dead. They've gone for a while because they don't like the rain, but they'll be back."

Behind her, Taran'atar seemed to be grinding his teeth together. Obviously, he didn't think much of Jem'Hadar who didn't like to get wet.

"Again I ask: Why are you here?" the figure repeated. "And why did you bring *him?*" He raised an arm and pointed a long-fingered hand at Taran'atar. "He wishes to kill us. They all do."

"No, he doesn't. He isn't like the others, I swear it. He simply doesn't yet understand that you aren't a threat to him. It's a complicated story," Ro said, dropping down on her haunches so she was as low to the ground as the other. "I'll be glad to tell you the whole thing, but I don't think we should do it here. Is there anyplace safe we can go?"

Again, the humorless *ack-ack-ack*. "Safe?" the figure asked. "This is Sindorin. No place is safe, not anymore. But perhaps we can find someplace a little more sheltered." He casually scratched the back of his head. "And there are others who will want to hear what you say." He stopped scratching and stood a little straighter. "Wait here until I come back."

From his crouched position, the figure leaped straight up into the air, easily clearing four meters, and grasped a low-hanging vine. Soundlessly, he pulled himself up, hand over hand, into the canopy. Ro listened carefully to see if she could tell which way he was going, but she heard nothing. Then, she turned slowly and walked to where Taran'atar was standing. "Can you tell where he went?" she asked.

Taran'atar nodded to his right. "He went south by southwest about two hundred meters. He is speaking to three others like himself. Who is he?"

"Him, personally? I don't know his name. But he's an Ingavi."

The Jem'Hadar shook his head. "The name means nothing to me. I was under the impression this planet was not populated by any sentient species."

"No *indigenous* sentients, no," Ro said. "Listen, I want to thank you for your forbearance, and your trust in me. I realize it can't be an easy thing for you."

Taran'atar inclined his head, accepting her statement. "You live dangerously," he noted, "but not recklessly. I will not challenge your authority. However, if you wish to avoid any further . . . misunderstandings, you would do well to brief me now on everything you have been withholding about this planet." Ro was surprised to realize that she felt no sense of threat. Taran'atar was not trying to intimidate her; he was attempting to gather information, though how he might use that information was another issue entirely.

"Here's what I know," she said. "The creatures, the Ingavi, were native to one of the worlds that fell under Cardassian control about seventy-five years ago, just as the Cardassian Union was beginning the same wave of expansion that eventually swallowed up Bajor. The Ingavi were still a young warp culture—they'd only had it for about fifty years—and a group of about two thousand fled before the Cardassians could completely annex their planet. They were forced into the Badlands to avoid pursuit, lost their primary drive, and were lucky enough to make it here relatively unscathed. They made a controlled reentry—barely—and managed to unload a few bare necessities before the ship sank in the ocean.

"The Ingavi family I stayed with the last time I was here said about twelve hundred refugees survived the first month after the crash, but after the initial shock wore off, they realized just how lucky they were. Sindorin is similar enough to their own world and many of the survivors decided there was an almost mystical connection between them and their new planet."

"So," Taran'atar asked, "they came here from a moderately sophisticated world?"

Ro nodded. "Tech-wise, Ingav was a lot like Bajor had been when the Cardassians arrived. But Ingav's occupation never ended. More than that, I don't really know. I haven't had the chance to do any research about their homeworld."

"But the being we spoke with did not smell like he comes from a technological society," Taran'atar commented.

Ro, impressed by the observation, said, "He doesn't. They aren't technological. Not anymore. From what I could piece together, the survivors decided to abandon as much technology as possible when they integrated themselves into the environment. They knew certain technological emissions were detectable from a distance; it was how the Cardassians found the Ingavi in the first place. By then they'd become obsessed with avoiding detection, concealing themselves from outsiders. And as I've already explained, conditions on Sindorin make it damn hard to find anything or anybody most of the time."

Taran'atar furrowed his brow. "They gave up technology out of fear."

"It's understandable," Ro said. "They'd been through a lot. The ship they arrived in crashed off shore. They probably got some basic supplies off before it sank, but not much. And these people were in shock—first they were forced off their planet and then crashed on an uncharted world. The wonder is that they didn't sink into barbarism. From what I saw, in the seventy-five years they've been here, the Ingavi have devised a very stable, very balanced civilization. They have some technology, but they use it judiciously. As you saw, they're arboreal; they cultivate fruit- and grain-producing vines in the canopy, and rarely come down to the ground."

"And these circles of large trees?" Taran'atar asked.

"They tend to build settlements in them. The older trees are more stable, less likely to fall over if struck by lightning or die if there's a ground fire."

"That is why the Jem'Hadar destroy them." It was a statement, not a question. "Target practice."

Ro said nothing.

"But this still does not explain how you know so much about them," Taran'atar said, looking around at the clearing.

"I'll get to that," Ro said, then looked back over her shoulder. "Are they still up there?"

Taran'atar shook his great horned head. *He must look gigantic to the Ingavi,* she thought.

"They've moved farther away. I cannot hear them now. They move quickly through the treetops. I do not think even a well-trained Jem'Hadar could keep up with them."

"That explains why there are some still alive."

"Yes," he said, and turned back to look at her. "Continue."

"Right," Ro sighed. "Most of what I said was true: The Maquis were looking for a new base and we thought Sindorin looked like a good candidate, so I came here with two others and we did a survey. The part I left out was the mudslide. They have a lot of those here. The heavy rains and loose soil can be treacherous. My two companions were killed—suffocated or drowned, whatever you call what happens in a mudslide—and I was in pretty bad shape. The Ingavi found me, took me back to their village, and nursed me back to health. I stayed with them for about three weeks until I was strong enough to find my ship." Ro sighed and craned her head back to look up at where the canopy would be, though she could see almost nothing more than a few feet away from the beam of her light. "I learned a lot about them during my convalescence, and I promised them I would never reveal to anyone that I had discovered them." She paused, shaking her head bitterly. "Problem was, the Dominion came anyway. Then Section 31. I kept my silence to protect them, and it didn't matter. It didn't matter."

Taran'atar tilted his head. "I don't understand. They were weaker than the Maquis, surely. What did it matter what they wanted?"

"What are you saying? We should have killed them or conquered them, is that what you're suggesting?" Ro asked coldly.

"But the Maquis were at war, and had need of this place."

"That's not good enough," Ro snapped. "I wasn't going to do to them what the Cardassians did to Ingav, or to Bajor. They've suffered enough."

"Yes. We have," said a familiar voice from directly overhead. Ro shined her lamp straight up, directly into the large round eyes of the Ingavi they had been talking to earlier. Hanging head-down, he flinched away from the light, then released the vine he was clinging to and dropped lightly to the ground at Ro's feet. This time, he did not stay crouching, but drew himself up to his full height—about the center of Ro's breastbone—then swept one arm forward in what she interpreted to be a courtly bow.

"My name is Kel. I am to serve as your guide while you are here. Those among us who remember Ro Laren speak of you with honor and affection. The heads of the families say you owe us an explanation as to why you are here, but we've decided to believe you mean no harm."

Then he turned to Taran'atar and said, "On the other hand, they all wanted to kill you, but I told them that you heeded Ro Laren when she asked you to lower your weapon. They have decided this means I have spoken for you, Jem'Hadar. So, if this is a trick and you plan to kill us all, slay me first. Otherwise, I could not bear the shame."

Taran'atar listened attentively, then nodded once.

Ro took the opportunity to take a closer look at Kel and found that she did not, in fact, recognize him. Like the rest of his kind, his head, arms, and legs were covered in short, coarse green hair—not their natural coloring, but the result of a colonial microorganism that clung to Ingavi fur, a harmless parasite that helped to camouflage them in the forest. He wore mottled green shorts, a close-fitting vest of the same color that had many sealed pockets of several different sizes down the front, but no shoes because the Ingavi used their long, prehensile toes while climbing as much as they used their hands.

Like most of the Ingavi males she'd seen during her previous visit, Kel had large eyes, a flat nose, and a wide, down-turned mouth. There was, to Ro's eyes, something about their habitual expression that made her think of a perpetually put-upon civil servant and, as far as she could tell, there was nothing about Kel's personality that would dispel that illusion.

Lifting one long arm, Kel pointed into the forest and said, "We have a shelter in this direction. Some of my friends are attempting to distract the Jem'Hadar—the *other* Jem'Hadar—who are searching the forest for you, so we must hurry."

Taran'atar looked back over his shoulder as though he was thinking about going back to face the other Jem'Hadar, but shook it off and returned his attention to Kel. "Lead on."

The Ingavi turned to Ro and said, "Talk to me while we walk. I will have to explain to the others why you are here when we arrive." He glanced at Taran'atar. "And why we should believe that this one is different from the others."

"Taran'atar isn't one of those who have been menacing you," Ro said. "He . . . works with me, and accompanied me in returning to Sindorin because what threatens you now also threatens our worlds." Ro told Kel an abbreviated version of the tale that brought her to Sindorin.

When she was finished, Kel asked, "So do you think your comrades perished?"

Ro puffed as they climbed a long, steep slope, but managed to say, "There's no way to know. It's possible, though I doubt it. There was no explosion when our ship went down, as far as I could tell. And Bashir and Dax, they seem a resourceful pair."

"That's not a reason," Taran'atar commented, chugging steadily up the hill. "It's an opinion."

"I agree," Kel said, loping along at an easy pace, "but I hope you are right, Ro. If this madman, this Locken, is the one responsible for these latest atrocities, then I hope your friend finds him and stops him."

"I think he could," Ro said, stopping to catch her breath when they reached the crest of the hill. Dawn was beginning to turn the sky to the east pink. "Or, anyway, he stands a better chance than anyone else. And Taran'atar and I will do whatever we can. It's the least we can do."

"The least you could do," Kel corrected, "is nothing, so anything you will do is welcome."

"But now you tell me of your fortunes, Kel," Ro said. "How have the Ingavi fared since I was last here?"

Kel looked up at her from under lowered brows. "Very little has occurred that I would call fortune, Ro. We have endured, but little else, though my wife tells me I am inclined to take the dark view. Now, come," he said, pointing the way down the hillside. "It's best not to be above ground when the sun rises."

There were caves where there should not have been any. Ro knew a little bit about geology, enough to know that the loose, shallow topsoil usually associated with rain forests could not support a system of caves as extensive as those the Ingavi refugees were hiding in. A surreptitious check with her tricorder revealed the truth: they were not in a cave at all, but inside the hollowed-out remains of a massive petrified root system. Sometime in Sindorin's distant past, its ecosystem must have supported the existence of gargantuan trees, plants so immense that they would have cast a shadow over half the area now covered by the Ingavi's rain forest. Ro didn't feel like she knew enough about botany to be sure of her idea, but she felt the blood rush in her veins at the thought of bringing a Starfleet survey team back to the planet to confirm the finding.

And then Ro felt ashamed. *Another* disturbance, *another* group of outsiders to harass the Ingavi? It wasn't right. She'd restrain herself, though she was surprised to find that the urge to explore—something she thought had atrophied forever when she had fled the *Enterprise*—was still there. How odd.

Kel introduced Ro to his extended family, most of whom seemed to already know who she was. Then, he grudgingly indicated Taran'atar, who took this as a signal to glide into a corner, where he hunkered down to watch the door, apparently making a sincere effort to appear as harmless as possible, although the Ingavi all jumped nervously whenever he shifted his weight or moved his hands. It was painful for Ro to watch, not in the least because the Ingavi had to know there was nothing they could do if Taran'atar took it into his head to open fire.

There were about twenty Ingavi in the bunker, and though it appeared to Ro that they had made themselves as comfortable as possible, it was clear they were miserable. They wanted to be swaying under the treetops, but here they were in these dank, dark, windless holes.

"How long have you been down here?" Ro asked, taking the small bowl of food Kel's wife, Matasa, offered. It looked like grubworms mixed with sawdust, but Ro ate it gratefully. She knew from her previous visit that she could digest Ingavi food (indeed, their digestion was considerably more delicate than the average Bajoran's) and that what she had been given was a generous portion by their standards. Ingavi ate many small meals every day and eating was usually an invitation to talk.

"One dry season and most of this rainy season," Kel said.

The better part of a year, Ro translated. "And before these Jem'Hadar, there were others?" she guessed.

Kel nodded. "The others were worse in many ways. They looked, acted, more like him." He pointed at Taran'atar, who was, Ro saw, silently declining the bowl he'd been offered.

Kel's family finished their meal, then invited Ro and Taran'atar into a small circular chamber where the air was fresher. Ro inspected the ceiling and saw that the Ingavi had inserted into the loose soil some kind of long, narrow tube that was drawing down air. Someone lit a small oil lamp and Ro turned her lamp off. Something shifted at the edge of the room and Ro realized there was an elderly Ingavi sitting there, wrapped in a heavy cloth. He had almost no hair left on his head, very little on his forearms or legs, and Ro noticed a milky white film over his eyes—cataracts, a severe handicap in an arboreal species.

"Hello, Ro," the old Ingavi said. "I hope the years have been kind to you."

Ro was surprised and delighted to realize she recognized the voice. "Hello, Tan Mulla," she said, bowing at the waist. "Passably kind, sir, and the same to you. I'm sorry we meet again under such circumstances." She turned to Taran'atar and explained that the Tan was one of the Ingavi who had rescued her after the mudslide.

"Yes, I was," Tan Mulla agreed. "And it is an action I have never regretted, though I confess I came close to despair today when I heard you had returned accompanied by a Jem'Hadar. But my nephew"—he nodded at Kel—"says you vouch for him."

"I do," Ro said, trying to sound certain. "We have a common goal. These other Jem'Hadar are not like him and he has been ordered by our leader to help us fight them." *Close enough to the truth without getting complicated.*

"I think we understand," the Tan said, but shook his head in mild disbelief. "You'll forgive us if we are suspicious. Not long after you left came the first Jem'Hadar, they and the pale ones who speak so well but smell so bad."

"Vorta," Taran'atar offered, the sound of his voice causing several nearby Ingavi to flinch.

"Yes," the Tan agreed. "Them. We did not like them, but they assured us they meant no harm and we believed them . . . for a time. Then they began to tell us, 'No, don't go there,' and 'Not allowed here,' all the time explaining why it was for our own good. We tried to respect their wishes as best we could, but then they began to harm the trees." He paused and inhaled deeply and let out a long wheeze. The air underground obviously did not agree with him. "We knew this did not bode well, so we ran and hid."

"We saw some of those trees," Ro said.

"There are worse areas, places where the forest floor is open to the sky for as far as I could see," Tan Mulla said, then pointed to his eyes. "When I could still see, that is. They built a very large structure and ringed it round with fences. Then, when they were secure, they came into the forest and hunted us. My family—those you see around me—once numbered in the dozens. Now, we are no more than those you see here. It is the same for all the other families, if not worse. We were fortunate to find this place. The Jem'Hadar never discovered that we hid underground."

Ro asked, "And then the Jem'Hadar left?"

"Yes, very suddenly. But their stronghold did not stay empty for long. Others came, men and women not unlike yourself, but with smoother noses. They began to create new Jem'Hadar, but these new ones seemed . . . less efficient than the previous ones. More brutal. I would even say clumsier, in some ways."

"Do you know how many there are?" Taran'atar asked softly.

"We think perhaps ten score now. But their creator, whom they call the Khan, is making more. We have done our best to stay hidden from them. Although there are many among us who would prefer to fight, even if it means we will die, because our lives now have become unbearable."

"I understand," Ro said sincerely. "As I told you when we first traded stories, my world was once occupied by the same aliens who conquered Ingav. I knew the anguish you felt then, and I know it now."

"I remember. You said then that you were fighting the Cardassians. Did you win?"

"No," Ro admitted. "I lost."

"What happened?"

"The Cardassians allied themselves with the Jem'Hadar, and together they waged a war against the entire quadrant. They eventually were defeated, in part because they turned against each other. But many died on all sides of the conflict, and my original cause was made moot. By the end, the Cardassians themselves suffered the most." She wondered if this news would come as some comfort to the Ingavi. She doubted it.

"But if there is peace now," Kel asked, "why has this horror come to Sindorin? Did you break your vow of silence?"

"No!" Ro said. "The people who started breeding these Jem'Hadar are renegades and opportunists. What they're doing violates the laws where I come from, threatening many beyond Sindorin. We've come to stop them, to rid this place of them. I'm just sorry, so very sorry that you found yourself trapped between all these forces. It's not right . . ." But she found that she didn't have words, couldn't find a way to define her anguish.

Beside her, Taran'atar uttered a word that Ro could only assume was a curse, then stood and marched out of the chamber. The startled Ingavi watched him leave, but no one questioned where he was going. Ro was compelled to make excuses and follow the Jem'Hadar, both worried and not a little curious about what had disturbed him. She found Taran'atar standing in the next chamber near the exit. He had opened his weapons satchel and was inspecting its contents.

"What's wrong?" Ro asked.

Taran'atar did not reply, but began checking the charge on his phaser.

"Taran'atar?"

"Nothing," he snarled. "Nothing is wrong." The power cell was fully charged, so he checked the edges on his throwing knives. Not looking up at her, he continued, "And everything is wrong. *You* are wrong. All this is wrong. The Founder—how can I say this?—he must be ill, possibly deranged from living among you for so long. Or a deviant. Why am I here? Why should I care about these . . ." and he said a word that Ro could not understand, the same word he had uttered in the small chamber. "Why do *you* care about them? They are weak. If they die now, *what does it matter?*"

Ro knew the philosophical gulf between them was too vast to bridge in one conversation, so she didn't try. Instead, she kept it as simple as possible. "They want to live."

"As do I," Taran'atar said. "As do all things. But what has any of this to do with our task here?" Taran'atar rose and slung his weapons onto his back. "If we die fighting Locken, then we die. I do not regret giving my life for my duty, Lieutenant, but I still do not understand what my duty here is."

"We're here to stop Locken."

"Then let us be about it!" Taran'atar hissed.

Ro sighed. "All right then. Let me put the question to you. What can we do in our present circumstances? What would you want to do to stop Locken?"

Taran'atar's shoulders relaxed and he seemed to give the question serious consideration. "A campaign?"

"Call it what you will."

"If I am to wage a campaign, I need supplies and troops."

"I can get you troops, I think. The Ingavi will fight. And not for us. They'll fight to win back their world."

"These creatures are no match for the Jem'Hadar," Taran'atar stated flatly. "Not even *these* Jem'Hadar."

"Neither were humans," Ro pointed out. "Or Bajorans. Or Klingons. Or Romulans. Or anyone else in the Alpha Quadrant. That *was* what the Dominion once believed, wasn't it?"

Taran'atar stared back at her, his pebbled brow knotted in turmoil. Finally he sat on the ground cross-legged, elbows on his knees, palms spread. He looked, Ro thought, strangely like a Bajoran monk in meditation. "We will need more supplies," he said. "And weapons. I do not have enough here to outfit an army . . . not even *this* army."

"Then, we'll have to find some more," Ro said, feeling hope rise in her for the first time since they beamed down to the planet's surface . . . how many hours ago? She had lost track of time.

"What about the ship?" Taran'atar asked.

"What about it?"

"You yourself thought it unlikely the runabout was destroyed, and I tend to agree. I've been considering the matter since you first brought it up. The runabout was little more than a conveyance, not a real threat, even to the limited forces at Locken's command. And those forces *are* limited. Especially if he must resort to gathering wreckage for his spacecraft."

Ro was following Taran'atar's train of thought. "Locken wasn't trying to destroy the runabout," she realized. "He just wanted to disable it so he could salvage it for himself."

"Precisely," said Taran'atar. "And if he hasn't yet recovered it—"

"He has not," a voice said. Kel again, standing in the opening between the root chambers. He had, she realized, been standing there for some time, listening to her debate with Taran'atar. "I believe," he said, "that there may still be time to find your ship. And we can help."

Chapter Twelve

"How many crash landings is that for you now?" Ezri asked.

Bashir rolled to the edge of his bunk and looked down at Ezri, who was stretched out on hers a meter below. He thought for a moment, then said, "Four."

"Only four?" Ezri asked, surprised. "Are you sure?"

"Actual contact between a ship and a planet's surface? Yes, just four: the *Yangtzee Kiang;* the *Rubicon;* that time in the stolen Jem'Hadar ship; and now."

"Huh. I guess I thought it was more than that, you being such an adventurous fellow."

"I'm adventurous," Bashir replied, "but careful."

"Ah. Well, that must make all the difference." She climbed out of her bunk and stretched, rolling her shoulders from side to side.

"How's your collarbone?" Bashir asked.

"A little stiff, but all right." She had cracked it in the crash, the worst of their combined injuries. He had been permitted to treat the break as well as various cuts and bruises, but then the Jem'Hadar had relieved him of his equipment—communicator, medical tricorder, hypo, and all the medication—and he felt slightly naked without them. "How are you?" she asked.

Bashir sighed, then sat up, almost hitting his head against the ceiling. "Annoyed. Angry. Fearful for . . ." He almost said "Ro and Taran'atar," but changed it to "the future." There was no sense in openly discussing their comrades since, in all likelihood, the cell was being monitored. A small black dome in the center of the ceiling was obviously the decoy, with the real surveillance device probably hidden among the needlessly complex-looking lighting fixtures in the corner of the room opposite the bunks. Bashir made sure to act as if he didn't care whether the cell had cameras or not, scrutinizing every part of the room with equal emphasis. It wasn't bad as cells went, he decided. Hot and cold running water. Even a small screen around the toilet for privacy's sake.

The Jem'Hadar had left them alone since they had been brought in and Bashir suspected their jailers were attempting to unnerve them, make them anxious about when Locken might arrive. Pitching his voice low, he asked, "Did you ever find your combadge?" When the Jem'Hadar had searched them, Ezri's had been missing.

"No," she said ruefully. "It must have fallen off during one of the bumps."

"Too bad. Did you have a chance to check the status of the runabout before they beamed in?" This was a safe topic since their captors undoubtedly knew more about the current condition of their craft than they did.

"Not really," Ezri said. "I think the fuselage was intact and I didn't hear any warning alarms from either the warp nacelles or the coolant system, so there weren't any leaks. Other than that, the only thing I remember is my board giving a funny little burp just before we crashed—some kind of power surge through the system just before the emergency shutdown. Did you see that?"

Bashir shook his head. "No, sorry. Missed that. Any idea what it was?"

She shrugged. "Can't say. Wasn't consistent with a burned-out system, though."

Bashir was struck by a suspicion, but he decided not to voice it just then. Changing the subject, he asked, "Did you get a chance to look out the viewports before the Jem'Hadar beamed in? Any idea about the crash site?"

Ezri opened her mouth to reply, but was interrupted before she could speak by a calm, clear, reasonable voice. "You were," it said, "extraordinarily lucky." Dr. Ethan Locken was standing in the cell door, beaming rapturously. He was wearing the same coat and smock they had seen him in on the Romulan ship, though in every other regard he appeared much less threatening than he had in the recording. Indeed, he seemed nervous and was unconsciously picking at the cuticle of his left thumb with his right one. "Dr. Julian Bashir," he said with undisguised admiration. "I can't tell you how delighted I am to finally meet you. Never in my wildest imaginings did I think Section 31 would be stupid enough to send you after me."

Bashir stood up. "Why stupid?"

"Because you're probably the one person who will truly understand what I'm trying to do here."

"And that is . . . ?"

"Save lives," Locken said simply, his cheerful smile never wavering.

"You said we were lucky," Dax said suddenly, before Bashir could inquire further. "In what way?"

"There's a salt marsh about a hundred meters to the north of where you crashed," Locken said, still addressing Bashir. "If you had gone down there, you would have sunk. Even assuming you didn't have any hull breaches, it would have been hard to get you out. To the north and west, there were much larger, much stronger trees. You would have dashed yourself to pieces against those. The grove you landed in, the trees are all young and much more flexible. They acted as a kind of crash net. Now there's an ancient word for you: 'crash net.' Do you know what I mean?"

Bashir nodded. "We used them on the station, in case the tractor beams failed when a ship was coming in hot. Our former chief of operations installed them."

"Yes, of course," Locken said. "O'Brien liked his low-tech solutions, didn't he?"

Bashir felt himself visibly start at the mention of his old friend's name and saw by the expression on Locken's face that he knew he had scored a direct hit.

"Don't worry, Doctor. Nothing sinister. I made it my business to keep tabs on you. Someday soon we *must* discuss your little obsession with the Alamo."

Ezri almost smiled despite herself.

"You might be interested to hear," Locken continued, "that I have a similar fascination with the Battle of Thermopylae."

"The three hundred Spartans against the army of the Persian Empire," Bashir recalled.

"Very good, Doctor," Locken said, smiling. "It's always a pleasant surprise to meet a well-rounded scholar. Is it only me, or have you also found that most people in the medical profession aren't really interested in the liberal arts?" He spread his arms expansively and exulted, "This is already better than I'd hoped. I feel like I know you, that we are simpatico."

"Except, of course," Ezri interjected, "that we're in a cell and you aren't."

Locken did not respond to the barb, but only walked away from the frame of the cell door. Seconds later, the forcefield was deactivated and Locken stepped into the cell. Sketching a quick bow, he asked, "Would you please accompany me to my chambers? I've prepared a light supper."

"Good," Ezri said, heading for the door. "I'm starving." For a second, Bashir thought that Locken hadn't planned on including her in the invitation, but then their "host" nodded and lifted his hand, giving her permission to pass. Ezri smiled ever so slightly, then waited for the two doctors in the corridor.

Bashir saw only a single Jem'Hadar posted at one end of the hall. There were no other obvious surveillance devices in sight, suggesting that Locken's resources were limited, and that he hadn't yet been able to begin full-scale production of his troops.

Though the place had a very "Dominion standard" look to it, Bashir couldn't overlook that the walls were all hung with paintings and art in other media, all obviously executed by the same hand: Locken's. There was a pair of gigantic, but well-balanced and aesthetically pleasing, pots standing guard beside the door to Locken's quarters. When Bashir stopped to admire them, Locken smiled and said, "Don't touch, Julian. The glaze isn't quite dry."

Bashir was surprised. He knew a little about pottery, enough to know how difficult it was to throw such large pieces. He had assumed they were replicated. "You did these?"

"Oh, yes. A hobby."

"I'm impressed." *A little fine art, a little galactic oppression,* Bashir thought. *When does he find time to sleep?* But then he considered his own all-too-frequent bouts of insomnia and realized that the answer to the question was *He doesn't,* and filed the fact away for later consideration.

Locken's private rooms were an understated mix of opulence and functionality. The living area was large, almost fifteen meters on a side, and Bashir assumed it had once been the compound's communal area, the place first the Vorta, then the Section 31 agents, had gathered to work as a group whenever necessary. There were no groups now—only Locken—so he had taken over the entire space.

One wall was dominated by a large computer workstation, probably the primary link to the computer core. Bashir made a mental note of this. On the wall opposite the door was a small but apparently well-equipped kitchen flanked by a large dining table set for one. *No replicators.* Bashir didn't see anything in the room that stamped its occupant as a megalomaniacal dictator, no life-size portraits or graven images. In fact, the room's most notable feature was its lack of personal touches, except for a small end table that displayed a selection of artwork created by children of different ages, from preschool to prepubescent, most of it addressed to "Doctor Ethan." Most of the pictures were either water-damaged or charred, and, Bashir realized with a small shudder, most of the children were probably dead, killed on New Beijing.

Amid the children's artwork, Bashir found a single holo, a group of men and women, all wearing lab coats, all smiling nervously. Locken was easy to pick out in the group. Next to Locken stood a blond-haired gentleman who had a very paternalistic arm around his shoulder. "Nice holo," Bashir said. "Was this the staff at your clinic?"

Locken's overly alert and attentive gaze relaxed into a genuine smile. "Yes," he said. "My colleagues."

"Obviously you were good friends with this gentleman," Bashir said, pointing at the blond man.

"Dr. Murdoch," Locken replied. "He was my closest friend, my . . . my mentor. I knew the *techniques*. It was all up here. . . ." He tapped his forehead. "But I didn't know how to treat patients. The children, a lot of them were afraid of me somehow, but Murdoch showed me how to set them at ease."

"It's a difficult skill to master," Bashir said. "Especially with children."

"I expect you two never met," Locken said, a questioning note in his voice.

Bashir shook his head. "No, never."

Awkwardly, as if he didn't know precisely how to continue the conversation, Locken pulled out a small control unit something like a tricorder and said, "But I promised dinner, didn't I?" He tapped a couple of keys and the lamp over the dining room table lit up. A moment later, an automated trolley covered with a selection of covered dishes trundled in and stopped before the table.

"I've prepared several things," Locken said shyly, indicating where Bashir and Dax should sit, then realized that there were no place settings. "I'll get you some tableware and napkins from the kitchen," he said apologetically, and ducked into the kitchen. When he returned, he continued, "Just take whatever you want from the trolley. No serving staff, I'm afraid. Even I wouldn't dream of using Jem'Hadar as domestics."

"But you're a god, aren't you?" Ezri asked, peeking under covers. She settled on a small salad and some rolls. "Doesn't that mean they'd wear an apron if you asked them?"

"I've never asked," Locken said. "You're a vegetarian, aren't you, Julian?"

"More or less," Bashir said, lifting the cover off a small bowl. He sniffed the contents. *"Plomeek* soup?"

"Yes," Locken said, taking the cover off what looked like a plate of lamb chops.

"Replicated or homemade?"

"Oh, homemade, of course," Locken said, returning to the table. "It's awful if you replicate it. The herbs just don't come out right."

"Yes, I know," Bashir said. "I've tried. This smells . . . good."

"Thank you. It's taken me a lot of years to perfect the recipe. A Vulcan colleague in my postgrad days said mine was superior to her mother's."

"You must have been so proud," Ezri said, sitting down at the table.

Locken did not respond, but as Bashir sat down beside Ezri, he saw the corner of Locken's eye twitch.

The soup was sublime. Locken ate at a stately pace and seemed to prefer to keep his peace, which surprised Bashir. In his experience, people who typically ate alone usually ate too quickly and tended to prattle on when they had company. That role, unfortunately, fell to Ezri, who seemed prepared to hold up the conversation for the entire table, gabbering merrily as a magpie about whatever entered her head.

When Locken carried the dishes into the kitchen, Bashir asked her, "What are you doing?"

"What do you mean?"

"The way you're acting—the nonstop talking. Why are you doing that?"

"To keep him off balance," Ezri explained. "To keep him from engaging you in conversation. He wants to win you over."

Bashir shook his head in consternation. "He's not going to 'win me over.' I'm not that easily persuaded, Ezri."

"He's very charming," Ezri said. "You have a weak spot for charm, Julian."

Bashir was stung by the observation and said, more sharply than he intended, "You obviously don't know me as well as you think you do."

"I still remember when you first met Garak . . ."

"Garak?" Bashir said. "I always thought of Garak as more mysterious than *charming.*"

"He was both. It's a potent combination—charm and mystery—particularly for you. . . ."

"That's beside the point," Bashir interrupted. "And not true, either, but we'll discuss that later. The important thing is I want *him* to talk. I'm supposed to be trying to *understand* him. How can I empathize with the man if you won't be quiet?"

"What are you saying?" Ezri asked, narrowing her eyes. "I'm a trained counselor . . ."

". . . Which would be fine *if* we're dealing with someone who needs help getting over a nasty breakup, but this is an entirely different order of being."

"Oh, of course, Julian," Ezri said icily. *"He's just like you."*

Bashir was staring at her openmouthed, stung by the retort, when Locken returned from the kitchen carrying a bowl of fruit. "Something wrong?" he asked. "I don't want to interrupt . . ."

"No," Bashir said, "nothing serious. A difference of opinion."

"Well, that happens," Locken said, picking up a pear-shaped fruit with a mottled purple skin. "Even with people who have a lot in common." He smiled at Bashir, then began to tear at the fruit's rind with his thumbs. "Try some of this," he said. "It's wonderful. I found a grove of them out behind the compound."

Bashir accepted the section of fruit, trying to imagine the neo-Khan picking fruit after disposing of the Section 31 agents. Locken was right. The fruit was delicious: lively and tart. Ezri refused any, claiming she had lost her appetite. When they were finished, Locken wiped his hands on a napkin and said, "I guess it's time for the tour now. What's the fun of having a secret base if you can't show it off?"

Locken looked at them both, obviously waiting for a smile. "You Starfleet types don't have much of a sense of humor, do you?"

Against his will, Bashir felt the corner of his mouth curl up. Ezri was right: charm and mystery *were* a potent combination.

Locken took a delightful pride in his complex, and, Bashir thought, justifiably so, it being both elegantly refurbished and well maintained. As they walked, Locken pointed out areas of special interest or pieces of art he had created. As they talked, Bashir and Locken played at a subtle cat-and-mouse game, each of them attempting to draw information out of the other without revealing too much about himself. Ezri walked half a step behind the two men.

"You've always been interested in the arts?" Bashir asked.

"Interested? Well, yes, I suppose, ever since the enhancement procedure, though I've only recently put my hand to anything. I was always afraid of drawing too much attention to myself. Being too good at too many things . . . it seemed dangerous. It was all right to be a good doctor, but only because I always tried to look like I was working very hard at it. Do you know what I mean?"

Bashir nodded, remembering the nights in the med-school library when he had to pretend to read the same page over and over again even after he had memorized an entire textbook.

"I suppose," Locken continued, "if I had received some encouragement from my parents, it might have been different, but they were always so concerned about my keeping the treatments a secret. It was difficult; they were so frightened of what might happen to *them,* though they never seemed to think very much about what I might be going through."

Bashir paused to take a closer look at a holographic sculpture, though it wasn't long before he realized he wasn't really seeing it. Instead, he was thinking about a lecture he had received from his father when he was thirteen about letting the other boys win in games sometimes, about the need to give the wrong answers on tests sometimes, about *not letting anyone know.* "The Secret Life of Jules Bashir," he had come to label it in his own head. And now here he was speaking to someone who understood, *really* understood.

"But I decided," Locken said, "to try to make the best of things, to create a meaningful life for myself. After I finished medical school, I accepted a position at the New Beijing Pediatric Center. They were doing some very interesting work in correcting prenatal microcellular damage. Did you ever read any of it?"

Bashir nodded absently. "A little," he said. "But I don't have much use for obstetrics on DS9. It isn't that kind of place."

Locken smiled as if he knew better. "I'm sure Colonel Kira and Captain Yates would beg to differ. Oh, and let's not forget Lieutenant Vilix'pran. No matter what else I accomplish here, I can safely say that the best work I ever did was back on New Beijing. We helped mothers bring new lives into the world . . ."

Bashir glanced at Ezri and watched her roll her eyes.

Locken had not missed it, either. "Mock if you will, Lieutenant," he said. "But one of the reasons settlers came to New Beijing was because of the work we did at the center. I treated more than a couple of Trill there, which means I have to ask myself why they didn't find what they needed at home. Do *you* know?"

Ezri didn't respond.

"I thought so," he said, and Bashir had to wonder at the change in his tone. Perhaps the shyness and humility were a little more calculated than he had thought. Or perhaps the differences in his personality existed side by side . . . ?

"And I'd still be there," Locken continued, his voice rising. "If it weren't for the damned war. *Starfleet's* war."

"Starfleet didn't start the war," Ezri retorted.

"Or the Dominion's war," Locken countered. "Or the Romulans' war or the Breen's war. It doesn't matter. The only thing that matters is it came to New Beijing and we didn't want it. We didn't *deserve* it, but there it was."

"Do you know *why* the Dominion invaded New Beijing?" Bashir asked, trying to break some of the tension, but keep Locken talking. "Starfleet could never make sense of it."

"Why?" Locken repeated, his bitterness growing. "Apparently it was all a mistake. They'd been misinformed."

Bashir frowned. "What do you mean?"

"I mean the Dominion apparently had erroneous intelligence that we were developing biogenic weapons on New Beijing. At one point while I was hiding from them, I managed to capture one of their Vorta. We . . . *spoke,* and he explained that they had learned we were developing a pathogen that would be effective against the Jem'Hadar. I didn't know this at the time, but I could tell them today that the idea is ludicrous. Any pathogen potent enough to kill a Jem'Hadar couldn't be released into a planetary environment without killing anything else it came into contact with."

"I agree," Bashir said.

"Ah, yes," Locken replied. "You know whereof I speak, don't you? You were able to observe a Jem'Hadar go from newborn to full adult a few years back, so you have a fairly complete genetic sample, don't you? Impressive, isn't it?"

"The Founders are extraordinary genetic engineers," Bashir said, but thought, *He doesn't know about Taran'atar. That means he and Ro are still free.*

Locken went on, "Remind me to show you some notes I've been developing for a paper suggesting the possibility that the Founders were once solids themselves and their current state is the result of genetic engineering."

"I'd like to see that," Bashir said. "Later. Continue with your story."

Locken stopped in front of a large window and stared out unseeingly into the night. They were on the second or third story, Bashir saw, overlooking a short, muddy lawn, and the lights in the corridor were low, so most of the illumination came from a pair of lampposts outside at the perimeter of the fence. "It was a nightmare," Locken said, his voice coming harsh and raspy. "The colony's automatic defenses went down and Starfleet was spread too thin. They couldn't—or wouldn't—send anyone."

"If they could have, they would have," Bashir said. "You must realize that."

Locken sneered, but did not respond to Bashir's claim. "And then the Jem'Hadar began beaming down," he continued. "They were everywhere—in homes, offices, clinics, parks, in the children's ward. . . . There was no warning, no request for surrender. They weren't an occupying army—they were *butchers*. Have you ever seen Jem'Hadar in combat? I don't mean against Starfleet or Klingon troops. Have you ever seen them tear into a civilian population?"

"No," Bashir said, his voice catching in his throat. "No, I haven't. And I never want to."

"No," Locken agreed, shaking his head. "You never do. And if I have my way, you never will. Not you or anyone else."

"How did you survive?" Dax asked.

Locken turned toward her, seemingly surprised to find she was still there. After a lingering pause, he answered, "I kept my head, Lieutenant. I hid when I could hide, fought when I had to fight."

"Against Jem'Hadar?"

"Jem'Hadar are mortal. They can be killed if you know where to strike them. One of the things I learned on New Beijing is that I can deal death quite efficiently when I must."

I know that feeling too, Bashir thought.

"But you weren't able to help any of the others?" Ezri asked. "Your colleagues? Your patients?"

Cocking his head to one side, Locken stroked his eyebrow thoughtfully and said in his mildest tone, "You know, Lieutenant, it strikes me that you've been attempting to sow some sort of discord. I wish you'd stop. It's really rather annoying and stands no chance of succeeding. But to answer your question, by the time I had recovered from the shock of the initial attack, my patients and my colleagues were all dead. They had a weapons platform in orbit."

"Like the one that shot us down," Bashir observed.

"Yes," Locken said. "Like that one. By the way, you wouldn't have had a problem approaching Sindorin if you had only announced yourselves sooner. You *were* planning on announcing yourselves, weren't you?"

"Right after we fired the quantum torpedoes," she said.

"*Ezri,*" Bashir said through gritted teeth. "I think that's enough for now." She didn't respond out loud, only glared at him.

"Yes, I quite agree," Locken said. "Would you like to see the rest of the facility?"

"All right," Bashir said. "And I'd like to hear some more about how Section 31 approached you. I have to confess I'm a little surprised you cooperated with them as long as you did."

"I cooperated with them as long as it suited me," Locken said, turning down a short corridor to stop before a pair of large, utilitarian double doors. "This leads to the Jem'Hadar barracks," he explained, laying his palm on an identity reader. "They won't be able to see us where we'll be, but try not to make too much noise anyway. There are some young ones in here and they tend to be ... irritable." The ID reader pinged and the doors swung open slowly, revealing a long dark corridor. Bashir glanced at Ezri, but she wouldn't meet his eyes.

"I'll keep that in mind," Bashir said. "You were saying about Section 31—"

"I wasn't," Locken replied, "but since you seem to want to hear it anyway ..." He waited for the doors to close, then pulled out his control unit again and pointed it at a row of black glass panels that made up one long wall of the corridor. At his touch, the entire wall lightened to transparency. "After the Dominion forces left New Beijing," Locken explained, "Federation relief teams arrived to help the survivors, to scrape dirt over the wreckage and to bury the dead. When they realized who I was, they asked me to stay on and help." He shrugged. "What could I say? Part of me desperately wanted to leave, but it was my home, so I stayed. I became friends with another one of the workers, a woman named Merra. We often found ourselves working on the same teams. Somewhere along the line, I realized she had been arranging that."

"She was a Section 31 agent," Bashir said.

"Of course," Locken agreed. "But she was also my friend. I still miss her."

"What happened then?"

"Sometime after the last of the dead were interred, Merra told me about Section 31—her version of what it was, at least—and told me that they had asked her to watch me, to learn about me. Merra was, I think, a true acolyte. She fervently believed in Section 31's mission and her superiors must have thought she could transfer her faith to me."

"Did she?"

Locken smiled. "I agreed," he said slowly, "that there needs to be a single, intelligent, unifying force organizing the quadrant. Section 31, by its very nature, cannot be that force, but I admire the organization, their ability to muster resources. I learned a lot from them."

"I've been meaning to ask you," Bashir said. "Where are the agents who accompanied you here? I haven't seen any other humans."

"My former colleagues are now my guests," he said. "If you'd like to meet them later, I'd be happy to arrange it. I'm not a murderer, Julian."

"Not a murderer?" Ezri flared. "What about the crew of that Romulan ship? That wasn't murder?"

Locken turned on her, his face flushed. "That was war, Lieutenant," he said. "The first volley in a new war that will bring about a permanent peace."

"That wasn't war," Ezri hissed. "In war, the victor takes prisoners when they've defeated an enemy. What I saw was a total and complete disregard for any universally recognized rules and conventions. What I saw was *sadism.*"

"Those are *your* rules and conventions, Lieutenant," Locken said. "Your limited concept of right and wrong. I've moved beyond your outmoded ethics. I see the universe as it really is and I see my place in it. Being the limited creature you are, you couldn't comprehend what I'm saying, but Julian understands." He spun back to face Bashir. "Don't you, Julian?"

Bashir was shocked by the transformation he had just witnessed. Until now, Locken had come across as traumatized, even deluded, but now here was the spark of megalomania that lay at the core of the neo-Khan's recent actions. Locken and Ezri stared at him as if he were about to judge the value of their arguments. The pulse of the world seemed to slow as the seconds ticked past, until Bashir finally said, "I think I'd like to see the rest of the facility." Dax just stared at him. And Locken, once again full of courtesy and goodwill, gestured toward the observation windows.

"Take a look," he said. "I think you'll enjoy this."

They were looking down through the transparent ceiling into a series of large chambers. In the room immediately below them, a trio of adult Jem'Hadar was drilling a group of youngsters in weaponry. "I like to keep the birth groups together whenever possible," Locken explained. "It promotes unity."

The youths appeared to be about twelve or thirteen, which meant, Bashir knew, that they were probably not more than two days old. Within the week, they would be adults, battle-ready and disciplined. That was not quite the case today, however; when one of the instructors handed a student a short sword, the boy lifted it over his head and would have brought it crashing down on the head of his "brother" if the instructor had not cuffed him in the mouth.

"You haven't begun to give those six ketracel-white yet, have you?" Bashir asked.

"No, not yet," Locken said. "My experiments show that if you give it to them too soon, it makes them harder to handle. Too late and they sometimes develop a histochemical response, and die."

"An allergic reaction?" Bashir asked, interested despite himself.

"A protein-inhibitor reaction. I suspect it has something to do with my formula for ketracel-white. The only sample I had to work with when I was duplicating the biochemistry was a little old, so I suspect something degraded. I'll show you my data logs later. You've done some work in that, haven't you?"

"Yes. Well, no. Not the real thing." Bashir was impressed. Locken had just casually—perhaps *too* casually—revealed that he had learned to synthesize ketracel-white, a problem that had eluded some of the best minds in the Federation.

"Another peculiarity: My Jem'Hadar go through white much faster than the Dominion's Jem'Hadar did," Locken continued. "They need to replenish as often as six times a day. Naturally I've dispensed with ritualizing the administration of white. I let my troops control their own intake. Pipes from the distillery actually lead directly to dispensers in the barracks.

"At first, I wasn't sure I understood why the Founders decided to create a species with a biochemical dependence. It seemed counterintuitive, especially since the Jem'Hadar were genetically programmed to think of them as akin to gods. But then, I began to see the sense of it. In addition to nourishing them, the ketracel-white also relieves them of any unnecessary concepts of guilt or innocence. In their view, there is only order or disorder. It is a very . . . liberating perspective."

"I'd imagine it is," Dax remarked, unable to help herself. "It enables one to justify almost anything."

Locken ignored the gibe, indicating with a wave of his hand that they were to continue down the narrow corridor. The second chamber, much larger than the first, was a shipbuilding bay and contained the fully functional composite ships that had attacked the runabout, plus four others in various stages of construction.

"We've turned necessity into a virtue," Locken said, indicating the ships. "When we began, all I had was the ship we came here in. I used it to salvage wrecks littering the area, then studied the components until I was able to piece together a working fighter craft."

"You assembled a high-performance fighter by *studying* the components?" Bashir asked, impressed despite himself. "But none of the ships had the same computer systems, or structural systems, or anything. Something like that shouldn't have been possible."

Locken gave a not entirely convincing shrug. "It was an interesting challenge, I'll admit that. But once I devised the proper algorithms, well, not so much a problem."

More of the false modesty, Bashir thought. *I begin to perceive a pattern.*

"You didn't have any use for our runabout?" Dax asked pointedly, noticing that it wasn't in the bay.

"Oh, I plan to put it to excellent use, Lieutenant," Locken said, favoring her with a supremely confident smile. "In time. But there's no hurry. It'll keep very nicely where you set it down until I'm ready to get to it. Besides, I didn't want it close enough to serve as a temptation for either of you."

The next chamber, smaller than the previous two, was a dimly lit lab. The doorframe, Bashir noted, glowed faintly blue in the low light. "This is where I manufacture my ketracel-white."

"A forcefield on the doors," Ezri said. She had evidently noticed the blue glow, too. "You don't trust in your own godhead?"

"I'm a very cautious individual," said Locken, "and though I don't think my Jem'Hadar would ever succumb to the temptation to break in, better to be safe than sorry. But this is a very dull stop on the tour. Come see the last chamber. This is where things get interesting."

Looking down into the chamber, Bashir felt his gorge rise and his stomach drop. There was nothing at all interesting about what was below them unless you could consider hell an interesting place.

It was a Jem'Hadar factory.

Bashir knew that he should use the word "hatchery" or "crèche" or something that could justifiably be applied to living organisms, but there was nothing about the place that hinted at anything resembling an organic process. It was a production line. At the center of the room was a machine that vaguely resembled the incubation chamber Quark had discovered among some ship wreckage he'd purchased several years ago, except much, much larger. Perhaps the unit Bashir had studied back on the station had once been part of a larger machine, or, just as likely, Locken had improved on the Dominion design.

"Look over there," Locken said, proudly pointing at a large translucent tube attached to the underside of the incubator. "There's a pupa coming through now."

Bashir watched as an oblong blob about the size of a soccer ball slid into the tube. Then, the tube contracted spasmodically, each convulsion pushing the shadow a little farther along. When the small bundle reached the end of the tube, it slipped out into a netted bag, still steaming from the warmth of the incubator, a thin stream of ooze dripping through the mesh.

"A pupa?" Ezri asked. "You call them pupa?"

"It isn't really in the mature form yet," Locken explained. "There's a short gestation period and then it enters the larval stage and begins to grow very rapidly."

"You mean it's a baby," Ezri said.

Locken began to laugh, giddy with delight. "That's wonderful, Lieutenant. Really. Never lose that sense of humor and you'll be fine, but also be sure you don't confuse it with unnecessary sentimentality. The Jem'Hadar don't care."

A pair of robotic arms yanked the netting tightly around the infant, then lifted it high and carried it away deeper into the factory. Bashir guessed it was placed in some sort of feeding chamber where it was maintained until it entered the "larval" stage.

"How quickly can you produce them?" Bashir asked, struggling to keep his voice steady.

"Not as fast as I'd like," Locken said. "I've improved the process to the point where a new batch—usually a couple of dozen—is produced every week."

Bashir watched Ezri flinch at the use of the words "process," "batch," and "produced," but he felt he was getting valuable information and he didn't want Locken to stop talking. "Usually?" he asked. "But not always?"

"There are problems sometimes," Locken explained. "We do a quality-control check just before the incubation period ends and I've found that the reengineering I've worked into the genetic code doesn't always take. It's strange—it's almost as if the Founders knew someone would try this someday and configured the code to fight off any restructuring."

"You're talking about the sequence that makes the Jem'Hadar obey you?" Bashir asked.

"Yes. It's the main sequence I check, but not the only one," Locken said. "Have you seen any information about transcription error rate in the Dominion? I imagine Starfleet would be very interested in something like that."

Bashir said no, and began to ramble on about Starfleet attempts to get information out of Vorta while simultaneously calculating how many Jem'Hadar Locken could have produced in the weeks since he took over Sindorin. "So you have, what, two hundred adult Jem'Hadar now?"

"One hundred eighty-two," Locken corrected. "And about fifty immature units. The incubator is very, well, I guess 'fussy' is the word, and I haven't been able to train the Jem'Hadar to tend it. It's not the sort of thing they excel at. But that will be changing soon. I've been distracted by other problems, but it won't be much longer before I go into full production. Soon, there will be more Jem'Hadar here than I'll know what to do with. Though, naturally, I know *exactly* what I'll do with them." He glanced at Ezri and asked, "What's wrong, Lieutenant? No pithy comments about not counting my Jem'Hadar before they're hatched?"

Ezri, who was still staring into the first chamber, trying to see where the robot had taken the unborn Jem'Hadar, turned to Locken and stared at him, her face locked into a rictus of loathing. Her mouth opened and she struggled to speak, but, finally, all she could do was turn her back to the incubation chambers, her shoulders hunched, her arms wrapped around herself.

Locken followed without comment, stopping only to glance at Bashir with an expression that said, *What shall we do about her?* "She doesn't understand," Locken said, amused by Ezri's revulsion. "She thinks genetic engineering is perverse, unnatural. Yet, I would be willing to wager she doesn't have any problem with traveling the cosmos in a faster-than-light ship or using medical technology to cure diseases or correct birth defects." He raised his voice to make sure Ezri could hear him. "But let me ask you both this: Does anyone in your immediate family have an artificial limb or organ? Perhaps a device that augments their hearing or vision? How about something as basic as a heart monitor?"

Ezri said nothing, but Bashir could tell that Locken had her attention.

"But genetic engineering—what is that? Isn't it just another advance in technology? We'll use it on plants. We'll even use it on animals, the lower-order animals at any rate. Am I wrong or don't many terraformers use algae ponds filled with genetically enhanced microorganisms that hyperproduce oxygen? Aren't there a million similar examples of controlled genetics throughout the Federation?"

Ezri turned, but her face was set, implacable.

"Everything changes, Lieutenant, everything evolves," Locken said, his voice calm and even, as if he were lecturing a slow, disobedient child. "Sometimes, we need to give evolution a boost, a little tweak, and most of the time we decide that's fine—unless it's ourselves we're doing it to. Then, it's unnatural and immoral. Do you know what I think, Lieutenant? I think the *laws* that govern these areas are unnatural and immoral, not to mention hypocritical and absurd. What is it they call these laws, Julian? A 'firewall'? What an evocative word that is. Fairly enflames the senses, doesn't it? And do you know what I see going up in flames?"

Bashir, as if caught in a hypnotic spell, could not resist answering. "No," he said. "What?"

"Our genetic potential," Locken said softly. "We *could* be better than we are, but only if we're not afraid. The Federation has grown feeble, its strength sapped by weak-willed politicians who are too concerned with public opinion to make the tough decisions. The Klingons, the Romulans, the Breen—they can all smell the Federation's fear, taste its weakness. It's only a matter of time before the barbarians descend on the Federation and tear it apart like the Huns overriding Ancient Rome. It *will* happen. It's only a matter of time—and afterward it's only a matter of who's left to pick up the pieces."

Locken turned to look down into the chambers beneath his feet, then pressed his hands and face against the glass. "Plato had the right idea. You've read *The Republic*. The Federation—or this miserable rabble that the Federation has become—needs us, Julian. It needs philosopher kings—enlightened men and women who will rule wisely, but with courage and daring.

"'Philosopher kings'?" Ezri asked mockingly. "'*Enlightened* men and women'? Like Khan, you mean, and his genetically engineered elite. Right—*there* was an enlightened group. I've seen the two-dees, read the histories: the food riots, the 'genetic cleansings,' the camps. Do you *really* think . . . ?"

"Winners write history, Lieutenant," Locken interrupted, pitching his voice low and cutting through Ezri's vehemence. "I thought you knew that. And no one knows anything with absolute certainty about that era. Yes, Khan made some mistakes, but think about what he might have accomplished *if* he'd had a chance. Think about what might be different today."

"Like *what?*" Ezri asked, exasperated. "Precisely *what* would be different?"

Locken's face flushed a deep scarlet. He clenched his teeth and Bashir saw tears spring into his eyes. Locken turned away and took several deep, shuddering breaths. When he turned around, Bashir saw no sign of emotion in his face. The rage or sorrow or regret—whatever it had been—was gone, replaced by a pure, crystalline light. "Like what, Lieutenant? How about all the lives that would have been saved if Julian and I were the norm and not the exception?" He faced Bashir, making his case directly. "Think about all the human lives that have been lost since Khan's time in battles with the Romulans, the Klingons, the Cardassians, the Tzenkethi, the Borg. If Khan had won, the Federation would be much more powerful today, the Dominion would never have stood a chance, and New Beijing would never have happened."

Ezri flashed Bashir a look that said more than words ever could. If she had been holding a phaser, Bashir suspected, she would have shot him on the spot. Not for personal reasons, not for the sake of vengeance or hatred, but for the same reason anyone would kill a diseased wild animal that had found its way into a nursery school: because it was the only thing to do.

Locken was still looking at Bashir. "It isn't too late, though. That's my point in all this. We can't fix the past, but we can learn from it to shape the future. We could do it together, Julian. You and I together could re-create humanity in our image."

Bashir felt something rise up within himself, and was as surprised as Locken when it expressed itself in an incredulous laugh. "You can't be serious," he said. "That's the most ridiculous thing I've ever heard. You're just mouthing words. You sound just like the villain in every bad adventure serial ever written. Why would I ever consider helping you in this *insane* scheme? What could you possibly have to offer humanity that would make them want to follow you? Some vague promises of genetic improvement? Of invincibility?" He shook his head. "It's not that simple, you know. You want to offer people some hope that genetic manipulation might improve their lives or the lives of their children? They have that now; the people of the Federation have those options available to them, but they've chosen not to take them. Perhaps the rest of humanity doesn't have our lightning-quick minds or our sharp reflexes, but they *do* possess the ability to make moral decisions—and this is the decision they've made."

Locken's expression didn't change as Bashir spoke, not a blink or a wince showing that the man had heard or understood a word he had spoken. But then he shook himself, strode forward, and brushed past Bashir. "Follow me," he said. At the very end of the corridor, he pulled the control unit from inside his coat and pressed it into a recessed panel on the wall. After keying in a code sequence, a section of wall slid open and Locken beckoned for Bashir to look inside.

"You said that I had nothing of value to give to humanity," he said proudly. "How do you think humanity would respond to *this?*" He must have activated another key on his control unit, because the lights came on and Bashir suddenly found himself facing a duplicate Locken.

He was standing, or rather floating, in a large transparent tube. There was a breathing mask over his face and several monitoring devices were stuck to his arms, chest, and groin, but there was no mistaking the red hair and the dark eyes, despite the fact that the eyes were empty of intelligence. Then Bashir stepped to the side and saw behind the first tube another just like it with another floating body. And behind that tube was another and behind that another. He could not see to the back of the room, but there could be no doubt that Locken had been busy.

"Clones?" Bashir asked. "Have you lost your mind, Locken? *Clones?* Who cares? Cloning technology has also been available for hundreds of years. It doesn't mean anything if you can't transfer the intelligence, and that sort of engrammatic work is ..." He hesitated, then, in hushed tones, said, "You've figured it out."

Locken grinned. "Almost," he said. "I have the theory worked out. The Dominion left behind traces of the technology they use to copy Vorta minds into their clones, but Vorta and humans—the physiology is very different. It almost looks like their brains were designed to facilitate the transfer process, but I think I know what needs to be done. The work you did with the Klingon—Kurn, I think his name was—that might be key."

Bashir's mind began to race. It was a fascinating concept and he could see exactly how his work on Worf's brother would be useful. Against his will, Bashir began to ponder the possibilities. What wouldn't humanity agree to in exchange for the promise of immortality?

And then there was a stir behind him as Ezri stepped forward, her gaze locked on the tube, her jaw clenched. "He'll never help you," she said, turning the full force of her disdain on Locken. "He'd never set himself apart like you have and try to tell humanity that he knows what's best for it. And he'd *never* engineer a race of beings to worship him like a god. You obviously don't know *anything* about him." She turned to look at Bashir, obviously expecting a cocky grin, a thumbs-up, or some other mark of solidarity . . . and found herself instead seeing the last thing she expected.

Uncertainty.

Locken, amused and triumphant, said only, "Obviously, Lieutenant, you don't know him as well as you thought you did."

"Oh, gods . . ." Dax whispered, then spun on her heel and ran down the corridor.

"Don't worry," Locken told Bashir. "She can't go far. I locked the other door."

"I wasn't . . . worried," Bashir mumbled. "I . . . I'm just very tired now."

"I understand," Locken said gently. "It's been an eventful day and you obviously have a lot to think about. Sleep on it and we'll see how things look in the morning."

Bashir listened to the sound of Ezri's footsteps echoing down the corridor. He knew he should run after her, confront her, try to explain what had happened, but all he could think about was how weary he was of always having to explain *everything* and how it seemed it always took so long for everyone to understand even the simplest things. And now, a new sound: Ezri pounding on the door. She wanted out. She wanted to go away. She didn't want to listen. He couldn't see her at the other end of the dark corridor, but he could feel her anger, her frustration, her fear.

He felt something inside him begin to slip loose, to tumble forward, to slide into the dark expanse. "Yes," Bashir said, staring into the abyss. "I guess we'll see how things look in the morning."

Chapter Thirteen

"What is this place?" Ro called up to Kel. "It seems familiar."

The Ingavi released his grip on the branch he was dangling from and dropped headfirst ten meters, snagging another branch a mere two meters above the ground and swinging himself up into a seated position. "Do not speak too loudly," Kel said. "The Jem'Hadar have claimed this area for their own and though they do not come here every day, they come often enough."

The sun would rise soon, Ro knew, and soon they would have to make a decision: stay under cover until nightfall and rest or continue to the spot where the Ingavi thought the runabout had gone down. Kel said it was still a few hours' hike, and while it seemed sensible to stop and rest, part of her wanted to press on.

"If the Jem'Hadar come here, why are we going this way?" Taran'atar asked, stepping into the clearing and dropping his shroud. He had been slipping away about once an hour—"reconnaissance," he said, though Ro wondered what he could be finding out that their arboreal spies could not.

And spies they had—in abundance. Kel had been true to his word; he had found them an army, though there was still a question about how effectively Ro and Taran'atar could use them. In the end, they could end up being nothing more than cannon fodder and that thought tore at Ro. What right did she have to ask these people to die? Certainly, they seemed willing enough to fight, but could they truly understand what they were about to face? She shook her head and tried to focus.

"There is something here," Kel said, "that you need to see."

"Quickly," Taran'atar snapped. Kel dropped to the ground and bounded up the trail a couple of dozen meters, then suddenly veered to the right. Above them, in the highest branches of the canopy, Ro heard their Ingavi army take a collective breath, then release it in low, grunting hoots that reverberated in the branches and seemed to shake dew from the leaves.

They walked through the dense brush over uneven terrain for several minutes, Kel first, followed by Taran'atar, then Ro last. Even in the dim predawn light, she saw signs that this narrow trail had once been well traveled by the standards of the forest. There was something familiar about the place, too; she had been here before, on her previous visit, though there was something dreamlike about the memory.

The trail opened out into yet another grove of huge trees. There must have been a cold spring nearby, because a heavy mist clung to the place, cloaking the ground up to the height of two meters. The fog didn't drift, but seemed only to ripple in the breeze like heavy gray curtains.

"Do you recognize this place now, Ro?" Kel asked softly.

"Yes," she said. "I remember now. I was brought here once. This is the oldest grove, the place where your people first settled when you came here." She explained to Taran'atar: "The Ingavi chose to live in the kinds of groves we saw earlier because they felt they were all connected to this spot."

"Physically or spiritually?" Taran'atar asked.

Ro was surprised by the question, but decided not to comment. Also, she didn't know the answer. "I don't know," she said. "I was never clear on that. All I know is that this is an important place for them, the forest at the heart of the forest."

"I understand," Taran'atar said. He turned to Kel and asked, "Why did you bring us here?"

In response, Kel only lifted his arm and pointed into the mist, directing Ro and the Jem'Hadar to enter.

"You won't come with us?" Ro asked. "Show us what you want us to see?"

"My people do not enter this place anymore." It was all he would say.

"Let us get this over with so we can continue our journey," Taran'atar said.

"He wouldn't lead us into danger," Ro said.

"Not intentionally, no." It was, Ro realized, almost a compliment coming from the Jem'Hadar. She wondered if Kel would care.

They strode into the mist and Ro quickly felt herself grow disoriented. The trees were closer together than they seemed from a distance and loomed up out of the fog, massive and somber.

"When you were here before," Taran'atar asked, "was this place tended?"

"Yes," Ro said. "They treated it like, well, a public garden, if you know what that is."

Taran'atar nodded.

"Any group that passed near here would stop and groom it, keep it tidy."

"But not anymore," Taran'atar observed.

"Yes," Ro said. "I see what you mean." Dead branches and leaf litter crackled under her feet and the sound—or possibly the mist—gave her a chill.

They stopped, each realizing that they were near the center of the place, and looked around at the trees. The canopy overhead was so dense that Ro sensed it would be dim in here even at high noon, but enough predawn light was filtering through the branches that she was now able to make out a few details. Something at eye level winked, but then was gone. *An insect?* she wondered.

Ro peered closer and saw it again—a faint glimmer. Reaching out, she touched a tree trunk, brushing away a piece of loose soil or moss, and found what she had seen from the corner of her eye: the flat head of a nail. Now that she knew what she was looking at, she saw another, perhaps a meter to the left of the first. A small, pale stick was wedged between the nail's head and the tree trunk. She reached up, touched it with the tip of her finger, then pulled back, shaken.

It wasn't a stick.

Ro knelt down and turned on her palm beacon. Here were more, many more, a jumble of tiny bones. They were too small to have been an adult's. Ro felt the bile at the back of her throat, but she willed it back down. She would not further dishonor this place.

She stood, a little light-headed, and walked around the tree, studying it carefully. Yes, there were more nails, most in sets of two, some high, some low. Here and there bits of bone and fur clung, and Ro tried not to think about the bit of moss she had brushed away earlier.

Moving faster, willing herself to be calm, she walked from tree to tree and studied each, wanting to check them all, but desperately wanting each one to be the last. There were more nails, many more. Most of the bones were small, but not all. It quickly became obvious that not all the victims had been brought here at the same time. The atrocities that had been committed in the grove had happened over the course of many weeks, possibly even months. The insects, the molds, and the elements had done their work; they had reclaimed the raw materials for another cycle of life, but not all the evidence had been erased yet.

It didn't occur to her until she reached the spot where they had come into the grove that she hadn't seen or heard Taran'atar since they'd entered the grove.

"Taran'atar?" she whispered.

He shimmered into view halfway down the trail. "Are you finished?" he asked.

"Finished?" she asked irritably. "Yes. I've seen what he wanted us to see. What about you?"

"What about me?" he asked as she fell into step behind him.

"Did you see?"

"I did not have to see anything," Taran'atar said. "I could smell it."

"What? Smell what?"

"Fear," Taran'atar said. "Uncomprehending dread. An echo of horror. The trees are saturated with it."

"They were children," Ro said. "Most of them. Why would they do that to children?"

"'They'?" Taran'atar repeated.

"The Jem'Hadar."

"Jem'Hadar did not do this," Taran'atar said. "Or if they did, they were very poorly trained Jem'Hadar. It was not . . . orderly."

"Then who?" Ro asked. "The Section 31 agents? If so, why? What would it prove?"

"Isn't it obvious, Ro?" Kel called from a branch overhead. They had reached the spot where they had turned off the main trail. "It was him, the one you are here to find: Locken. The Khan."

"Locken?" Ro asked incredulously. This did not fit the mental picture she had formed of the man. He was ruthless, but she hadn't imagined him capable of such casual brutality. "But why? It makes no sense. He was . . . he was a pediatrician. He treated children, all kinds, from every species in the Federation . . . I don't understand."

"What don't you understand?" Kel asked. "Why he would order his Jem'Hadar to kill the adults, the parents, but would tell them to save the children and bring them here? Why he would press their limbs against the trees and then . . ." But it was more than he could stand. Kel cupped his hands over his eyes and lowered his head. Above them, invisible, dozens of voices hooted and cursed. "And then," Kel finished, "he would sit on the ground and watch them. For hours sometime. However long it would take and sometimes it would take so very, very long. We tried to save them, every one of them, but the Jem'Hadar . . ." Here his voice cracked and he stared at Taran'atar. "They ringed the place around, faces pointed outward, not hearing the cries of parents or children."

Kel fell silent and Ro waited for him to speak again, but it was clear he had no words for what he was feeling, not even an inarticulate cry of rage.

"But why?" Ro asked again.

"Why?" Taran'atar asked. "Isn't it obvious? *Because he could.* Because he knew that whatever he once had been, he was no longer. Because there was no one who could tell him he could not. Because it is what unchecked power will always do."

There was something about the way Taran'atar said these words—so knowing, so serene—that rankled Ro. "You would know, wouldn't you?" she asked. "Isn't that what the Dominion is all about? Don't the Founders do pretty much whatever they want? Isn't that what they wanted to do to the Alpha Quadrant? Nail us all up to a tree?"

Taran'atar stared at her impassively, then slowly shook his head. "You don't understand," he said. "You obviously know nothing of the Founders. They . . ." But he checked himself. "This is not the place or the time. We have much to do still, if we can do anything at all." He looked up at Kel. "We have seen what you wanted us to see. Now, lead on."

Kel nodded and leaped up onto a higher branch, then swung forward, moving gracefully, almost carelessly. It was a breathtaking display of athleticism and Ro could not help but admire it for its simple beauty. When she looked around, she found that Taran'atar was also gone, having either shrouded or slipped away into the jungle unnoticed. For all Ro could tell, she was alone in the forest, the only humanoid creature for hectares around. The wind shifted and something fell rattling through the branches to the ground. Readjusting the straps of her pack and setting off down the trail, Ro tried not to think of bones.

"Commander, a call for you. Colonel Kira."

Vaughn, sitting in the center seat and studying a padd with the specs for the command/control module, looked over at Bowers and said, "Put it through, Lieutenant."

"You'll have to use the controls next to your chair, Commander. I can still only transmit text from this console."

Vaughn looked at the panels and cursed under his breath. Whoever it was who designed these things never seemed to be content to follow the layout of the previous generation.

"Comm channel three-eight-five, sir."

Vaughn found the contact, pressed it, and said, "Vaughn here." No response. "Nothing's happening," he told Bowers.

"You have to hold it down until the connection is made, sir."

Vaughn pressed hard on the contact with three fingers. "We're going to do something about this later," he said ominously to the entire bridge, but before anyone could respond the main viewscreen lit up.

"Do something about what?" Kira asked.

"About the whole ship, Colonel," Vaughn replied. "I'm beginning to think it doesn't care much for me."

Plainly amused, Kira shrugged. *"Sorry to hear that. I hope you both can work it out. I'd hate to have to choose between the two of you."*

"Ouch," Vaughn said. "Noted."

"I imagine the Defiant *isn't much like the last few ships you served on, is she?"*

"Not very," Vaughn said, smiling. "She reminds me of the ships of my younger days—all engine and weapons, halls too narrow to walk two abreast, and junior officers sleeping two or three to a room." He inhaled deeply, smelled burning insulation and lubricant, grateful that the *Defiant*'s bridge did *not* remind him of a hotel lobby.

"Those were the days, eh, Commander?" Kira said. *"So how's it coming? Admiral Ross is expecting a progress report."*

Vaughn found the proper contact on his left armrest, calling up a status screen and dropping the data as an inset in one corner of the viewscreen, which would be duplicated on the colonel's own monitor. "Fairly well," he said. "All things considered. What I should have said earlier was that the *Defiant* seems to occasionally resist refitting. She warmed right up to the new biochem lab, but she's being positively cranky about the new stellar cartography equipment. Shar thinks he has the problem sorted out, although we blew a main when we tried to reroute power for the new navigational controls earlier today. How's that coming, Tenmei?"

Prynn Tenmei, the conn officer, checked her status board and replied, "Repair team estimates three hours fifty minutes, sir."

"It'll be fixed by the end of the day, Colonel. And we've swapped out one of the old short-range probe launchers for a long-range tube. That seems to have gone all right. No worries on the weapons systems, of course. And where are we with the upgrades to the conn, Ensign?"

"Module one has arrived and is being unpacked, sir," Tenmei said. "Module two failed the primary test cycle and we're checking it for bugs. Anticipate completion at twenty-thirty hours tomorrow."

"Did you catch that, Colonel?"

"Yes, Commander. You should also know we received a revised ETA for the new warhead module. The U.S.S. Gryphon should be arriving with it in tow inside of seventy-eight hours."

"Thank you, Colonel, that's excellent news."

Kira nodded. "Oh, and Ensign? I've manned that station. Be good to her."

Tenmei grinned at Kira. "Of course, Colonel." She stroked the main panel of the conn and said, "Though we're still in the 'getting acquainted' stage."

"Maybe you should give the commander a lesson when you have a minute. He seems to make a bad first impression."

Tenmei's face snapped shut. "Yes, Colonel," she said curtly, but would say no more. There was an uncomfortable pause as Kira tried to figure out what she had done wrong, but Vaughn rescued her.

"Anything else, Colonel?" he asked.

"No, that's fine. Admiral Ross should be satisfied, thank you."

"Any word from our friends?"

Kira shook her head. "Not since yesterday." She didn't need to add since they signaled they were about to enter the Badlands. Vaughn could read the concern on her face. "Are you coming back to ops?"

"Later," he replied. "After I finish here, I'm going to get some dinner. Are you free?"

Kira considered, then said, "No, not tonight. I don't think I'd be very good company. Tomorrow?"

Vaughn nodded. "Tomorrow." Kira signed off and Vaughn absently stared at the blank screen for several seconds.

"Commander," Bowers called, crawling out from under the aft tactical console. "I've gotten as far as I can with this until the new units arrive. If you've no objection, I'm going below to check the installation of the industrial replicator."

Vaughn rubbed his temples, then felt his stomach rumble. "No, let's call it a day. We're making good time. Go relax, Sam. You can check the IR system tomorrow."

"Thank you, sir," Bowers said, "I'll be sure to get on it first thing." The lieutenant packed up his tools and exited the bridge, leaving only Vaughn and Tenmei. The ensign was struggling to lift the faulty conn module out of the panel.

"Can I help you there, Ensign?"

"No, sir," Tenmei said, without looking up. "Thank you, sir."

Vaughn stood and walked around to the front of the conn. "No, really. That looks heavy."

"It's not, sir. I'm fine." She had poked the tips of her fingers under the lip of the module and Vaughn could see that the weight had turned them deep purple.

"Are you sure? If you need help . . ."

"I'm fine, Commander," Tenmei said icily. "Thank you." She yanked her fingers out and the module clacked back into its grooves. "Dammit," she whispered, sucking on her fingers.

"Are you hurt?" Vaughn asked, holding his hand out, beckoning her to show him her fingers.

"No," Tenmei said. "I'm fine. I don't need any help." She refused to look up at him, but when he looked at her more closely, he saw there were tears in the corners of her eyes.

"Ensign," Vaughn said, employing his command tone. "Show me your fingers."

Tenmei reluctantly pulled her fingers out of her mouth and held them out for Vaughn's inspection. They were bruised from the weight of the module and there was blood oozing out from under three of the nails.

Vaughn scowled. "Report to the infirmary, Ensign."

"Yes, Commander," Tenmei said and walked stiffly to the exit. The doors opened as she approached them, but before she stepped through, Vaughn decided to take a chance. "Prynn?"

Tenmei stopped, but refused to turn around. "Yes, Commander?"

"Would you care to have dinner with me?"

Tenmei's head snapped around, the look of cold fury on her otherwise lovely face painful to see. She held his gaze as she spoke. "Permission to speak freely, sir?"

"By all means," Vaughn said quietly.

"I accept the reality that you're my CO on this ship, and the first officer of the station. I respect and honor your rank, and I'll follow your orders without question. I'll even carry on the pretense in mixed company that I can stomach being in the same room with you. But beyond that . . . you can go to hell. *Sir.*"

Tenmei turned and stalked out, the doors snapping closed in her wake, leaving Vaughn alone on the bridge of his ship.

"I'll take that," he said, "as a no."

Chapter Fourteen

Ro had carefully crawled up the side of the fallen tree trunk and peered out into the clearing. The runabout was nestled snugly in a small grove of crushed saplings about eighty meters dead ahead. It had looked surprisingly intact, and it appeared that Taran'atar had guessed right. But it only made her wonder why Locken had made no move as yet to transport the craft to his base. *Maybe those patchwork ships of his aren't good for surface-to-air towing. Maybe he thinks he can take his time, because he doesn't know about Taran'atar and me. Or maybe the ship is much worse off than it looks, and he's already judged it a lost cause.*

The last thought had troubled her . . . until she saw the first red-uniformed Jem'Hadar, then another, and another. She counted five in all, a figure Taran'atar confirmed when he unshrouded beside her, saying that there were strong indications that a larger group of soldiers was encamped some distance off. *That settles it,* Ro thought. *You don't post guards around something unless it has some value. The ship is still viable.* The only questions now were how soon would Locken want it recovered, and could they take out the five guards without alerting any others?

And, of course, had Dax and Bashir really survived? Assuming they had, they'd probably been captured, taken to Locken's stronghold about fifteen klicks to the east. If they'd escaped into the forest, the Ingavi would have known about it.

"How do you think we should do this?" Ro asked.

By way of response, Taran'atar holstered his phaser and readied his throwing knives.

"You have got to be kidding," said Ro. "We could pick them off from here before they knew what hit them."

"Possibly," Taran'atar said. "But energy weapons are loud. Even if we got them all before they could return fire, which I think unlikely, the sound of our phasers alone would attract attention from the rest of their unit."

"Oh, and they won't shoot at you while you're throwing knives at them?"

"Watch and learn," Taran'atar said.

"I thought that was supposed to be your job," Ro said.

Then Taran'atar gave her a look that she could have sworn bordered on mild amusement, and was gone.

Ro shook her head and resumed watching the patrolling guards. She hadn't had the opportunity to get a good look at Locken's Jem'Hadar until now, but she was finding them to be an interesting contrast to the ones she'd fought in the war. These seemed younger somehow, as if they wanted very badly to be fierce, but weren't entirely certain how "fierce" was supposed to look.

While she waited for Taran'atar to make his move, she once again tried to make sense of something that had been nagging at her since they'd set out for the runabout. Ostensibly, Section 31 sent Bashir against Locken because they believed that while their rogue agent could withstand an all-out assault against Sindorin, they didn't think he'd respond to Bashir as a threat.

But according to the Ingavi, Locken had created no more than two hundred soldiers. Locken's resources and manpower were so limited, in fact, that he was using technological scraps to build spacecraft. His orbital weapons platform notwithstanding, it wouldn't take more than a few dozen well-targeted quantum torpedoes to reduce his ships to the wreckage they came from, and the entire southern continent to a lifeless wasteland. So why hadn't they done it? Was it that Locken was more powerful than she knew . . . or was Section 31 less powerful than everyone had assumed?

Only an hour past dawn, the sun was just now high enough in the sky to send a few stray beams slanting through the dense canopy. Ro saw that the two Ingavi that had come with her—Kel and one of his cousins—were doing their best not to be seen or heard while waiting for Taran'atar's plan to unfold. The rest of their party, about three hundred Ingavi armed with blowguns, slings, and spears, were camped a kilometer away awaiting word, downwind from the Jem'Hadar.

Ro wasn't sure what she would do with three hundred Ingavi, but she was dead set against throwing their lives away in a frontal assault. Taran'atar had agreed, and her confidence in him had risen considerably. *At least, until he decided to start throwing knives.*

"Do you see him?" Kel whispered.

Ro started to shake her head when, without warning, Taran'atar was there in the guards' midst. He'd managed to find a spot in the center of the group where no one was looking, their attention all focused on the surrounding terrain. It was a sloppy mistake, very amateurish, and Ro wondered how much training these Jem'Hadar had received. They were bred for ferocity and strength, but there were other qualities—cunning and guile—that could only be gained through experience of the sort Taran'atar had.

Everything happened very quickly.

He was holding throwing knives in both hands and, with a terrifying grace and economy, he flung them at the opponents to his immediate right and left. The one to the left, closer by about three meters, was struck in the back of the head just below the base of the skull and crumpled to the ground without uttering a sound. The Jem'Hadar immediately to Taran'atar's right spun around just in time to see the second knife as it shot through his eye and pierced his brain. The soldier was dead before he hit the ground.

The other three guards were turning also, but Taran'atar had already planned his attack, had already visualized the deaths of these other Jem'Hadar. In his mind, Ro knew, they were already dead.

The soldier nearest him, less than two meters away, was raising his Federation phaser even as Taran'atar ran toward him, bringing down his *kar'takin* one-handed from its place behind his back. Ro winced as the blade bit deep, and Locken was short one more Jem'Hadar.

Taran'atar leaped into the air, spun to gain momentum, then threw his *kar'takin* at the acme of his arc. He landed lightly on all fours, rolled forward, and jumped up in front of a fourth Jem'Hadar just as the soldier was coming to terms with the fact that he had the *kar'takin* buried in his chest. As the soldier fell over backward, Taran'atar drew his phaser with inhuman speed and pointed it at the last of the guards, who was staring at him, ten meters away, paralyzed. Seconds after it began, the battle was over.

"Leave," Taran'atar told his target. "Or die. It makes no difference to me."

Ro's eyes widened in disbelief and she found herself pointing her own phaser directly at the last guard.

The guard threw down a Breen disruptor, his only weapon, and ran into the forest.

Kel and his cousin followed Ro down and onto the battlefield as Taran'atar walked from body to body calmly collecting his weapons. "What the hell was that?"

This time Taran'atar didn't need to have the question rephrased. "I told Colonel Kira I would not kill if I didn't need to," he said, tugging his *kar'takin* free from its victim. "These Jem'Hadar are a disgrace, badly trained by other Jem'Hadar who were badly trained by a human. They fear death. That whelp was no threat, and he will be a living witness to what happened here so the others will know what they face. It will cause unease within the unit, and perhaps others as well. We can use that."

Kel and his cousin were stripping the dead soldiers of their weapons. "Leave the bodies," Taran'atar told them. "They will serve as a warning."

Ro shook her head, and began jogging toward the runabout, Taran'atar following. "I almost shot him myself. You took a big chance that I wouldn't."

"You told me you were once in the Maquis," Taran'atar said.

"That's right."

"And you were one of the few that neither the Cardassians nor the Dominion could kill."

"So?"

"That means you are a good soldier. I was not worried."

It was, Ro reflected, one of the strangest compliments she'd ever received. She shook her head again and started to check the runabout.

At first glance, the ship looked bad. It had gone down nose-first into the young trees and the bow was buried up to the viewport in a bog. Closer inspection, however, was more encouraging. There were no hull fractures, the warp nacelles were intact, and a careful examination of the terrain around the main hatch revealed that several people had walked into and then out of the ship. She keyed the door to open, and it responded. *Some power left, then.*

The interior was a mess, though Ro was relieved that there were no bodies aboard. Her initial assessment was looking more and more likely: Dax and Bashir were still alive and had been taken prisoner.

The deck was tilted forward at a precipitous angle and so thickly spattered with mud that it was difficult to keep her footing. She sat down in the pilot's seat and tried to access the onboard computer. She wasn't surprised to be rewarded with silence.

"All right," she muttered. "Then let's just spin the *dabo* wheel." Ro started tapping the power plant activation sequence, and a few key panels lit up. Speaking clearly and precisely, Ro said, "Computer, this is Lieutenant Ro. This is a priority-one command. Begin restart sequence on my mark. Authorization Ro-Epsilon-Seven-Five-One."

There was no immediate response from the computer, but a couple of standby lights on the main control panel went from red to yellow.

"Mark."

One of the engineering boards sparked and blew out. Somewhere in the mud under the runabout's bow something vented and the ship began shaking. Ro grimaced, expecting a burnout at any second. Instead, the rest of the runabout control cabin lit up. For the first half-dozen seconds, all the lights were red, but then, as the computer completed a cursory diagnostic, they flashed to yellow, some directly to green.

Ro patted the console fondly. "Good girl. Computer, how much time is needed to complete restart sequence?"

"Four minutes, fifty-five seconds."

"Are the main thrusters functional?"

"Affirmative."

"Antigravs?"

"Stern antigravity units are fully functional; bow antigravity unit has been damaged and must be considered unreliable."

"Okay," Ro said to herself. "So, we'll be using the main thrusters." She rose, then inched back up the mud-smeared deck to the main hatch, her mind now working on the next question—namely, now that they could go somewhere, where would they go? The Ingavi knew the location of Locken's stronghold, but was that necessarily the best destination? Wouldn't it be more sensible to go back to DS9 and get help? Just as she reached the hatch, it seemed to open of its own accord. The air shimmered and Taran'atar appeared.

"We are discovered," he said.

"Jem'Hadar?"

Taran'atar nodded. "Will the ship fly?"

"Yes, but we need four minutes. How many are coming?"

"Impossible to be certain. They are shrouded."

"Then how do you know they're coming?" Ro asked.

"They are loud. Assume at least twenty."

"Will we have four minutes before they arrive?"

Taran'atar took the safety off his phaser and set it on high. "I will get you four minutes," he said, then tapped his combadge. "Keep our link open. I will keep you posted."

Before Ro could say a word, Taran'atar was out the door. He shrouded three steps from the hatch and was gone, not a leaf or twig stirring. The Ingavi were nowhere to be found. Taran'atar must have sent them back to warn the others. "Computer, time to completion?"

"Two minutes, fifty-two seconds."

"Can we fire phasers?"

"Negative."

"Can we raise shields?"

"Negative."

Ro heaved a sigh, rubbed her eyes, now burning from exhaustion, and when she looked up, saw two Jem'Hadar suddenly appear in midair, one flying to the left, the other to the right, both of them trailing streamers of blood. Just as the bodies were dropping to the ground, Ro heard Taran'atar's voice through her combadge. *"Shield your eyes,"* he said.

Just in time, she screwed her eyes shut and twisted her head to the side, but even with them closed, Ro saw a brilliant white flash. A second later there came a sharp crack and she felt a wave of intense heat on the exposed side of her face.

Voices cried out in agony, but only for a moment. When Ro opened her eyes again, there were four more bodies lying on the ground. Survivors had all unshrouded, the concentration needed to maintain their invisibility broken. She still couldn't see Taran'atar, but she heard his steady breathing through her combadge.

"Computer, how much longer?"

"Forty-five seconds."

She couldn't be sure that Taran'atar heard the computer over the sounds of battle, but she wanted to give him *some* warning, if possible. Leaving the hatch open, she climbed back down the slanted deck to the cockpit, slipping once and almost cracking her head on the engineering console. *Maybe fifteen seconds left,* she decided.

Checking her board, Ro decided that most of the main systems were back online, though she noted a couple of troubling red lights. Unfortunately, she didn't have time to check which systems were still out because the runabout was suddenly rocked by disruptor fire.

"Damage to port bulkhead," the computer announced. *"Recommend raising shields."*

"Raise shields!" Ro shouted, her hands dancing over the main board.

"Complying."

The runabout was rocked by another explosion, but since the ship didn't have a hole in the port bulkhead, she guessed the shields went up in time. Deciding her time was up, Ro eased power into the antigravs, but felt only the runabout's stern rise. Even if the bow antigravs were one hundred percent functional, the ship's nose was too deeply dug into the slope for the ship to rise horizontally. "Didn't think that would work. Time for something a little more dramatic."

Ro shut down the antigravs and the stern settled back onto the ground. As she strapped herself in, she instructed the computer to reroute power from the deflectors to the structural integrity field. She might be hit by another disruptor blast in the second and a half she needed to fire the fore thrusters, but it was a chance she had to take. It wasn't like she had any other options.

On the battlefield, Taran'atar crouched behind the largest of the young trees and waited for his opponents to finish shooting in random directions. He had just killed one by bouncing a rock off the underside of a tree bough so that it landed at the feet of one of his opponents. Three or four soldiers spun around at the sound and opened fire on their own man. Taran'atar shook his head, shamed by the idea that he might share genetic material with these amateurs.

His foes ceased fire and shrouded. Taran'atar waited, fixing his gaze on a narrow space between two saplings, then saw a blade of tall grass sway as if something invisible had brushed against it. Drawing a throwing knife from its sheath, he rose and smoothly threw the weapon into the gap. It halted in mid-air between the trees, the blade disappearing into a semicircle of amber-colored fluid. A Jem'Hadar fell forward, unshrouded in death, the knife embedded in his forehead.

Taran'atar heard the unit's First order his soldiers to move from cover and head for the runabout. *So, they aren't complete idiots after all.* They were doing what he would do if the situations were reversed—ignore the emplacement and advance to the main goal. Looking around, he saw leaves and blades of grass rustle and stir. Most of the remaining soldiers were within fifty meters of the runabout and he was at the edge of a clearing about halfway between them and their goal.

Someone became visible and opened fire. The runabout rocked.

Ro needed another ten, maybe fifteen seconds, but she wouldn't have them. . . .

Crouching low, Taran'atar ran to the center of the clearing, drawing his phaser as he ran. He'd studied the pattern of flattened grass; even as his chest hit the ground and he skidded to a stop behind a large stump, he opened fire, aiming low. Two more Jem'Hadar unshrouded and fell to the ground screaming, cut off just below the knees. A third briefly solidified, staggered by a graze to his hip. He quickly reshrouded, but Taran'atar fired again before the soldier could either roll aside or drop to the ground. Another dead.

The ground rumbled and surged. Taran'atar felt the runabout's antigravs beat uselessly against the ground. He could have told Ro that wouldn't work. *Maybe this is a futile battle after all.* A volley of shots from several points around the glade hacked at the stump. Splinters raked the side of his face and it was only luck that kept him from losing an eye.

Taran'atar raised his head, fired five quick shots at random points around the glade, then ducked back down, covered his head with his forearms, rolled to the left, and tried to shroud. Something was wrong; he couldn't focus his will. Reaching up to his forehead, he found a large gash and a sliver of wood as big as his thumb. He felt no pain, but he knew shock would be coming on quickly. There was blood in his eyes now, but Taran'atar didn't need to see. He heard the runabout's thrusters roar and he felt heat on his face, but Taran'atar could not decide if it was the heat of blood or backblast.

He cleared his eyes and watched as the runabout tore itself out of the steaming earth, clods of dirt sliding down off the bow, vines clinging, as if the planet were reluctant to let it go. Then a half-dozen Jem'Hadar soldiers unshrouded around him, all of them pointing their weapons at his head.

The last vine snapped and the runabout rose rapidly into the air. Some shots hit the belly of the ship, but couldn't pierce the shields. "Computer," Ro called as she swung the runabout's nose around. "Activate transporter. Lock on to Taran'atar's signal."

"*Unable to comply,*" the computer said. "*Transporter is offline.*"

"What?" she yelled, then glanced at the status board. She cursed and saw that one of the red lights she hadn't had time to check was the transporter. "Can you reroute power?"

"*Negative. Pattern buffers have been damaged. Risk to transportee would be unacceptable.*"

"Phasers?"

"*Phaser banks have not had time to charge.*"

She was climbing fast—fifteen hundred meters—and decided it was time to level off. *And time to pick a direction, too.* Taran'atar was either dead now or captured. Bashir and Dax were probably prisoners. The Ingavi had seen her take off and must be wondering whether she was coming back. Locken's fighters would be deploying soon. If she landed someplace, they'd have a hard time scanning for her—the one good thing about Sindorin.

No choice? she wondered, and knew precious seconds were ticking away. More than anything, Ro hated feeling like she had no choice. It was a long way back to DS9, assuming she even made it out of the Badlands, much too long a way for her to stare at her reflection in the console and think about what might be happening on Sindorin. So there were choices, but only one good one.

Ro programmed in a new course and the bow of the *Euphrates* dipped back down toward the planet.

The cell seemed much smaller now. Objectively, Ezri knew, nothing had changed: same walls, same bunks, same sink, probably the same Jem'Hadar standing outside watching them, but everything was crowding in much closer now. Even so, Julian felt farther away than he ever had before.

He hadn't moved since they'd been brought back to the cell: on the lower bunk, his back to her, facing the wall. For a while, Ezri had tried to pretend he was asleep, but she could hear him breathe. In every couple, there's the one who falls asleep first, and though she suspected that Julian liked to think of himself as the bedclothes-tossing, careworn one, he was, in fact, the one who usually fell asleep first. Ezri knew what Julian sounded like when he was asleep and this wasn't it.

Before she had been joined with Dax, Ezri had learned enough about herself and the men she found attractive to know that it was best to let a relationship find its own level, not to be too demanding. She knew better than to push too hard with Julian, especially when it came to issues relating to his genetic enhancements.

And Julian, to his credit, had seemed to understand her circumstances, too. He knew the bare facts about her joining, but hadn't asked for a lot of details, obviously preferring to give her time to tell her story when she wanted. They were a peculiar couple and they knew it—two people who were simultaneously very experienced and surprisingly naive, especially where it came to matters of the heart.

And all that had been fine, she concluded, until the Jem'Hadar attack on the station. Somehow that tragedy had set Ezri on a personal voyage of self-discovery, one on which she was determined to learn her true potential as Dax's reluctant ninth host. The slow realization that she would take that journey had widened an already growing distance between her and Julian, and it wasn't until she'd almost lost him forever that they'd regained their equilibrium, each perhaps a little wiser and more sensitive to the needs of the other. They still took great comfort and great delight in their togetherness . . . but they had quietly agreed to move at a very cautious pace.

But now . . .

Something else had changed since this mission began, something that—for all her certainty that she'd come to understand the man who now shared her bed—was eluding her comprehension. Locken had spun such terrifying scenarios with a wink and a smile, and Julian had listened as if on some level he could actually rationalize what the so-called Khan was proposing. And if that was true, did she really know him anymore?

Had she ever?

"Julian?" she called, her voice sounding a little sharper than she had intended.

He didn't answer right away and for a moment Ezri wondered if she had been wrong, if he *had* been asleep, but then, before she called again, he asked, "What is it?"

"I need to talk."

Julian sighed, then stirred on the bunk as though he wanted to get up, but didn't have the strength. "Wait a second," he said. "My arm's asleep." He slapped his hand against the wall to get the circulation going again, then rolled over slowly, taking his time to get his feet on the floor. Head hung low, Julian rubbed the bridge of his nose and asked, his tone low and weary, "What do you want to talk about?"

Ezri felt a tiny growl blossom at the back of her throat. "I want," she started, "I *need* to hear you say that Locken was wrong."

"About what?" Bashir asked irritably.

"About you," Ezri said. "About . . ." Her voice trailed off and Ezri found she wasn't exactly sure *what* she wanted to say, let alone what she wanted to hear. Then her mind latched on to the image of Locken's self-satisfied smile and she rallied. "About who you are," she said.

"Don't you mean," Julian asked, "about *what* I am?"

"That's not fair, Julian. That's not what I was thinking at all."

"No?" he asked. "It's what I was thinking. It's what I would be thinking if I were you." He stood, stretched, but refused to make eye contact with her. "Please don't pretend that it isn't," he said, his voice louder. "Because I really can't take it anymore, the pretending."

Sensing the rising tide of Julian's despair, Dax understood it wasn't her he was accusing of pretense, but himself. "Julian," she said softly. "No one has ever asked you to pretend . . ."

"Don't say it," Julian snapped. *"Everyone* has asked me to pretend. Even after you all discovered the truth about me, you all wanted me to keep being the same old Julian. It was all right for me to show off a little bit, but that was all. It was fine just as long as I didn't remind anyone of what I *really* am or what *they* really are."

"And that is?" Ezri asked.

Bashir inhaled deeply, then let it out slowly, obviously struggling to rein himself in. His voice calmer, he said, "I don't know exactly."

"Or you don't want to say. Go ahead, Julian. If you can think it, you can say it."

The lines around his eyes tightened, but then he relaxed the grip he held on himself. "A beginning," he said slowly. "And an ending, perhaps. I'm a doctor, Ezri, a very, very good doctor. I've studied the issue very carefully and I've come to some conclusions. The frightening thing is that I think others have, too, but are afraid to say anything about it."

"Julian, I'm not following."

Bashir sighed. "Have you ever read a paper on human physiology, published a couple of hundred years ago by Tanok of Vulcan? He was an ethnologist who lived on Earth for fifty years during the twenty-second century. Tanok observed that human evolution had plateaued, that our cranial capacity and efficiency of neuronal activity had effectively reached its maximum unless we began to manipulate our genetic code."

"I know about Tanok," Dax said. "He deliberately published his paper only on Vulcan—and in a privately circulated journal—because he knew how the humans would react. This was less than two hundred years after Khan was deposed and he and his genetic supermen fled Earth."

"True," Julian said. "But Tanok also said that he thought the humans would eventually calm down and see that while Khan's methods might have been too extreme, the basic concept was sound. And he posed the same question Locken did: What if Khan had won? How different would the quadrant, the galaxy, be today? What would *humanity* be today? And can we really know that it might not be a better place?"

"Julian," said Ezri, "I can't believe I'm hearing this." At first, she had thought Julian was engaging in some intellectual brinkmanship, trotting out arguments he knew Locken might use to see if she could poke holes in them. Now she wasn't so sure.

"You can't believe what you're *hearing?*" he said, his voice rising. "I can just barely believe I'm finally *saying* it. Do you have any idea how many nights I've lain awake thinking about these things?" Julian spun around and faced the cell door, though he didn't appear to be actually seeing anything, so deeply was he burrowing down into himself. "Do you want to know something else about me, Ezri? I don't have to sleep very much. Did you know that? But I've always felt like I had to pretend, like I had to go to bed when everyone else did, wake up when everyone else did, complain about being tired because everyone else does. . . . But the cruel truth is that I lay there every night, willing myself to sleep, but finding my thoughts wandering. In the pit of the night, in my darkest moments, I *have* thought all those things Locken said: I *could* cure all of the Federation's ills. I *have* wasted my life pretending to be less than I am because the society I live in considers my very existence to be illegal, even immoral. It's all true, Ezri, every word, and I'm tired of lying."

Then Julian turned and, with a single, well-placed blow, struck the steel brace that held the bed on the wall. The brace cracked and the upper bunk sagged forward.

Ezri was a good enough counselor to recognize a soul unburdening itself of long-denied emotions, but she was also frightened by the unexpected burst of violence. More, she was stung by the discovery that her lover had for months been literally lying next to her, silently seething and keeping such a secret. She felt guilty and not a little embarrassed. With a struggle, she set aside the shame, rose and moved toward Julian, hoping to offer comfort. But before she could close the distance, he was there—Locken—standing in the doorway. It was almost as if he had been waiting for those words to come out of Julian's mouth.

"Of course you are, Julian," he said. "And now the question is simply this: Will you allow yourself to act on those thoughts now that the opportunity has come to do something for the common good?"

"The common good?" Ezri asked, the snarl rising in her again. "Just what would *you* know about the common good?"

But neither Locken nor Julian was listening to her. Julian was standing at the cell door, his eyes locked on their captor. "What about Ezri?" he asked.

Locken glanced at her, then returned his gaze to Julian. "She may join us if she likes," Locken said, "but she has to cooperate."

"Cooperate?" Ezri scoffed. "Cooperate? Like I would *ever* join your new order, your elite minority . . ."

Locken grinned, delighted. "What a very amusing attitude," he said, "coming from a joined Trill." Then he turned away from her, completely dismissing her from his thoughts. To Julian, he said, "So, what's it going to be? What's your answer?"

Julian looked at him, then turned to Ezri and studied her expression. She sensed uncertainty and confusion and though she wanted to be steadfast and supportive, she felt herself responding with outrage: *Damn you, Julian! How dare you not know what to do?* Julian nodded, as if confirming a conclusion he had come to during an inner argument, then straightened his back and lifted his shoulders, as if a great weight had just been lifted. He looked at Locken and said, "My answer is yes."

Exuding triumph, Locken pulled out his control unit and pointed it at the cell. The forcefield faded and Bashir stepped out into the hallway, then half-turned toward Ezri. He said, "Ezri, you'll understand someday . . ." but stopped when her fist connected with his jaw. It was a poorly timed punch. She didn't have a chance to wind up and the angle was all wrong. Ezri doubted that it would even leave a mark. He grabbed her arm, immobilized her with a gentle twist of her wrist, then twisted her around so that she was back inside the cell, her back to Locken.

"You son of a—" she started, but he lifted his hand and covered her mouth superhumanly fast, silencing her.

"Don't fight me, Ezri. You'll see I'm right . . . soon." He took his hand off her mouth and gave her a small shove so that she stumbled back onto the lower bunk. She stared at him with loathing, her lips curled back over her clenched teeth.

"It's all right, Julian," Locken said gently, favoring her with a smile. "Maybe she'll come around. She seems very bright. And spirited. That counts for a lot." A touch on his control unit, and the forcefield was back up. Locken turned and started down the hall.

"Yes," Bashir said sadly. "It does." Then he too turned away, following Locken.

Ezri listened as the footsteps grew fainter, her body shaking as she heard the double hiss of the hall's security door opening and closing. Then she turned and curled up on the bunk, facing the wall, her body racked with sobs. She raised her hands to her mouth as if to stifle her cries, and then, feeling certain she was safe from any surveillance devices . . . she spat out the object Julian had shoved into her mouth.

She kept up the pretense of crying as she turned it over in her hands, recognizing it instantly as the primary circuitry module for a Starfleet communicator. The Jem'Hadar had taken Julian's, so this one must be hers. He must have found it on the floor of the runabout, probably cracked open just before they had been captured by the Jem'Hadar. Freed of its combadge casing, the circuitry module was small enough to conceal easily, inside his cheek, even in his hair. He must have been working on it the entire time he'd been lying in his bunk. The questions were, what had he been working on it *with* and what had he been trying to do?

She discreetly felt around the edge of the bunk pressed against the wall and found what she'd hoped for—a small shard of metal, undoubtedly from some damaged part of the runabout's control cabin.

So, Julian had been working on a plan. *Too bad he couldn't tell me what it was.* But then, lying down on the bunk, trying to look as dejected as possible, she decided that she would be able to figure it out. After all, she knew him better than anyone.

Chapter Fifteen

Vaughn decided to take his evening meal at Quark's, on the balcony level. The place had been fairly subdued when he'd walked in, which fit his mood perfectly, but by the time he was finished with his *hasperat*, a reasonably rowdy round of socializing had begun on the main floor.

Somehow, Quark had tapped into the S.C.E.'s surveillance feed of the work on Empok Nor and he was dumping the pictures into several monitors he'd installed around the bar. His stated reason was so that everyone could keep an eye on the work as it progressed, though it was obvious from the amount of interest displayed by the crowd that there was some heavy wagering going on. Vaughn only hoped that the Starfleet engineers were betting *against* one or the other station blowing up.

Though he had been ignoring most of the action, when he pushed his plate away Vaughn looked up from the report he'd been working on and glanced at the monitor nearest his table. The EVA crews had been working all day on the delicate job of aligning and inserting the new reactor core into Deep Space 9, and a collective cheer went up in the bar as the final connections were made. Tomorrow the task of repairing and restarting the six fusion reactors would begin, but that was tomorrow. For now it was enough for the crew to be able to celebrate this clear glimmer of light at the end of a very dark tunnel.

The commander was less than encouraged to hear that Quark was giving odds that even after everything was hooked up, the new core still wouldn't work. A chill ran down Vaughn's back and he tried to pretend that it was entirely attributable to the problems they were having with the heating plant and nothing whatsoever to do with his age. He sipped the very passable bock beer (where did Quark *get* this stuff?), and the hoppy aroma reminded him of something, but he couldn't remember exactly what.

Below him, the off-duty engineers and other crewmen were all doing whatever they felt was necessary to fight off the chill. Some were talking animatedly, most were imbibing insulating beverages, and not a few appeared to be on the verge of attempting to share some body heat. Prynn Tenmei was at the center of one of the latter groups at a table, ringed by a platoon of S.C.E. engineers, all of them either impressed with her knowledge of large-scale fusion reactors or dazzled by her smile or, most likely, a little of both. Tenmei was amused by their attention—that much was obvious—but Vaughn could see by the tilt of her head that not a single one of them was going to make a ding in her shields.

Vaughn raised his mug in mock salute and said, "Good luck, lads. You're going to need it." Then, he drained the last half-inch of his beer and set the mug down on the table. Before the bottom of the mug had a chance to make a damp ring on the tabletop, it was lifted off and replaced by a full one.

Without looking up, Vaughn said, "Hullo, Quark. I didn't ask for another drink."

"I know," Quark said. "But you looked like you were about ready. A good bartender knows these things."

Vaughn smiled ruefully and accepted the drink. "Thanks. Put it on my tab."

"Oh, it's there already." Quark, well-practiced in determining the focus of barroom stares, studied the angle of Vaughn's chin, checked the cant of his brow, and correctly triangulated on the top of Tenmei's head. "Come on, Commander," he said. "Don't do this to yourself. I sympathize, but it's not worth it—getting fixated like that—and I know whereof I speak. Not that I fault your taste. I've had a chance to observe Ensign Tenmei myself and there's definitely something special about that one."

"Quark . . ." Vaughn said, taking the mug and sipping off the head. "That's enough."

"No, really, I understand. And she's your conn officer, too, isn't she? That must be hard, working in close quarters that way." Quark wiped up an invisible speck of dirt. "But, listen, this is what you have to do: You have to get her off your mind. If you start obsessing, that leads to nothing but trouble. The sleepless nights, the gray days, the restraining orders . . ."

"Please, Quark," Vaughn said. "I'm asking you to stop now."

"But I have an idea," Quark continued. "A visit to the holosuite. I can make you a reservation right now so you'll be the first one in when they re-open. I don't think you've had a chance yet to peruse my wide selection of Lonely Nights programs—"

"*Quark,*" Vaughn said, slamming his mug down, beer slopping over the rim. He inhaled deeply, resigning himself to the fact that the truth was going to come out eventually. Why not now? "Prynn's my daughter."

Quark didn't respond for several seconds. Then, he picked up Vaughn's mug, wiped up the spilled beer, and set it down again. "On the house, Commander."

"Thank you, Quark."

"Well, *that's* going to cost me," Quark said to no one in particular as he descended the spiral stairwell. "And it started out to be such a pleasant evening, too." He had been doing that—talking to himself—a lot lately. "Because there's no one else to talk to," he decided, then realized he was doing it again.

Things had changed too much in the recent past for his taste. Kira had gone from being a zero on the fun scale to a negative number. Quark secretly blamed Odo, but he didn't feel comfortable voicing that opinion. Sure, they *said* there were no more changelings in the Alpha Quadrant, but who could be sure? And they might all be working for Odo now. Quark shuddered. It was all so unfair.

Threading his way back through the crowd, he tossed his tray behind the bar and dropped the empty beer glass into the recycler. He was frustrated;

there was nothing to vent his embarrassment on. Even Frool—the only one of his waiters he'd been able to bribe into staying on during the core transfer—was too busy keeping after the engineers for Quark to subject him to the abuse he was contractually obligated to endure.

And the *dabo* girls were all busy, too. The Federation types weren't usually interested in gambling, but the whiff of danger in the air must have been making them feel lucky. It was still no substitute for the civilian freighter crews who'd been flooding the bar almost daily since the station had become the Cardassian relief checkpoint. But with the last such freighter for the next few days gone since this morning, relying on a smattering of Starfleet officers for most of his business was killing him.

"What's on your mind, Quark?"

Quark looked up, but saw no one.

"Over here, Quark."

He looked down the length of the bar and found himself staring into a pair of golden eyes set in a broad green face. He smiled his "Neutral Smile #7," usually reserved for persons unknown who appeared to be well dressed and were not holding a weapon to his head.

Looks like not all the civilians have left, after all. "Good evening, sir," he said, strolling toward the man. "If we've met, I don't believe I remember when. And there haven't been too many Orions around these days."

The small, dapper Orion grinned winningly. "We haven't met, sir," he said. "But your reputation precedes you."

Insincere flattery. I smell a business proposition. He pulled a glass from under the bar and set to polishing it. "You are too kind," he said. "What can I get for you, Mister . . . ?"

"Malic," the Orion said, and held out his hand to be shaken. Quark quickly catalogued the stones in the settings of Malic's rings and decided that whatever business he was currently in was doing pretty well. "And what I would like is to meet a businessman with an open mind."

Quark took Malic's hand and they shook. *You can tell so much about a person from a handshake.* For example, he decided, this deceptively small man could probably crush all of Quark's fingers into paste if he wanted. "I believe I might have one of those," Quark said. "For the right price."

Malic grinned and Quark was intrigued to see there was something shiny embedded in his rearmost molar, something that twinkled merrily and, more important, expensively. *There's something that you almost never see anymore,* he thought. *I do so like a pirate who pays attention to detail.*

Taran'atar had experienced many different flavors of pain. Almost twenty-one years ago, in his first campaign against a species called the v'Xaji, he had been burned across most of the left side of his body. It had been agonizing, beyond anything his training had prepared him for, and though he had found the flavor bitter, he had learned to take comfort in it, too. Pain, no matter how intense or disabling, told you one thing: *You are alive.* To a Jem'Hadar, being alive meant one thing: *I can still serve the Founders.* But, privately, Taran'atar had also decided it meant one other important thing: *I can still deal death.*

So, Taran'atar took the pain he felt now—this careless but precise agony—and embraced it. He made it a part of himself so he would not forget it. He inhaled once, slowly, and though he thought the pain might stop his hearts, he let it slowly sink down through his flesh and into his bones. He exhaled, then inhaled again, then caught the scent of blood—his blood—mingled with sweat.

He heard voices—two, no, three—and focused past the pounding in his ears. The first voice was saying, "His blood's not the right color."

"No, it's not," said another. "Not dark enough."

"That's dried blood you're looking at," said the third. "It might be the right color. Let's get some fresh." Something touched Taran'atar's chest and he felt a bolt of white light arc through his body. His arms and legs, he noted, were numb. That would be a problem later when it was time to escape. He tried to flex his toes, but wasn't sure if they were moving.

"I think he's awake," said the first voice.

"He's *been* awake," said the third. "Parts of him, anyway."

"Maybe he was being run by a handler. You saw the communications device he had. Maybe the one in the ship was telling him what to do."

"But look at his neck. He takes no white. How is that possible?"

"Keep your place," the third warned.

Taran'atar lifted his head and opened his eyes. He saw three Jem'Hadar, all wearing the red-and-silver uniforms of the Khan.

The third—no, the First—looked down at him curiously. "Awake again? Good. I was beginning to think we'd damaged you too much."

Again? This was strange. Taran'atar didn't recall being conscious since the battle in the glade, but a quick glance around the interrogation room made it obvious that he had been there for some time. There were implements strewn around, most of which had clearly been used. He recognized a few of them, had even seen one or two used in his time, though information extraction was a specialized field, one Taran'atar had never developed a taste for. There were some who seemed to derive satisfaction from it and he wondered if he had fallen into the hands of one of those.

"Not so damaged," Taran'atar rasped through cracked lips.

The First touched something to his side and Taran'atar felt his hearts spasm. He couldn't breathe for five, ten, twenty seconds and the blackness began to close in around him. When he regained consciousness, the First was standing very near to him wearing an expression of genuine concern. Taran'atar attempted to summon the strength to lift his head, but he couldn't control his neck muscles.

"Still there?" the First asked. "Impressive. I doubt any of my own men could take so much."

His breath coming out in ragged gasps, Taran'atar forced himself to look his torturer in the eyes. "You . . . are . . . fools," he muttered. "And your Khan . . ."

The two soldiers who had been standing behind the First drew their weapons and stepped toward Taran'atar, but the First held up his arm and signaled them to step back. The soldiers, he noticed, were glaring at him, but the First's expression was something closer to curiosity. "Go," he told his men. "Attempt to contact the Khan again and inform him that we have taken this prisoner."

The soldiers were confused. "We've already tried to report to the Khan," one said. "We were told he was not receiving messengers tonight."

The First's eyes grew cold. "You are young, so I will excuse you this time—the only time. Do as I say. If the Khan will not receive you, leave word with the chief of guards, then return to barracks."

The two soldiers glanced at each other, but neither was prepared—or equipped—to argue. With one last curious look at Taran'atar, they turned and left.

He struggled to remain alert, but Taran'atar could feel his eyes fluttering, his vision dimming. Looking up, he saw the First leaning in close. "Do not take false hope," the First said. "You *will* die, but there are good deaths and bad deaths."

"I know that," Taran'atar managed, and would have liked to add, *better than you could ever know.* Instead, he asked, "What do you want?"

"What are you?"

"Exactly what I seem," Taran'atar managed. "A Jem'Hadar."

"You lie."

"You deny the evidence of your eyes? Scan me, if you have the technology. You will see I am exactly what I say. A Jem'Hadar of twenty-two years."

"I already have. The readings are not possible."

"So you deny your eyes *and* your instruments," Taran'atar said.

The First grabbed at the knot of black hair behind Taran'atar's head and forced him to look up. "Do you know who I am? I am First. First among my men, and the First born of the Khan. Whatever you may be, you were not created by him."

"Very astute," Taran'atar said, intrigued despite his agony. "Then how do you explain me? Either I am lying, as you say . . . or I am telling you the truth, in which case there must be other Jem'Hadar not of your Khan."

Taran'atar saw that he'd scored a hit. Suddenly the First leaned in closer. "Earlier, you spoke of the Founders. Do you remember?"

Surprise kept Taran'atar focused. Here was a Jem'Hadar *asking* him for information about the Founders. "I don't remember speaking of the Founders, but if you say I did, then I believe you."

"Who are they?" the First asked.

"The Founders are the givers of life and of purpose. They are the true creators of the Jem'Hadar. Your Khan . . . is not what you think he is. He has only corrupted the Founders' work."

The First seemed to consider this statement with some care for several seconds. "You seem very certain of this," he said. "How can you be sure what you have been told is true? Is it not possible that these Founders have lied to you? Perhaps they fear the Khan . . . which is as it should be."

"Then explain my age. I am not the first of my kind. The Founders have been creating Jem'Hadar for centuries. How many changes of season have you seen on this world? Do you truly believe that a life serving this human is all there is?"

The First shook his head. "You are misinformed. The Khan is not human. He is something else, the next step beyond humans. He was born to *rule* the other humans."

"So he says," Taran'atar agreed. "The human I came here with is the equal of your Khan in every way, perhaps even better, but he is not a ruler. He is a medic."

"Then obviously he is *not* the equal of the Khan," the First said. "Perhaps *he* is the fool."

"No," Taran'atar said. "He is no fool. I believe he *could* rule the humans if he wished to—some of them at any rate—but he chooses not to. He is a soldier of a sort, but he fights a different war. . . ." He barely understood his own words, but couldn't deny the truth he felt lay at the center of them.

The First stared at him as if he were mad or rambling from withdrawal, but then returned to his own topic as if impatient to be done. "But what are the Founders? Giants? Columns of shimmering light?"

"All of these things," Taran'atar replied, grateful to be able to return to the known. Here, at last, was a question he could answer without hesitation. "And more. They can be anything they wish. They are not trapped by flesh."

The First seemed interested. "Are they immortal?"

Taran'atar had to hesitate. He knew that the Founders could die, had even heard that Odo himself had once killed one of his own kind. He knew too that the Founders were ravaged by a plague not so long ago. And still, some Jem'Hadar had speculated that there were not truly any Founders at all, merely a single great being that could subdivide itself whenever and however it pleased, each of the parts having the knowledge of the whole. Did that mean if one Founder killed another, then he was killing a part of himself? The more he thought, the more he felt trapped by the First's questions, as much as he'd tried to trap the First in his own. "No," he conceded. "The Founders are not immortal."

The First listened without comment, waiting to see if Taran'atar had anything to add, then said flatly, "The Khan is immortal."

"What proof of that do you have?"

"One does not ask a god for proof."

"Even if you have doubts?"

"I have no doubts," the First said. "It sounds rather as if *you* might have reason to doubt, but I do not. You say these Founders are gods, but they do not sound very godlike to me. They sound like mortals who have somehow tricked you into believing they created our kind."

The First turned to go, leaving his captive alone with his pain, but offered Taran'atar a final thought. "Whatever you are, whatever you may believe about your origins . . . it seems your gods have forsaken you."

Chapter Sixteen

Returning to Locken's quarters that evening, Bashir discovered within himself a peculiar prejudice: he found that he could not believe that anyone who could cook well was entirely, irredeemably evil. Locken's potato-leek soup was astonishingly piquant and he whipped together a lighter-than-air cheese soufflé with as little effort as it would cost Bashir to make toast. Bashir worked hard to beat back the envy he was feeling; he had never had the time to develop much in the way of culinary abilities. And the kitchen—it had seemed so small, but it was unbelievably well equipped.

"Where did you get all these utensils?" Bashir asked, looking at a rack of exotic kitchen tools. "The Dominion couldn't have left them all behind. Jem'Hadar don't need to eat and Vorta can barely taste."

"They're mine," Locken said, cheerily chopping potatoes. "I brought everything I could salvage from my home when I came here with Section 31. We were going to be here for a while and everyone is always happy to find a cook in their midst. The plan was that I would cook for everyone . . . which I did. It's how I managed to take them prisoner. A little extra dash of something in the morning omelets."

"So they're all still here?" Bashir asked, slightly surprised. He had imagined all the Section 31 agents were dead.

"In stasis," Locken said, scraping up potato chunks with his knife and dropping them into a pot of boiling water. "Less trouble that way."

"But long-term stasis can be . . ."

". . . Very detrimental. Yes, I know. Don't worry. I've worked out some of the kinks in that. They should be fine for a while longer."

Bashir sat at the kitchen table, watching the chef work. There were four chairs at the table, but only one placemat when they came in. Locken had taken an absurd amount of pleasure in pulling out another place setting and putting it down before Bashir. The food preparation had been almost like performance art and Locken's ongoing banter had been upbeat and witty. It was all so civilized, sad, and desperate that Bashir felt like he was going to scream.

"I'm impressed," Bashir said. "Not only have you worked out the cloning process, but you've had time to do other work, too."

"Oh, I did the work on stasis a long time ago," Locken replied. "I just couldn't publish it because . . . well, you know."

"Professional jealousy. Didn't want to draw too much attention to yourself. Yes," Bashir said, drawing a breath and releasing a genuine sigh. "I understand."

"Of course, all that will be different now. Think of it, Julian. Someday, years from now, maybe decades from now, we'll look back on this night and remember it as the beginning of a Golden Age."

"We could make sure it's made into a holiday."

Locken laughed. "You're joking. I know you're joking, but maybe someday you'll say that and you'll be serious. Or maybe that's the sort of thing we should leave to others . . ."

"Maybe we should," Bashir said. "It would be presumptuous to begin declaring galactic holidays. There are a few obstacles between . . . us and our goals."

"A few," Locken agreed, rinsing his hands at the tap. "Would it make you feel better if we discussed some?"

"It might," Bashir agreed, then paused as if pondering. "For example—and I'm sure you've already thought about this—there's the problem of sheer numbers. Even the Dominion, with their dozens of hatcheries, weren't able to defeat the Federation. Now, granted, they're weakened and we'll be able to outthink them on most fronts, but you're only turning out a handful of Jem'Hadar a week . . ."

"Which will soon change," Locken agreed, "especially now that we're working together, but you're right. This is a key factor—but one I've been preparing for." He checked the timer on the oven, then covered the soup pot and lowered the heat. "We have enough time for this," he said, beckoning Bashir to the door. "Come with me."

In the main room, Locken pulled out his control unit and used it to activate the computer console and a large holographic display tank. He clicked through several layers of security, entering passwords too quickly for Bashir to follow. Finally, colors swirled inside the holotank and an image formed: a protein model, accompanied by streams of data. "You recognize this," Locken said.

Bashir studied the model and the data for several seconds, then realized what he was looking at and a cold shudder went down his back. "A prion," he said. "But not like any I've ever seen."

Locken grinned with satisfaction. "It gave me trouble. I admit it. But I'm a pretty good cook. I'd never done work like this before, but once you get the knack, it's a great deal like making a good soufflé: mostly just following the recipe, but there's artistry and luck involved, too."

"You made this?" Bashir asked, genuinely awed despite himself. "It's astonishing." He wanted to add, ". . . and insane," but he dared not. He had to find out what the—and there was no other expression for what Locken was—mad genius had in mind. "If I understand correctly what you've done . . ."

"And you do, of course."

". . . then this could infect almost every form of humanoid life in the quadrant."

"As long as it has a central nervous system," Locken explained. "There are one or two intelligent species it might not affect, but they're inconsequential in the long run."

Bashir continued to stare at the rotating image, at once impressed and appalled. This chain of proteins, he realized, could transform the brain of almost any creature in the quadrant into a mushy pastelike consistency. "How is it transmitted?"

"Airborne, waterborne, through sexual contact," Locken said smugly. "It's versatile."

"But your Jem'Hadar are immune?" Bashir guessed. "And you, too, I assume?"

"Of course. And since your arrival I've taken care to make sure you are, too. I haven't tested it extensively, but I didn't think I would have to. It's the beauty of simple things; they're foolproof. But, just in case," Locken smiled, "I have a planet picked out already—the Romulan protectorate in the Orias system." He touched a control on his handset and another section of wall slid open to reveal yet another computer console. A large monitor lit up, presenting a medium-range shot of a missile-launching platform with a single completed gantry and two others under construction. Several Jem'Hadar soldiers stood around the gantries, weapons drawn and alert, while in the background a trio dressed in protective armor were busy fueling a medium-size missile. "I had to cobble the missile together out of components my Jem'Hadar salvaged from the ships and outposts we raided," Locken explained.

"Outposts?" Bashir asked.

"Nothing very large," Locken said. "I suspect they were secret bases set up by the Romulan Empire in case the Federation began to flex its muscles. Probably the Empire hasn't said anything to the Federation about the attacks, though I'm sure it has left them feeling very suspicious."

"And you plan to fire one of their own missiles at the Romulans?"

"Modified missiles," Locken agreed. "Yes. There will be some parts on the missile that they may find afterward that will make them suspect the Federation."

"But there won't be enough evidence to make them act immediately."

Locken smiled. "Julian, I can see you have a gift for this sort of thing. No, not immediately, but the Romulans *will* begin to arm themselves. They'll begin to prepare. And then, assuming my prion weapon is as effective as I know it will be, shortly after the first launch, we'll begin a full-scale assault. We'll have at least six gantries completed by then and I have plans to outfit my ships with similar devices. I suspect I'll be able to drive the Romulans from the entire sector within a week."

"Drive?" Bashir asked skeptically.

Locken smiled, then almost giggled. "Excuse the euphemism. All right. They'll be dead. Most of them, in any case. A few will escape, but not for long. I engineered the prion to lie dormant for a short time in certain genotypes—just long enough for survivors to get home and spread it around a bit. It won't really matter, though, because by then the war will have begun."

"A conflict between the Romulans and the Federation," Bashir concluded. "And soon after, the Klingons will be drawn into it. Then, possibly the Breen, at which point the entire Alpha Quadrant will become engulfed. And when they're finished savaging each other, the genetically enhanced humans will step in, the New Federation will rise out of the ashes of the old, and the quadrant will be united at last."

"I couldn't have put it better myself," Locken said, beaming.

Bashir thought about trying to smile, but he was afraid the best he would be able to do was a grimace, so he gave up the attempt. "And the timetable for all this is . . . ?"

Locken brightened even more, if that were possible. "Didn't I say? Tomorrow we launch the first missile. Now, you'll have to excuse me. I think the soup is overboiling." Locken slipped the control unit back onto his belt and ran for the kitchen. Bashir stayed behind for several seconds and studied the console, but then hurried after. After all, it wouldn't do to look too interested.

Ezri knew that on some level she should be insulted that the Jem'Hadar guard wasn't standing right outside the cell door anymore—obviously, she presented no *real* threat—but she was too busy working with the combadge module to let it bother her. Much. She had been fairly certain *what* she had to do, but not exactly sure *how* to do it. In the end, she had consulted Jadzia's memories and learned that her predecessor not only knew the techniques, but had what amounted to a fascination for this kind of technological trickery. Ezri wondered if Julian knew this and had counted on it.

The metal shard wasn't the ideal choice for altering the combadge's circuitry, but she kept at it and eventually found the settings she needed. And then, there was the *other* problem, the question of what to do once she managed to get her cell open. Only one idea suggested itself—not a great one, but the best she could come up with under the circumstances.

She jiggled the circuit's broadcast cluster with the shard until she found the correct frequency. The cell's forcefield flickered, then stabilized. Ezri swore and tickled the frequency key again. The forcefield emitters surged; then the door flared and collapsed.

The temptation was to leap up and make a run for it, but Ezri sat tight. Seconds later, the guard was there, glaring, disruptor drawn. When he saw her, he pointed his weapon at her head. She expected him to be smiling for some reason, but then she understood that this wasn't fun for him; it was his job. It was his job to stop her from leaving the cell, however possible. And it was her job to escape. Simple.

Ezri jiggled the tool and the signal cut off. The forcefield emitters snapped back on. The guard was standing in the threshold, and as the forcefield closed around him, every muscle in his body—including his trigger finger—spasmed. His arm jerked and the shot singed the air just above Ezri's head. The Jem'Hadar pitched forward, dropped onto the floor, and curled into a ball at Ezri's feet as the forcefield emitters shorted out and the field collapsed for the last time.

Ezri rose, walked quickly to the door, then prodded the Jem'Hadar with her foot. He didn't move. She stripped him of his weapons and communicator, then crept down the corridor.

After twenty meters of careful prowling she found an unmarked door. Opening it carefully, Ezri found a maintenance room that was obviously meant, among other things, to service the air-duct system. She opened a grate, climbed inside, and began to move as silently as she could, unable to suppress a wicked grin as she crept through the dark.

"Do these Founders then not give you the white?" asked the First.

Taran'atar's mind felt clearer and he wondered if it was because the First had administered some kind of drug while he had been unconscious. "They *created* the white," he said. "And, yes, they do. Your Khan merely stole the formula and re-created it. Badly, I might add."

"Badly?"

"Your soldiers, First, are either very weak or badly trained. I killed ten of them myself. No single soldier should be able to kill ten Jem'Hadar."

The First frowned and it seemed for a moment that he was about to strike the prisoner, but then restrained himself. "Thirteen," he said.

Taran'atar did not understand him. "Thirteen?"

"You killed thirteen. Your grenade landed in the midst of three soldiers. None of them had the sense to pick it up and throw it back."

Taran'atar felt a strange desire to make some sort of comment—either an expression of regret or a point of advice—but he refrained. It would not be well received and he knew that his life still hung by a thin thread. This soldier, this First, had come back to talk to him not because he felt Taran'atar had any valuable information to contribute, but because something they had discussed earlier had cut deep and was now festering. Though he was not a true Jem'Hadar, this First seemed to have some worthwhile qualities. He might grow up to be a respectable soldier someday.

"Then how do you take the white?" the First said, continuing his earlier line of inquiry. "You have a shunt, but we found no evidence of a tube in your possessions. And you have been here many, many hours. Explain this."

"I am not like most Jem'Hadar. What you obtain from white my body can produce naturally."

The First's turmoil was growing by the moment. He suddenly drew his disruptor and placed the weapon at Taran'atar's temple. "I should kill you. You have no useful information and the time I spend speaking with you might be better used training the soldiers who still remain under my command." He flicked a switch on the weapon and Taran'atar heard the charge build. The First watched his face. Then, slowly, he lowered the weapon and said, "But you have courage. I'll grant you that. And some of the things you've said . . ." He walked back to where he had been standing and holstered his weapon.

Turning, he pointed at the tube that pumped white into his throat. "You say you do not need this. Is that true?"

"It is true."

"Is that how Jem'Hadar are meant to exist?"

Taran'atar hesitated. Once again the First had surprised him, raising a question that stirred the Elder's own growing uncertainty. "I don't know," he said, the words tearing at his throat like poison. "A Jem'Hadar lives only to serve the Founders and I have served them well and yet, *and yet,* as soon as they discovered my flaw they sent me *here,* to this blighted corner of the galaxy. I am a *deviant.* I am unfit to live among my kind and so I must die here among you weaklings and traitors. It is what I *deserve.*"

The First listened dispassionately until Taran'atar finished his diatribe. Then, he reached up as if to touch the tube, though he could not seem to bring himself to do it. "Yes," he said. "I see. You are correct about one thing: Your Founders and my Khan are very different. The Founders made you so that you hate the fact that you do not need the white, while my Khan . . ." Struggling mightily, the First managed to wrap his fingers around the tube and looked almost as if he would tear it from the shunt, but Taran'atar knew he would not, *could* not. Instead, panting heavily, he snarled, ". . . he made me well enough to make me willing to do *anything* for him, but not so well that I look upon this chain . . ." He let go of the tube. ". . . as a benediction."

Stepping close, putting his face in Taran'atar's, the First hissed, "I am not a soldier. I am not a servant. I am a *slave,* but at least I know it. *Why don't you?*"

Chapter Seventeen

"We don't have much time to talk, Joseph," Kasidy Yates said to her father-in-law. The image on the viewscreen snapped and popped as the signal faded, then grew stronger. "They're taking the subspace net down all across the province later this afternoon to put in some new equipment."

Joseph Sisko scowled. *"Well, they can just wait until we're finished,"* he said. *"I've been trying to get through all day."*

"I understand," Kasidy sighed. "It's harder here than it was on the station. Sometimes, it's easy to take for granted how efficient the Federation is."

"All right, all right," Joseph grumbled. *"I guess I just thought that all this 'wife of the Emissary' business would have given you some sort of . . . I don't know . . . special status."*

"It *does*," Kasidy exclaimed. "More than I know what to do with. Do you have any idea how many people have come to my door over the past couple of days just asking if they can help out? And they're all so earnest and polite, I can't turn them away! I've had furniture movers, kitchen cleaners, garden weeders."

"Sounds all right to me," Joseph said, something approximating a smile crossing his lips. *"The kitchen-cleaning part, at any rate. Besides, you should take it easy."* The picture cleared up and Kasidy took a moment to study Joseph's face and saw her fears confirmed: there were lines of weariness around his eyes and mouth that had grown more pronounced since Ben's disappearance. It was the ravaged look of a parent who'd come to believe he'd lost his child, despite Kasidy's conviction that her husband, Joseph's son, would someday return.

"Joseph, I'm in the middle of my second trimester—the best part of being pregnant according to my doctor—and I've never felt better. I *want* to do things. In fact," she laughed, "I'm feeling pretty broody."

Joseph's smile broadened and it took years off his face. *"I remember that,"* he said. *"When my second wife got to that phase. There weren't enough hours in the day to do everything she wanted. I was grateful to go to the restaurant every day where I didn't have to work so hard."*

"Well," she said, smiling back, "things will be better when Jake returns. He's good at handling the visitors. He has a gift for putting people at ease."

"Ah, he gets that from me. Never was one of his father's strengths . . ." Then, Joseph's expression went sober again. *"Well, where is he? Not back on the station again, I hope. I'd much rather he stayed there with you on Bajor."*

Kasidy stared at the monitor, confused. What could Joseph mean? Jake was on Earth. He'd left . . . how long ago? Two weeks. Could they be teasing her? But, no, that wasn't like Joseph. He would never joke about something like that. She said, "What do you mean? He's there with you, isn't he?"

Joseph's smile slipped away and even with the poor connection, Kasidy could see the blood drain out of his face. *"What? No . . . Of course not. What made you think he was here?"*

"He *told* me he was going there," she said almost angrily. The surges of hormones came on that way sometimes; she occasionally found herself growing misty and weepy over strange things—a dew-covered spiderweb in the garden or a hand-thrown clay bowl that Ben had used to stir together a batch of mole sauce. Kasidy reined in her emotions and said, "Wait. Maybe we're talking about the same thing and getting ourselves confused. Two weeks ago, Jake took a ship from DS9 straight to Earth."

Joseph's lips moved for several seconds and Kasidy began to think that the signal was breaking down, but then she realized he was having trouble forming words. He clutched his chest and sat down, the camera automatically tracking. *Good Lord, no,* she thought. *Please, not now. Not when I'm so far away.* But then he seemed to take hold of himself and said, *"I . . . I swear to you, Kasidy, Jake never called, never told me that he was coming here. Two weeks ago?"*

Kasidy nodded. "But if he didn't go there, then where could he have gone? And why would he have lied?"

"He wouldn't have . . . Jake would never lie to you . . . Unless . . ."

"Unless what?"

"Unless he was going to do something he knew we wouldn't want him to do."

Kasidy felt herself grow light-headed and had to lean over so she wouldn't faint. When she looked up again, she looked into the old man's eyes and knew that whatever she said next would only make him look older and more fragile. "Joseph . . . where can he be?"

Ezri stifled a sneeze, wiped her eyes against her sleeve, and desperately wished that she had an antihistamine. Why was it, she wondered, that in all the holonovels and two-dees of her youth, whenever the plucky young heroine had to clamber through ventilation shafts, she never seemed to get dirty? Ventilation shafts, she had discovered, were *filthy* places. And dark. And small. And things *lived* in them, the sorts of things that usually tried to get away from you, but sometimes grew confused and lost their way and came back *to* you.

She guessed she'd been sitting still and trying not to make any noise for more than two hours. Enough was enough. Either they had discovered what she had done and were on her trail, or the other, more intriguing possibility had come to pass—the one she had devised once she'd figured out where the ketracel-white distillery was located. One way or another, it was time to get out of the air ducts.

But there were problems.

The first was that she no longer had any idea where she was. Ezri was fairly certain that the duct was sloping downhill and had been for quite a distance. She had, she realized, been unconsciously braking with knees and palms after every switchback. She must be quite a way below the holding cells by now.

The other problem was that Ezri was afraid to push open a grate without first checking out what might be below, which meant shining the palm beacon she'd found into a dark room. The other option was simply dropping down into the darkness without checking first, an idea that held even less appeal than staying in the ducts. Sooner or later, she would have to do *something,* but, for now, crawling along in the dusty darkness was an acceptable alternative to making a decision.

Wait.

She backed up. Something had caught her eye in the dark. *There.* A flash. Red. Ezri reached out toward it and found a slightly open louvered grate. She poked at it and the louvers opened wider, creaking slightly, but there was no alarming noise from beneath her, so she assumed she was all right. For now. Lights, most of them very small. Control panels and lab equipment. There were no overhead lights, but the panels were casting enough glow that she could see the floor, not *too* far beneath her. The question was whether or not the room was safe. Nothing seemed to be moving, but Jem'Hadar could shroud themselves and stay *very* quiet if they so chose. But no, it seemed unlikely that a Jem'Hadar would be waiting shrouded in a dark laboratory.

She pushed on the grate and was satisfied to discover it was on a hinge. No large piece of metal crashing to the floor, at least. Moving slowly, listening for anything, Ezri lowered herself through the opening and let herself dangle at arm's length before releasing her grip.

"You're alone, Ezri," she said, trying to settle herself. Her words echoed strangely and she amended her original estimate of the size of the room. Either it was bigger than she had thought or she had spent too much time in the air ducts.

"Lights?" she called, but nothing happened. "Computer?" No response. Maybe that was for the best. No computer monitoring, at least, or it might be authorization-code–protected. Ezri had a vague idea about tapping into Locken's main computer and trying to cause some trouble, but she knew that her chances of accomplishing that were fairly slim. Locken—or Section 31 or the Dominion before them—were probably ultra-paranoid about security. She had managed to perform her earlier piece of skullduggery only by tapping into Audrid's extensive knowledge of humanoid biochemistry, Jadzia's scientific acumen, and her own recent research into Starfleet's Jem'Hadar database, when she'd been trying to gain some insight into Kitana'klan.

She flicked on her lamp and played the beam over the control panels. The consoles and equipment looked like the sort of thing that she would see in a sickbay: sequence analyzers, tissue regenerators, even a small surgical bay. Ezri frowned. Why situate a medical facility so far away from the living quarters? It didn't make sense.

She continued to pan the light over the consoles, but not so slowly or methodically now. She had an idea what she was looking for now and, moments later, found it against the far wall.

Stasis tubes. Two banks of four. Seven were active.

Ezri felt the hairs on the nape of her neck stand up.

What would Locken want with stasis tubes? It wasn't a happy thought. It obviously wasn't Federation technology and she didn't like the idea of trying to figure out Dominion control systems. And it was possible that whoever was inside the tubes had a very good reason for being there—sick or injured beyond the abilities of the facility to heal. Or they might be Jem'Hadar. This was less likely, though. Why would Locken keep Jem'Hadar in stasis? Unless they were really *bad* Jem'Hadar. She brushed aside the thought. Anyone Locken would want kept out of the way would be her ally, even if only in the short run.

"Logs," she said. "There have to be log files."

The main workstation was a stand-alone, with dedicated memory and processing units. That spelled the end of any lingering plans for crashing the system, but Ezri let the idea pass unmourned. She was more interested in finding out what Locken had been doing in this room.

There was no security on the system, not even a password. Locken had made no attempt to conceal his activities, which made sense to Ezri in retrospect. He was too arrogant to believe anyone would breach his security. There was one directory labeled STASIS, with seven files, named consecutively: SUBJECT 1, SUBJECT 2, SUBJECT 3 . . . No names, no identifying marks. They might have been petri dishes filled with mold.

Another directory was labeled FAILURES, with many, many more files, some of them arranged into subdirectories. After a cursory review of both sets of files, Ezri concluded that the Failures had been the lucky ones: they were dead.

Not all the test subjects had been humans. At least one of the Section 31 agents had been a Betazoid and another appeared to have been an Andorian, though it was difficult to say because of the poor quality of the recordings. The subject's skin was blue, but he was hairless and didn't have antennae, though there were small, dark patches on the skull where antennae might once have been.

There were others: a pair of Romulans that must have come from the pirated starship; three small, furry beings that didn't belong to any species Ezri knew; a Cardassian who screamed into the camera until he passed out or died. Each holoclip was preceded by several pages of notes and formulas, but Ezri could only guess at the connection between them. Had Locken been testing a mutagen, a nerve gas, a spectrum of radiation, possibly all of the above? There was no way to know. She ran a search and found that there were over seven hundred individual clips, though there was no way to know how many subjects the number represented.

There was a detached, clinical tone about the proceedings, but there was something even worse underneath it all, something that made Ezri want to shut everything off, crawl back into the snug, safe air vents. Beneath the clinical veneer, there lurked the horrifying spectacle of an emotionally arrested young boy taking a shivering pleasure in pulling the legs off bugs.

She did not know why Locken had put these seven individuals into stasis and she wasn't sure she wanted to dig deep enough into his "work" to find out now. Neither could she be sure that it was within the power of Federation science to restore them. Ezri wavered for a moment, wondering whether she should try to see if there was some way to cut power to the tubes and terminate the poor, damned monsters Locken had created.

But, no, she decided. It wasn't her call to make. When all this was over, she would bring back help. But dealing with Locken would have to come first.

As quickly as she could, she climbed back into the air duct, eager to put herself as far from Locken's chamber of horrors as she could.

Security officer's log. I'm leaving this record in case I don't survive the assault on Locken's stronghold.

It's still a few hours before dawn and we're camped out approximately two kilometers east-southeast of Locken's compound. We plan to leave as soon as the Ingavi have eaten and made whatever other preparations—physical or spiritual—they need to make. It occurs to me that I know almost nothing about Ingavi theology, whether they're ancestor worshipers, monotheists, atheists, or something else entirely.

I'm guessing there are about fifteen hundred Ingavi left, down from about five thousand when I was here last. That's an unbelievably high mortality rate and it's possible there are too few of them left for them to survive here on Sindorin, even if Locken and the Jem'Hadar left today. I don't even know what else to say about that.

Last night, we had an army of about three hundred. This morning, I counted one hundred sixty. The rest have seen what was going to happen and melted away into the forest. Wise, wise Ingavi . . .

They were watching me just a little while ago, waiting to see what I do to prepare myself. When I pulled out this tricorder, they left me alone. This, they must think, is what I do, and I suppose they're right. This is what I always did just before going on a mission with the Maquis. Everyone did it—left a will or, at least, a list of things you wanted divided up among your friends. I would do that now, but who would I leave anything to? All my friends from the Maquis are gone and there's no one back on Deep Space 9 that I feel any compulsion . . .

Well, wait, yes there is. Whoever finds this, please tell Colonel Kira to search the mainframe in the security office very carefully. I found some things in it that she might find useful someday. Oh, and if anyone finds my . . . my things, please give the fractal blade to Taran'atar. He's the only person I know who might appreciate it.

I'm going to attack Locken's fortress with about one hundred sixty Ingavi, most of whom are armed with slings, blowguns, and spears. A few of them have phasers and disruptors. It's not much . . . hell, it's not anything really, but if we can slow down Locken even a little, it might give Bashir and Dax a chance, assuming they're still alive. And if we can help them, maybe it will help the Ingavi. If you're Starfleet, try to find the Ingavi and help them. They might not make it easy— they don't owe us any trust—but do what you can.

One last request. If I'm found dead . . . please, take my bones back to Bajor.

This is Lieutenant Ro Laren, chief security officer of Starbase Deep Space 9, over and out.

"This is going much too well," Ro whispered to Kel.

The Ingavi, hanging upside down from a vine at that moment and looking over Ro's shoulder, shrugged, then suggested that Ro might not want to say anything that would endanger their good fortune. "There are always ears willing to listen to complaints of too much luck. What would you like us to do next?"

They were within seven hundred meters of the outer wall of the compound and, as anticipated, they had encountered opposition, but the Jem'Hadar they had fought were nothing like the soldiers Taran'atar had combated.

"How many soldiers have we killed so far?"

"Eight."

"Then we missed one. They usually patrol in three groups of three. He's either still on patrol or he's heard us and gone back to the base for reinforcements."

Kel asked, "If the latter, then why haven't we been attacked?"

Ro shook her head. "I don't know. Something strange is happening. How many Jem'Hadar have your people managed to defeat in the past?"

Kel hooted sardonically. "One or two. Maybe. No one ever stayed long enough to check. Believe me, we are as aware as you are that there is something wrong here."

"Could it be a trap?" Ro asked.

"Baiting a trap with one or two trained soldiers, maybe—but *eight?* Unless this Khan has bred thousands upon thousands—and we would know it if he had—there is something wrong with them. My people say they fight as if in a dream . . . if Jem'Hadar do dream."

"They don't," Ro said, running another scan of the forest before them. The missing ninth soldier was bothering her. "You can't dream if you don't sleep."

From above, there came a soft hiss and Kel scampered up the vine he had been hanging from. Looking up, Ro barely made out a pair of figures huddled together exchanging words.

Moments later, Kel dropped down again and the other Ingavi climbed higher into the treetops. "We found him," Kel reported. "The ninth Jem'Hadar."

"And?"

"He was asleep."

"*What?*"

"He was asleep. Standing at guard, gun drawn, with his eyes closed. When my soldiers approached him, his eyes opened, but by then it was too late. Even at the last, he did not seem to understand what was happening."

Ro was baffled, but she didn't want to waste the opportunity. "All right, they'll notice the guards not reporting in soon enough. We can't assume this stupor is going to last. Tell your people we may still have a fight on our hands."

"I'll ask everyone to move up, then," Kel said, already heading back up the vine. "See you soon."

What a polite army I have, Ro thought. *"I'll ask everyone to move up."* She laughed quietly, the first real laugh Ro remembered having in days. She fished her binoculars out of her bag and trained them on the forest even though they weren't much use in the dense foliage. Even the infrared setting was flummoxed by the shifting bands of hot and cool air being pushed around by the treetop breezes.

"What the hell is going on here?" Ro asked herself. And why couldn't she shake the feeling that Bashir was somehow behind it all?

"Bashir," Locken whispered through clenched teeth, stalking down the corridor from the main lab to his quarters. "It must be Bashir." Too many things were going wrong all at the same time. First, even as he was preparing the new cloning chambers, came word that the Trill had escaped. The security logs showed that the forcefield had been opened with some kind of electromagnetic pulse. And now there was something wrong with his Jem'Hadar, something to do with the white. The tests showed traces of a foreign substance, tainting it, making the soldiers sluggish. There was the puzzle of how the Trill had managed to get into the lab and Locken cursed himself for not taking internal security more seriously. Clearly he had underestimated Dax and Bashir both.

At least he had been suspicious enough to keep Bashir in his personal suite of rooms. If he had been allowed into the laboratory, there was no telling what kind of damage he might have done. The computers in his quarters, especially the units that controlled the missile launch mechanism, were protected by the most complex encryption programs he could conceive. Bashir might be clever, but he was no match for Locken's genius with coding.

And yet . . .

Locken stopped at the next check station and inspected the two Jem'Hadar who were on guard duty. One had the same glazed, numb expression he had seen on many of the other soldiers, but the second seemed alert, even eager. "You," Locken said. "You're feeling all right?"

The Jem'Hadar responded promptly. "Ready to serve, my Khan."

Locken nodded, noting the sputtering tube in the soldier's neck. Maybe the contaminant hadn't dispersed evenly through the white supply. Some of his men might still be as healthy as this one. He would find out after he'd dealt with the good doctor. "Come with me," he said, and the Jem'Hadar fell in smartly behind him. "We're going to my quarters. There will be a human there. Don't kill him until I order you to do so. Understood?"

"Understood."

Locken found Bashir precisely where he expected to find him: stooping over the master command console. His hands were flying over the controls, his brow furrowed with frustration.

"Stand away, Julian," Locken ordered.

Bashir's hands froze, but he didn't step away from the console.

"Soldier," Locken snapped. "Aim your weapon. If he doesn't move in three seconds, shoot him." The Jem'Hadar's rifle rose instantly and was pointed unwaveringly at Bashir's head.

Bashir lifted his hands off the console and took two steps back. "Over against the wall," Locken said. Bashir complied. It was hard to read his expression and that worried Locken, so he moved to the command console, entered his codes, and ran a quick diagnostic on the missile firing system. While the diagnostic ran, he checked the command system for viruses or other less elegant forms of sabotage.

Both checks reported finding nothing amiss. The command system was clean and the missile delivery system had not been tampered with. Locken almost laughed. Bashir must have had less time to work than Locken had assumed, or, possibly, he wasn't quite as clever as Locken had once suspected. "That was really foolish, Julian," he said. "All you've succeeded in doing is killing the inhabitants of the Orias system a little sooner." He keyed the launch code and activated the firing sequence. "I was going to do this after we had some breakfast, maybe a glass or two of ambrosia, but, well, sometimes it's best to do things without ceremony."

Locken punched up the exterior cameras and turned them toward the missile silo. The top of the silo opened, and, seconds later, a slim, matte black shape came forth on a point of blue-white flame that cut through the night sky. It rose swiftly, gained speed at an astonishing rate, then disappeared into the east.

"Honestly," Locken said. "I expected better of you. If you insisted on being my nemesis instead of my ally, the least you could have done was make it *interesting*. This was hardly worth getting out of bed for." He shrugged. "Well, at least we have the hunt for your little pet slug-girl to look forward to. Seeing as she managed to accomplish more than you did just by poisoning my Jem'Hadar ..."

The barb did not seem to sting Bashir as much as he had expected. In fact, despite the implicit threat to someone Locken knew full well was dear to Julian, his captive looked not just unperturbed, but positively pleased with himself.

"I have to admit," Bashir said, "that the encryption on the missile console was more than I could handle ..."

Locken nodded, graciously accepting the compliment.

"... but it was surprisingly easy to alter the orbit of the weapons platform."

It seemed to Locken that the universe became frozen in amber. His muscles, his memory, his mind, all were immobilized for exactly the span of time it required for everything, *everything* he had been planning to begin to tip forward, to crumble, to topple into the void that had just opened beneath his feet. There came a voice—whining, cajoling, exhorting—*why hadn't he been a little quicker, a little more clever, a little tougher . . .*

He was five again and there was the ring of faces standing around him, the boys who had taunted him for being slow, for being stupid. And here again was the desire to hurt them, to make them pay for what they said, except . . . except . . . he hadn't known how to do it . . . He *was* slow. He *was* stupid . . .

. . . And then time, stretched as far as it could, snapped back again. He looked down at his hands and saw that they were moving over the console, flying, his fingers a blur of motion, checking the sensors, checking the telemetry of the weapons platform, sending the disable code, but, no, somehow Bashir, damn him, had anticipated every move. The platform wouldn't do what he asked, though it *did* allow him to see Sindorin with its onboard cameras. Here came the missile, arcing up silently from the planet's surface, its blue-white flame bright against the black of space, unfettered, unstoppable, and then there came a dazzling flash of ruby light.

Then there was nothing, not even a trail of fragments.

Locken imagined what he hadn't been able to see: an explosion that consumed the missile and its biological payload, a chain reaction of blown power systems that was, even now, ripping his weapons platform apart. Locken stared at the monitor, stared and waited for some kind of meaning to emerge, but there was nothing. It was only space, only the void, only an abyss.

Behind him, he heard Bashir say, "It's over, Locken."

Locken composed himself and turned toward Bashir. He willed himself to remain calm, then slowly reached up and turned off the blank monitor. "You don't know what you're talking about, Julian. This was nothing. A minor setback, at best. I admit it—this stings, but that's all it is. A bug bite. I'll scratch it and by the time I'm finished, I'll have a new missile and a new payload. The Romulans on Orias III will live to see a couple more sunrises." He turned to look at Bashir. "But that won't mean anything to you, Julian. You won't be here to see it."

Bashir sighed. "Maybe," he said. "But I expect you won't be far behind me. You really don't get it, do you? You think you're so bloody intelligent, that you're always pulling everyone else's strings, but you haven't seen that you're really the puppet. This whole war—this decision to 'unite the Alpha Quadrant'—it wasn't *your* idea."

He stared at Locken as if waiting for comprehension to dawn, but Locken only stared at him blankly. Bashir shook his head, massaged the bridge of his nose, then continued. "During your time with Section 31, did you ever meet a man named Cole?"

Locken felt off-balance and found that he could not refuse to answer. "No. Who is he? And why should I care?"

"He's the one who sent me to stop you," Bashir said, then confidently walked back into the living area. Locken wondered if Bashir was going to try to make a run for it, then decided if he did, he would let him have a bit of a head start. It would make things more interesting. Bashir stopped in front of the small table that held the holo of the medical staff at the New Beijing Pediatric Center and pointed at the figure of Murdoch, Locken's friend and mentor. "That's him."

"You're lying," Locken said, a little too quickly.

"Am I?" Bashir asked. "Consider this: The Dominion was supposed to have obtained erroneous intelligence that New Beijing was producing biogenic weapons. But where did that information come from? I've been thinking about that," he said. "I've had a lot of free time on my hands lately, and here's what I believe: Section 31 wanted you badly. They desperately wanted an enhanced agent and since I'd already turned them down, they turned to you."

Locken felt himself begin to snarl, but then realized that Bashir was trying to make him angry, trying to make him make a mistake. He glanced to the right and saw that his Jem'Hadar was still tracking Bashir with his weapon, awaiting the kill order. Locken grinned.

"So, they assigned Cole to New Beijing," Bashir continued. "He obviously had some kind of medical training, enough at least to fool you and the others. As Dr. Murdoch, Cole had time to assess you and the colony. When he finished his assessment, he conceived a plan. He fed information to the Dominion that would guarantee they'd come in with weapons blazing, then made sure that the colony's defenses were disabled before he found a deep enough hole to crawl into until his ride home arrived."

"You don't—you can't—know if *any* of this is true."

"No, I don't," Bashir agreed. "But it all does fit, doesn't it? Even you can see that. Even you can see that Section 31 sacrificed five thousand men, women, and children—Federation lives—just so they could convince *you* to join their little crusade. They wanted that fantastic mind of yours working for them; it didn't matter how they got it. And all they had to do was let you think it was *your* crusade."

"No . . ." Locken said hoarsely.

"Yes," Bashir replied, his tone now quiet, even sympathetic. "You said it yourself: New Beijing changed everything. As much as you might have thought about it, you never would have done anything like this before. Think about it, Ethan: a missile . . . a *disease-laden* missile. Genetically engineered soldiers. What have you become? You were a *doctor.*" He let the words hang in the air for several seconds, then concluded, "But now you're their creature, their monster. . . . And I've been looking so hard to pry into your head, to try to *think* like you so I could stop you, that I almost convinced myself I was *like* you." Bashir rubbed the cuff of his sleeve over his eyes and Locken was surprised to see that his eyes were wet with tears.

"I want you to listen to me now, Ethan," Bashir continued. "It's still not too late. You wanted us to work together, and we can still do that. We could stop them, the two of us, bring Section 31 to justice. We can make sure they never again . . ."

Though Bashir could not have known it by any outward sign, Locken quickly and coolly processed all the possible outcomes that could be borne out of the option of joining forces with the Federation and crushing Section 31. It was a tantalizing prospect and offered, if nothing else, the twin pleasures of companionship and revenge. If he went with Julian, he would, Locken knew, have to undergo some form of discipline and punishment, but he also knew that Starfleet would not be permitted to parade him before a public tribunal. Word would never be allowed to leak out either about Section 31 or the attacks on the Romulans. He would be allowed to pursue vengeance and then, probably, be put somewhere out of the way. He might even be allowed to continue his research, to find new ways to help children, which was, in the end, the thing he wanted most to do. . . .

But Locken knew too that they would never, *ever* leave him alone. Already, he felt their gaze on him, their prying eyes, their meddlesome, ever-vigilant cow-eyed scrutiny. He closed his eyes and felt the blank, uncomprehending stares, and, worse, the tiny, smug smiles for the would-be conqueror. Something inside him crumbled and withered. It was more than he could stand; he deserved better.

But he didn't know how to say any of it, so instead he let the fear and anger speak for him. "The quadrant," he said, "the *galaxy*, still needs order. When people learn what I've been doing here, they'll flock to my cause. I'll deal with Section 31 in my own good time."

Bashir looked up at his flag, Khan Singh's flag, the merged sun and moon symbol dominating one wall of the room, and sighed. "Maybe you're right. Maybe you *are* just like Khan, after all." He caught Locken's gaze with his own and for the first time, Locken felt the power of the fury Bashir had been holding in check. "A deluded failure."

Locken flushed with loathing and finally turned to the Jem'Hadar guard, giving the order through clenched teeth: "Kill him."

The Jem'Hadar didn't move.

Locken screamed at him. "I gave you an order, guard!"

The guard turned to look Locken in the eyes. "My name," he said, "is Taran'atar."

One hundred meters from Locken's front door, it finally turned into a real fight. Either someone had roused the troops or all the wide-awake Jem'Hadar were just inside the front doors. Whichever it was, the bulk of the Ingavi troops were pinned down in the lee of a low hill. They were keeping their heads low and that meant the majority of the shots weren't dangerous, but every tenth or fifteenth bolt came at just the right angle and Ro heard an Ingavi die. She knew it was only a matter of minutes before the Jem'Hadar shrouded themselves, moved out to better positions, and caught them in a cross fire.

One way or another, she had to make a choice soon: charge or fall back.

The Ingavi could still melt back into the forest, though she knew it would spell their doom. If Locken and his Jem'Hadar won today, even if they never took control of the Alpha Quadrant, they *would* control Sindorin long enough to wipe out the Ingavi. She turned and looked at Kel, who was huddled down by her side, working hard to be as small a target as possible.

"What do you think?" she shouted. To their left, an Ingavi broke and ran for the edge of the forest, but was cut down before he had gone ten meters.

"I think," Kel said, grimacing, "that we may die soon, whether we flee or fight."

"I'm afraid I agree."

"So," he said, gripping the stock of his phaser more tightly, "we might as well die fighting."

Ro nodded in agreement and checked the charge on her phaser.

"You do not understand me, Ro Laren," Kel said. "I am saying that the *Ingavi* should stay and fight, not you. We are not your people, and this fight is not yours. If we are distracting the soldiers, you might stand a chance to escape in your ship and warn your brothers and sisters, might you not?"

Ro was surprised by the idea. She had been preparing to die. She thought about the recording she'd made and realized that she had been hopelessly optimistic when she thought someone might find it before Locken had been defeated. This was his home base; no one would be able to make it down to the surface. It might be important that she make it back to the Federation with the information she had gathered . . . which was exactly what? That Locken was a genuine threat? And what would make that more obvious than *not* returning?

But this was all just rationalization. Ro Laren was too brutally honest with herself to continue in this vein. She wanted to stay because she felt she owed these people a debt. Someone had to try to make things right. She held out her empty hand and after looking at it curiously for several seconds, Kel took it and they pressed their palms together. "In my culture," she explained, "this means we have made a pact."

"In mine," Kel said, "it means you have agreed to watch over my children while I go look for something to eat."

Ro considered it and finally said, "All right. Good enough. Now, go over there and find out how many of your cousins will attack the gate with us."

Kel nodded and crept away. Seconds later, a bolt creased the turf where he had been sitting.

They must be using tricorders now, Ro thought. *We don't have much time. . . .*

Chapter Eighteen

Locken ran.

He was fast, much faster than Bashir could have expected, faster even than he himself was, and it made him wonder if Locken had made some additional enhancements to himself. Nerve and motor-system tweaking, though illegal on Federation worlds, were far from unknown.

Bashir watched as Taran'atar raised his disruptor and coolly tracked Locken as he sped across the room, but before the Jem'Hadar could fire, Bashir barked, "No! Don't!" Taran'atar jerked his arm up and the energy bolt sizzled across the lab to shatter one of the large picture windows overlooking the lawn. The Khan never looked back, but bolted through the door, disappearing from sight.

"Why did you tell me to do that?" the Jem'Hadar asked.

"Because I want him alive."

Taran'atar moved to the doorway, then glanced outside to make sure Locken wasn't waiting in ambush. "But he's insane," Taran'atar remarked.

"Yes," Bashir agreed, following Taran'atar down the hall. "But it may be treatable. He was . . . I think he might once have been a great healer. I owe it to him to try . . ." Immediately in front of them, two small panels opened in the ceiling and a pair of lightly armored fighting drones dropped down.

Taran'atar calmly sighted first one, then the other, and blasted them out of the air before either had a chance to lock on to their targets. Then, before they moved again, he checked the rest of the corridor's ceiling and walls for traps. "This will slow us down," he said. "We'll have to check every corridor before we can move. We could go faster if I knew his likely goal."

Bashir pondered, then answered, "The barracks. No, wait. The lab. He said Ezri poisoned the white."

"Someone assuredly did." The thought seemed to remind Taran'atar of something. He tore at the tube of white on his neck and tossed it on the floor. Bashir saw that it was a fake, rigged to loop the flow so that it only appeared to be working. "The other Jem'Hadar have become slow, semiconscious."

"That makes sense. I suspect she probably concocted a powerful sedative and added it to the reservoir. That means Locken will head to the distillery and barricade himself inside with as many soldiers as he can, then see if he can cure them."

Taran'atar nodded. "Then we must hurry."

"I agree. It won't take him long to figure out what Ezri did to the white. It can't have been too complicated. . . ."

"No, you misunderstand," Taran'atar said, moving quickly, but alert for traps. He was favoring one side, Bashir noticed. "If you want him alive, we must find him before any other Jem'Hadar do, especially the First."

Bashir retraced the route to the reinforced double doors. "We have to find another way in," he said. "Perhaps the ventilation ducts . . ." Before he could finish, Taran'atar had entered a passcode into the security system.

"Inside information" was all he would say.

As they turned the next corner, another pair of security drones dropped from a shadowy corner. One succeeded in firing before Taran'atar could destroy it and the wall above his head exploded into shards of molten metal. He dropped to one knee, gulped air, and groaned. Bashir knelt beside the Jem'Hadar and tried to steady him with a hand to his back. When he pulled it away, he noticed it was damp with blood.

"You're hurt," the doctor said.

"It can wait," Taran'atar hissed. He pushed himself away from the wall, wavered once from side to side, then straightened. Pointing down the hall, he asked, "That way?"

"Yes, that way," Bashir nodded. "One way or another, let's end this."

Crouching low, Taran'atar peered around the corner that led to the lab door, disruptor at the ready. Bashir stood behind him wishing he had some kind of weapon—a club or even just a sharp stick to fend off attackers—but then he almost laughed. *If whoever we're going to fight gets past this Jem'Hadar, how long could I possibly last? Better to go forward unarmed,* he decided. *It will help me resist the temptation to do something stupid.*

Then Bashir was distracted by an unexpected sound: Taran'atar grunting in a tone that sounded like satisfaction.

"What is it?" Bashir whispered.

Taran'atar straightened, groaned slightly, then cupped his hand over the side where Bashir had seen the blood stain. *Broken ribs,* Bashir decided. *Possibly a collapsed lung.* "Come and see," Taran'atar said, beckoning to Bashir.

In huge letters, someone had painted the word "False" across the lab door. "The situation is worse than I thought," Taran'atar commented.

Bashir examined the "paint" more carefully. "Is this blood?" he asked.

Taran'atar leaned forward and his nostrils flared. "Yes," he said. "Locken's Jem'Hadar are coming out of their stupors. They're beginning to mutilate themselves. Soon, they'll begin to fight. I've seen this before. . . ."

"Then we have to hurry," Bashir said, stepping forward and tapping the entrance controls. Just as the doors parted, Taran'atar leaped forward and shoved the doctor to the ground. Multiple disruptor shots erupted from inside the lab. Taran'atar kept Bashir covered with his body until the first volley was over, then dragged him out of the line of fire. His ears ringing, Bashir realized how stupid he had been. There might be as many as two hundred enraged Jem'Hadar ranging throughout the complex. Bumbling into a room was an invitation to be shot.

One of the disruptor bolts must have destroyed the door mechanism, because it remained ajar. Bashir could hear cries from within, a chorus of Jem'Hadar soldiers bellowing, *"False! Faaallllssssse!"*

But as pathetic as were these groans of the lost and fallen, more pitiful still was the single voice raised against them. Locken was trying to sound commanding, but there was, to Bashir's ears, more than a little desperation in his every word. Determined to know what was happening despite the danger, Bashir dropped onto all fours and carefully peered around the corner.

He could see Locken's head above the throng of Jem'Hadar, so he must have been balanced on the narrow platform the cloning tubes were resting on. Bashir couldn't get an exact count from his vantage point, but he thought there must have been almost two dozen Jem'Hadar in the room, most of them milling about randomly, not looking where they were walking. Bashir could see their eyes and they were dull, heavily lidded, dead, but still there was a palpable feeling of dreadful expectation. The room was literally a powder keg and it would only be a matter of time until something touched a light to the fuse.

Perhaps Locken would even do it himself.

Only one of the Jem'Hadar did not move. He stood stock-still before Locken, studying his face and demeanor. Bashir guessed from the bit of collar brass he could see that this must be a First, perhaps even the same one who had freed Taran'atar. As if to confirm the doctor's suspicions, the Jem'Hadar held up his hand and made a complex gesture. The others froze in place.

"Yes," the First said softly, as if he were piecing together the syllogism as he spoke each word. "Perhaps you are our god. But if you are, then you must be a weak god, because you have had to use the white to keep us faithful." He paused and seemed to collect his thoughts. "And if you are weak and we are your creatures, then we are weak, too." A throaty growl rumbled through the room. The First raised his hand again and the growl died away. "But we will not be weak now," he continued. "We are Jem'Hadar. *True* Jem'Hadar!" And a shout went up, a roar from every throat.

Bashir looked at Locken and saw in his face the first pencil-line crack in the façade. The corner of his eye twitched and there came from his throat a sound somewhere between a whine of terror and a cry of defiance.

"We are *strong,*" the First concluded. "So you cannot be our god. You . . . are . . . *false!*"

With this, Locken reached into his pocket and drew a hand phaser. He moved deliberately, without haste, and pointed it at the First's head. It was, Bashir realized, either because he did not expect anyone to defy him or because he no longer cared. As he lifted his arm, Locken said simply, "I am your Khan," as if it would explain everything.

Two dozen disruptors came up. There was a massive *thrum* as they fired in concert. The Jem'Hadar, for reasons known only to them, continued to fire long after Locken had been reduced to atoms. The incubation tubes ruptured and the gestational fluids boiled away in the intense heat.

When he opened his eyes, Bashir realized that Taran'atar must have pulled him away from the door. There before him were two pairs of booted feet. One pair belonged to Taran'atar. The other belonged to the First.

"He's dead?" Taran'atar asked.

"Yes," the First replied.

"Good," Taran'atar said.

Angry, Bashir surged to his feet. He knew he would probably regret saying what he was preparing to say, but he could not countenance their callous attitude. A man had just died, after all. He might have been insane, but he had also been brilliant and, if not a god, then certainly a creator. Bashir was prepared to say all these things and more. He wanted the Jem'Hadar to feel as humbled and ashamed as he himself felt for his part in the tragedy—because surely there was some element of tragedy in this situation—but then he saw their eyes.

Bashir had studied Jem'Hadar anatomy closely enough to know that their faces didn't have the flexibility of some of the thinner-skinned humanoid species, so it was frequently difficult to "read" their expressions. But in the First's eyes he saw the truth. He saw a grim acknowledgment that the universe was without foundation. After all, if God could be killed, what other horrors might be possible?

Bashir clamped his jaw shut and looked back into the room. . . .

The Jem'Hadar who had been in the lab—the same soldiers who had been gripped by a killing frenzy only seconds before—were once again become passive, like sleepwalkers. The First and Taran'atar stared at the group, then looked at each other only long enough to nod, a suspicion confirmed. Bashir was about to ask him what this meant when he heard a loud crash behind him.

Bashir spun around, but, surprisingly, neither of the Jem'Hadar reacted. A grate fell out of the ceiling, and, seconds later, two legs dangled in the gap. Ezri Dax dropped to the ground, absorbed the impact with a roll, then came up on her feet. Her hands, face, and uniform were filthy, covered with the dust, dirt, and mold that accumulate in ventilation shafts and out-of-the-way corners, but, at that moment, she was the most welcome sight Bashir could have imagined.

Bashir helped Ezri to her feet and saw that though her face was almost gray with soot, her eyes shone bright with pleasure. Bashir embraced her so fiercely that she yelped. "Sorry," he muttered into her hair, then wrapped his arms around her more tenderly. Even as he enjoyed the feel of her warm body molding into his, Bashir was stabbed by a pang of guilt: why hadn't he been more concerned about her over the past several hours? For all he had known, she might have been lying in a dungeon or trapped in a narrow ventilation shaft or even dead, shot by a Jem'Hadar soldier who was standing at the wrong place at the wrong time. He released her, held her at arm's length, and began to ask, "Are you—?"

"I'm fine, Julian," she said, smiling. "Fine. Don't worry. How are you? And what was all that weapons fire? It sounded like it was right here."

"In the lab," Bashir said, glancing behind him at the still open door. "Things haven't gone exactly like . . ." He stopped. "I'm afraid . . ." He became frustrated with his inability to form a coherent thought. *Shock,* he thought. *I'm in shock,* and realized that the only thing he really wanted to do was wrap his arms around Ezri and sleep for three or four days. She seemed to read the thought on his face; without speaking, she pulled his head down onto her shoulder and rubbed the back of his neck. Bashir closed his eyes and inhaled deeply. She smelled of sweat and grease and mold, but yet, underneath all that, he still could find the essence of Ezri. He let it sweep through his senses and, briefly, Julian Bashir was comforted.

"I'm sorry," she whispered. "Truly sorry . . . for you. But not for him, Julian. Not for him."

He pulled away from Ezri and saw that she was weeping, but not, he thought, from sorrow, but anger.

"If you had seen . . ." she whispered, her voice cracking. "If you had seen some of the things he did . . ."

Bashir pulled the cuff of his sleeve up over the heel of his hand and wiped away her tears, taking several layers of dirt with it. "It's all right," he said softly. "I understand. It's all right. I don't think . . . I don't think anyone could have helped him. Not even me."

"Hey," a voice said from the other end of the hall. "Break it up, you two. I'm getting embarrassed just watching you."

Ezri spun around and Bashir looked up. It was Ro looking, if possible, even more weary and begrimed than Ezri, but smiling, obviously relieved to find her companions alive and well.

"Ro!" Ezri cried, and threw her arms around the Bajoran's neck, almost dragging her to the ground. This turned out to be a mistake. Suddenly, half a dozen small green-furred humanoids appeared from out of the shadows behind Ro, each of them hefting an energy rifle of some kind. Behind him, Bashir heard Taran'atar and the First stir. From all around him there came the unmistakable sound of weapon chambers beginning to charge.

"Ro," Bashir said evenly. "Please tell me these are friends of yours."

"Doctor," Ro said, then swallowed dryly, "these are my friends, the Ingavi." She turned around and waved her hands down, speaking softly and quickly in clicks and long, guttural fricatives. Without his combadge, Bashir couldn't make out what she was saying, but the response was reassuring. The Ingavi lowered their weapons and shuffled back into the shadows. Ro flicked a look over her shoulder at Ezri. "Don't do that again," she said.

"Right," Ezri said. "Noted."

Obviously deciding it would only be appropriate to respond in kind, Taran'atar pointed at the lab door and he and the First slipped inside. It was still ominously quiet within, but Bashir sensed that the two Jem'Hadar knew this would not last much longer.

When Ro returned, she was escorted by one of the aliens who moved, Bashir thought, with a jaunty nonchalance. "This is Kel," Ro said. "He's the leader of these Ingavi. Most of the others are outside watching the perimeter."

"And the Ingavi are . . . natives of this world?" Bashir asked.

"It's a long story, Doctor. I'll try to explain later. But they deserve our help if only because of what they've done for me today."

"All right," Bashir said, and that seemed to settle things. The little Ingavi hunkered down on his heels, phaser rifle on his lap, eyes locked on the open lab door.

"So, what's been happening?" Ro asked.

Ezri launched into her tale. "After I broke out of our cell, I wasn't sure at first what I could do. I found the air duct and started nosing around. Eventually I found the white distillery and got inspired to do a little creative chemistry. After that, I spent most of my time avoiding Jem'Hadar patrols. It wasn't much fun the first few hours, but then the tainted white began to affect them and it got easier. Sometime after that, the shooting started." Turning to Bashir, she said, "I figured you would be here—one way or another."

Then Ro took up the tale of what had happened since she and Taran'atar had beamed off the runabout. Bashir was beginning to feel like too much time was slipping away, but he was soon caught up in her tale. "By the time we got within fifty meters of their main emplacement," Ro recounted, "at least half the Ingavi had either been shot or forced to retreat. Then the firing let up. Nobody dared to move until one of our snipers picked off a Jem'Hadar at the gate. When we got to the gate, we discovered he was the only one there. It didn't make any sense, but we weren't going to pass up the opportunity, so we kept moving. All we found was dead Jem'Hadar, all of them obviously shot by *other* Jem'Hadar." She looked at Dax with a curious combination of respect and apprehension. "What did you *do* to them?"

"More than I intended, obviously," Dax said. "I just wanted to knock them out. . . ."

"You couldn't have known," Bashir said. "Ketracel-white is a tricky bit of chemistry, one of the reasons it's impossible to replicate. Any impurity will eventually lead to aberrant behavior, eventually escalating into uncontrolled violence. If I can access Locken's records, I should be able to—"

Suddenly, Bashir became aware that Taran'atar was standing directly behind him. *How long has he been there?*

"I do not think you will have time to perform tests," he said. "We must leave here soon or we will very likely die along with the Khan."

"Leave? What do you mean?" Bashir asked. "We have to download records, find evidence . . ."

From the lab, there came a deep, snarling yell, then the crash of something large and delicate crashing to the ground. Bashir saw the First's back in the narrow gap, then his face when he turned around. "Close this door," he ordered Taran'atar. "Now." Taran'atar rushed, gripped its edge and began to push in concert with the First. Before they could budge it more than a centimeter, Bashir heard a disruptor discharge and the First had to turn around. "Jem'Hadar!" he shouted. "Stand at attention!" The noise within died. Jem'Hadar conditioning died hard. The First turned back to the door and spoke quietly to Taran'atar. "The need grows strong in them . . . in all of us."

"But we can fix the white," Bashir said.

"No," the First said. "It's too late for that . . ." A tremor ran through his body.

Taran'atar grabbed his shoulder through the narrow space. Already, the Jem'Hadar inside were beginning to stir again. "Give them a good death," Taran'atar said.

The First nodded. Gripping the stock of his disruptor, he shook himself as if to turn away from the door. Without another word, Taran'atar finished shoving the door shut.

Moments later, from within the lab came sounds of death.

Chapter Nineteen

Taran'atar turned to the others. "We must go."

"The runabout is only about a half hour from here on foot," Ro said.

Ezri stared at her in surprise. "It survived the crash?" she asked.

Ro nodded. "She's tough. If we can get off planet, she'll get us home."

"No," Bashir said suddenly. They all looked at him. "We're not finished. We have to get his data. It's the evidence we need to expose Thirty-One. And the only place left now is his quarters." Bashir broke into a run.

Taran'atar and Ro looked at Ezri as if she were responsible for explaining Julian's behavior. "We have to stay with him," she said. "He's not armed."

"He's not *thinking*," Ro added.

"No," Ezri corrected her. "He's thinking too much. He almost can't help it." Something large and metallic crashed against the lab door and the floor vibrated underfoot. "Let's go."

In Locken's quarters, Bashir had already beaten the encryption codes on Locken's log files, but now he was furiously yanking open cabinets and cupboards and tossing their contents out onto the floor.

"Dammit!" he yelled. "Nothing!"

"What are you looking for?"

"A tricorder. A memory solid. Something I can record this data on!"

Ro opened her pack and pulled out a tricorder. "Here," she said, tossing it to Bashir.

Once Bashir found the correct frequency, he quickly developed a search strategy that discarded extraneous material while flagging files with key words and terms. An expert searcher would have required two hours to complete such a task, but Julian was finished in minutes, after which he was downloading the relevant data as quickly as the tricorder would allow.

The immediate task addressed, he began to browse through some of the other directories until he found a schematic of the entire complex. Ezri saw Julian's brow wrinkle. Something was bothering him. Wiping her hands, she walked toward him and saw that he was studying a corner of the compound where power lines and plumbing were leading into a seemingly empty space.

"What could that be?" she asked.

"I don't know," Julian said. "But I have some ideas, and they all bother me."

"Only one way to find out for sure," she said. "Want me to come with you? I know where all the entrances to the ductwork are just in case we have to avoid pursuit."

Julian smiled. "Wedged into a small, dark space with you? What more could I ask for?"

Ezri snorted. "You *are* feeling better, aren't you? Well, believe me, it's not nearly as interesting as all that. You can hear things moving around in those vents. Every once in a while, you surprise one—"

"Now you're just trying to impress me," Julian said. "Whatever we do, we have to do it quickly." He called to Ro and said, "When this is finished, call me, then head for the runabout. There's something we want to go check."

"I don't think it's a good idea for us to separate now," Ro protested. "Especially if the Jem'Hadar break loose."

"Locken might have left something behind. Possibly more Jem'Hadar cloning tubes. If we don't shut them down, there's no telling what they'll do after we're gone. We wouldn't want anything to happen to your native friends."

Ro surrendered. "All right. We'll leave when the download finishes. Take this with you," she said, handing the doctor her phaser rifle. "Watch your back. I have a feeling this place has a few more surprises left."

"You know," Ezri said as they made their way back toward the main lab, "that was quite an act you put on back in the cell. You almost had me convinced."

Bashir stopped and leaned against a wall and rubbed his eyes. "I had you convinced," he said, sighing, "because I wasn't lying. Not entirely. Don't misunderstand—I would never have joined him, Ezri. But those sleepless nights—they *do* happen and they scare the hell out of me. I just don't know how narrow the line is between what I am—" He glanced down the shadowy hall in the direction of Locken's lab. "—and what he was." They stood staring into the darkness and listening to the ominous silence. "What would it take, I wonder, for me to cross that line?"

Ezri reached up and touched his cheek. "Nothing that I can think of," she said reassuringly. "You're not him, Julian. You never will be."

Bashir grasped her hand with his, then pulled her toward him for a gentle kiss on the lips. He smiled and said, "Let's finish up this mission. I want to go home with you."

"That is the best idea I've heard in days," Ezri replied.

Bashir counted off a dozen paces and they found themselves facing a blank wall. "Nothing here," he said. "Nothing obvious, anyway." He laid his fingertips on the wall, then paced back and forth, feeling for some kind of bump or imperfection. He checked the seams to see if there was a raised area, then the joints between wall and floor. "Still nothing," he said.

"Might be voice-activated," Ezri said. "Or more likely, that control unit he carried everywhere."

"Hmmm," Bashir hummed. "Good point. Well, I'm not going into the lab to retrieve it, so it looks like we do this the hard way. Let's go back around that corner," he said, pointing back toward the intersection.

He set the weapon for moderate impact—he wanted to damage the wall without bringing the roof down on their heads—and fired. The wall cracked, but did not shatter. With the second shot, chunks of plasteel crumbled and fell onto the floor. The third shot blasted away large pieces. They coughed and waved their hands in front of their faces until the dust settled and they could see well enough to pick their way through the debris.

Three meters from the wall, Bashir said, "Stop," and pointed down. Something in the dark sparked and writhed. "Power lines."

Ezri pointed at the floor. "And some kind of liquid. You must have hit the plumbing. Not a good combination."

Without a tricorder, it was impossible to check whether they could proceed without danger, so they stood together for several seconds considering options until Ezri slapped her forehead and yelled, "Computer! Lights!"

A trio of fixtures flickered on and they could dimly see what was inside the room.

"More cloning tubes," Ezri said. "More Jem'Hadar."

A chill crawled down his spine. "No," he said. "Not Jem'Hadar." No longer thinking about the possibility of electrocution, he stepped lightly through the rubble, then climbed through the hole in the wall. Moments later, he heard Ezri climb in behind him, then a gasp, then a Klingon curse that would have made old Martok blush.

"When did he have time to do this?" she asked. "We've only been here two days!"

There were four cloning chambers, all of them full. The tube closest to the hole in the wall was cracked, obviously the source of the fluid on the floor. The body was slumped against the inside of the tube, the front of the head pressed flat against the glass. It was a young face, unlined by care or worry, but there was no question who it was.

It was him—Bashir.

He was immobilized, transfixed with shame and a sick kind of wonder. Ezri seemed compelled to peer into each tube. Stepping carefully, almost reverently around the cracked tube, she stared into the somehow unformed faces of the other three clones, each younger than the last, the smallest obviously no more than three years old.

"Oh, no—" she groaned.

Bashir seemed to snap out of the trance he was in and turned toward her. "What—what is it?"

"Julian— He must have been— Locken did some genetic manipulation—this one—is a female."

Bashir almost doubled over, staggered by the almost physical power of his revulsion. He leaned against the wall and felt his legs go numb.

"But, *why?*" Ezri asked. "What was he thinking?" But she already knew, Bashir thought. It was obvious. Cloning was a reliable technique, but nothing worked better than nature.

"Breeding stock," Bashir whispered. "For the new, better Federation." As he said the words, he felt the disgust well up inside his gut, threatening to detonate inside him, to destroy him. There was only one thing he could do. He said, "Get away from there, Ezri."

"What?"

"Get away." He hefted the phaser rifle.

"But, Julian—this is evidence. We can *use* this."

"It's not evidence, Ezri," Bashir said. "It's atrocity."

And she must have seen something in his eyes—something bitter and unwavering—because she didn't say another word, but crept back out over the rubble and stood beside him. When he pressed the trigger, he thought he heard a scream and some distant part of his mind wondered if it could be one of the clones. Was that even possible? He thought he heard the same noise every time he fired, as each phaser bolt cut through plastic and metal, plumbing and electrical conduit, as the tubes exploded, as flesh burned, and fluid boiled away.

It was only much later—when he realized how raw his throat was—that he realized it had been him.

When they stumbled back out into the hall, Bashir and Ezri were surprised to find a Jem'Hadar waiting for them, disruptor drawn, but not raised. Bashir hefted his own weapon, but he knew that if the soldier were to attack, they were as good as dead.

"Why are you still here?" the Jem'Hadar asked, and then Bashir and Ezri simultaneously exhaled. They recognized the voice; it was the First.

"We were taking care of some last-minute business," Bashir said coolly. "What about you? Were you successful? Did you complete your mission?"

"I have done my duty," the First said, glancing back at the lab. "But I have had communication from another squad, one that was on patrol and was not affected by the tainted white. There is something happening outside and I must go to them."

Bashir's mind raced. What could be happening now? Could it be the natives Ro had brought? No, that didn't seem likely. They were obviously not interested in confronting Jem'Hadar if it wasn't necessary. He quickly considered all the other possibilities and realized there was only one likely candidate. "Come with me," he said to the First. "I think I know what's going on."

When they reached Locken's quarters and the doors parted before them, Ro was struggling with the computer console.

"Doctor!" Ro called. "Get over here! Something's wrong." She was frantically working the controls. With a quick glance, Bashir saw that something was happening to the data stored in Locken's computer. The tricorder indicated that they were disintegrating at a precipitous rate.

"A virus?" he asked. "Did we set off a defense mechanism?"

"That's what I thought at first and I spent five minutes running virus-protection routines. I thought it was going after backups first and I had time, but that was just a mask. Meanwhile, most of the primary files were being slagged while it ran these phony displays." She punched in a series of commands. "It *looks* like a virus, but it's really a targeted EM pulse weapon. Someone outside, close, or the damned thing wouldn't work."

Suddenly, Ro's tricorder alarm sounded and she turned away from the console. "Damn!" she shouted, and reached for the tricorder just as its power coupling blew out. She jerked her hand away, grunted in pain, then ran for the kitchen, where she began running water over her fingers. Bashir ran to follow her, but was stopped by the sight of the tricorder. It was a blob of molten metal and plastic swimming with bits of gleaming circuitry.

Before Bashir could inspect Ro's injury, Taran'atar called, "Look here," and pointed at the surveillance monitor. At first, Bashir couldn't make sense of what he was seeing. His first thought was that he was looking at the rays of dawn, but then he caught sight of small animals and birds breaking cover. Through the heavy shadows and bright lights, he saw a sapling, then two larger trees, crash to the ground. Then came the men, most of them wearing camouflage or night suits, though a few of them were carrying phaser rifles with searchlights.

A cluster of Ingavi burst from cover and ran at the soldiers. The men with phasers turned toward them and began firing, cutting them down with almost casual ease. There was no sound, but Bashir could hear the little aliens screaming in his mind.

Bashir knew who the newcomers were. He'd done what they asked of him; now they were moving in to finish the job. And that meant wiping out any evidence that they'd ever been to Sindorin. And any witnesses.

Bashir sensed Ro and Kel come up behind him. The Ingavi cried aloud when he saw the images on the screen, then ran for the door. Ro called out to him, "Kel! Wait! We can help."

"No," Taran'atar said. "We can't. It isn't a battle we can win. This mission is over."

"I'm not talking about winning," Ro said. "I'm talking about keeping a promise."

Kel had little patience for their debate, but Bashir sensed that he understood and sympathized with the conflict raging inside Ro. Fighting his desire to join his comrades, he stayed long enough to say, "You have already kept your promise, Ro. You have freed us from the Jem'Hadar. It was much more than we could have hoped for." He pointed the muzzle of his rifle at the monitor. "Do not make the mistake of believing it is your responsibility to resolve this. Not *everything* is your responsibility. The weight of so much guilt would crush you."

And then he was gone.

Ro tried to grab her weapon from Bashir, but she was no match for him with her burned hand. "Doctor," she said. "I'm begging you . . ."

Bashir shook his head. "No," he said. "Taran'atar's right. We have to go. If we stay . . ."

"If we stay," Ro spat back, "we die. But if we go, the Ingavi will die. Maybe not all of them, maybe not immediately, but they can't survive much longer if we don't *do* something." She lurched toward the door, but Taran'atar put his hand on her shoulder, not restraining her, only reminding her of his presence. Ro seemed to sag within herself.

"How," he asked Bashir, "do we get out of here?"

Bashir mentally scanned the complex's layout and had begun to plan an escape route when he was distracted by the flash of disruptor fire. But something was different. "Look here," he said, calling to the First, pointing at the monitor. "This is disruptor fire, isn't it?"

The First barely glanced at the images. "My soldiers," he said. "They must be the ones who called me earlier. I've lost contact with them." He checked the grid coordinates on the surveillance feed. "Who are they?" he asked, referring to the humans with phasers.

"They're Locken's accomplices," said Dax, who had been silently watching the Jem'Hadar for the past several minutes. "They're the ones responsible for all this."

The First gritted his teeth. "Then," he snarled, "I will gather my soldiers and we will greet our makers appropriately." He glanced at Bashir, but then spoke to Taran'atar. "There is a transporter pad in the room at the other end of this corridor. You can use it to get to your ship. Go now."

Taran'atar nodded once, but the First wasn't even thinking about him anymore. As they ran down the corridor, Bashir heard the sounds of phaser fire slashing through walls and doors. The Section 31 operatives didn't seem to be encountering any resistance, though he suspected that would change as soon as the First reached his men.

They'd monitored events from inside the plasma storms as best they could. Cloaked surveillance probes had recorded some very interesting images on most of the frequencies in the EM spectrum, detailed enough that they knew the moment Locken was dead, but not the exact circumstances, save that somehow Bashir had turned the would-be Khan's own Jem'Hadar against him. But once the kill was confirmed, Cole gave the order to deploy.

He took off his night-vision lenses and glanced around to get a better look at the spot he had staked out as his observation post. The sun had just barely climbed over the top of the tree line and he would have to switch to the standard binoculars now. *The worst part about dawn operations,* he reflected, *is that sooner or later you have to see everything that was done under cover of darkness.* There were bodies everywhere, most of them Jem'Hadar, but some of the local ape creatures, too. A few of his men had gone down, but not many, and well within acceptable losses.

But Cole knew some things about this rain forest. It wouldn't be long before things started to smell bad. And there were scavengers crawling over some of the bodies. These would disappear as soon as the sun came up, but then the insects would begin to appear and they would lay eggs and the eggs would turn into larvae and then the larvae would begin squirming—

Cole was glad he would be gone within the hour. He was here to make sure the cleanup operation was well under way, but he had no intention of staying for the whole thing.

One of his runners ran up beside him and waited to be acknowledged. Cole made him wait for a few seconds, then spoke without turning. "Yes?"

"Sir, sensors report a Starfleet runabout lifting off to the northwest of us. You gave orders to be alerted if we picked up on anything like that."

"Right. I did, didn't I?" He picked up a pair of standard-issue binoculars and studied the battlefield—no, the killing field. Cole shook his head in wonder at how careless Sloan had been to let Bashir get away. He would have been an astonishingly effective field agent. Not that he didn't have other uses . . . Well, that explained where the locals got phaser rifles. He wondered how many of Bashir's team were making it off alive.

"Orders, sir?" the runner asked.

Cole lowered his binoculars, and stared into the northwest sky, almost convincing himself he could spot the fleeing runabout with his naked eyes. "Let it go," he said.

"Sir?"

"Let it go." He studied the front of the compound and wondered how many quantum torpedoes it would take to level the place once they had cleaned out the useful bits.

The *Euphrates* would, as Ro had said, get them home, but she wasn't the same ship she had been when she left DS9. Ezri was fairly sure she could get them out of the Badlands, but if they ran into any major plasma-storm activity, it would be a near thing. Once clear of the Badlands, they would activate the distress beacon and head for home at a conservative pace.

Julian was in the back treating Taran'atar's wounds, which were already healing at an astonishing rate. According to his readings, Taran'atar had suffered a punctured lung, but it was completely healed now.

Ro was back in the aft compartment. She wanted to be alone.

And then there was Julian. She had seen him in some black moods, but nothing like this. In his eyes, the fact that they had probably just saved the quadrant from months or years of struggle and strife didn't mean anything. The only thing that mattered was that he hadn't been able to slay his dragon. Section 31 was still out there, still three steps ahead of all of them.

The sensor alarm blipped and Ezri glanced at the readout. The short-range sensors had begun to act up shortly after liftoff and she was tempted to just shut them down, but she was worried about encountering another orbital weapons platform. She checked the display and found—what? A sensor ghost of some kind. She reset the master grid and the ghost disappeared.

Steering to starboard, giving a plasma plume a very wide berth, she wondered why so many of their missions didn't have happy endings.

Chapter Twenty

"Deep Space 9, this is the *Euphrates*. Come in, Deep Space 9." Ro waited for several seconds for a response, then repeated the message.

"Are you sure the transmitter is working?" Ezri asked.

Ro stared at her, expressionless. "Would you like to try?" she asked.

Ezri smiled guiltily. "No, sorry. Go ahead. I'm just getting worried."

"We're all worried," Bashir said from the engineering station behind them. "But there's no way to be sure whether the scanning problem resides in the runabout's systems or in the diagnostic programs. Everything *looks* like it's working, but we could be transmitting on the wrong frequency . . ."

"Or the station's comm system could be offline," Ro added.

"But shouldn't we be able to pick up one of the patrolling starships?" Ezri asked.

"There may be subspace interference," Ro suggested. She didn't elaborate; she didn't need to. Everyone aboard knew that only a massive explosion was capable of causing that much interference—the kind of explosion no one wanted to think about.

"Can we get any more speed out of this thing?" Bashir asked.

Ro shook her head. "Without knowing whether the diagnostic programs are functioning properly—and I'll say again that I don't think they are—then, no. Warp two is the maximum and we're taking a big chance there. If it were up to me, we'd drop to impulse and send out a distress call."

Bashir didn't want to admit it, but he knew that what Ro was suggesting was not only proper protocol, but the sensible thing to do. The problem was he didn't feel like being sensible—he wanted to go home. "Best speed, Lieutenant," he said, rising from his chair. It was his turn to get some sleep. "But do whatever you think is best."

"Yes, sir," Ro said flatly, and it was clear from her tone that if they had done what she thought best they would still be on Sindorin. *A problem to deal with after I've had some sleep,* Bashir decided.

Bashir was so weary that when he lay down he thought for a moment that Ezri had suddenly doubled the gravity, but then realized, *No, it's only my body surrendering.* He closed his eyes and a gruff voice asked, *"So, what did you learn, Doctor?"*

Bashir struggled feebly to open his eyes, but it was too late, his system had been too abused. He couldn't rouse himself and he couldn't refuse to answer. *What did I learn? I learned that it's always possible to feel more alone than you thought you could ever feel.*

And from up out of the dark came the approving voice of Sloan. *"Excellent, Doctor. You've learned your lesson well."*

"Julian, you have to come see this."

Bashir's eyes snapped open. He didn't remember closing them, which was unusual for him because most of the time sleep was an elusive thing. He tried to sit up, but his arms felt numb, his legs rubbery. "What? Yes. . . . Coming." His mouth felt like a dried-up tennis ball and his eyelids were grating over the surface of his eyeballs. He had been dreaming about . . . something disturbing. What? Oh, the clones . . . just before he had triggered the phaser, the clones had come to life and pressed their faces against the tubes. . . .

He stumbled to the cockpit and felt the runabout shudder as they switched over from warp engines to impulse. "What's happening?" he asked, his eyes still not clear. "Where are we?"

But then he looked out through the main viewport and he knew where they were. It hung there—a glistening jewel, an ornament against the night— Deep Space 9. Nog had done his job: all the lights were on, much brighter even than usual, blazing so brilliantly that the stars themselves seemed dim.

Ezri, seated in the copilot's chair, reached up, took his hand, and said, "We're home, Julian."

Ro repeated, *"We're* home," and it was clear that the betrayal of the Ingavi was still foremost on her mind. Bashir felt it, too, but didn't begrudge himself the wave of relief that swept through him.

"Can we contact them?" he asked.

"No," Ezri said. "It's definitely our subspace transmitter. The diagnostic program sorted it out while you were asleep. It also said we were safe to go to warp four, so we got back a lot faster than we had expected."

Bashir did the calculations. "So I was asleep . . . ten hours?"

"Twelve," Ro said. "The rest of us took turns. We figured you needed the sleep."

He didn't know how to respond, so he said only, "Thank you," and gripped Ezri's hand more tightly. A shadow crossed between them and the station and he looked up. Directly above them, a Klingon attack cruiser shed its cloak.

"They're challenging us," Ro said.

"Come to a halt," Bashir said. "And release the emergency beacon. They'll figure it out."

Ro did as he asked, and several minutes later the attack cruiser grappled the *Euphrates* with its tractor beam and set them down on a runabout pad. Suddenly her combadge—the only one to survive the mission—chirped for attention. *"Ops to Lieutenant Ro."*

"Ro here. Go ahead, Nog."

"Lieutenant? Is everyone all right? I have no other combadge signals from your team."

"We're all okay, Nog."

"That's a relief. Colonel Kira would like you all to report to her office directly."

"Of course she would," Ro said quietly.

"So," Nog continued, *"doesn't the station look great?"*

Even Ro smiled a little at that. "Yeah, Nog," she said softly. "It sure does."

• • •

"That's a hell of a story," Kira said when the companions finished delivering their report. "My only question is: How much of this can you tell to Starfleet Command?"

The question seemed to surprise Dax, but Bashir understood what she was asking. "I think we can tell Admiral Ross most of the tale," he replied. "Though I expect he'll have to edit it heavily before Starfleet shares it with any other Federation worlds. I'd like to be able to tell the Romulans *something* about their missing ships. But the part about what happened on New Beijing ..."

"That'll never come out," Kira sighed. "On the bright side, now that we know what was done, Starfleet can take steps to ensure that such a thing never happens again."

Ro sat stone-faced, arms crossed over her chest. "I can't help but notice," she said, "that none of you has said a word about the Ingavi. What are we going to do about them?" She looked from face to face. "Colonel? Doctor? Any thoughts? Do you even *care?*"

"You're being unfair," Dax said. "Of course we care. And it's not like we didn't accomplish anything. If we hadn't gone to Sindorin, probably all the Ingavi would be dead by now."

"Most of the Ingavi probably *are* dead by now," Ro muttered.

"That's enough," Kira snapped. "This is hard enough without everyone sniping at each other." She turned to Ro, modulating her tone. "You're welcome to make your thoughts on the subject clear in your formal report, but otherwise I think that's the end of the topic for now. We'll do what we can."

"Right," Ro said. "When things cool off. When the Romulans stop searching the area for the missing ships. When no one will have any reason to suspect anything terrible has happened on Sindorin." She leaned forward and slapped the top of Kira's desk with the flat of her hand. "When they're all dead."

"Ro ..." Dax began, but Kira signaled for her to be silent.

Unable to listen to any more, Ro rose from her seat without asking leave. "I'm going back to my office to check on some things. Sir."

"When you get there," Kira said, "contact Commander Vaughn. He left me a message saying you should get in touch with him. He's on Empok Nor with one of the engineering teams."

"Where *is* Empok Nor?" Bashir asked.

"Nog towed it into orbit of Cajara."

Cajara. The Bajoran system's seventh planet, Bashir recalled. *Currently on the same side of the sun as DS9. A short trip by runabout.*

Ro sighed, picked up her travel-stained bag, and headed for the door.

As soon as she left, Bashir rose. "Well, you'll have to excuse me, too."

"No, wait. Stay right there," Kira said, pointing Bashir back into his seat. "I already know what you're thinking."

Bashir sagged back into his chair. "What am I thinking?" he asked.

Kira folded her arms. "One: You're thinking that you utterly failed because you weren't able to bring back the evidence you wanted in order to expose Section 31 and bring it to justice."

Bashir smiled wanly.

"And, two," Kira continued, "you're pondering ways you could slip back to Sindorin while no one is looking and save the Ingavi. 'It should be simple,' you're thinking. 'I'm ever so much smarter than everyone else. And, oh, while I'm there, I'll look around for some more evidence that I can someday use to crush Section 31. And, no, I don't need to bother telling the colonel because she would just try to tell me I'm being an idiot.' "

Bashir's smile turned into a weary grin. "You've been listening at my door," he said. "That's pretty good, though I'm not nearly that humble."

Kira almost smiled in return. "I've ordered ops to keep a close eye on all outgoing traffic. I already have one missing person; I don't want another." Then, she filled in Dax, Bashir, and Taran'atar on the situation regarding Jake Sisko.

When she finished, Dax rose and said, "I'm going to call Kasidy. She must be frantic."

"She seemed all right when I spoke with her," Kira replied.

Dax shrugged. "And she probably was at the time. But the hormones kick in at unexpected times. Pregnancy, you know. I remember—"

Kira nodded, also remembering. "All right. Thank you, Ezri. Yes, please call her and tell her we'll come down to Bajor to see her as soon as possible."

Dax nodded and left.

Bashir rose to follow, but before he could leave Kira stopped him and said, "I know this must have been difficult for you, Julian. So let me just say thank you. If you have trouble sleeping tonight, think about how many people you saved on this mission."

Bashir nodded gratefully and said, "You're getting good at this command thing, Nerys. That almost makes me feel better. It almost helps me forget the ones I *didn't* save."

"I don't want you to forget them, Julian," Kira said. "I just want you to forgive yourself for not being the superhuman you sometimes think you are."

Bashir locked eyes with her for several seconds, unblinking, then bowed his head, the tension that he had been holding in his shoulders and neck melting away. Finally, he nodded, and with a heartfelt "Thank you, Nerys," he left.

That left only the colonel and Taran'atar.

He had been sitting in the corner, in the seat farthest from her desk, and though he had not said a word during the debriefing unless asked a direct question, Kira had sensed his interest in the proceedings.

Even after Bashir had left, he did not speak for some time, but only stared at her from beneath his brow. She waited for him to speak, but finally decided that Jem'Hadar weren't accustomed to speaking first. "Dr. Bashir said that the mission would have failed without your assistance," she said. "Thank you for that. It must have been difficult for you to be here so short a time, and already finding yourself having to face other Jem'Hadar in combat, twice now."

"These were not the first times Jem'Hadar have fought Jem'Hadar. They will not be the last."

Kira mentally filed that statement for later consideration. "The doctor also said that you were badly injured and that some of the injuries might not have been battle-related. Again, if that was the case, I appreciate how you might have suffered. I know a little bit about torture—"

"How to take it or how to give it?" Taran'atar asked.

Kira hesitated. "I don't think I want to answer that question," she finally replied. "Let's just leave it at that."

"All right," Taran'atar replied. "We will."

When he did not rise to leave, Kira asked, "Is there anything else we can do for you right now? Do you want to send a message back to the Dominion? I could arrange it if you like."

"I was not instructed to make reports, so I will not. The Founders will contact me when they wish—if they wish."

Again, he did not rise to leave, so Kira asked again, "Something else?"

Taran'atar inhaled deeply, then slowly released it. She could see that he was trying to make up his mind about something, but she resolved to wait it out in silence. At last, he leaned forward in his chair, balled up one fist, and cupped it with his other hand. He said, "Lieutenant Ro told me that she has never met anyone who has as much faith in her gods as you. Is this so?"

Kira was more than a little surprised to find out that Ro had any opinions about anyone's spiritual life, let alone Kira's own, but for the sake of discussion, she decided to agree. "It's hard to measure such things, but, yes, I believe my faith is very strong."

"How did it get to be so strong?" Taran'atar asked. "How can you . . . not doubt?"

Kira leaned back in her chair. She hadn't been prepared for a theological discussion today, especially not with a Jem'Hadar. She resolved to cuff Odo the next time she saw him . . .

. . . if she ever saw him again.

But she said, "I do doubt. Every day, I doubt everything. I doubt that I'm doing this job right. I doubt that I'm a good and decent person. I even doubt that we'll all be here tomorrow. I doubt, and doubt, and doubt. But through it all, I draw strength from the idea that the Prophets are weaving a tapestry in which my life is a thread, and that my faith helps bring me closer to understanding my part in the whole. It's become my belief of late that the Prophets have no use for blind devotion. They want us—their people—to question our beliefs every day, because the only way our faith can grow stronger is by having it challenged." Kira stopped then, slightly embarrassed. "Does any of that make sense?" she asked.

Taran'atar mulled it over. "This," he said at length, "is all very paradoxical."

Kira shrugged. "At best," she said, "it's paradoxical. On its bad days, it's just complete nonsense."

The Jem'Hadar grunted his assent.

"If nothing else," she concluded, "have faith in Odo. I know I do."

He looked up at her then and the glaze of confusion in his eyes seemed to lift and he nodded. "Then perhaps that," he said, "will be our common ground."

The corpse of Empok Nor was growing cool; and though several of DS9's emergency generators had been transferred over to keep the chill out of a few sections, Vaughn found something sad about it, but he seemed to be the only one who did. Perhaps it was a function of having seen so much death over the years. *Old people,* he reflected, *think about death more.* Well, nothing profound there. *They also think about being cold more,* he decided, and zipped his coat up to the neck and flipped up the collar.

It was one of the old-issue Starfleet field coats, probably one of the best garments the quartermaster's office had ever issued, and Vaughn, like most officers who had been cadets eighty years ago, had held on to his. They were sturdy, had deep pockets, and the heating cells were well placed.

Vaughn was standing at the docking port in one of the station's lower pylons, watching the stars through the airlock viewport. He appreciated that about Cardassian station design, being able to actually *see* the ship approaching the dock rather than relying on a monitor or a holotank. He was thinking about the term "mothball." Many, many years ago, he had looked the word up in one of the older editions of the *Oxford Dictionary of Terran Languages* and had been surprised to find that it had something to do with a substance that was stored with clothing to kill insect larvae. The definition still made him shake his head and smile in wonderment; what a wonderfully flexible language Late English had been.

"Mothballed," he said aloud, letting the word roll over his tongue. How long would it be before someone somewhere decided it was time to mothball *him?* He glanced out the viewport at the huge docking ring above him and decided, *Well, a little longer, anyway.*

Someone was coming up behind him. It was in itself unusual enough that Vaughn hadn't heard the approach. There were only two or three possibilities for who it might be. One of the three would have killed him by now. The second . . . well, he knew it couldn't be her, because he always knew exactly where she was.

"Dr. Bashir," Vaughn said without turning. "What can I do for you?"

Bashir stopped walking, obviously puzzled. Vaughn heard him take a deep breath, then release it slowly. *He's angry,* Vaughn decided, *but trying to keep it under control. Almost doing it, too.*

"I need to ask you some questions," Bashir said, obviously struggling to remain polite. "And I'd like some straight answers, please." Then he added, "For once."

Vaughn turned around to look at him, then leaned back against the airlock portal. "Of course, Doctor."

Bashir closed the distance between them, then stopped, set his feet as if he was expecting Vaughn to throw a punch at him. "You knew what was going to happen."

Vaughn cocked his head to one side. "That's not a question."

Bashir sighed and began to turn around to leave.

Vaughn held up his hands. "All right, all right. Sorry. Evasion is a difficult habit to give up. The answer is, no, I didn't know exactly what was going to happen. I had suspicions. I know how Thirty-One works, Doctor, and there's always more than one meaning to anything they say." He pulled his combadge off the front of his uniform and held it up for Bashir to see. Then he curled his fingers around it, shook his fist in the air, and opened his palm. The combadge was gone. "And always remember," he added, "whatever it is they let you see, no matter how interesting it might be, they're only letting you see it so you won't pay attention to something else." He held out his other hand and showed Bashir a combadge. Bashir shrugged and then Vaughn pointed at the front of the doctor's uniform. His own combadge was gone.

Bashir held out his hand and Vaughn dropped the combadge into it. "Section 31 needed Locken out of the way. And while they most likely could have mustered a force capable of reducing him, his Jem'Hadar, and the hatchery to ashes, they would have lost what they were really after all along."

"His data," Bashir guessed.

"Yes," said Vaughn. "But the only way to accomplish both goals, get rid of Locken and obtain his data, was to put someone on the inside, something Section 31 couldn't do. Cole needed you to do it for him. Once you took care of this for him, their job would be simpler. They got what they wanted, and they covered their tracks. Section 31's first principle is to protect the secret of their existence. Any other motivation they might espouse is secondary and serves only to reinforce the first principle. It may have been different once, but not anymore. It's their greatest strength and their greatest weakness."

Bashir studied Vaughn carefully. "Are you telling me, then, that you *aren't* one of them? Another Starfleet officer on a short leash—"

Vaughn's eyes narrowed dangerously. "I'm not on anybody's leash, Doctor. And I've *never* worked for Thirty-One."

Bashir saw the truth then, and the revelation left him breathless. "You've been fighting them, too."

"Longer than you've been alive," Vaughn said. He turned to look out the viewport again. "I think, Doctor, that you've always been and always will be a bit of a romantic. Your latest romantic fantasy is this idea that you're the solitary opponent to this gigantic conspiracy. It feeds your ego."

Bashir began to protest, but Vaughn waved him to silence. "There's nothing wrong with having an ego, Doctor," he said. "It's a necessity if you're going to survive this. The truth is that there are only a few of us. The other much sadder truth is that the only ones among us who have survived opposing Thirty-One are the ones who are patient, and who can think even more moves ahead than they do."

"A lot of good any of that did the Ingavi," Bashir muttered.

In response, Vaughn tapped a command code into the companel on the wall. He pointed up to Empok Nor's docking ring, where an odd-looking, blocky starship suddenly decloaked.

"What the hell is that?" Bashir asked.

"That, Doctor, is a mobile environment simulator—a holoship, for want of a better word. The only one of its kind, in fact. It was custom-built in secret and illegally equipped with a cloaking device. It's a relic from a failed Section 31 operation in the Briar Patch last year. Thirty-One was never implicated, unfortunately. The blame went instead to a single rogue admiral, now dead, who was working with the Son'a. But those of us who have made it our business to oppose Thirty-One knew perfectly well who and what was pulling his strings.

"After the operation failed, the holoship was officially confiscated by Starfleet Command and destroyed." A small smile made its way into Vaughn's beard. "At least, that's what the paperwork says."

"Are you telling me you stole it out from under the noses of Starfleet Command *and* Section 31? But why?"

Vaughn shrugged. "For a rainy day. The idea of using one of Section 31's own instruments against them appealed to me. This one was designed specifically to relocate a small colony—in secret."

The last piece clicked into place for Bashir, and he started laughing. "You got the Ingavi off Sindorin!"

Vaughn nodded. "Most of them. As many as we could find in the time we had. And I didn't do it personally. But as I said . . . you aren't alone."

"Ezri mentioned that we picked up a sensor ghost while leaving the planet."

"Nothing is perfect, Doctor," Vaughn said. "Not even one of *my* plans. You'll learn that as we work together."

Bashir suddenly smiled, a roguish, almost boyish grin. He looked like he might climb through the airlock without an e-suit to get to the ship. "But—Ro! You have to tell her! She was devastated!"

"She's already up there," Vaughn explained. "Trying to make it clear to the Ingavi what happened. With only mixed results, I'm afraid. They're pretty shocked by this whole affair, though she seems to be getting a lot of help from one in particular."

"Is it Kel?" Bashir asked. "He made it?"

"I didn't catch the name. All I can tell you is that whoever he is, he seemed very pleased with himself."

"It's Kel!" Bashir shouted. "I have to tell Ezri! I have to explain it to Kira! Otherwise, she'll start making plans—"

"The colonel knows," Vaughn said. "We couldn't have done this without her looking the other way at the proper time. And as for Lieutenant Dax—I think you should wait."

"Wait? Wait for what?"

"Wait until you've gone over there and started doing some medical assessments on our guests. Then, you help me explain that they're to be resettled on Ingav—which, incidentally, is a Federation protectorate these days. And then . . ." He clapped Bashir on the shoulder. "Then you come back to DS9 with me and I'll make you a cup of good twig tea, and together, *together,* we'll begin to make plans."

DEMONS OF AIR AND DARKNESS

Keith R. A. DeCandido

For David Henderson,
the world's most professional fan.

Historian's Note

This novel takes place about two weeks after the events of the *Star Trek: Deep Space Nine* novel *Section 31: Abyss,* and also after the events of the *Star Trek: Voyager* episode "Pathfinder."

The doors of heaven and hell are adjacent and identical.

—NIKOS KAZANTZAKIS

Chapter One

The Delta Quadrant

"Shields one and two are now down, shield three is buckling, and warp drive is down!"

Controller Marssi of the Malon supertanker *Apsac* snarled at Kron's report.

For years, she had heard stories of this ship and its strange alien crew. Some had called it the "ship of death." At least two other Malon export vessels had encountered it, and neither had come out of the experience intact.

Now it was attacking the *Apsac*. They'd already been forced to drop out of warp, dangerously close to a star system. Marssi had no idea what had prompted the attack, nor did she care. She just wanted it to stop.

"Return fire," she snapped, moving from her small circular console in the center of the bridge to Kron's larger one against the starboard bulkhead.

"We *have* been," Kron said. "Our weapons have had no effect."

Marssi rubbed her nostrils. The smell of burning conduits was starting to fill the bridge. "I take it they aren't answering our hails?"

"Of *course* not. They don't want to talk, they want to destroy us, same as they do everyone else." Kron turned back to his console. "Shield three is now down. Our weapons banks are almost exhausted and we still haven't even put a dent in their hull. They're coming in for another pass." As he spoke, more weapons fire impacted on the *Apsac*'s hull.

Kron spit in anger. His saliva was tinged with green. He motioned as if to wipe hair off his face, which under other circumstances would have made Marssi smile. Kron had been making that gesture during times of stress in all the decades they'd served together, but the old man's gold-brown hair had long since thinned past the possibility of ever actually impeding his vision.

"Shield four just went down and shield five is at critical levels," he said. "They're on a parabolic course—they'll be back in weapons range in two minutes."

Marssi cursed. She had designed the *Apsac* herself, supervising its entire construction personally. The vessel was groundbreaking—it had seven separate shields in addition to the reinforced tanks. If that redundancy wasn't enough, the shields were strengthened by an enhancer of her own design. (In truth, designed by someone to whom she'd paid a considerable sum, but as far as she was concerned that made it hers.) Her ship had the lowest incidence of thetaradiation poisoning of any export vessel on Malon Prime and she'd set several records for hauling. Perhaps best of all, her core laborers had a survival rate of sixty percent—twice that of most other export vessels—and she was able to pay them well above the already-lucrative going rate.

Her profit margin was huge—the cost of constructing the ship and designing the shield enhancer had been recouped by her second run. With this latest trip, she would clear enough to finally buy that house in the mountains that she and Stvoran had had their sights on all these years.

And now, Marssi thought, *these be-damned aliens are going to ruin it.*

From the big console behind her, Gril said, "Controller, look at this." Gril was a new hire—this was his first run. *He's certainly getting more than he signed on for,* Marssi thought bitterly. *We all are.*

The controller walked over to the young man. "What is it?"

"We're getting an analysis of their hull—it's made of monotanium! Can you imagine that? No wonder our weapons have had no effect. If we could make our ships out of that—"

Rolling his eyes, Kron said, "Do you know how much it'd cost to mass-produce enough monotanium to build a tanker, Gril?"

"I know, I know, but think of it! We'd never have another tank rupture."

"We've never had one in the first place, you idiot," Kron muttered.

Defensively, Gril said, "You know what I mean."

Marssi looked more closely at the readouts as they scrolled across Gril's black screen in clear green letters. In addition to the powerful hull, the small, squat ship had a very efficient dicyclic warp signature, decades ahead of anything the Malons had developed for faster-than-light travel.

"You're right, Gril," she said. "Those aliens do know how to build a ship."

An alarm sounded. Marssi heard the staccato rhythm of Kron's boots on the bulkhead as he ran to one of the other consoles. She turned to see that he seemed a bit blurry—a green haze was starting to descend upon the bridge. *One of those burning conduits must be leaking* arvat. *That's just what we need.*

Kron pushed a few buttons and then pounded the console with his fist. "Dammit! The warp core containment field is showing signs of collapse and the impulse drive is down." He turned to look at Marssi, his yellow eyes smoldering with anger, his golden skin tinged with sweat. "We can't even move now. And they'll be in range in one minute."

Wonderful, Marssi thought. *If the tanks don't rupture and the shields don't go down, we could still die from a containment breach.*

"Who *are* these people, anyhow?" Gril asked as he nervously scratched his left nostril. "What do they want with us?"

"The Hirogen are hunters," Marssi said grimly, walking back to her center console and running a check to see if she could get the propulsion systems back online. "No one knows where they come from, but they've shown up in every part of known space. Supposedly, they'll hunt anything and everything. This particular ship has been reported in this sector at least twice."

"From what I hear," Kron said with a nasty look at Gril as he moved back across the bridge to his own console, "there's only one way to survive an encounter with them: don't be their prey."

"But—but we *are* their prey."

"Smart boy," Kron said with a grim smile, then glanced at a readout. "That's interesting, they've slowed down. They're still closing, but it'll be another minute or two before they're in range." He snorted. "They probably realize that we can't fight back, so they're going to take their time with us now."

Gril shook his head. "I don't get it. Why hunt *us?*"

"It's what they *do,*" Kron snapped.

"Yeah, but whatever they do to us will kill them, too, if the tanks rupture or the core breaches. What's the good of being a hunter if you don't live to enjoy the fruits of the hunt?"

Marssi turned to Gril. "That's a good point. Maybe he just doesn't know." She looked at Kron. "Open a channel to them."

Kron snorted. "They haven't answered a single hail yet."

"They don't have to answer, they just have to listen. Open the channel."

Scowling, Kron pushed three buttons in sequence. "Fine, it's open."

Marssi took a deep breath—then regretted it, as the burning-conduit smell had gotten worse. "Attention Hirogen ship. If you continue with your present course of action, this ship will be destroyed and our cargo will be exposed to space. We are currently carrying over half a trillion isotons of antimatter waste. We have heard stories of how Hirogen hunters can weather anything, but I doubt that even you could survive being exposed to those levels of theta radiation. Over half our shields are down and a warp core containment breach is imminent. There's a danger of physical damage to the tankers as well. Any one of these can lead to this entire star system being irradiated and will result in the instant death of you, us, and anyone else in the immediate vicinity. Please, break off your attack—for your own sake, if not for ours."

Kron's eyes went wide. "They're replying."

"You sound surprised," Marssi said dryly.

"That's because I am," Kron said, shooting her a look. "On screen."

A face appeared on the console in front of Marssi. The creature fit the descriptions from the stories she'd heard of the Hirogen: a face of rough, mottled skin, with the rest of the body covered in metallic, faceted body armor. The helmet had four ridges that began close together at the forehead and spread out and around to the back of the head. This one also had a streak of white paint on either side of each middle ridge. As he spoke, he reached up to his forehead with a gloved hand. Red paint dripped from the index finger, and the Hirogen applied it to the section of the helmet under the leftmost ridge.

"Prey. You will surrender."

The screen went blank before Marssi could say anything in reply.

"Either they're immune to theta radiation, or they don't believe you," Kron said. "Or maybe they just don't care."

Again, Marssi cursed. "Any luck getting the propulsion systems back up?"

"No. The Hirogen ship's velocity is still pretty leisurely. Rumor has it they like to deal with their prey one on one. My guess is that they're going to try to board us."

Since the Hirogen ship was only a fraction of the size of the tanker, this seemed reasonable to Marssi. *There is no way I'm going to surrender to that monster.*

I've heard about what they do to people they capture—weird experiments, dissections, and worse.

So, even if they surrendered, they were going to die.

If that's the way it's going to be, fine. They told me a woman could never be a controller. They told me the Apsac would never work right. I didn't let that stop me then, and I damn well won't let it stop me now.

She looked at the image of the Hirogen ship on her screen. *And if I don't, at least I'll have the satisfaction of knowing you'll die too, you waste-sucking toad.*

Kron announced, "They're firing again," and the *Apsac* lurched. "That did it. Shields five and six are both down and seven is buckling. One more shot, and we've got serious problems."

"Yes, Kron," Marssi muttered, shaking her head, "our problems until now have been quite droll."

"Controller, I'm picking up something!" Gril cried before Kron had a chance to reply. "Something just appeared a hundred and fifty *hentas* off the nose!"

"I'm picking it up, too," Kron said, much more calmly. "It's—a hole."

Marssi blinked. "I beg your pardon?"

"A hole."

"Can you be a *little* more specific, Kron?"

"No," Kron snapped. "That's the only way I can describe this. It's an opening of some kind, and based on the readings I'm getting—huh. There are stars and planets and such on the other side, but it's not matching anything on our star charts."

Another impact. Gril said, "Shield seven will go on the next shot!"

"So it's a wormhole," Marssi said to Kron.

Kron shook his head. "No, it's completely stable, and it doesn't have any of the properties of a wormhole. In fact, it doesn't have the properties of much of anything. I'm not picking up any particulate matter that wasn't there before, no changes in the chemical composition of the area around it. It's just—a hole." He looked over at Marssi, and the controller was amazed at the look of disbelief on her old comrade's face. "It's like it's some kind of—of gateway to another star system."

"What the *tuul* is it doing here?" Gril asked.

"Who the *tuul* cares?" Marssi said with a grim smile. *Maybe I will see Stvoran and Ella again.* "Kron, use maneuvering thrusters—I want the *Apsac* positioned so that the openings to the tanks are facing that hole."

Kron returned her smile, though his was less grim for a change. "Consider it done. Thrusters online."

Marssi nodded. She remembered one controller who had once been the most profligate of those who disposed of Malon's industrial waste. He had found, in essence, a hole to dump the waste into—a hole located in a starless region known simply as the Void. Unfortunately, another ship full of irritating aliens—the *Voyager*—had forced him to stop by cutting off his access to the Void. Marssi hadn't minded, as that opened the field a bit—his success was in danger of putting several controllers out of business—and it gave her the opportunity to secure the funds to build the *Apsac*.

Now she'd found her own version of that Void.

"Preparing to eject the tanks," Gril said.

"No," Marssi snapped, whirling on the young man. "We're just ejecting the contents into the hole."

Gril blinked. "But—but Controller, that'll expose the waste! The radiation—"

"We'll only be exposed for a short time, not enough to have any lasting effect. I'm not losing the tanks down that hole as well. Unless, of course, you want to replace them out of your earnings?"

"N-no," Grill said quietly, and turned back to his console.

"That may be academic," Kron said. "Shield seven just went down and the Hirogen is at four *hentas* and closing."

"Maybe. But even if we die, I want it to be just us who do. I won't let Stvoran and Ella live with the disgrace of being the husband and daughter of the woman who destroyed a star system."

"Very considerate," Kron said dryly. "We're in position now."

"Begin ejecting the waste."

Marssi stood at her console and saw the external camera's image of the green-tinged toxic material start to jet its way into the vacuum of space.

Soon enough it'll be in the hole and someone else's problem. My problem is the Hirogen. Once we no longer have to worry about the tanks rupturing, maybe we'll have a better chance against them.

Right on cue, the Hirogen ship came into view.

An errant cluster of waste material tumbled right toward it. It collided with the hunter's small vessel with sufficient impact that even a monotanium hull couldn't save it.

Like all explosions in space, it was brief, but no less spectacular for all that. It blossomed evenly, then contracted into nothingness—aside from the green mass that had caused the explosion, which continued to tumble toward the hole.

To Controller Marssi, it was the most beautiful sight she'd seen since the completed *Apsac* was first unveiled on Malon Prime.

She still had no idea what that hole was or where it came from, and right now she didn't care. All she knew was that if it hadn't shown up when it did, she never would have ejected her payload, and the Hirogen ship would still be in one piece.

"Looks like you beat the odds again, Controller," Kron said with a smile, his words mirroring Marssi's own thoughts.

Laughing, Marssi said, "Did you ever doubt it?"

"Yes, every second. But, like all the other times you've proved me wrong, I'm glad you've done so."

"Controller," Gril said, his voice shaking, "I must protest this! We don't know what's on the other side of that hole! What if—"

Marssi knew exactly what Gril was going to say, and so was happy to interrupt him. "Gril, what is the mission statement of this vessel?"

"To—to dispose of the waste that accrues from our use of antimatter in a manner that will not be harmful to the Malon community as a whole," he said as if reciting from a textbook—*probably,* Marssi thought, recalling Gril's age, *read recently.*

"Exactly," she said, advancing slowly on the young man who, for his part, started to cower as she moved closer. "And we have done that, and also kept this star system from being contaminated. We've saved millions of lives today—most notably our own—eliminated one of the scourges of this sector, *and* we've done our job. Not to mention the fact that we've made an astonishing discovery that could very well spell even more profit for us down the road. So what, precisely, are you protesting, Gril?"

Gril swallowed, and once again scratched his left nostril. "Well, when you put it that way, Controller, I guess—nothing."

"Good. Keep an eye on the waste, and tell the core laborers to keep on their toes." Blinking a few times, she added, "And get someone to fix that damn *arvat* conduit—I don't know what's worse, the haze or the smell."

"Yes, Controller." Gril returned to his console.

Kron shook his head and chuckled. "Were we ever that young?"

"I was," Marssi said. "But not you. When you were born, you were already a cranky old man." Placing an encouraging hand on her old friend's shoulder, she said, "We need to get the warp drive fixed. As soon as the last of the waste has gone through that hole, I want to get back home and file a claim on this little discovery of ours."

"The drive'll take at least a day or two to fix."

Marssi shrugged. "It'll be at least that long before all the the tanks are emptied."

"Good point," Kron said, and with a nod to Gril, sent the younger Malon down to engineering to surpervise the repairs.

Marssi turned back to her console, and watched as the first bit of waste material approached the event horizon of the hole and then disappeared from sight. Even if she wanted to know what was on the other side, she'd have a difficult time getting a proper sensor reading now, with all the radiation in the way.

Besides, she didn't want to know. She didn't care. She'd done her job. *I can't wait to tell Ella about this,* she thought with a smile. Her ten-year-old daughter always loved to hear stories about her mother's trips. Marssi predicted that this one—where she defeated one of the most brutal foes imaginable and also made an astounding new discovery—would quickly become Ella's favorite.

Chapter Two

The Gamma Quadrant

"The communications array is now online, sir."

Commander Elias Vaughn didn't smile at Nog's report, but the lieutenant hadn't really expected him to. In the month since Vaughn had been assigned as the first officer of Deep Space 9 and commanding officer of the *U.S.S. Defiant,* Nog had seldom seen the human smile while on duty.

But when the young Ferengi turned to look at Vaughn in the *Defiant's* command chair, he did notice a slight curling of Vaughn's lips under his gray-and-silver beard.

Vaughn turned toward the bridge's port side. "Excellent work, gentlemen," he said to Nog and the Andorian sitting at the console to Nog's right.

Ensign Thirishar ch'Thane didn't smile, either, but Nog had learned to read the young science officer's facial features well enough to see that he, too, was pleased with himself. Nog and Shar had spent the last week going over every square millimeter of the communications array, and they were quite proud of the work they'd done.

Now, at last, everything appeared to be ready to go.

"Address intership, please, Lieutenant," Vaughn said to Nog.

Nog couldn't resist smiling as he complied. "Yes, sir. Intership open."

"Attention all hands, this is Commander Vaughn. Starfleet's primary mission has always been one of exploration. Over seven years ago, Benjamin Sisko and Jadzia Dax discovered a stable wormhole in the Denorios Belt, one which opened the door to an entire quadrant of new worlds for us to seek out. Five years ago, Starfleet, Bajoran, and Cardassian personnel worked together to install a subspace array on the Gamma Quadrant side of the wormhole to provide communication between the quadrants. Unfortunately, that array did not survive the hostilities of the Dominion War—a war that, sadly, also closed the door that Benjamin Sisko opened.

"But the war's over now. And thanks to efforts by the crew of the *Defiant* and Deep Space 9, a new communications array has been successfully deployed and is now online. As of this moment . . . we're back in the Gamma Quadrant."

Nog's smile broadened, and he drummed his hands against the edge of his console in applause. At conn, Ensign Prynn Tenmei clapped, and Lieutenant Sam Bowers at tactical let out a celebratory whoop. Over the comm system, Nog could hear other expressions of jubilation from all over the ship.

Looks like we're finally putting the war behind us, Nog thought with satisfaction. The repairs and upgrades to the station and the *Defiant* had been completed, and now the communications array was up and running—the prelude to the *Defiant's* upcoming mission of exploration to the Gamma Quadrant. Things were finally starting to get back to normal.

Shar, meanwhile, had turned back to his console. "All systems are functional, and the silithium receptors are aligned. We're ready to send our first message to DS9, Commander."

"Very well," Vaughn said, standing and walking toward the viewscreen. "Open a channel and transmit the following: 'Watson, I need you.' "

Shar's antennae lowered slightly. "Sir?"

Vaughn's lips curled again. "Old joke. A human one, so Colonel Kira won't get it, either. Send the message please, Ensign."

Shar nodded. "Yes, sir."

After a moment, Colonel Kira Nerys's sharp voice sounded crisply through the speakers. *"Who the hell is Watson?"*

"Excellent," Shar said, letting out a breath. Then he muttered some kind of supplication to the Andorian deity.

I guess he wasn't sure it was going to work, Nog thought with a smile. Nog, on the other hand, had known in his lobes that the array would function just fine.

"Old joke," Vaughn repeated. "Just a little test, Colonel. The new array seems to have passed it."

"Glad to hear it. Your timing is perfect. Get back over here right away, Commander. We have a meeting with Admiral Ross in half an hour."

Nog's lobes pricked up at that, and he felt a phantom twinge in the biosynthetic that had replaced his left leg, lost in the war. Ross had been the commander of Starfleet's forces against the Dominion. They'd already had one near-miss with renegade Jem'Hadar trying to start hostilities again.

The war's supposed to be behind us, dammit.

"Starfleet's declared a state of emergency," Kira went on to say, *"we've received a distress call from Europa Nova, and both the* Tcha'voth *and the* Makluan *have been recalled."*

Nog frowned at that. Those two ships had been posted to Deep Space 9 by the Klingons and Romulans, respectively, to bolster the station's defense, along with the *Defiant.*

"I want you to go to yellow alert. We're doing the same on the station."

"Acknowledged," Vaughn said, calmly sitting back down in the command chair. "We'll be back at the station in ten minutes. *Defiant* out." He turned to tactical. "Signal yellow alert please, Lieutenant Bowers. All hands to general quarters." Looking forward, he said, "Ensign Tenmei, set course for the wormhole, full impulse."

"Yes, sir," Tenmei said, and Nog noticed, not for the first time, the change to the ensign's voice that occurred every time she had to address Vaughn. It was subtle—a slight alteration in timbre that only a Ferengi would notice, but it happened only with the commander.

Although it had become common knowledge among the crew that Prynn was Vaughn's (apparently) estranged daughter—Uncle Quark had hardly been able to contain the information once he'd found out—Nog wondered what the source of that estrangement was. Generally, Tenmei was friendly and out-going off duty—Nog had even talked her into trying a tube grub in the mess hall yesterday. (Like most humans, she didn't have the stomach for it and spat it back out.) On duty she was an exceptional pilot and a consummate profes-sional, and apart from that slight shift in her voice that no one else seemed to notice, there was no obvious indication that she had any issues with Vaughn at all. And yet . . . Nog was certain there was something there, something that made him wonder if the *Defiant* bridge didn't have a serious problem on the horizon.

As the *Defiant* came about, Nog's thoughts changed course as well and he turned to Shar. "I told you we could do it."

Shar was hunched over his console, making sure that the automatic set-tings on the array were running properly so that it would continue to function after the *Defiant* was out of range. "I never doubted it."

"Oh really? Who was the one who thought the alignment of the subspace antenna was wrong?"

"That was me," Shar admitted.

"Who was the one who said that we'd need twice as many flux capacitors as we actually did need?"

"That was me, too."

"Who was the one—"

Shar finally looked up, brushing a lock of his coarse white hair off his face. "Nog, just because I was critical of some details doesn't mean I doubted that we'd get the array online."

"Hah. You say that now."

"Yes, and I would've said it then if someone had asked."

The young Ferengi chuckled and relaxed for the first time in a week. While no words to the effect had been spoken, Nog knew that no one was entirely sure about whether or not he and Shar could get the job done. After all, from the time the station was turned over to Bajoran and Starfleet control by the Cardassians, over seven years earlier, the responsibilities of science offi-cer and chief of operations had belonged, respectively, to Jadzia Dax—a Trill scientist with three centuries' and eight lifetimes' worth of experience—and Miles O'Brien—a Starfleet veteran of over twenty years. They'd now been replaced by a recent—albeit brilliant—graduate of Starfleet Academy and a junior-grade lieutenant who owed his rank to battlefield commissions rather than full Academy experience. Nobody had forgotten that, when Chief O'Brien first took over, Nog was a child being arrested by Odo for stealing from the assay office.

From the conn position, Tenmei said, "Entering the wormhole."

Nog looked down and made sure that all the ship's systems were within expected parameters for a trip through the wormhole. Most of the time, they were, but more than one such trip had been fraught with danger, from Kira and Dr. Bashir's unexpected jaunt to a parallel universe to the aliens who resided in the wormhole causing an entire Jem'Hadar fleet to vanish. Nog didn't want something like that to happen to them now because he was too busy rib-bing Shar to notice an anomalous reading.

However, everything seemed to be fine. Nog set the viewscreen on his console to show the wormhole as they passed through it.

For a long time, Nog had thought of the wormhole solely as the thing that brought Uncle Quark all the new business. Then it was something they talked about in school occasionally. But he'd never really looked at it until Jake Sisko dragged him to the catwalk over the Promenade to watch the wormhole open and close one afternoon. It was then that he truly started to appreciate it. He hadn't admitted it to Jake—nor to anyone else—at the time, but it was the most glorious sight he'd ever seen, and he wanted to know more about it. Nog often suspected that that moment, when he found his mind flooded with questions about the wormhole, was probably the first step on his journey to the Academy and Starfleet.

Studying the wormhole in school didn't prepare him for seeing it, and seeing it didn't remotely prepare him for what it was like to go through it.

His studies told him that the streams of white and silver light were verteron particles and silithium streams and various other bits of particulate matter, but that only mattered to Nog when duty required it of him. Times like this, he liked to just sit back and watch the dance of lights as the ship shot through seventy thousand light-years in a matter of minutes.

As they emerged from the Alpha Quadrant mouth of the wormhole into Bajoran space, Shar spoke up, apparently not willing to let the subject die just yet. "It's actually quite intriguing the way you keep doing things that don't match the specifications. Especially since you're always right."

Nog chuckled. "Well, not *always.* But when I'm wrong, I've gotten very good at making it seem like it was what I meant to do all along. I met Captain Montgomery Scott recently, and he said something great." Shar didn't seem impressed by the name-dropping, so Nog added, "You've heard of him, right?"

"Oh, sure, I know Scotty," Shar said.

Nog felt his jaw drop open. "You call him 'Scotty'? I don't think I'd ever have the lobes to do that."

"My *zhavey* introduced us, and he insisted I use the nickname."

Nog shook his head. He kept forgetting that the unassuming young An-dorian had a parent on the Federation Council. "Anyway, he said, 'The estab-lished norms are just guidelines, and your job as an engineer is to find a better way around them.'"

"That certainly sounds like Scotty."

From behind him, Nog heard Vaughn's rock-steady voice say, "Deep Space 9, this is the *Defiant* requesting permission to dock."

"Granted," came the reply from Selzner in ops.

Something caught Shar's attention on his console. "Commander, we're getting a message from the array. It's relaying something on a Federation civilian frequency from the Kar-telos system, just a few light-years into the Gamma Quadrant."

"Put it on screen, please."

"It's audio only, sir," Shar said quickly.

Vaughn looked over at Shar and fixed him with an intense, calm gaze that was as scary as anything Nog had ever seen. "Then put it on speakers, Ensign ch'Thane."

"Yes, sir."

"This is Captain Monaghan of the Mars freighter Halloran. *I need some help here. I was doing the Jovian run, and now—well, I think I'm in the Gamma Quadrant. I haven't the first clue as to how I got here. Someone please help me!"*

"You said it was a civilian frequency, Ensign?" Vaughn asked Shar.

Shar nodded.

"That explains it, then. Open a channel."

Manipulating his console, Shar said, "Channel open."

"Freighter *Halloran,* this is Commander Elias Vaughn, first officer of Deep Space 9. You are, in fact, in the Gamma Quadrant."

"How the hell did I wind up here?"

"That's a very fair question, Captain. I wish I had an answer for that. What I can tell you is that we will dispatch a runabout to your position right away and lead you back to DS9 through the Bajoran wormhole. Is that acceptable?"

Captain Monaghan started to sound panicky. Nog's sensitive ears noticed the change in the timbre of her voice, even over the communications system. *"I guess so. Isn't this where the Dominion came from?"*

"Yes, ma'am, it is."

"Should I be worried about the Jem'Hadar?"

"No," Vaughn said with calm confidence that Nog—remembering the recent attack on the station—didn't share. "You're quite safe, I can assure you. Nonetheless, we'll dispatch the runabout immediately."

"Thanks, Commander." Nog noticed that the timbre of her voice had changed again. Vaughn's words had obviously reassured her. *"Halloran out."*

Vaughn turned to Bowers. "Lieutenant, when we dock, prepare the *Sungari* for departure and take it to the Kar-telos system."

Bowers nodded.

Shar was staring at his panel. "How is it possible that a ship in the Terran system suddenly found itself in the Gamma Quadrant?"

"Let's hope, Ensign, that it relates to why we're at yellow alert right now."

Nog frowned. "Why would we hope that, Commander?"

This time, Vaughn's hard stare was turned on Nog. "Because, Lieutenant, I've been through more Starfleet states of emergency than I care to count. And the last thing you want to have to do during one is split your focus."

Chapter Three

Deep Space 9

Elias Vaughn hated meetings.

Oh, he understood the need for them. There were times when such things were vital, and it was good for groups of people who worked together to gather regularly and keep each other abreast of their duties, lives, or anything else of import.

But the ideal meeting was short and to the point. Vaughn's long years of experience had shown him that most meetings were neither, and were primarily an impediment to actually getting anything accomplished. One of the many—although lesser—reasons Vaughn had declined so many promotions over the years was the surety that a higher rank would result in more meetings.

As he and Kira approached Quark's bar, Ensign ch'Thane's voice sounded through Kira's combadge. *"Ops to Colonel Kira."*

Tapping her combadge, Kira said, "Go ahead, Shar."

"Colonel, we're receiving detailed information from Europa Nova. It isn't good, sir."

They entered the bar, occupied solely by a few civilians—including Morn in his usual seat toward one end of the bar. With the station at yellow alert, the Starfleet and Bajoran Militia personnel were either at their duty stations or on standby, and most of the rest of the station's population probably felt safer on their ships or in their quarters.

"Anything new I should know?" Kira asked as she walked up the tightly winding staircase to the second level.

"They are primarily confirming the original distress call—theta radiation is appearing in orbit from an unknown point of origin and will reach lethal levels within fifty-two hours. The only new data is that the source of the radiation appears to be some kind of antimatter industrial waste."

Kira frowned. "That's odd."

Vaughn searched his memory for anyone in the quadrant who still generated waste from their matter-antimatter power sources, and couldn't find any. Every warp-capable species he knew of that used such reactors had conquered the waste problem in fairly short order.

"Lieutenant Bowers has rendezvoused with the Halloran. *He reports no problems, and should be back within the hour. We've also received several odd reports in the usual dispatches."*

"Odd in what way?" Kira asked.

"Apparently, Orions have been sighted on Ferenginar, near the Grand Nagus's home, the Deltans and Carreon have mutually broken their treaty in a manner that defies logic, there's a medical crisis on Armus IX thanks to an unauthorized alien pres-

ence—the list is quite extensive, and has a common element of people not being where they should be."

"Keep a log of the odd reports, Shar," Kira said. She and Vaughn arrived at the door to one of Quark's holosuites on the bar's third level. Nog was already there, making some adjustments to an outer panel. "We're about to go into the meeting—maybe we'll find out what this is all about. Kira out." She looked at Nog and said, "Report."

"Just a second, sir." Several seconds later, Nog stood up and turned off the polarizer he had been using. "It's ready, Colonel. The connection to Starfleet Headquarters is functional. We just need them to activate it on their end."

"Any problems?"

Nog gave a lopsided smile. "None, sir. My uncle's off-station, after all."

Kira gave an equally lopsided smile in return.

"I take it Quark would have been something of an impediment to using the holosuite this way," Vaughn said dryly as he followed Kira through to the presently inactive holosuite.

"A small one. He would've complained and asked for compensation and generally made a nuisance of himself—the usual. But, whatever Quark's failings," she said in a tone of voice that implied that she found those failings to be legion, "he's a good Ferengi. His underlings are usually competent enough to keep the business from going under while he's away, but not good enough to be a danger to his position as the boss."

"So they're easy to intimidate."

Nodding, Kira said, "Especially by the son of the new Grand Nagus."

Nog's voice came from over the intercom. *"Signal coming in from Starfleet now, Colonel."*

The holosuite environment didn't change, but Vaughn suddenly found himself in a room full of red-trimmed uniforms, his ears assaulted by several simultaneous conversations all being piped in at once. It was as if a cocktail party had suddenly been beamed aboard the station. However, the noise almost immediately dropped to near-silence as people realized that they were "on."

In recent years, holographic technology had been refined to the point where it could be combined with subspace communication, allowing two people to converse while each appeared to be in the same room with the other, even though they were in fact separated by light-years. What Starfleet had done here was take that to the next step by linking the holocoms of various ships and starbases to the one at Starfleet HQ on Earth so that dozens of people from all across the quadrant could meet. Just as it appeared to him that these men and women were standing in the holosuite, Vaughn knew it appeared that they were all standing on the holodecks of each officer in attendance.

All of those present were of command rank, but only one—William Ross—was from the admiralty. *These are some of Starfleet's most prominent leaders,* he thought, *but not the ones who run it. This is a room full of "doers." Interesting.*

Just as interesting was Kira's distinction within the gathering as the only non-Starfleet command officer present, her Bajoran Militia uniform standing out in stark contrast to the others. Vaughn knew there were those at Starfleet Command who were less than pleased with the idea of a non-Federation officer commanding Starfleet personnel and a facility as important as DS9 was strategically. As far as Vaughn was concerned, the naysayers were simply ignorant.

Not this group, though. Kira had worn the Federation's uniform once, he knew, during the final weeks of the Dominion War and under extraordinary circumstances. But Vaughn wondered how many in the meeting actually knew that, or if their clear and unflinching acceptance of Kira as part of this very special circle of officers stemmed rather from the strength of her reputation and her record. She stood next to him, her arms folded expectantly as she studied the faces of the other officers, exchanging nods with the few that she knew, secure in her own authority and ready to get down to business. Not for the first time, Vaughn found himself uncharacteristically impressed with his commanding officer.

For his part, Vaughn knew most of the people in the room personally, including Captain Solok of the *T'Kumbra* (not a bad ship commander, as Vaughn recalled, but something of a jerk personally); Commander Ju'les L'ullho of Starbase 96; and Captain Walter Emick of the *Intrepid*. A few—Captain Elizabeth Shelby of the *Trident;* Captain Elaine Mello of the *Gryphon;* and Captain Mackenzie Calhoun of the *Excalibur*—he knew only by reputation. Some, of course, had more of a reputation than others, and Calhoun's was fairly bizarre. He had, Vaughn knew, done quite a bit of work for Admiral Nechayev's little corner of Starfleet Intelligence. Vaughn had thought that Calhoun was a bit too much of a loose cannon for that kind of work, but Alynna seemed to find him useful. Calhoun was also supported by Jean-Luc Picard and intensely disliked by Edward Jellico, both points in his favor.

Speaking of Jean-Luc, the *Enterprise* captain stood in the center of the room next to Bill Ross. Picard seemed strangely unreadable as he surveyed the gathering, but Ross had a hangdog look that spoke more than anything to the gravity of the situation. The admiral hadn't looked this bad since the worst days of the Dominion War.

"Good afternoon," Ross said. Gestures and muttered returned greetings filled the room momentarily before he went on. *"It's nice to know our relay systems are fine-tuned enough to allow holoconferences like this to occur. It certainly beats trying to find parking orbits for all of you."* Ross attempted a smile, but the joke fell flat. *"I'm placing you all on yellow alert until further notice."*

Next to him, Kira's eyes smoldered. Vaughn immediately recognized her "gee-how-brilliant-of-Starfleet-to-do-something-I-already-thought-of" expression.

Ross continued. *"As for why we're doing this, we have a new problem. A few days ago, the Federation Council was approached by a group of beings who identified themselves as the Iconians."*

Vaughn watched the reactions of the others around the holosuite. Some nodded in understanding—ones probably familiar with the two on-record Iconian encounters and/or the legends that had surrounded that ancient, and supposedly extinct, species—others looked confused, still others asked people off-circuit to check up on the name.

Once the brief commotion settled down, Ross turned to the *Enterprise* captain. Vaughn remembered that Jean-Luc had always had a fascination for Iconian legend. *"Captain Picard, would you please detail what we know of the Iconians?"*

"Of course, Admiral. The Iconians were known to exist in this quadrant of space some two hundred millennia ago. Their culture and technology were unparalleled in that time period but records about them are scant. About a decade ago, Captain Donald Varley of the U.S.S. Yamato determined the location of their homeworld in the Romulan Neutral Zone, but was lost along with his ship when a destructive Iconian computer program inserted itself into the Yamato's mainframe. Even after all that time, the technology on the homeworld remained functional—including the gateways.

"These gateways provide instantaneous transport between two points that could be meters or light-years apart. Two functional gateways have been found over the last few years: one on the homeworld, which I myself destroyed rather than allow gateway technology to fall into Romulan hands; and one discovered by the Dominion in the Gamma Quadrant, which was destroyed by a joint Starfleet/Jem'Hadar team from the U.S.S. Defiant."

Ross nodded. *"Thank you, Captain. The Iconians who have come forward now have offered us the gateway technology for a price. The Council is considering the offer, but it's a bit more complicated than that. First, they are offering the technology to the highest bidder. Similar offers have been made to governments throughout the quadrant. Clearly, this could have a devastating impact should any antagonistic or ambitious government obtain the technology exclusively.*

"Second, and most immediate: the Iconians have chosen to demonstrate how useful the gateways can be by activating the entire network. Gateways have opened up all over the quadrant and beyond. The Iconians have seen fit to withhold how to control them and have chosen not to provide us with any form of useful map."

Once again a brief commotion broke out, as the officers present reacted to the news. Vaughn scratched his salt-and-pepper beard thoughtfully. *That,* he thought, *would explain the* Halloran *and all those odd reports of Shar's. And, quite probably, what's happening to Europa Nova.*

"As the gateways came online," Ross continued, silencing the group, *"we immediately began studying their output, trying to get a handle on how they work."*

As Ross spoke, another figure came in. Vaughn almost smiled. This was another captain, and probably the only human in the room older than Vaughn himself.

"We became rather alarmed at some of the readings, and so turned the study over to the Starfleet Corps of Engineers. We now have a preliminary report." Turning to the new arrival, he said, *"Captain Scott, thank you for joining us."*

"It's not a problem," Montgomery Scott said, after giving a quick, affection-

ate glance to Picard. Vaughn remembered that the *Enterprise* rescued Captain Scott from the *U.S.S. Jenolen,* where he'd been trapped in a sort of suspended animation for over seven decades as a transporter pattern. In the years since, the man out of time had traveled far and wide and performed a variety of tasks; most recently, however, he'd been assigned to serve as the liaison between the Starfleet Corps of Engineers and the admiralty.

Scott continued. *"Those gateways, to be blunt, are behavin' in ways we never imagined. It seems that when they exhaust their power, they tap into any other power supply that's available. Like pussy willows here on Earth, that seek water and break into pipes to find it. These gateways are so beyond our ken tha' figuring out how they tick and stoppin' them will be almost impossible."*

"Do you mean, they could tap an entire planet's resources and drain them dry?" Ross asked.

Scott took a deep breath. *"Aye. Worse, for those worlds using predominantly geothermal or hydraulic power. Their ecosystem could be compromised. We don't have all the figures in yet, but one o' my ships is measuring solar consumption. My fear is some stars might be destabilized by additional power demands. It's a very nasty bit o' business."*

Turning back to the assembled commanders, Ross said, *"All the more reason for us to mobilize the fleet. Duty packets are going out now with specific sector assignments. We'll need to maintain the peace. Some of our scientific vessels will be working with the S.C.E. to determine just how severe the problems might become. Captain Solok, I will want you and your crew to begin monitoring all incident reports from gateway activity. If the Iconians won't give us a map, I want us to make one."*

Speaking gravely, the Vulcan captain said, *"Understood. I should point out that it will not be complete and therefore not entirely accurate."*

"Noted," Ross said. *"I'll take whatever we can get since it's better than the nothing we have right now."*

Ross then looked directly at Vaughn and Kira. *"Colonel, Commander, our scientists have done some preliminary mapping based on the gateway power signatures and we've discovered something very interesting out your way. We're estimating no gateway activity within ten light-years in any direction of Bajor."*

Interesting, Vaughn thought. *Europa Nova's ten light-years from here.* Aloud, he said, "The wormhole."

"We think so, yes."

Kira said, "It could be the Prophets protecting this region."

"That's certainly a possibility. Vaughn, given your experience with the gateways, I want you out there, finding out why there aren't any gateways near Bajor. Is it something natural? Is it the doing of the aliens—that is to say, the Prophets?" he amended with a conciliatory glance at Kira. *"What properties are being displayed, and can they be harnessed beyond your sector?"*

"You're hoping we can turn it into a practical countermeasure."

"Exactly."

Picard then said the words that Vaughn had been half-expecting from the moment the Iconians were mentioned. *"I was unaware, Admiral, of any encounters with gateways beyond those by the* Enterprise *and the* Defiant."

Next to him, Kira was giving Vaughn a rather penetrating gaze. "Neither was I."

"It was a few years ago," Vaughn said neutrally. The mission to Alexandra's Planet had been classified, and Vaughn had yet to be given any reason to disregard that.

Ross gave Picard a reassuring look. *"The relevant portions of Commander Vaughn's mission will be declassified in light of the present emergency."*

Picard nodded. *"Good."*

Vaughn gave Kira a quick nod that he hoped matched Ross for reassurance. Kira seemed dubious, but willing to table any further discussion.

Particularly since there were more pressing matters. "Admiral," she said, "we have another problem. Europa Nova is suffering a planetwide catastrophe, possibly a result of this gateway problem. Some kind of antimatter waste field is appearing in orbit, seemingly out of nowhere. We need to evacuate the settlement immediately, and we're going to need the *Defiant* and as many more ships as possible to assist. The *Tcha'voth* and the *Makluan* were recalled suddenly, so we're even more shorthanded. Lieutenant Dax is assembling a task force of Bajoran and civilian ships, but—"

"Say no more, Colonel. We're aware of the situation on Europa Nova. There's a Federation Councillor there right now negotiating with their parliament, and we received the same distress call you did. Since the Klingons and Romulans have recalled their ships, I've assigned the Gryphon *and the* Intrepid *to be at your disposal."* Turning to Captains Mello and Emick, he asked, *"Captains, your ETAs?"*

"Two and a half hours, Admiral," said Captain Mello, a short, robust woman with a round face and curly brown hair. The *Gryphon* had delivered the *Defiant*'s replacement warhead module over a week earlier, but Vaughn hadn't had the chance to meet her captain then.

Captain Emick—a man who came from a long line of Starfleet officers dating back to the founding of the organization—turned to Kira and said, *"DS9 is actually on our way there, so with your permission, Colonel?"* Kira nodded. *"The* Intrepid *will rendezvous with the* Defiant *in two hours."*

"Good," Ross said. *"I only ask that you hold back one runabout to investigate the wormhole, Colonel."*

Kira inclined her head. "Of course, Admiral. The *Sungari* will handle it as soon as it returns from the Gamma Quadrant."

At Ross's frown—at present, only the *Defiant* had authorization to go through the wormhole—Vaughn quickly explained the situation with the *Halloran.*

"Understood. Keep us posted on Europa Nova." Ross then turned to Captain Calhoun and started to detail the *Excalibur*'s assignment.

Vaughn looked at Kira with a raised eyebrow; she inclined her head, and the commander then stepped aside so he wouldn't disturb the rest of the meeting. Kira would keep track of what was going on while her first officer started getting all the balls that needed rolling into motion. Possibly Ross might have preferred that the highest-ranking Starfleet officer on Deep Space 9 be the one to participate in all aspects of the meeting, but, Bajoran Militia or not, Kira was in charge.

Besides, Vaughn *really* hated meetings.

"Vaughn to Dax."

"Go ahead."

"Lieutenant, add the *Intrepid* and the *Gryphon* to our list and take the *Sungari* off it. As soon as Lieutenant Bowers returns with the *Halloran,* have the runabout prepped for Lieutenant Nog and Ensign ch'Thane to take it back to the wormhole. And assemble the senior staff in ops. The colonel and I will meet you there shortly."

"Yes, sir. Uhm—Starfleet's only sending two ships?"

"That's correct, Lieutenant."

"I take it there's more going on than just Europa Nova's crisis?"

Vaughn turned and looked back at the meeting. Calhoun had apparently just cracked a joke, and several of the assembled officers guffawed—pointedly, Bill Ross was not among those laughing. "Quite a bit more, yes."

"Well, it's been almost an hour since the galaxy was last in danger of destruction." Vaughn could almost see Ezri's wry grin. *"By the way, the Bajoran Militia has detached the Lamnak fleet to us for the crisis—that's their ten biggest ships under the command of Colonel Lenaris Holem. I've also signed up the* East Winds."

"The *East Winds?*"

"It's a ship out of Risa. Cassandra—she's the captain—had some kind of deal going with Quark, but since he's not here, she's at loose ends."

"So she's agreed to help?"

"Yup. She's, ah, an old friend of Curzon's."

Vaughn decided that he didn't want to know. "Very well. Carry on, Lieutenant."

"Dax out."

As Vaughn turned back to the meeting, Ross was saying, *"These will be some trying days ahead of us all. I want to keep in constant contact and I'll be reachable any time you need me. Good luck."*

Then the room turned back to the default holosuite setting, leaving Vaughn and Kira alone.

"I've called a briefing in ops," Vaughn said as he followed Kira out of the holosuite.

"Good."

"I love you, too."

Both Vaughn and Kira looked up at that.

Nog, still standing by at the holosuite control panel in the hallway and now holding an isolinear rod, had heard it, too, through the open door. At the two officers' questioning glances, he shrugged. "The connections didn't all break at once. It's impossible for them to coordinate that perfectly. That was probably a stray transmission."

"That sounded like Calhoun's voice," Kira said.

"Well, my understanding is that he and Captain Shelby recently married," Vaughn said.

Kira snorted. "Let's hope she got the message." Shaking her head, she moved toward the staircase, Vaughn and Nog following. "Two ships. It's a good thing we heard the entire briefing, otherwise I'd accuse Starfleet of shortchanging us again. Now, though, I'm wondering if they can even spare those two."

Vaughn nodded as they went downstairs. As the trio exited Quark's, Captain Kasidy Yates approached them. The skipper of the civilian cargo vessel *Xhosa* quickly fell into step with them as they moved across the Promenade.

Yates, now five months pregnant, was living on Bajor, in the house that had been begun by her husband, Benjamin Sisko, before his disappearance. Vaughn was surprised to see her on the station.

"How're you doing, Kas?" Kira asked.

"Fine. I was up for my monthly prenatal with Dr. Bashir—you'll be happy to know that everything's fine—when I heard about Europa Nova. The *Xhosa*'s ready to volunteer for evac duty."

Nog winced, and looked down at the captain's belly. "Captain Yates, with all due respect—is that really a good idea in your condition?"

Yates fixed the young Ferengi with a reproachful glare. "Nog, you say one more condescending word about my 'condition,' I swear you will *not* live to regret it. I'm pregnant. I'm not dying. And I'm still perfectly capable of doing my job."

Nog's eyes went wide and he stammered, "Of—of course, Captain, I didn't—I didn't mean—"

Kira, who had a huge grin on her face, said, "Thanks, Kas. Coordinate with Dax; she'll fill you in on the details." Nog looked relieved at the interruption.

"I'll be ready, Nerys," Yates said. Nodding cordially to Vaughn, she said, "Commander," then gave Nog another withering look before she turned and walked off.

As they entered the lift, Kira said, "Ops," then turned to Nog. "Safety tip, Lieutenant: don't treat pregnant women like they're made out of glass. I know whereof I speak."

"Yes, sir," Nog said crisply.

"Besides," she said more gravely, "we can use all the help we can get."

"Of course, sir."

The lift arrived at ops, which marked the first time in days that Vaughn had set foot in Deep Space 9's nerve center. The arrangement of personnel was somewhat different—and more chaotic—than it had been when he was last here. One thing, however, remained constant: Taran'atar. He stood in the exact same spot in the exact same position on the upper level of ops with the exact same expression on his face. The Jem'Hadar had been sent to the Alpha Quadrant by the Founders of the Dominion as a cultural observer, and it was in precisely that capacity that he maintained his frequent presence in ops. By now, the crew had gotten used to his almost statue-like presence. Sergeant Gan Morr, whose sensor maintenance station was right next to where Taran'atar stood, had been most distressed at first, but now he seemed completely oblivious to the Jem'Hadar's presence.

As Kira, Vaughn, and Nog proceeded to the table on the lower level, Dax, Bowers, and ch'Thane did likewise from their stations. Bashir was already sitting on the edge of one of the chairs, portable medikit over his shoulder, poised as if ready to leave at a moment's notice.

"As you know," Kira said once everyone had settled, "the planet of Europa Nova is suffering a global catastrophe. What appears to be antimatter industrial waste is appearing in increasing quantities in orbit around the planet and the level of theta radiation is rising steadily. We don't know where it's coming from, and right now that's a secondary concern to evacuating the planet. There are three million people on Europa Nova, and they're all in danger of lethal exposure to the radiation within fifty-two hours." She turned to Dax. "Lieutenant, what's the status of our convoy?"

Dax consulted a padd. "We've got the *Defiant,* the *Intrepid,* the *Euphrates,* and the *Rio Grande* from Starfleet, with the *Gryphon* meeting us at Europa Nova. We've also got four civilian ships: the *East Winds*—"

"Cassandra's ship?" Kira asked, and Vaughn noted the distaste in Kira's tone.

Grinning, Dax said, "Yup."

"You did say we can use all the help we can get," Vaughn deadpanned, which earned him a glare from Kira.

"Fine," she said with a nod to Dax, "go on."

"The other civilian ships are the *Ng,* the *Goldblatt's Folly,* and the *Halloran.*" She looked up and smiled. "I convinced Captain Monaghan that it was the least she could do after we rescued her."

"Add the *Xhosa,*" Kira said. "We bumped into Kasidy on the Promenade."

"Okay," Dax said, making notes on her padd. "We can leave here as soon as the *Intrepid* arrives in two hours. The Lamnak fleet—that's ten Bajoran Militia ships—will rendezvous with us at Bajor on the way."

"So that leaves us with twenty ships?" Kira asked.

Dax nodded. "A lot of them are cargo ships, or at least ones with plenty of space. I also talked with Minister Lipin and Vedek Eran about arranging for emergency housing for the majority of the refugees on Bajor, and Ensign Ling has started working with Ro's people to get temporary accommodations set up here."

"Good work." Kira said. "Let's hope it's enough ships to get three million people off within fifty-two hours."

Bashir leaned forward. "It might well be. Assuming the reports we have on the number of ships available on Europa Nova itself are accurate, and based on the capacity of each of the ships in the convoy, and assuming the current rate of radiation increase, it's mathematically possible for us to complete the evacuation before we reach fatal exposure."

From anyone else, the statement would have been arrogant and presumptuous, but Vaughn was sure that Bashir's genetically enhanced brain was more than capable of making all the calculations necessary to back the claim up. Turning his gaze on the doctor, Vaughn said, "The problem with mathematical predictions is that they involve variables. And this particular equation is littered with them." Before Bashir could reply to that, Vaughn added, "Speaking of fatal exposure, Doctor, what's our medical status?"

Taking only an instant to switch mental tracks, Bashir said, "I've had the lab replicating arithrazine nonstop since we first received the distress call. The *Defiant*'s dispensary is already full, and I should have enough for the *Intrepid* by the time they arrive."

Bowers frowned. "I thought hyronalin was the standard for radiation."

"Usually, yes, but arithrazine specifically deals with the peculiar side effects of theta radiation. Hyronalin will do in a crunch, but in a case like this, arithrazine is preferred."

"Colonel," ch'Thane said, "I'm not familiar with Europa Nova. They're not a Federation world?"

Shaking her head, Kira said, "No, but it's a human colony. They settled there about a hundred years ago, but never joined the Federation. They actually managed to repel a Breen attack during the war."

Several eyes widened at that bit of information.

"I'm surprised," Vaughn said, "that you're not familiar with the world, Ensign. Andor has several trade agreements with Europa Nova."

"I haven't been home for some time, Commander," ch'Thane said quietly.

Vaughn filed the fact away for future reference. Now wasn't the time or place to pursue this, but there was significant weight to the ensign's statement, especially given who his mother was.

"What about the *Sungari?*" Bowers asked. "I mean, I realize that runabouts won't be all that helpful in evacuation compared to the others . . ."

"No, they won't," Kira said. "In fact, the main purpose of the runabouts will be to try to figure out where the radiation is coming from."

"And," Vaughn added, "how it might relate to the gateways."

"Gateways?" Bashir and Dax both asked simultaneously.

Vaughn very quickly summarized the salient portions of the meeting with Admiral Ross, concluding with: "Lieutenant Nog, you and Ensign ch'Thane are to take the *Sungari* to the wormhole and investigate this phenomenon. There are two encounters with gateways on record: the *Enterprise* and the *Yamato* in the Romulan Neutral Zone on Stardate 42609; and the *Defiant*'s mission to Vandros IV on Stardate 49904. A third, on Alexandra's Planet on

Stardate 44765, has been partially declassified for this mission. There are also extensive research notes taken by a Professor Chi Namthot at Memory Alpha. You should both become as familiar with those records as time will allow. Your task is to try to figure out why there are no gateways within ten light-years of Bajor and determine if that reason is something we can harness for practical use. At the moment, we have no control over the gateways, and it's resulted in no small amount of chaos throughout known space."

"Those odd reports," Shar said, nodding. "The presence of Iconian-type gateways would explain most of them—if not all of them, including Europa Nova."

"Exactly. If your mission succeeds, we may be able to get some control of our own."

"Uh, Colonel?" Nog said tentatively.

"Yes, Nog?" Kira said.

Nog held up an isolinear rod he'd been carrying. Vaughn peered at the markings, and saw that it contained a replicator pattern. "I, ah, have something that might help. It's a shield modulator that I—acquired from the Shelliak."

Everyone whirled and stared at Nog. Dax's mouth was hanging open.

Bashir asked, "Aren't the Shelliak among the most xenophobic species in the galaxy?"

"Xenophobic's the wrong word," Dax said. "More like xeno-disdainful. They don't really fear other species, they just don't think all that much of them."

"How the hell did you manage to make a deal with them?" Bowers asked.

Nog smiled. "A good Ferengi never reveals his methods."

"What does this modulator do?" Kira asked, yanking the discussion back on track.

"It strengthens shields against the effects of radiation."

"That's handy," Dax said.

Nog continued, "The problem with it—and it's one of the reasons why it isn't used much—is that it weakens shields' effectiveness against weapons fire."

Bashir said, "That's *not* so handy."

"Still, in this case," Kira said, "we need protection from radiation a lot more than we need protection from phasers. Good work, Nog."

Beaming, the young Ferengi said, "Thank you, Colonel. We were lucky. I've been working on this deal for four months now. I figured this type of modulation might be useful for navigation in the Badlands. It finally arrived while we were in the Gamma Quadrant."

A pity Dr. Bashir didn't have use of it on his mission to Sindorin, Vaughn thought, and he could see by the pensive look on the doctor's face that he was thinking much the same thing.

Nog continued. "I can have the modulators replicated and installed on the *Defiant* and its shuttles, the *Euphrates,* and the *Rio Grande* by the time the *In-*

trepid gets here, and their chief engineer should also be able to install one with no problem."

"All right, get to work on that, then report to the *Sungari.*"

"Yes, sir," Nog said, and he moved toward the lift. Then he stopped and turned back to Kira. Vaughn noticed that the young Ferengi now had a rather pained expression on his face. "Colonel? If we're committing all these ships— does this mean we've given up searching for Jake?"

That pained expression flew around the table, particularly to Dax and Bashir. Kira looked like she'd been gut-punched. Where the room previously had the crackling tension of a group of trained professionals about to embark on a complex mission, now ops felt almost like a mausoleum.

For the past two weeks, Deep Space 9 had been coordinating a sector-wide search for Jake Sisko, the son of the former station commander and also, Vaughn knew, a close friend of Nog. Young Mr. Sisko had last been known to be on his way to Earth to visit his grandfather. But when Captain Yates had contacted Earth, Joseph Sisko had professed no knowledge of any visit from his grandson.

However, as continued searches had turned up negative, the efforts, of necessity, had diminished. The *Defiant* was needed to set up the communications array, and Nog—who had been at the forefront of the rescue attempts—was needed to assist Shar in the engineering thereof.

"We haven't given up anything, Nog. But we've done everything that we can do to look for him. We still have an open call to all ships to look out for him, and Ro's people have been questioning everyone who comes on-station. The authorities on Earth are looking, too. We'll find him. But right now, we have to give priority to the three million people on Europa Nova." As she spoke, Kira's face hardened up again, and by the time she reached the words "Europa Nova" she was back to her firm, commanding self.

Kira's words—and, more important, her tone—had an effect. Nog, Dax, Bowers, and Bashir still looked concerned, but the crackling tension of the immediate crisis had returned.

Turning to Dax, the colonel said, "Lieutenant, you'll be in charge of the station while we're gone. Keep coordinating with Lipin and Eran—we'll need housing set up for the refugees within the next twelve hours or so."

Dax nodded.

"Commander Vaughn, you'll take the *Defiant*. I'll take Ling and the *Euphrates*. Bowers, you'll go in the *Rio Grande* with Roness." She looked around the table. "Let's get to work, people. Dismissed."

Good thing we haven't reopened the wormhole for business yet, Vaughn thought. If that had been the case, the station would probably be full to bursting with ships bound for the Gamma Quadrant. Not that they weren't dealing with considerable traffic as it was, especially with all the relief ships going to and from Cardassia, but all things considered, their position could be much more difficult.

As the meeting broke, everyone headed for their stations or the lifts. Vaughn followed Kira up the stairs toward her office. They were intercepted by Taran'atar. "Colonel, request permission to join the mission."

Kira seemed to size up the Jem'Hadar. "Any particular reason?"

"I may be of some use."

"How?"

"I don't know. Nor did I know how I might be of use on Dr. Bashir's mission to Sindorin, yet you yourself said that the mission would have failed without me. For that matter, I've yet to comprehend how I may be of use on this station at all, yet Odo said that I would be. It seems reasonable that I continue seeking ways to make myself useful. Your mission to Europa Nova seems like such an opportunity."

I guess he's getting bored standing around ops, Vaughn though bemusedly. *But he makes an interesting point. And it might do him some good to see a Federation rescue mission.*

Kira turned to Vaughn with a questioning glance. Vaughn looked in the colonel's eyes, and saw that Kira had already made up her mind. She wasn't looking for his approval, just wanting to know if he had any objection. He shook his head slightly.

"Fine, you'll come with me on the *Euphrates.* Commander, see to it that Lieutenant Bowers knows that Ensign Ling is to remain on the station."

Vaughn nodded. "Yes, sir."

Taran'atar inclined his head. "With your permission, then, Colonel, I will report to runabout pad A and prepare the *Euphrates* for our journey."

Chapter Four

Farius Prime

"This is *so* exciting!"

Quark tried to ignore the bleating of the blond, scantily-clad Bajoran woman walking alongside him down the corridor of the Orion starship. *Why did I ever think taking a* dabo *girl along for show would be a good idea?*

Then he looked at their two escorts, a pair of tall, burly, green-skinned Orion men who kept their eyes primarily focused on the outfit his companion wasn't wearing, so to speak, and thought, *Oh, right—that's why.* The next time he saw Garak he had to once again thank the Promenade's erstwhile tailor for his amazing work on the *dabo* girl outfits—every one a masterpiece of textile engineering, they managed to show everything yet reveal nothing.

Especially useful when you're dealing with Orions—after all, they appreciate sexy women.

The only parts of the outfit he thought were a little much were the four large, round tassels that dangled from the waistband of the pants—two on either hip. Those pants had slits on both sides of each leg, showing a generous display of flesh, with the waistband just below the pelvic bone. To Quark's mind, the tassels detracted from the effect. *Still, I suppose they serve a purpose.*

They had just disembarked from an Orion transport that had taken them from Deep Space 9 to the Clarus system. It had taken no time at all to get from there to Farius Prime. Quark had, in fact, been stunned at how fast the trip had been—it should've taken several hours at warp six, but was over in less than five minutes.

Now they traversed the corridors of a large vessel that appeared to be based on Vulcan designs, albeit with some modifications. Besides, Quark knew the sound of a Vulcan impulse engine—their Cochrane distortion spiked much higher than on any other vessel. *That's the Orions for you,* he thought with admiration, *always stealing from the best.*

To one of the Orions, he asked, "So how'd we get here so fast, exactly?"

"You'll find out soon enough, Ferengi." The Orion did not take his eyes off the generous display of cleavage that they'd been fixed on since they'd left Deep Space 9 a day earlier. The *dabo* girl wore a necklace with a Spican flame gem at its center—the necklace acted as an arrow that pointed to her chest, and the flame gem did a marvelous job as that arrow's rather prominent point.

The *dabo* girl grinned widely and said, "I can't *wait* to find out. This is so unbelievably amazing!"

They arrived at a meeting room that was much more lavishly decorated than one would expect on a Vulcan-designed ship. Most of it consisted of low-quality (in Quark's informed opinion) erotic artwork, ranging from paintings to holosculptures. There was also an impressive display of jewels—including a remarkably good fake of the Zateri emerald—under directed floodlights that cast odd shadows about the room. At the center of the room was a table made of what appeared to be real oak, which couldn't have been cheap.

A small, sour-faced, stoop-shouldered, elderly Orion man whom Quark had last seen on the station sat at one end of that table. His name was Malic, and he had been the one to recruit Quark for this particular endeavor.

His gnarled green fingers moved furiously about the controls of a padd. Said speed was astonishing, given that he wore a ring with a heavy precious stone on each of those fingers. The padd itself was quite impressive, too—its border had an ornate pattern of fighting Aldebaran serpents, and the back had a relief representation of a nude Orion female carved into it. Several more or-dinary-looking padds sat on the table in front of him.

"Ah, Quark," Malic said without looking up from the padd. "Glad to see you've arrived in one piece. We're almost ready to begin." Finally, he looked up, and, typically, his eyes went straight to Quark's companion. "And I see you brought company."

Indicating the blond Bajoran with an exaggerated flourish, Quark said, "This is Tamra, one of my finest *dabo* girls."

"You expect to be playing *dabo,* Quark?" one of the huge Orions said with a laugh.

"No, but Malic indicated that this might be a protracted negotiation. If I'm going to be away from home this long, I'd like to have some—compan-ionship." On that last word, his hand brushed across his right lobe.

The Orions chortled knowingly.

"Of course," Quark continued as he walked to the other end of the table, "it would help if I knew just what it is I'm supposed to be negotiating. It's hard to prepare to do business when I don't know what the business is."

He sat down on the seat opposite Malic. Malic frowned—or, rather, his perpetual frown deepened—at that action. A chair had been set out at the ta-ble to Malic's left, which Quark knew was intended for him. However, he preferred to be on an equal footing—or, in this case, seating—to Malic, so he sat at an equivalent spot rather than the inherently subordinate position that had been set aside. Tamra moved into place behind Quark.

Perhaps in response to Quark's symbolic gesture, perhaps just to generally reassert his superior position here, Malic remained hunched over his padd for a full minute. Quark waited patiently, though Tamra shifted her weight from foot to foot. *I've been stalled by the best,* Quark thought with pride at the Orion. *I can wait as long as you want.*

Finally, Malic placed the padd in the inner pocket of the lavishly patterned dark green jacket he wore.

"Have you ever heard of the Iconians, Quark?"

"Sure. Ancient species, conquered most of this part of the galaxy some two hundred thousand years ago. I've auctioned some artifacts and relics of theirs over the years." *Some of them might have even been authentic.* "They're ex-tinct, though."

Malic's wrinkled lips pulled back into a rictus that one could charitably call a smile. The jewel in one of his rear molars twinkled in the glow of one of the floodlights. "Not so extinct, it would seem. The Iconians have returned, Quark, and they want to deal. And they've activated all their gateways."

"Gateways?" Quark asked.

"Portals that provide instantaneous transportation from one point in space to another. It's how the Iconians created and maintained their empire. There are thousands of them throughout the galaxy."

Nodding, Quark said, "That's how we got here from Clarus so fast."

"Exactly. There are two types of gateways—the older ones that can move ships across great distances and are usually located in planetary orbits; and the later, smaller ones on planets that can take people from one place to another in the time it takes to step through them."

"So they're like wormholes?"

"The orbital ones are similar, but they're completely stable—and I don't just mean stable the way your wormhole is stable," Malic said with another of his pseudosmiles. "I mean stable in every sense. And you arrive at your destination with much greater dispatch and less risk."

Several possibilities danced through Quark's head. He thought about the economic boom that had resulted from the opening of the Bajoran wormhole—increased traffic to Deep Space 9 and his bar; new resources to exploit and riches to obtain; more profit for Bajor, which meant more wealthy Bajorans who liked to spend money at his bar; trade with the Dominion, which increased his profit margin, since he was the first to open relations with the Dominion; and so much more. True, the war had upset much of that, but one needed only to remember the Thirty-Fourth Rule of Acquisition: "War is good for business."

From what Malic was saying, this was like the opening of the wormhole, but increased by a factor of thousands.

"Where do I come in?"

"The Iconians are auctioning off the rights to the gateways to the highest bidder. We've been able to secure private negotiations on this ship with one of their mediators."

"What are the terms?"

Malic looked up at one of the two big Orions, who walked to the table, picked up one of the padds, and handed it to Quark.

Quark took it and thumbed it. It contained three lists.

"The first list is the initial offer," Malic said, "followed by the secondary offer—"

Putting the padd down, Quark finished, "And the third is the last-resort add-ons when the bidding gets fierce, I know. This isn't my first negotiation, Malic. If it was, you wouldn't have gone to the trouble of asking for me." He picked up the padd again and held it screen-out toward Malic. "And this list needs work."

Again, Malic's frown deepened. He removed his fancy padd from his jacket pocket and looked at the screen—presumably he had called the same list onto it that Quark was speaking of. "What do you mean?"

Looking back down at the list, Quark said, "You've got rights to the dilithium mines on Dozaria in the second list. The Iconians are *getting rid* of a method of instantaneous transportation. Do you really think that dilithium mines are going to be a sweetener for them? It's just a source of extra profit, but not a compelling offer in and of itself."

"It was extremely—difficult to obtain those rights from the Breen," Malic said. "We're reluctant to part with them so easily."

"Then don't part with them at all. They're a minor component of this deal, and if they're that precious to you, save them for some time when you'll really need them. On the other hand, the acribyte futures should move to the second list—maybe the third. Acribyte wasn't discovered until long after the Iconians were last seen in this quadrant, and it only exists in one star system. It's something brand new to them, and also something immensely profitable. That's much more compelling to this type of client."

Quark suggested other rearrangements of the list before Malic finally said, "Have a care, Ferengi. Don't presume to—overstep yourself."

"I'm just trying to complete my task, Malic," Quark said, opening his arms wide.

"Your task is to negotiate with the Iconians."

"On your behalf," Quark added, "and in order to do that, I need to negotiate from the best possible position. Now if you don't want my advice, why bring me here?"

Malic said nothing.

"Fine, I'll answer my own question, then. You need me."

"The Orion Syndicate needs no one."

Quark made a "tchah" noise. "Posturing now? C'mon, Malic, I expected better from you than that." He leaned back in his chair. *Have to play this carefully.* The fact of the matter was, the syndicate could crush him like a tube grub, and Quark knew it. The Orions had their grubby green fingers in most of the illegal activity across half the quadrant—and a decent amount of the legal activity, too. They'd stayed one step ahead of Starfleet Intelligence, the Tal Shiar, the Obsidian Order, Klingon Imperial Intelligence, and the Ferengi Commerce Authority for decades.

Taking a breath, Quark continued. "Look, I freely admit that I owe you for not exposing my little scheme back on the station. It's true, you've done me a favor—but you're not doing me any favors, if you know what I mean. I can turn right around and walk out of here and take my chances back on Deep Space 9." The two guards moved forward menacingly. "Metaphorically speaking, of course," Quark added hastily. "The point is, I can handle Starfleet, and I can handle the Cardassians. Been doing it for years."

"Really? Shall we test that theory?" Malic asked nastily. "All it will take is a simple command on this padd, and all the details will be transferred to a

Commander Ju'les L'ullho on Starbase 96 and to certain individuals on Cardassia Prime."

"That won't be necessary," Quark said quickly. "What I'm trying to say here is that—well, no offense, but, you're pirates. You're used to taking what you want, not asking for it. That's why you need me—I know how to get you a bargain. So are you going to take advantage of my skills—which were the whole reason why you talked me into coming here in the first place—or are you going to guarantee that you'll lose the gateways before I ever even walk into the negotiating room?"

Malic glowered at Quark for several seconds. Quark didn't move, didn't even blink. *I've sat through Odo's interrogations, I can sit through this old slug's stare.*

Finally, Malic looked down at his padd and said, "What other changes would you like to make?"

Smiling, Quark proceeded to continue with his suggested changes to the list.

Once they'd gotten everything to a satisfactory level, Malic said, without looking up, "Bring some tube grubs for our negotiator—and see if there are any Bajoran hors d'oeuvres left for his companion." One of the two Orion landmasses moved toward the door.

Quark inclined his head toward Malic. "I admire a man who knows how to treat the hired help."

Another Orion entered the room. "The Iconians have arrived, along with their mediator. I've installed them in the conference room."

"Good." Malic looked up at Quark. "Do well for us, Quark. The syndicate does not tolerate failure."

The implication came through quite clearly: if the Orions did not wind up with control of the gateways, Quark would be held responsible. Never mind exposing his scam on Cardassia—Quark suspected that the syndicate's ideas of retribution would get a good deal more unpleasant.

The oversized Orions stood on either side of Quark. "Let's go," one of them said.

"Don't I get my tube grubs?" Quark asked, looking up at one of the Orions—who was actually staring at Tamra as he spoke.

"We'll bring 'em to the table. Move."

"Fine."

Quark got up, and he and Tamra followed the Orion out the door, then down a corridor to another conference room.

This one was somewhat larger than the previous room, and much more tastefully decorated. No erotica here, but an impressive array of paintings lined the walls, including the best fake of T'Nare of Vulcan's *ShiKahr Sunrise* Quark had ever seen. *If I'd had fakes that good when I was selling that alleged lot of T'Nare's work, I wouldn't have had to pay that fine.* This table also appeared to be made of oak, but Quark's practiced eye recognized it as an Ordek transformer table, which could take on different appearances. At its center was a pair of opaque pitchers and two mugs.

Personally, Quark thought, *I'd have chosen something a bit more friendly. There's something foreboding about oak.*

Then Quark looked at the people in the room, and tried to keep his jaw from dropping.

Standing around the table were two tall, skinny bipeds with yellowish skin. Their features seemed unfinished, almost like Odo's. They wore outfits of green satin similar to the type favored by the more well-to-do members of the Orion Syndicate—light green cape with dark green brocade, a loose-fitting tunic and tight pants the same color as the brocade.

All of that registered in Quark's mind peripherally. Most of his attention was focused on the person sitting at the head of the table. It was a Ferengi with small beady eyes and sporting a huge sneer. He was dressed in a suit of the finest Tholian silk. The Forty-Seventh Rule of Acquisition came to mind: "Never trust a man wearing a better suit than your own."

And this Ferengi was definitely not one to be trusted, regardless of his suit.

"Gaila." Quark said the name in a dull monotone.

"Pleasure to see you, cousin," Gaila said. His sneer widened.

Gaila, to whom Quark had made a loan years ago to help him start his business. Gaila, whose subsequent success as an arms dealer was profitable enough to allow him to buy his own moon. Gaila, who gave Quark a ship in order to repay that loan, but sabotaged it, an incident from which Quark, his brother, and his nephew barely survived. Gaila, who brought Quark into the weapons business to help alleviate Quark's near-destitute state after he'd been banned by the Ferengi Commerce Authority.

Gaila, whom Quark had betrayed to General Nassuc of Palamar, which had resulted in Gaila becoming a target of the general's "purification squad." Gaila, whom Quark had last seen on Deep Space 9 as a wreck, a shadow of his former self, aiding Quark on a lunatic mission to rescue Quark's mother, Ishka, from Dominion forces.

"I was wondering where you've been keeping yourself," Quark said.

"I've been busy. But we're not here to talk about old times, cousin. Please, have a seat. Let's get started." Gaila smiled. "We have a *lot* of work to do, if we're to hammer out any kind of deal here."

"Of course," Quark said agreeably, and sat at the place opposite Gaila.

He could feel in his lobes that Gaila was going to make sure that this deal would, in fact, be as much work as possible.

The preliminary negotiations were just that—nothing ever got accomplished during an initial session. Generally, it was just an opportunity for the negotiators to get a feel for each other, and for the precise nature of the deal to be spelled out. The Iconians were offering exclusive rights to, and complete instructions on how to operate, all the gateways in the galaxy. Not just the Alpha Quadrant, but the entire galaxy.

Mentally, Quark had had to rearrange the order of the list. He had not realized quite how far-flung these gateways were, and certain items would need to be moved further up the list if they were even going to have a hope of negotiating with these aliens.

Of course, the negotiator wasn't alien at all. Quark and Gaila had known each other since they were boys cheating the younger kids out of their lunch money so they could buy the latest Marauder Mo action figures.

The question is, will Gaila take advantage of this negotiation to get some of his own back? After all, the last two times he and Quark had been together, Gaila had almost gotten himself killed, and Quark had also been more or less directly responsible for Gaila hitting absolute bottom. Ferengi generally didn't let personal grudges get in the way of business, but Quark couldn't really count on that.

Now they were taking a half-hour break—ostensibly for a meal, but truthfully so each side could figure out what their offer was really going to be. As soon as Quark, Tamra, and the two giants entered Malic's private conference room, the elderly Orion said, "So he's your cousin, is he?"

"Yes, Gaila's my cousin. We've known each other since we were kids. He and I have even done a few business deals together."

"Is that going to be a problem?"

Quark shrugged, and lied. "I don't see why it should be. Gaila's a businessman. I'm a businessman. We're both going to do the best we can for our clients. And, before you ask, I won't be able to prevail upon him to give me a break because I'm family."

"I wasn't going to ask that," Malic said sourly. "I've done my research on you, Quark. The last person I would expect to give you a break is someone who's known you since you were a child."

Nodding, Quark said, "It's possible that Gaila's presence will slow the negotiations down a bit. After all, Gaila and I know each other's tricks—it just means we'll each have to come up with new tricks, so I wouldn't be *too* concerned. As a matter of fact—"

"Quark, the more you try to convince me that there won't be any problems, the more convinced I am that there will be. So kindly shut up, and take a look at this." He indicated a padd on the table, and one of the Orions picked it up and handed it to Quark.

The display showed a report from a Starfleet vessel called the *T'Kumbra*. Quark remembered that as Captain Solok's ship—*the ones who defeated us in that silly human bays-ball game of Captain Sisko's.* The report was incomplete, but one of the items in it was that there were no gateways at all in the Bajoran system—a twenty-light-year-diameter hole in the gateway lattice, in fact.

Smiling, Quark said, "Interesting that the Iconians didn't mention this when they were carrying on about how there were gateways *all* over the galaxy."

"Very interesting. I think it's worth mentioning at the next session, don't you?"

Quark nodded.

A half an hour later, Quark didn't even sit down before he said, "You told us that these gateways were in every sector of the galaxy."

Frowning, Gaila said, "They are."

"Really?" Quark stood next to his chair and looked down at Gaila on the other side. "Then why is it that there isn't a single gateway within ten light-years of Bajor?"

Gaila, to his credit, barely missed a beat. "What need is there for one? You have the wormhole, after all."

"Which was discovered less than a decade ago." Quark finally sat down. "Whereas the Iconian gateways were—apparently—built around it long before anyone knew it was there. Seems to me that this should have been mentioned at some point."

Gaila leaned back. "We're under no obligation to explain ourselves to you, Quark."

"No, but it does make me wonder what other little facts you've managed to leave out."

"We've left nothing out, Quark."

Quark regarded his cousin with what he hoped was a penetrating gaze. "You've said that before."

"It should be pointed out," Gaila said, "that the Breen, the Romulan Empire, and the Klingon Empire don't much care if there aren't any gateways around Bajor. After all, with the gateways reactivated, the strategic value of the wormhole will plunge to nothing. And they've all made very competitive offers."

"You forget, cousin, that I'm not here on my behalf, but as a representative of the Orions. They don't care about Bajor, either—they do care about being lied to in a good-faith negotiation."

Smiling, Gaila said, "Quark, you're always working on your own behalf—one way or the other."

Quark swallowed, but said nothing.

"Hig."

"Hig here. What is it, Kam?"

"There's a problem."

"Another one?"

"This is serious, Hig."

"I'm always serious. What's the problem?"

"There's apparently some kind of flaw in the gateway network. There aren't any gateways within ten light-years of System 418—the natives call it Bajor."

"That's where that stable wormhole is, yes?"

"Yes. I want you to head over there right away."

"Why?"

"Two reasons. One, see if you can figure out why there aren't any gateways there. Two, see if the Bajorans or Starfleet or anyone else is trying to figure out why there aren't any gateways there."

"What if they do find out?"

"Do whatever's necessary to stop them. We can't let anything slow these negotiations down. We're going to have enough problems as it is—the Orions have already complicated things by bringing a Ferengi of their own in. Those two will likely go at it for days. The longer this takes, the harder it will be to maintain the illusion."

"Fine. I'll take the gateway to System 429 and head to System 418 from there. I'll let you know what I find out."

"Good."

Chapter Five

The Wormhole

"Nog, can I ask you a question?"

At Shar's words, Nog turned to look at the Andorian sitting in the *Sungari*'s copilot seat. Shar had waited until they had come to a relative stop near the mouth of the wormhole before posing his query.

"Sure."

Shar was still working his console as he spoke. "Why haven't you asked me about my *zhavey?*"

Nog broke into a smile. Shar's *zhavey*—apparently, the Andorian equivalent of a *moogie*—was a Federation Councillor, a fact that had come to light around the same time as that mess with the Jem'Hadar.

"To be honest, I've gotten so sick of people asking me what my father is like, I didn't think you'd appreciate being pestered with the same question."

"Sensors are calibrated—beginning sweep." Once that was done, Shar finally looked up at Nog. "Interesting. So people ask you about your father?"

"All the time. Well, mostly asking how he's changed. See, that's the thing, Father lived on the station for ten years before he became Grand Nagus, so everyone knew him."

"Interesting," Shar repeated. Then he looked back down at his readouts. "I've done a full scan of the wormhole. Everything's within established norms. So far I'm not detecting anything that would explain the lack of gateways in this sector."

"So it's probably something natural to the wormhole?"

Shar's antennae quivered. "We don't even know for sure that the wormhole is connected—it's a vague hypothesis based on circumstantial evidence. I've read the data from Starfleet on the Iconian technology and programmed the *Sungari* computer to compare that to what we receive from these scans to see if there's any correlation. So far, there's nothing showing up on sensors that would prevent the gateways from functioning."

Nog shot Shar a look. "You went over *all* the data?"

"No, I *read* all the data. Twice. Commander Vaughn did ask us to be familiar with it."

Nog blinked. "You read fast."

Shar shrugged.

Nog tried not to let his frustration show. He'd barely had time to look at the data, what with replicating and installing the Shelliak shield modulators, though the latter, at least, he had been able to delegate to other engineers on his staff. Of course, Ezri had to remind him that he *had* a staff to delegate it to. *I'm still thinking like a cadet. . . .*

"With your permission, Nog, I'd like to try a few more specialized scans," Shar said.

It took Nog a second to remember that he needed to actually give the order. "Okay," he said. That didn't sound like an officer, so he quickly added, "Ensign."

Yup, definitely still thinking like a cadet.

After a few moments, Nog asked, "Actually, I do have a question. What's it like?"

"My *zhavey*, you mean?"

"Not exactly. What's it like for *you?*" When Shar hesitated, Nog added, "It's just that, all my life, Father's just been a regular Ferengi—not even that, really. Now he's the most important Ferengi in the galaxy. It's kind of—well, daunting."

"That is a very good word for it," Shar said. "The magnetron scan is negative. Trying a positron scan now."

"Okay," Nog said. "It's funny, but part of the reason I joined Starfleet was so I wouldn't turn out like my father."

That got Shar's attention. "How so?"

"Well, at the time, my father was working for Uncle Quark. He was the assistant manager of policy and clientele."

Shar looked as befuddled as everyone else did whenever they heard that particular title. "What does that mean, exactly?"

Chuckling, Nog said, "In practical terms, it meant that Father did whatever Uncle Quark told him to do." He turned and looked at Shar. "My father is an engineering genius. And he was trapped under my uncle—I didn't want to be like that. I knew I could do better."

"So you did. In fact, I'd say you probably did better than your father."

Nog frowned. "What do you mean?"

"I'm sorry, sir, I spoke out of turn." Shar turned back to his console.

"It's okay, Shar, please—tell me what you meant."

Shar hesitated. "I've seen what your father accomplished once he joined the engineering staff on the station. Those self-replicating mines of his that they put in front of the wormhole probably kept the war from ending badly two years sooner. I just don't see why he would abandon that to go into politics."

Nog adjusted the runabout's position as it started to drift away from the wormhole. "My father has a chance to change the face of Ferengi culture!"

Shar looked back up. "Really?"

"Yes. My father was entrusted with the nagushood and a mandate from former Grand Nagus Zek to bring about major reforms in Ferengi business practices."

At that, Nog thought he saw Shar's antennae move back slightly. Nog wondered if it was an expression of surprise. Shar said, "Well, my *zhavey* was elected to the position of Councillor with a mandate from the Andorian people to improve our trading positions with non-Federation worlds. It hasn't happened yet, and she was elected eight years ago. May your father have better luck." And then Shar smiled.

"I hope so," Nog said in all seriousness. "I think he has the potential to make our society even greater."

"How so?"

Shar seemed genuinely curious, so Nog checked the *Sungari*'s position, and then began to go into a lengthy explanation of the reforms that Grandmother Ishka and Zek had devised and that Father was supposed to put into action.

They spent the better part of the day working and talking about it, interrupted by the occasional monitoring of short-range sensors and Shar's reports of his scans—none of which were of any help regarding the gateways. They paused for lunch—Nog convinced Shar to try a tube grub, which the Andorian didn't like any more than Prynn Tenmei had—and Shar asked more questions about the reforms.

"So women are allowed to wear clothes now?"

"Allowed, yes," Nog said as he washed a tube grub down with a swig of root beer. "Not all of them do, particularly once you get out of the capital city. But more and more are. If nothing else, it's cut down on illnesses—which has the doctors in an uproar."

"I don't understand."

Nog smiled. "Ferenginar in general and the capital city in particular have a very damp climate. Women got all kinds of bronchial infections and things regularly when they'd go out. With more women wearing clothes, they don't get sick as often, so the doctors do less business."

Shar took a bite of his *jumja* stick. The Andorian had made a point of trying other worlds' cuisines—which was why he'd been willing to sample the tube grub—and he had developed a particular taste for *jumja,* much to Nog's abject confusion. "I have to confess, I never would have thought of the economic implications of women wearing clothes on the medical profession."

Laughing, Nog said, "Unfortunately, Father has to. According to his last letter, he's had to sign off on all kinds of concessions to the medical association."

Once they finished eating, they went through the wormhole and ran a few more scans inside, then the same ones on the Gamma Quadrant side. The end result was more of the same.

It took a while for Nog to notice that Shar had never actually answered his question. *That's the second time he's danced around it,* Nog thought. He considered trying again, then decided that, if his friend didn't want to talk about it, Nog would respect that.

As Nog piloted the runabout back into the wormhole, Shar said, "Wait a moment. Computer, is the Kar-telos system within ten light-years of the Gamma Quadrant mouth of the wormhole?"

"Affirmative."

"We are fools. All of us. It cannot be the wormhole that is causing that gap. The *Halloran* fell through a gateway in the Kar-telos system."

Nog blinked. "You're right. It's got to be something else. Well, wait a minute, it could be an unscientific reason." As Nog spoke, the *Sungari* came out the Alpha Quadrant side.

Shar looked at the Ferengi. "What do you mean?"

"We don't know what this area of space was like when the Iconians were around. For all we know, there was some kind of treaty with the people who lived here to keep out any gateways."

Shar nodded. "Good point. Still, I hope they're not putting too much hope in this. The chance that we'll find the one thing—"

"It's not our place to assume anything, Ensign," Nog said sharply. "We just do what we're told."

"I know, and we're doing it. But it's getting us nowhere. I've done every scan the *Sungari* is capable of."

Nog couldn't help but agree. They'd spent too long at this as it was. "I'm setting course back to DS9. We can look at the data just as easily there—this way we'll free up the runabout for Europa Nova if we need it."

"Wait."

Frowning, Nog said, "What?"

Shar was touching his left antenna. "The Denorios Belt. It's full of tachyon eddies, isn't it?"

"Yes."

"That might be it, then." Shar called up a record on the viewscreen. It was a Starfleet data record—with, Nog noticed, some information removed. "This is the declassified portion of Commander Vaughn's mission to Alexandra's Planet. Tricorder readings showed that for a fraction of a second, there was a disruptive effect on the gateway right around the time they were trying to detect a cloaked Romulan ship."

Nog put it together. "Tachyon bursts are used to detect cloaked ships."

"Exactly. And it makes sense. The wormhole is a local phenomenon. At its absolute worst, it never has any impact on the space around it outside the range of the Denorios Belt."

Picking up the ball, Nog said, "But tachyons move faster than light." He snapped his fingers, a sudden gesture that made Shar jump. "Sorry, but I just remembered something. A couple of years ago, Captain Sisko re-created a Bajoran solar sailing ship."

"Yes, I remember reading about that," Shar said. "What of it?"

"That ship got caught in one of those tachyon eddies and wound up in the Cardassian solar system. Later, the Cardassians admitted that the ship the captain based his design on did the same thing centuries ago."

Shar's antennae pulled back again. "Cardassia is within ten light-years of Bajor. Nog, I believe we have a workable theory."

"Now we just need to test it," Nog said. "And it makes a lot more sense than the wormhole. The belt has always been a navigation hazard. That's why it took so long for anyone to discover the wormhole in the first place." He smiled and added, "Just don't tell Colonel Kira I said that."

Shar frowned. "Why not?"

"Adjusting position for best scanning vector," Nog said, then turned back to the Andorian. "As far as the Bajorans are concerned, the Celestial Temple went undiscovered until seven years ago because the Prophets were waiting for the Emissary."

Shar seemed to consider that. "That's actually a perfectly valid interpretation of the facts. In fact, you could even argue that the Prophets made the Denorios Belt such a navigation hazard in order to keep the temple hidden until the right moment."

Nog grinned. "Do you believe that?"

"Well, I'm not a Bajoran, and I wasn't raised in that religious tradition, so no, but it's an interesting hypothesis."

"So there's no way I'm going to convince you that you need to live a profitable life so you can go to the Divine Treasury when you die?"

Shar said in all seriousness, "Probably not, no. The Andorian afterlife is a bit more—complicated than that, I'm afraid." He turned to his console. "Computer, do a detailed scan of the Denorios Belt and then run program ch'Thane Gateway One using that data."

"*Acknowledged,*" said the pleasant, mechanical voice.

"*Sungari* to Deep Space 9," Nog said, opening a channel to ops.

"*Dax here. Go ahead, Nog.*"

"Lieutenant, Ensign ch'Thane and I have developed a working theory for the lack of gateways in this sector. He's running tests now to confirm it, but we're pretty sure it has something to do with the tachyon eddies in the Denorios Belt, not the wormhole."

"*Good work, Nog. I'll let Commander Vaughn know.*"

"Thanks, Lieutenant. How's the rescue mission going?"

"*Slowly but surely. The first contingent of refugees are expected within the hour.*"

"Great. I don't think we'll be at this more than another hour, so the *Sungari* should be available if they need it."

"*I'll let Commander Vaughn know that, too,*" Dax said. Nog could almost see her smile.

Sighing, he thought, *Dr. Bashir is a lucky man.* Aloud, he simply said, "*Sungari* out."

"I think I have something, Nog," Shar said, looking over a readout on his console. "Based on the records from Alexandra's Planet, and also some of Professor Namthot's notes, a compressed tachyon burst *should* disrupt the gateways, if combined with certain noble gases." With a smile, he turned to Nog. "All those gases are present in the Denorios Belt. We just need to figure out some way to harness them and combine it with the burst. I'm not sure how we could do that, but—"

Nog peered at the readout. "Oh, that's easy. Rig the Bussard collectors on the *Defiant*—or some other starship—for those gases, modify an intermix chamber to infuse the tachyon burst with them, and then run it through the phaser banks—oh, wait." He took a closer look at Shar's display. "No, something like this, we'll need to run it through the deflector array—the phaser banks would burn out after two seconds."

Shar stared at Nog. "If you say so," he said slowly.

"One question, though—you said 'disrupt.' Disrupt, how?"

Sighing, Shar said, "I wish I could answer that. We just don't know enough about how the gateways *really* work. All of this is pure theory, but at least it's consistent with the available data. The problem is the unavailable data. That could easily come along and slice off our antennae."

"So for all we know, this tachyon burst will make the gateways belch fire or something?"

Shar's antennae quivered. "Let's not be silly. Still, it's a concern."

"Yes, but it's not our concern. That's Colonel Kira and Commander Vaughn's problem. Are you done here?"

Taking one last look at the data he'd accumulated, Shar said, "Yes, I think I've done all I can."

"Then let's get back. Setting course for DS9."

That's when a strange vessel came out of warp and fired on the *Sungari*.

"Damage report!" Nog cried as he quickly put the runabout's shields up. *What is it* this *time?* he wondered. It all happened incredibly fast. One moment they were alone, the next an odd-looking, oblong vessel ten times the size of the runabout blasted out of subspace.

"Heavy damage to the starboard nacelle," Shar said. "Nothing critical, but we can't go to warp."

"Returning fire." Nog targeted the phasers on the newcomer. *I'm just glad I put off installing the shield modulator on the* Sungari, *or this damage would be a lot worse.*

"Minor damage to their shields," Shar said. "There's no match for this ship in the databank, although parts of it are similar to known ships. Length, two hundred meters, hull composed of a variety of rodinium alloys—except for the secondary hull, which is duranium. Their weapons are some kind of directed ladrion pulse."

"Whatever that is," Nog muttered.

Another impact. "Shields at sixty percent. Structural-integrity field weakened."

"Send out a distress call to the station."

"Aye, sir."

Looking down at the console, Nog programmed a random firing pattern that Worf had taught him. It was designed to score multiple hits on enemy shields as hard as possible. The pattern was designed for the *Defiant,* which had more powerful phasers, but the *Sungari* was more maneuverable. After that, he set a course that the computer knew as Kira-Three.

"What are you doing?" Shar asked, sounding concerned.

"Something Colonel Kira taught us about taking on a big ship with a small one."

"Lieutenant, I don't think the SIF can handle this kind of maneuvering."

Another impact. "I know we can't handle sitting here. Implementing pattern."

The runabout moved in a zigzagging spiral pattern around the larger vessel, phasers firing at multiple points on their shields.

"SIF holding," Shar said. "Their shields are weakening."

Just as the *Sungari* came about on its last pass, the enemy vessel fired again.

Several of the aft consoles blew out. Nog's console stopped responding to his commands. The runabout continued forward on its own momentum, Nog unable to control the vessel's movements any longer.

"Shields down!" Shar said over the din of the alarms. "Impulse engines and weapons offline, transporters down, and SIF at fourteen percent." Shar looked over at Nog. "One bit of good news: their shields are down as well. Your maneuver worked."

Nog ground his teeth. "That might mean something if we still had weapons. Did the station get our distress call?"

"Impossible to be sure, but considering that all of our other ships are at Europa Nova . . ." Shar trailed off, then glanced at his console as it beeped. "They're coming around for another pass."

"Ready thrusters," Nog said.

"We can't evade their weapons with thrusters," Shar said.

Nog's left leg started to itch again. "It beats sitting still and waiting for it. Transmit the specs for the tachyon burst to the station in case we don't make it."

"Done," Shar acknowledged. His console beeped again. "They're charging weapons."

Nog closed his eyes.

Chapter Six

Europa Nova

"Coming out of warp, entering standard orbit."

Colonel Kira Nerys's fingers flew over the console of the *Euphrates,* suiting actions to words as she led the convoy of nineteen vessels into orbit of the Class-M planet. The world was a bit smaller than Bajor, and looked more blue from orbit than the greener tinge of home—or, at least, parts of it did. As the *Euphrates* and the other ships entered orbit, antimatter waste became visible. Amorphous green material, it clustered in chunks in a close orbit, hanging menacingly over the exosphere.

Kira then looked back down at the screen on her console. She'd been studying the library records on Europa Nova. The planet was pastoral—like Earth, covered in oceans; like Bajor, awash in vegetation.

Or, at least, she thought, *like Bajor was before the Cardassians.* Seven years later, even with the best efforts of the planetary government and the Federation, Bajor still bore the scars of the previous half-century.

But Europa Nova had been spared those scars. The colonists had built carefully, constructing their small cities in places that could handle the inevitable environmental damage of urbanization with minimal impact on the overall ecosystem, and utilizing the arable land for farms. Five cities were festooned about the landmasses, including one on a remote island. Smaller villages, towns, military bases, and research centers dotted the rest of the two continents.

Kira had been especially fascinated by the cities. Generally, the architectural progression of a city—if it had one at all—was to emanate from the old in the center to the new as it expanded outward. Bajor, for instance, had several cities with millennia-old temples and other older buildings in the middle of town, surrounded by more modern architecture. Europani cities, however, went the other way around: dull, modern, prefabricated structures formed the hubs of the cities—the original, simple constructions of the twenty-third-century colonists who of necessity favored functionality over aesthetics. As the cities expanded and the colony prospered, the buildings became more elaborate and artistic. According to the records, the style was a melding of Earth Gothic and Tellarite *Churlnik*—both involving elaborate decorations on stonework.

The world also had gained an impressively rich cultural and scientific reputation during its first hundred years. Europani duranium sculpture had become especially popular in the last decade or so—there had been an exhibit at the Akorem Laan Museum on Bajor a few years back—and, according to Keiko O'Brien, some of the most important breakthroughs in botany and agriculture of the last fifty years were by Europani.

And these people repelled the Breen. Where Bajor at the height of its renaissance still fell victim to the Cardassian occupation, where Earth itself had been unable to prevent the sneak attack that had devastated Starfleet Headquarters, this group of humans, who had barely been on their world for a full century, managed to stay out of the Dominion War.

Next to her, Taran'atar said, "I am reading an *Akira*-class Starfleet ship already in orbit. It registers as the *U.S.S. Gryphon*. There are also several non-Starfleet transports—and an increasing amount of theta radiation originating from the antimatter waste field dead ahead."

Kira nodded, then opened a channel. *"Euphrates to Gryphon."*

Turning to the small viewscreen on her left, Kira found herself once again facing the round visage of Captain Elaine Mello.

"Glad to see you, Colonel," Mello said. *"I've been in touch with the Europani authorities, and we started bringing up the sick and injured who can be transported."*

"Good," Kira said.

"Otherwise, they're implementing an evac plan. Wicked efficient, from what I've been able to see so far. They've already gotten most of their children off-planet by using their own civilian vessels, as well as their military transports. We're only going to have to handle the adults."

Kira breathed a sigh of relief at that—both because the children were already safe, and because it would cut the load the convoy would have to deal with by a third.

Mello went on. *"I'm having a copy of the plan sent to you, the* Defiant, *the* Intrepid, *and the* Rio Grande." Then she frowned, as her gaze moved past Kira. *"Colonel, is that—"*

"Yes, he's a Jem'Hadar. He's a cultural observer, here on my authority."

"If you say so," Mello said, a dubious expression on her face. *"President Silverio said she wanted to talk to you as soon as you were in orbit."*

"Thank you, Captain. I'll be in touch shortly. Kira out." She had been grateful that Mello was going to defer to her command. Since Kira wasn't Starfleet, she had been concerned that the captains would take charge, but it seemed both Mello and Emick considered her the mission commander. She probably had Ross to thank for that, and she made a mental note to mention it the next time they spoke.

Mello also obviously had a war veteran's distrust of a recent enemy, but she was apparently willing to defer to Kira's judgment about Taran'atar as well. Kira could understand the captain's concern, but she also understood the importance of Taran'atar's mission. *Odo sent him to begin bridging the gap between the Dominion and their enemies—former enemies,* she amended. That bridge needed to be built. Kira herself had learned the hard way that not all Cardassians were evil, conquering sadists—*though the species has their share of them,* she thought, an image of Dukat floating unwelcome into her mind. But there were good Cardassians—Ghemor, Marritza, Damar in the end, even Garak, to a degree—and Kira had even helped Damar's resistance movement against the Dominion. If she could put aside her lifelong distrust for all things Cardassian to help Damar, she could put aside the last few years of conflict against the

Dominion to help Taran'atar's mission succeed. She owed Odo that much, and more.

Pushing thoughts of her faraway lover to the back of her mind, she opened a channel to the surface. Soon after, a tired-looking human face appeared on the screen.

Had Kira met President Grazia Silverio on the Promenade, she would have pegged the older woman as someone's kindly aunt or grandmother, not a head of state. She had short, curly, paper-white hair, a wrinkled if pleasant face, a bulbous nose, and a jowly neck. The deepest wrinkles were next to the eyes and bordering the mouth, indicating someone who smiled a lot.

She was not, however, smiling now. Her face was long, and her eyes were tired.

"You're Colonel Nerys?" she said without preamble.

"Colonel Kira, actually. Bajoran tradition puts the family name first."

"I'm sorry, Colonel. I'm afraid things are a bit hectic right now."

"Understandable, ma'am."

Silverio waved her right arm. *"Apf. None of this 'ma'am.' Call me Grazia. I've gotten enough 'ma'am' the last few days to last me until I die. Which probably won't be too long now. And before you say anything, I'm not being fatalistic about the radiation—I'm old, that means I'm going to die soon. That's the way of the galaxy. But I'm not going to die today, and neither is anyone else. We didn't fight off the Breen just to let some radiation do us in. You've seen the evacuation plan?"*

"Not yet." She looked over at Taran'atar, who nodded. "We're receiving it from the *Gryphon* now."

"Good. We've gotten most of the children off, as well as about a thousand adults. Altogether that's about a million that have already made it off-planet."

"That's good to hear," Kira said with a small smile. "They can proceed to Deep Space 9. The station's acting commander, Lieutenant Dax, is coordinating housing efforts both on the station and on Bajor—tell the ships to contact her when they arrive."

Silverio nodded. *"Our treatment facilities could use some assistance, also—we're running out of hyronalin, and our surgeon general tells me that isn't even the best treatment."*

"No, it isn't. *Euphrates* to *Defiant.*"

"Vaughn here. Go ahead, Colonel."

"Commander, have Dr. Bashir contact the Europani surgeon general—"

Silverio said, *"Dr. Martino DeLaCruz."*

Nodding, Kira continued, "Their hospitals need arithrazine. I want him to organize a distribution program. Have him coordinate with the *Intrepid*'s CMO—the *Gryphon*'s handling the evac of the sick and injured, so let them deal with that."

"Understood. Anything else?"

"That's it for now. I'll be in touch shortly. Kira out."

Silverio said with a tired smile, *"Thank you, Colonel. Right now, the remaining population is gathering in each of the five major cities for mass transport."*

"Good. We'll use transporters for as long as is practical. Most of the ships can land—" Kira had made sure that the ten Bajoran ships had atmospheric capability, and the runabouts, most of the civilian ships, and the *Intrepid* all could land as well "—and we'll do that, once the radiation gets past the point where we can use transporters. We also hope to figure out how to cut off the radiation."

"That'd be good. This is our home, Colonel, and we don't abandon it easily."

"You won't have to, ma—Grazia," she amended with a smile. "You have my word, I'll do everything in my power to restore your world."

At that, the president's face blossomed into a smile. *"I appreciate that, Colonel. One other thing. We'd like to get Councillor zh'Thane out of here before the radiation gets much worse. She's our invited guest, after all, and it's bad form to give your guests radiation poisoning. She allowed us to use her own ship to transport some of the children off."*

Kira was impressed—politicians didn't often make that kind of sacrifice, though she supposed the councillor would put the goodwill gesture to use in negotiations. *Not that I'm cynical or anything,* she thought wryly. "Understood. We'll beam her to the *Defiant* as soon as possible."

"Excellent."

"I'll contact you again once I've gone over the evacuation plan. *Euphrates* out."

President Silverio's face disappeared from the screen.

Kira glanced over the evac plan, which was refreshingly well-ordered, and also similar to a standard Federation evacuation agenda—which they no doubt based it on. "Taran'atar, open a channel to all the ships in the convoy."

"Channel open," the Jem'Hadar said after a moment.

"This is Colonel Kira. At the moment, the theta radiation is within tolerances of the transporters, but the level is increasing and we'll lose that ability pretty quickly. For now, we've got five major cities and a lot of other, more rural areas to cover. The *Defiant* will handle L'Aquila. The *Gryphon* will take Spilimbergo, the *Xhosa* will handle Chieti, the *Intrepid* and the *Goldblatt's Folly* will take Padilla, and—" she sighed "—the *East Winds* will take Libre Pista." L'Aquila was the capital city, though the least populous of the five major urban areas—in any case, Kira wanted Vaughn to deal personally with the VIPs who'd be coming up from there, including Councillor zh'Thane. Padilla was the most populous city, and would require two ships. "The *Rio Grande* and the *Halloran* will take the smaller towns on the northern continent, and the *Ng* and the *Euphrates* will take the smaller towns on the southern continent. That still leaves a wide range of rural and pastoral land. Colonel Lenaris?"

The commander of the Lamnak fleet said, *"Yes?"*

"I want you to divide the remaining land into nine areas and dispatch nine of your ships to seek out and transport personnel in those areas. Use your remaining ship to scan the islands."

"Will do."

Kira smiled. Lenaris Holem had been a member of the Ornathia cell during the resistance, and had been involved in the historic Pullock V raid. Later, he'd been instrumental in defusing a crisis in Dakhur Province over the disposition of some soil reclamators. Lenaris himself hadn't made much of his role in that crisis, but those events had led to Shakaar Edon running for, and winning the position of, first minister of Bajor. Kira's former resistance-cell leader had had a most successful reign thus far, and Lenaris's actions had a lot to do with allowing that to come about.

Lenaris was also deeply religious, she knew, as most of his people must also have been, and he probably wasn't entirely comfortable dealing with Kira as one Attainted by the Vedek Assembly. But Kira also knew that Lenaris was too professional to allow any personal feelings to obstruct his duty, especially if lives were on the line. Kira was grateful that the Militia had assigned him to the evac mission. If anyone could get out all the Europani who might still be in the assorted nooks, crannies, trees, and caves of the planet, it was Lenaris.

"You have your assignments—let's get to work. Kira out."

"Colonel, a moment, please?" Vaughn's voice.

"Be right with you, Commander." She closed the general connection, then went ship-to-ship with the *Defiant.* "All right, go ahead."

"Lieutenant Dax relayed a communication from Farius Prime. According to our source there, the Iconians are, in fact, peddling two kinds of gateways. Besides the ones we're familiar with, there are also large orbital ones. Apparently, the original Enterprise *encountered one a century ago on Stardate 5720. I think it's safe to say we've got one in orbit here."*

"All right. Try to get a sensor reading through the theta radiation and see if you can detect the gateway—maybe we can find a way to shut it down before the situation gets worse."

"Aye, sir. Vaughn out."

Kira closed the connection, and said, "Setting course for the southern continent."

"Shields raised for atmospheric entry," Taran'atar said. "There is no indication that the Ferengi's modifications will have any deleterious effect." Then he turned to Kira. "Colonel, may I ask a question?"

"Of course," Kira said, surprised.

"Why did you take command of this inferior vessel instead of the warship?"

Kira smiled. *It figures he'd pick up on that. Sure, I could have taken the* Defiant *myself. It's part of my command, after all. But part of being in command is delegating responsibility.*

She said none of this to Taran'atar, saying instead, "I've always been more comfortable with the runabouts. They remind me of the flitters we flew during the occupation. The *Defiant*'s too much like the Cardassian ships we fought against."

"You prefer the weapon you are used to."

Kira almost smiled. "Something like that. Entering atmosphere."

The viewscreen became all but useless as the *Euphrates* entered a thick cloud layer.

Of course, there was another reason, which she felt it was impolitic to mention directly to Taran'atar. While the Jem'Hadar had proven as good as his word so far—and indeed had been useful both against the renegade Jem'Hadar who attacked the station and on Bashir's enforced errand for Section 31—the fact was that most of the crew didn't yet trust him entirely. Kira had thought it best to have Taran'atar where she could keep an eye on him, and also keep him from interacting directly with Starfleet personnel who until recently might have shot Taran'atar on sight.

A Starfleet captain would have had Taran'atar on the Defiant, a voice in the back of her head said. *Probably alongside a speech about how we'll never learn to trust each other until someone takes the first step.*

Kira slapped the voice down. *I'm not a Starfleet captain.*

But that single thought brought with it another—one that had been recurring ever since Starfleet had first come to the station more than seven years ago. The thought had become more prominent since Shakaar had informed her how close Bajor was again to joining the Federation. When that happened, the Militia would be absorbed into Starfleet, and all Bajoran officers and enlisted personnel who chose to stay would have to trade their uniforms for another, one that stood not just for one world, but a plurality. It was, she knew, what DS9 had been about from the beginning. In part it was also what Bajor's role in the relief efforts to Cardassia was about, and this mission to help the Europani—Bajor was learning to think outside the confines of one planet and one people. And if that were true, then the next logical step for Kira would be to put on a Starfleet uniform again, as she'd done to help the Cardassian resistance. She recalled vividly that at the time, it had been a strange fit.

But was it the right fit?

Her musings were interrupted by Taran'atar. "I have another question, Colonel. You and President Silverio indicated that you intend to restore Europa Nova."

"Of course."

"There's no known way to dispose of theta radiation on this scale. The most efficient course would be to relocate the inhabitants to another planet."

"This is their *home.*"

"I don't understand." Taran'atar seemed genuinely confused. "It is simply a planet. To try to restore it is a waste of resources."

Kira shook her head. "There's nothing 'simple' about it, Taran'atar. Saving a home is never a waste."

"Please explain."

She had expected the request to be phrased disdainfully, but Taran'atar seemed genuinely curious. *I guess that comes with age,* she thought with mild amusement. Taran'atar was twenty-two years old, which made him an "Honored Elder" by Jem'Hadar standards. Bred solely for military combat, few Jem'Hadar lived past the age of ten.

Kira started several sentences in her head before finally committing to one. "I've spent my life fighting for Bajor. It isn't just a planet I happened to be born on. It's *home.*"

"You keep using that word. My home has always been where the Founders tell me to be. A Jem'Hadar's home is his unit."

Seizing on that statement, Kira said, "A people can be defined by where they come from. Who the Bajorans are is shaped in part by our world. It's part of what ties us to the Prophets. The Cardassians didn't belong there, so I fought them. All my life, I've fought *for* Bajor because that is *my* unit."

She thought Taran'atar would grasp the analogy, but he seemed to focus on something else. "You believe caring for your home brings you closer to your gods?"

"I suppose that's one way of looking at it," she said neutrally.

"Yet your gods cast you out."

On reflex, Kira's hand went to her right ear, which had gone unadorned since she'd been Attainted. "Not my gods," she said, quietly but firmly. "Only a few men and women who claim to represent them."

She thought Taran'atar would challenge her statement. Instead, as the clouds outside the viewport cleared, he reported, "Entering lower atmosphere. Setting course for the southern continent."

As the *Euphrates* scanned for life-forms and began beaming people up, nothing more was said about homes and gods. Kira was both annoyed and grateful. Annoyed, because it was in her nature to argue and defend her position, and she was damned if she'd let some Jem'Hadar make light of her devotion to her homeworld. Grateful, because her being exiled from the Bajoran religious community was still an open wound, and the conversation was taking a direction that would surely pour salt in it.

Part of the problem was her own inability to convey her feelings about faith properly. She remembered something Istani Reyla had said to her when she was a child: "One does not explain faith. One simply has it or does not."

And Kira did have faith—in Bajor, and in the Prophets. She always had. It had kept her going during those cold winter nights in the caves, hiding from the Cardassian patrols, with not enough clothes to keep her warm, unable to build a fire for fear of being detected. It would keep her going now, too. *After all, the Prophets didn't "cast me out," Vedek Yevir did. If I learned nothing else from Kai Winn's thankfully brief reign, it's that even the clergy isn't perfect.*

Part of it might also have been that Taran'atar was struggling with his own crisis of faith ever since he returned from Sindorin. Questioning Kira about her own spiritual dilemma was the only way he had to at least attempt to resolve it. He simply wasn't equipped to cope with the doubts that had taken root in his mind. She understood his turmoil; to some degree, she even shared it. But she would never lose faith, never give up.

She wouldn't give up Europa Nova, either. These people, in their own way, fought for their home, same as she always had, whether against the Cardassians or the Dominion, and she would make sure they wouldn't lose it, either.

"Ready to transport the first wave, Commander."

Vaughn nodded to Chief Jeannette Chao as she manipulated the controls in transporter bay one. The *Defiant's* primary bay was fairly small—there was barely room for Vaughn, Chao, and Ensign Gordimer. The other transporter bay on deck two, as well as the cargo transporter on deck three, were performing similar functions. They would keep going until they had approximately a hundred and fifty refugees, then head back to Deep Space 9 to drop them off.

Getting so many people onto a ship with a normal complement of forty was going to be something of a challenge, particularly when most of them would be the upper echelons of the Europani political structure. The burden on life-support would be considerable. *Still,* Vaughn thought, *"needs must as the devil drives."* Vaughn had also made sure that Ensign Gordimer had issued hand phasers to the security staff, just in case.

Chao manipulated the controls, and seven humans materialized on the platform, along with one tall, familiar Andorian: Charivretha zh'Thane. Her feather-like white hair had been styled in a manner that made her head look like a negative-image *zletha* flower, complete with antennae substituting for the stamen, a blossom with blue petals and a white stem.

At the sight of Vaughn, she broke into a smile. "Elias? Is that really you?"

Vaughn nodded. "Councillor zh'Thane."

"Please, Elias, I'm in no mood for formality," she said in her mildly accented voice as she stepped down from the platform.

Before responding, Vaughn turned to the Europani, most of whom were well dressed and carried themselves with the arrogance Vaughn had come to associate with politicians. *Of course, they're the first to beam out.* To her credit, President Silverio was not among them.

"Greetings and welcome aboard the Federation *Starship Defiant.* I am Commander Elias Vaughn, in charge of this vessel. If you will all please follow Ensign Gordimer, he'll escort you to the mess hall. As soon as we're at capacity, you'll be taken to Deep Space 9."

"The mess hall?" one of the men said—a short, rotund man with receding brown hair and a neatly trimmed beard. "I had assumed we would be getting quarters."

"You will on the station, sir," Vaughn said. "However, the *Defiant* is not equipped with such facilities."

"I've seen Federation starships—you can't expect me to believe that you don't have proper quarters!"

"The *Defiant* is primarily a warship, sir," Vaughn said calmly.

"I'm sure the mess hall will be fine," a tall woman with long, straight, jet-black hair said as she moved toward the door. Others followed suit.

The balding man, however, stayed put. "Commander, do you have any idea who I am?"

"I'm afraid not, sir."

"I am the minister of agriculture, one of the most important people on this planet—"

The long-haired woman rolled her eyes. "Give it a rest, Sergio."

Disregarding this request, the minister put his hands on his hips. "I refuse to be transported on this vessel! I demand to be taken to one of the other starships! One with proper facilities!"

Keeping his gaze fixed on Sergio, Vaughn said, "Chief Chao, prepare to transport the minister back to the surface. Minister, I'm sure you can arrange ground transport to Spilimbergo, which is not very far from L'Aquila. At that point, you can no doubt get on the list for transport to the *Gryphon*. Ensign Gordimer, please see the rest of these good people to the mess hall."

"Yes, sir. If you will all follow me, please," Gordimer said as he led the assorted politicians out of the room.

The minister, meanwhile, had gone pale. "On the list?"

"Someone as important as you can surely arrange for something, sir."

The minister sputtered for a moment, then quickly ran after the departing crowd.

Vretha zh'Thane had remained behind. "Very nicely handled, Elias, as always. But then, you never had any patience with politicians, did you?"

"Chief Chao, please prepare to beam the next wave up. Energize as soon as Ensign Gordimer returns."

"Yes, sir."

Indicating the door, Vaughn said, "Councillor?"

Chuckling, Vretha said, "Of course, *Commander.*" She inserted her arm into the crook of Vaughn's, and walked out the door with him.

"You haven't changed much since the last time I saw you," Vaughn said as they proceeded down the narrow corridor. Allowing himself a small smile, he added, "Except for the hair, of course."

"I needed a change, and I thought a floral hairdo would be fitting for negotiations with a world that prides itself on work in the biological sciences. Where are you taking me?"

"The bridge."

"Really?" Vretha said with a wry smile.

"You're a Federation dignitary. It seems only appropriate."

Again, Vretha chuckled. "The ironic thing is, I was going to make a side trip to DS9 in any case. I wanted to see my *chei.*"

"You'd be very proud. Ensign ch'Thane is a fine officer."

The smile fell, and Vretha's arm tightened in Vaughn's. "Yes, I'm sure he is. However, there are other—" She hesitated.

Vaughn remembered ch'Thane's comment in ops about not having been home in a while. For the first time, he spoke in a gentler tone. "Vretha, if there's a problem, you can tell me."

They arrived at the bridge. "We'll talk later, Elias," Vretha said with finality—yet also with certainty. Vaughn recognized the tone of a parent whose child was a source of consternation.

Ensign Tenmei vacated the command chair as Vaughn entered. Without even looking at Vaughn, she said, "Sir, we've detected something of interest on the surface." As she took her position at the conn, she activated the viewscreen to show a sensor log. "This is near one of the small towns on the east coast of the northern continent—a place called Costa Rocosa."

The viewscreen displayed a familiar image: the energy signature of a gateway.

Costa Rocosa was on the *Rio Grande*'s agenda. *"Defiant to Rio Grande."*

"Bowers here."

"Lieutenant, have you reached Costa Rocosa yet?"

"Not until the next trip, sir."

"Very well." Turning to the crewperson at ops, he said, "Contact the local authorities on Costa Rocosa. Tell them I'll be beaming down to the coordinates of that gateway." Turning back to the conn, he said, "Good work, Ensign. You're in command until I return. Alert Colonel Kira and the other Starfleet vessels to what you've found."

"Yes, sir," the young woman said.

To Vretha, he said as he approached the rear exit, "Councillor, I think it would be best if you waited in the mess hall with the others."

"Of course, Commander." Vaughn was relieved that she didn't protest, but simply followed him off the bridge.

"Colonel, I have good news and bad news."

Vaughn stood on a large, craggy rock, waves from a reddish-blue ocean crashing only a few meters to his right. Wind blew through his silver hair, sometimes hard enough to cause him to stumble on the uneven ground. That wind also forced him to raise his voice in order for Kira to hear him through his combadge.

Costa Rocosa was aptly named. Spanish for "rocky coast," this fishing town consisted of several well-built stone houses near the coastline, which was composed entirely of rock. *No beachfront property here,* Vaughn observed. The locals had constructed an extensive marina around one of the larger stony outcroppings.

Vaughn's present location was a much smaller outcropping about fifty meters south of that dock. The town had a population of less than a thousand, and it seemed like all of them had gathered near this outcropping since Vaughn had beamed down. One, a tall, skinny, black-haired and -bearded man named Nieto, had identified himself as the mayor and had offered to render any assistance necessary to the commander. Vaughn had thanked him politely and then ignored him and the others while he examined the strange phenomenon on the rocks.

Sitting on the next rock over was, for lack of a better phrase, a hole in space. Through this hole, Vaughn saw not the rocks and breaking waves of Costa Rocosa that he knew to be on the other side of it, but instead an arid expanse of blue sand being blown by winds even harsher than those buffeting Vaughn. A heavy cover of dark red clouds in an even darker sky obscured the sun. At the moment, there was no sign of any life, but Vaughn's tricorder had indicated a thin-but-bearable oxygen/nitrogen atmosphere.

After the tricorder completed its analysis, Vaughn had contacted Kira on the *Euphrates*.

Vaughn continued. "The good news is that this is indeed a working gateway, and it's programmed for a single location." The other gateways that had been discovered tended to be on random settings, jumping from one location to another. Had that been the case, it would have been potentially dangerous for evacuation purposes.

"What's the bad news?"

"As far as I can tell, the location in question is Torona IV—the homeworld of the Jarada."

"And they are . . . ?"

"A fussy, somewhat xenophobic people that insist on very specific protocols. During first contact, the Starfleet captain mispronounced a word in their language, and they went into a twenty-year snit. Relations reopened about twelve years ago, but it's been a struggle to maintain those relations—and they've steadfastly refused to let any aliens set foot on their homeworld. The last people to try were the crew of a transport that needed to make an emergency landing about five years ago. The Jarada fired on the ship and all four crew members died in the resulting explosion. Things have been a trifle sour since then."

Kira spoke sharply. *"Commander, we have to use that gateway. I just got a report from the* Gryphon *that the transporters will be useless in eight hours, which is sooner than we thought. We have to get two million people off-planet with twenty ships that, filled to capacity, will take less than five hundred thousand at a time."*

Vaughn refrained from pointing out that he knew that already. "I don't believe we can risk sending people through the gateway without contacting the Jaradan authorities first."

A pause. *"Agreed. But make it fast, Commander. Do whatever you have to do to convince them to take the refugees."*

"Aye, sir. Vaughn to *Intrepid*."

"Emick here."

"Walter, I need a favor. Your library computer should have records of all the contacts with the Jarada, yes?" The *Defiant*, built for combat, had a very limited library computer, generally only used for temporary storage of mission-specific data. That would change soon enough when the *Defiant* returned to the Gamma Quadrant, but for now, the only permanently stored material tended to relate to military and intelligence matters, not diplomatic ones.

"Of course."

"Could you download it to my tricorder, please?" Quickly, Vaughn explained the situation.

"I don't envy you your task, Elias. The Jarada won't be easy to negotiate with."

"There's no such thing as an easy negotiation, Walter. If there was, you wouldn't need to negotiate in the first place."

"You've gotten cynical in your old age, Elias," Emick said with a chuckle. "You should have the data now."

"Thank you. Vaughn out."

As Vaughn looked over the material, Nieto approached him again, being helped up the uneven surface with the aid of a young blonde. "Commander, if I may intrude—this thing is a portal to another world, yes?"

"It would certainly appear so, Mayor Nieto," Vaughn said without looking at the taller man. He continued to study the data, running through the pronunciation of the ritual greeting in his head.

"I assume this world is habitable?"

"It reads as Class M, yes."

Smiling under his thick beard, Nieto said, "Then, if I may ask—why the delay in allowing my people to go through it? There would appear to be plenty of space."

"It's an inhabited planet, Mr. Mayor. We need to make contact with the local government and obtain their permission first."

Nieto scratched his beard thoughtfully. "I see. And how long will this take?"

"I can't say at the moment," Vaughn said honestly, frowning at his tricorder. "Sir, if you'd be so kind as to return to your people. I need to finish my preparations for making contact."

"Of course, Commander, my apologies, but please understand my position," Nieto said, and his smile fell. "There is deadly radiation in our sky. Our entire world is rapidly becoming uninhabitable, perhaps permanently. We are a small town, often ignored even during the height of the fishing season. In times like these, it is the small ones who are forgotten. I will not allow that to happen to the good citizens of Costa Rocosa."

Vaughn finally turned to look at Nieto, and he could see the concern in the man's eyes. "I can assure you, Mayor Nieto, that we intend to get everyone off this planet long before the radiation becomes lethal, regardless of how large the town is. However, the Jarada will need to be contacted first. Now please, if you could tell your people what I told you and let me complete my work."

"Very well, Commander. I appreciate everything you are doing for us."

"You're quite welcome, sir. Now, if you please?" He indicated the crowd of Costa Rocosan people, who, Vaughn noticed, were buzzing with more chatter and looked anxious.

With any luck, he can reassure them the way I reassured him, Vaughn thought. *Let's hope that reassurance was warranted.*

Again helped by the blonde, Nieto moved back to his constituency. Turning back to the gateway, Vaughn set his tricorder to boost his combadge's signal. *Here goes nothing,* he thought.

"Attention Jaradan authorities. This is Commander Elias Vaughn of Starfleet, representing the United Federation of Planets." Remembering the Jarada's preference for dealing with those in charge from his recent crash course in Jaradan relations, he added, "And commanding officer of the *U.S.S. Defiant.*" He took a deep breath, then said, *"Ârd klaxon lís blajhblon ârg níc calníc ârd trasulâ rass tass trasulâ."* Wishing he'd thought to ask Kira to beam him down a glass of water, Vaughn cleared his throat before continuing. "As you may be aware, there is an interspatial gateway linking your world with another, a human colony known as Europa Nova. It is through that gateway that I am contacting you now. Europa Nova is suffering an ecological crisis and needs to be evacuated. We respectfully request permission to bring people through the gateway to your world."

A lengthy pause ensued. The sound of the wind combined with the crashing of the waves might have sounded idyllic and peaceful to Vaughn's ears, had they not also been intermingled with the sounds of Nieto speaking to the Costa Rocosans. Vaughn couldn't make out the mayor's words over the din of the natural noises, but the buzz from the crowd itself had dulled, which Vaughn chose to view as an encouraging sign.

"You honor us with the proper greeting," came a haughty voice from Vaughn's combadge. *"For that reason, we will grant you the consideration of a proper warning. Do not set foot on our world, or you will be killed."*

"To whom have I the honor of speaking?"

"You have been given your warning, commander of the Defiant.*"*

Accepting that the Jarada would not identify him- or herself, Vaughn said, "I ask that you rescind it."

"These gateways you describe have caused incursions on our worlds. Three hostile aliens attacked one of our hives on Torona Alpha and destroyed it. No one may step on our soil and live."

Vaughn thought quickly. A humanitarian appeal would do no good— these people had no compunction about firing on a ship in distress. For that matter, during the contact with the *Enterprise,* Jaradan actions almost resulted in the death of four people, including Jean-Luc Picard. Their strategic importance to the Federation had lessened with the alliance between the Federation and the Romulans during the Dominion War, and no formal treaties had ever been signed.

So what Vaughn was about to do was, strictly speaking, against regulations.

"If you agree to help us, we will share all our intelligence about the gateways. We have encountered them before, and devoted considerable resources to studying them. That study is still ongoing, and we will also share any subsequent data with you. I can tell you this much—the gateways do present a long-term danger to your technological infrastructure, and possibly your very ecosystem. The nature of that danger will also be shared—but only if you agree to accept Europani refugees and guarantee their safety until Starfleet can arrange their transport off your planet."

Another pause. The wind howled louder. Nieto had stopped talking. An especially large wave crashed against a nearby rock and Vaughn—who had gained a fine layer of mist on his person in the time since he beamed down— was splashed with a bit of backwash from it.

"You will share this intelligence before we allow any to step on our soil."

"I will share some of it. The rest will come after the first refugees have passed through the gateway unmolested."

Yet another pause. *"Very well, commander of the* Defiant. *A forcefield has been erected in the area proximate to the gateway. It will accommodate five hundred thousand members of your species. You will send that precise number through and no more, or the agreement will be considered in abeyance."*

Vaughn noticed that the winds on Torona IV had suddenly stopped. "Very well. If any harm comes to those five hundred thousand, we shall likewise consider the agreement in abeyance."

"Any who step outside the boundaries established by the forcefield will die."

"Understood," Vaughn said. *Let's hope Mayor Nieto and his people aren't partial to taking long strolls.* "My thanks to your government. *Trasulâ ríss blajhblon ârd."*

"Again, you honor us with an appropriate salutation, commander of the Defiant. *See that you continue to do us honor and we will not do you harm."*

Letting out a breath he didn't know he was holding, Vaughn tapped his combadge to fill Kira in.

Bill Ross will probably have a seizure when he finds out I agreed to share intel with a semi-hostile government, Vaughn thought grimly. He felt no concern about it, however. It was the only way to save these people's lives.

Chapter Seven

The Denorios Belt

I'm going to die, Nog thought.

It was, on the face of it, a stupid way to go: only a few thousand kilometers from Deep Space 9, in a runabout, under fire from an unknown ship. But if AR-558 had taught him anything, it was that the universe was stupid and cruel and arbitrary. So Nog was completely at peace with the fact that—after surviving the taking of the station by the Dominion, a covert mission into Dominion territory, the attack on AR-558, the destruction of the previous *Defiant,* and so much else—he would die under such ridiculous circumstances as this.

His only regret was that he would never find out what happened to Jake.

"Picking up another ship!" Shar said urgently, then looked sharply at Nog and smiled. "It's the *Defiant!*"

Nog looked at his own sensor display. Half the systems were offline, but he could see the *Defiant* bearing down on the enemy vessel.

"I can't get a specific life-sign reading," Shar continued, "but it looks like the *Defiant* is filled beyond its capacity."

"Probably Europani refugees," Nog said in a steely voice. He expected to feel a sense of gratitude that he was likely going to survive. He was relieved that there was still a chance he might find Jake, but for his own survival, he felt nothing.

"Attention unidentified ship," came Vaughn's steady voice over the comm system. *"You have fired on a Starfleet vessel. Surrender or suffer the consequences."*

In response, the ship fired its forward weapons on the *Defiant* and its aft ones on the *Sungari.*

"Matter-antimatter containment field weakening!" Shar said over the din of exploding consoles. "And *Defiant* shields are at forty percent!"

Nog winced. His Shelliak modulator weakened the *Defiant*'s shields against directed energy fire, and this ladrion weapon of theirs was a particularly nasty example of the type. And the *Sungari,* of course, no longer had shields. "Eject the core."

"Ejection systems offline." The lights went out. "In fact, at this point, I would venture to say that the entire ship is offline."

Nog looked down at a dark console he could now barely see. Even the emergency lights weren't working. The only illumination came through the porthole from the external lights of the *Defiant* and the unidentified vessel. The *Sungari* was dead in space. If even the emergency systems were out, then the containment field was also down. *Which means that this runabout is a big duranium bomb about to go off. Maybe that's why I didn't feel relieved—I'm not alive yet.*

More illumination as the *Defiant* fired its pulse phasers. Thanks to the

Sungari's attack, the enemy ship was also without shields. The phaser bolts tore through the hull as if it were tissue paper, and the ship exploded a moment later.

Good, Nog thought, urgently slapping his combadge, *they can lower shields for transport now.* "*Sungari* to *Defiant*. Emergency beam-out."

The room started to fade into a silver haze, then coalesced into the main transporter bay of the *Defiant*. He looked to his right, and saw Shar, who let out a long breath.

From the console, Chief Chao tapped her combadge. "Got them, sir."

"Are they injured?"

Tapping his own combadge, Nog said, "We're fine, Commander."

"Good. Report to the bridge."

"The *Sungari*'s about to breach, Commander. You need to—"

"We're aware of the situation, Lieutenant. Remote shutdown isn't working, so we're using the tractor beam to push the ship as far away from the station and the wormhole as possible."

"Still inside the belt, though?" Nog asked.

"Yes. Why?"

Nog turned to Shar. "Will that affect the gases in the belt for the burst?"

Shar shook his head. "It shouldn't."

"Good," Nog said, then he moved to the transporter bay door.

As soon as the doors opened, his sensitive ears were assaulted with a cacophony of sound. Dozens of human civilians were standing in the hallways, along with a few security guards. Nog noticed that the guards were carrying phasers, which he thought might have been a tad excessive. The humans—presumably the Europani refugees—looked tired and scared. Nog couldn't bring himself to be surprised at that.

Shar had an odd look on his face, and one finger brushed against his right antenna. "You okay?" Nog asked.

"Yes, it's just something in the air. This many people crowded together, it changes the nature of the atmosphere. It's usually a bit more—well, sterile than this."

Nog nodded in understanding as he and Shar entered the bridge. Some debris from the enemy ship was visible in the lower right-hand corner of the viewscreen, but its focus was on the *Sungari*. The runabout's running lights were extinguished. A blue tractor beam engulfed the runabout and thrust it away from the debris.

Vaughn fixed his steely gaze upon the two junior officers. "Did they identify themselves at all?"

"No sir," Nog said dutifully. "They attacked without any warning."

The young Ferengi turned back to the viewscreen to see the *Sungari* moving farther away and deeper into the Denorios Belt—before exploding. Sighing, Nog found himself wondering how much longer Starfleet would continue replacing the station's runabouts.

"Set course back for DS9, Ensign," Vaughn said to Tenmei. "We'll collect and examine the debris once we've offloaded the refugees."

A thought occurred to Nog. "Sir, with all due respect—you took a very big risk, engaging in battle with all these refugees on board."

"We were the only option, Lieutenant. There aren't any ships docked at DS9 at the moment, and the station itself is out of range. In any event, there was every chance that the vessel would have turned its attention to the station after disposing of you two. We couldn't take that risk, even with so many civilians on board."

"Thank you, sir." Then remembering the whole reason for their trip to the Denorios Belt in the first place, he added, "Uh, sir, I'm not sure if Lieutenant Dax told you, but Ensign ch'Thane and I have determined a course of action that might disrupt the gateways."

"Thirishar, there you are."

Shar felt like a *grelth* had started weaving a web in his stomach. The voice spoke in Andorii, and it was one he hadn't heard in person for five years.

He turned to take in the unexpected sight of Charivretha zh'Thane, his *zhavey*. She had changed her hair since their last communication, and was as overdressed as her position always required her to be. She was walking with a group of Europani refugees who were being escorted onto the station by Ensigns Gordimer and Ling.

"I wasn't expecting to see you here, *Zhavey.*"

She broke off from the crowd to approach her only child. Gordimer gave her a look, then saw Shar. Shar nodded quickly at the security guard, who simply shrugged and resumed his escorting duties.

"I was on Europa Nova. We're trying to convince them to join the Federation, and I was negotiating. Ironically, the Federation's response to this crisis may help me solidify my argument—assuming there's a Europa Nova left when all is said and done." She stared at him. "I didn't realize you were on board. I would've thought you'd have been on the bridge when Elias brought me there."

"I was on the *Sungari*. They beamed me over before it blew up."

"Blew up?" Her voice raised an octave. "Obviously, I should have stayed on the bridge."

Shar's antennae quivered. "It's all right, *Zhavey,* everything turned out fine." He hesitated, and then lied. "It's good to see you."

Vretha's own antennae did likewise. "It's especially good to see you given what happened to your runabout. I was actually going to come to the station after I was done on Europa Nova in any case. We need to talk, Thirishar."

What would be the point? Shar almost said aloud, but he kept the respectful mask plastered to his face. "I'm afraid I can't right now, *Zhavey.* The crisis is not—"

Waving her hand in what appeared to be a dismissive gesture, Vretha said,

"Of course not now, Thirishar. You have duties to perform, and I need to check on my ship—I lent it to the relief efforts so they could get the children off-planet right away. We'll talk when we both have time to do so." She stared Shar directly in the eye. "But we *will* talk. We have danced around this subject for far too long."

"Yes, *Zhavey,*" Shar said dutifully.

"You always say 'yes, *Zhavey*' in that respectful tone," Vretha noted, "yet you never change, Thirishar. It is a stalling tactic I will not tolerate any longer."

"I'm sorry, *Zhavey.*"

"No, I don't think you are." Vretha's voice sounded sad now. "And that is a pity." She closed her eyes. "But enough of this. We will speak later. Be whole, Thirishar." With that, she walked off.

Shar struggled to keep his emotions in check. *It would not do to smash a bulkhead right now with all this security and these civilians around.* He latched on to the anger, wrestled with it, and forced it down into the dark corner of his mind where it normally lived—and from which it inevitably clawed its way out every time he talked to Vretha.

Once he felt he was under sufficient control, he also walked off the *Defiant* and into the docking ring corridor, where he saw Nog. "There you are," the Ferengi said. "Was that your—what's the word? *Zhavey?*"

"Yes, it was."

Shar himself hadn't noticed any alteration in his voice at first, but Nog almost flinched from Shar's tone. *Perhaps I haven't buried my anger as efficiently as I believed,* he thought with a sigh. "I'm sorry, Lieutenant," Shar said quickly. "I'm afraid that she does not bring out the best in me."

Smiling, Nog said, "That's all right. C'mon, we need to head to ops to brief everyone on our brilliant theory." As they walked toward a turbolift, Nog added, "Mothers can be difficult. Mine took Father for all he was worth before the marriage contract ended, then remarried a richer man."

Frowning, Shar thought back to the conversations about Ferengi mores that they'd had in the *Sungari.* "I thought Ferengi women couldn't do that sort of thing before the reforms."

"Well, it was her father's doing, really. I think. Honestly, I don't remember most of that—I was very young. Father was destitute after that, and took me here to work for Uncle Quark."

"And now he's the Grand Nagus." Shar considered, then smiled. "It seems to me that your mother should have cause to regret her decision."

Nog laughed. "Probably. I wonder if Father's gotten in touch with her since going home to Ferenginar."

Shar smiled, and he already felt better, the anger well and truly buried now. *This is where I belong,* Zhavey, *not back on Andor—no matter what you or anyone else says.*

He also had to admire Nog's grace under pressure. He hadn't let their life-or-death situation get to him at all. *I suppose that comes of spending most of the war on the front lines.* Shar himself had been fortunate enough to miss any direct combat, spending most of the war working feverishly in a lab.

As they entered the turbolift, Shar said, "Let us go and be brilliant, my friend."

Nog grinned. "Ops."

Chapter Eight

Europa Nova

"Take all transporters offline."

It was an order Kira had not looked forward to giving, but she'd known all along it was inevitable. Antimatter waste now made up an entire orbit of Europa Nova, forming a deadly green ring around the planet. The ring was thickest at the gateway, of course, the point from which the cloud of hazardous material originated, and it thinned as it arced above the planet surface. Now every ship needed to keep its shields up to protect them from the radiation. The concentration was such that, even at the polar regions, transporters were unreliable.

At least Nog's shield modulator is working, she thought, thanking the Prophets for her operations officer's impeccable timing in consummating his business deal just when they needed it most.

The *Gryphon,* the *Halloran,* and the *Xhosa* were on their way to Deep Space 9 to drop off more refugees, and the *Defiant* was already there doing the same. The *Xhosa* had somehow managed to make some extra room, relieving the *Euphrates* of the refugees it had picked up, allowing Kira to remain in charge of the evacuation.

Europa Nova's surface transporters—still operational for the time being—were being used to bring the five hundred thousand the Jarada were allowing to Costa Rocosa to make use of the gateway there.

"Transporters offline," Captain Emick acknowledged, and Colonel Lenaris echoed the reply a moment later, followed by the civilian captains.

"Implement plan B," Kira ordered.

"We've found a landing site for the Intrepid," Emick said. *"It's right outside Padilla. I think we can take the city's remaining population on this run."*

"Good."

"Colonel," Taran'atar said, "I'm detecting a dense concentration of theta radiation in the upper atmosphere."

The voice of one of the officers on the *Intrepid* came through the comlink. *"Confirmed,"* she said. *"A solid mass of waste material has fallen out of orbit. On its present course, it'll land four kilometers due west of Spilimbergo."*

Kira checked the configuration of the convoy. The *Gryphon* had been evacuating Spilimbergo. Between the starship and the assorted private craft, not to mention the earlier evac of the children, a bit less than half of the city's population of three hundred and fifty thousand had been evacuated thus far. Right now, with the *Gryphon* on its way to the Bajoran system, the *Euphrates* was in closest proximity to the threat.

Without hesitating, Kira changed course and reset the shields for an atmospheric entry. "Kira to Bashir."

"Bashir here," said a very tired-sounding chief medical officer.

"Doctor, what would be the effects of a meteoric collision of a mass putting out"—she glanced at her console—"a hundred thousand kilorads of theta radiation four kilometers from a population center?"

"In a word, devastating. I could give you precise figures if you want, but the short version is the population center would be as good as dead."

"That's what I thought you were going to say."

Emick spoke up. *"Colonel, what are you doing?"*

"Saving lives," Kira said. "Doctor, how far from the population center would the waste need to be to minimize the danger?"

"Well, on another planet would be ideal."

"Julian . . ."

"Sorry, Colonel. I would estimate a minimum of a hundred kilometers."

Next to her, Taran'atar said, "I have reconfigured the tractor beam with additional power from the warp drive." He turned to Kira. "I assume your intent is to divert the meteorite."

Grateful for the Jem'Hadar's instincts, she said, "That's the plan. Activate the beam on my mark."

"Why not just destroy it?" Bashir asked.

Emick replied, *"Doctor, if we could just destroy the antimatter waste with phasers, we wouldn't be in this mess in the first place. Colonel, you sure you know what you're doing?"*

"*Euphrates* is the only ship close enough, Captain," Kira said as she guided the ship through the cloud cover. "Our new modulated shields are protecting us against the radiation. As it is, we're cutting it close."

The other *Intrepid* officer said, *"Colonel, I've found a lake about a hundred seventy-five kilometers northwest of Spilimbergo. You should be able to divert the mass there. The only life-form readings I'm getting within a hundred kilometers are flora."*

Kira found that lake on her sensor display. The locals called it Lago De-Bacco. "Got it. Thanks."

"Good luck, Colonel," Emick said. *"With your permission, I'll inform President Silverio."*

"Thank you, Captain. Kira out."

As the *Euphrates* came out of the cloud cover, Kira quickly ran her fingers over the console, calculating the course she'd need to take. She had to angle her approach just right so that, when the tractor beam was activated, she'd be able to divert the meteorite to the lake in question. It was a delicate piece of navigation, made more challenging by having to account for prevailing winds—which, it turned out, were pretty fierce near Lago DeBacco.

Just like the good old days, she thought with a half-smile. Piloting skimmers around Dakhur Province in the dead of winter, avoiding the Cardassian patrols. No sensors worth mentioning, wind shear way beyond the skimmer's capacity, flying by the seats of their collective pants. All she had to worry about was keeping alive and watching the other cell members' backs, with the assured faith that the Prophets would guide them to freedom if they just kept fighting, kept *believing.* Politics didn't matter. You didn't have to say the right thing or not step on the appropriate toes or go through a chain of command—it was just you, the cell, and the enemy.

As the *Euphrates* neared the mass—which was careening toward the surface at an alarming rate, cutting a trail of green death across the sky as it fell—Kira shook her head at her own wistfulness. *Great, now I'm getting nostalgic for the occupation. What does that say about my life?*

"Tractor beam ready," Taran'atar said.

It's so simple for you, she thought at her Jem'Hadar companion. *You have your duty, and you perform it. You don't have to worry about what Starfleet will think or what the Vedek Assembly will think or what the Ministry will think or what the Bajoran people will think. You just have to do what you're told.*

Sometimes Kira longed for that kind of simplicity.

The console beeped—they were in range. She waited until the angle of approach was just right, then said, "Activate tractor beam."

As she spoke, she changed course.

Her stomach lurched violently as the runabout—which had been accelerating toward the surface of the planet at maximum impulse—altered its flight path upward.

"Tractor beam holding," Taran'atar said.

Kira could only nod. The bitter taste of half-digested *hasperat* started to well up in her throat. *It's been way too long since I did something like this,* she thought. *Stomach's not used to it. Been spending too much damn time sitting at a desk.*

Taran'atar, of course, did not look in the least bit put out. "We are exceeding the tractor-beam tolerances."

Forcing the *hasperat* down, she said, "Just another six seconds."

The *Euphrates* continued to arc away from the surface, the ship fighting against the momentum of the antimatter waste to which it was tethered. The impulse engines strained, but held.

Then, finally, when the mass had changed course sufficiently to land in Lago DeBacco, Kira said, "Disengage tractor beam."

The *Euphrates* lurched as, no longer burdened with the tremendous mass, its velocity jumped suddenly. Once again, Kira's stomach heaved, but she kept her hands on the controls. Something blew out in one of the aft consoles. She couldn't afford to slow the runabout down, as any moment . . .

A shock wave rocked the *Euphrates* as the meteorite collided with the westernmost side of the lake. Kira was able to remain in her seat, but only barely. *All those years of bouncing around in Bajoran skimmers pays off,* she thought with a bitter smile. The shock wave was considerably less than a direct impact would have been—the *Euphrates*'s tractoring also served to retard the meteorite's rate of descent, greatly reducing the force of its landing.

"Shields have held," Taran'atar said. "No radiation has penetrated. We remain uncontaminated. But this vessel's tractor-beam generator has burned out."

Kira smiled. *We did it.*

Then she put Lago DeBacco on the main viewer.

The smile fell.

Five minutes ago, Lago DeBacco had been a lush, thriving lake. Reddish-blue water flowed gently across, fed from several local rivers that acted as tributaries. An entire ecosystem had lived in it—a teeming mass of plant life.

Now, in spots where the runabout's optical sensors could penetrate the billowing green mist that filled the valley—irradiated water vapor from the lake—the terrain was reduced to blasted ruin. Trees and bushes proximate to ground zero that weren't vaporized were already showing signs of decay from the theta radiation. No one would be able to approach Lago DeBacco without decontamination forcefields for many years to come.

Europa Nova had its first scar.

Kira swore an oath right there that it would also be the last.

"We are receiving a communication from L'Aquila, Colonel," said Taran'atar. "It is President Silverio."

Sighing, Kira said, "On screen." *Here it comes. The outrage at destroying such a beautiful piece of nature. The anger at not being consulted. I so hate politicians.*

Grazia Silverio's pleasant face appeared on the screen, looking even more haggard than before. The bags under her eyes had doubled in size since Kira had last seen her, and her jowls seemed to droop even more. The theta radiation that they were flying through interfered somewhat with the communication, and the image blinked in and out. *"Colonel, Captain Emick tells me the town of Spilimbergo owes you a debt of gratitude."*

Kira blinked. "Uh—"

"I understand you diverted the meteorite that was endangering the town at considerable risk to yourself."

"Honestly, ma'am, the only risk was that it would fail to divert far enough to save Spilimbergo. Starfleet makes its runabouts pretty sturdy." That much, at least, was true. The structural integrity field had held up with no sign of strain. If she'd tried that move with one of the old Bajoran skimmers, it would have torn itself apart.

"Apf," she said, waving her arm. *"Don't give me false modesty. The point is, you took the risk, and saved lives. And you got us that gateway at Costa Rocosa. You have my gratitude for that."*

"Thank you, ma'am, although Commander Vaughn found the gateway."

"Grazia, it's Grazia," she said with a tired smile. Then she was distracted by something off-screen. *"What? Oh, all right. I must go, Colonel—there is still much to do, but I wanted to thank you personally. As long as you're in charge, I'm sure we'll get through this."*

With that, she signed off.

As the *Euphrates* came out of the atmosphere and back into orbit, a signal came through from Vaughn, back on the station.

"Go ahead, Commander."

"Good news, Colonel. Lieutenant Nog and Ensign ch'Thane have devised a method of disrupting the gateways—possibly even shutting them down permanently. It's a modified tachyon burst that can be easily done from the Defiant."

"Glad to hear it, Commander. Would we have to do this on a gateway-by-gateway basis or would it knock out the whole network?"

"Ensign ch'Thane seems to think that activating it at one gateway will cripple the entire network at once. That might cause more problems than it solves, of course."

Kira let out a breath through her teeth. Vaughn was right—who knew what kind of uses the gateways were being put to? Yes, the sudden mass opening of the gateways was causing chaos all over the quadrant—if not the entire galaxy—but shutting them down just as suddenly wouldn't necessarily improve things.

On the other hand, the Iconians were, from all reports, lording this technology all over the Alpha Quadrant. It was about time the tables were turned. Besides, the reports Kira had been monitoring from Starfleet indicated that the situation was just getting worse—problems ranging from vandalism to murder to the rekindling of hostilities between governments were rampant. All-out war might well have been the next consequence unless something radical was done soon to stem the tide. Shutting down the gateways might well be it . . . especially if doing so stopped more antimatter waste from coming into orbit of Europa Nova.

Then again, it would also cut off what was rapidly becoming their most important evac point: the gateway at Costa Rocosa.

So, with extreme reluctance, Kira decided that she had no choice but to do something she rarely did: pass the buck. "Run this by Admiral Ross, just in case there's something going on we don't know about that would preclude shutting down the gateways. Besides, we can't do anything until we've evacuated Europa Nova, and that gateway you found is the only way we'll be able to get it done before the theta radiation gets fatal."

"Understood and agreed. I've got a message in to the admiral now."

"Good." She changed the Euphrates's course. "In the meantime, I'm not just going to sit here waiting for another meteorite to endanger the planet."

"I beg your pardon?"

Kira quickly explained about the irradiated mass that had nearly destroyed Spilimbergo. "Since this crisis started, we've been reacting. It's past time we acted. The runabout isn't going to help much with the evacuation—but I can take it through the gateway to the other side and try to cut this off at the source. Somebody's using Europa Nova as their personal dumping ground, and it's going to stop now—before something comes through that we can't stop from killing anyone."

"Very well, Colonel. Lieutenant Nog is modifying the Defiant's deflector array right now. It'll be ready to emit the tachyon burst as soon as the evac is completed."

"Good. Captain Emick will be in charge of the task force when I'm gone."

"Understood. Vaughn out."

"Kira to Emick."

"Emick here, Colonel. We've just landed on Europa Nova and are about to begin our evac of Padilla's population. We've also been monitoring your communications. Do I gather that you intend to go through the gateway?"

"Yes, you do," Kira said, getting ready for an argument.

However, it wasn't forthcoming. *"Very well. Anything we can do to help?"*

Breathing a sigh of relief, Kira said, "Actually, yes. You sent a probe into the gateway when we arrived, right?"

"Yes, we did. I'll have my second officer send over the probe's data. The star system on the other side is in the Delta Quadrant. Hang on a second, we might be able to get you some help."

As Kira moved the runabout into a position proximate to the gateway, she said, "I beg your pardon?"

"You familiar with the U.S.S. Voyager, Colonel?" Emick asked.

"Of course. They left DS9 before they went missing."

"Right—and they wound up in the Delta Quadrant. I'm having my second officer look up the data from Starfleet's Project Pathfinder— Ah, damn. Voyager's last reported position is nowhere near where this waste is coming from."

"Let's hope she runs across another gateway that'll get her home," Kira said.

"Shields are holding against the radiation," Taran'atar said.

"Good," Kira said. "Setting course for the gateway . . ."

Before she could start the runabout moving, however, Lieutenant Bowers's voice came over the comm. *"Rio Grande to Euphrates."*

"Go ahead, Lieutenant."

"Sir, I'm picking up a ship entering this star system—Colonel, it's Cardassian. Galor-class."

Kira heard Emick curse. *"What the hell's a Cardassian ship doing here?"*

Kira looked down and saw the same sensor readings that Bowers had picked up. "I haven't a clue, Captain, but I intend to find out. Lieutenant Bowers, status?"

"We're about to head back to DS9 with our refugees, Colonel."

"Stay in-system until we determine what these Cardassians want."

"Aye, sir."

Emick asked, *"Do you want me to cut short our evac?"*

Tempting as it was to add the *Intrepid's* firepower to her conversation with this Cardassian, Kira had to say, "No, the evacuation takes precedence. Don't worry, Captain, I know how to deal with Cardassians."

"Of that I have no doubt, Colonel. Keep in touch. Emick out."

As Kira brought the *Euphrates* about to intercept the Cardassian, the sensors got a better read on it. As Bowers said, it was *Galor*-class—registry identified it as the *Trager*—and it had seen better days. It was pocked with phaser scarring and had several hull breaches, only two of which were actually sealed with forcefields. The structural integrity field was at about sixty percent of capacity. *Looks like it took a beating during the war,* Kira thought. *And Cardassia doesn't have the resources to do proper repairs, it would seem.* That didn't surprise her. Between the internal strife, with half of the Cardassian fleet turning against the Dominion, the war damage inflicted by the Alpha Quadrant allies—much of the war had been fought in Cardassian territory, after all—and the horrendous retaliation taken against Cardassia Prime by the Dominion, the war had left the Cardassian Union in what could kindly be called a shambles.

The *Trager* took up a position in orbit around the sixth planet. That was, at present, the closest planet in the system to Europa Nova, and also outside Europani space.

She opened a channel. *"Trager,* this is Colonel Kira Nerys in command of this joint Federation/Bajoran task force. What business do you have in this solar system?"

After a moment, a reply came on a standard Cardassian military frequency. A face appeared on the viewscreen.

It was the face of the man Kira Nerys hated more than any other sentient being who'd ever lived—and might ever live. The former prefect of Bajor, the man who had killed millions of Bajorans during the occupation, the filth who had taken Kira's mother from her family, and the man responsible for the Dominion/Cardassian alliance that led to years of bloody conflict. It was a face she prayed she'd never see again, one that still came to her in nightmares.

"Greetings, Colonel," he said.

"Dukat," Kira said with a snarl, and armed the runabout's phasers.

Chapter Nine

Farius Prime

"Kam, we've lost the signal from Hig's ship."

"Verify that."

"I already have. Their last communication indicated that they were about to destroy the Starfleet ship that was gathering intelligence on the hole in the lattice when another Starfleet ship showed up."

"Then what?"

"Then nothing."

"That's not good."

"I'm fully aware of that."

"Let's hope they were destroyed rather than captured. Do we know what intelligence Starfleet gathered?"

"Hig's ship intercepted a transmission, but they weren't able to forward it to us. All I know is their Ferengi engineer reported that they came up with a way to sabotage the gateways."

"They have a Ferengi engineer?"

"Yes. In fact, he's the nephew of the one negotiating on the Orions' behalf."

"Really? Interesting. Keep monitoring System 418, just in case. The negotiations here are taking far too long."

"Then why bother with them? There are others."

"Because the Orion offer is several orders of magnitude better than anyone else's."

"It may not be worth the risk."

"I'll be the judge of that. You just do as you're told."

Quark popped a tube grub into his mouth. *Things are going well,* he thought. His instincts told him that the Orions had the best offer on the table to the Iconians. *Why else allow it to drag out so long?* Quark knew that people all over the quadrant were clamoring for this technology. Plenty of governments would have made overtures. But no government had the resources of an underworld syndicate—or, rather, they did, but weren't willing to part with them. Quark knew that, and so did Gaila. At this point, the negotiations had boiled down to piddling over minor points. The deal was all but done. Quark could feel it in his lobes.

Indeed, the deal might have been done already, but for Gaila's picking at every point. While Gaila hadn't actively tried to sabotage the negotiations, he hadn't made it easy, either—and there was more to it than simply trying to get the best deal possible. He enjoyed making Quark squirm.

But that only went so far. Like Quark, Gaila was working on behalf of another party, and there was no getting around the quality of the Orions' offer to his client.

They were taking another break before going into what Quark predicted would be the final session. This time, Malic had decided to lay out a buffet of Ferengi food in deference to both negotiators, with some other food for those, like Bajorans and Orions, who preferred blander fare.

Gaila approached the huge ceramic bowl of tube grubs and took a few for himself. "So Cousin Rom is the Grand Nagus now," Gaila said in a conversational tone.

"That's right," Quark said, wondering where Gaila was going with this. *Somehow, I can't imagine he just wants to catch up on family gossip.*

"Grand Nagus Rom. Sounds funny, doesn't it? Aunt Ishka's on Risa with the former Grand Nagus. And I understand Nog's been promoted. All these changes—and yet you still own the same bar you've had for over fifteen years. How many different governments have controlled that station since you set up shop? Three? Yet you've managed to thrive."

"More or less," Quark said, popping another tube grub.

"You'll probably still be running that bar long after your dear brother has been ousted."

That got Quark's attention. "What do you mean?"

"Oh, nothing," Gaila said, pouring himself a glass of Slug-o-Cola. "Just call it—speculation on my part. Zek was able to put forward his reforms because he's Zek. He had the weight of years and experience, and decades of prosperity behind him. What does Rom have?"

A history of being an idiot, Quark thought, but said nothing. Gaila's expression was already saying it quite eloquently.

Gaila took a swallow of Slug-o-Cola. He smiled, wiping some of the green slime of the beverage from his upper lip. Gaila had several smiles that Quark had learned to quantify when they were kids. This was Gaila's "I know something you don't, and I'm not going to tell you what it is" smile. "Mark my words, cousin," he said, leaning close enough to Quark so that the Tholian silk jacket brushed against Quark's own suit. "You can count the years of Rom's reign as Nagus on the fingers of one Daluvian hand."

Daluvians didn't have fingers. Quark grabbed another tube grub.

Not wanting to dwell on this subject, Quark asked, "So how did you wind up negotiating for a dead civilization anyhow? Last time I saw you, you only had seven bars of latinum to your name." That had been the reward Zek had offered for the rescue of Ishka: fifty bars of latinum, which had been split evenly among the six Ferengi who participated in the rescue (after Quark skimmed off a sixteen percent finder's fee, of course).

Smiling his "I'm more clever than you think" smile, Gaila said, "You'd be amazed what you can do with seven bars of latinum." The smile fell. "Unfortunately, my old contacts had dried up. Did I ever tell you how I got that purification squad off my back?"

Quark shook his head.

"I gave General Nassuc weapons—free of charge. That's why I was destitute when you found me in that holding cell. I bankrupted myself so that mad female could complete her takeover of Palamar. I went through all my cash reserves—I even had to sell my moon before I got enough weaponry to get her to call off the squad." Gaila now took on the "I'm moving in for the kill" smile as he leaned in even closer to Quark and whispered, "She killed ten million people before the civil war was over. The Regent had many friends, it turned out."

The tube grub felt like ashes in Quark's mouth. Quark had set in motion a chain of events intended to keep that very civil war from happening. The death toll was still far less than it would have been if Quark had helped Gaila and his partner Hagath obtain biological weapons for the Regent of Palamar to use against the general. *But still, ten million people. Their deaths . . .*

Quark stopped that train of thought. *Those deaths are not on my conscience. Nassuc and the Regent were at each other's throats long before I came along. One way or another, there would have been a war on Palamar. I just did what I could to keep the death toll down.*

Now if I can just believe that, everything will be fine. He grabbed another tube grub, then put it down uneaten.

Gaila was no doubt of the opinion that Quark had let sentiment get in the way of business, but Quark simply could not bring himself to trade millions of lives for personal profit. *Maybe it's years of exposure to the Federation—or maybe that's just the way I am.*

"Sorry, cousin," Gaila said insincerely. "But it was that or death. Not really so difficult a choice."

"Well, it was nice chatting with you, Gaila." Quark started to walk away.

"You know," Gaila said, "the gateways are a lot more valuable to the Orions than they are to the other governments."

Quark stopped. *Now he's going back to business. Interesting.*

"After all, who better to take advantage of the gateways than a decentralized group? It's tailor-made for the Orions. The Klingons, the Breen, the Romulans, the Federation—they'd have to completely readjust the way they live their lives to properly take advantage of the gateways. But the Orions wouldn't have to change a thing. They don't have a homeworld as such, just a network of bases—like this one."

Smiling, Quark said, "If this is an attempt to drive the price down—"

"Merely another observation, cousin."

"You've been full of observations, haven't you?" *Or full of something, anyhow.*

Gaila's shrug was as eloquent as his smile. Then he walked off.

Malic approached, gnawing on some kind of cooked poultry leg. "What was that all about?"

"Just catching up on some family gossip."

Glowering at Quark, Malic said, "I hope that's all it is, Quark. These negotiations have taken far too long. I was under the impression that you were *good* at this."

"I am. So's Gaila. That's why it's taking so long."

"That had better be the only reason, Quark. I'm fast running out of patience."

Only then did Quark notice that the two burly Orions had appeared behind Malic and were now gazing down on Quark. *Is it my imagination, or are their biceps bigger than they were yesterday?*

"Don't worry," Quark said, holding up his hands in as reassuring a manner as he could manage. "I'm confident that this will be the final session and you'll have possession of the gateways within the hour."

"You'd better hope that's the case, Quark. I still have the details of your scheme on my padd, and all it takes—"

"—is a simple command, yes I remember," Quark said with a sigh. "I'm aware of the terms of our agreement, Malic, and rest assured I'll honor it. Seventeenth Rule of Acquisition: 'A contract is a contract is a contract.' " Quark left out the subsequent clause: "But only between Ferengi." It was generally wise to leave that clause out when quoting that Rule to non-Ferengi—it just annoyed them.

Soon, everyone was ready to resume negotiations. Malic, to Quark's surprise, remained in the room, taking a seat in a corner of the meeting room, the two Orions on either side of him. Perhaps because of Malic's presence, the two Iconians—whom Quark hadn't seen since the initial session—also remained, standing behind Gaila. Malic took his personal padd out of his jacket pocket and started making notes onto it.

Tamra took up her position behind Quark, running her hand seductively across the outline of Quark's left ear. *Not now,* he thought, *I don't need the distraction.*

Another Iconian came in and handed a padd to Gaila, then went to stand with the other two.

Unbidden, the image of Rom standing in the bar came into Quark's head. Leeta by his side, Rom was holding the staff of the Nagus. Quark had publicly railed against the Zek reforms that Rom intended to continue. *Maybe that will be enough to keep me from going down with him when . . .*

He cut the thought off and glowered at his cousin, who was reading something on the padd. *I can't believe I fell for that,* he thought, admonishing himself. *I don't know what's worse, that Gaila stooped to try it, or that I almost succumbed to it.*

Aloud, he said, "So, shall we bring this negotiation to a close?"

"Just a moment, Quark," Gaila said without looking up from the padd. Then he finally set the padd down, folded his fingers together, and smiled.

It was the "I'm moving in for the kill" smile again. Quark folded his arms in an attempt at impatience and defiance—but mainly to cover his trepidation. *I don't like this one bit.*

"Tell me, Quark," Gaila said, "how long have you been working for Starfleet?"

Quark burst out laughing. "Working for *Starfleet?* Me? That's ridiculous!"

"Really? Then why is your nephew—an officer in Starfleet—working to sabotage the gateways?"

Quark frowned, genuinely confused. "What're you talking about?"

"We've intercepted a message from a Starfleet vessel called the *Sungari*," Gaila said, holding up the padd. "Lieutenant Nog in command. The message claims to include the specifications for something that will disrupt the gateways." Looking up at Malic, Gaila said, "Nog is Quark's nephew. Quark is also a known collaborator with Starfleet."

"What?" Quark couldn't believe his ears.

"Three years ago, he worked with Starfleet on a sting operation to bring down a weapons dealer named Hagath. Two years ago, he bartered a prisoner exchange on Starfleet's behalf involving a Vorta named Keevan."

"Those are lies," Quark said to Malic. Starfleet had nothing to do with either instance, and Gaila knew it—he was there for both incidents, after all.

"Are they?" Malic said quietly. Quark felt his blood freeze. "It would explain why you've been dragging out these negotiations—it allows your friends on Deep Space 9 to find a way to destroy the merchandise."

"They're not my friends," Quark said. His lobes started to ache. This was not going in the direction he'd hoped.

"Really?" Gaila's smile widened, which was never a good sign. "These are the people who kept your bar going when the Ferengi Commerce Authority banned you."

Quark sighed. Technically, of course, that was true—Captain Sisko and the others on the station, even Odo, had provided him with the resources to keep the bar going even when he was forbidden from doing business with any Ferengi.

Malic made notes onto his own padd, then stood up and moved toward the table. "I've been growing more and more suspicious of you, Quark. I have been unhappy with the length of these negotiations—and I was unaware of all these connections you have with Starfleet."

"The negotiations are almost complete," Quark said.

Gaila's smile changed to one of pure viciousness. "I wouldn't presume that if I were you, Quark."

Ignoring Gaila, Quark continued, "And I don't have 'connections' with Starfleet. Yes, my bar is on a station that is jointly operated by the Bajoran Militia and Starfleet, and *yes,* my nephew is an officer in Starfleet—a career path I strenuously objected to, I might add, and which I have never, ever supported. If Nog remained working for me, he'd be making more money and still have the left leg he was born with."

Malic looked at Gaila. "Let me see this transmission."

"Of course." Gaila got up and, smiling his "you're doomed" smile at Quark the entire time, handed the padd to Malic.

Putting his own padd back in the jacket pocket, Malic took the padd from Gaila and examined it. "This is definitely Starfleet, and definitely from one of the runabouts assigned to DS9."

Malic nodded to his bodyguards, and they moved forward and removed sidearms from holsters inside their jackets. Quark recognized the weapons as modified Klingon disruptors, each pointed directly at his head.

Tamra made a squeaking noise.

"You'll either tell the truth, Quark, or you'll die."

As a general rule, Quark found it best to keep negotiations as complicated as possible. It made it easier to find loopholes and get a better deal for himself. This negotiation, however, had just gotten depressingly simple: either tell Malic the truth, or be killed.

For Quark, that was no choice at all.

"All right, all right—I'm working for DS9 security. They sent me here to drag out the negotiations for as long as possible."

Malic shook his head. "And I thought having leverage over you meant I could trust you. I should've known better than to trust a Ferengi."

An Orion pirate is talking to me about trustworthiness? Quark thought, but wisely did not say aloud. At this point, saying anything else could prove fatal.

After making a few more notes on his padd, Malic said, "Kill him anyway."

Chapter Ten

Europa Nova

"I believe you've mistaken me for someone else, Colonel."

Now that Kira had a moment to take a good look at the Cardassian on the viewscreen, she had to agree. The face and voice were frighteningly similar to Dukat's, but there was a slightly less arrogant timbre to the voice, and his facial ridges, while similar, were arranged a bit differently. Most distinctively, this Cardassian had facial hair, something Kira couldn't remember seeing on any member of the Cardassian military. Two dark tufts extended from the corners of his mouth to his chin in small crescents.

"I am Gul Macet," he continued. *"Skrain Dukat was my cousin, and I can assure you, the family resemblance is not something that's done me any favors."*

"Surprised to hear a Cardassian say that," Kira muttered.

"I suppose you would be. But my relationship to Dukat has not been a beneficial one—especially of late. It seems that our resemblance has become more pronounced over the last few years. The more famous—or infamous—he became, the more people mistook me for him." He leaned forward. *"I know you have a history with Dukat, Colonel. I would ask only that you no more hold it against me than you would hold it against his daughter."*

Ziyal. "I wouldn't go there if I were you, Macet. What do you want?"

"Simply stated . . . I want to help, Colonel. The Trager is at your disposal to aid in the evacuation of Europa Nova."

Letting out a bark of derisive laughter, Kira said, "Out of the goodness of your heart?"

"You've been willing to make use of my services in the past, Colonel—though, come to think of it, you wouldn't be aware of it." Macet's face formed a smirk that was eerily similar to that of his cousin. *"The Trager is the ship that destroyed the cloning facilities on Rondac III."*

Blinking, Kira said, "You were part of Damar's resistance."

Macet smiled. Unlike Dukat's smile, which always carried an air of superiority and arrogance, Macet's smile seemed genuine, even warm. *"Why do you think the Trager looks like this?"*

Taran'atar finally spoke. "You were one of those who betrayed the Dominion."

The smile fell. *"That would be your view. You must be Taran'atar, the so-called observer from the Dominion I've heard about. I admire your courage in allowing that creature on your station, Colonel, if not your common sense."*

Ignoring the gibe, Taran'atar said, "Treachery is a poor foundation for trust."

"The traitors were the Cardassians who subsumed our empire to—"

"That's enough!" Kira snapped.

"My apologies, Colonel."

Taran'atar said nothing.

Kira considered Macet's offer. Every instinct told her not to trust him. He was part of Dukat's family. He was a Cardassian gul. *And he had to bring up Ziyal, the bastard.*

That, in turn, was precisely why she couldn't let Macet's accidental relationship—and unsettling resemblance—to Dukat influence her now. She remembered her thoughts upon arriving at Europa Nova the day before, regarding Taran'atar and her feelings toward Cardassians.

She knew the size of a *Galor*-class ship, and had a good idea about the number of evacuees it could probably take on, even one as damaged as the *Trager*. And she thought about the rising levels of theta radiation, the extra time it was taking to get the refugees off-planet, and the scores of people in the rural areas who had proven harder to locate than originally anticipated. Europa Nova apparently had a good-sized contingent of "back-to-nature" types among its population, who were apparently ignoring the orders to abandon their homes, despite the danger, and were proving difficult to find.

"All right, Macet. I can't say I understand why you're doing this, but I'm in no position to refuse, and I don't have time to discuss it. I accept."

"Very well, Colonel. I believe it would be best for all concerned if I remained here and accepted refugees that are brought up from the surface by your task force. The Trager *cannot land, of course, but it would speed up the process, and alleviate the need for your ships to evacuate to another star system once they've reached capacity. I assume you're bringing them to Deep Space 9?"*

"And to Bajor."

Macet nodded. *"Then that would be our wisest course."*

Kira silently agreed. With transporters no longer an option, she had intended to use the *Gryphon* and *Defiant* just as Macet proposed: position them at a safe distance while the *Intrepid,* the *Rio Grande,* and the other landing ships relayed refugees from the surface. The *Trager* would be a big help in that effort.

"Colonel," Taran'atar said, "sensors are showing that the *Trager* is equipped with Dominion technology."

Kira glanced down at the sensor readings. "I didn't know that had been done to any Cardassian ships."

"Some twenty ships were equipped with Dominion transporters and sensors," Taran'atar said. "It was intended to be the first step toward integrating the Central Command vessels with the Jem'Hadar warships. For obvious reasons, the project was never completed, but the *Trager* was apparently one of those twenty ships."

"Your observer speaks true, Colonel. We do in fact have sensors and transporters on par with those of a Jem'Hadar vessel—at least, that was what the Dominion told us," Macet added with another smirk.

Again ignoring Macet, Taran'atar said, "Colonel, if the *Trager* is equipped with Dominion transporters, they will still be viable for another six hours, based on the current rate of increase in theta radiation."

Shooting the Jem'Hadar a glance, Kira said, "Are you sure?"

"Quite sure."

"In that case, Macet," she said, turning back to the viewscreen, "you'll be much better off transporting people from the rural areas. We've had trouble locating all the people in the outlying territories. If you've got better sensors *and* can beam them out . . ." As she spoke, Kira did some quick calculations on her console. *This should cut the evac time considerably.* She was growing ever more concerned as to whether or not they'd be able to get everyone off-planet before the concentration of theta radiation in orbit reached fatal levels.

"I don't think that would be wise, Colonel."

"Why the hell not?"

"Let us just say there is a—history between Cardassia and Europa Nova. Transporting Europani onto a Cardassian vessel without warning would be provocative to say the least. So, for that matter, would be entering orbit of the planet."

"Macet, what are you talking about?"

"I must insist that we proceed with my proposed plan."

"These people are going to die if we don't get them off-planet within the next day or so, and we can't do it without your help."

"You have my help, Colonel. The only way you will get more help is if you talk to the local government. If they approve of our orbiting Europa Nova and transporting their citizens, I will be happy to do so. But, last time I checked, their military had standing orders to shoot down any Cardassian vessel entering their space. The Trager *has taken enough damage lately, I'd rather not add to it while trying to commit an act of kindness."*

Kira had no idea about any of this. "I'll contact the surface and get back to you. Hold your position until then."

"Of course. And Colonel?"

"Yes?"

"It's a pleasure to be working with you once again."

"I hope I can say the same when this is all over, Macet. *Euphrates* out." She then opened a channel to the *Intrepid.* "Captain Emick, did you monitor that?"

"Yes, Colonel," said Emick, *"and I'm as in the dark as you. I had no idea that there was even any contact between Europa Nova and Cardassia."*

Biting her lip, Kira said, "I'll talk to President Silverio."

She opened the channel, and then was politely told to wait a moment. The president was busy with other duties, but would be with her as soon as possible. While they waited, Kira told the *Rio Grande* to proceed to DS9 with their refugees.

As soon as she closed the channel to the *Rio Grande,* Taran'atar said, "You should not trust him."

"Why, because he worked for Damar's resistance?"

"In part."

"I worked for that resistance movement, Taran'atar. Yet you follow my orders."

"I follow your orders because a Founder has instructed me to. I have received no such instructions regarding trusting Cardassian guls who are known betrayers of the Dominion. You don't trust him, either—yet you are willing to give him this responsibility."

"Yes, I am," Kira said. "Because I don't have a choice. Look at the numbers, Taran'atar—we're *not* going to get everyone off Europa Nova in time. We've only got twenty ships and one gateway, and that gateway can only take five hundred thousand people. There's a good chance we won't get everyone off the planet in time. If we accept the *Trager's* help, then maybe—*maybe*—we'll be able to do it. I made President Silverio a promise, and I'm damned if I'll renege on it because of a Cardassian who reminds me of someone I hate."

"Colonel Kira, I have President Silverio for you," said a voice from the comm channel.

Still glaring at the Jem'Hadar, Kira said, "Go ahead."

Silverio looked just as haggard as she had when Kira spoke with her only a few minutes before. *"Colonel, I'm told there's a Cardassian ship in our system."*

"Yes, and they've offered—"

"I want that ship gone, Colonel. I don't care how you do it, but get rid of them." For the first time, there was a hard edge to Grazia Silverio's voice. Gone was the pleasant, grandmotherly tone. Now she sounded like—

Like me seven years ago, whenever the subject of Cardassians came up, Kira thought ruefully.

"Ma'am—Grazia—they've offered to help with the evacuation."

"I don't care if they've offered to scrub out the theta radiation with their teeth, I don't want them in my home."

"They have better sensors and transporters than any of the other ships in the task force—they can still *use* their transporters. If you allow them to go into orbit, they can transport the people in the rural areas that we've been having so much trouble with."

"Colonel, are you familiar with the asteroid belt between the sixth and seventh planets in this system?"

Kira shrugged. "I know it's there."

"When we first colonized this planet a century ago, that was a planet. The only other Class-M planet in the system. We seriously considered starting a second colony there. Thanks to the Cardassians, that's now an asteroid belt. Our military has standing orders to—"

"Shoot down any Cardassian ship that enters your space, I know."

"You know?"

"Gul Macet told me. He knew that, and he came anyhow. Grazia, I spent the first twenty-six years of my life fighting Cardassians—more than that, I spent all that time hating them. Nobody knows more than me what horrors they're capable of, and what they've done. And I'm telling you, we have to let them help. If you turn them away, people are going to die—people who trust you to lead them." She took a deep breath. "Look, if you tell me you don't want them here, I'll tell Macet to go back to Cardassia. But you're going to have to answer to the people who don't make it because you turned away a starship that could've rescued them."

Silverio closed her eyes for a moment. Then she shook her head and waved her arm. *"Apf. Let the ship in."*

Letting out a breath, Kira muttered a quick phrase of gratitude to the Prophets. "Thank you, Grazia."

"No, Colonel, thank you for knocking some sense into this old head of mine. You're right, now's hardly the time to let old hatreds get in the way of good sense. I always thought I had more brains than that."

"As long as you made the right choice in the end, it doesn't matter how you get there," Kira said with a gentle smile. "And call me Nerys. Let me put Gul Macet on." She opened a channel. "Gul Macet, I have President Silverio."

"Gul, I hereby give you permission to enter Europani space. And I thank you for your generous offer."

"You're welcome, Madame President. And may I say that I hope this marks a new beginning in relations between our people."

Kira shook her head. Macet was definitely going to take some getting used to—his voice was *so* like Dukat's. Yet those words out of Dukat's mouth would have had the listener waiting for the other shoe to drop. Macet, though, spoke with a sincerity that Dukat was, as far as Kira was concerned, congenitally incapable of.

"We'll begin scans and beam-outs immediately," Macet continued.

"Good," Kira said. "We're going to investigate the gateway, see if we can stop the radiation at the source. Captain Emick of the *Intrepid* will be in charge of the rescue operation while I'm gone."

"Understood, Colonel. Trager out."

Silverio signed off as well.

"Colonel, I have Commander Vaughn on subspace," Taran'atar said.

"Good timing," she muttered. "Go ahead, Commander," she added in a louder tone.

"Colonel, we're on our way back to Europa Nova. Admiral Ross has given us the go-ahead to attempt the disruption as soon as all five hundred thousand Europani have been evacuated through the Costa Rocosa gateway."

"Good. It'll be at least another three hours before they're all through. That should give Taran'atar and me enough time to check the other side of the orbital gateway."

"Lieutenant Nog says it will take two and a half hours to modify the Defiant. *We can aid in the evacuation in the interim."*

"Do that. I'll keep in touch. Oh, and we're getting some unexpected help here."

"Colonel?"

"Captain Emick can fill you in. Kira out." Turning to Taran'atar, she said, "Shield status?"

"Modulator is performing as expected."

"Good. Put them on maximum. Setting course for the gateway. Let's see what's on the other side."

Chapter Eleven

Deep Space 9

"Lieutenant, we're getting a message from Vedek Eran."

Ezri Dax stood at the table in ops, looking over the distribution of refugees to the open quarters on the station. Luckily, they had plenty of room to spare, though it meant utilizing some of the quarters that had belonged to station staff and crew who had died in the Jem'Hadar attack a month earlier. Since the quarters weren't needed, the processing of the possessions had been given a comparatively low priority, and had only seriously been tackled in the last week or so. Yesterday, however, Dax had assigned a detail to take care of it, thus providing them with maximum availability.

She had just discovered an anomaly, but set it aside to take the call from Eran Dal. "Yes, Vedek?"

Eran was an older man with a pleasant, round face and a completely shaved head who managed to look exactly like Benjamin and nothing like her old friend at the same time. *Maybe if Benjamin added fifty pounds,* Ezri thought, and had to conceal a smile.

"Lieutenant, we've been having some troubles with the Federation industrial replicators we've been using to fabricate the temporary shelters for the Europani. Is there any way you can provide us with someone to repair them?"

Most of the Starfleet Corps of Engineers crew that had aided in the refurbishing of the station after the Jem'Hadar attack had departed, and the station's own engineering staff was busy with their own duties. Ezri was about to check the duty roster to find a loophole, when she remembered something.

"Hang on a moment, Vedek." She called up a station manifest. Sure enough, there was an industrial replicator on board, tagged for delivery to Cardassia Prime by the *U.S.S. Hood* next week. *If it's just going to sit in a cargo bay for a week, we may as well put it to good use.* She checked another display, and saw that the *Ng* was an hour away from finishing offloading refugees onto the station before heading back to Europa Nova.

"Vedek, I can't spare personnel, but I can give you a temporary replacement. Wait for a signal from Captain Hawkins on the *Ng* in about two hours, and he should be able to bring you a new replicator."

"Excellent. Thank you, Lieutenant."

"Not at all," Ezri said. "It's the Vedek Assembly we should be thanking for making so much of its land available to the relief efforts."

"It is our pleasure to help those in need, Lieutenant. It was not long ago that we were relying on others for help when our world was devastated. We should never forget that. Eran out."

Eran's face winked out from the screen.

"Are you all right, Lieutenant?" Cathy Ling asked from the operations station.

Frowning, Ezri said, "I'm fine, why?"

"It's just—well, when you were talking to the vedek, your voice seemed to get—deeper. And scratchier."

Smiling her most reassuring counselor smile, Ezri said, "I'm perfectly fine, Ensign. Probably a little rough from all the talking I've been doing." She picked up a padd. "Before the vedek called, I noticed something—the atmosphere was never changed in the suite of rooms the Plexicans were in. We'd better do that before the *Ng*'s refugees try to set up there and find they can't breathe the methane."

Ling nodded quickly. "I'll get a team right on it, sir."

Ezri went back to looking over the status reports. Most of the refugees had settled in as well as could be expected. Many were scared, concerned about what they'd had to leave behind. Some expressed concern about their children—all of whom had been relocated to the Tozhat Resettlement Camp on Bajor. Ezri made a mental note to try to set up a schedule that would allow people to communicate with the camp.

Several had made specific complaints that had been forwarded to Ezri. "Computer, time?"

"The time is 1409 hours."

She still had almost an hour before her subspace meeting with First Minister Shakaar. As far as she could tell, all the fires had been put out. Ling reported that the off-loading of refugees was proceeding apace. Vaughn had left on the *Defiant* with Nog and Shar's gateway disruption scheme ready to go. Dr. Tarses's last report from the infirmary was that all the cases of theta-radiation poisoning were minor and easily treated—as were the assorted other bumps and bruises that people had suffered during evacuation. She was actually free for the next fifty minutes.

"Ensign, I'll be in the habitat ring until my meeting with First Minister Shakaar," Ezri said as she moved toward the turbolift and grabbed a padd with the list of complaints. *May as well give these people's complaints the personal touch. With all they've been through, they deserve the station commander's direct attention.*

Station commander. Ezri surprised herself with how much she liked the sound of that. Most, though not all, hosts of the Dax symbiont gravitated toward positions of authority. In some cases—notably Ezri and Jadzia—that desire didn't seem to come until after joining with the symbiont. Ezri wondered if this inclination was congenital to Dax, or just the combined weight of all those memories of being an authority figure.

Just as she reached the top step of ops's upper level, Ling said, "Lieutenant, there's a personal communiqué here from a Dr. Renhol on Trill."

Damn, Ezri thought. With everything that had been going on, she hadn't made her check-in call with Renhol.

Renhol was a member of the Trill Symbiosis Commission. Ezri had not been a candidate to be joined, and had united with the Dax symbiont in order to save its life. The commission had asked that Ezri check in on a regular basis with Renhol—ideally once a week, but at least once a month, duties permitting. Of course, many on the commission would have preferred to keep Ezri on Trill and have her adjust to a joined life under close supervision, but Ezri was a free citizen and could do as she pleased. *And right now, I'm pleased to be here on the station, thank you very much.* She sighed. *Still, it's been over six weeks.*

"I'll take it in the colonel's office," Ezri said, changing direction.

Ezri went in, took a very deep breath through her nose, let it out through her mouth, and then sat down in Kira's chair. "Put it through," she said, tapping her combadge.

Renhol's angular face appeared on the small viewscreen on the desk. As always, her brown hair was tied severely back. *"Lieutenant Dax. It's good to see you."*

Holding up her hands, Ezri said, "I know why you're calling, Doctor, and I'm *very* sorry, but things have been a little crazy on the station."

"So I've heard. For that matter, so I see—I seem to recall that your uniform was a different color when last we spoke."

Involuntarily, Ezri's hand went up to the collar of her uniform, which was now command red instead of the sciences blue she'd worn ever since graduating from the Academy. "I've switched over to the command track."

"Really? That's rather a major step, don't you think?"

"Yes, it is. But I think this is the right thing for me to do. About a month ago, I wound up in command of the *Defiant* during a combat situation. I realized then that I needed to stop assing around in a fog and put these centuries of experiences to better use."

"Don't you think that's a decision you should have consulted us on?"

Ezri rolled her eyes. "Young lady, I don't need the commission's permission to hold my hand and walk me through every major life decision. I'm a grown woman, and I'm completely capable of making my own choices. Or do I have to consult the commission when I brush my teeth every day?"

Renhol's lips pursed. *"Of course not. But are you aware of the fact that each of those three sentences came from a different host?"*

Frowning, Ezri said, "What?"

"You modulated from Lela to Ezri to Jadzia. For that matter, Torias was fond of the phrase 'assing around,' if I recall correctly. That isn't the way the joining is supposed to work, Ezri, and you know that."

Taking another deep breath to compose herself, Ezri said, "Look, Doctor, I appreciate your concern, but right now I have to deal with a huge influx of refugees from Europa Nova." Quickly, she outlined the situation.

"So you're in charge of the station?"

"At the moment, yes, and I really don't have time to bring you completely up to speed on my life. I promise that I'll contact you again within the next two days, assuming the crisis is resolved."

"I apologize, Lieutenant, I didn't realize my timing was so bad," Renhol said, though Ezri didn't think she was sincere. *"Get back in touch with me again at your convenience—but soon, please. We* do *need to discuss this."*

"Of course, Doctor. Dax out." She cut the connection.

Stupid, meddling commission. Why can't they just let me live my life?

As she exited the office and headed to the turbolift, she caught sight of Ling. She then remembered what she had said about Ezri's voice getting deeper and scratchier. *That was when I was talking to Vedek Eran—and giving him the speech about how we should thank him. Which,* she realized suddenly, *I did in Curzon's classic "diplomatic mode."*

She shook her head as she entered the turbolift. *I'm just tired—*

—like I was last month when I tapped into Jadzia's memories during sex with Julian? Renhol was right about one thing: it *wasn't* supposed to work that way. Ezri had been content to chalk it all up to a transitional phase she was going through—from a year of stumbling her way through a labyrinth of past lives, to really taking control for the first time. More and more, ever since that terrible day on the *Defiant,* she found herself drawing from the wellspring of her previous hosts to take on greater and greater challenges. And the more she took on, the more she seemed to crave.

What's wrong with that? she wondered, not without some resentment. *Isn't that the point of being joined? To harmonize those life experiences and use them to live up to their combined potential? To be greater than the sum of my past hosts?*

As the turbolift arrived in the habitat ring, she looked over the list, her mind returning to the issues at hand. She decided to simply take the complaints by order of quarters.

On her way, she passed by Ensign Gordimer, who had remained behind when the *Defiant* left, leading a group of refugees toward section nine. She smiled at the line of people who shuffled in a more-or-less orderly manner toward the empty quarters there.

She walked up to Gordimer. "Ensign," she said quietly, "make sure that the last two quarters in this section have been readjusted for humans."

In a whisper, Gordimer reported, "I've already been in touch with Ensign Ling, sir. This group won't need those two quarters, but they should be ready by the time the *Xhosa* arrives with the next batch."

Ezri nodded. "The *Ng*'s refugees are going to section twelve, right?"

"Yes, sir."

"Good. Carry on, Ensign."

"Excuse me?"

Ezri turned to see a very short older man. His face was wrinkled, his neck jowly, his snow-white hair thin and wispy, and his skin liver-spotted. Despite this, he did not seem at all decrepit—he walked with as much vitality as Vaughn, even though Ezri figured he had to have thirty years on Elias.

"Can I help you, Mr.—?"

"Maranzano." The deep, rich voice belied the fragile form it came out of. "I just wanted to know—are you in charge?"

Smiling, Ezri said, "Well, I'm presently in command of the station."

"I just wanted to thank you all for your help. I know how difficult this must be for all of you, keeping track of all of us and herding us around . . ."

Ezri couldn't help but laugh. "Difficult for *us?* Mr. Maranzano—"

A woman standing in the queue said, "Oh, don't listen to him, young lady. He just thinks you're pretty and wants to make nice."

Mr. Maranzano turned and gave the woman a dirty look. "I'm not allowed to be nice to a pretty young woman?"

Should I tell him I'm over three hundred years old? Ezri thought mischievously. *No, that wouldn't be fair.* "Well, thanks all the same, Mr. Maranzano, but I think you're the ones who should be thanked. Now please, if you'll go with Ensign Gordimer here, he'll take you to your temporary quarters."

She saw them off, then continued to the nearest one containing someone who had relayed a problem to ops.

The first two were minor complaints about the size of the quarters—mostly from people who lived in houses on Europa Nova. Ezri made appropriately conciliatory noises that boiled down to *tough luck,* and moved on.

A heavyset woman answered the third door. "Is everything all right, Ms. DellaMonica?"

"The replicators don't work. I've been trying to make an espresso for the last hour."

"Oh, I'm sorry. Let me take a look." She went inside the quarters, which were also occupied by four other people, all male. All five of them had similar facial features, and Ezri assumed they were related. "Computer," Ezri said to the replicator, "one espresso, unsweetened."

A demitasse cup appeared in the replicator, filled with steaming black liquid. Ezri picked it up. "Looks okay to me."

"Taste it."

Ezri tasted it. It seemed to taste right. But then, Ezri had never been much of an espresso drinker—she put it in the same category as *raktajino,* which she detested—though Jadzia loved it, having been a regular customer at the Café Roma on Earth, with its magnificent brew, when she was at the Academy. But then, Jadzia also liked *raktajino.*

"It seems fine," she said tentatively.

"It's horrendous!" Ms. DellaMonica cried.

"Ms. DellaMonica, I realize it may not be up to your standards, but replicators are sometimes—"

Holding up a hand, Ms. DellaMonica said, "Lieutenant, I know what you're going to say. 'This espresso is good enough.' Well not for me." She took a deep breath. "Look around you, Lieutenant. What *don't* you see?"

Looking around the quarters, Ezri saw what one usually saw in such places—but saw very little by way of personal effects, which was presumably Ms. DellaMonica's point. "I know that things are difficult, Ms. DellaMonica, but—"

"Do you know what a pietà is, Lieutenant?"

"No."

"It's a religious icon of a woman holding her dead son by the artist Michelangelo. We have a replica of it that's been in my family since Earth's eighteenth century. My *nonna* gave it to me on her deathbed. That pietà means more to us than anything—but we left it behind, because we only had to take the essentials with us. I may never see that statue again, Lieutenant. That's the way the universe works, and I accept that. But, all things considered, I don't think it's too much to ask that at least I can get a decent espresso. This is *not* decent espresso."

Casting her mind over the duty roster for the engineering staff, Ezri tapped her combadge. "Dax to McAllister."

"Go ahead, Lieutenant."

"Could you report to the habitat ring, Level Four, Section Forty-Eight and have a look at the replicator, please? The people in the quarters will explain the problem."

"On my way."

The faces of all five DellaMonicas brightened with smiles. "Thank you," Ms. DellaMonica said, clasping her hands together and shaking them over her heart.

"Anything else?"

"Nothing a good espresso won't cure. Without my caffeine, I get cranky."

"Trust me," one of the other DellaMonicas added. "You wouldn't like her when she's cranky."

Ezri smiled. "I get that impression. Don't hesitate to call me if there are any other problems. And Ms. DellaMonica?"

"Yes?"

"We're doing everything we can to get you back together with your pietà and your espresso maker."

"I appreciate that, Lieutenant."

After bidding them a cheery good-bye, she went to the next door.

Without preamble, the occupant, Mr. Pérez, said: "It's too hot in here."

"I'll have the temperature reduced. The last occupants were Ovirians—you know how they like it hot."

"What's an Ovirian?"

"They're from the planet—"

"Aliens? You put aliens in my room?"

"They're simply the ones who had the quarters last."

"I don't want to share my space with aliens."

Ezri took a deep breath. "You won't be. The Ovirians were in here over a month ago."

"If there are any aliens in here, I want to move."

"There are no aliens, Mr. Pérez. It's just you and your brother and sister in here."

"It better be."

The next door: "I've got a terrible rash!"

"Have you been to the infirmary?"

"There's an infirmary here?"

Sighing, Ezri asked, "What type of rash is it?"

"A bad one."

Remembering something Julian had mentioned earlier, Ezri said, "It's probably just an allergic reaction to the arithrazine you were given on the *Defiant*, Mr. Amenguale. You should report to the infirmary right away."

"Where is that?"

"The computer can direct you."

"What computer?"

Ezri quickly described the shortest route from this section of the habitat ring to the infirmary, then moved on.

The next door: "Where's the kitchen?"

"These quarters have food replicators."

"What're they?"

Sighing, Ezri tried not to dwell on the irony of explaining the concept of food replicators to someone who lived in a society that relied on them.

"Oh, okay. So how do I cook food, then?"

Ezri explained the concept a second time, which seemed to take, and she took her leave.

The next door: "The lights are too bright."

Next: "These beds are terrible!"

Next: "I can't get the sonic shower to work."

Next: "The lights are too dark."

Next was Ms. Bello, a small, timid-looking woman who said, "Lieutenant, someone stole my necklace."

Before Ms. Bello could elaborate, some insensitive jackass cried out, "How could you let someone steal your necklace? Why were you wearing a necklace anyhow? You knew you'd be crowded in with a bunch of other people and going to a space station! Any idiot knows to keep an eye on your belongings when you come to a space station like this! I can't believe you'd be so *completely* idiotic!"

Ezri realized two things as this diatribe went on. One was that Ensign Gordimer had just turned the corner. The other was that the insensitive jackass was in fact Ezri herself.

"Lieutenant," Gordimer said quickly, "are you okay?"

Catching her breath, feeling like the most horrible person who ever walked the halls of the station, Ezri said, "Yes, I'm fine. Can you do me a favor, Ensign? This woman has had some jewelry stolen. Can you take her statement?"

"Of course, Lieutenant," Gordimer said quickly.

Turning to the small woman, who looked like she wanted desperately to curl herself up into a ball, she said, "I'm very, *very* sorry, Ms. Bello. My behavior was *completely* uncalled for."

Ms. Bello simply flinched and nodded.

Gordimer gave a reassuring smile. "I promise we'll try to get to the bottom of this theft, ma'am."

Again, she flinched. Ezri decided to get the hell away from the woman before she did any more damage.

I desperately need a break, she thought, wondering if perhaps Dr. Renhol didn't have a point.

No, that's silly. I've been dashing about full-tilt since we got the distress call from Europa Nova. I've barely slept in the last fifty hours. I just need to relax. "Computer, time?"

"The time is 1445 hours."

Damn, she thought. *Only fifteen minutes until Shakaar.*

Ezri entered a turbolift. "Wardroom," she said after a moment. That room was likely to be empty—she could get a cup of tea, compose herself, and still make it to ops in time.

As the turbolift wended its way mid-core, she wished Julian had stayed behind. After all, the *Intrepid* and the *Gryphon* had full medical staffs that could work just fine with the Europani medical authorities. But they decided to play it safe and have as many medical personnel available on-site as possible, which certainly made sense. Besides, Simon Tarses and Girani Semna were handling the load back here just fine.

Speaking of medicine, I wonder if Mr. Amenguale actually found his way up to the infirmary. She tapped her combadge. "Dax to Tarses."

"Go ahead." The doctor sounded exhausted.

"You okay, Simon?"

"Nothing eight days of sleep won't cure. What can I do for you, Lieutenant?"

"A Mr. Amenguale should be reporting to you with a case of arithrazine rash. If he isn't there in the next five minutes or so, send someone from security to find him—I think he might get lost."

"Got it. And hey, you don't exactly sound hale and hearty yourself."

"I promise to get some sleep as soon as I can, Simon."

"Why am I not reassured?"

Ezri chuckled as the turbolift arrived at the wardroom level. "Dax out."

As she exited the lift, she heard the familiar voice of Shar.

"I understand, *Zhavey.*"

"No, Thirishar, I don't think you truly do. You mustn't, if you're going to insist on acting like this."

The second voice wasn't immediately familiar, but given the way Shar addressed her, it must be the infamous Councillor Charivretha zh'Thane. They were obviously right around the corner from where Ezri was walking—or, rather, standing, since she had stopped short of proceeding once she heard the voices.

"I am acting like myself, *Zhavey.* I don't know any other way *to* act. I am sorry for that, but—"

"In Thori's name, Thirishar!" zh'Thane cried out in a voice that, Ezri suspected, had intimidated many on the Federation Council floor, "you cannot afford to take such risks when you *know* what is at stake!"

"Exploring the Gamma Quadrant is hardly a 'risk,' *Zhavey.*"

"Please don't tell me you're that naïve. If you want, I can quote casualty figures on starships exploring unmapped space for the last two hundred years."

"That won't be necessary."

"Then what will it take?" zh'Thane snapped. "To what part of you should I appeal? Clearly you feel no sense of duty to your own kind, nor to me. You have no fear of what may befall you before the window is closed. Have you even considered what your obstinancy is doing to Anichent, to Dizhei, to Thriss? Are you even thinking about anyone besides yourself?"

There was an unexpected sound, like a bulkhead being struck, and Dax almost moved to see what had happened, to intervene, but the sound of Shar's voice, raised to a hiss and seething with emotion, stopped her in her tracks.

"I have thought of everyone *but* myself my entire life, *Zhavey!* That's how you raised me, isn't it? How *all* Andorian children are raised? We don't live for ourselves, we live for the whole, always the whole.

"You ask me if I love them . . . as if I had a choice. As if every cell in my body didn't long to be among them *every day.*"

"Then why are you doing this?"

"Because it isn't working! I've kept track, *Zhavey,* more closely than you imagine. I've seen the numbers, and I see what we're doing to ourselves as a people because of them, because of our desperation to delay the inevitable. We're so consumed with keeping ourselves alive, we have no conception of what we're living *for.*"

"And so your answer is to turn your back to us? On everyone and everything?"

"You don't understand. You never did," Shar said in a deadly whisper.

The last time Ezri had heard an Andorian use that tone of voice was thirteen years earlier, when she was Curzon. The person to whom the Andorian had spoken was dead five minutes later.

There was a terrible silence. And when zh'Thane broke it, her voice was firm. But also, Ezri thought, tinged with sorrow. "Don't force me to act, my *chei.*"

"Stop meddling in my life, *Zhavey.*"

"Don't walk away from me, Thirishar!"

Uh-oh, Ezri thought, and she immediately started walking forward in a pointless attempt to cover up her eavesdropping.

Shar turned the corner just as Ezri approached it, and the two almost collided. Shar's antennae were standing straight up, and his eyes—normally the inquisitive eyes of the scientist that Ezri knew quite well from Tobin and Jadzia—were smoldering with emotions Ezri couldn't begin to read.

At the sight of Ezri, though, the antennae lowered slightly, and he regained his composure. "Lieutenant! I'm sorry, I didn't see you there."

A tall Andorian woman with an impressively elaborate hairdo came around the corner, and she was similarly brought up short by the Trill's presence.

Well, this is awkward, Ezri thought. She supposed she should have turned and walked away the minute the first words came within earshot, but her own curiosity—and her counselor's training—had kicked in.

Finally, after the pause threatened to go on for days, Ezri offered her hand to the tall woman. "You must be Councillor zh'Thane. I'm Lieutenant Ezri Dax."

The councillor took it. "Dax—you used to be Curzon Dax, yes?"

"Two hosts ago, yes."

Sourly, she said, "Well, I'll try not to hold that against you." Turning around, obviously unwilling to air her family's private affairs in public, she said, "If you'll excuse me."

She walked off. Idly, Ezri tried to recall what, exactly, Curzon might have done to offend Andor's representative to the Federation Council. She couldn't remember ever having met her, but that was hardly conclusive—Curzon had annoyed plenty of people he had never met.

Shrugging, she turned to Shar, who looked as unhappy as Ezri had ever seen him. In fact, it was really the first time Ezri could ever remember seeing him unhappy.

Based on the conversation, she could guess why.

"Do you want to talk about it, Shar?"

"I'm afraid I can't, Lieutenant, but thank you for asking."

Ezri thought a moment, then decided to go for broke. "I take it there are three people on Andor waiting for you to come home to take part in the *shelthreth?*"

Shar whirled around, his antennae raised. In a quiet, stunned voice, he asked, "You know about that?"

"I've been around for three centuries, Shar—I've known a few Andorians in my time."

Nodding, Shar said, "Yes, of course you have."

"And I know how important the *shelthreth* is."

Shar's face hardened. "Not you as well, Ezri. I know that I have a duty to Andor. And whether anyone back home understands this or not, I'm fulfilling it in my own way. But now *Zhavey* is making threats."

"What can she do?"

"She can have me reassigned to Andor."

Ezri frowned. "Last time I checked, Federation Councillors didn't have any influence over Starfleet personnel assignments."

"Respectfully, Lieutenant, I don't think you fully appreciate the power of politics. And she knows Commander Vaughn."

Dax's frown deepened. "You think she'd convince Vaughn to transfer you? I think you underestimate him, Shar. You've been doing superlative work. I ought to know—I sort of used to have the job," she added with a smile.

"Thank you, but unfortunately, I think you underestimate Charivretha. It would be just like my *zhavey* to talk him into transferring me. She might even go so far as to explain why."

"Even if that's true, Vaughn doesn't strike me as the type who'd authorize transfers for personal reasons. And even if he did, I can't see Kira approving it."

"Your confidence is touching, but I've only been here a few months. I haven't done anything to command that kind of loyalty—certainly not enough to refuse the request of a Federation Councillor. Besides, why do you think I'm not on the *Defiant?*"

"That's a good point," Ezri said. "Why aren't you on the *Defiant?*"

"Because *Zhavey* asked the commander to leave me behind so we could talk." Some of Shar's coarse white hair fell into his face, and he brushed it out of the way. "Although the talk accomplished nothing that we haven't already said in our private communications."

Remembering how much more painful it was to deal with her own mother in person than over subspace, Ezri could see Councillor zh'Thane's logic in believing that an in-person plea might be more effective. Saying that, however, would not help matters, so she tried another tack:

"Shar, maybe you should consider what she's saying." At the Andorian's sharp look, she added, "I'm not taking her side. Believe me, I can quote you chapter and verse on the subject of parental guilt and not doing what they expect you to do. I'm not saying you should reconsider your position because it's what your *zhavey* is telling you to do. What I *am* saying is that you should examine the situation without considering her at all. Forget about what she wants. Think about yourself—and think about the three people waiting for you back home. They deserve *some* consideration, yes?"

Shar said nothing.

"Just think about it, okay?"

Sighing, Shar said, "I *have* thought about it. I appreciate what you're trying to do, Lieutenant, but I've already made up my mind. Being in Starfleet is what I want—it's all I've ever wanted, since I was a child. I'm not going to give it up now, and I'm certainly not going to let *Zhavey* hold me personally responsible for the fact that the Andorian species is dying."

Chapter Twelve

The Delta Quadrant

The stars are wrong.

Kira had that same thought every time she left the Bajoran sector. For years in the resistance, she had depended on the stars in the sky over Bajor. It was better to move at night when they were on the run from Cardassian patrols. Scanners could fail or be jammed, but all she had to do was look up to know precisely where she was. Even when most or all of the moons were visible, she still could see enough of the constellations to orient herself.

In space, it was the same thing. Navigational equipment wasn't always reliable, particularly when you were being fired on. Again, the stars were always there for her—as long as the Prophets provided a view of the other suns in the galaxy, she could find her way.

Before becoming first officer on Deep Space 9, she had spent very little time out of the Bajoran system, and even when she did, she'd had other things on her mind—picking up supplies, or some other errand related to the resistance. For most of the first twenty-six years of her life, the stars as they were seen from Bajor were her anchors. It was something she could depend on in a life that had precious little of that.

The first time she went through the wormhole and into the Gamma Quadrant, the disorientation had been almost painful. Her anchor was gone. Everything was arranged differently, and Kira—at the time, still not accustomed to working with reliable Starfleet equipment—found herself in the uncomfortable position of being forced to depend on technology far more than she was used to.

Now, seven years later, it was hardly an issue. She'd made dozens of trips to the Gamma Quadrant, and had traveled all over the Alpha Quadrant, from Cardassia Prime to Earth. Still, every time she found herself far away from home, there was that feeling that the sky was somehow lying to her.

As the *Euphrates* came careening through the gateway, piercing the thick green jet that choked the passage, the sky told her a new lie, one as big as the one it told her when she went through the wormhole.

She kept going at full impulse when they cleared the gateway—she wanted to get away from the radioactive waste as quickly as possible. Taking up a position about a hundred thousand kilometers from the gateway, Kira did a sensor sweep.

Her eyes went wide and she felt her jaw go slack. "Oh no . . ."

"I assume," Taran'atar said, "that you have just noticed the waste concentration bearing 273 mark 9."

Kira nodded. "That single mass is putting out more radiation than everything that's in orbit of Europa Nova right now combined. If we let that go through, the planet's as good as dead."

"Can we destroy it?"

Kira shook her head as she studied the readings. "Best we could do is blast it into smaller pieces. Impact damage might be less, but it wouldn't alleviate the radiation." She didn't have to remind Taran'atar that they no longer had a tractor beam, so trying to alter its course as they'd done before wasn't an option.

"Colonel, I'm picking up a vessel," Taran'atar announced. "It's the source of the jet."

"Do you recognize it?" Kira asked.

Taran'atar said, "No. It does not match anything in Starfleet records, nor any ship I have knowledge of." He peered at his sensor readings. "Length, seven thousand meters. Hull is made of an unidentified alloy that appears to include elements of duranium and holivane." Kira had no idea what holivane was and, just at that moment, didn't care. Taran'atar continued, "Indeterminate weapons capacity. They appear to operate on channeled matter-antimatter reactions but, based on what I have been able to read through the interference from the radiation, it's an inferior engine design."

"If they're producing antimatter waste on this scale, that's not surprising. Anything else?"

"Fully ninety percent of the ship is dedicated to cargo space. Based on its size and configuration, I believe the ship is a barge for the hazardous material."

"And they decided they had a perfect dumping ground." Kira felt revulsion build up in her gut and work its way to her extremities, which she had to keep from shaking. Even at their absolute worst, the Cardassians never did anything so repugnant as to dump highly toxic material into a populated region. "It must've thrilled them when the gateway opened. I wonder if they even bothered to see if there was an inhabited planet on the other side." A brief urge came over Kira to lock the runabout's phasers on the ship and destroy it just to teach these people—whoever they were—a lesson. She set the impulse aside. "What else?"

"There are no docking ports. They also have an unusual shield configuration."

"Unusual how?"

"There are seven of them, though most are offline right now. They appear to have been enhanced in some way. I've never seen a design like this."

Kira noticed that there was none of the scientific curiosity she would expect from, say, Nog or Shar in Taran'atar's tone. He was simply reporting the facts as he saw them.

The Jem'Hadar continued, "At present, most of their systems are offline. I am not reading any life signs."

Blinking, Kira said, "None at all? That ship's got to have a crew of at least several hundred. Could the radiation be interfering?"

"The radiation could not interfere so much as to mask that many life signs, Colonel."

Shaking her head, Kira looked down at the display. They had a little over two hours before the mass would go through the gateway, so there was time to figure something out. *But what? With no tractor beam and no way to destroy it effectively . . .*

Then she noticed something. "I'm reading some debris. Sensors say it's primarily irradiated monotanium—along with organic matter. Looks like a ship was destroyed by the waste."

"A ship with a monotanium hull," Taran'atar mused. "Even the Dominion was never able to refine enough monotanium to make spacecraft from it."

Kira couldn't resist. "Looks like the Dominion doesn't have the market on high technology."

"It would seem so."

Growing serious once again, Kira said, "Still, if even a monotanium ship couldn't hold up to that waste, Europa Nova won't, either."

"There is a Class-M planet in this system," Taran'atar said, "less than a million kilometers from our position. There are, however, no high-order life signs."

Kira took a deep breath. "All right, I'm going to assume that *someone* is alive over there." She opened a channel. "Unidentified vessel, this is the Federation runabout *Euphrates*. Respond please."

There was no reply.

"This is the Federation runabout *Euphrates* contacting unidenti—"

"The tanker's systems are coming online," Taran'atar said suddenly. "Weapons are powering up—"

"Raise shields," Kira said half a second before the weapons fire struck the runabout. She immediately sent the *Euphrates* onto an evasive course that would take them farther away from the radioactive waste.

"Shields at sixty percent," Taran'atar said. "Shall I return fire?"

Kira hesitated only for a second. The Jem'Hadar was bred for combat. *So why not let him do what he does best?*

"Do it," Kira said, and as she piloted the *Euphrates* away from the tanker, another salvo of weapons fire struck the runabout.

"Shields are down," Taran'atar called over the din of alarms. "Shield generators offline."

"Lucky shot," Kira muttered.

"No, Colonel," Taran'atar said. "That shot was carefully aimed and modulated. Our opponent knew precisely where and how hard to strike."

Before Kira could respond to that, the runabout faded into an incoherent jumble. Her body suddenly felt disconnected from reality. The sounds of the alarms in the runabout faded, the feel of the cushioned seat under her dissolved. It was akin to being transported, but that didn't come with such a feeling of disorientation—of removal from reality.

For a brief instant that felt like it would never end, she was nowhere, felt nothing, *was* nothing.

Then, slowly, her senses returned. Except what she now felt beneath her was hard, cold metal; she was lying down instead of sitting, and her hands were now bound behind her back. Instinctively, she struggled against her bonds, but they did not yield.

She no longer heard alarms, but she did hear the constant thrum of a ship's systems. The ship, however, was not the *Euphrates*. The silvery-blue colors that Starfleet favored had been replaced by dark browns and greens—the latter accentuated by the dim green lights on the ceiling. She saw unfamiliar interfaces and a smaller, cruder style of screen—a rounder design than the usual flatscreen displays Kira was accustomed to. A green-tinged miasma hovered in the very air of the ship, and it smelled like someone was burning plastiform. The gloom was palpable.

Adding to it were the three humanoid corpses which also lay on the deck. Golden-skinned, wearing bulky uniforms, and most in pools of their own greenish-blue blood, these, Kira suspected, were the life signs that the *Euphrates* could no longer read. One appeared to be female, the other two male, one of the latter with thinning hair. All three had been cut to pieces.

If these were members of the crew, they'd certainly paid for the act of dumping their lethal payload on Europa Nova.

Of Taran'atar, she saw no sign.

Then a huge figure stepped into view, walking purposefully toward her. The figure—whom Kira guessed was at least two and a half meters tall, though her worm's-eye view gave her a skewed perspective—wore an imposing uniform of dark metallic armor. Most of its head was covered by a helmet with ridges that began close together at the forehead and spread out and around to the back of the head. The only displays of color beyond the blue-black of the armor were the alien's mottled brown face, the streak of white on either side of the helmet's middle ridge, and the streak of bright red under the leftmost ridge.

The alien stopped, looked down on Kira, and spoke one word in a deep, resonant voice that carried the promise of a painful death.

"Prey."

Chapter Thirteen

Farius Prime

So this is it, Quark thought. *We're going to die.*

What galled him the most was that it was Gaila who engineered this. The beloved cousin to whom he had lent that latinum to get his arms business started—*and this is how he repays me. He undermines a business deal just to take some misguided revenge on me. How could Gaila, of all people, forget the Sixth Rule of Acquisition?* "Never allow family to stand in the way of opportunity."

No, Gaila just sat there, smiling his "I won" smile as if he hadn't just ruined things for his own client. The Iconians would never get a better offer than this. The Orions were not likely to engender much confidence as a potential buyer after killing their own negotiator.

He probably had that same smile on his face after he had Quark's Treasure *delivered to DS9.* Gaila had always claimed that the malfunction that caused the ship to be transported over four hundred years into the past wasn't the result of sabotage, but Quark had never believed it.

One of the two burly Orions looked over at Tamra and smiled lasciviously. "Just so's you know, Quark—after I kill you, I'm takin' the *dabo* girl for myself."

Tamra smiled right back.

The Orion's face fell. This was not the vacuous facial expression of a woman whose main purpose was to provide distracting eye-candy for the customers. This was closer to one of Gaila's smiles.

Then Tamra grabbed one of those idiotic tassels from her waist and threw it into the middle of the room.

Quark quickly closed his eyes and covered them with his hands. When the flare went off, a huge flash of light filled the room. Quark could see the glow even through his eyelids and hands.

A hand grabbed his left arm and yanked him out of his chair.

He opened his eyes to see the room in chaos. The Iconians, the Orions, and Gaila were all blinking, trying to clear their vision and obviously failing miserably. For his part, Quark was being dragged toward the door.

The only person standing between the two of them and that door was Malic, crying, "Kill them! *Kill them!*"

"I'm blind! I'm *blind!*" one of the burly Orions screamed over Malic's voice. He had, Quark noticed, dropped his disruptor.

The other Orion, though, still had his disruptor, and took Malic's instructions to heart; he fired. Luckily for Quark, he was as blind as his panicky comrade: the shot went about a half a meter over Quark's head.

The blond Bajoran, still dragging Quark with one hand, clipped Malic with her other arm, knocking the Orion to the floor. In the same motion, she bent over and picked up the dropped disruptor.

Another shot flew over Quark's head, closer this time.

"Quark! You won't get away with this, cousin!" Gaila was, Quark noted, facing away from Quark, yelling at a bulkhead.

When they reached the corridor, Quark yanked his arm free. "What took you so long? I was starting to think you were going to wait until he actually pulled the trigger."

Lieutenant Ro Laren glowered at him from under her unnaturally colored hair. "You're welcome, Quark."

Deep Space 9 (four days ago)

"I've got a little bit of a problem."

It hadn't been easy for Quark to come to the security office. He had, in fact, spent the last day staring at the door to Ro's office, trying to figure out what to do.

Normally, of course, he wouldn't even need an excuse to go to the security office. After all, Ro was there, and that vision of Bajoran loveliness was more than enough reason for Quark to contrive a feeble excuse to drop in.

But this was different.

It had seemed innocent enough when it began nearly two weeks ago. An Orion named Malic had entered the bar with a business proposal: he wanted Quark to negotiate a deal for the Orion Syndicate on his behalf. The terms had been pretty vague at first, as had the payment—all Malic had said was that it would be "worth your while." It wasn't as if the syndicate in general didn't have money, and Malic in particular was obviously a wealthy man, so Quark wasn't terribly concerned on that score. The syndicate had, in fact, turned down Quark's long-ago overtures for membership, so the fact that they were coming to him with a business proposition was enough to get Quark's lobes tingling.

Then came the kicker. Malic explained in very plain, simple terms why this was an offer Quark couldn't refuse. Then Malic departed, promising to return "soon."

Now Quark was scared. He hated being scared—so much so that it rather irritated him how often he wound up feeling that emotion.

In the past, he'd have no one to turn to. His brother had never been the most useful person in a crisis—though even Quark had to admit that Rom occasionally had his moments, for an idiot—and Odo was as likely to toss him into a holding cell as help him out.

But there was a new constable in town, so to speak, and Quark felt confident that he'd be able to appeal to her better nature. *As opposed,* he thought, *to Odo who, let's face it, doesn't* have *a better nature.* Besides, when the renegade Jem'Hadar attacked the station a few weeks back, Quark had saved Ro's life. *It's time I collected on that debt.*

"A problem, huh?" Ro said with her toothy smile. "This ought to be good." She stood at the rear wall monitors, looking over the current inhabitants of the holding cells. Quark saw the usual bunch of criminals, deadbeats, losers, ne'er-do-wells, and regular patrons of his bar in the screens. Ro turned off the surveillance and the screens went blank.

As she did, Quark started, "There's this Orion—"

"Malic." Ro sat back in her chair and touched the control that closed the door to the security office. "He came to you a few days ago to extort your cooperation in a business venture, and you're expecting him to return at any moment so you can get started."

Quark sighed. He hated when security people did that. They never understood the importance of not letting the person on the other side know that you know more than they think you know.

"Right. And that's my problem."

"Don't want to work for the Orions?"

"Don't want to work for *this* Orion." Quark finally sat down in the guest chair. "You see, I have this friend on Cardassia named Deru. He used to be a glinn in the military, and he was assigned to the station back when the Cardassians ran it. He retired about eight or nine years ago to go into private enterprise. The two of us entered into a business deal about two months ago. We've been arranging to get supplies to people who need it in Cardassian territory."

"Very noble of you." Ro sounded almost sincere. "Or it would be if I didn't know you better than to think you're doing this out of the goodness of your heart."

"I *am* doing it out of the goodness of my heart!" Quark said indignantly. "What is it about Bajorans that you think that doing a good deed and turning a profit are mutually exclusive?"

"So what's in it for you?"

"Land. See, we divert shipments of relief supplies to certain individuals in return for their land."

Ro's face distorted into a frown. "You kick people out of their homes?"

Quark rolled his eyes. "Don't be ridiculous. We're not doing this to anyone who can't afford it. No, we're getting supplies to the people with excess land. Nobody's being kicked out of their home. Besides, most of this property was damaged during the war. It'll only be useful again with a lot of work—which, I'm sure, some entrepreneuring buyer would be willing to invest in."

"And a Cardassian landowner who's starving to death wouldn't be willing to invest in it, but he might be willing to sell it to somebody like Deru, in order to stay alive," Ro said, showing a keen grasp of the economics.

"Exactly!" Quark said, grateful that she understood. "I knew you had the lobes for this sort of thing."

"Keep my ears out of this, Quark. So let me get this straight. A bunch of Cardassians, who used to be rich, now find themselves stuck with a ton of land, but no way to make use of it. They're also starving to death because the Cardassian economy is in a shambles, or maybe they're sick or injured from the devastation because relief hasn't reached them yet. Along comes Quark—"

"Actually, it's my associate who approaches them."

"Along comes *Deru*," Ro said obligingly, "who goes to these people, who are used to feeling like they belong to the greatest civilization in the galaxy, and now can't even get a working replicator. And Deru tells them he can get them black-market food and supplies, courtesy of his anonymous, big-lobed accessory—"

"Hey!"

"—and all they have to do is give up all this extra land that they can't do anything with anyhow."

"You make it sound like I've committed a crime," Quark said.

Ro laughed. "If you didn't *know* you'd committed a crime, Quark, you wouldn't be here right now. Because you know damn well that if Malic informed Starfleet or the Cardassian authorities about this, they'd rip your ears off."

"It isn't Starfleet or the Cardassians I'm worried about," Quark snapped. He looked over his shoulder as if he expected someone else to be listening, then turned back to Ro. "It's Garak."

Ro shrugged. "So?"

Quark threw up his hands. "You ever *met* Garak?"

Ro shook her head. "I know he's very involved in the rebuilding of Cardassia Prime. I also know him by reputation, and I honestly don't think we'd ever find your body."

"You see the problem."

"Should've thought of that before you got mixed up with Deru."

"How was I supposed to know that some old Orion would come along and blackmail me with it?"

"Isn't there a Rule of Acquisition about knowing your customers *before* they walk in the door?"

Quark rolled his eyes. "I come to you for help, and you quote the Hundred and Ninety-Fourth Rule at me. Some friend you are."

Ro leaned forward and got serious. "What exactly does Malic want you to do?"

Sighing, Quark said, "He wants me to negotiate a purchase on behalf of the syndicate. I don't know what for."

"I've heard of worse deals," Ro observed. "Maybe you should just take it."

"You don't understand—this is the Orion Syndicate!"

"I know who they are, Quark. I went through Starfleet tactical training, remember? We spent a week just on the syndicate." Ro picked up a padd and started fiddling with it—constantly turning it ninety degrees with her hands without actually looking at it. "You're worried that once the Orions get what they want, they'll tell Garak anyway."

"Something like that."

Now she looked genuinely amused. "You're really scared of him, aren't you?"

"For Gint's sake, Laren, he used to be in the Obsidian Order! Didn't you spend a week on *them* in Starfleet tactical training?"

"No," she said gravely, "it was two weeks." She set down the padd. "All right, Quark, I'll help you. But you have to help me in return."

Quark's eyes narrowed suspiciously. "How?"

"By going through with Malic's negotiations, and helping me to infiltrate the syndicate."

Quark felt his ears shrivel. "Infiltrate? Are you insane?"

Ro keyed a file on her padd and held it up so Quark could see the display. "Look at this—Malic is on about a dozen wanted lists. Getting close to him—"

Quark stood up abruptly. "I'm *not* going to infiltrate the Orion Syndicate, Laren!"

Ro rose and glowered down at him across the security desk. "Oh yes you are. Because if you don't—I'm going to tell Starfleet *and* Garak you've been exploiting Cardassian citizens."

Falling more than sitting back into the chair, Quark said, "I don't believe this. I save your life, and this is how you pay me back? You help me get out of being blackmailed by Malic by blackmailing me with the same thing?"

"Yes, I know, the injustice of it all." Ro smiled. "Don't look so glum, Quark. Think of the points you'll score with Kira and Vaughn when I tell them that you helped me bring down a major player in the syndicate *and* turned in a Cardassian who is illegally diverting relief supplies to wealthy patrons."

Quark put his hand over his heart. "Are you telling me I have to turn in Deru? Betray my comrade and business partner in order to save my own skin?"

Ro nodded.

"He'll turn me in!"

"Let me worry about that."

Quark knew then that it was over. He had no bargaining position this time. Ro had him by the lobes. *Not the worst position to be in, when you think about it, but still . . .*

"All right, fine. What do I have to do?"

"Exactly what Malic wants you to do. The only difference is, you'll have a *dabo* girl with you."

Aghast, Quark said, "You want me to expose one of my *dabo* girls to those Orion lunatics?"

Ro glowered. "Don't be an idiot, Quark. *I'll* be disguised as a *dabo* girl."

Suddenly getting a very pleasant mental picture, Quark smiled. His right hand brushed across his lobe. "Really?" From the moment he'd met her, Quark had wondered how Ro would look in a *dabo* girl's outfit. *Maybe this won't be so bad after all.*

When his glazed eyes refocused on Ro, she was scowling at him. "Get your mind out of the waste extractor, Quark. This is business. I'll be by your side at all times. The Orions won't care—their attitude toward women is even worse than the Ferengi's, so they won't see me as anything more than decoration. If things go well, you'll be out of there with no problems, I'll have some useful dirt on Malic, and I'll make sure Starfleet and Garak don't give you any grief over your little land scheme."

"You're not exactly giving me much of a choice," Quark said pointedly. "All right, it's a deal."

"Good."

"But I think this is insane."

Farius Prime (the present)

"I *still* think this is insane."

Quark ran after Ro through the corridors of the Orion ship. Alarms blared loud enough to hurt Quark's sensitive ears.

Two Orions came around a corner. Ro took them out with two well-placed shots before they had the chance to fire their weapons.

"Nice shooting," Quark said. He noticed that they were headed farther away from both the ship's transporter and the hangar bay. "Where are we going?"

"We need to be near an outer bulkhead. The inner sections of the ship are shielded against transporters."

"Why not just go to the ship's transporter?"

"Because then there'll be a record, and they'll know where we went."

"Oh."

Ro bent over and took the Orions' disruptors. She stuck one in the waist-band of her slitted pants and handed the other to Quark.

The Ferengi looked at it as if it were someone asking for a handout. "What am I supposed to do with this?"

"Take a guess."

Reluctantly, Quark took it. Since it was of Klingon design, it didn't have a safety, so Quark handled it as if he feared the slightest touch would trigger it.

While Quark weighed the risk of putting the weapon in his jacket against holding it and accidentally blasting a hole in the bulkhead, Ro took a moment to admonish him. "Oh, and by the way, the reason it took me a minute to throw the flare is because I frankly didn't expect you to cave in so easily."

"What're you talking about? I was following the terms of Malic's oral agreement. Malic said to tell the truth or die, so I told the truth."

Ro shot him a dubious look.

Quark sighed. "Fifteenth Rule of Acquisition, Laren: 'Dead men close no deals.' It's not my fault that Malic changed the terms of the deal at the last minute and decided to kill me anyhow."

They turned a corner. A turbolift door opened on an Orion male, escorting a scantily clad Orion female. The female—who was a full head taller than the male—was practically draped all over him. She wore what appeared to be rags, but Quark recognized the custom tailoring at work. *Obviously the male has a thing for women in dirty rags and she's dressing for the part.*

At the sight of Ro's disruptor, the male screamed, which surprised Quark—he'd expected the scream from the female.

"Back inside," Ro snarled.

The female quickly backed into the turbolift. The male just stood there, screaming. He was worse than the alarms.

"Stop," Ro said, putting the disruptor to the Orion's head, "screaming."

The male fell silent and went into the turbolift. He did blubber a bit, though.

Once the doors closed, Ro said, "Take us to deck seventy-one."

Quark frowned, confused—then he remembered that the ship's computer would probably only accept commands from certain Orion males. No female, and no Ferengi—not even one working for the Orions—would have access.

At first, the male didn't reply, busy as he was with his blubbering. Ro again put the disruptor to his head. "D-d-d-d-deck seventy-one," he finally said.

The turbolift moved. As it did, Ro removed another of her tassels. There was a small button on it, which she pressed.

"What's that do?" Quark asked.

"Scattering field. It should block any attempts the Orions make to divert the turbolift."

"Should?"

Ro shrugged. "If this were an ordinary Vulcan ship, it would, but I don't know what kind of modifications they made."

Soon, the question was academic. They arrived on deck seventy-one—the ship's lowermost deck—and the doors opened.

Half a dozen Orions were waiting for them.

Ro immediately put the disruptor to the female's neck. "Let us go or the slave gets it."

"Are you insane?" Quark whispered. "She's just a female."

Snarling, one of the Orions said, "Lower your weapons."

Slowly, and to Quark's abject shock, the Orions did so.

"Try anything," Ro said, "and I blow her pretty head off, understood?"

"Just don't hurt her," the Orion said.

Ro moved down the corridor, guiding the female in front of her with the disruptor still at her neck, and pulling the male along behind her. Quark followed behind the male.

As soon as they got close to the Orions—who parted to let them pass— Ro tossed the male in the direction of three of the Orions.

One of them immediately punched Ro's former hostage in the gut. "Alhan, you idiot!" another one said. "How could you let Treir be captured like that?"

Alhan was unable to reply, as he was too busy coughing up blood.

Quark quickly followed Ro and Treir. Now he understood Ro's logic— Treir was valuable merchandise. The Orions couldn't afford for her to be harmed. Alhan, on the other hand, was just another Orion male, and by allowing himself to be captured, his value to his fellows had plummeted to nothing. Once again, he admired Ro's grasp of business matters. *So rare to find a female who understands—especially a female Bajoran.*

From behind him, Quark heard one of the Orions' voices. "Malic, they've got Treir." A pause. "I *know* she's not to be harmed, but they're going to get away."

They turned a corner, out of sight of the Orions. Quark could still hear the Orion talking to Malic.

"All right," the Orion was saying as Ro stopped walking and—still holding the disruptor to Treir's neck—removed the last two tassels from her waist. She threw the first one back around the corner toward the Orions. The one speaking to Malic was suddenly cut off by a noise that sounded to Quark like five phasers firing at once.

Then silence.

"What was that?"

"Concussive grenade. Should keep those six out for a while."

"You couldn't do that before he told Malic we were here?"

As she pressed a control on the final tassel, which caused its base to split open, Ro said, "You really can be a whiner, can't you? We had to get out of range."

Ro removed a Bajoran communicator from inside the tassel and tapped it.

As soon as she did, the corridor shimmered, faded, and re-formed into the flight deck of a small spacecraft of Bajoran design. About the size of a small Starfleet shuttlecraft, the ship seated two fore and two aft.

A Bajoran woman in a red Militia uniform and with the rank insignia of a sergeant vacated the pilot's seat. "Who's your friend, Lieutenant?"

"She was a hostage," Ro said, removing the disruptor from the woman's neck. "Luckily, they didn't call my bluff when I said I'd blow her head off."

Treir, for her part, had kept a remarkably calm expression on her face from the moment she first saw Ro with the disruptor. Once she dropped out of the role of being Alhan's lover, her face had gone surprisingly neutral.

Quark asked, "Where are we?"

"A Bajoran Militia flitter," the sergeant said.

"I *know* it's a Bajoran Militia flitter," Quark said impatiently. "I mean *where?*"

"Farius Prime's innermost moon." Ro touched the flame gem on her necklace. Her hair returned to its natural black color. "Ychell Mafon, this is Quark—Quark, this is Sergeant Ychell. I had her hide out here as our escape route."

"Nice of you to tell me ahead of time," Quark muttered.

"Don't push it, Quark, or so help me—"

Quark rolled his eyes and shut up.

Turning to Treir, Ro said, "As for you—you're free to come with us. You can start over in the Federation or on Bajor. You don't have to be a slave anymore."

Treir smiled. "Did it even occur to you that I liked being a slave?"

Ro blinked. "Honestly? No, it didn't."

"You're lucky, then, that I didn't. On the other hand, no one ever gave me a choice in the matter. Besides, Malic treated me very well."

"Well, Malic doesn't own you anymore."

Again, Treir smiled, this time a wry one. "Malic may have something to say about that."

Ro settled into the pilot's seat. "He has to find us first." She indicated the two rear seats. "Get in the back. You too, Quark. We need to get back to DS9."

"What's the point?" Quark asked, taking his seat. "I'm doomed anyhow. You may as well give me back to the Orions."

"What are you talking about?"

"You heard Malic. All it takes is one command into his padd, and Garak will know all about my role in that land deal."

Ro reached behind her back and took something out from under the rear part of her waistband. She smiled broadly. "You mean this padd?"

Quark saw fighting Aldebaran serpents and a nude Orion woman. His mouth fell open.

So did Treir's, but unlike Quark, she was still able to formulate words. "That's Malic's padd! How did you—?"

"I grabbed it out of his pocket when I knocked him down in the meeting room. Not only are you safe from the Orions, Quark, but I'm betting there's enough information in this thing to bring Malic down—and maybe the whole syndicate."

A huge sense of relief spread over Quark. "So Garak won't find out?"

"Well, I never said *that.*"

Quark's eyes went wide. But before he could pursue the matter, Ychell announced, "Lieutenant, the Orion ship has started a search pattern. They're going to find us soon. We need to get out of here. I've got a course set for that hole that your transport came through—the one that goes to the Clarus system."

"Let's do it," Ro said, getting into the pilot's seat. She touched a few controls, then turned back to Quark and smiled. "I wonder if Malic made a copy ..."

Quark felt his lobes shrivel.

Chapter Fourteen

The Delta Quadrant

"They were diverting prey."

The giant indicated the fallen aliens with one gauntleted hand. Kira looked once again at the three butchered corpses she shared the floor with. *Diverting* wasn't the first word that came to mind. It was possible, of course, that these aliens were tougher than they looked, but Kira couldn't imagine they were so vicious that it was necessary to slaughter them.

"But only just," the being amended. "It was their ship that was the true enemy. I had hoped that a vessel capable of withstanding an attack such as mine and causing my own vessel's destruction would be crewed by the worthiest prey."

That explains the debris, Kira thought.

He started to pace around the bridge. "Instead, I found them to be soft and weak. Not worthy of a hunt." The creature pounded a fist on a nearby console, denting the metal. "My ship was destroyed. My trophies, my weapons, my *life*—all of it wiped away by these insignificant creatures."

"They were fighting for their lives, what do you expect?" Kira found herself saying.

As if she hadn't spoke, the alien went on. "After I killed them all, I waited. I knew this ship would not stay unmolested for long—not with such volatile cargo. So I awaited fresh prey." He once again looked down at Kira. "Then you came."

"You tie up all your prey before you 'hunt' them?" Kira mocked, testing her bonds. "Some predator."

The insult slid right past the alien. "No, you are bait. Just as this ship sat idle as a lure, so will you."

"A lure for what?" Kira asked angrily, already knowing the answer.

"The other one. I beamed two over from your ship, but only one is here. The other one is somewhere on the ship. Eventually it will show itself."

Taran'atar, Kira thought. *He must've shrouded when we were beamed off the Euphrates.* Jem'Hadar were born with the ability to cloak themselves, rendering them invisible both to the naked eye and most scans. The ability required most of their concentration, which meant they couldn't actually fight while shrouded. Kira hoped Taran'atar was scouting the ship, then waiting for the right moment to attack. "You're wasting your time," she said. "He's probably long gone."

"He's near," the hunter said with certainty. "I can feel it in the— *Ooof!*"

That last word was spoken as he was tackled from behind by Taran'atar, who solidified half a second before striking.

While both aliens crashed against the deck and began struggling for the upper hand, Kira managed to roll over to a nearby console. Bracing her back against it, she pushed herself upward to get into a crouching position, and then stood upright, quickly taking stock of her surroundings.

The room, which she assumed was the tanker's bridge, had two entrances—one, a closed door on the far side, the other, an open hallway right behind her.

A very large handheld weapon, easily twice the size of a Starfleet phaser rifle, was lying on the deck beyond the combatants, out of her reach. *Not that I could use it with my hands tied behind my back, but . . .*

The alien had gained the advantage, pinning Taran'atar to the deck. Kira saw an opportunity and sprang forward, pivoting on her left leg, spinning and landing a kick to the alien's helmeted head.

Her teeth clenched. It was like kicking a stone wall, and she suspected only her boot's padding kept her from breaking her foot.

It did, however, surprise the alien enough so that Taran'atar could fling him off. The alien crashed against an instrument panel, sending sparks flying. The Jem'Hadar leapt and stood in front of Kira, deliberately placing himself between her and their foe.

The alien slowly rose and faced them. Now that they were all standing up, Kira saw that the self-styled hunter was indeed tall, but not quite the giant she had thought him to be—Kira estimated he was a bit more than two meters in height.

The alien smiled in a manner that reminded Kira far too much of Dukat. "At last," he rumbled. "Worthy prey."

To Kira's annoyance, Taran'atar had thrown the alien closer to where his rifle lay. If he grabbed it while they were in the room, they were dead.

"Move!" she barked, leading Taran'atar to the open hallway behind them. Without an instant's hesitation, Taran'atar followed.

"I had the chance to explore this deck before I attacked the Hirogen," the Jem'Hadar said as they ran side by side down the corridor.

So that's what he's called. "Fine, take point."

He led them through a maze of corridors. Everywhere they went, Kira found more bodies like the three on the bridge: gold-skinned, wearing the bulky uniform, and bleeding from dozens of wounds each.

Taran'atar led them into what appeared to be a maintenance tunnel. He shut the hatch and locked it, showing an impressive aptitude for equipment he'd never seen before today.

Once the door closed, Kira turned around. "Can you do something about these bonds?"

Taking Kira's wrists in his scaly hands, Taran'atar said, "I believe so. This may hurt."

"Just do it."

Taran'atar grabbed the bonds, the sides of his hands pressing up against Kira's wrists. He pulled for several seconds. She gritted her teeth against the pain that shot through her shoulders as the bonds finally gave in to the Jem'Hadar's strength, and her arms were suddenly wrenched apart.

She flexed her shoulders. "Thanks. Now then, you obviously know who this guy is."

"I know of the species from an encounter a Jem'Hadar unit had with a Hirogen ship several hundred years ago. Back then, they were nomadic hunters with an impressive level of technology."

"Judging from what I've seen and heard, I'd say they still are," Kira said. "I take it from the way you shut the door so easily that you had a chance to examine some of the ship's systems?"

"Those that still function, yes. It did not take long, as very few of the systems are functioning at all. Propulsion, weapons, and tractor beams are inoperative."

"So we can't try to draw the waste back into the cargo hold?"

"No, Colonel."

Kira pounded the bulkhead with a fist. "Dammit!" She reached for her phaser—and found that it wasn't there. "I don't remember him taking my weapon."

"He didn't. My rifle didn't materialize with me when we were taken to this ship. Our energy weapons are either still on the *Euphrates* or dispersed."

Kira tapped her badge. "Kira to *Euphrates*. Computer, two to transport to the runabout."

The computer's voice was barely audible through a burst of static. *"Unable to comply due to theta radiation interference."*

Kira muttered an Old High Bajoran curse that her brother Reon had taught her when they were kids. "Computer, scan this vessel. Is there anywhere aboard we can go where the interference is weak enough so transporters can penetrate?"

"Negative."

She thought a moment. Obviously the transporters on this ship could penetrate the theta radiation, otherwise the Hirogen could never have beamed them over. Besides, these people had reason to make their transporters more resistant to radiation interference than Starfleet ever did, if they lived with this toxicity every day. "Can you locate the transporters here?"

"Affirmative."

Kira looked around. There were no working terminals, and she didn't have a tricorder. "Locate the nearest one to these coordinates."

"The nearest transporter to your location is in the fore section of deck twelve."

"And where are we right now?" Kira asked impatiently.

"In the middle section of deck two."

"Can you read any life-forms aboard this vessel?"

"Life-sign scan inconclusive. Two life-forms are assumed based on combadge signals of Colonel Kira Nerys and Taran'atar."

Kira repeated the curse, and cut off the transmission. Then she looked at Taran'atar. "Do you still have your *kar'takin?*"

"Yes." Taran'atar reached behind his back and unsheathed the thin-bladed weapon that Jem'Hadar generally carried as backups in case their energy weapons failed or were sabotaged.

"Good. We don't have any way to track the Hirogen—and he's a trained hunter. Do you know any way to go down ten decks from here?"

"No," Taran'atar said, "but I believe it should not be difficult to find one. With respect, Colonel, I should take the point."

Kira was unaccustomed to letting others put themselves in danger on her behalf. Unfortunately, in this particular instance, Taran'atar was the only one who was armed. "After you."

Taran'atar led them down the corridor, his *kar'takin* held in a defensive position. Kira followed close behind, feeling naked without a weapon. No rifle, no hand phaser, not even a blade. *Hell, at this point, I'd take a club.*

Finding access to the lower levels proved easier than she expected; they discovered a narrow, vertical shaft that was propped open by the corpse of one of the tanker crew.

"Were you able to find any working terminals?" Kira asked as she and Taran'atar moved the body out of their way and onto the deck. "Find out who these people are?"

"No."

Shaking her head as she peered into the shaft, she said, "It's ironic. When we first arrived, I wanted to kill these people. Now that they're dead—I actually feel sorry for them." A ladder on the far wall of the shaft went up one level to deck one, and went down farther than Kira's eyes could see. The shaft was illuminated only with the same dim green lights that the rest of this deck was bathed in.

"Whoever they are," Taran'atar said, "their battle is done, and they did not reclaim their lives. Our battle is not yet over."

"Damn right it isn't," she muttered as she clambered into the hatch and set her feet down on one rung of the ladder. Taran'atar followed a moment later.

Kira couldn't read the writing on the shaft wall—in the dim light, she could barely even see it—but she counted her way down past each of the identical hatchways until she reached what should have been the twelfth deck from the top.

Unfortunately, this hatch was not propped open by a gold-skinned corpse. Simply pushing on the handle didn't budge it. She tried pulling it, but that didn't work, either.

"Give me your blade," she said, reaching up.

Taran'atar handed the *kar'takin* down, hilt-first, without comment. *There are times when his unquestioning obedience is really refreshing.* For all that Starfleet insisted on military protocol, their officers had a tiresome tendency to question everything. It was a nice change to work with someone who just did what he was told.

Hooking one arm and one leg through the ladder's strut, she used the thin blade to try to pry the door open. Her leverage was awful, and the best she could do was bend the metal slightly outward.

That should be enough, though. Handing the Jem'Hadar his weapon back, she asked, "Taran'atar, do you think you can pry the door open with that handhold?"

"I believe so."

Kira climbed down several more rungs to allow Taran'atar access. Grimacing slightly, the Jem'Hadar grabbed at the bent metal and pushed against it. He peeled back the hatchway, the sound of the distorting metal disturbingly loud in the shaft. He then went through the opening he'd made, the edges of the torn metal tearing at his dark coverall. Kira, who was much smaller, was able to get through a moment later without any damage to her uniform.

Deck twelve looked very much like the one they had just come from: same green lights, same browns and greens in the décor, same nonfunctioning equipment, same miasma. The only improvement was that the burning smell didn't make it down this far.

As Taran'atar led the way toward the ship's fore, Kira tapped her combadge. "Computer, can you pinpoint the exact location of the transporter room on deck twelve of this vessel?"

The static was less here than it had been on deck two. *"Negative. Theta radiation prevents a precise reading."*

"Figures," she muttered. "We'll just have to try all the doors in the forward section until we find one."

The first two doors they came to seemed to be locked. Taran'atar pried them open to find that they were storage rooms.

The third opened when they approached. At the sight of what was inside, Kira gasped. She tapped her combadge again. "Computer, can you scan the equipment in this room?"

"Negative."

"Is the shield generator somewhere in the forward section of deck twelve?"

"Affirmative."

She looked at Taran'atar. "If this is what I think it is . . ." She knelt down in front of one piece of equipment.

The room was lined with machinery that looked enough like a shield generator to satisfy Kira—especially given the device that was attached to one of the consoles. The device was very obviously of a different design than the rest of the ship. It had a sleeker interface, a different control layout, and a different type of display screen from everything else on the tanker.

It was also very familiar.

"I was right," she said after examining it. "This is just like the shield enhancers we had in the resistance." She looked up at Taran'atar. "Under normal circumstances, our little ships couldn't hold up to the Cardassian warships, but we were able to enhance our shields. This is very similar to something that one of the other cells came up with for our sub-impulse raiders."

"With respect, Colonel, we must find the transporter and—"

"Help me remove this."

"Colonel, the Hirogen may arrive at any time to—"

So much for unquestioning obedience. "Taran'atar, this may be what we need to save Europa Nova! Now help me remove it!"

Taran'atar glared, then said, "As you command."

As she started undoing connections, she said, "It'll still be another three hours before all the Europani going to Torona IV will be through the gateway at Costa Rocosa. The *Defiant* can't disrupt the gateways until then. That huge mass of waste will go through in less than two hours. If we attach this shield enhancer to the *Euphrates,* it may just boost Nog's shields enough so that we can use the ship to block this gateway completely. It won't just stop the mass, it'll stop more of the irradiated material from going through and give our people more time to evacuate." She had removed all the rear connections by the time she finished the sentence.

Taran'atar undid the last of the side connections, and the two of them gently set the enhancer onto the floor. Kira looked around, and found a handle. Awkwardly, she picked it up with both hands. *These people also designed it to be portable. Smart move.* When Kira's resistance cell acquired the enhancer, the first thing Kira had said was it needed to have a handle on it so it could be carried more easily—without that handhold, it needed two people to move it. This one was heavier than the one they'd had in the resistance, but still manageable.

The Jem'Hadar moved to assist her, but she shook her head. "No. I'd rather you kept your hands on your weapon. Let's find that transporter."

The fourth door opened as they approached, and it appeared to be the transporter. Kira lugged the enhancer to the platform while Taran'atar sheathed his *kar'takin* and went to the controls.

"I have locked on to the *Euphrates.*"

"Good. Get up here."

The Jem'Hadar did not move. "If we both beam off the tanker, the Hirogen will simply beam us back. One of us must remain behind to distract the hunter while the other installs the shield."

Kira stared at Taran'atar. The Jem'Hadar, typically, betrayed only one emotion: resolve. Taran'atar knew that there was only one decision Kira could make here. He was armed and could shroud, and therefore had the best chance against the Hirogen. Kira knew the shield enhancer and how to install it—she'd done so once while under fire from Cardassians, she could certainly do it in a Starfleet runabout that was much more receptive to adaptive components than Bajoran sub-I's.

But she hated the idea of leaving someone behind. With the runabout's transporters unable to pierce the radiation, she'd be unable to beam him back to the *Euphrates,* or even return to help him once her task was done. "That thing out there will probably kill you."

Unsheathing his *kar'takin* and holding it across his chest, Taran'atar said, "I am already dead. I must go into battle to reclaim my life. This I do gladly because I am Jem'Hadar."

As if I needed reminding, Kira thought.

"You must fulfill your oath to President Silverio, Colonel. And I must fulfill the one I made when the Founders gave me life."

Kira took a deep breath, then nodded. "Energize."

Taran'atar set the controls. Then he looked up. "One more thing, Colonel. When the Founders sent me on this mission, I thought that my gods had cast *me* out. I have since learned that I was wrong."

Then he finished the sequence, and both the Jem'Hadar and the tanker's transporter room disappeared, replaced by the interior of the *Euphrates*.

Sighing, Kira thought, *Every time I think I have that Jem'Hadar figured out, he goes and surprises me.*

"Computer," she said, then hesitated. She was about to ask for a full damage report, but that would take too long. "Status of shields and propulsion."

"Shields inoperative. Warp drive functioning at eighty-two percent of capacity. Impulse drive functioning at seventy-four percent of capacity."

"Reason for shield failure?"

"Power conduits one through four have been irreparably damaged. Six microprocessors have failed."

"If the conduits are replaced, will the shields function?"

"Affirmative."

"Do we have four replacement conduits on board?"

"Affirmative."

"Thank you, Nog," she muttered. Then, removing her uniform jacket and setting it on one of the chairs, she set to work.

Within twenty minutes, she had replaced the conduits. "Computer," she said, "prepare shield generator for installation of additional equipment."

This certainly brings back memories, she thought, as she looked for an appropriate access port. The last time she had to install one of these, it was in the midst of a firefight. She, Furel, Lupaza, and Mabrin were supposed to rendezvous with Shakaar at Singha when the Cardassian scout ship found their flitter. They had just obtained the enhancer, and Kira had been forced to connect it and use it without testing—all in about five minutes, while under fire. It only worked part of the time, but that was true of everything on that ship.

Unbidden, the voices of her fellow resistance fighters sounded in her head.

"They're coming around for another pass. Hurry up with that evasive course, Lupaza."

"I'm moving as fast as I can, Furel. The controls are sluggish."

"I'm gonna slug you in a minute."

"They're firing!"

"Shields are down to fifty percent!"

"Nerys, if you don't get that damn thing installed in another minute, there won't be any shields for it to enhance."

"I'm working as fast as I can, Mabrin. Anytime you want to climb under here and help out . . ."

Kira smiled as she attached two more leads to the generator. So many memories—liberating Gallitep and freeing those poor laborers from their deadly mining duties, the attack on Gul Pirak, the destruction of the Seltran mine. Most of all, she remembered Lorit Akrem taking her twelve-year-old self to meet Shakaar Edon for the first time in the caves of the Dakhur Hills.

It was all so much easier, then. Shakaar gave us our orders, and we fought. We knew who the enemy was, and we went after them.

She stopped what she was doing, and shook her head.

"What the hell am I thinking?" she said.

"Please repeat instruction," the computer droned.

Ignoring the computer, Kira snarled and threw herself back into the shield enhancer. *How screwed up is my life that I'm looking back* fondly *on the resistance? Now I'm feeling nostalgia for Gallitep?*

I wish Odo were here.

She stopped working. *Dammit,* she thought, furious at her own weakness. *I promised I wouldn't let myself do that. Odo did what he had to do. I know that.*

But she could always talk to Odo. Even before they became lovers, he had always been there for her when she needed him. And if he wasn't available for whatever reason, there had always been someone—Jadzia Dax, Bareil Antos, Tiris Jast, even sometimes Captain Sisko, when she could get her mind around his being the Emissary.

But Odo and the captain were gone, perhaps never to return. Jadzia, Antos, and Tiris were dead. Ever since becoming station commander, Kira had been putting more distance between herself and her officers, even the ones she'd known for years. She admired and respected Vaughn, but they were still getting to know each other. She'd also recently put a huge strain on her friendship with Kasidy.

And since I became Attainted, most Bajorans can't even bear to look at me.

What was it Benjamin once said? "It's lonely at the top." But dammit, even he had Dax—either one. Not to mention Jake and Kasidy. Who've I got?

"Warning—power requirements of enhancement module exceed current capacity."

"Dammit," she muttered. She had been hoping that Starfleet's adaptable engines would be able to handle it. But this enhancer was designed for that beast of a tanker out there, not something as small as the *Euphrates.*

That can't be it, she thought. *There's got to be another way.* "Computer, is it possible to divert enough power from other sources to the shield generator to allow it to function?"

"Affirmative."

Another thought occurred. "Can it still be done if impulse power is left active?"

"Affirmative."

"Good. Do it."

"Unable to comply."

She closed her eyes. *Take it easy, Nerys, you can't punch the computer.* After taking a deep breath she asked, "Why not?"

"In order to comply, life-support must be terminated."

"There's always a catch," she muttered.

"Please restate request."

"Never mind." She searched around the enhancer, and found an inhibitor switch that would keep it from activating when it was hooked up. "Computer, time?"

"The time is 1242 hours."

She stood up. *Little more than an hour before that mass goes through.* "Computer, begin recording a message."

"Recording."

Placing her hands on the back of one of the side console's chairs, Kira took a moment to compose her thoughts. "This is Colonel Kira Nerys on the *Euphrates* contacting all vessels at Europa Nova. The radiation is coming from a cargo tanker that's dumping antimatter waste from its hold into the gateway. The crew of the tanker is dead, killed by an alien who is currently engaged in combat with Taran'atar. There's a concentration of toxic material bigger than anything that's gone through the gateway so far, coming through in one hour. I'll be using the *Euphrates* to block that and any further waste with the help of a shield enhancer I salvaged from the tanker." She took a deep breath. "In order for this enhancer to function, I'll need to shut down life-support. I'll therefore be evacuating the *Euphrates* and taking my chances on the fifth planet in this system, which is Class-M." *Not much choice; with the transporter useless and no docking ports on that thing, there's no way for me to return to the tanker on my own.* "As soon as it is feasible to attempt the disruption of the gateways, do it, regardless of whether or not Taran'atar or I have returned. That's an order." She took another deep breath. "Computer, end message. When the *Euphrates* approaches the gateway, broadcast the message every two minutes."

"Affirmative."

She sat at the helm and set a course for the fifth planet.

As the runabout descended into the atmosphere, Kira programmed a course that would take the *Euphrates* on autopilot back to the gateway. The ship would take up position at the threshold, then activate the enhancer and expand the shield envelope to maximum, with the impulse engines working to hold the runabout in position regardless of any force arrayed against it. After all, it would do no good to have that chunk of waste push the runabout through the gateway.

The viewport showed an arid desert of a planet. The vegetation was sparse at best, and there were few bodies of water around. Kira did an intensive scan, and found a location that was near a freshwater lake and that also registered a survivably low temperature. Unfortunately, that spot was currently in the early morning, so the temperature would probably increase significantly before long, but she didn't have time to search for the perfect place to land.

Once she set down, she got up to inspect the runabout's emergency kit. Everything seemed to be present and accounted for, and then some. *Starfleet does believe in overcompensating, don't they?* A small army could subsist on the combat rations, and Kira had to wonder if both a temperature control unit *and* an expandable shelter were necessary. The quick diagnostic she ran showed that the small communications module was in working order, and the medikit had been stocked with arithrazine. The Hirogen had indeed dispersed her phaser, so she took a Starfleet-issue one from the weapons cabinet—then took a second for good measure, as well as a tricorder.

She opened the hatch. A blast of heat assaulted her face, a dry wind pushing her back from the hatchway. The air smelled stale and uninviting, and Kira was grateful that she hadn't bothered to put her uniform jacket back on, though she had tied it to her waist.

Everywhere she looked on the ground was sand, broken very rarely by bits of plant life, and the one freshwater lake that she had made sure to land near. It was flat land, with the only variations being the curvature of the planet itself. Not even any hills or mountains or sand dunes in sight. It was almost like a negative image of Europa Nova—where that world was the picture of luscious beauty, this was quite possibly the bleakest planet Kira had ever seen.

And I'm stuck in this place in order to fulfill my oath to save the other one. To think, some people believe the Prophets don't have a sense of humor. Well, they do, and it's a black one. My life is proof of that.

She tapped her combadge, and her hand almost slid off it, it was so covered in sweat. *And I've only been here a minute.* "Computer, activate program Kira-One."

At those words, the hatch to the runabout closed. As soon as it locked into place, the runabout lifted off into the cloudless blue sky. Kira watched it ascend for as long as it was in sight, then tracked it with her tricorder while it remained in range—which wasn't long at all.

Now I just have to hope that my plan works.

She checked the tricorder. Theta radiation was already contaminating the atmosphere—that clear sky was working against her—and with the gateway blocked up, it was only likely to get worse.

Kira gave herself a dose of arithrazine, then got started setting up the shelter.

Within two minutes she had to stop. Sweat plastered her uniform to her body and dripped down into her eyes. Kira worked hard to keep herself in shape, and so little physical effort should not have exhausted her so quickly. She grabbed a bottle of water from the emergency kit and drained the entire thing in one gulp. It helped only a little.

This is gonna be fun, she thought grimly. Then she got back to work on the shelter, moving more slowly this time, conserving her energy, praying that Taran'atar would win his battle.

And that she would win hers.

Chapter Fifteen

Europa Nova

"Commander, we can't do this."

Vaughn didn't bother to turn the *Defiant's* command chair around at Bashir's outburst. "What in particular is it that we can't do, Doctor?"

Bashir stepped between Vaughn and the conn. He was holding a padd in his left hand and pointed at the viewscreen with it as he said, "This! All of it! I had hoped that the *Trager* and the gateway to Torona IV would make a difference, but I'm afraid they won't. The *Trager* is transporting people more slowly than anticipated. Each wave of evacuation is taking twice as long as the previous one. This relay method of the *Trager* and *Intrepid* picking people up and passing them off to the other ships is not what one would call expedient."

"We're not exactly overburdened with alternatives, Doctor," Vaughn said dryly.

"I'm aware of that, but—" Bashir sighed. "We had a chance when we started, but with the tortoise-like pace we've been going at, I'm afraid those chances have dwindled to nothing. People are going to die!"

Vaughn simply stared at him. "We had this conversation in ops, Doctor. The chances were poor to begin with. We don't give up because the math is bad."

"I understand that, sir, but we have a bigger problem. Have a look at this." He handed Vaughn the padd.

Looking down at the padd, Vaughn saw a familiar-looking sensor reading from the *Gryphon,* then handed it back to Bashir. "Yes, I know. Captain Mello told me about this an hour ago."

Bashir looked incredulous. "If that mass comes through the gateway—"

"I'm aware of the danger to Europa Nova. Tell me, Doctor, do you have any actual business on the bridge besides telling me things I already know?"

"I'd like to know why I wasn't informed of this! And I'd like to know what's being done!"

His voice as calm as Bashir's was frantic, Vaughn said, "Colonel Kira and Taran'atar have gone through the gateway to try to stop the radiation at the source. Since you've been occupied with coordinating relief efforts, keeping you briefed wasn't a priority. Neither is panicking, nor flailing about in outrage. We'll deal with the problem."

A voice sounded over Bashir's combadge. *"DeLaCruz to Bashir."*

"Bashir here. What is it, Martino?"

Vaughn was impressed—and grateful—that Bashir and the surgeon general of Europa Nova were on a first-name basis. His predilection for histrionics notwithstanding, Bashir was a damned efficient doctor, and the treatment of the sick had been handled very well on this mission.

"Julian, did you remove the arithrazine stock from Spilimbergo's hospital?"

"Of course not."

"Well, it's gone. And I've got hundreds of people here that need treatment."

"Doctor, this is Commander Vaughn. The *Intrepid* is supposed to be landing within the hour to take the remaining population of Spilimbergo." While Kira's diverting of the waste to Lago DeBacco saved Spilimbergo from any immediate danger, the level of exposure made that city's evacuation a priority. Unfortunately, the proximity of that waste meant that even the *Trager*'s transporter wasn't reliable, so the *Intrepid* was tasked with evacuating Spilimbergo as fast as possible.

"I'm aware of that, Commander, but some of these people can't wait an hour."

Bashir looked over at the command chair. "Commander, with your permission, I'd like to have the *Chaffee* bring down some of our arithrazine stock to Spilimbergo."

Vaughn nodded. "Granted." He turned to the conn. "Ensign Tenmei, can you please handle that?"

Prynn said nothing, but simply nodded, got up, and approached Bashir.

"Martino, one of our shuttlecraft will deliver your arithrazine within twenty minutes," Bashir said.

"That's fine, Julian, but I'm also a bit concerned with who might have stolen it. Arithrazine has to be administered very carefully. If some amateur is passing it out . . ."

"We'll keep an ear out for it, Doctor," Vaughn said. "Thank you for bringing that to our attention, however. *Defiant* out."

Bashir then spoke with Prynn about the particulars of bringing the arithrazine down on the *Defiant* shuttlecraft.

Nog announced, "Incoming message from the *Gryphon*, sir."

"On screen, Lieutenant."

The viewscreen shifted from a view of the planet to the face of Elaine Mello. "What can I do for you, Captain?"

Mello broke into a smile. *"You can enjoy the good news I'm about to give you, Commander. Colonel Kira did it. The toxic stream coming through the gateway has reduced by ninety percent."*

"That *is* good news."

Bashir, having finished his conversation with Prynn, said, "That'll improve the chances that we'll be able to evacuate in time." For her part, Prynn left the bridge without a word.

"We're not sure exactly how she did it—sensor readings are still pretty spotty—but Dr. Bashir's right in that it should buy us some more time."

Nog looked up from his console. "Commander, we're getting an incoming message from the *Euphrates*."

"On audio, Lieutenant."

Kira's voice was barely recognizable—and not consistently audible—over the static from theta-radiation interference. *"This is Colonel Kira Nerys on the Euph . . . all vessels at Europa Nova. The radia . . . antimatter waste from its hold into the gateway. The crew of the tanker is dead, killed by . . . ger than anything that's . . . using the Euphrates to block that and any further waste . . . eed to . . . fifth planet . . . soon . . . it is feasible to attempt the disruption of the gateways, do it, regardless of whether or not Taran'atar or I have returned. That's an order."*

"Can you clean that message up, Lieutenant?"

"I'm afraid that is the cleaned-up version, sir. It's broadcast twice since the radiation levels decreased, and the first transmission was the better of the two."

Vaughn scratched his beard thoughtfully. "Keep an ear out for more repetitions. With the radiation decrease, we might get a better signal. Some of those gaps were too damn long."

Nog nodded. "Yes, sir."

"Captain Mello, I assume you got that message, as well?"

"Yes, Commander. And to answer your next question, we've still got two hours before we've hit our quota for the Jarada." The *Gryphon* security chief had taken over supervising the evacuation at Costa Rocosa.

Turning back to Nog, Vaughn asked, "Will the tachyon burst be ready by then, Lieutenant?"

"It should be, sir." Nog hesitated, then added, "Sir, I'd feel better about it if Ensign ch'Thane were here to look over the specs one more time. It was his design. May I ask why he didn't accompany us?"

"You may *not* ask, Lieutenant," Vaughn said without looking at the engineer. That was all he planned to say on the subject. He had ordered ch'Thane behind as a favor to Vretha. He wasn't happy about it, and Nog's concern was understandable. But then he thought about his just-departed daughter. *I'm not going to keep a parent from trying to reconcile with her child. Especially given what's at stake. I just wish it were that easy for me to order Prynn to talk to me off duty.*

"Spillane to Mello." The voice was coming through the bridge speakers.

"Mello here."

"Captain, we've, ah, got a bit of a problem down here."

Lieutenant Ann Spillane was Mello's chief of security, so "down here" was Costa Rocosa. *That's not encouraging,* Vaughn thought.

"There's a Europani down here," Spillane continued, *"holding five people hostage along with six crates of arithrazine."*

Bashir looked up at that. "There goes Martino's arithrazine," he said quietly.

"He just showed up with a ship and the drugs, grabbed five people who were about to go through the gateway to Torona IV, and blocked the way. He says he'll release the drugs and the people if we let him and his family through to Torona IV."

Nog muttered, "So why not just let them through?"

Mello apparently heard him, because she said, *"Because the five-hundred-thousand-person limit the Jarada put on us is pretty strict, and all those slots are taken. I take it no one's willing to give up their slot, Lieutenant?"*

"That's the kicker," Spillane said. *"He won't let anyone give up their slot—says he doesn't want anyone else to suffer because of him. He just wants to add him, his wife, his mother, his five kids, and his sister to the group—and he'll kill the hostages and destroy the drugs if we don't let him."*

"Interesting method of not letting people suffer," Bashir said. "Especially if he's blocking the gateway."

Vaughn stood up. "With your permission, Captain Mello, I believe I can handle this."

"*Granted.*"

As he moved to the door, he said, "Doctor, you're with me. I'll need you to deal with the arithrazine when we're finished. Lieutenant Nog, you have the conn."

It only took forty minutes for Vaughn to fly the *Sagan,* the *Defiant's* other shuttlecraft, to Costa Rocosa. Bashir spent the time contacting Dr. DeLaCruz to inform him that he had a promising lead on that missing arithrazine, and then checking the radiation levels to make sure that none of it penetrated the shuttle's enhanced shields.

Vaughn scanned the area in search of a decent landing spot. When he had beamed down the last time *(Was that only yesterday?* he thought; *seems like decades . . .),* there seemed to be a paucity of places to land on the uneven ground near the gateway. *And if this hostage-taker has a ship, he's probably used one of those places already.*

That last assumption turned out to be false. The Europani hostage-taker had landed his ship—a small atmospheric pod about five meters long—right on the rocky outcropping and was using it to block the gateway.

I see how this got out of hand. He was sure Spillane was a completely satisfactory security chief, but one person with a hand phaser, no matter how talented, was hardly in a position to stop an unannounced pod from landing wherever it wants.

A quick sensor scan revealed that the pod had four landing struts meant for resting on solid, even ground, and that only two of them had any kind of solid support. One plan immediately presented itself: destroy that support—either by phasering the struts or the rock under them—and get the hostages out in the confusion. That was a last-resort plan, as it carried the greatest risk, and one Vaughn dearly hoped he wouldn't have to implement.

He picked up approximately five thousand human life signs in the vicinity. Most were congregated just to the east of the gateway outcropping. There were another nineteen near the gateway, one of whom wore a combadge whose signal corresponded to Lieutenant Spillane.

He landed the *Sagan* in a clearing about twenty meters from the gateway in a flat area atop a rock. Then he rose and went to the weapons locker. As he removed a hand phaser, Bashir said, "Do you think it's wise to go into a hostage negotiation armed, Commander?"

Vaughn ignored the question as he opened the hatch. The early-evening wind blew fiercely into the cabin. Bashir approached the hatch alongside Vaughn. He peered out and saw the almost sheer drop. The flat part of the rock on which they'd landed was no bigger than the *Sagan* itself.

To Bashir's credit, he kept pace with Vaughn as they clambered down the steep incline without once making a tiresome comment about the first step being a doozy—a remark which Vaughn had fully expected the doctor to make. Bashir found handholds with all the assuredness and athleticism of a well-trained climber. Idly, Vaughn wondered how much of that was truly training and how much was Bashir's genetic enhancements—then decided that it didn't really matter.

Once they reached bottom, it was a short walk to the scene. The crowd was being kept at bay and in relative order by the Costa Rocosan police force. Based on the reports, they were the only locals still present. Mayor Nieto had been the first one through the gateway, along with other members of the police force, and they had taken over the organization of the refugees on the Jaradan side of the gateway. The thousand inhabitants of the city were next. After that, there had been a steady flow of Europani from the nearby principalities, organized by the local police and Lieutenant Spillane.

Spillane herself stood with two Europani police officers about ten meters from the pod. As the *Sagan's* sensor readings had indicated, the pod was right in front of the gateway.

Standing in front of the pod was a short man with long black hair. He looked determined. Behind him were eight other people, ranging in age from midthirties to about eight years old—presumably the family he wished to take with him—who all looked more worried than anything. Next to him were five adults—three men, two women—who looked scared to death.

"What is that he's holding?" Bashir asked, squinting at the hostage-taker.

"I think it's a Starfleet phaser," Spillane said. She was a slim human woman. Her long blond hair, currently tied back in a ponytail, had been matted down by the local humidity. "But I don't remember ever seeing one that—well, bulky before."

"That's because its type was taken out of service before either of you were born," Vaughn said. "That's a standard-issue Starfleet hand phaser from around the turn of the century." He turned to Spillane. "Report, Lieutenant."

"Nothing's changed since I contacted the *Gryphon,* Commander."

Nodding, Vaughn said, "Very well. Doctor, I want you to take a precise sensor reading of the vicinity and tell me the concentration of theta radiation in the area in front of the gateway. Triple-check your findings before you report them to me, understood?"

"Of course," Bashir said, sounding confused.

Keeping his phaser holstered, Vaughn stepped toward the outcropping. "Good evening, sir!" he called out.

"Uh, hello," the man said after a moment.

"My name is Elias Vaughn. I'm with Starfleet. We seem to have a bit of a problem, and I was hoping you could help us out with it."

"There's—there's no problem. Are you—you in charge?"

"Yes, sir, I am. May I ask your name?"

"M-my name is—is Tony Fusco."

Vaughn inclined his head. "A pleasure to meet you, Mr. Fusco. Where are you from?" As he spoke, Vaughn took a closer glance at the weapon. *That's definitely an old Starfleet phaser. Looks just like the one I was issued when I graduated from the Academy, almost eighty years ago.*

"My—my family and I are from Spilimbergo. We—we just want to go through the portal!"

Letting out a breath, Vaughn said, "That may be difficult, Mr. Fusco. You see, the people on the other side of the gateway are a bit—fussy. Dangerously so, in fact. The *Intrepid* has been evacuating Spilimbergo, I'm sure—"

"I—I—I—I *can't* go *up* there." Fusco shook his phaser with each emphasized word. "You don't—you don't know what it's *like* up there."

"Up where?"

"*Space!* It's all so—so—so *open!* There's—there's nothing around you, you just get billions of kilometers of nothing before you even come—come close to getting near anything and I *can't* go *up* there."

Hell and damnation, Vaughn thought, *a space case.*

"We're going to try to work this out, Mr. Fusco. Just wait here and please don't hurt anyone."

"I—I don't want to hurt anyone, b-but I *can't* go *up* there, d-do you understand?"

Holding up his hands in a conciliatory gesture, Vaughn said, "I understand completely, sir. If you'll just give me a moment to consult with my people, we'll see what we can do to accommodate you."

He climbed back down the outcropping. Bashir, Spillane, and the police gave him an expectant look.

"Agoraphobic. Violently so. The idea of being in space terrifies him so much that he'll do anything to avoid it."

Bashir nodded. "He must have seen this gateway as a golden opportunity."

"Until he realized that nobody from Spilimbergo got on the list of five hundred thousand going through. What did your tricorder readings tell you, Doctor?"

"Hm? Oh, the radiation levels are at seven hundred rads at the moment, though that amount is climbing, obviously."

Vaughn let out a small sigh. "Oh, good, I was worried that this was going to be difficult."

He turned around, saw that no one was standing closer than half a meter from Fusco, raised his phaser, and fired.

In the instant it took the beam to reach him, Fusco's expression changed from agitation to shock. Then he fell to the ground.

Spillane and Bashir had similar looks of shock on their faces. The latter spoke. "Commander, with all due respect, you took a terrible risk! What if his finger had spasmed on the phaser and fired?"

"I'm sure it did." With that, Vaughn walked back toward the pod.

Bashir frowned as he followed. "What?" Behind him, Spillane and the two officers did likewise.

"I told you, that phaser is Starfleet issue from eighty years ago. Those models were especially susceptible to ambient radiation—anything over five hundred rads and they misfire."

They arrived at the pod. The officers immediately escorted the Europani—both the hostages and Fusco's family—off the outcropping.

Vaughn took the phaser out of Fusco's hand, which still had a surprisingly firm grip on the weapon considering the wielder was unconscious. He pointed it at Bashir and fired. As expected, nothing happened, though the doctor did flinch. "You see? That design flaw's not in later versions, of course . . ."

Shaking his head, Bashir asked, "Why didn't you say that's what you were planning in the first place?"

Vaughn smiled. "Because, Doctor, when they make you a commander, they take the bone out of your head that makes you explain orders."

"Point taken," Bashir said.

Vaughn looked at the pod. "Lieutenant Spillane, do you think you can fly this thing?"

With a wry smile, the young woman said, "It's been a few years, sir, but I think I can hop it out of the way at least."

"Good, get to it." He tapped his combadge. "Vaughn to Lenaris."

After a moment, the Bajoran's voice came over the speaker. *"Lenaris."*

"Colonel, when are you scheduled to return to Bajor?"

"We're receiving refugees from the Trager *right now. We'll be at capacity in about ninety minutes."*

"So what's your ETA to deliver the refugees to Bajor itself?"

"Call it 2530 hours."

"Thank you, Colonel. Dr. Bashir will be bringing you nine additional passengers, one of whom will be fully sedated for the journey."

"Understood. I'll notify Gul Macet of the change."

Turning to Bashir, Vaughn said, "Doctor, I want you to find something that will keep Mr. Fusco sedated until at least 2530. I don't want him to wake up until he's back on a planet."

Understanding, Bashir smiled and nodded. "I'll take care of it, sir."

"Good. Let's get out of the pod's backwash so the lieutenant can take her up."

It took a moment for Vaughn to convince the Costa Rocosan police to remand the Fuscos into Starfleet custody, but ultimately they didn't want to deal with any more than they already had on their hands. By the time Bashir and Vaughn had gotten the entire Fusco family and the crates of arithrazine onto the *Sagan,* the evac had resumed under Spillane's watchful eye, the Fusco family pod tucked safely out of the way.

The Fuscos themselves were abject in their apologies for their patriarch's behavior. Vaughn listened patiently to their complex explanations of his rather simple psychosis. Soon enough, they were transported to Lenaris's ship, and Vaughn took the shuttle back home.

"The arithrazine we recovered can replace the stock Ensign Tenmei brought down from the *Defiant,*" Bashir said.

Vaughn just nodded as he guided the shuttle into the bay.

As soon as Vaughn walked onto the *Defiant* bridge, Nog vacated the command chair and said, "We just received a message from the *Gryphon,* Commander. The last of the five hundred thousand allowed by the Jarada have been evacuated through the gateway."

Settling into the chair, Vaughn said, "Were you able to get a clearer message from Colonel Kira?"

Nog shook his head. "No, sir."

Vaughn sighed. "Very well. Prepare the tachyon burst."

"Sir, Colonel Kira—"

"Colonel Kira," Vaughn interrupted, "specifically said to try the tachyon burst as soon as it was feasible, regardless of whether or not she and Taran'atar had returned. Are you questioning her orders, Lieutenant?"

"No, sir," Nog said reluctantly.

"Good." Vaughn was grateful that Prynn hadn't yet returned from the surface. No doubt she'd have some choice words on the subject of condemning people to their deaths. To the officer who'd replaced her at conn, he said, "Take up position forty thousand kilometers from the mouth of the gateway."

"Aye, sir," the conn officer said.

Nog manipulated the controls of his console. "Tachyon burst ready on your orders."

"Consider the order given, Lieutenant."

A burst of light shot from the *Defiant*'s deflector array and struck the mouth of the gateway.

As soon as it did so, the gateway seemed to light up with a rainbow's worth of bright colors. Vaughn had to avert his eyes from the viewscreen.

Then the gateway went dark.

"Radiation levels at the gateway's perimeter have reduced to zero percent," Nog said, "and we're no longer reading the Delta Quadrant. Power output of the gateway is zero." He checked another reading. "Power output on the Costa Rocosa gateway is also nil, sir." Turning toward the command chair, Nog smiled. "We did it. The gateways have been shut down."

Chapter Sixteen

The Delta Quadrant

Kira looked down at her tricorder readings. *Not good,* she thought. The radiation levels were increasing dangerously. If she stayed here too much longer, no amount of arithrazine was going to help her.

She had drained the emergency kit's water supply. The cooling unit in the shelter was at maximum. Kira knew she would have to leave the confines of the shelter to get more water from the lake, but just the act of walking would drain her—she had barely been able to get the shelter constructed, as the heat only intensified with the passing of time. Soon it would be midday. Kira wondered how well the cooling unit would hold up.

She hadn't heard anything from Taran'atar. The Jem'Hadar was far too much a creature of duty—the moment he was able, he would contact her to announce his victory. The fact that he hadn't done that yet meant either the fight was still going on—or he had lost.

Damn you all, she thought at the Hirogen and the owners of the tanker and everyone else in this quadrant. *Didn't the Borg come from this area of space? Damn them, too. Hell, the Iconians also probably came from around here.*

Checking her tricorder again, she saw that the radiation would be at fatal levels in two hours. The intensity had been rising exponentially, and her arithrazine would be all but useless before those two hours were up. A blister started to form on her hand, and she injected another dose of arithrazine, figuring she had nothing to lose.

Kira then did something that the Vedek Assembly had judged her unworthy to do with other Bajorans: she prayed.

Or, rather, she tried to.

On many occasions in her thirty-three years of life, Kira Nerys had been sure she was going to die. From the resistance to the Dominion War, her life had been fraught with danger, and she had long ago made peace with the fact that she was not likely to die of old age in her bed.

When circumstances permitted, Kira had always prayed on those occasions. She had faith in the Prophets, and in prayer she took comfort in the idea that her life had some meaning to them, that she had made some contribution to their grand design. And she always believed that if the path they had guided her on had finally come to its end, her death wouldn't be a vain one. Those prayers were always heartfelt and came easily to her.

But this time, the words wouldn't come. She had been a devout follower of the Prophets her whole life. *Is this how I'm to have that faith rewarded? Dying on an arid wasteland, alone in a Starfleet shelter tens of thousands of light-years from home, theta radiation chewing up my cells and spitting them out?*

True, her actions might well lead to saving Europa Nova, something she swore she would do no matter what.

But I don't want to die like this. Not here, not this way—and not Attainted.

Then her tricorder beeped.

Worried that it would show her that the levels of radiation had increased yet again, she was surprised to discover that it was instead registering a familiar energy signature half a kilometer distant.

A gateway.

A gateway here, on the surface of the planet where she'd taken refuge. A gateway that didn't exist a moment ago, suddenly appearing in her hour of need.

Why? What does it mean?

Ultimately, it didn't matter. Whether it was dumb luck from the Iconians or deliverance from the Prophets, Kira had a way off this death trap of a planet.

It took only a minute to compress the shelter into its backpack form, but Kira almost succumbed to heat exhaustion just by performing the act of picking it up and shrugging into it. She walked slowly to the lake and proceeded to refill the kit's water containers. The lake was, of course, warm, but Starfleet built its kits well. Within seconds, any water she bottled would be refrigerated to five degrees.

She then set off in the direction the tricorder had indicated.

Five minutes later, Kira was ready to collapse. But she soldiered on. The gateway would take her away from here.

After another five minutes, she did collapse. She only took one moment to compose herself, then gathered every muscle in her sun-battered body and hauled herself to her feet.

Her vision blurry from the sweat that poured into her face, she finally gave up and dropped the shelter from her back, hanging on only to the water.

Ten minutes later, she collapsed again.

The Prophets have given you a sign! her mind yelled. *They haven't abandoned you! But you have to get to the gateway. So move it!*

Again, she gathered every muscle. Again, she got to her feet.

She didn't know how long it was before she drained the water supply. Or, for that matter, when the blisters started breaking out all over her skin. She didn't have the wherewithal to check her tricorder to see how bad the radiation was. Every fiber of her being was focused on the overwhelming task of putting one foot in front of the other.

After what seemed like an eternity, she saw it.

It floated in the air over the endless expanse of sand.

Dimly, in the small part of her mind that was able to focus on something other than moving forward, Kira remembered that the ground-based gateways tended to do one of two things: jump randomly from vista to vista every couple of seconds, or, like the one at Costa Rocosa, stay fixed on one location. This one, however, was different: it jumped back and forth between only two destinations.

The first was ops on Deep Space 9.

The other was the comforting light that Kira Nerys knew in her heart belonged to the Prophets.

Each time the vista switched to the light, Kira felt her heart beat faster. *This is it. The Prophets are calling to me. My road is at an end.*

But when it switched back to DS9, she wavered. *You can go back home.*

To what? Pain and hardship? The disdainful stares of most Bajorans? The headaches of running the station? Making life-or-death decisions about everything from attacking Jem'Hadar to Section 31 nonsense to rescue operations? To a life of losing everyone I care about?

When she was within a meter of the gateway, it lit up with a rainbow's worth of colors. Kira had to avert her eyes from it.

Then it went away. Kira saw nothing in front of her but the endless sand.

Her outrage giving her strength that the heat of the planet had drained out of her, she took out her tricorder and scanned the area in front of her. The gateway's power reading, according to the tricorder, was nil. The hand that held that tricorder was now covered in cracked skin and red-and-green blisters.

On many occasions in her thirty-three years of life, Kira Nerys had been sure she was going to die.

This time, it seemed, she was right.

Chapter Seventeen

Farius Prime

"Approaching the hole."

Smirking at Ychell's choice of words, Ro said, "It's called a gateway, Sergeant."

Ychell shrugged. "Whatever. So far, no sign of pursuit, but that could change at any moment."

Ro nodded, then looked back at her two passengers. Quark was fidgeting nervously, no doubt still worried about Malic. Ro supposed she shouldn't have said anything about the possibility of copies—from all accounts, Malic was the type to keep information to himself as much as possible.

Treir sat passively, looking surprisingly unconcerned.

Ychell obviously noticed Ro staring, because she asked, "What're you going to do with that one?"

Shrugging, Ro said, "Not sure. It's funny, she didn't even flinch when I put the gun to her neck. I mean, she couldn't have known I was bluffing."

"She's been a slave all her life, Lieutenant. She may not know how to be anything else."

Ro sighed. "Maybe. For now, let's just go through that gateway and—"

Suddenly, the gateway lit up with a rainbow's worth of colors. Ro winced.

Then it went dark.

"I'm not reading any power signature from the gateway," Ro said, looking down at her instruments.

Ychell looked at hers. "I'm not picking up the Clarus system anymore, either."

"Dammit."

"It gets better," Ychell said. "The Orions have found us. Two of their fighter ships are on an intercept course."

Chapter Eighteen

The Delta Quadrant

The alpha smiled for the first time in a long time. *At last,* he thought, *worthy prey.*

As the alpha worked his way through the corridors of the Malon tanker in search of the Jem'Hadar, he chastised himself for his own carelessness. He had grown overconfident.

For far too long, he had been on his own. He had had no real choice—everyone with whom he'd crewed had been too weak, too slow. They hadn't been worthy of his hunting skills and made the hunts so much poorer.

So he had chosen to fly alone. And he had been much more successful.

There was no sign of the Jem'Hadar on this deck. He climbed down the access shaft to the next one, holstering his rifle on his left shoulder.

After a time, the thrill of the hunt had started to wane. It became too easy. He'd hunted for so long that no prey presented a true challenge. He had grown soft and careless. So careless that he had allowed the cargo of those Malon fools to destroy his ship.

Everything he had was in that ship: his trophies, his food, his triumphs, his war paint, most of his weapons—his entire life. All he had left was his rifle, his armor, and himself.

Perhaps this is all I truly need. Perhaps this will allow me to restore my own glory, by reducing the hunt back to its essence.

He saw a shadow move behind one of the bulkheads.

Prey.

The alpha moved slowly toward the shadow.

As he approached, the shadow took on the form of one of the Malon fools.

I thought I had destroyed all of them, the alpha thought angrily.

"Please, gods, don't kill me, please don't kill me!" the Malon cried as he stepped into the open. He had blisters on his skin.

This prey is weak to be susceptible to so minor a thing as theta radiation, the alpha thought with disgust. *It isn't even worthy of being hunted.* This one was as bad as the tanker captain—she had pleaded to the alpha about a mate and offspring, as if the family structure of prey was of any relevance. He had particularly enjoyed slicing her open.

However, the alpha did not have time to kill this one with his blade as he did the others. With the press of a button on his rifle, he blasted the Malon into atoms. The Malon screamed for as long as he could before he discorporated.

The alpha forgot about the Malon and turned his mind back to thoughts of the Jem'Hadar.

How long has it been since we hunted one of these magnificent creatures? Engi-

neered by their primitive gods to be the perfect soldiers. They are among the worthiest prey the Hirogen have ever sought.

They were from a part of the galaxy where few Hirogen had traversed. Their presence here was a surprise, since the portal that had opened in this star system did not open to the region where the Jem'Hadar came from. Either their empire had expanded, or these portals were more widespread than the alpha had thought.

When the alpha came to the room with the shield generator, he noticed that a component was missing. *The prey has been in this room.*

The prey had also been in the next room over. The transporter logs showed that someone had transported one person and one piece of equipment to the prey's vessel. The Malon computer did not recognize the life signs, but the alpha knew that it was not the Jem'Hadar. No doubt the other, less significant prey had taken the shield modulator.

The alpha cared little for the petty concerns of prey. He no more cared about what it was doing with the shield modulator than what the Malon prey did with their meaningless cargo. All that mattered was the hunt.

The prey has been here. But the trail is cold now.

The alpha moved on to the engineering deck. Here, he found plenty of the corpses he had left behind on his last trip through this ship.

But of the Jem'Hadar there was still no sign.

Soon, the alpha had checked every cranny of the Malon tanker. *How has the creature managed to evade me? Not only is there no sign of him, there is no sign he has been anywhere, save the bridge and the transporter.*

It has been too long since we hunted these creatures. There is obviously missing intelligence about them that I need for the hunt.

If he still had his ship, he could check records of previous hunts. But that was lost to him. All he had was his instincts.

That should be all I need.

He returned to the bridge. Some of the equipment on this ship still worked. The alpha would make use of it to find his prey and destroy it.

Taran'atar had followed the Hirogen throughout the ship, watching as the alien hunter tried in vain to track the Jem'Hadar. He had watched as the Hirogen checked every portion of the tanker, pausing only to kill one native who had somehow escaped the predator's prior rampage.

Remaining shrouded had proven to be the right course of action. The Hirogen had an extraordinary tracking ability—without any apparent aid from mechanical devices—but could not detect Taran'atar as long as he remained shrouded.

What had started as a simple stalking strategy soon became a handy delaying tactic. After all, the important thing was to keep the Hirogen occupied while Kira installed the shield enhancer onto the *Euphrates* and used it to block the gateway. The only flaw in the plan was that Taran'atar could not contact

Kira to keep her apprised of his progress—the Hirogen could easily have had some way of detecting transmissions.

Still, this was the way that best served Kira. Ultimately, that was what mattered.

His assignment to the Alpha Quadrant had been a difficult thing for Taran'atar to accept, particularly being assigned to the command of Colonel Kira. After all, she had fought hard against the Dominion, and was even instrumental in its defeat. Kira was also like no Vorta Taran'atar had ever served under. Most Vorta were weak fools—self-serving at best, incompetent at worst. Taran'atar had obeyed them only because the Vorta served as the voice of the Founders. But Kira was no one's functionary. She did not just command, she led. She did not react, she acted. She did not direct battles, she fought them.

Taran'atar had fought alongside thousands of Jem'Hadar, and grown to respect many of them, for they had been true soldiers of the Dominion. Kira Nerys was the first alien he had ever met that he could truly call a soldier.

The Hirogen had gone through the entire ship. Taran'atar could not be completely sure of what the alien's facial expressions signified, but he was fairly sure that the creature was growing frustrated. He headed back up from the engineering section toward the bridge.

This may require a change in strategy. It was possible that the Hirogen was planning to use the ship's equipment to supplement his own tracking skills. Taran'atar's understanding about this ship's level of technology was still incomplete, but considering that it had transporters that could penetrate Starfleet shields, sophisticated tactical equipment was not unlikely.

Of course, he thought, *they also have such primitive warp engines that they still produce antimatter waste.* This was why the Dominion's way was so much better: everyone in the Dominion benefited from the technological advances of all its component parts. Such inefficient disparities as the owners of this tanker had did not exist.

Sure enough, the Hirogen arrived at the bridge and began to manipulate the controls of one of the consoles. He had holstered his rifle across his left shoulder.

The rifle is the key, Taran'atar thought. *With it, the Hirogen has the clear advantage.* The Jem'Hadar's sole weapon was his *kar'takin,* which the Hirogen had thought so little of that he hadn't bothered to remove it from Taran'atar's person as he had his phaser.

The initial strike was the most important: to land as devastating a blow as possible while he had the element of surprise. Striking at the armor would be pointless—as strong as his blade was, Taran'atar seriously doubted it could penetrate. The rifle itself was probably similarly difficult to damage. That left only two viable alternatives: the Hirogen's face, and the strap holding the rifle.

Possibly they are the same alternative, he thought as he studied the battlefield. The Hirogen currently stood at the center of the bridge, operating what appeared to be a general-purpose operations console. The console was a circular island in the middle of the control room—which, like those of Jem'Hadar ships, had no chairs.

Taran'atar took up position on the side of the console opposite where the Hirogen stood. Then he stepped backward as far as he could and unsheathed his *kar'takin,* directing his thoughts at the Founders.

I am Taran'atar, and I am dead. I go into battle to reclaim my life. This I do gladly, for I am Jem'Hadar. Victory is life.

He ran toward the console, leapt on top of it while lifting his *kar'takin* over his left shoulder, unshrouding as his concentration shifted to combat mode, and brought the weapon down.

The Hirogen fell back, one hand reaching up to cover his lacerated face, the other groping for the rifle that fell clattering to the deck, its shoulder strap severed cleanly.

Little blood flowed from the wound, and Taran'atar didn't allow his foe a chance to respond. He leapt onto the Hirogen, dragging him down and away from the fallen rifle. The pair fell to the deck, much as they had the last time Taran'atar attacked, only this time the Jem'Hadar was on top.

Again he attacked the Hirogen's face with the blade, but this time he thrust straight downward, aiming for the alien's right eye.

Unfortunately, the Hirogen clapped his gauntleted hands over the *kar'takin,* halting its downward motion. Taran'atar struggled to push the blade downward, but the Hirogen's strength was tremendous.

The hunter swung both arms to one side, pushing Taran'atar off balance and forcing him to release his hold on the *kar'takin.* The blade spun away as Taran'atar tumbled off his opponent and fell into a roll. He came up to his feet as the Hirogen did likewise.

The rifle was on the far end of the bridge out of reach of both combatants. The *kar'takin,* however, was close enough that the Jem'Hadar was willing to take the extra second he needed to reach it and arm himself, especially given how he expected the Hirogen to respond.

Sure enough, the Hirogen got to his feet and pressed a control on his right wrist. A long, straight blade extended from the underside of his gauntlet. The part closest to the Hirogen's palm was shaped differently—a grip, Taran'atar realized as the Hirogen's large hand clasped around it. *Clever design. The blade is still attached to his armor, so there's no risk of him dropping it, but it has a grip that provides him with better leverage.* The blade had to be either flexible or collapsible, but Taran'atar could not count on that meaning that it was weak. The Hirogen were an ancient species, that much he knew, and Taran'atar had to assume that any civilization capable of refining monotanium into hull metal could also manage comparable metallurgy in the creation of hand weapons.

Holding his *kar'takin* in front of him, ready to strike or parry at a moment's notice, the Jem'Hadar focused on his primary advantage: Hirogen were more interested in the hunt than the victory—but Jem'Hadar knew better. In a hand-to-hand fight, the Hirogen's size and armor gave him an edge over Taran'atar. Armed combat leveled the playing field to some extent—how much would depend on the Hirogen's skill. Taran'atar had already known that the Hirogen carried an edged weapon—it was what he used to kill the owners of the tanker—and Taran'tar also knew that if he came at the Hirogen with a blade, the Hirogen was likely to respond in kind.

The two circled each other on the spacious bridge, each ready to strike at a moment's notice, neither willing to make the first move.

"Curious prey," the Hirogen said. "You yourself set the terms for combat with blades, yet you do not attack. Instead you wait—try to gauge my own attack even as I wait to gauge yours."

Taran'atar said nothing. Speaking during battle was pointless unless one was giving orders to one's troops. Taran'atar had no troops, so he remained silent.

"Do you not speak, prey?"

Again, Taran'atar said nothing. *Let the hunter rant all he wants.*

They continued to circle each other. Taran'atar watched for any sign in the Hirogen's eyes that he would strike, but all the Jem'Hadar could read was curiosity.

Then the Hirogen did something unexpected: he smiled.

"Very well, prey. If you will not strike first, I will."

In the back of his mind, Taran'atar had wondered if perhaps this hunter was simply incompetent. After all, he had lost his ship to an inferior foe. And now he announced his attack so that Taran'atar had plenty of time to parry the downward strike at his head.

Another thirty seconds of sparring, however, disabused him at least of the notion that the Hirogen had no weapons skills. He was as good as Taran'atar with his weapon, and the Jem'Hadar found himself unable to move onto the offensive. He was able to counter each of the Hirogen's attacks, but his foe was too fast to allow Taran'atar ever to strike back.

The weapons clanged against each other, the sound of metal colliding with metal ringing through the otherwise silent bridge. The combatants soon fell into a rhythm. The Hirogen's thrusts were fast, strong, and powerful, but predictable. He never varied the pattern—a simple right-left-forward progression that he stuck to without deviating. Unfortunately, being able to predict the strike only meant Taran'atar could raise a defense against it. The Hirogen presented no opening to take the offensive.

Taran'atar soon realized that—collapsibility or flexibility notwithstanding—the Hirogen's blade was as strong as the Jem'Hadar's own weapon, and since it was attached to the armor, there was no way Taran'atar would be able to disarm him. *So I must turn his unity with his sword to my advantage.*

Looking around, Taran'atar saw that the Hirogen was maneuvering the fight toward the rifle. *I cannot allow that.* The minute one of them was able to get his hands on the rifle, the battle was over.

When the Hirogen made one of his right swings, Taran'atar overstumbled to his left after parrying, and continued backing away in that direction. This also sent Taran'atar in the direction of one of the secondary consoles against the wall. *Ordinarily, backing into a wall would hardly be an optimum strategy . . . but this might provide me with a path to victory.*

Right-left-forward, right-left-forward.

The first Vorta that Taran'atar had served under as a Sixth had been fond of dances performed by a minor Dominion species known as the Thepnossen. When he first saw them, Taran'atar had thought their movements to be foolish and wasteful, and he had been equally foolish in voicing these thoughts in the presence of the Second. He had been reduced to Seventh for the infraction—had the First or the Vorta herself heard him, he might well have been killed. He had learned that day to be more prudent when speaking his mind. Until now, he had only thought of those dances as a reminder of the discipline.

Now, however, he and the Hirogen were engaged in a dance that was eerily similar to that of the Thepnossen.

But unlike those choreographed moves, which were consistent and constant, Taran'atar was, as he was backed closer and closer to the console against the wall, noticing a change to the Hirogen's pattern: each forward thrust was lower than the last. The lower thrusts made Taran'atar's parry—which, on the forward thrust, required him not to just block the strike but push the sword away—more difficult, and gave him less time to mount a defense against the next, right thrust.

Right-left-forward, right-left-forward, right-left-forward, left—

Left!

Taran'atar had thrown off the forward thrust and had already raised his *kar'takin* to block the expected attack on the Hirogen's right. But the Hirogen switched to a left thrust. Taran'atar attempted to switch over, hoping that the Hirogen's enforced right-handed attack (thanks to his sword being attached to his right arm) would slow his attack to the left enough so that Taran'atar could block.

The Hirogen's blade cut through the Jem'Hadar's coverall and into his scaly skin, slashing his right bicep.

But, while there was pain, it was not enough to be distracting. While Jem'Hadar could, of course, feel pain—it was necessary to insure survival—the Founders had designed their nervous systems with a very high threshold for it. A cut to the arm was nothing.

So it was a simple matter for Taran'atar to thrust his *kar'takin* forward with his left hand toward the Hirogen's face. The hunter saw the attack coming, but with his blade still embedded in Taran'atar's arm, he could not back away in time. Taran'atar made a second gash across his foe's face, but again, not deep enough to kill.

The Hirogen pulled his sword out of Taran'atar's arm as if he were sawing the limb off, causing more damage, and then backed away. The arm felt sluggish, and Taran'atar knew that he could not depend on it. He switched from using the *kar'takin* two-handed to holding it in his left hand.

Taran'atar was now standing directly in front of the console he'd been backing toward.

They stood facing each other for a moment once again. "Clever prey," the Hirogen said as dark blood trickled down his cheek.

He then thrust his sword forward, even lower than he had in previous strikes.

Rather than parry it, Taran'atar instead leapt into the air. The Hirogen stumbled forward, and his sword went straight into the console.

The Jem'Hadar came down from his leap onto the Hirogen's head, using it to flip through the air and land on his feet behind his opponent. His hope that his foe's embedded sword would carry an electrical charge through the armor was not realized—either the Hirogen missed a power junction or the metal was nonconductive. But for the moment, at least, the Hirogen was stuck.

And Taran'atar now faced the rifle on the far side of the bridge.

Knowing he only had seconds before the Hirogen pried his sword out of the console, Taran'atar ran for the energy weapon, which he estimated to be ten meters away.

At eight meters, the Hirogen growled.

At six meters, he heard a metallic snap that rang through the bridge even louder than the clashing blades had.

At four meters, the Hirogen's armored form collided with Taran'atar's back, sending them both sprawling.

The Hirogen grabbed Taran'atar's good arm and twisted, forcing the Jem'Hadar around and onto his back. Taran'atar could see that the Hirogen had broken the sword off—a very short, jagged edge protruded from the hilt.

His mouth spreading into a rictus, the Hirogen started pummeling the Jem'Hadar's face with both hands. Blood from the alien's face dripped onto Taran'atar, mingling with his own.

Taran'atar's vision began to blur.

Suddenly, the pummeling stopped. Through a haze, Taran'atar saw the Hirogen get up.

No.

The Hirogen was moving toward the rifle. *I won't allow that. I won't be defeated.*

Taran'atar gathered every bit of strength he had left as he forced his arms to brace himself. He gathered every millimeter of faith in the Founders and willed his legs to move. He gathered every shred of duty and made himself stand upright.

The image of the Hirogen was still blurry to his eyes, but Taran'atar could see that the alien had stopped and was regarding the Jem'Hadar with surprise. "Resourceful. But this hunt is over."

For the first time during the battle, Taran'atar spoke. "Not . . . while . . . I . . . live."

And then he leapt at the Hirogen. The attack was without grace, without subtlety. It was simply brutal.

The hunter again fell to the deck. Taran'atar punched the Hirogen at the alien's face wound.

Taran'atar kept on, kicking the alien twice in the face and chest. Growling, the Hirogen twisted the Jem'Hadar off balance. Taran'atar toppled to the deck—

—and saw the rifle within reach.

Reaching out with his good arm, he managed to snag the broken strap in his fist. But before he could pull the weapon toward him, the Hirogen's boot came down on his arm.

A klaxon started to blare. He had no idea what it signaled, and it hardly mattered now.

But the sound caused the Hirogen to turn, shifting his weight just enough for Taran'atar to yank his arm free and pull the rifle toward him.

But then the Hirogen knelt down hard, his knees impacting Taran'atar's chest. The Jem'Hadar found it hard to breathe.

"I repeat," the Hirogen said, "this hunt is over."

With that, the Hirogen stabbed Taran'atar in the chest with the jagged edge of his broken sword.

Chapter Nineteen

Farius Prime

"I don't like this."

"I'm not really interested in what you like, Gen. We've come this far."

"Kam, the gateways have gone offline! And I haven't the first clue as to why."

"Probably that sabotage they developed in System 418. Have you had any luck getting them back online?"

"No. That's why I said I didn't like this. I think it might be prudent if you return to the ship."

"It would be dangerous to leave now. The Orions are a suspicious people by nature, and they've already been betrayed by their own negotiator. We can't risk their discovering our deception."

"If you say so."

"Yes, I do. Meanwhile, get those gateways working again. Coordinate with the other pods—we can't permit a perception of anything other than complete control."

"Of course, Kam. I'll keep you posted."

"Good."

"Sensors are picking up a Bajoran Militia craft near the gateway—pursuit ships have been dispatched. And the gateway has gone offline!"

Vincam's first sentence was the only piece of good news Malic had received since before the "final" negotiation with the Iconians had begun. He stood on the bridge of his ship, having left the Iconians and their Ferengi in the conference room under the watchful eyes of his two bodyguards. Up until they'd allowed Quark and his *dabo* girl (or whoever she was) to escape, the guards, Werd and Snikwah, had been Malic's most trusted employees.

The bridge had a simple, logical layout—one would expect no less from Vulcan ship designers—with three tiers. Command was on the top tier, with primary operations on the second tier closest to the commander, secondary operations on the third—near enough to be accessible but out of the way when not needed. Vincam sat at the communications console just under the command chair next to which Malic was standing. He had chosen not to sit in the chair, as he didn't intend to remain on the bridge for all that long.

What had started out as a simple business transaction was getting irritatingly more complicated. Quark had betrayed him. That *dabo* girl was either Starfleet security or Bajoran Militia—given the class of ship they'd just detected, not to mention the fact that she took Treir hostage, the latter was more likely. Hostage-taking wasn't Starfleet's style.

Now this.

"What do you mean the gateway has gone offline?"

Vincam finally looked up from his console and turned around to face

Malic. "Just what I said. There's no power reading from the gateway, and we're not reading the Clarus system on the other side." His console beeped and he looked back down at it. "Gatnir is reporting—that gateway he took to Ferenginar went offline, too." Looking back up, he continued, "And I've monitored half a dozen other communiqués—Starfleet, Klingon Defense Force, Federation civilian, Ferengi Alliance, Romulan—that indicate that other gateways have gone dead. I've picked up one message on a Starfleet frequency—this appears to be the result of something one of their ships is attempting at Europa Nova."

Damn them, Malic thought. *No doubt this is the very same sabotage that Quark's accursed nephew dreamed up.* "It's time I had a conversation with these Iconians. I'll be in the conference room."

Loga spoke up from the sensor console. "Malic? I'm getting life-form readings on the Bajoran ship—two Bajorans, one Ferengi, and one Orion. They're also retreating into the asteroid belt."

Snarling, Malic said, "They still have Treir." Turning back to Vincam, he said, "Make sure the pursuit ships are told that the Bajoran ship is to be disabled—not destroyed. If any harm comes to Treir, the person responsible will be expected to compensate me for her full value, understood?"

Vincam nodded.

Malic turned toward the lift and reached into his pocket to make notes into his padd.

His hand felt only the fabric of his inner pocket.

For almost a hundred years, Malic had thrived. He'd started out as a simple deckhand on a ship belonging to the famed pirate Tu. Nobody there would take him seriously—he was viewed as being useless owing to his lack of height. Determined to prove himself, he quit Tu's ship and went to Finneas XII. He started working for Zil, one of the more talented enforcers in the syndicate and the man who controlled pretty much the entire planet. Malic had made his height work for him by his ability to fit into odd places to scout and spy. What Zil had never suspected was that Malic didn't just spy on people Zil had told him to spy on, but also on Zil himself. Soon enough, he had gathered enough information to take Zil—who had been skimming off the top of his fare to the syndicate for years—down.

Malic's only mistake had been to trust others. Although technically he was the one who brought Zil down, others had taken the credit by altering the data he had gathered to make it appear that it had been someone else's intelligence. Malic had been rewarded in other ways, but not with the credit he deserved.

So after that, he made sure that all the information he gathered was all in one unimpeachable source. He had spent all the money he had and more on a special padd that was genetically coded so that it could not be used by anyone but him. The information on that padd was sacrosanct, and could only be traceable to him. He upgraded the padd every chance he got, making sure that its security was the best that money could buy. And, with the information he gathered on it used to his own ends, the amount of money in question soon became considerable.

Still, no security was perfect, and Malic had been careful to guard the padd with his life. He'd never let it out of sight in the near-century that he'd owned it except when the upgrades were performed. Besides a record of all his transactions and business arrangements, the padd contained dirt on several other prominent syndicate members, half a dozen officials from virtually every major Alpha Quadrant government, most of the people Malic had done business with over the years, and Malic himself.

So to not feel it in his pocket now . . .

While quickly checking his three other pockets, he whirled and bellowed, "Loga! Turn on the tracer for my padd, now!"

Loga nodded and operated his console. Then his face went almost yellow. "Uh—you're not going to like this."

Clenching his fists hard enough that he could hear his rings scraping against each other, Malic said, "Where is it?"

Turning to Malic, Loga said, "You're *really* not going to like this."

"I like your procrastinating even less," Malic said in a low, menacing tone.

"It's on the Bajoran ship."

Several thoughts went through Malic's head at once, from disbelief to outrage to anger. *That damn* dabo *girl, whoever she truly is.* She had knocked the wind out of him when she tackled him, and had apparently managed to make off with his padd. *If she is Starfleet—or if she turns it over to Starfleet—it will be the end of me.*

Looking at the communications console, Malic said, "Vincam, add this to the message regarding the penalty for any harm coming to Treir: the pilot responsible for disabling the Bajoran ship and bringing its contents directly to me will be rewarded with a hundred bricks of gold-pressed latinum."

Vincam's eyes went wide, and it took him a moment to recover his wits enough to send the message.

Malic then left the bridge, ordering the turbolift to the conference room. Initially, he had been concerned with how to conclude these negotiations in light of Quark's sabotage. However, the Ferengi, damn his ears, had actually negotiated a good deal for them. True, the actual process had taken longer than necessary—and Malic had his suspicions as to how that was accomplished—but the deal itself was a solid one.

This new wrinkle about the gateways, however, gave Malic a concern regarding the Iconians themselves. From the first time they approached him two weeks previous, Malic had never gotten the feeling that they were as—well, *old* as they said they were. Admittedly, one could hardly judge what a member of an ancient civilization would truly act like—Malic hadn't met all that many, after all—but something about these Iconians felt wrong.

Let's see how they react to this latest news.

He arrived at the conference room to see Werd and Snikwah standing on either side of the doorway, Klingon disruptors in their hands, though lowered.

That was on Malic's instruction—he was taking no chances. The head Iconian, Kam, and his aide Pal, were standing in the same spot in the back of the room where they had been when Malic left. The Ferengi Gaila was currently at the buffet table, stuffing tube grubs into his mouth.

"Would you care to explain," Malic asked the room in general—he didn't care if it was Gaila or the Iconians who answered, as long as someone did, "why the gateways have all gone offline?"

The Iconians' facial expressions were as bland as ever, but Gaila's eyes went wide. "What?" he said through a mouthful of grubs.

Kam spoke up quickly. "It is nothing to be concerned over. We wish to conclude these negotiations."

"These negotiations will not be concluded until I have a satisfactory answer as to why the gateways are all dead."

Smiling a small smile, Kam said, "We said from the beginning that we would not reveal all the secrets of the gateways to you unless and until you consummated the deal."

"And I'm telling you now that no deal will be consummated until you explain to me why a relative of your negotiator has sabotaged your product."

Gaila, who had by this time swallowed the tube grubs, actually smiled at that. "If you're referring to young Lieutenant Nog—why would you assume that our family relation is meaningful?"

"For the same reason you assumed that his relationship to Quark was meaningful. You proposed that as sufficient reason to discredit him as my negotiator—I am starting to wonder if it is equally sufficient to discredit you."

"*Malic.*" It was Vincam's voice.

"Excuse me a moment," Malic said. "I must speak with my bridge. In the meantime, see if you can concoct a compelling reason for me not to have all three of you shot."

With a nod to his bodyguards, Malic moved toward the exit. As the doors parted, the two large Orions raised their weapons, and Malic could hear Gaila gulp.

Malic went to an intercom. "What is it, Vincam?"

"*The gateways just came back online. They were only down for about ten minutes. As far as Loga can tell, they just seemed to reboot.*"

"Very well."

"*There's more. We've been monitoring the Iconian ship. They've been doing the exact same thing we've been doing—examining it with sensors. And they've been in constant contact with the two in the conference room.*"

"That's to be expected."

"*Yes,*" Vincam said, and Malic could hear the pride in the younger man's voice, "*but we finally were able to break their code.*"

For the first time in several days, Malic smiled.

"*Kam, the gateways are back online.*"

"Good work."

"It wasn't my work! I think they just rebooted and came back online."

"We'll take what we can get. The Orion is suspicious of us. We have to inform him that this was our intention all along."

"How you coming along with that code, Ychell?"

Ro asked the question as she maneuvered the fighter through the asteroid belt. Already a skilled pilot, she had learned every trick in the book for evading capture during her time with the Maquis—and, in fact, had taught them a few tricks before the Jem'Hadar all but wiped them out.

Memories of a raid on a Cardassian supply depot came unbidden to Ro—piloting that ancient crate that was called the *Zelbinion* for reasons no one in her cell could adequately explain. They had been chased into an asteroid belt then, too, the depot's guard ships flying around in a standard search pattern while Ro kept the *Zelbinion* out of their sensor field.

That in turn led to another memory, of piloting another ship—one that didn't even have a name—through a field of antimatter mines laid by the Jem'Hadar en route to Osborne's World. They lost a lot of good people on that mission. In fact, if it hadn't been for Jalik's sacrifice, they all would have died . . .

Ychell suddenly spoke, forcing her to put those bad memories aside. "I don't think I can do it, Lieutenant," she said.

"You need a code broken?"

Ro looked back briefly to see that Quark had moved to stand between the pilot and copilot seats, then turned back to her console as she said, "Quark, get back in the rear."

"I need something to do, Laren. Besides, I'm an expert codebreaker."

Ychell made a dismissive noise. "Expert? I spent most of my time in the resistance cracking Cardassian codes."

Quark waved a hand dismissively. "Any idiot can crack Cardassian codes."

Before Ychell could respond, Ro said, "Sergeant, let him have a shot at it. We've got nothing to lose, and I'd really like to know what's in all the comm traffic we're picking up."

Glowering at Ro, Ychell said, "Fine. I'm transferring access to the comm systems to the aft panel." With a sneer at Quark, she said, "Have a party, Ferengi."

Quark gave her an equally mocking smile in return and went back to the aft compartment.

"Why do you allow him such familiarity? Hell, why do you let him stay in business? He worked for the Cardassians—and for the Dominion when they took over."

"You should know better, Ychell. He was part of the resistance movement that kicked the Dominion off the station," Ro said as she maneuvered around one particularly large asteroid. Sensors said it had a high enough magnetic content that it should confuse the hell out of the Orions. "And his bar serves an important social function."

"If you say so. I never went much for the type of socializing that goes on in those establishments." She checked her console. "I'm picking up two Orion pursuit ships nearby—the others are still outside the asteroid belt."

Ro studied the sensor readings. "Well, if they've found us, they're hiding it well. That's a pretty standard search pattern. We ought to be okay here for a few more minutes at least."

"I broke the code!" came a triumphant voice from the rear of the fighter.

Ychell whirled around. "What!? That's not possible!"

"Let me rephrase," Quark said as he bounded triumphantly back to the fore. "I broke one of the codes. That's why you were having trouble, Sergeant, there were two different codes there—the Orions' and the Iconians'."

"Which one did you break, the Orions'?"

"No," Quark said, to Ro's surprise, "the Iconians'. You should be getting a translation of the last five minutes' worth of comm traffic on your panel, Sergeant."

Ychell looked down. "Looks like it, yes. It—" Her eyes went wide. "Interesting."

"What?" Ro asked.

"If I'm reading this right, Lieutenant, these aren't the Iconians at all."

Ro repeated, "What!?"

"They're still transmitting—I'll put it on audio."

"You're lying."

Kam had just spent several minutes explaining what had happened to the gateways, that it was a simple maintenance cycle, and Malic's reaction had been those two words.

He stood between Werd and Snikwah in the conference room. The bodyguards had their disruptors trained on the two Iconians and the Ferengi, who were now all standing against the wall together. The Iconians looked as unconcerned as ever, but Gaila seemed a bit panicky.

"I don't think you even were the ones who opened the gateways," Malic continued. "I think this was all part of an elaborate plot on the part of the two Ferengi, the Bajoran Militia, and perhaps Starfleet to undermine the Orion Syndicate. Well, your accomplices will be captured soon enough." *They had better be, at least,* he thought, remembering his stolen padd. "And we have our weapons trained on your ship."

"There's no need for these hostilities," Gaila said. Malic could hear the Ferengi attempt to keep his voice calm, but he was failing. "We can discuss this like rational beings."

Malic snorted. "The time for discussion is over. It's obvious that you withheld intelligence on the gateways, not as a bargaining tactic, but because you didn't have that intelligence. It's also obvious that you didn't know about the gap in the gateway lattice in the Bajoran sector—otherwise you wouldn't have dispatched a ship there as soon as we brought it up. And it's equally obvious that you have no idea why the gateways went offline, nor why they came back online. You've lied to us. The syndicate doesn't appreciate being made fools."

"We haven't made fools of you!" Gaila said quickly. "It was Quark! He made fools of all of us! He's a crafty one, my cousin. But I can assure you—"

"Be silent, Ferengi. I have learned the hard way not to trust the mouthings of anyone from your wretched species." He turned to the Iconians—or whatever they truly were. "Well, Kam? Have you nothing to say for yourself?"

Kam simply regarded Malic with the same calm expression that never seemed to leave the alien's face. "Are you familiar with subvocal communication?"

Frowning, Malic said, "No."

"We perfected it some time ago. I have been in constant communication with my ship while we have been speaking. They have armed their weapons. You will allow us safe passage back to our ship and then allow us to leave the Farius system, or we will destroy you."

Malic didn't need a century of experience in business to know when someone was talking a better game than they could truly play. "Don't be fooled by the fact that this vessel was constructed by pacifists, Kam. It is more than armed enough to eliminate your ship." He turned to Werd and Snikwah. "Kill them all."

Then the lights went dead.

The darkness was short-lived, as the room was lit by a rather spectacular explosion from one of the walls. Malic heard someone scream, but he couldn't tell if it was the Ferengi, one of his own people, or one of the aliens.

Vincam's voice sounded over the speakers. *"We're under attack!"*

"We've got to save Gaila."

Ro turned in surprise at Quark's statement. "I beg your pardon?"

"He's still on that ship," Quark said, pointing to Ro's tactical display. "The Orions and the Iconians—or whoever they are—"

"They're called the Petraw," Ychell put in, "based on these comms we've been intercepting."

Nodding in acknowledgment, Quark said, "They can kill each other for all I care, but we have to save Gaila."

"Not that I disagree with the sentiment or anything, Quark," Ro said, "but why this sudden outburst of compassion? Gaila was the one who betrayed you in there."

Quark just shrugged. "That was just business. He's still family."

"Isn't there a Rule about how family should be exploited?"

Smiling, Quark said, "And how am I supposed to do that if he's dead?"

"Lieutenant," Ychell said, "the pursuit ships are breaking off—they're heading back toward Malic's ship. Probably to help out against the Petraw. That firefight is getting worse. Both ships have taken heavy damage."

Ro looked down at her own console. As it happened, the most direct course from their current position in the asteroid belt to the gateway—which had gone back online only ten minutes after shutting down—involved going straight through the battle between the Petraw and the Orions. The only way to go fast enough to escape their notice would be to go in a straight line at near-lightspeed. *So that works out fairly nicely anyhow . . .*

"Sergeant, can this crate do a near-warp transport?"

Ychell whirled toward Ro. "You're kidding, right?"

"I'm dead serious."

Snorting, Ychell said, "Bad choice of words, Lieutenant." She took a deep breath. "I suppose it's possible, but I've never done it."

"I have," Ro said confidently. Of course, that was on the *Enterprise*—a top-of-the-line Starfleet ship that was designed for those kinds of maneuvers. In fact, the operation had been performed at least once before she'd signed on. In addition, back then she'd been working in concert with Miles O'Brien, an expert in transporter technology.

She set the course she'd need to take in order to make this work. *I just hope the gateway doesn't wink out on us again.* "Can you get an accurate life-form reading from the Orion ship?"

Ychell nodded. "Scanning for Ferengi life-forms now." A pause. "Got him."

"Good," Quark said, "let's move while he's still alive."

Without looking up, Ro said, "Quark, get back aft. The ride's gonna be a little bumpy. You and Treir need to strap in."

Quark didn't look terrifically pleased by the notion of a bumpy ride, but said nothing as he moved back aft.

"Course set," Ro said and looked over at Ychell.

"Transporter standing by."

Ro took a deep breath, and remembered something one of her Academy instructors always said right before flight simulations. "Here goes nothin'."

Gaila ran.

He had no idea where he was running to, but he thought remaining in a dark room waiting for one of the two moon-sized Orions to shoot him was not in his best interests. So he made a dash for where he remembered the door being, was favored by that door opening at his approach, and proceeded to run down the hallways, which were now lit only by green emergency lights.

Escape pods, he thought. *That's what I want. They have to have them here. No self-respecting Vulcan would build a ship without escape pods. Wouldn't be logical.*

Gaila did not allow himself to think that getting rid of them might have been one of the (several) modifications Malic had made to the ship.

This is all your fault, Quark. Every time I turn around, you're there to thwart me.

A small voice in the back of Gaila's head reminded him that it was Gaila's own actions that led to this particular state of affairs, in his attempt to take his revenge for Quark's indignities. After all, if it hadn't been for Quark, Gaila would still own a moon. But if it hadn't been for Gaila, the Orion ship probably wouldn't be falling apart around him right now.

And then there's the Iconians. If they really are the Iconians. Not only did I break the Sixth Rule to get revenge on Quark, it's looking like I broke the the Ninety-Fourth as well. Cost me a perfectly good client, too.

Or maybe not so perfectly good, if Malic's suspicions were right. Frankly, Gaila didn't really care much one way or the other if they really were the Iconians or not. They'd paid him half up front, and that—along with most of the other seven bars of latinum he'd gotten from Zek—was safe in a despository. *All I need to do is live to get off this ship, and everything will be fine. I'll live without the rest of Kam's fee. I won't live if I stay here any longer.*

He turned a corner to see a male Orion who looked like he'd been worked over by a particularly cranky Klingon standing there.

Regarding him with two eyes that were half-swollen shut, the Orion asked through his split lip, "What're you doing here?"

"Trying to find the escape pods. Didn't you hear the order to abandon ship?" The first sentence was truthful, the second somewhat less so.

"Abandon ship?" The Orion started to quiver. Gaila supposed his eyes might have widened in shock if they weren't so swollen. "No, I didn't hear that! Follow me, the escape pods are this way."

Gaila smiled. *That's more like it.*

As they moved as one toward a turbolift, a voice from behind Gaila cried, "There he is! Good work, Alhan."

It sounded like one of Malic's bodyguards. *Damn,* Gaila thought. *Almost made it.*

He turned around and saw that it was indeed one of Malic's two mountains. He was aiming his disruptor right at Gaila's head.

So this is it, he thought. *I'm going to die.*

Then, suddenly, Gaila found himself looking down at the bodyguard from what felt like inside the ceiling.

That rather bizarre sensation only lasted an instant. Then the world dissolved into a confused mess before coalescing into the very face Gaila had imagined himself punching repeatedly only moments before.

"Quark."

"Good to see you too, Gaila."

He looked around to see that he and Quark, along with a Bajoran sergeant, an Orion slave girl, and Quark's *dabo* girl—who was a brunette now—were crammed into the flight deck of a Bajoran Militia flitter. "Where are we?"

"A Bajoran Militia flitter," Quark said.

"I *know* it's a Bajoran Militia flitter," Gaila said impatiently. "I mean where?"

"On our way to the Clarus system, and then to DS9. Oh, and Gaila?"

"What?"

"You're welcome."

Gaila's stomach hadn't felt this unsettled since the last time he had to eat cooked food in order to suck up to a potential client. He looked past Quark's self-satisfied smile to the viewscreen to see that they were indeed heading to the gateway in this system—which would take them to Clarus.

The Bajoran sergeant spoke up. "The Orion ship's shields just went down. The Petraw are firing again."

Then she touched a control and the image on the viewscreen changed to an aft view, showing the small ship commanded by Kam doing as the sergeant had indicated.

"Petraw?" Gaila asked.

Quark's oh-so-smug smile widened. "You mean you didn't know that you weren't working for the Iconians? Well, I'm surprised, Gaila. These Petraw were running such a weak scam that I thought for sure you'd be involved."

"Very funny, Quark. Their latinum was good enough regardless of—"

Gaila was interrupted by the rather impressive sight of Malic's ship exploding in a fiery conflagration.

"Well, if Malic did have a backup of that padd, it's gone now."

"Any sign of the Petraw ship?" the erstwhile *dabo* girl asked the sergeant.

"Negative. They could've warped out under cover of the explosion." The sergeant then looked up. "Entering the gateway now."

As usual, there was no real sensation of travel. Unlike wormholes or transporters or warp drive or any other method of getting somewhere fast, the Iconians had built their portals with a minimum of bells and whistles. One moment they were in the Farius system, the next they were in the Clarus system. No disorientation, no disruption of the very air, just a simple movement from one place to the next.

"Set course for DS9," the *dabo* girl said, holding up a padd. "I want to get to work on cracking this thing." Gaila realized after a moment that it was Malic's padd, thus explaining Quark's comment about a backup.

He then looked at his most hated cousin, who still hadn't lost the smug smile. "You saved my life."

"Looks like I did, yeah." Quark put his hand on Gaila's shoulder. Gaila looked at it with all the disdain he could muster—which right now was considerable—but Quark did not remove it. "Don't worry, Gaila. I promise not to ask for too much to settle the debt."

"And you have Malic's padd."

"Mhm. All in all, it's been a good day for me."

"If it's all the same to you," Gaila said, taking a seat next to the Orion slave woman—who had been watching the exchanges between Gaila and his cousin with a level of amusement that Gaila found inappropriate in a female—"you can drop me off at Clarus IX. I have no interest in accompanying you to that wretched station."

The *dabo* girl turned and smiled in a way that Gaila hated even more than he hated Quark's. "This isn't a ferry service, Gaila. We're heading to DS9, so that's where you're heading. If you have a problem with that, we can always send you back where we found you."

"Look—" Gaila started, but Quark interrupted him.

"I don't think you've been properly introduced. Gaila, this is DS9's new security chief, Lieutenant Ro Laren."

Gaila shot Quark a look. "Security chief?"

Quark nodded.

Sighing, Gaila leaned back. *I suppose it won't be so bad. I don't have any outstanding warrants or bad business contacts on Bajor.* "Fine," he said. "I'll arrange transport on DS9."

"Good luck with that," Ro said, still smiling. "Right now, DS9 is chock-full of refugees from Europa Nova. I doubt there are any quarters available."

"Oh don't worry, cousin," Quark said quickly. "I'd be more than happy to put you up in my quarters for a very reasonable fee."

Gaila looked up at his cousin for a long time before coming to a realization.

"I hate you, Quark."

Chapter Twenty

Europa Nova

"Commander Vaughn, the last of the refugees have been evacuated from Europa Nova."

At Nog's words, a cheer went up from all around the *Defiant* bridge. Vaughn did not join in that cheer, but he did smile. There had been several hundred cases of theta-radiation poisoning, but—between the efforts of Bashir and Dr. DeLaCruz on the surface and the sickbays of both the *Intrepid* and the *Gryphon*—none of those cases were fatal. The combined efforts of the five Starfleet ships, ten Bajoran ships, one Cardassian ship, one gateway, and the assorted civilian and Europani military vessels had resulted in a complete evacuation of the adult population.

And not a moment too soon, as the regions directly beneath the mouth of the gateway—which included the large cities of Spilimbergo and Chieti and half a dozen smaller towns—were at fatal levels of exposure at this point.

The cheering continued for several seconds. Prynn got up from the conn and gave Nog a hug. When the embrace broke, Prynn found herself looking right at Vaughn in the command chair.

Vaughn was expecting a look of disdain or annoyance, so he was rather surprised when Prynn actually smiled at him and nodded her head.

He returned both the smile and the nod, and with that, she went back to the flight controls. Vaughn had no idea if Prynn was just feeling giddy from the success of their mission or if she was truly softening in her attitude toward him. He hoped for the latter, but he was cynical enough to believe it was more likely the former. *Still,* he thought, *it's a step. And not a small one, either.*

When the din finally quieted enough to speak over, Nog said, "According to Captain Emick, President Silverio was the last person to board the *Intrepid.*"

Vaughn nodded. *Good for her,* he thought. *The captain should be the last one off the sinking ship.* "That's excellent news, Lieutenant. Open a channel to the entire convoy, please."

"Yes, sir," Nog said, returning to his console. "Channel open."

"This is Commander Vaughn. Excellent work, all. We still have a long way to go, but the most important thing—getting the Europani out of danger—has been accomplished. At this time, we will prepare to bring the last remaining refugees to Bajor and Deep Space 9. Lieutenant Bowers, you and the *Rio Grande* will remain behind and await any new signals from Colonel Kira or Taran'atar."

Vaughn hesitated. It galled him that he could do no more than that. It had also galled Nog that the gateways had come back online after only being off for ten minutes. While it did leave the door open, so to speak, for Kira and the Jem'Hadar to return, it also meant that Ensign ch'Thane's solution was not the cure-all they'd hoped for. He wished he could inform Nog of the eyes-only communiqué he'd gotten minutes before from Bill Ross, telling him that the disruption of the gateways had been useful in exposing the "Iconians" for the frauds they truly were. Apparently, the people peddling the gateways—under false pretenses—were known as the Petraw, and their helplessness in the face of the temporary disruption proved their undoing.

At least, when the gateways had come back online, the *Euphrates* was still there blocking the radiation, keeping the Europa Nova situation from getting even worse. There was still the matter of somehow disposing of all this theta radiation—but that was a solution for more scientifically bent minds than that of Elias Vaughn.

Prynn said, "The convoy is getting into formation for the return voyage, Commander." A pause. "Except for the *Trager*."

They weren't part of the original convoy, Vaughn thought. "Open a channel to the *Trager*," he said, standing as he faced the viewscreen.

Gul Macet's image was suddenly looking back at him. *"What can I do for you, Commander Vaughn?"*

"I merely wish to confirm that you'll be joining the convoy back to DS9, Gul."

"Of course, Commander, I simply was not sure where, precisely, to align myself."

"Have your conn officer coordinate with Ensign Tenmei."

Macet nodded. *"Very well."*

Vaughn was about to order the connection cut, then hesitated. *Oh what the hell,* he thought, *you've been wanting to ask him since they got here.* "If you don't mind my asking, sir—why are you here?"

At that, Macet threw his head back and chuckled. *"Not an unreasonable question under the circumstances, Commander."* His face grew more serious. *"Are you familiar with a former Starfleet captain named Benjamin Maxwell?"*

In fact, Vaughn had known Ben quite well when the latter was a junior officer, though he'd lost track of him by the time he made captain. The erstwhile commanding officer of the *Phoenix* had been court-martialed and imprisoned following his attacks on several Cardassian ships. Maxwell had been convinced that they were carrying weapons, in violation of treaty, and had taken matters into his own hands.

Aloud, Vaughn simply said, "Yes. And to answer your next question, I know why he's now a former captain."

"I was assigned by Central Command to work with a Starfleet ship to track Maxwell down when he went rogue. That ship was the Enterprise.*"* Macet took a deep breath. *"I did as I was told, and we were eventually able to stop Maxwell before he murdered any more citizens of Cardassia. But the strange thing was—Maxwell was right. Those ships were carrying weapons. I did not agree with the actions of Central Command in that case, but I was a good soldier, and said nothing, not even when Captain Picard told me that he knew the truth.*

"I learned an important lesson that day, Commander, and that lesson is why I am here today. You see, both Maxwell and Picard knew that we were violating the treaty.

But where Maxwell's reaction was to madly destroy our ships, Picard's was to work to preserve the peace."

Macet took another deep breath and folded his arms. "My people have been too much like Maxwell of late. We have worked against the galaxy. At a time when the entire Alpha Quadrant united against a common threat, we alone stood with the threat—well," he added with a smile, "we and the Breen. We did not realize our mistake until it was too late. Now many of us—including myself—believe that we are better off trying to become part of the quadrant once more. We were a nation to be reckoned with once, Commander. If we are to be so again, we must work with our neighbors to preserve peace, not against them in conflict. You may consider this," he said, holding his hands outward, as if to encompass the entire convoy, "the first step on that road."

Vaughn nodded. At worst, it was a good speech. At best, it was an encouraging sign for the future of both Cardassia and the Alpha Quadrant. "Thank you for your candor, Gul Macet."

"You're welcome."

"And perhaps when we arrive back on Deep Space 9, we can discuss future steps on that road of yours."

"I would like that, Commander. Trager out."

Macet's image disappeared. As Vaughn returned to his chair, a voice from his right said, "Weird."

"What's 'weird,' Lieutenant?" Vaughn asked Nog.

"He looks so much like Dukat. When I first moved to the station as a boy, Dukat was the prefect of Bajor. He was always coming into Uncle Quark's bar. I used to be scared of him. Later on, I hated him. Seeing someone who reminds me so much of him . . ."

"There's an old human saying, Nog—don't judge a book by its cover. You of all people should be aware of that. Give Macet a chance to prove himself."

Nog nodded. "Oh, I will, sir. But it's still going to be weird."

"Convoy is in position, sir," Prynn said before the conversation could continue.

"Very well, Ensign. Ahead warp six."

Chapter Twenty-One

Cardassia Prime

"This price is outrageous, Deru."

Deru sighed at the face of the Kobheerian on his personal comm unit. He'd been going around in circles with him for almost an hour now over the price of the land he and Quark had acquired on Chin'toka IX. He got up from his chair—which was comfortable in theory, but after sitting in it for an hour his back was starting to ache. He paced around the sitting room of his large house, the maroon walls covered with Bajoran paintings he had taken during the occupation.

Riilampe was an entrepreneur Quark had brought in. He claimed to be looking for landowning opportunities, and was therefore perfect for the operation Deru and Quark had going. The price he had offered was of course three times what Deru and Quark had paid that retired gul for it (they had paid in *kanar* and *taspar* eggs).

"The price is commensurate with the value. Think about it, Riilampe—this land is arable. Cardassians all over the union are starving. Replicators can't handle all of it—farmland is going to be immensely valuable. In fact, I could easily justify charging more, if it weren't for—"

"If it weren't for the battle damage," the Kobheerian interrupted.

Deru sat back down. "And the amount we lowered the price is about what it would cost to restore the scarred topsoil to proper form. I know Quark went over all this with you before, and when you arrive at Deep Space 9—"

"The Ferengi hasn't gone over anything with me. I haven't been able to get through to him for a couple of days. I've also been turned away from DS9. Some kind of crisis—they're not letting anyone on-station."

Frowning, Deru said, "That's odd. Perhaps—"

"I'll be on Cardassia Prime in two days, Deru. We'll finalize the deal then, all right?"

"So you accept this price?"

The Kobheerian hesitated. *"Provisionally. Let me look over the deal memo one more time."*

"You won't regret this, Riilampe. You're getting in on the ground floor of one of the best land-development deals of the century."

Laughing, Riilampe said, *"You've been hanging around that Ferengi too long—now you're starting to sound like him. Screen off."*

Deru's comm went dark. He then entered some commands into his computer.

Odd, he thought, *that he couldn't get through to Quark. Wonder if it has to do with that emergency. Not to mention all those rumors of strange portals opening up all over the galaxy . . .*

Ah, well. Not my concern.

In the middle of his file update, the screen went out. So did the lights, plunging his house into utter darkness.

Damn, another power outage. I thought they'd solved the power problems. That, he supposed, was wishful thinking. The Dominion had inflicted obscene damage onto Cardassia Prime, and even well-to-do citizens like Deru had had to live with this sort of thing. He walked toward the window—

—to see that the other nearby houses all had power.

The emergency power kicked in. It wasn't enough for him to get his computer back, but at least now there were lights, albeit dim ones, and the doors would work. *I can't believe that just my house had an outage. It's not like I haven't kept up with my payments. Somebody's going to answer for this.*

He walked out to the hallway, and thence to the front door.

It opened to reveal the smiling face of a Cardassian that Deru recognized immediately. He'd never met the man, but it was impossible for anyone living on Cardassia not to know him.

Former agent of the Obsidian Order. Living for almost a decade in exile on Terok Nor—or, rather, Deep Space 9. And the man now spearheading the rebuilding of the Cardassian Union.

"Garak." Deru's voice sounded hollow to his own ears.

"Good evening, Mr. Deru," Garak said in a most pleasant, affable tone. "I've only just become aware of your charming little enterprise here . . . and I believe we need to have a little chat."

Deru swallowed hard.

Chapter Twenty-Two

Deep Space 9

"Excuse me, but how long am I supposed to stand here?"

Ro Laren rubbed her temples. Never a particularly religious person, right now Ro would happily worship the great god Ho'nig if they would just take this damn Orion woman away from her.

They'd returned to DS9 to find absolute chaos. Intellectually, Ro had expected this—Ychell had received coded updates from Dax on the Europa Nova situation, and Ro had talked with the lieutenant directly when they were en route from Clarus—but she hadn't been emotionally prepared for the reality of the station being so completely inundated with refugees. From the minute she arrived, all her deputies had questions and Dax had half a dozen tasks that needed Ro's attention.

Pointedly, none of the Starfleet security people came to her with questions or requests. Most of them treated her with indifference at best, which was to be expected given Ro's somewhat rocky Starfleet career—and just at the moment, it meant that one less set of people was harassing her.

Unfortunately, every time she looked up, she saw a green torso standing in front of her desk. The Orion woman who dressed in a skimpy outfit carefully tailored to look like rags would not leave her office.

"Treir, I'm really busy now. Can't you go somewhere else?"

Indicating the Promenade with one hand, Treir asked, "Where, precisely? I'm not exactly dressed for walking around in public."

Ro looked up. Treir had a point. Although the outfit did technically conform to Bajoran decency statutes, about seventy percent of the Orion's green flesh was exposed, and her presence on the Promenade would cause a stir to say the least.

"And," Treir continued, "I don't have a change of clothes. In fact, I don't have much of anything now, thanks to you."

Ro ran her hands through her increasingly tousled black hair. "If you want to go back and sift through the debris of Malic's ship for your personal belongings—"

"Very funny. The point is, Lieutenant, I had a life until you hijacked me into your harebrained scheme."

Aghast, Ro said, "You were a slave!"

"I was well treated, fed four exquisite meals a day, given luxurious quarters, and I was damn good at what I did. Then some Bajoran woman needs a hostage, and my life's turned upside down." She put her hands on her hips and glowered at Ro with a stare that reminded the security chief that this woman was almost two heads taller than Ro.

"Look, I'm sorry about that, but—"

Treir snorted. "No you're not. I know your type, Lieutenant. You think you've done me a big favor. Well, you haven't."

Throwing up her hands, Ro said, "You're right, Treir. I should've left you on Malic's ship so you could've died when the Petraw blew them up. What was I thinking?"

"Oh, please," Treir said, rolling her eyes. "You didn't take me hostage to save my life, you took me hostage because it was the only way you could get off the ship safely. And you knew damn well that I'd be more valuable as a hostage than Alhan. Did you for one second think about what your actions would mean to me?"

During Treir's tirade, Quark approached the entrance to the security office. "Lovers' spat?" Quark asked as he entered, smiling lasciviously.

Glowering, Ro said, "Quark, I really don't have time for—"

"Actually, I have a solution to your problem."

Indicating the pile of padds on her desk with a sweeping arm gesture, Ro asked, "Which one?"

"This one," he said, putting his arm around Treir.

That one gesture had a remarkable effect on Treir. Her face transformed from angry to seductive—even though it looked to Ro like all she did was lower her eyelids slightly. She draped herself over Quark, which was no mean feat, since the height differential between her and the Ferengi was even greater than it was with Ro.

"What did you have in mind?" Treir asked. She had lowered her voice half an octave, and spoke in a breathy whisper.

Quickly, Ro said, "Quark," in as menacing a tone as she could manage.

Quark straightened—at least, as much as he could with a two-meter-tall woman hanging all over him. "Calm down, Laren. I actually have a business proposition for you, Treir, if you're interested."

As quick as that, Treir extricated herself from Quark's embrace and took a step back, transforming from a seductress into something more akin to a Federation negotiator. Ro found herself wondering which one was the real Treir, suspecting it might well be something else entirely.

"Go on," Treir said expectantly.

"Well, as it happens, I haven't been able to find a decent *dabo* girl to replace the one who married my brother and moved to Ferenginar. How'd you like a job?"

Ro couldn't believe what she was hearing. "You want to hire her as a *dabo girl?*"

"Why not? She's definitely got sex appeal, which is the only skill she'll need. She'll earn her keep. Plus it gets her out of your hair."

"And you get to fulfill your lifelong dream of having an Orion *dabo* girl."

Grinning, Quark said, "Exactly. So everyone wins."

"Excuse me," Treir said, "but I haven't said yes yet."

"Oh, come on," Quark said in what Ro was quickly coming to recognize as Quark's best wheedling tone, "what could possibly be better?"

Treir laughed. The breathy whisper a thing of the past, she said sharply, "Listen to me, you little troll, I was the most respected of Malic's women. I had my pick of clients, I had the second-best quarters on the ship, I had clothes, jewelry—"

Quark grinned. "No you didn't. Malic had all those things, and he let you use them."

Ro almost cheered.

"Maybe." Treir seemed to concede very reluctantly. "But now you're making me work as a *dabo* girl on some backwater station run by Starfleet and Bajorans."

This time, Ro rolled her eyes. "Nobody's *making* you do anything, Treir. You're free to go wherever you want, do whatever you please." Grabbing a padd at random off her desk, she added, "And the only condition to that is that it isn't in my office. Now, if you'll both excuse me . . . ?"

Treir went back to standing with her hands on her hips. Ro looked up at her face, which seemed to be wrestling with the decision, even though, to Ro's mind, she really only could make one.

Finally, Treir threw up her hands. "Fine. It's not like I've got a lot of alternatives, thanks to you," she said with a glare at Ro.

Biting back a retort, Ro said, "Good luck."

Quark's grin widened so much that Ro was sure his head would split in half. "Come along, my dear," he said, offering his arm. "We'll get you a proper *dabo*-girl outfit and get you started."

Smiling a vicious smile right back, Treir said, "No, you'll get me some real clothes and then we'll talk about the terms of the employment contract—over a dinner that you're buying."

Ro chuckled as she opened the door to let them out. *At least she's not letting Quark play her for an idiot.* Whatever Treir's other qualities, she wasn't just a mindless slave. Hell, she seemed to enjoy it.

Treir stopped in the doorway and turned around. "Oh, Lieutenant?"

Looking up at her, Ro said, "Yes?"

"Have you ever heard of the Hinarian coding system?"

Ro frowned. "It rings a bell."

"You may want to use it when you're trying to crack the code for Malic's padd."

With that, she and Quark exited the security office.

Ro stared after them for several seconds. *Damn it all, I'm starting to like her.*

Then she put the Orion out of her thoughts. The convoy was due with the last of the refugees within the hour, and she had to find somewhere to put them. . . .

"You've got a message."

Quark sighed. He had gotten Treir settled temporarily in his brother Rom's old quarters. He'd been forced to bribe its current occupants, two Europani officials, with ten free holosuite hours, before returning to the delight-fully overcrowded bar, only to have Frool announce what the blinking light on his companel already told him.

It was happy hour, and the place was near to bursting with Europani refugees. Apparently they preferred socializing, eating, and drinking to sulking in their assigned quarters, a philosophy Quark could easily get behind and happily exploited.

Ideally, of course, Quark would have brought Treir to his own quarters, but Gaila was there—and paying a princely sum for the privilege of rooming with his cousin, an amount that more than made up for the lost holosuite time. *But this'll do. And she'll melt before my charms before too long—and even if she doesn't, she'll definitely take the job. An Orion dabo girl! I may have to start charging admission.*

Quark's hand brushed against his lobe as he went to his private area behind the bar to take the message. *First Odo's gone from the station, replaced by the lovely Ro Laren, then I get to save her life, then I save Gaila's life, the station is full to bursting with Europani who are filling the tables in the bar, and now I have an Orion dabo girl. Life is good.*

The message was from Cardassia Prime. *Uh oh,* he thought, hoping it wasn't Deru.

Instead, it was Garak.

The always-smiling face of the former Obsidian Order agent smiled warmly at Quark from the viewscreen. *"Good day, Quark. I hope this communiqué finds you well."*

Oh, this is not good. Quark felt his lobes—which had been all tingly from the moment he'd entered Ro's office with the proposition for Treir—shrivel to the size of a human's.

"I just wanted you to know I recently spoke with Deep Space 9's new security officer, Lieutenant Ro. A delightful young woman. I can see the Promenade is in good hands. I hope you're treating her well—unless I'm mistaken, she seems to have a soft spot for you. But then, I suppose no one is perfect.

"The lieutenant was kind enough to suggest I look in on an acquaintance of yours from before the Cardassian withdrawal from Terok Nor—a gentleman named Deru. Perhaps you remember him from his days working in the military. Well, he's done quite well for himself in the private sector—made a sum of money that is, frankly, envious. Distressingly, though, he seems to have been involved in some, shall we say—illicit activities. Some kind of black-market dealings. A most unpleasant business for all concerned. Now he's fallen on hard times, the poor fellow. Most shocking of all, he's been saying the most slanderous things about you, Quark, suggesting you were somehow involved in the entire affair. You can rest assured, however, that I set him straight, explaining that Lieutenant Ro had vouched for you, and I had known you to be such an upstanding individual during our time together on the station.

"Such a pity about Mr. Deru, isn't it, Quark? Fortunes can change so quickly." Garak heaved a sigh, then said, *"Well, I must be going. A pity we couldn't chat di-*

rectly, but affairs of state have kept me extremely busy of late. Perhaps at a later date we can catch up on old times—and new ones. Good-bye for now."

Garak had said it all in the most pleasant tone imaginable. He never lost his genial smile or his affable demeanor.

It was the most terrifying thing Quark had ever experienced.

Chapter Twenty-Three

The Delta Quadrant

The alpha twisted his blade into the prey's chest, then removed it. The Jem'Hadar's blood stained the broken sword end.

A most satisfying hunt, he thought as he rose from the prey's now-motionless form. *Now, however, it is time to see what that alarm is about.*

He went to the console. Sensors were working only intermittently, but he was soon able to determine a rather ugly truth: the power core was experiencing a malfunction. The tanker was likely to explode within the next fifteen minutes.

The alpha pounded the console with his fist. *To lose my ship was bad enough. Now I lose this one as well.*

Still, all was not lost. A quick check of the ship's inventory—which took longer than it should have, with the console flickering in and out of power—showed that they had plenty of escape pods.

The deck seemed to disappear from under the alpha's feet as the tanker rocked to the side. The ship righted itself soon enough, but a quick check showed that the stabilizers were working at only forty percent of capacity.

It is time I took my leave, the alpha thought. He had had one disappointing hunt, but one great one with a foe he never thought he'd face. Ultimately, that was what mattered. The Jem'Hadar had been most worthy prey.

He was about to turn when a clattering sound drew his attention. The alpha spun to see the Jem'Hadar struggling to his feet, the Hirogen's rifle in hand.

The alpha smiled. *Truly this is worthy prey.*

Blood trickling out of his mouth, the Jem'Hadar spoke, every word sounding like an effort.

"Victory . . . is . . . life . . ."

Then he pulled the trigger.

It was a struggle for Taran'atar to make his limbs work. His right arm was completely useless, and his left arm was slow to respond as well. He felt a weakness in his chest, and his legs were by no means steady.

But the Hirogen was finally dead. Killed by his own weapon.

Oddly, the alien died with a smile on his face. Taran'atar did not understand how one could take joy in losing a battle.

Dropping the heavy rifle to the deck, he moved to the central console. While his body was gravely injured, his mind still functioned at peak efficiency. The Founders had made him well. It was the work of only a few minutes to figure out that the warp drive containment field was in danger of collapse. Within ten minutes, the tanker would explode.

Then he scanned the fifth planet. Readings were difficult, but he did detect a Bajoran life sign—however, theta radiation on the planet was at fatal levels, and the life sign was very weak. It was only a matter of moments before Kira died.

Then the sensors went down. Taran'atar quickly manipulated the console and got them back online.

He no longer saw the life sign. And the theta radiation was increasing by the minute.

"No!" Taran'atar pounded futilely at the console. *It was my duty to die for her, not the other way around!*

I have failed my duty. I have failed the Founders.

A part of him was tempted to simply remain on the tanker and die when it exploded. But no, he still had a duty to perform. The same sensors that told him that Kira was gone also told him that the gateways were online—apparently ch'Thane's attempt to shut them down permanently had failed.

Taran'atar had to return to the Gamma Quadrant and inform Odo of his failure. For that matter, Kira's comrades on Deep Space 9—they too deserved to know how she died.

The ship rocked once again. *The stabilizers are failing. There are only minutes until the warp core breaches.*

The Hirogen had called up a schematic that showed the fastest route to the escape pods—no doubt intending to make use of one himself. Taran'atar ran in that direction, as fast as he could make his legs move.

Chapter Twenty-Four

Europa Nova

"Lieutenant, something's coming through the gateway."

Sam Bowers set down the birch beer he'd been drinking on the *Rio Grande*'s console and checked the runabout console. Ensign Roness's words were accurate—something was coming through. *About time something happened.* He'd enjoyed the relative calm after the chaos of the Europa Nova evacuation—for about twenty minutes. Then the restlessness kicked in. Roness hadn't actually said anything, but it was obvious from the looks she gave him that she was about ready to kill him.

She, of course, liked the quiet. Bowers hated it. He had always been a man of action. That was why he went into tactical when he joined Starfleet.

"Looks like an escape pod," he said. "I think. It's just managing to squeak past the blockage created by the *Euphrates.* I don't recognize that configuration."

Roness said, "It doesn't match anything in the database. But I am reading a life sign." She looked up, a surprised expression on her face. "It's Jem'Hadar."

"Taran'atar?"

Shrugging, she said, "That'd be my guess."

"Trying to get a transporter lock," he said, manipulating the controls. The theta radiation was still too intense, unfortunately. "Damn. Can we get a tractor beam?"

Roness nodded. "Yes, sir."

"Do it." Bowers then set a course for the next planet over.

"Tractor beam engaged. We have the pod."

"Good." Bowers took the *Rio Grande* forward. As soon as they were far enough from Europa Nova to engage the transporter, he did so.

Bowers had to admit that the sight on the runabout's small transporter platform was one that, in the past, he had enjoyed tremendously: a broken, bloody Jem'Hadar soldier. A part of him wanted to take pleasure in it now, but he forced that out of his head. *Taran'atar's on our side—hell, it was Odo who sent him. He's part of the team now.*

Intellectually, he knew that. It was convincing his gut—and his instincts, which had spent the last several years being trained to shoot Jem'Hadar on sight—that was the problem.

As he got up from his chair, grabbed a tricorder, and approached the unsteady form of the Jem'Hadar—who collapsed to his knees as soon as he materialized—he asked, "What about Kira?"

"Colonel Kira . . . did not . . . survive," Taran'atar said.

Bowers felt like the temperature had lowered in the runabout. *Dammit, no, not another one,* he thought. First they lost Captain Sisko—and not even to the war, but to some ridiculous thing with those damn wormhole aliens—then they lost Commander Jast when those rogue Jem'Hadar attacked the station. To lose the colonel . . .

"I . . . must . . . return . . ." Taran'atar couldn't finish the sentence. Bowers could see why. The tricorder indicated that he'd suffered half a dozen internal injuries, not to mention the obvious stab wound to the chest. He needed Bashir's services posthaste.

"Set course for DS9, maximum warp," he shouted to Roness.

"Yes, sir." After a moment: "Course laid in."

"Engage."

It wasn't until after the runabout went into warp that Roness turned to Bowers. "What about Colonel Kira, sir?" Her tone implied that she wasn't entirely willing to take a Jem'Hadar's word for it that she was dead. *On the other hand,* he thought, *she did wait until after we went to warp to ask.*

"For now?" he said. "Hope to hell he's wrong."

Chapter Twenty-Five

The Delta Quadrant (fifteen minutes earlier)

Blisters had now broken out on every millimeter of Kira's skin. The tricorder told her that the level of exposure was beyond what would be fatal to a Bajoran. Her life could be measured in seconds.

There was no word from Taran'atar.

Breathing became harder with each second. Her vision started to cloud over.

Then, miraculously, the gateway came back online. It once again went back and forth between Deep Space 9 and the comforting glow of the Prophets.

Now the choice was easy. She was already dead. It was just left to her to take the final step.

Colonel Kira Nerys stepped into the gateway, determined to face what lay beyond . . .

HORN AND IVORY

Keith R. A. DeCandido

Chapter One

The ax nearly took her head off.

Its wielder was large by the standards of the Lerrit Army, but she still stood half a head taller. The plate armor he wore on his chest was too small for him, and it slowed him down, making it easier to anticipate his movements, and therefore just as easy to duck the attack.

That it still almost decapitated her spoke to how long she'd been fighting. How many hours had they clashed on this grassy plain just outside the capital city? She'd long since lost track, but however long it was, the fatigue was taking its toll. Her muscles ached, her arms and legs cried out for respite.

She ignored the pleas of her limbs and fought on.

The ax-wielder probably thought the sacrifice of movement was worth the protection his armor afforded. The problem was, it only covered his chest and groin, leaving his arms, legs, and head exposed: still plenty of viable targets. So as she ducked, she swiped her staff at his legs, protected only by torn linen. She heard bones crack with the impact—the staff was made from a *kava* tree, so it was as hard as they came—and the Lerrit soldier went down quickly, screaming in pain at his broken leg.

She stood upright and surveyed the battlefield. The smell of mud mixed with blood combined with the faint tinge of ozone left from the morning's rainstorm to give her a slight queasy feeling, but she fought it down with little difficulty.

As they'd hoped, the Lerrit Army's formation had been broken. *As last stands go,* she thought, *this is pretty weak.* The war had been all but won on the seas, after all. Lerrit had lost all control of the port, and without the port, there was no way they could hold the peninsula, even if they somehow were able to win today.

Based on the number of Lerrit Army bodies on the ground, that wasn't going to happen.

She caught sight of General Torrna Antosso, the leader of the rebel army for whom she fought, and who looked to be the victor this day. As she ran toward him, one man and one woman, both much shorter than her, and both unarmored, came at her with swords. She took the woman down with a swipe of her staff, but the man was able to strike, wounding her left arm before she could dodge the blow.

Gripping the upper part of the staff with her right hand, she whirled it around so that it struck her attacker on the crown of his head. He, too, went down.

Tucking the staff under her injured arm, she put pressure on the wound with her right hand and continued toward Torrna.

As she approached, she heard the reedy sound of a horn.

Torrna, a wide-shouldered bear of a man with a full red beard and bushy red eyebrows that encroached upon his nose ridges, threw his head back and laughed. "They retreat!" he cried.

She came up to his side, and he stared her in the eye—easy enough, as they were the same height. "We've done it, *Ashla,*" he said, his yellowed, crooked teeth visible in a smile from behind the beard. "We've driven the last of them off!"

"Yes, we have," she said, returning the smile with her perfect white teeth. The nickname *Ashla*—which meant "giant"—was given to her shortly after she joined the rebel army, since she was taller than all the women, and as tall as or taller than most of the men.

Torrna's words were prophetic: the horn was indeed the sound of retreat. The Lerrit soldiers who were able ran as fast as they could northward. No doubt they were returning to the base camp the Lerrit had set up on the other side of the hills that generally demarcated the border between the peninsula and the rest of the mainland.

Raising his own ax into the air, Torrna cried, "Victory is ours! At last, we are free!"

The remaining soldiers under Torrna's command let out a ragged cheer.

Next to him, Kira Nerys did the same.

Chapter Two

The meeting room needed a paint job, but at least it didn't smell like a charnel house anymore, Kira mused. A particularly brutal battle had been fought here when the rebel army took over the capitol building. Even with the tide of war turning, the building was still the most heavily guarded, and the fight to take it was a brutal one with excessive casualties on both sides.

But someone had done their job well enough to make the place habitable, if not aesthetically pleasing. The meeting table had been scrubbed, the chairs repaired, and the floor, walls, and ceiling washed.

Looking around at the assorted happy-but-tired-looking faces in the meeting room, Kira wasn't entirely sure what she was doing here. It was, after all, for the high-ranking members of the rebel army. At best, she was a soldier—hardly what anyone would consider important.

And she didn't want to become important. She'd done enough time-traveling—both voluntary and involuntary—to know the risks.

Flexing her left arm, Kira winced slightly. The wound from the sword had been long, but not deep, and was proving maddeningly slow to heal. Unfortunately, Deep Space 9 and Julian's infirmary wouldn't be built for many millennia, leaving Kira to heal naturally, just like when she was in the resistance. Her tendency to scratch at her wounds and not give her body a chance to heal properly hadn't changed with age. In fact, she remembered a snide comment Shakaar had once made about how symbolic it was that Kira always picked at her scabs....

Kira had met most of the people in the room only once or twice. The ones she'd gotten to know thus far were Torrna and the tiny, short-haired woman who entered the meeting room last: Natlar Ryslin.

"Thank you all for coming," she said as she approached the seat at the head of the table. "Please, everyone, be seated."

It soon became apparent that there were far more people than chairs, by a factor of two to one.

With a small smile, Natlar amended, "Or stand, whichever you prefer."

Soon enough, many were seated around the table, with the rest standing against the wall. Kira was among the latter—Torrna, though, sat in the seat opposite Natlar, at the foot of the table.

Her expression serious, Natlar said, "I hereby call to order the first meeting of the government of the Perikian Republic."

A cheer, much less ragged than the exhausted one Kira had participated in on the battlefield, met that pronouncement. Periki Remarro had first agitated for independence against the oppressive Lerrit regime years earlier. The nation of Lerrit had ruled the peninsula with an iron fist and a hefty tax burden, and, though she was not the first to desire the removal of their yoke, she was the first to say so publicly.

Periki had died soon after she began that agitating, hanged by Lerrit authorities. Her cause had lived on, and was now, finally, victorious.

I always wondered how the Perikian Peninsula got its name, Kira thought with a smile.

As Natlar went into the details of what needed to be done next, Kira found herself tuning out. She had been to plenty of meetings just like this—hell, she'd *led* meetings just like this. But those meetings were far in the future and, paradoxically, in her own subjective past. She saw no reason to involve herself now.

She stared out the window, seeing the people of the capital city—which would no doubt also be renamed at this meeting—rebuilding their homes and places of business. The window faced south, so she could also see the docks and the large port beyond the city—the true heart of the peninsula.

Docked there were several warships, armed with massive cannons, that carried the flag of the nation of Endtree.

Kira turned back to the table just as Natlar was saying, "Admiral Inna, once again, we thank you for all you have done for us."

Inna Murent, a short, stout woman with salt-and-pepper hair severely tied back and braided, nodded her head. Kira noticed that she gripped the edges of the table—no doubt a habit from a life aboard a seafaring vessel where the surface beneath her feet was never steady. "We simply followed the road the Prophets laid out for us," she said.

Kira's eyes automatically went to the admiral's right ear, which was adorned with an earring. Though it was nowhere near as elaborate as those worn by Kira's time, Kira knew that it symbolized devotion to the Prophets—a way of life that had not become as widespread in this era as in hers. Kira wasn't completely sure how far back she had gone, but, based on the clothes and weaponry, it had to be over twenty thousand years in the past. *Which means,* she thought, *the first Orb won't even be found for at least ten thousand years or so.* Still, though no Lerrits she saw wore earrings, a few from the peninsula did, as did most of those from Endtree.

And, of course, Kira, though a believer herself, didn't wear one either, thanks to a decree by a religious authority that did not yet exist.

The admiral's comment elicited a snort from Torrna. "I doubt that the Prophets were the ones who put those cannons on your ships, Admiral."

A chuckle spread around the table.

"Be that as it may," Natlar said before Inna could reply, "I am afraid we have more business with our neighbors in Endtree."

Inna seemed to shudder. "With all due respect, Prefect—" Kira blinked; she had missed Natlar's assumption of that title "—I'd rather leave any other business to the diplomats and politicians. I was happy to aid you in casting out those Lerrit leeches. Their shipping tariffs were an abomination. But whatever further relationship there is to be between our governments, it is not for me to arrange. I would simply like to return home and await new orders."

"I, however, would rather you did not return home just yet." Natlar folded her hands together. "While General Torrna has assembled a fine army, and one that I would pit against any other nation's in the world, we are still vulnerable at sea. Lerrit does have a navy of their own, after all, and the moment we lose the protection offered by your fleet, they will return and take us back with little difficulty."

"Perhaps," Inna said cautiously. Kira knew that tone of voice. The admiral knew that Natlar was absolutely right, but to admit it would mean going along with something she did not want to do.

"I therefore would like to request that Endtree leave a delegation of five ships behind to protect the port."

Torrna slammed his fist on the table. "Prefect, no!"

"Is something wrong, General?" Natlar asked, her tone never changing from the reasonable calm she'd been using all along.

"We've just fought for our independence."

"With our help," Inna added with a small smile.

Sparing the admiral a glance, Torrna said, "For which we thank you, Admiral. But if we allow them to stay here, we become as dependent on them as we were on Lerrit! We'd be exchanging one oppressor for another!"

"My people do not 'oppress,' General," Inna said sharply. "The Prophets—"

"I'm fully aware of your people's religious beliefs, Admiral. They don't change the fact—"

"*Many* worship the Prophets," Natlar said. "It is not a reason to dismiss Endtree as a potential ally."

"I still think—"

"General, can we adequately defend the port with our current forces?"

Torrna grimaced. "Given a few months, we can assemble a fleet that—"

"And until that fleet is assembled?"

Kira winced in sympathy for her friend. She understood all too well the difficulty Torrna was having.

Some things never change, she thought.

Inna was speaking now: "One of my ships is setting out for home with a full report at first light tomorrow. I will include your request, which will be put before the Council."

Nodding, Natlar said, "Thank you, Admiral. General Torrna will serve as your liaison to me—and, should the Council see fit to honor our request, he will continue in that duty."

Torrna stood up. "What!?"

Before Torrna could argue further, a young girl came in. "Excuse me, but three men are here claiming to represent the Bajora."

Kira blinked. *Just when I thought this couldn't get more interesting.*

Natlar barely hesitated. "Send them in." To Kira's ear—well used to the nuances of politicians—the prefect sounded relieved that her argument with Torrna had been interrupted.

For his part, the general sat back down, but glowered at the prefect. Kira knew Torrna well enough to be sure that he would pick up this argument sooner rather than later.

Three men entered. They wore red robes that reminded Kira a bit of those of a vedek in her time, though these were shorter and tighter about the sleeves.

They also wore earrings in their right ears.

"Greetings to you from the Bajora," said the one in the middle, the oldest of the three. "Do we have the pleasure of greeting Natlar Ryslin?"

"I am Prefect Natlar, yes."

All three bowed their heads. "We would like to extend our respects to your provisional government, and—"

Torrna stood up again. "There is nothing 'provisional' about our government! We are the Perikian Republic, and we will be treated with the respect we deserve!"

The envoys looked a bit nonplussed at the general's outburst. *Good,* Kira thought. They seemed a bit too obsequious to her.

"My apologies for my imprecision in speech. Regardless, we do come to you with an offer."

"Really?" Torrna said with a laugh. "The battle has been won less than three days, and already the Bajora have sent their envoys. Were you flown here by *remla* bird with this offer?"

"General, please," Natlar said in her usual calm tone, but it was enough to induce Torrna to take his seat. The prefect then turned back to the envoys. "General Torrna's point is well taken. You cannot have received word of our victory and composed any offer in so short a time."

The envoy smiled a small smile. Kira noted that the envoy had yet to provide a name for himself or his two aides. "You are correct. We have been in the city for several weeks now, awaiting the outcome of your war. If you were victorious, as our intelligence reports indicated you likely would be, then we were prepared to offer you entry into the Bajora. If you lost, then we would simply return and await a more felicitous time to add this region to the glory of the Prophets."

"The Prophets?!" Torrna's voice was like a sonic boom. "You wish to make us part of your theocracy?"

In a snippy tone that Kira recognized from certain vedeks back in her time, the envoy said, "We are not a theocracy, sir. The Bajora is a democratic government of the people of this world. Our goal is to unite the planet once and for all."

"Really?" Torrna's tone was dubious.

"For too long," the envoy said, and now he was addressing the entire room, not just Torrna or Natlar, "we have squabbled and bickered in conflicts much like the one you just finished."

"That was hardly a 'squabble,'" Torrna said angrily.

"True," the envoy said, sparing the general a glance, "many lives were lost. And they need not have been, for if we were a united world, there would *be* no such conflicts. Sister need not fight against sister, blood need not be spilled recklessly—we would all be free to follow our *pagh* without worrying about who rules us or who we will fight tomorrow." He turned to Natlar. "I urge you, Prefect, to consider our offer. The Bajora can only bring benefit to you in these difficult times. You would have the service of our navy to guard your port, you would have the benefit of our assistance in repairing your soil—"

"And all we'd have to do in return is worship your Prophets, yes?" Torrna said. "A small price to pay, I'm sure."

The envoy turned to the rest of those gathered. "And does this man speak for you all? Will you let one man stand between you and progress?"

Natlar suppressed a smile. "General Torrna does not speak for us all—he simply speaks loudest." A small chuckle passed around the table at that—though Torrna looked even angrier at the barb, and Kira couldn't blame him.

"The point is," the envoy continued, "you have been weakened by this conflict. True, the Lerrit have as well, but they have greater resources. The Bajora, however, have even greater resources still, and we're expanding. It is only a matter of time before we have united the entire planet—we urge you to aid in that process."

The envoy went on for quite some time, outlining in more detail what joining the Bajora would involve. Kira found her attention wandering. It reminded her a bit too much of the meetings with Federation dignitaries when they carried on about the joys of joining them.

Another parallel . . .

Finally, Natlar said, "You have given us much to think about." She signaled to one of the guards who was standing at the door, who sent the young girl in. "We do not have the finest accommodations, but Prilla will show you to a chamber where you may refresh yourselves while we discuss your proposal."

Prilla came in as the envoy nodded. "We thank you for your hospitality and your indulgence, Prefect." Then he and his two aides followed Prilla out of the conference room.

Silence descended upon the room for several seconds, before Torrna's booming voice, predictably, broke it. "You can't *possibly* be considering their request, can you?"

Natlar sighed. "Of course I am *considering* it, General. I would be a fool not to."

Torrna slammed a fist down on the table. "No, what would be foolish would be to accept their offer! We'd be trading one oppressor for another!"

One of the other people at the table, an older man, said, "You keep saying that, Antosso. What, you're saying the Bajora, Lerrit, and Endtree are all the same?"

"That's *exactly* what I'm saying."

"Then you're even more naïve than I thought."

Again, Torrna slammed his fist on the table. Kira half expected to see a dent in the wood at this point. "*I'm* naïve? *I* have been fighting for our lives out there, Morlek! Don't you *dare* tell me—"

"No one is doubting your accomplishments," Morlek said, "but the truth is—"

"The truth is, *we are free!*" Torrna looked at each person at the table as he spoke. "But we are not going to remain free if we just let someone else do exactly what Lerrit did! So many have died so that we could shape our own destiny—*not* so we can let someone else do the same thing. No matter who it is—Bajora, Lerrit, Endtree—we cannot let *anyone* direct our paths!" He turned back to Morlek. "You're right, Morlek. Lerrit, Endtree, and the Bajora are *not* the same. But from our perspective, they are all outsiders, and *that* is what concerns me—and should concern all of us. If we are simply going to allow ourselves to be subsumed by the next power that comes along, then I have to wonder what, precisely, we have been fighting for all this time."

Torrna strode purposefully toward the exit. "I will abide by whatever you decide in this room, Prefect," he said as he walked, "but I will not sit here and listen to any more foolish ramblings. Just remember this one thing." He stopped and gave the table one final glance. "Periki Remarro did not die so we could become part of the Bajora. Or part of Endtree. She died so we could be *free*. If we are to name ourselves for her, then we should *never* forget what she stood for."

And with that, he left.

Chapter Three

Kira found Torrna two hours later in his quarters. He was sitting on the windowsill, staring out the window at the port. Kira noticed that his quarters were clean, which was a first. *Guess that's how he spent the last two hours,* she thought with amusement.

"You want the good news or the bad news?" Kira asked as she entered.

Torrna didn't even look at her. "I find it impossible to believe that there is good news."

"Well, there is. Natlar rejected the Bajoran offer."

Shaking his head, Torrna said, "Amazing. I wouldn't have given them credit for thinking that clearly."

"Why not?" Kira asked angrily. "You think you're the only one who was fighting out there?"

Torrna sighed. "I sometimes wonder." He shook his head. "No, of course, you're right, *Ashla.* I simply don't want to see everything I—*we* fought for ruined by shortsightedness."

"Give Natlar a *little* credit, Antosso. She's not about to throw everything out the window."

"I suppose not."

Kira wasn't finished. She moved closer to Torrna and went on: "But give the Bajora some credit, too. What they're trying to do is important. I know you don't believe in the Prophets, but what they're doing is bringing—bringing the world together." She had almost said, "bringing Bajor together," but that word would not be applied to the planet as a whole until after the Bajora succeeded in uniting it many years hence. "Don't let a little bit of agnosticism blind you to that."

Chuckling, Torrna said, "'A little bit of agnosticism.' What a wonderful way of phrasing it. I may not be the most spiritual person in the world, *Ashla,* but—" He hesitated. "Perhaps you're right. But even if I thought the Bajora were the most wonderful people in the world, I wouldn't want to become part of them. Someday, maybe, but not today. Not after all we've fought for."

Kira put a soothing hand on Torrna's shoulder. "I know, Antosso. *Believe* me, I know. But you can't blind yourself to a good thing just because *you* don't like it."

"I know that." He smiled. "Well, at least, I sometimes know that."

Taking in the newly cleaned room with a gesture, Kira asked, "That why you had the cleaning frenzy?"

Torrna laughed. "It was either that or punch through the walls—and I do have to live here."

Wincing, Kira said, "Well, actually, no, you don't. That's the bad news—the prefect wants you to relocate to the port and set up your office there to serve as liaison to the Endtree fleet."

It took only a second for Torrna's face to go from amused contriteness to vicious fury. "An *office*? Inna hasn't even asked her government's permission yet, but Natlar wants me to set up an *office*?"

"She's hoping for the best," Kira said with a shrug. "Besides, after your performance today, I think she wants to keep you far away from the capitol building."

"Yes," he said bitterly, "to keep my voice from being heard."

Kira smiled. "Antosso, even from the port, *your* voice is going to be heard."

Torrna whirled on her, then let out a long, hissing breath that sounded like a deflating balloon—apt, since the crack seemed to deflate his anger. "How do you do that, *Ashla?*"

"Do what?"

"All of this."

"I haven't done anything, Antosso."

"You may not think so, but you have been a most valued right hand. And one I am reluctant to lose. If I am to be exiled to Natlar Port—"

"What?"

He smiled. "The resolution to pass the name change has been postponed until the prefect isn't in the room, since she'd never let it come to a vote otherwise. In any case, if that is where I am to be sent, I want you by my side. To guard my back and to keep me from making a complete ass of myself."

Kira hesitated. "Can I think about it?"

"Of course. Let me know tomorrow. It will take me that long to pack up my own belongings and inform Lyyra and the boys that we'll be moving."

"Moving where?" came a voice from the doorway.

Kira turned to see a large, stout woman with a mane of red hair to match Torrna's own standing in the doorway to Torrna's quarters. She had met the general's wife only once, but she was probably the only person who could stand up to Torrna and not be killed for their trouble.

"I am to be the new liaison with the Endtree fleet that will be occupying the port."

"Good. The change in climate will do some good. The humidity opens your pores, you know." She turned to Kira. "How are you, Nerys? Is the arm healing well?"

Lyyra was an apothecary, and the first time Kira had met her was when she'd given her a remedy to help heal her arm faster.

"Well enough," she said neutrally. *I'd kill for a dermal regenerator, but this'll do.*

"I still want to know what you've done to keep your teeth so perfect."

"Nothing special." Not wanting to pursue this line of questioning, she said, "I need to get going—and think about your offer. I'll talk to you tomorrow. Good to see you, Lyyra."

Chapter Four

Kira Nerys lay on the bunk in the barracks that she shared with a dozen other soldiers. It had been surprisingly easy to readjust to sleeping in uncomfortable beds or no beds at all. Since arriving here—

Whenever that was . . .

—she had either slept on cold ground or on uncomfortable beds, either way crammed into a too-small space with dozens of other soldiers.

Just like the good old days, millennia from now.

Kira's memories of arriving in Bajor's past were hazy. She often didn't bother trying to think about it, simply accepting what her senses told her as reality.

Tonight, facing the end of the conflict that had raged since she arrived here—

However that happened . . .

—and the start of something new, she once again cast her mind back to see how she should proceed forward.

The last thing she remembered with any clarity was that arid desert planet in the Delta Quadrant.

Everywhere she looked on the ground was sand, broken very rarely by bits of plant life, and the one freshwater lake that she had made sure to land near. It was flat land, with the only variations being the curvature of the planet itself. Not even any hills or mountains or sand dunes in sight.

She'd gone there and abandoned her runabout in order to block a gateway, a portal in space through which deadly theta radiation was flowing into orbit around the inhabited planet of Europa Nova, in the Alpha Quadrant. Kira's actions had prevented one lethal piece of radioactive waste from going through the gateway, thus saving the lives of the Europani as well as the task force she herself had assembled to evacuate the planet.

But to do that, she'd also had to abandon her companion, the Jem'Hadar named Taran'atar, who had stayed behind to fight a Hirogen hunter, keeping him occupied while Kira blocked the gateway.

After that, she couldn't recall what happened. She knew that she found a gateway on the planet where there had been none before. She knew that the theta radiation on the planet had grown to fatal levels.

And she knew that she was now many thousands of years in Bajor's past, fighting in a rebellion that the history of her time had long forgotten. She wasn't even sure how long it had been since she'd arrived in this time. All she was sure of was that she no longer had the radiation sickness she'd been afflicted with—

—and the Prophets had something to do with her sojourn to the past.

Maybe.

The gateways weren't built by the Prophets, after all, but the Iconians—in fact, there weren't any gateways within ten light-years of the Celestial Temple.

Based on the reports she'd read en route to Europa Nova, the gateways had not only come in all shapes and sizes, but types. Some even seemed to work interdimensionally—so it was quite possible that they could move through time as well.

(Of course, the Orb of Time had that capability, too, as Kira knew from more than one firsthand experience . . .)

Still, she hadn't questioned her odyssey, simply because it felt right. Once before, during the Reckoning, she had served as a vessel for the Prophets. That same feeling she'd had then, she had now.

Well, okay, she thought wryly, *it's not exactly the same—then I couldn't even control my own actions. But I can't shake the feeling that They're the reason I'm here, somehow.*

She lay awake on her pallet, listening to the sounds of the other slumbering soldiers. Some snored, some mumbled in their sleep, some simply breathed heavy. Until the Cardassians pulled out of Bajor, Kira Nerys had always slept in large groups of people, so tuning out the sounds came easily to her. In fact, when she'd first been assigned to Deep Space 9, one of the hardest things had been learning to sleep in a room by herself.

But sleep eluded her, not because of the noise, but because she wrestled with her conscience. Fighting with the rebels had been an easy choice. Agreeing to accompany Torrna to his new duties at the Natlar Port was somewhat less so.

On the one hand, she was concerned about altering the past. On the other, very little was known about the history of this region.

If the Prophets had sent her here—and she felt at the core of her *pagh* that they were involved *somehow*—then they'd done it for a reason. She needed to continue down the path that was set before her.

Dying didn't concern her. She had accepted the reality of her own death in the Delta Quadrant. As far as she was concerned, any living she did from this point forward was a gift. That was why she had no compunction about fighting alongside Torrna with weapons far more primitive and, in their own way, more brutal than any she used in the resistance.

Besides, she thought, *I have to believe that I'm here for a reason. There are far too many similarities to my own life for this to be a coincidence.*

She resolved to accept Torrna's offer first thing in the morning.

Within minutes of making that resolution, she fell into a deep, peaceful slumber, unbothered by the breathing and snoring around her.

Chapter Five

"Look, Torrna's *not* going to bite your head off if you take this complaint, to him."

"Are you *sure?*" The merchant looked dubious. More than that, he looked scared to death. "I've heard about how he drove off the Lerrit Army by breathing fire into their camp and setting them alight!"

Kira tried not to laugh, but she did at least keep an encouraging smile on her face. "I can assure you that his days of breathing fire are long in the past. Just go to him and tell him that you object to the inspections. I can't guarantee that he'll do what you ask, but he *will* listen. Just give him a chance."

The dubiousness did not leave the merchant's face. "If you say so."

"I say so. He should be back in the next day or two, and I'll make sure you get to see him, all right?"

"Fine. Thank you, ma'am."

Nodding, Kira excused herself from the merchant, leaving his quarters and going out onto the deck of the docked merchant trawler. It never failed to amuse her, this fear that people had of Torrna. Mainly because she knew that his bluster was worse than his bite.

She also had to wonder, though, if this was what people thought of her after the Cardassian withdrawal. Did people fear that she would breathe fire? Was that why she had been sent to Deep Space 9? After all, she'd been assigned as first officer and Bajoran liaison before the discovery of the wormhole turned the station into a major port of call. She'd never had any illusions that it had been done to get her out of the way of the provisional government, who found her intemperate ways to be too much for them to handle—at least nearby. So they sent her into orbit.

Natlar had all but done the same to Torrna. The disruptive influence he could have in the council chambers—as evidenced by the way he all but took over the meeting shortly after the Lerrit Army's final retreat—was probably seen by the prefect as an impediment to actually getting anything done.

Kira walked down the gangplank of the merchant's ship to the marina and took a deep breath of the sea air. She'd lost track of how long she'd been serving as Torrna's adjutant at the Natlar Port, but she'd been enjoying it immensely—particularly now that the weather was warmer, the sun was shining, the Korvale Ocean was a clear green, and a lovely breeze was pretty much her constant companion every time she walked outside. She hadn't spent much time near the sea prior to this, and when she did, it was during her days in the resistance. She had other things on her mind, then.

She nodded to the assorted dockworkers who passed her by, then whirled around when someone cried, "Look!"

The Perikian Peninsula jutted out into the Korvale Ocean along the southern end of the coast of the continent. Any ship that came down the coastline from the west would have to, in essence, come around a corner and therefore would not come into sight from the marina until it was almost ready to dock.

Right now, one of the largest and most impressive ships that could be found on the planet was coming into view around that bend. It stood at ten meters above the surface of the ocean, with the green-and-black flag of Endtree whipping in the breeze from the mast.

Kira peered more closely and noticed that there was a second flag under it: the flag of the Perikian Republic. *Interesting,* Kira thought. *That wasn't there when they left.*

The ship was Admiral Inna's flagship, the *Haeys,* returning a day early from their investigation of the reports of pirate activity.

Several people on the marina stopped what they were doing to see the flagship approach the dock. As it settled into port, a cheer started to break out, which spread all the way across the marina. Kira found herself joining in the cheer—and she wondered how much of it was general goodwill toward Admiral Inna's fleet and how much was the new presence of the Perikian flag.

Within half an hour, Inna and Torrna had extricated themselves from the admiring crowd. Kira noted that they had been chatting amiably as they approached the gangplank before they were set upon by the admirers. *Quite a switch,* she thought, *from all the sniping they've been doing.* The admiral went off to consult with the captains of the other fleet ships in dock, and Torrna walked with Kira back toward their office in the rear of the marina.

"So what happened?" Kira asked.

"We found the pirates and took care of them in fairly short order. They didn't have anything to match Murent's cannon."

Smiling, Kira said, " 'Murent'? That's new."

"I beg your pardon," Torrna said, a little indignantly.

As they approached the office, nodding to the sergeant at the desk, Kira said, "It wasn't that long ago that the only way you referred to her was as 'the admiral' or 'that damned woman.' "

To Kira's surprise, Torrna actually blushed, his skin turning the color of his hair and beard. "I suppose so. But she showed me something on this trip that I didn't expect. She was efficient yet merciful with the pirates, she was very effective in questioning the pirate leader without being unnecessarily brutal, and she agreed to fly the Perikian flag."

"I was going to ask you about that."

They entered Torrna's tiny office. The general sat behind his rickety wooden desk, which was cluttered with assorted pieces of paper that required his attention. Torrna ignored them and instead poured himself a drink from the small bar that sat under the window looking out onto the mainland. Torrna had specifically requested a north-facing office so he could look out on, in his words, "the republic that I fought for, not the ocean that is controlled by someone else."

He offered Kira a drink, which she declined. *They liked their drinks a little less smooth in the old days,* she had thought after the first drink she had shared with Torrna, and she made it a point to avoid the stuff when possible.

"It took surprisingly little argument," he said as he sat down. "I pointed out that her fleet was there at the invitation of the Perikian government and was there to protect Perikian interests, so it made sense that they should fly our colors. Not that she gave in completely, of course . . ."

"Let me guess, you wanted the Perikian flag on top?"

Kira had spoken with a modicum of facetiousness, but Torrna leaned forward and said gravely, "These are *our* waters, *Ashla.* We must never forget that."

"I haven't," she said with equal seriousness.

She also noted that she'd said "the Perikian flag," not "our flag." Perhaps a minor point, but, even though she had fought for the republic's independence, even though she now worked for Torrna, she still couldn't bring herself to think of this as home. She knew this was the right place for her to be, but in the back of her mind was the constant feeling that this was not her new home, that she was only visiting. It made no sense to Kira on the face of it, and she wasn't sure what to think of these feelings.

Deciding not to dwell on it, she leaned back in her chair. "So what did the pirate leader say when Inna questioned her so efficiently?"

Taking a sip of his drink, Torrna said, "Actually, the most interesting intelligence we received wasn't from the pirates, but from their slaves. The most recent conscripts they picked up were refugees from a disaster in the fire caves."

Kira blinked. "What?"

"Apparently the entrance to the fire caves collapsed—and completely destroyed Yvrig." Yvrig was a city on another peninsula west of Perikia but on the same continent; it, too, had a thriving port.

Torrna snorted as he continued. "Some of the slaves claimed there was some kind of blue fire when the caves collapsed, but I don't put much stock in that."

Kosst Amojan imprisoned . . . the Pah-wraiths banished to the fire caves . . . Shabren's Fifth Prophecy . . . the Emissary going to the fire caves to stop the Pah-wraiths from being freed . . .

Kira knew exactly what had happened, remembering her experience channeling the Prophets during the Reckoning, and now knew precisely *when* she was. Some thirty thousand years before she was born, the Prophets banished the Pah-wraiths to the caves, sealing them in there forever. Only their leader, Kosst Amojan, was imprisoned elsewhere, on a site that would one day be the city of B'hala. The others remained in the fire caves, until Winn Adami and Skrain Dukat attempted to free them only a few months ago, subjective time. Only the sacrifice of the Emissary—Benjamin Sisko—had thwarted the scheme.

Or, rather, will thwart it. I hate time travel. We need new tenses . . .

Until now, though, it never occurred to Kira that the Prophets' actions at the caves might have had harmful consequences for the people near the site.

"We've got to help those people. There may be—"

"Sit down, *Ashla*," Torrna said, which was when Kira realized that she'd stood up. As she sat back down, Torrna continued. "This happened over two weeks ago. There's very little we can do."

Right. Of course. There is no instant communication here. Kira nodded in acknowledgment.

"However, this does mean that we're going to see a significant increase in traffic in the port. Without Yvrig, we're the only viable port on the southern part of the continent."

Kira nodded. "Traffic's going to increase."

"That's an understatement." Torrna broke into a grin.

Yet another parallel, she thought. The discovery of the wormhole transformed Deep Space 9 from a minor outpost to a major port of call. This wasn't quite on the same scale as that, but Kira did remember one important thing from those early days on DS9.

Torrna continued speaking. "We'll need to work on expanding the marina to be able to accommodate more ships. Maybe now Marta won't close her tavern down the way she's been threatening to. For that matter, we'll probably need a new inn. Plus—"

"We'll need more ships from Endtree—or we'll have to start building some of our own."

Frowning, Torrna said, "What for? I mean, we'll need more people for the Dock Patrol, obviously—the number of drunken louts on the docks will increase dramatically—but I don't think we'll need—"

"We're going to need more ships to hold off the pirates—and the Lerrit Navy."

Torrna snorted again. "The Lerrit Navy is barely worth giving the title."

"Don't be so sure of that. We just got another report from Moloki." Moloki was one of the spies that the Perikian Free Army had observing the goings-on in Lerrit. In fact, the PFA had many such operatives, more than even Torrna or Kira knew definitively about. "He says that they've employed shipbuilders from Jerad Province to completely rebuild their navy from scratch. Within the year, they may well be a legitimate naval power—or at least legitimate enough for us to worry about. And with this change in the geography, they're going to be more interested in taking us back, not less."

Torrna frowned. "Isn't Jerad part of the Bajora?"

Kira nodded.

He shook his head. "Wonderful. We don't join their little theocracy, so they help Lerrit take us back."

"You can't blame them for taking on a lucrative contract like that," Kira said, trying not to examine how much that sounded like Quark.

"I can damn well blame them for anything I want!" Torrna stood up and drained his drink. "Damn it all, I was actually enjoying the good news."

"I'm sorry, but—"

Torrna waved her off. "No, that's all right. That's why I keep you around,

Ashla. You have the knack for dragging me back to reality when I need it most." He turned to stare at the view from his window. "There is a great deal of work that will need to be done."

Kira got up and walked to Torrna. "Then we'd better get up off our butts and do it, shouldn't we?"

"Definitely." Torrna smiled. "What else did Moloki have to report?"

"Nothing different from his last few. The official word is that the Queen is dying, but she keeps showing up at official functions. She hardly ever says anything, but she's there and smiling a lot. Moloki seems to think that Prince Avtra is doing all the real work."

Shaking his head, Torrna said, "That woman will *never* die. You know, she swore that she would live long enough to see the peninsula brought back under her rule. She's probably the one who contracted the Jeradians to build her a navy so she could fulfill that promise. I daresay she's clinging to life solely for that reason."

"Maybe." She hesitated. "I'm glad you and the admiral are getting along better."

"Yes, well, her tiresome insistence on giving those silly Prophets of hers all the credit for her work aside, she's quite a brilliant tactician." They both sat back down in their seats after Torrna poured himself another drink. "She was able to deal with those pirates with a minimum of fuss. You should have seen . . ."

He went on at some length, describing how she stopped the pirates, and her ideas for curtailing some of their activities in the future. Kira smiled and nodded, but naval battles were not an area of great interest to her—her tactical instincts for vehicular combat of that sort tended to be more three-dimensional.

She was just glad that Torrna and Inna were getting along. She had a feeling that that would be vital in the long run . . .

Chapter Six

The worst thing about the dungeon was the smell.

True, Kira had spent most of her formative years living in the caves of Da-khur Hills and other less-than-hospitable places. But even though she had been roughing it by the standards of her culture, it was still a world that had replicators, directed energy weapons, faster-than-light travel, near-instant communication over interstellar distances, and other luxuries that Kira had al-ways taken for granted. Such a world did not include a dungeon that smelled of dried blood, infected wounds, and the feces of assorted vermin.

She looked over at Torrna, sitting in the corner of the cell. The wound on his left arm was growing worse. If it wasn't treated soon, the gangrene would probably kill him.

Just hope our capture did some good, she thought.

Kira had no idea how long the war with Lerrit had been going on. At this point, she couldn't even say for sure how long it had taken the retreating troops to bring Kira and Torrna to Lerrit's capital city and the dungeon where they'd been languishing. On the one hand, in a world where communication and transportation was so slow, the pace of life was much slower than Kira was used to—on the other, it seemed like the rebellion had only just ended before this new war with Lerrit had begun.

Kira had been fearing this very thing since the collapse of the fire caves meant more business for the Natlar Port. The port had indeed thrived, giving the Perikian economy the shot in the arm it so desperately needed in order to truly start building itself into a legitimate power in the region, instead of an insignificant nation lucky enough to have a nice piece of real estate.

What she had not expected was the sheer strength of the Lerrit Army. The same army that Kira had helped repel had doubled its numbers and was much better armed. The navy was giving the Endtree ships a run for their money—and the war had been declared on both Perikia *and* Endtree, so there was also fighting in Endtree's territory, both on land and sea.

Still, they had won a major battle at Barlin Field, driving the army com-pletely out of the Makar Province.

All it had cost them was their best field general.

The door to the dungeon opened, and Kira winced. The place had no route of escape (Kira had spent the first six hours in the cell scouring every millimeter for just such a thing), and only one window, which was fifteen meters above them—just enough to provide a glimmer of light and hope for escape without any chance of that hope being fulfilled. A (very small) part of Kira admired the tactical psychology that went into the dungeon's design.

The flickering torchlight from the hallway, however, was far brighter than the meager illumination provided by the faraway window, so it took several seconds for Kira's eyes to adjust. When they did, she was confronted with the guard who brought them their food and waste buckets (not replacing them nearly often enough to suit Kira). The guard wore the usual Lerrit uniform of gray and blue, with the addition of a shabby black cloak that probably served to keep the stink and filth of the dungeon off the guard's uniform. Standing next to him was a very short man dressed in a white jacket and white pants, both with shiny gold fastenings, and a white cape that served the same function as the guard's cloak—and, being white, was more noticeably the worse for doing so.

Kira recognized him, barely, from the coins that sometimes changed hands on the docks: this was Prince Syba Avtra of Lerrit.

"You look better on your coins, Your Highness," Kira said.

The prince looked up at her. "Very droll."

Then he glanced at the guard, who rewarded Kira's comment with a slap to the face. All Kira could think was, *I've known some Cardassians in my time who would eat you for lunch.* She gave the guard a contemptuous look in reply.

Avtra, meanwhile, had moved on to Torrna. "You will rise in the presence of royalty, General."

Torrna looked up at Avtra with the one eye that wasn't swollen shut. "As soon as I'm in the presence of some, I'll consider it."

Again Avtra gave the guard a glance. Since Torrna was seated, the guard elected to kick the general in the stomach rather than bend over to slap him.

After coughing for several seconds, Torrna said, "I'm disappointed. I was hoping that Her Royal Highness herself would come to gloat over our capture. It is, after all, the only true victory you have won in this war."

The prince laughed heartily at that.

"Something amuses you?" Torrna asked the question with contempt and with a few more coughs, diluting the effect of the former.

"My 'dear' mother has been dead for some time, fool! Do you truly think *she* engineered this war? Or our alliance with the Bajora?"

This time Kira felt like she'd been kicked in the stomach, though the guard had made no move toward her. *The Bajora? No* wonder *they're so well armed!*

"I can see by the look on your face that you appreciate the position you're in, General. With the Bajora behind us, we will destroy Endtree, squash you upstart rebels, and finally control the entire southern coast." He moved toward Torrna, looking down on the general's dirty, bruised, swollen face with a sneer on his own clean visage. "Now I don't suppose you'll tell me what the troop movements are for your little band of spear carriers?"

"If I thought you were worth wasting the spit, I'd spit on you right now," Torrna said. His voice was more subdued than usual—not surprising after the ordeal they'd been through—but the tone was abundantly clear.

"I assumed as much. Besides, I can't imagine that even your soldiers are so stupid as to retain the same battle plan after one of their generals has been captured. Still, I had to ask. And I wanted to see the infamous General Torrna in our dungeon for myself. You will be publicly executed at dawn tomorrow. It was going to be yesterday, but the demand for tickets is simply outrageous, and we had to postpone so we could put in extra seating in the stadium."

Kira wondered if that was the same stadium that had been unearthed in this region during the occupation. After the Cardassian withdrawal, Bajoran archaeologists had speculated that sporting events had been held there as long as fifty thousand years prior to its rediscovery. That it was used for public executions was a fact of which Kira could happily have remained ignorant.

Avtra finally turned back to Kira. "As for this one—I suppose we should let Torrna have one final night of companionship before we take her to the front lines. She'll make fine arrow fodder."

With that, he turned and left, saying, "Enough of this. I need to get the stink of this dungeon off my person."

The guard closed the door, leaving Kira wishing she could get the stink of the prince off herself as easily.

"We have to get out of here," Torrna said.

Kira snorted. "I'm open to suggestions. The only ones who have free rein in and out of this cell are insects and rodents."

Torrna tried to stand up, but made the mistake of bracing himself with his left arm, and he collapsed to the floor.

Kira moved to help him up, but he waved her off. "I'm fine. Just forgot about the damn wound. Stupid arm's gone numb." He staggered to his feet. "Damn those foul Bajora—I hope those Prophets of theirs strike them down with lightning."

The Prophets don't work like that, Kira thought, but refrained from saying it aloud.

"We *have* to—argh! I'm fine," he added quickly, again brushing off Kira's offer of help. "We have to get this intelligence back to the prefect and to Inna. If the Queen is dead, and the Bajora are helping . . . You were right, the fire caves' collapse definitely made our land more attractive."

"I don't think that matters as much as we thought. From the way that kid was talking, he's been wanting to start a war with us for years, but his mother's been holding him back. The collapse of the caves probably made it easier for him to justify it, but I'm willing to bet that we'd have had a war on our hands as soon as the Queen died no matter what."

Torrna nodded, and Kira could see him wincing in the dim light. *He's more hurt than he'll admit, and the stubborn bastard won't let me help him.*

"We've got to find *some* way out of here! If we can get back, tell them about this, we can change our strategy, try to hit the supply lines the Bajora are using. . . ."

Sure, no problem. I'll just tap my combadge, order the runabout to lock in on our signal, and then we'll beam out of here. Then we can transmit a subspace message with our intel. That'll work . . .

The door opened suddenly again. A guard—a different one—came in with two buckets.

Then he closed the door. *What the hell—?* The guards *never* closed the door.

The guard dropped the buckets, then reached into his cloak and pulled out a set of keys. "C'mon, c'mon, we haven't got much time. Take these, take these."

"Who the hell're you?" Torrna asked.

"Right, right, the password." The guard then uttered a phrase in Old High Bajoran that Kira only recognized two words of.

Torrna's eyes went wide. "Moloki?"

"In the very frightened flesh, yes."

"We thought you dead."

"I probably will be after this stunt, *believe* me. Don't know *what* I was thinking coming up with this ludicrous plan. They'll use my guts for building material, they will."

Kira took the keys from Moloki. "What happened to you?"

"Nothing happened *as such.* I simply couldn't get any messages out. The moment Her Royal Senility dropped dead, all hell broke loose. Truly, a spy can no longer make anything like an honest living in this environment."

"Can you get us—" Torrna started.

"*Yes,* yes, I can get you out of here, just give me a moment to collect myself. I've never been much for impersonations, and I had to pull off being one of those imbecile guards that the prince likes to employ. Stomping 'round all day, bellowing at the tops of their lungs so loud you can't *think.*" He shuddered. "No style at all, more's the pity." He reached into his cloak. "In any case, here's a map that'll show you how to get out of here once I bring you to the surface, as well as a map that shows the supply lines the Bajora are using. Assuming you get home alive, that should be fairly useful." He put his hand on Torrna's shoulder. "Let me make something abundantly clear, General—it will *not* be easy to get home. It will involve going through a swamp and then across a mountain range. Deviate even slightly from the route I've mapped out, and you're guaranteed to be captured."

"And if we stay on the route?" Kira asked.

"Then you're just *likely* to be captured."

"I was afraid of that," Torrna muttered.

Kira looked at Torrna and winced. "He's not going to make it with his arm in the shape it's in."

"He has to, dammit!" Moloki said sharply, in marked contrast to his more affable tone. Then he composed himself. "Listen to me, and listen very carefully, because I'm only going to say this once. Years ago, I offered to help Periki Remarro in whatever way was necessary—not because I have any great love for that silly peninsula of yours, but because I want to see Lerrit great again. That isn't going to happen as long as those inbred mutants are in power."

"So you've been working to undermine them from within?" Kira said.

"Something like that, yes. It's been a bit of a chore, but I thought the end was near. Avtra is sterile, you see, and so can't produce any heirs. I had hopes that the Syba dynasty would *finally* end its pathetic chokehold over my home." He sighed. "This ridiculous alliance with the Bajora changes all *that,* of course. The Bajora know damn well that Prince Idiot is the last of his moronic line, and they plan to use this alliance to gain a toehold so they can take over once the Crown Imbecile dies." Moloki unsheathed the sword he had in a belt sheath. "You'll need this more than I will."

Kira took it and hefted it. It was a pretty standard design, average balance, nothing spectacular. *But it beats being unarmed.*

She looked at Torrna, who was now sweating rather more than was warranted by the temperature in the chilly, rank dungeon. "You okay?"

"No," Torrna said honestly, "but it doesn't matter. Moloki is right, we *must* return with this news or everything we've fought for will be lost!"

Chuckling, Moloki said, "You're as much of a crazed zealot as I suspected, General." He held up a hand to cut off Kira's protest. "I meant it as a compliment, my dear, believe me. I can say that as the craziest of crazed zealots. Now come, let us go over this map quickly before someone decides to check up on us . . ."

Chapter Seven

In over thirty-three years of life, Kira Nerys had been sure many times that she was going to die.

Thus far, she'd been glad to have been wrong each time, but as she crouched in the half-meter of snow, sweat pouring from her brow even as she shivered uncontrollably, checking to see if anyone was coming up behind them, she was starting to wish she would die, just so her present hell would end.

First they had spent two days trudging through a swamp. She had done what she could to keep Torrna's arm from getting worse, but it was an uphill battle, and she was no medic. Plus, they had no food—Kira had many skills, but foraging had never been one of her best. They'd scavenged a few animals here and there, but most weren't anything larger than a *paluku*.

Resistance had been less than expected, but as Moloki had explained, the castle itself was not very well guarded. Support from the Bajora notwithstanding, in order to fight, in essence, a three-front war—on the ground against both Periki and Endtree, on the sea against their combined navies—the prince had limited resources to keep an eye on things at home. Kira and her newly acquired sword had been able to take care of the few guards they had seen with little difficulty.

Then they'd gotten to the mountains.

From humidity and high temperatures to snow and frigidity. From her old wound feeling just fine to her arm stiffening up from the cold. And now, quite possibly, coming down with pneumonia.

If Julian were here, he'd give me a shot of something, and I'd be fine. Of course, I'd have to listen to a lecture about not taking better care of myself.

She shook her head. That part of her life was over now. She was here, and she had a duty to perform. The Prophets sent her here for a reason.

Right. To die on a mountain with a blowhard general who got himself captured, and was only able to escape imprisonment thanks to a spy. Makes perfect sense.

Sighing, Kira satisfied herself that they still weren't being pursued, despite the five corpses they had left behind in the castle and the obvious trail they had made through the swamp. She got up, hugged herself with her arms (wincing in pain from the wound), and, shivering all the way, went back to the small inlet where she'd left Torrna.

"Dammit!" she yelled when she saw that Torrna had fallen asleep. He'd been fading in and out for quite some time. Kira's medical knowledge was limited, but even she knew that going into shock would be deadly.

She slapped his face a few times. "Torrna. Torrna! Dammit, Antosso, *wake up!*"

He blinked a few times. *"Ash—Ashla?"* he said in as weak a voice as she'd ever heard him use.

"Yes, it's me," she said, plastering an encouraging smile to her face, hoping her teeth weren't chattering too obviously. "We're still not being followed. And we've only got a few more kilometers to go. Think you're up to it?"

He nodded. "I think so. I just—*arrrrrgh!*"

Torrna had started to rise, then collapsed back to the snow-covered ground. "Sorry," he said through clenched teeth. "Keep forgetting that the arm doesn't really work."

"Let me take a look at it," Kira said, moving as if to pull back his cloak—stolen off one of the guards they'd killed on the way out.

With his good arm, Torrna grabbed Kira's wrist. "No!" He took a breath. "I'm sorry, *Ashla,* but you fussing over it isn't going to change the fact that it feels like someone's driven a flaming hot poker through my shoulder."

"Once we get back home—"

"It'll be too late, then. *Ashla*—I need you to cut the damned thing off."

Kira laughed derisively. "Antosso, I'm not a surgeon. And I don't have anything to stanch the bleeding or cauterize the wound with. If I cut your arm off now, you'll bleed to death." *Not to mention that I'm shivering so much that I'll probably cut off your head by mistake . . .*

"And if you don't, I'll die from the infection. You yourself said that was a risk."

"A risk means the possibility of success. If I just hack your arm off right now with no alcohol, no bandages, no cauterizing agent—"

"All right! You've made your point." Smiling grimly, Torrna added, "I suppose this means I'll just have to make it back to Perikia, then."

Kira just nodded, and helped him to his feet.

They trudged their way through the snow-covered region, climbing over outcroppings, under crevices, and through chest-high snowdrifts.

She didn't know how long it was before she drained the water supply. Or, for that matter, when the blisters started breaking out all over her skin. She didn't have the wherewithal to check her tricorder to see how bad the radiation was. Every fiber of her being was focused on the overwhelming task of putting one foot in front of the other.

How long ago was it that she had been trudging through the hot, arid wasteland of that theta-radiation-racked planet in the Delta Quadrant? Days? Months? Years? Now she was engaged in the same mindless task, staying focused solely on moving forward, ever forward, in the hopes of reaching her goal. Then it was to reach a gateway. Now it was to make it back to Perikia.

Of course, the gateway took her to Perikia. *Is there some kind of symbolism here?*

Or maybe it's just nonsense. Maybe all of this is. Maybe I'm just here because it's where the gateway sent me. There's no purpose, no road the Prophets have put me on, I'm just here because some portal built by a bunch of aliens hundreds of thousands of years ago happened to show up when I needed it to get off a planet.

She closed her eyes and then opened them. *Focus,* she thought. *Just put one foot in front of the other and try not to think about the fact that your internal temperature is skyrocketing while your external one is plummeting. At this rate, I'll explode by nightfall . . .*

Kira trudged her way through the snow, willing the feeling to stay in her feet even though they were starting to numb again—the last time they did, they had stopped in the crevice.

"Yet your gods cast you out."

"Not my gods. Only a few men and women who claim to represent them."

Kira had no idea why the conversation she and Taran'atar had had in the *Euphrates* was coming back to her, but she tried to banish it from her head. "Shut up!" she cried.

"What?" Torrna asked from behind her.

"Nothing," Kira said, embarrassed. *Great, now I'm yelling at the voices in my head.*

"We will make it, *Ashla*. We *must*. There is no other way—if we do not, Perikia will be lost. It's *our* land—the Lerrit do not belong there, and I'll do everything I can to keep them out! But we can't do it if we don't get Moloki's information back to the prefect."

Kira looked back at Torrna, and saw the look of determination on his face even through the snow and facial hair, through the bruises, and through the pain he felt.

And she felt ashamed for doubting.

"We'll make it," she repeated.

One foot in front of the other, she thought. *You can do it. We can do it. We'll make it back.*

Half an hour later, she collapsed face-first into the snow.

Chapter Eight

"Major?"

"Sir?"

"Tell me another story."

. . .

"While you had your weapons to protect you, all I had was my faith—and my courage. Walk with the Prophets, child. I know I will."

. . .

"I was there."

"Sir?"

"B'hala. It was the eve of the Peldor Festival. I could hear them ringing the temple chimes."

"You were dreaming."

"No! I was there! I could smell the burning bateret leaves—taste the incense on the wind. I was standing in front of the obelisk, and as I looked up, for one moment, I understood it all! B'hala—the Orbs—the occupation—the discovery of the worm-hole—the coming war with the Dominion . . ."

. . .

"A people can be defined by where they come from. Who the Bajorans are is shaped in part by our world. It's part of what ties us to the Prophets. The Cardassians didn't belong there, so I fought them. All my life, I've fought for Bajor because that is my unit."

"You believe caring for your home brings you closer to your gods?"

"I suppose that's one way of looking at it."

"Yet your gods cast you out."

"Not my gods. Only a few men and women who claim to represent them."

. . .

"Why have you taken this woman's body?"

"This vessel is willing. The Reckoning—it is time."

"The Reckoning—what is it?"

"The end, or the beginning."

. . .

"But what do the locusts represent? And why Cardassia—?"

"You were dreaming—and dreams don't always make sense."

"This was no dream!"

. . .

"The captain is not going to die. He is the Emissary, the Prophets will take care of him."

"With all due respect, Major, I'd rather see Julian take care of him."

"Chief, I know you're worried, but the Prophets are leading the Emissary on this path for a reason."

"Do not attempt to convince them, Major—they cannot understand."

"Since when did you believe in the Prophets?"

"What I believe in—is faith. Without it, there can be no victory. If the captain's faith is strong, he will prevail."

"It's not much to bet his life on."

"You're wrong—it's everything."

. . .

"Major?"

"Sir?"

"Tell me another story."

. . .

"Nerys?"

Kira's eyes fluttered awake. "Where—where am—?"

"You're back home."

She didn't recognize the face. "Who—who are you—where—?"

"You're in the infirmary—"

Julian?

"—at Fort Tendro."

No, Fort Tendro's on the outskirts of the peninsula—practically the front lines. That's where Torrna and I were headed.

She looked up to see a pleasant, round face, partially obscured by a wispy white beard and equally wispy white hair. "I'm Dr. Maldik," he said. "How are you feeling?"

"Thirsty. And warm."

Maldik smiled. "That's good. Both very encouraging signs."

"Wait a minute!" Kira cried out as Maldik started to walk away. "What about Torrna? We were in the mountains, and—"

"Yes, you were in the mountains." Maldik turned back around. "Almost died there, too, based on the shape you two were in when you got here."

Pouncing on the words "you two," Kira said, "Antosso—General Torrna. Where is he?"

Tugging on his beard, Maldik said, "He's already gone back to the capital. You and he had been declared dead by the Lerrit, you see—they claimed to have executed you. It therefore came as something of a surprise to see him stumbling into the fort, carrying you on his right shoulder."

That bastard, Kira thought. *Avtra must've been annoyed that he didn't get his stadium receipts, so he decided to get some propaganda value out of pretending to kill us.* Musing over her present condition, she thought, *Of course, he came pretty close to calling it right that we were dead. . . .*

"In any case, he left immediately to pass on some news or other about the Lerrit, and also to let his wife and children know he was alive."

Letting out a breath, Kira said, "Lyyra must have been devastated."

"I wouldn't know. Oh, the general did ask me to pass on a message."

Kira gave Maldik a questioning glance.

The doctor tugged on his beard some more. "He said, and I think I'm quoting this precisely, 'Thank her for me.'"

Snorting, Kira said, "He's thanking me? What did I do, besides fall on my face?"

"Well, from what he said, you didn't actually come out and tell him you were dying of pneumonia while you were stupidly trudging through freezing mountains after wading hip-deep in a swamp."

In a weak voice, Kira said, "I didn't want to worry him."

Another beard-tug. "No, better to wait until you fall unconscious and then completely frighten him. Yes, good point, much better than simply worrying him."

Kira ignored the barb, instead asking, "What about his arm? Were you able to save it?"

"Barely. You did a good job of keeping the wound clean. If you'd continued your summer stroll for much longer, it would've been infected, but he got the two of you here in time." One last beard-tug, then: "Enough gossip. You need your rest."

"I'm fine," Kira said, and she started to sit up. The room proceeded to leap around, whirl in circles, and generally behave insanely—until she lay back down, and then everything was fine. "On the other hand, maybe rest isn't a bad idea."

In a tone that sounded irritatingly like Julian at his most smug, Maldik said, "Soldiers make such *wonderful* patients. Try listening periodically, it'll do you wonders."

Chapter Nine

Kira spent what felt like an eternity on her cot. Every once in a while she was able to sit up, but never for very long.

As time went on, news from the front lines, and from the capital, came in the form of messengers. Admiral Inna led a convoy of ships to the Kendra Valley River in an attempt to cut off the Bajora's supply lines. Natlar also sent an envoy to the Bajora, asking them to cease their support of Lerrit.

It turned out that the battle at Barlin Field had been more decisive than Kira and Torrna had realized, busy as they were being captured. It had been a major victory, and led to the complete reclamation of not only Makar Province, but also most of the Lonnat Valley.

By the time Kira was well enough to travel, a ship was coming down the coast—the fort was located near the Korvale Ocean—to bring injured troops home. Being, in essence, an injured troop as well, Kira went along.

The captain of the ship was a *very* short, no-nonsense woman named Tunhal Din. Kira noticed that she wore an earring in her right ear. "Who the hell're you?" was her way of introducing herself.

"Kira Nerys. I'm General Torrna's adjutant."

"Didn't know he had one. Well, find yourself somewhere to sleep. If you get sick, do it over the edge or clean it up yourself."

"How's the fighting going?"

Tunhal shrugged. "We haven't surrendered yet."

Kira had never traveled much by sea. Her initial assumption that it would be much like flying in an atmospheric craft turned out to be optimistic. She managed not to throw up, but that only through a supreme effort of will.

When they came around the bend into sight of Natlar Port, she had other reasons for being ill.

The port was on fire.

She stood at the fore of the ship, next to the wheel, watching in shock. Tunhal was next to her. "Well, that was damn stupid o' them Lerrits."

Kira looked at her. "What do you mean?"

"Port's what makes this land so damn desirable. Why'd they cannon it to smithereens like that? If they're trying to win back the land, why screw up the most valuable part of it?"

"It depends on your goal," Kira, who had spent her formative years as a terrorist, said after a moment's thought. "If you're trying to take land from the enemy, you're right, it is stupid. But if you're trying to do damage to your enemy where it hurts the most, that's the thing to do."

Tanhul looked at her like she had grown a second head. "That's insane."

Kira had to bite back her instinctive response: *You say that because the tactics of terrorism haven't really been invented here yet. They haven't needed to be. And you should thank the Prophets for that every night before you go to bed.*

Instead, she said, "It's actually a good sign, believe it or not."

"How's that, exactly?"

"They wouldn't have attacked the port directly if they had any intention of taking it. This was the final defiant act of a navy that knows it's lost. A kind of 'if I can't have it, no one can' gesture. This probably means the war's going well for our side."

"Your definition of 'well' differs from mine," Tanhul said dryly.

There were no obvious piers available for docking—half of them were damaged beyond usefulness, and the rest were occupied. The marina itself was a mass of chaotic activity, with small fires being put out and people coughing from the smoke.

Someone noticed them eventually, though, as a small rowboat approached the spot where Tanhul had dropped anchor. Kira recognized its occupant as the assistant dockmaster, Hiran. As he pulled up alongside the ship, Tanhul ordered a ladder lowered for him.

"Good to have you back, ma'am," he said upon sighting Kira as he arrived on deck. Then he turned to Tanhul. "I'm sorry, Captain, but as you can see, we're a bit shorthanded."

"I've got wounded here."

Hiran frowned. "Let me see what I can do. I might be able to get a few skiffs over to offload the worst of them." He turned to Kira. "Ma'am, you should know that General Torrna's in his office. You might want to see him."

Kira didn't like the tone in Hiran's voice. "Is he all right?"

"I really think you should see him, ma'am." Hiran's tone was more urgent. Kira also knew him well enough to know that he was unlikely to say anything else.

She accompanied him back in the rowboat to the marina. As Hiran stroked the oars, Kira asked, "What happened here?"

"Lerrit's last stand, you could say, ma'am," Hiran said, almost bitterly. "General Torrna pretty much beat them on the land. See, on his way back from Fort Tendro, he came across General Takmor's regiment—but Takmor'd been killed."

Damn, Kira thought. *She was one of the good ones.* "I'd heard that she was the one who reclaimed Sempa Province."

"Actually, that was General Torrna, ma'am. The general, see—well, he just plowed on in and led them to victory. They were ready to call it quits, but he rallied 'em, and they took Sempa back. Meantime, Admiral Inna came back here when she found out that the Lerrit Navy was gonna throw their whole armada at us."

Kira looked at the smoky, ruined port. "Looks like they did."

"Oh, the admiral, she threw back pretty good, too. Cost her her life, mind, but—"

"Inna's dead?"

Hiran nodded. "Just what we needed after everything else."

"What everything else? Hiran, I've been laid up at Tendro, and obviously I haven't been getting all the news."

"Oh, ma'am, I'm sorry," Hiran said in a sedate tone. "I guess you didn't hear that Prefect Natlar was killed, too. See, same time the Lerrit Navy did their last stand here, the Lerrit Army did likewise in the capital. Didn't work, of course—thanks to the blockade, they were underfed, understaffed, and under-armed. We beat 'em back mighty good, truth be told, but—" He sighed. "Not without a cost, if you know what I mean."

Kira shook her head. "So we won?"

"Yes, ma'am, if you can call this a victory."

They arrived at the marina. Kira disembarked from the rowboat, and couldn't help contrasting this with the last time she set foot on the dock. Then, the sun was shining, a stiff breeze was blowing, carrying the smell of fish and seawater, with the Korvale Ocean a sparkling green in contrast to the dull-but-solid brown of the dock's wood. Now, the sun was obscured by billowing smoke, and the wind carried only the smell of that smoke, occasionally broken by the stench of blood and death.

Then she saw the bodies.

They were arranged in a row just past the marina in a ditch that hadn't been there before. Many wore Perikian uniforms; many more wore Lerrit uniforms. A few—though even a few were too many—wore civilian clothing.

Nerys walked into the other chamber, Furel right behind her. Kira Taban's body was laid out on the pallet. She had seen far too many dead bodies not to know one now.

Her father was dead.

"He died calling your name."

It took an effort for Kira to pry her horrified eyes away from the array of corpses and continue her journey to the office where she and Torrna had spent so much time together.

The small wooden structure had held up remarkably well during the attack—only a few scorch marks differentiated it from Kira's memory of the building. Several familiar faces greeted her hastily; others ignored her completely. One person, a merchant who had set up a shop specializing in merchandise from Endtree, muttered, "Thank the Prophets she's here. Maybe she can talk some sense into him."

Nobody sat at the sergeant's desk.

She entered Torrna's tiny office. The general sat behind his rickety wooden desk, which was piled top to bottom with enough refuse and detritus to be a serious fire hazard, given the conditions outside. The small bar that sat under the window was full of empty, overturned, and broken bottles. Kira was therefore not surprised that the smoky stench that had filled her nostrils since Tunhal's ship came around the bend was now being overpowered by several different types of alcoholic beverage. At least three more bottles were visible on the desk, not to mention the large glass that Torrna Antosso clutched in his right hand.

The smoke obscured the view of the mainland, as it obscured everything right now.

The general looked like a zombie. His eyes stared unblinking, straight ahead. If not for the smell of alcohol—not to mention Torrna's atheism—Kira would have thought he was in the midst of a *pagh'tem'far* vision.

"They're *dead*," Torrna said without preamble, his voice barely more than a monotone. "Dead dead dead *dead.*"

"I know, Hiran told me about the prefect and Admiral Inna. But—"

Torrna made a sweeping gesture, knocking over one of the empty bottles. "No! Not them. I mean, they're dead, too, but tha's not who I mean."

"Who's—"

"Lyyra! She's *dead!*"

Kira found herself unable to reply at first. She had been prepared to console Torrna on the deaths of Natlar and Inna even as she herself struggled with the fact that the serene prefect and the no-nonsense admiral were gone.

"What about the kids, are they—"

"They're dead, too. All of 'em, dead dead dead dead *dead.* An' they didn' know."

Frowning, Kira prompted, "Didn't know what?"

"Th' I was alive! B'fore I could get home I found Takmor's regimen'."

"I heard."

"By time I got home, they were dead—an' I never got to tell 'em I was alive!"

"They probably found out from the dispatches," Kira said, not sure if, in the chaos of the end of the war, anyone would have the wherewithal to contact Lyyra about so trivial a matter as the fact that her reported-dead husband was still alive. *Especially if she and the kids were close enough to the fighting to be killed. Hell, knowing Lyyra, she was right in the midst of it. She was always a healer at heart.*

"Doesn' matter. Nothin' matters. They want me to take over now't war's over. Ain't gonna do it."

"What do you mean?"

"Gonna drink m'self to death. If that doesn' work, I'm gonna cut m' throat. Don't wanna live in this world without 'er."

. . . Odo "putting on" the tuxedo for the last time before descending into the Great Link . . .

"Listen to me, Antosso, you can't just give up."

"Why not?" He pounded his fist on the desk, rattling the bottles and knocking several papers off. "Haven' I done enough?"

. . . Bareil, his brain barely functioning, slowly fading away on the infirmary biobed . . .

"No, you haven't! You've spent all this time fighting, you *can't* give up now! Perikia *needs* you! They couldn't have fought this war without you, and they certainly wouldn't have won it without you."

"Doesn' matter. Without Lyyra—"

. . . Captain Sisko—the Emissary—traveling to the fire caves, never to be seen again . . .

"There are still hundreds of people out there who fought and died for

Perikia—including Lyyra. Without Natlar, without Takmor, without Inna—they're going to need your strength. They need the man who beat back the Lerrit Army. They need the man who trudged through the swamp and the mountains to get home. They need *you*."

. . . her father lying dead in the caves of Dakhur Hills . . .

Torrna shook his head. "Can't do it. Jus' can't."

Snarling, Kira got up and went to the other side of the desk. She grabbed Torrna by the shirt, and tried to haul him to his feet. Unfortunately, while they were the same height, he was quite a bit larger—and, in his drunken state, so much dead weight.

. . . Opaka lying dead after a shuttle crash on some moon in the Gamma Quadrant . . .

"Get up!"

"Wha' for?"

"I said get *up!*"

. . . Furel and Lupaza, only on the station to protect her, being blown into space by an embittered, vengeance-seeking Cardassian . . .

Torrna stumbled to his feet. Then he fell back into the chair. Kira yanked on his arm, which seemed to be enough to get him to clamber out of the chair again.

She led him outside. She propped him up on one of the wooden railings that separated the small office building area from the main marina and pointed. "You see that?"

"I don't see anythin' but—"

Losing all patience, Kira screamed. "The bodies! Look at the bodies! Those people died fighting for Perikia! So did Natlar, so did Inna—and so did Lyyra. You have no right to give up now—because if you do, Lerrit has won. There's no one else who can unite these people the way you can now—you're a hero! Without you, they'll fall apart, and either Prince Avtra or the Bajora will be able to come right in and take over."

Torrna stared straight ahead for several minutes. Then he turned back to Kira.

When she first entered his office, Torrna's eyes were glazed over. Now, they were filled with sadness.

In as small a voice as he'd used when they were traveling through the mountains, Torrna said, "I'm sorry."

Kira remembered that the ground-based gateways tended to do one of two things: jump randomly from vista to vista every couple of seconds, or, like the one at Costa Rocosa, stay fixed on one location. This one, however, was different: it jumped back and forth between only two destinations.

The first was ops on Deep Space 9.

The other was the comforting light that Kira Nerys knew in her heart belonged to the Prophets.

As she stared at the pathetic, drunken figure of Torrna Antosso standing in the midst of the wreckage of Natlar Port, Kira at once realized that she made the right and the wrong choice in stepping through the gateway when she did.

This, she thought, *is me. And whether or not Torrna decides to drink himself into oblivion or takes charge of the Perikian government—doesn't matter.*

Kira walked away, then. Away from Torrna Antosso, away from Natlar Port, away from the Korvale Ocean, away from the Perikian Peninsula.

Or, more accurately, under it.

She'd been in these caves before. The last time was when the Circle had kidnapped and tortured her thirty thousand years from now. She had no idea why she came down here, and yet she was never more sure of anything in her life.

Despite the fact that the Denorios Belt's tachyon eddies prevented any gateways from being constructed within ten light-years of Bajor, Kira was not surprised by the fact that an active gateway was present in the caves. She didn't know where it would lead her, but she felt supremely confident as she stepped through it, ready to face what lay beyond . . .

Chapter Ten

Kira Nerys stared at the galaxy.

She had to look up to see it in its entirety, its bright face filling half the sky. She'd seen images of the galaxy before, simulations and holos taken from deep-space probes launched centuries ago by any number of worlds. But nothing prepared her for the sight before her now.

The galaxy stared back down at her, a still and silent maelstrom that seemed to scrutinize her as she stood beneath it, and she knew that it was no simulation. She was as far from home as she'd ever been, and might ever be, and under the unblinking eye of the immense double spiral, Kira Nerys felt very, very small.

She was only partly aware of her surroundings: the smooth circular floor beneath her feet, the central console with its brown-and-blue color scheme and alien markings that registered dimly as matching the known designs of the Iconians.

And no walls. Only sky. She stood in a room without shadows, lit by a hundred billion suns.

Must be a forcefield, but—

"Ah, there you are."

She felt the voice more than heard it, as if it came from within her. Kira wanted to turn around to respond, but found herself transfixed by the starscape.

A finger seemed to appear from nowhere and point at a spot in the lower left quadrant of the vista spread out before Kira. The voice said, "It's here."

Kira finally tore her gaze away from the view and followed the finger back up the hand and arm it was connected to, and finally to the body. The figure was huge, though definitely bipedal and apparently humanoid, standing at well over two and a half meters tall, dwarfing even the immense Hirogen hunter that she and Taran'atar had faced in the Delta Quadrant. He—the voice *sounded* male, at least—wore a maroon cloak with a hood that obscured his features.

"Wh—what?"

"The world you come from is here. I believe you refer to it as Bajor."

"Who are you?"

The figure hesitated. "You might say I'm an emissary of the people who built this outpost, but that might have unfortunate connotations for you. Suffice it to say that I am the custodian of this place."

"You're an Iconian?"

There was a movement inside the cloak that Kira supposed could have been a nod. "You'll be pleased to know that I was able to cure you of that unfortunate energy."

Energy? It took Kira a moment to realize that he was referring to the theta-radiation poisoning. She had been on that arid desert of a planet in the

Delta Quadrant, theta radiation eating away at her, when the gateway beckoned. Her tricorder had told her that the radiation levels were fatal. . . .

Of course, the rational part of her brain said as she looked down and saw that she no longer wore the ancient clothing of Bajor's past *(did I ever?)* but was instead in her sand-soiled Militia uniform.

It was some kind of dream, she thought, *that's all. Or maybe a* pagh'tem'far. *That would certainly explain—*

She cut the thought short as she felt a mild stiffness in her left arm. Looking down, she saw the badly healed wound she'd received the day they drove the Lerrit Army out of the capital city. "How did—how did this get here?" She pointed to the wound.

The hood tilted a little to one side. "Presumably you received it at an earlier date."

"You're a big help," she muttered.

"I assume that you wish to take the gift that has been given to you and then go home?"

Kira almost asked the figure what he meant by that. But duty took over. Like Torrna Antosso, she had a role to play, a duty to perform, and a planet to defend—regardless of what obstacles had been placed in her path.

"Actually, I need to return to Europa Nova. I made a promise that I would do everything I could—"

Before she could finish the sentence, the custodian drifted—*walk* was too clumsy a word to describe how he moved—over to the center console.

"Ah, I see. One of our *hezlat* gateways is in orbit of that planet," he said after touching one of the triangular controls.

"*Hezlat?*" Kira asked as she approached. Two small holographic displays hovered on either side of the blue globe atop the console, each showing a star system. The sizes and magnitudes of the two stars matched those of Europa Nova's star and the star where they'd found the tanker in the Delta Quadrant.

"Many different types of gateways were constructed over time," the custodian said, "some large and inelegant, some small and functional, others that could be held in the palm of one's hand. The *hezlat*s were among the first, and also among the largest. Let's see, this one is stable—it links System X27πL with System J55ΔQ."

The custodian seemed to be just staring at the display, so Kira helped him along. "Someone decided to dump theta radiation into that—that *hezlat* of yours. We had to evacuate everyone from the planet on the other side before the radiation levels became fatal."

"Yes . . . I see that now. But there is something blocking part of the gateway."

Thank the Prophets, the Euphrates *is still there.* "Yes, that's one of our vessels. That's how we travel, by ship—and I used mine to block the radiation from coming through and—"

"I understand, Colonel. I observe your ships traversing the galaxy all the time from here. It is not a pastime shared by all my people."

"There are more of you, then?"

"Yes. Some of them are dealing with this crisis now. I have faith in the Sentries."

Kira had no idea what that meant, but she didn't want to get off topic. "What about Europa Nova?"

"Hm?"

"System—" She peered at the console screen, but couldn't read it. "X2-whatever," she said. Finally, she pointed at the holographic display. "That one!"

"Oh, yes. I am searching now. Ah, there we are. System O22ψT has a star that will suffice for the purpose."

A third star-system image appeared in the holographic display. From the brightness and magnitude, it had an O-type star.

"I can reprogram this particuar *hezlat* gateway to transport the matter that is emitting the energy on both sides into the star in System O22ψT. The star there will render the energy inert." He turned to Kira. "I will also remove the object blocking the gateway. Would you like it in System O22ψT, System X27πL, or System J55ΔQ?"

"Uh, the second one," Kira said. "Is the place where you're sending the waste uninhabited?"

"Of course," the custodian said as if the answer were self-evident. Kira had no such assurances, though. After all, according to most of the legends, the Iconians were conquerors.

The custodian made some adjustments on the panel. "I assume by the state you arrived in that your species is vulnerable to this type of energy."

Assuming that he meant theta radiation, Kira said, "Yes, very vulnerable."

"In that case, you must be careful. The gateway can remove the matter, but some of the energy will remain around that planet you were concerned with. You say it was evacuated?"

Kira nodded.

"Repopulating it will be a challenge."

"Like I said—I made a promise."

Again, the custodian made a gesture that might have been interpreted as a nod, then said, "It is time for you to leave." The Iconian touched a series of triangular panels. A blue light shot out from the globe and then a gateway opened near the edge of the floor. Through it, Kira could see the bustle of ops, with Dax giving orders to Sergeant Gan.

She looked at her host. "We thought there was a natural phenomenon preventing your gateways from functioning in the space around my planet," Kira said. "That isn't completely true, is it?"

"No," the Iconian confirmed. "But we respect the beings who watch your worlds. And we long ago promised never to interfere with them."

"Worlds . . . ?" Kira asked.

"Farewell, Colonel."

A million questions on her lips, it took a conscious effort to turn toward the gateway. Taking a deep breath, Kira walked around the console.

Before stepping into the gateway, she took one last look at the immense galaxy above her.

She once again found the spot where the custodian had indicated that Bajor was. From there she traced an imaginary line to the region she knew was the Delta Quadrant, and wondered whether or not Taran'atar had survived his battle with the Hirogen. Then her eyes drifted to the Gamma Quadrant, to the expanse that contained the Dominion, and the Founders' world.

You don't look so far away from here, Odo.

The custodian waited patiently while she took it all in, and eventually she turned away from the sprawling mass of stars.

Enough self-indulgence. It's past time I went back to work.

But as she approached the gateway, it seemed the custodian had one more thing to tell her. "One of the things that doomed the Iconian Empire, Colonel, was that the gateway technology meant that we could no longer travel. We lost sight of the journey in our desire to achieve our destination. Don't make that mistake."

Kira smiled at the cloaked figure. "I won't. And thank you."

Then she stepped through the gateway, knowing full well what lay beyond.

Chapter Eleven

Ezri Dax had, Kira knew, centuries of life experience thanks to the Dax symbiont, and she also knew that, among her nine lifetimes, she had probably seen everything.

So seeing her jump up, scream, and drop the padd she was holding when Kira walked into ops made for a fairly amusing sight.

As usual with the gateways, there was no feeling of transition from one point to the other. It was as if ops had been the next room over from the extragalactic outpost. The only change was that the Iconian outpost's gravity was a bit lighter than that of DS9, so Kira stumbled a bit upon her arrival.

Dax blinked several times. "Colonel?"

"Yes, Lieutenant, it's me."

Gan said, somewhat redundantly, "You're alive."

Kira resisted the obvious rejoinders. "Report."

"Europa Nova has been completely evacuated. Most of the refugees are on Bajor. The station's also filled almost to capacity. Lieutenant Ro, Sergeant Ychell, and Quark have returned, and Ro says she's got some good news regarding the Orion Syndicate. And Taran'atar's in the infirmary."

Kira's eyes widened. "He's all right?"

Dax winced. "I wouldn't go that far, but he'll recover. Whatever he fought gave him quite a beating." Then she smiled. "Apparently enough to cause delusions, since he reported that you were dead."

Probably didn't read my life signs on the planet and made assumptions, Kira thought. *Given the radiation levels, I can't really blame him.* "Let's just say I was able to make the gateway technology work for me. Go on."

Dax continued with her report, including the fact that the *Defiant* had gone off to rendezvous with the *Marco Polo* to help implement a plan to deal with the gateways; that the *Trager* was attached to upper pylon 1, Gul Macet having been invited to stay for a bit by Vaughn; the continued presence of Councillor Charivretha zh'Thane on board the station; and the fact that Lieutenant Bowers had taken the *Rio Grande* back to Europa Nova to keep an eye on the gateway there.

"It's been taken care of," Kira said. "There won't be any more antimatter waste in orbit of Europa Nova at all. Send a message to Bowers; tell him to do a full sensor sweep to determine how much contamination is still there. If we're lucky, it's little enough that we can work on repopulating sooner rather than later." She smiled. "And tell Bowers when he's finished to tow the *Euphrates* back. It should be in orbit." *With,* she recalled, remembering the shield enhancer she had salvaged from the tanker, *a nice piece of new technology.*

"Yes, sir," Dax said, moving toward a console. Then she stopped, and smiled. "It's good to have you back, Nerys. I don't think this place could've taken losing another commanding officer."

"Good to *be* back, Ezri. Don't worry, I'm not going anywhere. I've still got too much work to do."

Chapter Twelve

Kira sat in her office, looking over the historical records she had been able to scare up from the Perikian region. There was distressingly little from as long as thirty thousand years ago. She had found no record whatsoever of the Lerrit, aside from some archaeological indications of some kind of empire from that time period that looked Lerrit-like to Kira.

Kira had taken care of a variety of administrative duties—not to mention assuring everyone from station personnel to First Minister Shakaar that she was, in fact, alive, contrary to reports—and also been sure to visit Taran'atar in the infirmary. He was fairly weak, but recovering quickly, though Julian had made noises about even laboratory-bred supersoldiers needing their rest when they have the stuffing beaten out of them. For his part, Taran'atar had only one thing to say: "It is good that we have both reclaimed our lives."

"You don't know the half of it," Kira had said.

Afterward, she returned to her office and tried to find out what she could about the Perikian region thirty thousand years ago.

The name of Torrna Antosso did come up in several texts, as did that of others with that family name. Historians had debated just who Antosso was and what form his apparently tremendous influence had been in the peninsula, but given the number of landmarks and streets and such that had been named for him or other members of the Torrna family, it was obvious to Kira that he had taken her advice.

Assuming I was ever really there, she thought, as she rubbed her left arm, which still had the scar. Julian had offered to remove it, but she had refused.

Shutting down the computer terminal, Kira stared straight ahead for a moment, then picked up the baseball.

Benjamin Sisko had always kept that baseball on his desk. The central element of a human game that he'd been inordinately fond of, the white spheroid with red stitching was a symbol of Sisko's presence. When the station had been taken by the Dominion during the war, Sisko had deliberately left the baseball behind as a message to the occupying forces that he planned to come back—a promise he had fulfilled.

Even though the station was now hers to command, Kira had not been able to bring herself to remove the baseball. She wasn't sure why she had left it there.

No, I know why. I kept thinking in the back of my head that the Emissary was going to return—hoping that he'd return and take the burden off of me, that he'd take the station back just like he did two years ago, and everything would be back to normal.

But that's not going to happen. This station is mine, now. I may have lost the Emissary, Odo, Jast, and the kai, I may be Attainted—but I've got responsibilities, just like Torrna did.

And dammit, I'm going to live up to them.

She opened a drawer in the desk and placed the baseball in it.

I'll hold it for you, Benjamin, for when you come back.

But I need this to be my office now.

She got up and went back into ops, knowing her journey was far from over.

Two gates for ghostly dreams there are: One gateway of honest horn, and one of ivory. Issuing by the ivory gate are dreams of glimmering illusion, fantasies, but those that come through solid polished horn may be borne out, if mortals only know them.

—Homer, *The Odyssey*

About the Authors

S. D. PERRY has worked in a number of multimedia universes, novelizing videogames, graphic novels, and movies, as well as creating original fiction with characters established for television. She lives in Oregon with her family, and is currently working on a first novel entirely of her own creation, a thriller.

DAVID WEDDLE was a writer and executive story editor for *Star Trek: Deep Space Nine*. He is currently a writer-producer for *Battlestar Galactica*. He has written for such television series as *The Twilight Zone* and *The Fearing Mind*. His other books include: *"If They Move… Kill 'Em!": The Life and Times of Sam Peckinpah*, and *Among the Mansions of Eden: Tales of Love, Lust, and Land in Beverly Hills*. He has written articles for such publications as: *Rolling Stone*, the *Los Angeles Times*, *The Washington Post*, *The San Francisco Chronicle*, *San Jose Mercury News*, *Sight & Sound*, *Film Comment*, *Variety*, and *L.A. Weekly*.

JEFFREY LANG is the author of *Star Trek: The Next Generation—Immortal Coil* and *Star Trek: Voyager—String Theory, Book One: Cohesion*. He is also the co-author, with J.G. Hertzler, of the *Left Hand of Destiny* duology for *Deep Space Nine*. He has also written short stories for a number of *Trek* anthologies, including, most recently, *Constellations* for the original series. Lang lives in Bala Cynwyd, PA with his partner Helen, his son Andrew, and their two parasitic blobs, uh, cats, Kirby and Puff.

KEITH R. A. DECANDIDO is the author of a dozen other *Star Trek* novels besides *Demons of Air and Darkness* and ten other *Trek* novellas besides *Horn and Ivory*. However, he's still extraordinarily proud of these two works, and is grateful that they're reaching a new audience six years later. His other work being published in 2007 includes the *Star Trek: The Next Generation* 20th anniversary novel *Q&A*; *The Mirror-Scaled Serpent*, the *Star Trek: Voyager* portion of *Mirror Universe, Book 2: Obsidian Alliances*; the *Buffy the Vampire Slayer* novel *The Deathless*; short stories in the anthologies *Doctor Who: Short Trips: Destination Prague*, *Age of War: A Classic BattleTech Anthology*, and *Pandora's Closet*; the novelization of *Resident Evil: Extinction*; and the *Command and Conquer* novel *Tiberium Wars*. When he isn't writing, Keith is the editor of the monthly *Star Trek* eBook line, the percussionist for the parody band the Boogie Knights, and a student of *kenshikai* karate. Find out less about him at his official website at www.DeCandido.net, read his inane ramblings at kradical.livejournal.com, or send him snotty e-mails at keith@decandido.net.